THE PRESIDENT'S WOMEN

JUNE FLAUM SINGER

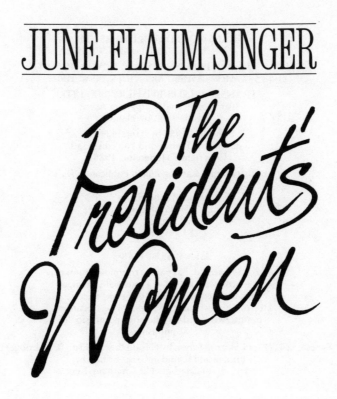

The Presidents' Women

BANTAM PRESS

LONDON · NEW YORK · TORONTO · SYDNEY · AUCKLAND

TRANSWORLD PUBLISHERS LTD
61–63 Uxbridge Road, London W5 5SA
TRANSWORLD PUBLISHERS (AUSTRALIA) PTY LTD
15–23 Helles Avenue, Moorebank, NSW 2170
TRANSWORLD PUBLISHERS (NZ) LTD
Cnr Moselle and Waipareira Aves,
Henderson, Auckland

Published 1988 by Bantam Press
a division of Transworld Publishers Ltd
Copyright © Jongo Inc. 1988

British Library Cataloguing in Publication Data

Singer, June Flaum
The President's women.
I. Title
813'.54[F]

ISBN 0-593-01486-3

Typeset in 10/11pt Linotron Sabon by Goodfellow & Egan (Cambridge) Ltd
Printed and bound in Great Britain by
Mackays of Chatham Plc, Chatham, Kent

For my son, Ian Jory . . .
When he was born I held him in my arms
and dreamed that someday he would be
President. He dreamed, in turn, that he
would be baseball player, astronaut, rock
star. He grew up to be his own man.

Special thanks to Betty Prashker, Mark
Barty-King and Herb Katz for their
friendship and unflagging enthusiasm, to
Gary Flaum for his friendship and
researcher's expertise, and to my Joe, for
his love and infinite wisdom.

About the Author

June Flaum Singer lives in Bel-Air, California with her husband, painter Joe Singer. They have three daughters, Sharon, Brett, and Valerie, and one son, Ian — all writers. Born and raised in New Jersey, she attended Ohio State University before experiencing a brief stint as a starlet in Hollywood. After the success of her first novel, the best-selling THE DEBUTANTES, she believed she enjoyed the best of all worlds. She is now working on her sixth novel.

PART ONE

The Party

I
1962

'Damned if you ain't prettier than a little red wagon, Frankie!' LBJ kissed Francesca full on the lips as he greeted her in the marble reception hall of La Casa del Presidente, the Sheridans' great white palace fronting on the Atlantic.

'Really, Lyndon!' Lady Bird protested. She smiled graciously which was meant to soften Lyndon's blunt, or even, sometimes, brusque manner. 'What kind of a compliment is that, comparing our darling Frankie to a red wagon, of all things?'

The Vice-President then gave Francesca one of his famous bear hugs, nearly squeezing the breath out of her. 'Bird's right as usual. What you are, Frankie, is beautiful. As lovely as the yellow rose of Texas. Ain't that so, Bill?'

And as a photographer's camera flashed, catching the four of them – Lyndon and Lady Bird, Bill and Francesca – Bill laughed heartily as Lyndon seized his hand in his two-pawed grip. Yet Bill's eyes reflected a certain wariness. Bill never took *anything* Lyndon said lightly. While the two had been friendly and often political bedfellows through the years, theirs was a guarded relationship.

Francesca reflected on how similar the two men were in certain outward appearances, in style. Both were big men, overpoweringly so, with personalities to match and a tough shrewdness shrouded in a personable, Southern backslapping conviviality, and both men had started life poor and grown up hungry for success. Now, both were rich and powerful and shared the same obsessive goal – the presidency of the United States.

Considering this, it was no wonder there was an underlying distrust of one another, and a shared, smouldering resentment of the President. Jack Kennedy was the rich boy, only a few months older than Bill, who had snatched, seemingly with such little effort, the golden ring from under both their noses two years before to become the youngest president ever to assume office.

Of course there were differences between LBJ and Bill, the most obvious being their physical appeal. While Lyndon was not unattractive, Francesca considered her husband stunningly handsome. The first time they met she'd turned to her sister Carlotta and breathed, 'Isn't he the bestlooking man you've ever laid eyes on?'

In the end, it hadn't mattered one way or another, but Francesca had never changed her mind. But then, she was deeply, as desperately in love with Bill Sheridan as she'd ever been.

Still, the most remarkable difference between LBJ and Bill was something else altogether and it wasn't obvious to anyone who hadn't known Bill for many years . . . before he had come to Florida to make his fortune. It was that while Bill and Lyndon sounded alike in public with that same colourful cornpone style, the Vice-President had been born to it and Bill, like John Kennedy himself, had been a congressman from Boston with an *A* every bit as broad as Jack's.

Musing, Francesca was startled to hear her daughter D'Arcy, whose sixteenth birthday was being celebrated that night, squeal indignantly, 'No one would believe this but I swear – the Vice-President of the United States of America just goosed me!'

Hoping that none of the many photographers floating around had captured *that* for posterity and trying to keep a straight face, Francesca mentally commiserated with her daughter. D'Arcy, after all, had never planned on having the Vice-President at her party. All D'Arcy had ever wanted was a 'great big gorgeous sweet sixteen' for herself and her friends with a ratio of five very neat boys to every girl.

But D'Arcy really didn't need those odds, Francesca thought. D'Arcy had her father's fantastic looks – the light blond hair, the midnight-blue eyes, and in addition, D'Arcy had the wonderful peaches-and-cream complexion of the true Southern belle. But having been born in Boston, like her father and mother, D'Arcy, however lovely, was but a transplanted Yankee flower.

Not that anyone would ever guess it from D'Arcy's speech or manner. D'Arcy, who'd read *Gone With The Wind* three times and seen the movie seven times, had Scarlett O'Hara fixed firmly in mind as a role model. This had all kinds of ramifications, one of them being that like the formidable Scarlett, D'Arcy never gave up on something once she decided that she wanted it. Rather, she became consumed with her fixation, as Scarlett had been consumed with wanting Ashley, as D'Arcy's father was consumed with wanting the presidency.

Well, this evening both Bill and D'Arcy were getting what they wanted, Francesca reflected. D'Arcy was having her great big gorgeous Sweet Sixteen complete to the gown she'd demanded, an almost exact copy of the one Scarlett wore to the barbeque at Ashley Wilkes' Twelve Oaks the day the War Between the States broke out – green-sprigged white muslin with a huge hooped skirt, and Bill had had his way with the guest list, turning the event into what he described as a 'smashing, nationwide neighbourhood block party. . . .'

Accordingly, tonight's gala would be graced by a plethora of politically prominent people chosen without regard for party affiliation, a good sprinkling of those eminent in the arts and letters, along with a large dollop of glittering society names plus a smattering of film personalities thrown in for additional sparkle and glamour. (Big Hollywood names were always useful in raising campaign dollars.)

When she and Bill had discussed who was to be invited, Francesca quickly realized that their daughter's Sweet Sixteen was not going to be so much a celebration of D'Arcy's birthday as a celebration of her father's political strength. A show of power. National exposure for the Florida governor who didn't intend to let anything stand between him and the presidential throne in '68 since there was no way he could buck the incumbent president for the party's nomination in '64.

With these goals fast in mind, the name Kennedy figured largely on the guest list. Bill wanted them *all* at the party, as many of them as he could get. But he particularly wanted the President and Attorney-General Bobby, even though he attempted to make light of it.

'What's more natural than inviting the boys?' he asked Francesca. 'They're our good Palm Beach neighbours and we're inviting all our good Palm Beach neighbours, aren't we?'

Despite his jocular tone, Francesca knew that having the Kennedys there was deadly serious business to Bill. Even more than a show of his political strength, it was a contest of power between him and the Kennedy faction in the party. Having the President attend his party meant that the Kennedyites acknowledged Bill's boast that he had the political South in his pocket, an admission that they needed Bill's full support in the '64 election.

'They damn well know they need my backing with the whole country screaming nepotism what with Teddy running for the Senate and after that Bay of Pigs fuck-up. Oh, Jack needs me all right and he damn well knows that if he wants me, he'd damn well better show up at our shindig.'

Since Bill planned on having representation from every major media outlet on hand to record the event for mass public consumption, Francesca could understand why having the Kennedys there meant so much to him and why the Kennedys, from their point of view, might well want *not* to attend. But Bill seemed sure they would come . . . that he'd win this particular tug of war.

'We're going to have the biggest and the best damn party the country's ever seen. I bet one of those magazines – *Life* or *Look* – will want to come down and do one of those articles. You know – "Life goes to a Sweet Sixteen" . . . Maybe they'll even put D'Arcy's picture on the cover. Wouldn't that be something?'

By then Francesca wondered if it was really D'Arcy's picture Bill wanted to see on the covers of magazines with circulation in the millions or his own, billed, maybe, as the king who was going to be President. . . .

Francesca had smiled her acquiescence to every name Bill proposed for the invitation list. But then she almost never opposed him. From the very first night they'd met.

He said, 'Look!' and she looked. He said, 'Jump!' and she jumped. And when he said, 'Marry me!' the very same day they learned of Carlotta's marriage, she only asked, 'When?'

But then after the invitation list was complete and *Look* said they would indeed like to make the party their cover story, Francesca was moved to voice a protest. It was when, almost as an afterthought, Bill said he wanted D'Arcy's cousins invited too. *The cousins!* Her nieces, Carlotta's daughters, Abigail Truesdale and Jade Boudin. And Judith Tyler Stanton who was her niece too but of her own generation, Judith being the daughter of a much older half-sister. And Rudyard Stanton, Judith's eighteen-year-old son.

'Why?' Francesca had demanded. 'Why in God's name do you want them? We don't even know Carlotta's daughters, and as for Judith, she's our enemy! She hates us! Why do you want to invite her? Or the girls?'

'Oh, just because they are D'Arcy's cousins.' Bill had remained smilingly affable even in the face of her displeasure. 'How can we have a great big neighbourly bash without a few relatives thrown in? It wouldn't look right. As for Judith being our enemy, what the hell? It's all in the past and the time comes when you have to forget old grudges, especially when it comes to family. Invite them!'

13

That was an order no matter how affably put, and Francesca had no choice but to do what Bill wanted. And so the invitations to D'Arcy's cousins went out with all the others. To Judith and Rud in Newport where they always spent the summer and to sixteen-year-old Abigail in Boston and to fifteen-year-old Jade in California.

But even as the invitations were mailed Francesca clung to the hope that all four would send their regrets . . . that Abigail's Truesdale guardians wouldn't allow her to accept . . . that Trace Boudin would be loath for his daughter Jade to attend. And Judith? Why *would* she accept? After all, it had been Judith who with all her money and influence had driven them out of Boston . . . out of the whole state of Massachusetts!

As for Bill's smooth rhetoric about forgetting old grudges, Francesca didn't believe that for a minute. If she knew anything about her husband she most certainly knew that he never forgave his enemies, old or new. In fact he kept a list of all the people who had ever crossed him and when the chance came for him to get even, it was zingo! Off with their heads!

Was that why Bill wanted Judith at the party? Francesca wondered. Because he was ready to send her to the guillotine along with her son, he being guilty by association? What other possible reason could there be? Still, it wasn't the invitation to Judith and Rud that disturbed her so much as those to Abigail and Jade. She felt she knew why Bill wanted the young girls there and it was for the very same reason she herself *didn't* – just because they were Carlotta's daughters. The very last thing in the world Francesca wanted was to think about Carlotta at all!

Then the RSVPs came back and all four cousins wrote that they would be pleased to attend. It was then that for Francesca the prospect of the party assumed the proportions of a nightmare, for only God alone knew how she dreaded seeing Carlotta's girls. . . .

Francesca shook hands with George Wallace but had little to say to him. While the word was that he would take Alabama's gubernatorial race in November, she couldn't very well tell him she hoped he'd do better than the state's current governor on the civil rights issues. Not that it mattered *what* she said to George since practically every politician in Dixie was committed to the fight against integration, except for Bill who had been one of the very first in the South to speak out against Jim Crow, and for that she was proud. Bill had declared himself and had still been elected, and no matter what his detractors said, *that* had been an achievement. More, that had been courage!

She turned to George's wife and enthused, 'I just love your gown, Lurleen.' This wasn't true but Francesca tried to say something nice to everyone. Besides, she always felt a little bit sorry for Lurleen Wallace who seemed to live only in the shadow of George's forceful personality.

'Your home's magnificent,' Lurleen said and Francesca knew that her compliment was sincere. La Casa del Presidente *was* magnificent, which was why Bill had insisted on buying and renovating the palatial white residence that sat on five acres of oceanfront and why Bill had insisted on having the party in Palm Beach even though the resort was out of season in September. (Bill had said that almost everyone who'd been invited would flock there

14

regardless, and of course he'd been right.) She herself had thought they should have the party at the governor's mansion in Tallahassee which was lovely with its French Impressionist paintings, but Bill had said nothing could compare in grandeur with La Casa del Presidente, the house which bore testament to everything Bill Sheridan was and hoped to be. The house of the president but a castle fit for a king. . . .

It *was* a contradiction in terms but not one that bothered Bill at all. He always said, 'Never defend, never explain.' Bill Sheridan was a law unto himself and that was why he was referred to as 'King Sheridan' by both his constituents and the power brokers in Washington. The truth was he didn't give a good goddamn what anyone thought, and Francesca thought that was one of the reasons she loved him so.

How do I love thee? Let me count the ways. . . .

She and Carlotta reading love poems to each other so very long ago. She herself thinking about Bill, and Carlotta? With Carlotta, one was never sure.

But whatever else the house might be, it *was* absolutely perfect for a party with a guest list that ran well over a thousand. The guests, arriving at the main portico graced by giant columns, mounted marble stairs appointed with enormous decorated urns, then entered the great hall where Bill, D'Arcy and she were receiving and where there was a marble and mirrored bar at one end and a branching staircase of Caen stone and bronze at the other. (The hall with its twenty-foot high ceiling had recently been described in an architectural review as being nearly as large as the main lobby of the Waldorf in New York.)

The action would then proceed to the ballroom where there was a raised platform for the orchestra and dozens and dozens of round tables ringed the dance floor. This room was especially splendid with its banquettes covered in Savonnerie tapestry and its seemingly endless wall of Roman-arched windows topped by François Boucher depictions of the Four Seasons. Mirrored panels were spanned by gilt-bronze sconces and the huge chandeliers, hung with enormous crystal drops, added a special sparkle. From there the party would spill over to the white and gold salon, the glass-domed, palm-filled conservatory and out on to the rear portico, the fountained patio, the manicured lawns and gardens. Dinner would be served from a buffet set up in the sixty-foot square green and gold dining room.

But no matter how splendid the estate, Francesca was very conscious of the large contingent of state troopers who stood guard tonight, a visible intrusion into the festivities within, the velvety, scented night without. They were stationed in doorways, on balconies, on the pink-tiled rooftops – a necessary presence, for King Sheridan was not without his critics and enemies. How could he not be with his influence extending far beyond Florida's borders and his rise to power founded on so many controversial issues? And there were always the envious who wondered how a man who had come so far as a 'man of the people' had accumulated so much money. . . .

Still, Francesca felt this presence, frequently called Sheridan's Standing Army by the press, an alien note in what was an otherwise glittering and elegant occasion. Alien and ominous . . . adding to the feeling of apprehension she was already experiencing about the evening ahead.

15

A dry cough interrupted Francesca's stream of thought and her eyes focussed on J. Edgar Hoover who stood solemnly in front of her waiting to be acknowledged.

'Oh, Mr Hoover . . . Edgar! How good of you to come,' she blurted, passing him quickly on to Bill with a 'Look, Bill! Look who's here!' She always found the head of the FBI a bit unnerving. Maybe it was because she'd never seen him smile.

She chatted with the president of one of the tobacco companies and his wife, still overhearing the Director say to Bill, 'I've been informed that the President and the Attorney-General will be here tonight.' The statement sounded more like a question and Bill replied with a non-committal, 'So I've been told.'

But that was a lie. Poor Bill, Francesca thought. The truth was that while all the members of the Kennedy clan had been invited along with many of the President's Irish mafia, not one had answered with a definite reply. Not the President and not Rose who was definitely in residence at the Kennedy compound on North Ocean Boulevard practically down the street from La Casa del Presidente in a manner of speaking. Francesca knew this because she'd seen Rose shopping on Worth Avenue just the day before last. Ethel and Bobby hadn't replied positively either. Rather, there'd been assorted, vague telephone calls from assorted vague secretaries or aides who rambled on in a cloud of ifs, maybes and perhapses.

'If the President is in Palm Beach for the Labor Day weekend. . . .'

'Perhaps if Mrs Kennedy's not away. Retreat, you know.'

'Bobby says maybe *if* the dog's back from the vet's. . . .'

A secretary had even called from the Coast. 'If Peter's not too tired from shooting all week maybe he and Pat will shoot down to the Beach for a few days. . . .'

Then another element had been added to the intrigue. Someone from Protocol had phoned to say that if the President was unable to appear, the Vice-President would certainly be dispatched in the President's stead. This call gave a different shading to the whole business. It was a subtle manoeuvre which in effect constituted a subtle put-down. If the President sent the V.-P. in his stead that turned what was a social invitiation into just another invitation to a mundane official occasion – a snub. And the snub was compounded by the fact that it was common knowledge in Washington circles that the V.-P. had received his own *personal* invitation. And even now that Lyndon and Lady Bird were here, and it wasn't clear whether they were here on their own or as the official representative of the President, it was still up in the air whether any Kennedy would actually attend. All they knew was that the Secret Service had been there to check things out 'just in case.'

It *was* a frustrating situation, Francesca agonized, as she went on greeting new arrivals by rote – shaking hands with this one, kissing that one, making the appropriate sounds. It was no wonder Bill was edgy tonight. Nearly as edgy as she herself.

Out of the corner of her eye Francesca could see Bill's gaze covertly stray to the entrance for at least the tenth time that evening though the party had hardly begun. She couldn't help wondering if it were just the question of the

Kennedy's attendance that had him in a stew, or the delayed arrival of the cousins.

While it *was* still early, the cousins had been expected to arrive during the day. Abigail, coming by train, had been expected at noon. Jade, winging in from the Coast, was supposed to have got in around three. And Judith's and Rud's anticipated time of arrival had been five o'clock. Then Judith's secretary had phoned that the Stanton private plane's takeoff had been delayed. And Abigail had sent a telegram that she'd been forced for some unexplained reason to take a later train than originally planned. From Jade, there'd been no word at all.

As the State Military Band broke into their first offering of the evening, a spirited rendition of the official state song, 'Old Folks At Home', D'Arcy let out a scream which pierced the air like a siren: 'Great balls of fire! It's Rock Hudson!'

While it was unlikely that D'Arcy, so avid a movie fan, could be mistaken about it being Rock Hudson, Francesca looked to check for herself since the actor's name hadn't been on the invitation list. But then Bill had invited several people by phone and she had no idea who they were or how many there were. She saw that it was indeed the handsome Mr Hudson arriving with their neighbours from Jupiter Island across the sound, the Harrimans. She thought that it was indeed a small world – Assistant Secretary of State Harriman was the godfather to young Peter Duchin whose orchestra was already positioned up in the ballroom. As for Rock coming to the party, Francesca recalled that she had once read in one of those gossip magazines that Rock was one of Carlotta's Hollywood friends. Is that why Bill had invited him? she wondered. And was that why Rock had come? A kind of courtesy call?

Everyone shook hands all around and Bill boomed, 'Glad you could come, Rock! We sure got a lot of clay-kickin' bastards here tonight and we damn well can use a little class to dress up the joint!'

Francesca shuddered. That remark was the kind Bill liked to use every now and then – one of his parlour tricks, sounding off like the son of a back country sharecropper who could match any son-of-a-bitch cuss for cuss, drink for drink, even punch for punch. In fact, one of Bill's most favourite claims was, 'I can lick any man in the room and failing that, I can certainly drink him under the table!'

That line never failed to bring down the house whether it was the State Senate, a congregation of dirt farmers, or even a bunch of rough and tough roustabouts on the Miami docks. It always brought a laugh but its message was always crystal clear – Bill Sheridan was a man of the people and don't you forget it! And sometimes even she found it hard to remember that Bill had received his law degree from Harvard.

Then Rock did one of *his* parlour tricks – he took one look at D'Arcy in her green-sprigged plantation gown and declared in a reasonably good imitation of Clark Gable: 'Frankly, my dear, I *do* give a damn!' Then he leaned down and kissed her. 'Happy birthday, dear Scarlett.'

It was an absolute triumph for D'Arcy. She was ecstatic, her friends who had come rushing up were stunned, and Francesca was very grateful. A birthday kiss from Rock Hudson was bound to make up to D'Arcy for Bill treating her celebration as his own, and also for not having Elvis Presley on hand to sing Happy Birthday to her. . . .

When Francesca had first explained that while it was her birthday party, about ninety per cent of the guests would be people her father was inviting, D'Arcy had pouted. 'Why can't he have his own old party and leave me mine?'

'Now don't act like a spoiled brat,' Francesca had told her. 'You know that you *love* being the governor's daughter and this is part of it. The bitter with the sweet. And I'm sure you won't mind *Life* or *Look* covering your party, will you? Maybe even put your picture on the cover? Hmmm?'

'Oh, Mummy, do you mean it? My party's going to be in *Life*? or *Look*? Wait till my friends hear about this! They'll just die of envy. I swear, they'll turn pea green! And we *will* have lots of rock and roll and not just all old fogey music? I mean I wouldn't put it past Daddy to get Lawrence Welk to play at my party or Perry Como to sing.'

'Who would you prefer?' Francesca teased. 'Chubby Checker?'

That was a mistake, for D'Arcy immediately seized on it. 'You mean I can have anyone I like? Well, I want Elvis! Promise me we'll have Elvis!'

'But why not? Everyone says that whatever Daddy wants, he gets. That nobody ever refuses a request from King Sheridan. Isn't that right?' she asked slyly. 'Well I want Daddy to *insist* that Elvis come and sing Happy Birthday just like Marilyn Monroe sang Happy Birthday to President Kennedy.'

Then remembering that the pastel-haired sex symbol who had been a favourite of hers was so recently and tragically dead, D'Arcy's voice dropped to a regretful whisper. 'Well, she did sing Happy Birthday to the President, didn't she?' And then Francesca was reminded of another actress of haunting beauty who too had lived too close to the edge, and resenting being reminded, snapped: 'You're being ridiculous, D'Arcy Sheridan! Of course your father can't command Elvis to sing at your party. What do you think he is? Royalty?'

But then they both laughed because sometimes even they forgot that Bill wasn't royalty, not really, and Francesca was already sorry she'd lost her temper. 'Well, they do call Elvis "The King" too, don't they? And I don't know what happens when one king gives a royal command to another.'

D'Arcy shook her head. '*Very* funny, Mother. But Daddy *can* ask, can't he?'

'We'll do our best but you have to remember that Elvis may very well have prior commitments.'

'OK. But one more thing. Besides a rock and roll band we have to have a rhumba band.'

'A rhumba band? I thought you were planning on doing the twist, not anything as old-fashioned as the rhumba.'

D'Arcy rolled her eyes. 'Not the rhumba, the *samba*!'

'The samba? But *that* went before the rhumba really came in!'

D'Arcy was patronizingly amused. 'Well, it's back and it's fun. I bet even your Palm Beach friends are doing the samba. Anyway, doing the twist does not preclude doing the samba, does it? Anymore than it precludes doing the Watusi.'

18

It was all too much for Francesca. 'Well, I think a rhumba band can be arranged. In fact, your father and I might surprise you. We used to do a pretty mean rhumba, if I do say so myself.'

But it was Carlotta who was the show stopper. Carlotta and Trace. When they did the rhumba, everyone else stopped dancing to watch. . . .

At first the thought of D'Arcy doing the twist or even the samba in her ante-bellum party dress made Francesca want to laugh. But then, inexplicably, her eyes filled with tears. Somehow, the very idea of it – D'Arcy, teenager of the sixties, doing all the things all teenagers did today, yet yearning to be Scarlett O'Hara, the teenager of the sixties one hundred years before, made her sad. She reached out a hand to touch her daughter's pale blond hair which had recently been cut in the Marienbad fashion – short and straight, tucked behind one ear, a sweep of bangs across the forehead – after D'Arcy had seen the film *Last Year at Marienbad,* and loved it.

Oh, my spoiled but very sweet daughter. May the years be kind to you. . . .

Then, suddenly, Francesca recalled thinking the very same thing about Carlotta once and remembering, a twinge of pain shot through her. And she laughed to chase away the pain. 'And what about your hair? How can you be Scarlett in a Civil War gown with your hair cut like that?'

'Oh, Mother, I swear! Sometimes I think you must be living in some other century. *Everybody's* wearing wigs this year, or haven't you noticed? What do you think? Should I get a blond wig or a red one?'

Not red! Certainly not red!

'You listen to me, D'Arcy Sheridan! You can wear a wig if you must but it better be the exact shade of your own hair or I'm going to flay your bare backside with a buggy whip straight out of the nineteenth century. I too have my limits.'

But D'Arcy only laughed and Francesca wondered whether her daughter, like her husband, knew her better than she did herself. *Did* she have her limits, or could she be pushed endlessly?

No, not endlessly. Once, she had been pushed to the wall, and had, finally, lashed out.

Francesca looked over at D'Arcy now with her long fake fall of pale blond curls cascading over her shoulders. Instead of greeting the still-arriving guests, D'Arcy was flirting effusively with a boy, who, apparently uncomfortable in his formal attire, was tugging at his bow-tie. Francesca tried to catch D'Arcy's eye to indicate that she still had her official duties to perform as hostess before she was free to fool around with her friends, but it was hopeless. D'Arcy wouldn't look her way, most probably deliberately so.

Francesca sighed. She really couldn't blame D'Arcy. It *was* her party and shaking hands with hundreds of people she didn't even know had to be a colossal bore. And now as the music of the Duchin orchestra was beginning to float down from the ballroom, D'Arcy was probably dying to leave the reception line and join the party. Not that the society orchestra's music thrilled her, but true to Francesca's word, there was also a Cuban band from Miami as well as a very 'hot' rock group on hand. Certainly between the three, in addition to the military band, there'd be enough of a mix to please everyone. Even D'Arcy.

Francesca welcomed Jimmy Hoffa from the United Teamsters Union. She'd only met him once before and their conversation was accordingly brief. But once Hoffa moved on to Bill it hit her. It was Hoffa's union that was under investigation by the Attorney-General's office and it was no secret that the union leader had it in for the Kennedys. He and Bobby had nearly come to blows on more than one occasion. And here was Mr Hoffa while they were expecting, or at least hopefully anticipating, the arrival of the Kennedys. *Wonderful*! This was all they needed tonight!

She had no recollection of Hoffa's name on the invitation list. Bill must have invited him on his own. Once Hoffa moved on, she sidled up to Bill and hissed under her breath, 'Why is *he* here? It's unthinkable that we'd have both him and the Kennedys here tonight!'

Bill gave her one of his mischievous grins. 'Don't fret, Frankie. I'm sure both gentlemen will remember that they are that – gentlemen, and that this is a party and not an arena.'

'That's not the point, Bill. Just having that man here is an affront to the President and his administration. For God's sake, Robert Kennedy is trying to send Hoffa to jail!'

'Tut, tut, Frankie,' Bill teased. 'You're getting yourself all excited over nothing. Anyhow, we're not even sure the Kennedy boys are coming, are we?'

Had Bill invited Hoffa just to get even with the Kennedys for not giving a definite reply as to whether or not they were coming? Just having a little spiteful fun?

'Really, Bill, this is no joke.'

'Look Frankie, this is no time to discuss it. Let's get back to our job of greeting our guests.' He turned away from her to say hello to Nelson Rockefeller who, Francesca noted, was alone.

Well, he had just divorced, she thought, and had probably decided it would be wiser this election year not to bring his soon-to-be-bride, Happy, with him. Making this kind of decision was part of being a politician . . . just as Bill had had to decide whether or not to invite Hoffa.

Bill was probably right and she was, as usual, being the naive fool. She knew damn well that although Bill tried hard to make good on every campaign promise, he hadn't got to where he was, and wouldn't get to where he had every intention of going, without the backing of men like Hoffa, or for that matter, the well-dressed men from the boardrooms of the nation's biggest industries. Nobody knew better than she that while Bill's candidacy for governor might have seemed the result of a grass-roots movement, it was more huge sums of money spent, an efficient political machine and countless back room deals with all kinds of interests. That's the way it was and certainly by this time she should accept it. A politician's wife had to be truly the other half of the man.

She saw Nelson, the present Republican governor of New York, shaking hands with Averell, the Democratic ex-governor of New York, whom Nelson had defeated. 'Governor, good to see you,' Nelson said heartily with his big warm grin and Averell, equally pleasant, smiled back, equally warmly. 'Governor, a pleasure, as always.'

This was the game of politics as played by gentlemen and she hoped that they only had gentlemen present tonight and that there'd be no ugly disruptions. God knew she already had enough inner turmoil churning away. . . .

Once again Francesca checked her slender wristwatch of rubies and diamonds – Bill's present to her on this anniversary of their daughter's birth. A quarter to eight. Only a little more receiving time and then it would be time to break ranks and move on to mingling. And still there wasn't a Kennedy in sight and ne'er a cousin either.

How wonderful if none of the cousins showed up at all, she thought. But that was too much to hope for, especially since Bill had insisted that all four be invited to stay on an additional week. 'It will give everyone a chance to really get acquainted. And since we won't be going back to Tallahassee until the ninth—'

She'd really been a fool to agree to that! A whole week of entertaining Judith! A whole week of looking at Carlotta's daughters, of being reminded of the past. . . .

2.

Francesca watched her secretary, Bess, make her way through the crowd towards her. *Now what?* Had the caterer's people suddenly gone out on strike? Maybe they'd even have to call on Jimmy Hoffa to iron out the dispute. . . .

'I just wanted you to know that your niece arrived about fifteen minutes ago.'

That feeling of dread again. 'Which one?'

'The one from Boston. Abigail. Emma took her upstairs. The poor thing had to freshen up and change into her party dress.'

Poor thing? 'Why do you say that?' she asked Bess curiously.

Bess shrugged. 'Oh, I don't know. She just seemed so tired and bedraggled. And worried. She said she left Boston yesterday afternoon and sat up the whole night. It seemed she was afraid to go to sleep because her grandaunt had told her to be sure and keep an eye on her purse at all times. The kid acts like she's afraid of her own shadow. I told her just to come down as soon as she was ready.'

Afraid of her own shadow? Carlotta's daughter?

'Aunt Francesca?' a hesitant, timorous voice. Her heart beating rapidly, Francesca swung around to face her niece. Long dark wavy hair. Dark, wet, supplicating eyes. A too pink dress that didn't fit properly. Yes, she could see why Bess had called her a poor thing.

Abigail lifted her arms up and out as if about to throw them around her aunt and without thinking, Francesca recoiled and stepped back . . . out of reach. Abigail dropped her arms looking as if she might burst into tears.

'No, she wasn't anything like Carlotta, Francesca thought. Not in any way,

21

not in face, form or style. She forced herself to smile, to lean forward and peck the girl on the cheek quickly. 'Abigail, my dear!' Even to her own ears, she sounded insincere.

Well, even though not a Kennedy has arrived, the first shoe has fallen. Now there are only three more to go.

Francesca turned to Bill, perversely eager to see how he'd greet Carlotta's elder daughter. Would a flash of recognition cross his face? Would he kiss her? Would he enfold her in a great big welcoming embrace?

'Bill! Look who's here! It's Abigail!' Then she was sorry she had given him her name. She should have let him guess.

Bill smiled warmly at the girl, extending both his hands to catch hers. 'Abby! How good to see you!'

Francesca, watching closely, thought she saw *something* in his eyes. But what? The flicker of recognition? Or was it disappointment that Abigail, after all, didn't resemble Carlotta one bit?

But then she saw Bill's face break into a really exultant grin. But Bill was looking *over* Abigail's head. 'Take a gander, Frankie. Do you see who's waltzing in? Nobody else but our President! Ha! I knew there was no way he wasn't going to show up. And look at how many of them there are,' he chortled. 'Practically every member of the tribe not to mention half of that Irish mafia of his!'

In his moment of triumph Bill all but forgot Abigail who stood there forlornly. *So!* It certainly wasn't Abigail whose arrival Bill had been so edgy about, Francesca reflected. But was it *only* that of the Kennedys?

'What should I do now, Aunt Francesca?' Abigail whispered.

Francesca looked at her niece wondering what on earth she was going to do with her. 'Well . . . you must go over and introduce yourself to D'Arcy. She's been dying to see you.'

'Really?' Abigail asked as if she couldn't quite believe it. 'Which one is D'Arcy?' she asked anxiously, looking over at the group of boys and girls laughing and talking boisterously, completely oblivious to the arrival of their President.

'You can't miss her,' Francesca said dryly, 'She's the one in the middle with the hoop skirt and the fake curls.'

She saw Abigail take a deep breath, square her shoulders as if she were about to beard a lion in its den, and march off valiantly. Francesca hoped that D'Arcy, at least, would make Abigail feel wanted even if she herself hadn't. She had wanted to but she just couldn't!

The band broke into 'Hail to the Chief' and Bill calmly watched the presidential party move as of one piece through the hall towards the reception line, stopping to shake hands here, exchanging a few words there, working the room. Jack and Jackie, surrounded by the ubiquitous Secret Service men, their profession obvious despite their correct black tie attire, followed by Bobby with Mother Rose on his arm, then Ethel with Andy Williams, a family friend. Then Jackie's sister Lee with Pat and Peter Lawford.

Francesca's first thought was how thin Lee was, so fashionably thin. . . .

Next came those men Bill called the President's Irish mafia. Francesca recognized some of them, and others not. Bringing up the rear was baby brother Ted and his wife Joan, both of them looking so incredibly young.

Then she heard D'Arcy's 'Great balls of fire! If you aren't the sweetest thing I've seen in years!' and she looked over to see D'Arcy squeezing the life out of Abigail who appeared pathetically grateful. Well, that's nice, Francesca was relieved. At least *someone* in the Sheridan family was pleased to see poor little Abby Truesdale from Boston.

Then came that great crushing feeling of guilt again. None of it, after all, was Abigail's fault. Still, she who had always thought of herself as a reasonably decent person, was unable to open up either her arms or her heart to this child . . . not even after the passage of so much time. Sixteen years and then some. . . .

Francesca shook hands with the President, told him how glad she was to have him join them and turned to greet Jackie, lovely as usual in a slim white beaded sheath with her pearls tucked into her neckline, a style she had started. Her gown was Givenchy, Francesca guessed, or perhaps Jean Louis. But she had read that Jackie favoured Oleg Cassini. But it didn't matter who the designer was, she thought. It was Jackie's own radiance shining through that made her appearance so special.

Tonight Jacqueline looked not much different from the very first time Francesca had seen her, when she and Bill had gone up to Newport for the couple's wedding. *Nine years . . . so much water under the bridge. So many changes for both of us. . . .*

'What a lovely night you have for your party,' Jackie practically whispered, and Francesca agreed. It *was* a stunning tropical night, typical of Palm Beach in the first week of September with the threat of hurricane hovering in the sultry air, adding a certain electricity, a certain seductive quality, a feeling of imminent danger.

'I do so love Palm Beach at this time of year . . . more so than at Thanksgiving or Christmas,' Francesca said, suddenly remembering New England Thanksgivings, Boston Christmases . . . the carolers wending their cheery way through the frosty night.

Another world, a long time ago.

A picture came to mind, vivid in retrospect. . . . She herself, seventeen, and Carlotta sweet sixteen but definitely already kissed, rushing out into the cold to join the carolers on their rounds. . . . Carlotta's young voice as sweet, perhaps sweeter, than the others.

Jackie leaned forward as to speak confidentially. 'I've heard you have a Latin band. Do you think we might have a conga line? Oh, how I love the conga!'

Francesca laughed wistfully. Jackie too had good memories of years gone by. 'It's a deal,' she said, 'if *you'll* lead the line.'

Bobby only smiled and nodded. It was well known he wasn't given to small talk. But when he moved on to Bill, she heard him say, 'I see you have an interesting mix of guests, Governor Sheridan,' which meant that he had already spotted Jimmy Hoffa talking to Mayor Daley of Chicago.

Francesca asked Ethel how things were at Hickory Hill and wondered if she

dared ask Andy Williams to sing *Moon River* for D'Arcy. She knew that the
song had been one of Andy's big hits that year and it was a particular favourite
with D'Arcy ever since she'd seen *Breakfast at Tiffany's*. She'd loved that
movie. 'It's so romantic, Mummy!' D'Arcy had enthused. 'I swear, *even you*
would love it.'

Francesca had been miffed by that 'even you.' What had she ever done or
said to make D'Arcy think she didn't believe in romance?

*My God, how I believed in romance. In kings and fair maidens, in fairytale
princes. . . .*

She wished Teddy luck on his forthcoming primary and marvelled again at
how young he appeared, too young to be a senator. And Joan! So bright-eyed
and innocent. . . . Had she herself ever been that innocent? Had Bill ever
looked that young when he'd been a Massachusetts congressman?

Younger than springtime. . . .

She asked Rose about her stricken husband and a picture of Joe Kennedy in
better days flashed through her mind, a dominant figure overwhelmingly
forceful. She couldn't think of him in any other way since both Bill and Jack
had been congressmen from Massachusetts and were of an age, and Joe had
played so active a role in his son's career. Bill, orphaned early on when his own
immigrant father had died of tuberculosis desperately poor in a damp Boston
cellar, had always envied Jack his father. And of course there had always been
the money. When it came to campaigning, there was Joe with his open bulging
wallet and Bill had always had to scramble . . . endlessly scrambling for
money. . . .

Rose, dressed every bit as stylishly as her daughter-in-law, smiled as if at
peace with herself. 'We live with hope and place our faith in God.'

And then Francesca envied the President's mother. To live with hope and
faith . . . never to have lain in bed wondering of whom her husband, beside
her, was dreaming . . . . Or had Rose, better disciplined than she, just firmly
banished all such distressing thoughts from her mind in order to achieve her
state of grace?

Francesca silently signalled Bill that receiving time was over and it was time to
move on to the next phase of the party. They would now proceed along with
the presidential entourage up the stairs to the ballroom.

Bill seemed startled. Hesitant . . . . And Francesca thought, he's reluctant to
leave the reception room. So it *was* true, that which she had suspected. It had
never been the uncertain arrival of the President that had kept Bill so
uncharacteristically jittery this evening. Like a cat on a hot tin roof. And it
certainly hadn't been Abigail's arrival. No, it was the delayed appearance or
the possibility of a non-appearance of another person . . . persons. . . .

There was no need to tell D'Arcy that *her* time on the receiving line was
over. She and her friends were already off and running, screaming delightedly,
D'Arcy pulling at Abigail who hung back, separate from the others. Abigail
had a natural reticence, Francesca decided, which gave credence to the theory
that it was environment rather than heredity that had the most influence on a

child's development. Whit Truesdale . . . Selena and George Truesdale, Abigail's guardians, were nothing if not reticent and reserved like all proper Bostonians. But Carlotta? Reticence had always been a stranger to her. Rather Carlotta had been heedless, reckless, and vital. As vital as life itself.

But she didn't want to think about Carlotta and she didn't want to think about Abigail. Still she was aware that even as D'Arcy tugged Abigail along, her niece was looking over her shoulder at her as if to say: 'Aren't you coming, Aunt Francesca? I want to be where you are. . . .'

Damn her! Isn't it enough for her that she's here? What does she want of me?

But Francesca knew. Abigail wanted love. Wasn't that what everyone wanted in one form or other?

As the presidential party and the Sheridans walked into the ballroom, the Duchin orchestra played *America the Beautiful*, presumably in honour of the President, and then *Tallahassee* in honour of the Governor. Then a small woman in a sequined tunic over narrow satin pants came on to the bandstand and spoke into the mike in an unmistakeable voice, 'And now friends, let's wish D'Arcy Sheridan, our Sweet Sixteen girl, the happiest of birthdays!'

With this, the orchestra began its medley of sixteen tunes all pertaining to a sixteenth birthday, accompanied by Judy Garland on the vocals, beginning with 'Sixteen Reasons Why I Love You' while D'Arcy stood awe-struck. It was Dorothy from the Land of Oz who had travelled through the sky to wish her a happy birthday in the very nicest way.

D'Arcy ran over to her father to take his arm and snuggle up to him. 'Oh thank you, Daddy for getting Dorothy . . . Judy . . . to come to my party. I didn't know you knew her.'

'I don't. She came as a favour to an old friend. You might say she's a friend of a friend.'

'Well now she's our friend too, isn't she? And Mummy never even let on she knew Judy was coming!'

D'Arcy turned around to look for her mother. At first she couldn't find her but then she did . . . in the far entrance at the other end of the room. Her mother's back was to her, stiffly erect as she conversed with a stately woman gowned in black. And next to her in a white dinner jacket was easily the most beautiful young man D'Arcy had ever seen!

'Daddy!' D'Arcy pulled at her father's arm.

'Hush, honey! Where are your manners? Judy's still singing to you.'

'I just wanted to know who it is Mummy's talking to,' she whispered. 'It's a lady with the handsomest boy I've ever laid my little old eyes on. . . .'

Then Bill turned to look, his face growing pale beneath his tan. 'That's no lady, honey, that's your cousin Judith.'

'So that boy's my cousin Rud?'

'Yes, I'd say so,' Bill said, running his tongue over dry lips. 'That young man is sure to be your cousin Rud.'

'Well, I do declare! I had no idea he was *that* goodlookin'!'

'Neither did I,' Bill mumbled. 'Neither did I. . . .'

25

3.

Francesca plucked a glass of champagne off the passing butler's silver tray. She needed it!

She felt that she was being faultlessly polite . . . a hostess talking to a guest she barely knew. Judith, for her part, was being coldly formal but then, she'd always been that way with the Collings sisters, her aunts Francesca and Carlotta, even when they'd all been girls, all practically the same age. She had never let her open hatred shine through.

They chatted idly, party chatter between two strangers, while Rud smiled at them both. He was friendly enough, Francesca decided, and seemed genuinely interested in everything – in her, in the activity going on all around them. Judith had changed quite a bit, she thought, even as she talked – a skill she'd developed through the years as a politician's wife, carrying on a conversation while her mind clicked on. Judith, who'd always been more ugly duckling than not, had emerged into, if not a beautiful swan, then at least an attractive one.

The once drab pale hair was now a silvery blond, fashionably arranged in a bouffant style. And the body which had once been lumpy and dumpy and flat in the wrong places, was now quite shapely as if it had been pounded and pummelled, exercised and dieted into submission. And what about those breasts? Francesca speculated. Judith must have had an augmentation. Not that that was so shocking or unusual, *but Judith?* Sour, dour Judith who had looked down her supercilious nose at that sort of thing? And speaking of noses, what about that nose? Judith had always been a little long in that department. The nose had definitely been bobbed. And the chin! There was definitely more chin now than when Judith had started out.

Who would guess to look at Judith now that she'd ever been anything but glamorous? Francesca marvelled. Clever, yes. Clever enough that, plain and only nineteen, she'd managed to snag one of the richest men in the country! But she'd been widowed for eighteen years. When had she glamorized herself and for whom? Was there a man in her life or was there only her son? Was it he for whom she was wearing coquettish black lace with tier upon tier of ruffle?

Francesca drained the last drop of champagne and Rud, gently removing the glass from her hand and flashing perfect white teeth, said, 'Here, Aunt Francesca. Let me get you a refill.'

He was back in half a minute with a sparkling flute for Francesca and one for Judith. 'Madame,' he presented it to his mother, bowing gracefully from the hips. 'But I warn you, Judith. I will not have you getting tipsy on me,' he chided, stroking her arm.

So courtly, Francesca thought. More than courtly. It was almost as if he was flirting with his mother, and she, glowing only when she looked at him, was obviously relishing it.

Outside of the superficial colouring of blue eyes and blond hair, Rud was nothing like Judith. *He*, unlike his mother, had definitely been born beautiful. He was most definitely a charmer, Francesca reflected, and charm had never been Judith's strong suit. In fact, she decided, there was absolutely nothing wrong with this boy. He was stunningly good-looking and very, very sexy.

26

Even she, who had never felt the pull of sexual appeal from any man other than Bill, could feel it so powerfully, she could almost touch it. His manners were impeccable. As for his smile – glorious was the word.

Still there was something about him that disturbed her. She couldn't quite put her finger on it. Maybe it was that he was too charming, too good-looking, too sexy.

She was running out of easy conversation. 'Well, it's really good to see that you're looking so well, Judith,' she said, commenting for the first time on her niece's appearance. 'Marvellous!'

'Well, it's good to see that you're *doing* so well, Francesca,' Judith came back at her, indicating the opulence of their surroundings with a significant tilt of the head. 'Who would have guessed that Bill Sheridan, that poor struggling congressman, would come this far?' Her lip curled in a smile. *Or is it more of a sneer?* Francesca decided that it was and she felt the muscles of her lower face tense as she gritted her teeth. 'Who? *I* did. Always.'

Stung, she was tempted to say more but this was not the time, she told herself. And as Bill had said, they were supposed to forget the past, old crimes, old grudges. Still he hadn't told her *how* to do that. It was difficult . . . very difficult . . . maybe *too* difficult to forget that it was Judith who had chased them out of the state they had called home.

All she could do was to spend as little time alone with Judith as possible. But again she asked herself why Judith had come? It was beyond her. Was it only to fence with her, to make her pointed, barbed remarks? And had Bill invited Judith just to show her how far indeed he had come? *Hey, Judy, look at me now! Look at my powerful guests, my magnificent home, my kingdom where I reign supreme. . . .*

No, that was too simple and Bill was never simplistic. Her original theory had to be the right one. Bill had invited Judith here to pay her back in some way. And that could have deadly repercussions. Judith herself was a master at the game of tit for tat.

Rud broke into the frigid silence with, 'It's just so terrific being here, Aunt Francesca. I can't wait to meet Uncle Bill and the birthday girl. But if she's anywhere as lovely as her mother, then we're all in trouble.' He smiled deeply into Francesca's eyes with his own – incredible violet-blue eyes fringed with thick, sooty lashes, as long as any girl would hope for. . . .

Judith was still the bitch, Francesca thought, but her son was absolutely devastating and she wouldn't be the least surprised if, indeed, they were *all* in deep trouble. D'Arcy was bound to be infatuated with Rud Stanton and she felt sorry for *any* girl who came near grizzly Judith's prize cub.

Oh, how she dreaded the week to come. . . .

'Now,' Judy Garland cried into the mike, 'everybody dance!'

While Bill ached to go over to where Frankie stood with Judith and her son, he had no choice but to hold out his arms to D'Arcy since the orchestra was playing *Daddy's Little Girl*. But then when he saw the President claim Francesca for this dance, leaving Rud and Judith standing by themselves, he couldn't contain himself. This was his chance to see them alone and he broke away from D'Arcy. 'Sorry, Princess, but I have to go welcome our new arrivals.'

'I'll go with you!'

'No!' he said brusquely but realizing how that sounded, he quickly said, 'I want *you*, Miss Sheridan, to find Miss Garland this minute and thank her. Your mother will be very unhappy if you don't do the right thing. You'll meet your cousins later. Now, go on,' he prodded her, patting her on the rump, and set off across the room before D'Arcy could protest further.

He'd been waiting for this moment for a long, long time.

As D'Arcy looked around trying to spot Judy Garland, her best friend, Muffy Galuten, came rushing over in a state of near-hysteria. 'D'Arcy, do you realize who's here at your very own party?'

'Yes, I know,' D'Arcy said, bored. 'The President . . .'

'I don't mean *him*, you ass. I mean, Rock Hudson!'

D'Arcy smiled in superior fashion. 'But of course, Muffy darling. Weren't you here when Rock first came in and *kissed* me?'

'He kissed you? Rock Hudson kissed you?'

'Well, naturally, he kissed me. Dear Rock . . . he *is* an old friend. And now that you mention it, I should go and talk to him. When he arrived I was far too busy. . . .'

'He's over there,' Muffy pointed. 'Talking to Judy Garland.'

'Well, good. I have to go over and thank her anyway. It *was* so sweet of her to come, don't you think? So if you'll excuse me, I'll just mosey on over. . . .'

'I'll just mosey on over with you—'

'Oh no you won't! I promised my mother that none of my dopey friends would make any of our celebrated guests uncomfortable with their infantile goofy attentions. So, just cool it, Muffy.'

'You know something, D'Arcy Sheridan? You suck, even if it is your birthday!'

D'Arcy shrugged and picked up her hooped skirt in two hands to work her way more expeditiously among the tables ringing the dance floor. Then she spotted Abigail pressed against the wall and she sighed in exasperation. *Someone has to do something about that girl!* She beckoned to Abigail who, thrilled to be rediscovered, came racing over.

'What are you trying to do, Abby? Hold up that wall all by yourself? Why aren't you dancing?'

Abigail flushed. 'Nobody asked me.'

'Don't be an asshole, Abby. You can't wait to be asked. That way you get left behind. You just have to put your little old foot forward and grab at the nearest boy! Well, now you might as well just come along with me and meet Judy Garland and Rock Hudson.'

She waited for a reaction from Abby at the mention of Rock Hudson's name but there wasn't any. Instead Abigail gestured. 'Your father's over there. Talking to Judith Stanton and her son Rudyard. Aren't we going over there to meet them?'

D'Arcy laughed knowingly. 'So you *have* noticed our cousin Rud, have you? He's something else, isn't he? But my father says I have to go thank Judy Garland first and then we'll go over to say hello to them.' Then she looked at Abigail curiously. 'You recognized Judith and Rud straight off? I thought you said you never met them. How did you know who they were?'

'Well, they *are* from Boston and I've seen Judith's picture in the papers lots of times. She's a very important person. They say she's one of the richest women in the United States. And I have seen Rud a couple of times. Once at a concert and once in Harvard Square.'

'Then you *did* meet him?'

'No. I *saw* him. I didn't *meet* him.'

'You mean to say you saw that gorgeous Rud who *is* your second cousin and you didn't go up and introduce yourself?'

'No,' Abigail admitted.

'For God's sake, why not?'

Abigail lifted her thin shoulders helplessly. 'I don't know. I guess I was afraid to—He's so—I don't know. Glamorous! And he was with a bunch of people. College kids, I guess. And I felt foolish, you know?'

No, D'Arcy didn't know. All she knew was that Rud was absolutely the cutest boy she'd ever seen and there was nothing like taking a bull by the horns. She shook a finger at Abigail. 'You're really going to have to change your style, Abby Truesdale. If you don't learn to be more aggressive, you're going to be left behind. And then how will you have any fun? Tell me that!'

Abigail ducked her head, but did not mind at all being scolded by D'Arcy. She figured that if D'Arcy scolded her, it meant she cared.

Bill was effusive and Judith cool but Rud was warm and forthcoming, shaking Bill's hand firmly. Good handshake, Bill thought. Handshaking was an art.

'You're looking mighty pretty, Judith,' Bill said, affecting his down-home cordiality.

Judith laughed mockingly. 'How would you have me respond to that? Shall I flutter my lashes and say, "Thank you kindly, sir!"?'

Bill felt himself flush. His meaningless remark had been a mistake. Pretty was hardly the word for Judith. He knew it and she knew it. Not even with all the changes that had been made in her appearance. She was now what people would call a handsome woman.

'Well, Judith, it's been a long time,' he ventured again while he tried to size the boy up. But Judith chose once again to pick up on his remark, to spar.

A little superior smile. 'Some might say time is relative. . . .'

He was annoyed. 'I guess what counts is what use one puts one's time to—'

'Ah. I suppose one might say you've put your time to good use. Yes, a most impressive roster of guests,' she allowed. 'You *have* made some friends in high places.' A condescending smile.

He shrugged modestly. 'You know how it is. Everyone looks for an opportunity to come down here. Even Ponce de Leon's wife said, "Don't think you're going to Florida without me, Ponce!"'

It wasn't much of a joke and Judith didn't even crack a small smile but Rud laughed heartily.

And what a wonderful laugh it is! The old master, Franklin Roosevelt, laughed that way – head thrown back, a wide flash of teeth. Very effective.

'Well, *I'm* glad I came to Florida, sir.' Rud reached out and touched Bill lightly on the shoulder. 'I've followed your career and have always admired you. It's great to meet you at last, Uncle Bill.'

Bill glowed, pleased with Rud's obvious sincerity. And he liked the way the boy had touched him on the shoulder. That was really wonderful.

Then Judith smiled that patronizing smile Bill remembered so well. 'My son has such beautiful manners. No matter what the situation or the person, he somehow always manages to say the right thing.'

Whether or not he means it. . . . That's what she's implying. With a few words, she had managed to make both Rud and him appear foolish. Bill felt himself grow hot with anger and saw Rud blush in embarrassment. Or was it anger too?

He felt an overwhelming urge to seize the boy and hug him to his breast, to tell him that it didn't matter what Judith said, but he knew he couldn't afford to do that, or let his anger show. All he could do right now was continue the idle chatter and wait until he got Judith alone.

The boy's *really* the pretty one, Bill reflected. The shock of yellow hair rising from the clear brow, the perfectly modelled nose, the straight dark eyebrows over the nearly purple eyes, and those lashes! Definitely a pretty boy and that could serve against him. Nobody took a pretty boy seriously. A pretty boy was either a movie star, a playboy or gay. But Rud was young. Only eighteen. He had plenty of time to outgrow that look. What was pretty now could be masculine dynamite in a few years, and who knew better than he himself how the average female voter was a sucker for a virile, ruggedly handsome candidate?

His physique was just about perfect. Broad shoulders, small waist, narrow hips . . . the long length of him. Rud was already just an inch or so shorter than his own six-feet-four. He might very well grow another couple of inches, and there was nothing the American public admired more than a really tall man. Height inspired confidence.

And his manner was special too, Bill thought. The way he carries himself . . . like a proud young lion. At ease with himself. Assured, the way men born to money usually were. And he seemed confident that people would like him. Ah . . . *that* was the key to popularity, knowing beforehand that you would be.

And Bill liked the way the boy spoke. Without hesitation. And the voice was fine and deep and resonant.

He was almost too good to be true. If only Judith didn't ruin him, over-refine him or cut all the guts out of him with her exquisitely sharpened manipulative knife.

Bill thought about that time back then – how precise her instructions had been, she knowing exactly what she wanted and how she wanted it delivered. . . .

Here . . . there . . . softer . . . harder . . . faster . . . now!

D'Arcy broke into Judy and Rock's conversation breathlessly, thanking the actress for the present of her singing and then without a pause, she told the actor how much she adored him in *Lover Come Back* with darling Doris Day. 'And needless to say, I loved you too, Miss Garland, in—Oh, darn, what's the name of that depressing movie I saw you in?'

30

Judy laughed and Abigail blurted out, '*Judgement at Nuremburg*. I thought you were wonderful in it too, Miss Garland.' Then, lowering her eyes, unable to bring herself to look directly at Rock Hudson, she murmured, 'You too, Mr Hudson. I mean in *Lover Come Back*.'

'Yes, thank you,' Rock smiled at her. 'I knew exactly which picture you meant.'

'Oh, my goodness,' D'Arcy cried out. 'My mother would absolutely kill me for so forgetting my manners. I haven't properly introduced you all. Mr Hudson, Miss Garland, may I present my cousin, my Aunt Carlotta's daughter?'

'Carlotta's daughter!' Judy said enthusiastically. 'I always wanted to meet you, Jade. After all, how many girls have a Vegas hotel named after them?' Judy laughed.

'Oh no!' Abigail blushed. 'I'm Abigail . . . Abigail Truesdale. I come from Boston, not California,' she said, sounding as if she were apologizing for not being Jade. 'Jade's my sister . . . my half-sister.'

'Really?' Judy was a little embarrassed. 'I had no idea . . . I didn't know Carlotta had another daughter. I—'

The colour drained from Abigail's face and she sucked in her breath, afraid she might cry. If people in Hollywood . . . people who had known her mother, didn't even know she had two daughters it meant just one thing – her mother, the person she had thought about practically every day of her life, hadn't even thought enough of her to mention her to her friends. It was true what her father and then Aunt Selena and Uncle George had told her – her mother had forgotten she'd ever existed!

Seeing the look of despair on the girl's face and hearing D'Arcy explain, 'Abby never met her mother,' Judy guessed that she'd said the wrong thing and looked to Rock for help, and then he quickly jumped in with, 'But I remember having a conversation with Carlotta when she talked about you a lot, Abigail. She said some wonderful things about you. In fact, she talked about how she planned on you coming out to California . . . how she wanted you to live with her. . . .' He shook his head as if remembering fondly. 'Carlotta! What a great gal! You must be very proud. . . .'

'Yes. . . .' Abigail looked down at her new pink high heels which almost matched her dress, and then up again. All three of them – D'Arcy, Judy and Rock – were gazing at her sympathetically and she realized that Rock was lying to her. Her mother had never mentioned her to him. He'd made the whole thing up. He'd just been trying to be nice, kind. He had told her a nice white lie.

But she could hardly call him a liar to his face, especially since he had been trying to be nice. 'My sister Jade is coming tonight,' she said instead. 'I've never met her either.'

'Isn't it weird?' D'Arcy laughed. 'I guess you might say we're a peculiar kind of family. I never saw Abby before tonight and neither had my mother and father. And the same goes for Jade. None of us have ever met her.'

'Well then,' Judy said, 'I guess tonight is a special night for all of you, isn't it?'

It would be if Jade ever got here, Abigail thought. Maybe then she might even find out the truth about her mother — why she never had even received so much as a Christmas card from her.

Maybe she and Jade would be good friends, would talk for hours about everything — their mother, even life! That was what sisters were supposed to be — best friends. And maybe they could make up for all the years . . . all the days of their lives they'd been apart. Maybe Jade longed to see her as much as she longed to see Jade . . . almost as much as she had yearned for Carlotta. . . .

But then, Abigail was immediately besieged by doubt. Suppose Jade was disappointed in her? Didn't like her one little bit? Just like Aunt Francesca. Before she'd arrived she'd been so sure Francesca would take her in her arms, loving her just a little . . . *almost* like a mother. But Francesca hadn't. In fact, Aunt Francesca had treated her like a stranger! But why? Why had Francesca been so cold to her?

Oh, please God, just let Jade get here! And let her, at least, love me!

'Football?' Bill asked after Rud told him that he'd completed his freshman year at Harvard. 'You *are* on the team?' There was nothing like football for a young man to cut his competitive teeth on. Rud *had* to get his letter in football.

For a moment Rud's eyes lit up but then the light went out and he shook his head regretfully. 'I was on the Freshman Squad last year but this coming year I'll be on the sailing team instead.'

Sailing team? What the hell kind of a sport was that for a leader of men?

Judith laughed. 'I . . . we, that is . . . decided we really didn't want to risk that nose on the football field. And what if he injured a knee or something, perhaps permanently? I don't intend for Rud to be anything less than perfect when he takes office as President of the United States.' She made a joke of it. 'Isn't that so, Rud darling?'

She kept her eyes fastened on Rud's face awaiting an answer. For a fragmented second Bill could see Rud's eyelids flutter almost imperceptibly but then he composed his features and smiled affectionately at his mother. 'Whatever you say, Judy. . . .' He winked at Bill.

So, Bill thought, that's the way it is. Judith's the same manipulative bitch and Rud's the charmingly obliging dutiful son. But at least one thing seemed clear — he and Judith were thinking on the same lines and that, at least, was encouraging. Still, there remained a lot of wooing to be done and it wasn't going to go easy. . . .

D'Arcy tucked Abigail's arm under hers. 'Now you must excuse us,' she told Judy and Rock. 'We're off to see the wizards, *our* wonderful wizards of Oz,' she giggled, pleased with her apt reference to Judy's famed role as Dorothy. 'Our wizards are our cousins, Judith and Rud Stanton, whom we've never met before either. 'Look,' she pointed. 'There they are, talking to Ted Kennedy. Judith and gorgeous Rud. Don't you all think he's gorgeous, Judy? Why, he's *almost* as gorgeous as old Rock here, isn't he?'

Abigail gasped at D'Arcy's incredible audacity but Rock Hudson threw back his head and roared.

'Cousin Rud!' D'Arcy threw her arms around the startled Rud and covered his face with kisses while Abigail looked on enviously. It wasn't the embrace so much as D'Arcy's total insouciance. D'Arcy wasn't struck speechless by Rud's dazzling presence, or even by Judith's imposing one.

'You're sweet too, Judith,' D'Arcy threw over her shoulder, wasting no time pulling the bemused Rud out on the dance floor. The rock group, The Beached Bums, was pounding out *Mashed Potato Time*, and she hadn't put in any dancing time yet. 'You *do* do the Mashed Potato way up there in Boston, don't you?' Her body began to move in a manner as provocative as her tone.

Rud grinned and thrust a hip forward. As a matter of fact he had never danced the Mashed Potato before but it was of no concern – if you did one dance you'd done them all. But girls were another story. *They* were all different and he'd been finding that out every chance he got ever since he turned fourteen. That is, whenever he was able to get out from under his mother's highly critical eye. *That* was the real challenge, not the girls. The girls were easy. As for his cute young cousin D'Arcy, she was a live wire, her dress was cut extremely low and as far as he could see, which was quite a lot, she had superb tits which was always nice.

Abigail, left alone with Judith, anxiously wondered what they'd talk about. She wished Judith would say something first but Judith was smiling faintly, appeared to be studying her. *She must think I'm a dope.* Her hands grew damp from nervous perspiration.

What an awful dress, Judith mused. Dowdy, and a size too large besides. Well, it was no wonder, what with Selena and George in charge of the girl ever since that fool, Whit Truesdale, bowed out of the picture. The Truesdales weren't only unbelievably stuffy, but the kind of 'first family' Bostonians who were infamous for keeping tight purse strings. George and Selena probably still had that first dollar George's Plymouth Rock ancestors had earned, multiplied at least a few million times over.

Unable to bear the silence, Abigail said the first thing that came into her head. 'D'Arcy has the most wonderful personality, doesn't she?'

Judith cocked an amused eyebrow. 'Does she?'

'Oh, I think so! I most definitely do!'

'Then I'm sure you're right. But can you tell me why she's dressed in costume?' Judith asked even though she thought she knew the answer. It was because Francesca's daughter was undoubtedly as tacky as Carlotta's daughter was mousy.

Abigail was bewildered. She hadn't realized that D'Arcy's beautiful dress was a costume but Judith Stanton must know. 'I'm . . . I . . . I don't know. . . .'

'Oh well, it doesn't really matter.' It *was* hard to believe that this timorous child was Carlotta's daughter. Apparently sometimes the apple did fall far from the tree. 'Tell me something about yourself, Abby.'

Abigail gulped. What could she possibly say about herself that would interest Judith Stanton who was so . . . so grand, even if Aunt Selena did call her an opportunist. Besides, Aunt Selena called anyone who married into great wealth an opportunist.

'Well, I go to the Beacon Hill School for Girls,' she finally said. 'I graduate next June and I hope to go on to Radcliffe. I'd like to major in English literature. I love English literature,' she confided shyly. But then she was embarrassed. 'I'm afraid that's not very interesting.'

'Oh but I'm very interested. I enjoy English literature myself.'

'You do?' Abigail raised her eyes in gratitude to find that Judith was smiling at her encouragingly . . . warmly, as if she were really, genuinely interested, and then Abigail's spirits lifted . . . *soared!*

Francesca was on her fourth glass of champagne. Only half concentrating, she checked the long buffet table in the dining-room to make sure the table looked as attractive now as it had in the beginning of the evening, with all the platters, bowls and silver trays fully replenished. Yes, it still appeared pristine as if no hungry horde had already partaken of its bounty – oysters on the half-shell, the caviar still in their cans buried in crushed ice, whole cold salmons, cracked crab, huge Florida crayfish, the giant pink prawns from the Gulf, the great ribs of beef and the turkeys from their own smokehouse, standing ready to be sliced to order by the waiters in their tall chef's hats.

She moved a platter of sugar-frosted grapes an inch to the right. The truth was she was reluctant to go back into the ballroom. She wanted to stay as far away as was possible from Abby who looked at her with those imploring puppy-dog eyes every time they were near each other, and she wanted to avoid Judith since it took so much effort to be civil to her.

For the time being, Judith was occupied with people she knew from Newport, sitting at a table with these so-called friends – the titled and the rich and those who lived off the rich by using their wits . . . like Elsa Maxwell who was one of the many who had not been invited but brought by someone else. In Elsa's case, it was one of the Vanderbilts, a Palm Beach regular. And sitting at the same table were the Duke and Duchess of Windsor who had come with Marjorie Post Davies May at whose magnificent Mar-a-Lago the Windsors were staying. ' . . . a brief layover on our way to New York,' Wallis had explained. According to Elsa, who was a great chum of Wallis's, the Windsors' presence officially stamped the Sheridans' party an unqualified success. 'Wherever the Duke and Duchess go, so goes the world. . . .'

'Really?' Francesca had enthused, trying not to laugh at the unattractive Elsa. (Alabama's darling, Tallulah Bankhead, passing by at the moment, had drawled in an aside in her wonderful whisky voice, 'Just another pretty face,' which hadn't helped.)

But Elsa wasn't far off the mark, Francesca mused. What excitement when the Windsors made their entrance, Wallis in a white silk peau-de-soie gown with a sweeping matching coat and her fantastic jewels and the Duke in white-tie tagging after her. They had generated *almost* as much excitement as Elizabeth Taylor, she in low-cut red silk peau-de-soie and *her* fantastic jewels plus her magnificent breasts, which the Duchess couldn't match for beans.

Elizabeth had won hands down with D'Arcy who had come racing over to report to Francesca that Liz was supposedly shedding husband Eddie for Richard Burton with whom she'd been having a hot and heavy during the filming of *Cleopatra*. 'It would have been so neat if she'd brought Richard with her! He's so groovy! But I'm not complaining. I'm just thrilled to have Liz at my party with or without Richard. And I'm thrilled that out of the five biggest box-office draws announced for 1961, two of them are here – Rock and Liz! Two out of five isn't bad!'

Francesca laughed. 'We did all right without Elvis then, didn't we?'

'Elvis!' D'Arcy sniffed. 'On that list of box-office draws, he was only *ten*!'

*

Francesca took a long sip of champagne, hiding behind a cluster of potted palms in a corner for a few minutes of solitude. She really couldn't blame D'Arcy for being impressed by movie stars and their glamour – she was only sixteen. But the others, those supposedly mature and sophisticated. What was their excuse? Here they were at a party with some of the most influential people in the country, with people who had enduring achievements to their credit and they were more impressed with Edward and Wallis, Liz and Rock and Judy, than with even the President or John Glenn. . . . At least those in the entertainment field made a contribution by the pleasure they afforded but what was the Windsors' great achievement? That they went to the world's best parties?

A faint flower-perfume breeze wafted in through the open French doors and Francesca walked out on to the terrace overlooking the sea. Oh, it *was* a gorgeous night. It was hard to believe that there might be a hurricane brewing out there, as a recent report stated. Perhaps the storm activity would blow itself out before it came anywhere near the Florida coast.

Francesca giggled, a bit giddy from the champagne. There might be a bigger storm brewing *inside* – maybe even *storms*, considering the volatility of certain guests and certain feuds that were already part of the public domain. It seemed prominent people didn't mind making their feuds public, which seemed like such a courageous thing to do. She had to admire them for that. They were so unlike herself who carried on her own feud in the secrecy of her soul. That was a sobering thought and Francesca lost all her pleasant champagne giddiness, and she thought, what a waste of time and good champagne. . . .

Well, drunk or sober, it was time for her to go back into the fray. After all, how long could she hide out? She took a last gulp of wine and marched bravely back into the ballroom.

Nelson Rockefeller was twirling Liz around and she appeared to be having fun. Lucky Liz! Francesca thought. She probably *always* has fun.

Then the President cut in on Nelson and danced off with Liz while the orchestra played *What Kind of Fool Am I?* Well, why not? Liz Taylor was one of the most beautiful women in the world and both Nelson and Jack were no sluggards when it came to recognizing a prize.

She glanced at her wristwatch again. Who would have thought the presidential party would linger this long? She'd expected they'd stay an hour or so and then would make their goodbyes. Well, at least *someone* was having a good time tonight.

She spotted Bill dancing with Judith. Not that she was counting but it *was* the third time and while she really didn't mind Bill was the host and should have been spreading his favours around. Why wasn't he dancing with Jackie or Rose or Liz, for God's sake?

Suddenly she felt a chill. The damn air conditioning! No matter what you did – turned it up, or down – it was never just right!

She saw Rud within a circle of admiring girls while D'Arcy stood next to him holding his arm possessively as if to proclaim: 'This is my cousin and this is my party, so hands off!' On D'Arcy's other side Abigail was hanging on to D'Arcy's hand as if for dear life. What was *she* proclaiming? As for Rud, he seemed to be having the time of his life even though there wasn't a girl there over sixteen and most likely, he was used to headier fare. It was as if without his mother standing by, controlling him, Rud had shed years of sophistication.

Lyndon grabbed Francesca around the waist from behind and whispered in her ear,'This is your Vice-President speaking, honey, and he wants a dance!'

Laughing, she begged off, said she had to mix . . . circulate. 'You know how it is, L.B. A political party doesn't mean Democrat or Republican, it means the three Cs – caviar, champagne and conversation.'

'Doggone! I thought you were going to say chasin', cuddlin' and com—'

Not wishing to be disrespectful to the office of the Vice-Presidency, Francesca cut him off with a grin and a wave of the hand as she moved away.

She saw Bill whispering in Judith's ear and it appeared most persuasive, for Judith was actually smiling. An ambiguous smile, half-amused and half-what? Francesca wasn't sure.

It seemed like the party was far from over. But if nothing else, she'd been spared the sight of Jade Boudin. Surely it was too late for her to show up anymore. . . .

They were posing for a family picture at the request of the photographer from *Look* – Francesca and Bill, Judith and Rud, D'Arcy and Abigail, when suddenly there was a hush in the huge room usurping the enormous din, followed by an excited squall of rising voices. A woman screamed out: 'Oh, my God! It's Carlotta Boudin!'

Then another voice responded: 'But it can't be! Carlotta Boudin's been dead for years!'

No, not years. Carlotta hadn't made movies in years, but dead? Three years . . . just three years. . . . Francesca knew that as well as she knew that this was the year 1962. She knew because she'd counted off every day since that fateful afternoon that the legendary Carlotta had ceased to be. . . .

Then, acting almost in concert all six – Francesca and Bill, Judith and Rud, D'Arcy and Abigail – turned towards the landing leading up from the reception hall. There, poised like an extraordinarily lovely butterfly stilled in flight, was a vision in an emerald-green satin gown, dripping white furs and blazing jewels. And then the vision tossed her head and a long sweep of red gold hair fell forward, seductively covering half her face. It was as if a scene from Carlotta's last and most successful triumph, *Born to be Bad*, was being enacted before their very eyes!

Then Francesca's heart pounded out a message: *Carlotta lives!*

'Great balls of fire!' D'Arcy's voice rang out. 'That must be Jade!'

36

'Wow!' Rud declared inelegantly and then, almost inaudibly, 'She's got to be the most beautiful girl in the world!'

He was talking to himself but Judith heard, frowned, and turned to glance at him sharply.

'Oh, it's Jade! Jade!' Abigail rushed forward, for once heedlessly pushing past everyone to get to her sister.

Francesca instinctively looked at Bill. He was pale, speechless, as if he'd seen a ghost.

And then D'Arcy's voice pealed out again. 'And I do declare! Look who's there! Right behind Jade! If my little old eyes don't deceive me, I believe it's Captain Rhett Butler who's come to my party!'

Francesca tore her eyes away from Bill. What nonsense of D'Arcy's was this? And then she saw to whom her daughter was referring – a slender figure as graceful in his formal attire as a professional tango dancer, with gleaming black hair and a trim black moustache, white teeth flashing! *Trace Boudin!*

How dare he?

Especially this evening with the house full of elected officials including the President himself, and the small army of reporters and photographers. Forgetting all the rest of it, Trace Boudin, professional gambler and known associate of mobsters, was a particular embarrassment tonight.

She heard Bill muttering, 'The bastard! The son-of-a-bitch!' He was clenching and unclenching his fists. It was her old nightmare being relived. The four of them together again! She, Bill, Trace and Carlotta, reincarnated in the body of her daughter, Jade. . . . And hovering over all, Judith!

Silently, as if turned to stone, Francesca, Bill and Judith looked on as Abigail hurled herself at Jade who was as emotionally responsive as her sister. Jade rained kisses on Abigail's face, pressing her convulsively to her, as Trace Boudin moved forward and kissed both his daughter and Carlotta's daughter by her first marriage.

Then, unable to contain herself a moment longer, D'Arcy reached out for Rud's hand. 'Come on, cuz, let's go say hello to our gorgeous California cousin!'

'We don't have to stand for this!' Francesca told Bill. 'We can ask that he leave! We can have him thrown out!'

'No! We don't want a scene! Besides, we have to find out why he's come.'

Judith didn't move a muscle although she thought she knew why Boudin had come . . . or at least, one of the reasons. Perhaps there were more. Boudin was the kind of man who didn't put all his eggs in one basket. But who knew? Maybe he was desperate.

Tallulah of Alabama, New York and Hollywood, and drunk to the gills, waltzed by unsteadily. In a loud stage whisper, she said, 'Watch out for Boudin, Frankie. He's excruciatingly attractive but take it from me, he's bad medicine!'

As if this were news to Francesca!

Jade, green eyes glittering, red lips moist, delicately placed her hands to

Francesca's cheeks, the long, fuschia-tipped fingers barely touching. Still, Francesca felt as if they were digging into her skin. 'Dear Aunt Frankie! It's so wonderful to see you in the flesh at long last. I just can't tell you.'

The voice too was Carlotta's, low and throaty.

'It's wonderful to see you, Jade,' Francesca said politely.

'Mother talked so much about you. She told me how close you two were . . . how you shared everything, even your secrets.'

Was there a stress on the word 'secrets'? Francesca wondered, or was she just imagining it? Was she just being foolish? Probably. What she had to do was act in normal, aunt-like fashion and say what any aunt would say on such an occasion. And she had to force herself to remember that this replica of her sister was *not* Carlotta but just a fifteen-year-old girl.

'I've thought about you often, Jade.'

Jade laughed that tinkling laugh, the sound fine crystal made when one flicked it. Carlotta's laugh. 'Oh, I'm sure you have, Aunt Frankie. And I about you. Often. Especially when I read through Mother's diaries.'

'Diaries? Oh, of course. Carlotta and I both kept diaries when we were children. I had no idea she saved hers.'

'Oh yes, she saved hers. But these aren't childhood diaries. They're most definitely *grown-up* diaries. From the time she was, oh . . . eighteen, maybe, till the—Until the very day she died.' Jade smiled at her aunt.

She's talking about her mother dying but her lips are smiling and her eyes are glistening, Francesca thought, shocked. *Is it malice?*

'I read them often. Over and over again. They're so revealing! All those secrets!'

There was that word again. And Jade was still smiling at her with those pretty, white teeth, the tongue tiptoeing over the lips as if she were relishing every word. . . .

No, I'm not just imagining things. She's definitely trying to upset me. She is being malicious!

Carlotta had never been that, Francesca thought. Not malicious. Many other things – self-centred, even selfish, but not intentionally malicious. Mostly she'd been careless . . . careless of other people's feelings, of other people's hearts.

Now she knew that her instincts had been right when she never wanted to see this girl, and she was glad to be rid of some of the guilt she had carried about that. About not going to see her when Carlotta had died. Maybe she'd been wrong about not seeing Abigail but certainly not about this one with her talk of diaries and secrets. But what did she care about Jade's insinuations? It was she, Francesca, who had been the victim and Carlotta the perpetrator. . . .

'I've brought them with me . . . Mother's diaries.'

Francesca was cool. 'Really? Why did you do that?'

'I thought it might be fun if you and I read them together. You and I and maybe D'Arcy. . . .'

'Why would D'Arcy want to read your mother's diaries?'

'Because they're so interesting . . . *so* revealing.'

What's she getting at? 'I would think Abigail rather than D'Arcy certainly,'

Francesca said and saw Jade's composure falter, the façade of her sophistication slip for a moment, and for that moment she looked like what she was, only a teenager.

'Abigail?' Jade said uncertainly. 'No, I don't think—'

The last thing in the world she wanted was for Abigail to read the diaries. She hadn't come here to upset her sister, to destroy whatever happy images Abigail managed to have of their mother. Her purpose in coming, above and beyond the primary one of settling certain scores, was to shower her sister with affection, to bring her a message of love from the grave.

She tried to settle her expression back into one of confidence, conscious that Francesca was watching her closely. 'Perhaps we won't show the diaries to either D'Arcy or Abigail. Maybe we'll just keep them between us.'

After all, Jade thought, I have nothing against D'Arcy. She's no more guilty than I or Abby, or Rud for that matter. . . . If she could, she'd protect them from the truth. She'd get the rest of them but she'd try and spare them – the children of the guilty.

'I think you'll find them fascinating. There's so much in them about you and Uncle Bill and—'

'No, thank you, Jade,' Francesca said coldly. 'I don't care to read your mother's diaries. And frankly, I don't think you should either. Diaries are personal and not meant for anyone's eyes other than the person's who wrote in them.'

Jade shook her head emphatically and the full wave of bright red hair fell across her face and again the familiar gesture brought a twinge of pain to Francesca. 'No. My mother *wanted* me to read her diaries. She left them to me specifically in her will along with her red Rolls-Royce and her dresses and furs and her jewellery collection.' Her fingers went to the diamond and emerald necklace at her throat as if to make sure that it was still there. 'They're my legacy. All that's left of Carlotta. I don't want to forget. I want to remember, always.'

Remember and make everyone pay for what they did, including you, Sweet Auntie.

'It's one thing to remember, another to dwell unhealthily on the past.' Francesca made no effort to keep the frigidity out of her voice.

'But Aunt Frankie, how can I face the present and look forward to the future unless I deal with the past first?' Jade asked ingenuously. 'Maybe you can tell me how. Mother always said you were so smart . . . Frankie, her very wise older sister who was so good to her always . . . who took such good care of her.'

Francesca laughed bitterly. 'Oh, I think Carlotta was very, very good at taking care of herself . . . always.'

Jade's smile faded and she said soberly, 'No, you're wrong, Aunt Frankie. Carlotta wasn't good at that at all. And I think that's what people say about other people – that they're good at taking care of themselves – while at the same time they're betraying them.'

A huge rage consumed Francesca. *How dare she stand here and taunt me with talk of betrayal? I could tell her about betrayal . . . about who betrayed whom!*

Francesca fought for control. She reminded herself how ridiculous it was for her to stand there trading barbs and veiled threats with a child. For that's all Jade was, no matter how malicious or mature she seemed . . . centuries older than any of them, just like all witches. . . . She had to remember, no matter how difficult it was, that this girl was only fifteen and *not* Carlotta. But then, watching her with Bill, Francesca began to forget quickly.

Jade slid pale white arms around Bill's neck, pressing her body insinuatingly against his. And Francesca knew definitely she wasn't imagining this since Bill's manhood was announcing itself indisputably. Not that she was surprised. Anguished, but not surprised. Jade was her mother all over again and how did the expression go? *The flesh remembers.* . . .

It was incredible, Bill thought, finding it difficult to breathe. In all his life he'd never seen a resemblance so startling. And all the little things. . . . Carlotta too had wrapped her arms around his neck, whispering in his ear in her husky, sexy voice. She too had pressed herself against him in just that way. . . . He closed his eyes and could feel the years dropping away. He could remember . . . feel . . . as if it were only yesterday. . . .

'It's no secret how much Mommy adored you, Uncle Bill,' Jade breathed in his ear. 'She always said you were the very best.'

The very best? How did she mean that? Bill made the effort to disengage himself from her and it was damn hard. So hard! How good it would be to forget everything and just go with it – the exquisite headiness, the instinctive response of his body . . . to relive the moment as if there were nothing else in the world but the two of them. . . .

But he couldn't. That was then and this was now and both Judith and Francesca were watching. And there were the children and all his guests, curious about Carlotta Boudin's startlingly beautiful daughter. A man in his position had his priorities. The trick was to keep those priorities in mind at all times. And above all, goddamn it, he *owed* Frankie. He owed it to her to protect her from the truth!

And there was Boudin. He had to keep his eye on Boudin . . . find out what the slimy bastard wanted. He was as slippery as a snake and probably twice as lethal. Oh, he'd warned Carlotta. He had pleaded with her. He had never begged any man for anything, but he had begged Carlotta.

Deliberately he removed his body from Jade's. 'What a great idea it was to bring your dad with you,' he said, testing the waters. 'I'm glad you thought of it.'

Jade blinked and for a second her gaze moved to Trace talking . . . being charming . . . with Abigail, D'Arcy and Rud. Then she smiled beguilingly at Bill again but she wasn't fast enough for in that instant, Bill – an old poker player – recognized the emotion he saw flash across her face. And it wasn't love or anything near it. It was naked hate.

'It wasn't my idea that Daddy come along. It was his. He said it would be so much fun to renew old friendships with you and Aunt Frankie and Cousin Judith.'

'Your dad mentioned Judith, did he?'

'Oh, absolutely. He said he and Judith were old pals. That's nice, isn't it? Everyone old friends. Well, I guess it's time for me to go and make friends with Judith too.'

But even as she turned away her eyes made promises the way Carlotta's always had. 'It's so wonderful that we're going to be here for a whole week. I know we're going to have a marvellous time really getting to know each other.'

Oh yes, Uncle Bill, you and I are really going to get acquainted. We just might get to know each other as well as you and Mother did.

Jade really didn't have anything against Bill. He, she knew, had never hurt Carlotta. But how could she square things with Francesca without involving him?

Jade kissed Judith on the lips, suspecting that Judith would find it distasteful. When Judith grimaced Jade dimpled at her. 'Judy! I may call you that, mayn't I? I know that's what Mother called you—'

When Judith neither confirmed nor denied, Jade went on blithely, 'Well, that's what it said in her diaries anyway. And how crazy she was about you. How you and she shared so many secrets.'

Judith smiled coolly at Jade. Her manner is challenging, she thought. And she's using key words – secrets . . . diaries. Were there diaries? Perhaps. That little fool Carlotta was idiotic enough to keep a diary and the bastard Boudin was stupid enough to let this little baggage get her hands on it. 'Secrets?'

'Oh yes, lots of secrets.'

Judith laughed. Maybe this sly little bitch is working with Boudin, she speculated. It wouldn't surprise her. She'd seen everything and done practically everything herself. Conspiracy, blackmail, bribery . . . she was no stranger to any of it. And when she'd been fifteen herself, she hadn't been too young to scheme and plot. It takes one to know one. But she suspected that Jade had a lot to learn. Did she know that when you played poker for high stakes, you'd better always have an ace in the hole? Like the one she had ready for Boudin if it came to it. And one for this daughter of Carlotta too. She wondered if Jade was any smarter than her mother.

'You're the picture of your mother, aren't you?'

Jade batted her lashes, knowing exactly how beautiful she was. 'That's what they tell me.'

'And you're just playing it to the hilt, aren't you?'

'Why, Cousin Judy, you don't pull your punches, do you?'

'I try not to. When I play I like all the cards on the table.'

'Good. So do I. And I like someone who deals off the top, like you.'

Judith smiled, shook her head. 'I wouldn't go that far, Jade. I'm not at all sure you're going to like me at all.'

'*Au contraire*, Judy. I'm sure I'm going to adore you. I do so admire cleverness and Mother said you were very clever . . . that a person would have to get up really early in the morning to get the best of you. But I expect that I will. Oh, I mean that I'm sure I'm going to love you . . . that we're going to be the best of friends and know everything there is to know about each other. Now will you excuse me? I really must go and get acquainted

41

with Rud and D'Arcy and Abby. I'll tell you a little secret. I've looked forward to meeting everyone but most of all, my sister Abby.'

'Yes, of course. And I was talking to Abby at some length. I like her. A very nice girl, sweet and innocent. I would hate for her to get hurt. She seems very vulnerable. Not at all like you who I suspect can take good care of yourself. Actually, the two of you aren't alike in any way. It's really strange. . . .'

The smile slipped off Jade's face. She was supposed to be baiting Judith, not the other way around. Her composure began to slip. 'What's so strange about that?' she asked defensively. 'We're only half-sisters.'

'Yes, of course you are. But look at her! Such odd colouring!'

'What's so odd about it?' Jade demanded, forgetting that the important thing was to act as if she had the upper hand. 'It looks pretty normal to me.'

'That dark hair and those dark eyes. . . .'

'Not *that* dark. . . .' Jade said inadequately.

'I just can't think of anyone in our family with that colouring. Not a single soul. Everyone blond and blue-eyed, as far as I know. Except for your mother and you. But when we know where *that* colouring came from. *Your* grandmother, Frankie and Carlotta's mother, who only married into the family, had the red hair and green eyes.'

'So what's your point?'

'The point, dear Jade, is that a child takes after either its mother or its father. And all the Truesdales are blond and blue-eyed too. Didn't you know? Now, look over there—' Judith indicated the grouping of Abigail, D'Arcy, Rud and Trace with a tilt of her head. 'What do you see? Rud, blue-eyed and blond like me. D'Arcy, blue-eyed and blond like her mother and father. And then there's Abby, the only exception in the crowd unless you count *your* father,' she laughed, 'which is silly of course because he isn't related to anybody but you.'

Did this little snip of a girl really think she was going to get the best of me with her hints of secrets? With Judith Stanton who's taken on giants and won? It's a joke!

But then Judith was startled to see the smile return to Jade's lips, her composure apparently recaptured.

'You certainly sound like an expert in genetics and all that stuff, Judy, and what do I know?' Jade shrugged. 'I haven't even finished high school. But I would like to know more about the subject and maybe you could straighten me out. Isn't it possible that my sister's colouring is a throw-back to some Collings on our side of the family, or a Truesdale on her father's side, way back when? Who knows what goes on in a family, if you get my meaning?' she giggled deliberately. 'And just so I can understand all this better, could we take you and Rud for an example? Obviously you're both blond and blue-eyed. But what about your husband, Rud's father? Was he blond and blue-eyed too, just like . . . say, Uncle Bill?'

When Judith, her blue eyes narrowed, didn't answer, Jade's laugh tinkled, clear as a bell. Here was one game Mrs Stanton wasn't going to win. In a game of hint and bluff, the one who won was the one who had the least to lose. And between the two of them, wasn't Judith the one who had the most to lose?

And then Jade turned over what she hoped was another telling card. 'As for me, Cousin Judy, I'm just crazy about these blond, blue-eyed boys, especially when the blue's the colour of violets . . . like Rud's. They absolutely make me weak. . . .'

Just at that moment, almost as if aware that he was being talked about, Rud glanced over at them and saw Jade looking at him in that special way girls did when they were very, very interested and his heart lurched in a special way it never had before.

Jade laughed again. 'I'm really looking forward to this week we're all going to be spending together, aren't you?'

Smooth as silk, Trace Boudin apologized to Francesca and Bill for turning up on their doorstep unannounced. 'I wanted it to be a surprise,' he grinned.

'It certainly was,' Francesca said grimly, 'and I am surprised our security men or the President's didn't consult with us before—'

'You mustn't blame those nice gentlemen. After all, I *was* with Jade who was expected and I *am* your niece's father. Besides, I can be very persuasive if you'll recall. . . .'

He's laughing at us. Francesca, who felt all the nerves in her body exploding, had an urge to reach out and scrape that infuriating grin off his face with her fingernails. She shot a look at Bill that shouted: 'Do something! Get this man out of our house!'

Bill took her hand and patted it reassuringly while he sent her a message with his eyes: Careful . . . slowly. . . .

He couldn't let Boudin push him into taking a position before he found out what it was the scumbag was after . . . why Jade had joined the legions of those who detested him.

'Listen, I don't want to be any trouble, Frankie. Hell, you can stick me anywhere for the week – in the servants' quarters, over the garage, a guest house. . . . You know me – obliging. The last thing I want to do is get in anybody's way.'

At least the kids were getting along, Francesca observed, watching Jade being as affectionate and giggly with D'Arcy and Rud as she was with her sister, who – now that Jade was here – was hanging on to her for dear life.

Of course D'Arcy was neglecting all her friends for her cousins and ordinarily Francesca would have spoken to her about the obligations of a hostess, but at this point it hardly seemed to matter. By now it looked like the party was a shambles, with every politician in the room with the exception of a congressman from Nevada and a councilman from Beverly Hills, trying to stay far, far away from Trace Boudin just to be sure that their picture wasn't taken with a known associate of the Mob. It was one thing to enjoy Boudin's company if a fellow was out his way on the Coast, or in Vegas, or to accept certain favours when the time and place was right, but tonight wasn't it. The problem was Boudin was courting exactly that which they were trying to avoid. As fast as they moved away from him, the faster he was on their trail.

'Oh my God!' Francesca moaned to Bill when, somehow, Boudin managed to get past the Secret Service and all Jack Kennedy's buddies to slip his arm around the President's shoulder just in time to be photographed by a nimble photographer.

43

But this time Bill laughed. 'Well, it's Jack's lookout. When it comes to public images, it's every man for himself.'

Francesca felt similarly irked when she saw Bill dancing with Judith *again*, and she wished she could have been amused when she saw Jade cut in on them. She *almost* felt like laughing when she saw the look on Judith's face. Judith was positively glaring at Jade which was funny since no one, to Francesca's knowledge, had ever upset Judith's cool equanimity. Somehow, Jade had done exactly that, and while Jade had done the same thing to her, it was still funny.

Then she saw Trace claim Judith as Bill danced away with Jade, and Judith was glaring at him too! Did Judith too, like the politicians, just want to avoid him publicly because of his unsavoury reputation, or was it something else more complex? Once, they too, had been business associates in a manner of speaking.

Bill howled as Jade pulled the startled J. Edgar Hoover out onto the dance floor as The Beached Bums broke into *Twistin' the Night Away*. Hoover didn't know what hit him and everytime he tried to get away, Jade dragged him back. The feared and formidable old fussbudget was obviously no match for Carlotta's teenage daughter.

Francesca, distraught, wandered around like a lost soul trying to find her bearings, checking out the different pockets of the party. In the conservatory she saw Bobby Kennedy and Jimmy Hoffa glaring at each other threateningly and she backed out of the room quickly and quietly, closing the door after her. She wanted to make sure the voracious phalanx of cameramen didn't descend upon them. What photographer worth his salt wouldn't prefer a picture of Bobby Kennedy facing Hoffa down to just another shot of D'Arcy Sheridan doing the Watusi with her cousin Rud?

The Hollywood contingent were banded together in the white and gold salon – Liz and Peter Lawford and Judy Garland and Rock . . . old friends. Old friends were the best friends, she thought. And she had left old friends in Boston thanks to Judith. But then she couldn't place her entire loss at Judith's doorstep. Carlotta had been her very oldest friend, and once, the very, very best.

Back in the ballroom, Jade was dancing with Rud, one hand playing with the back of his neck, her head thrown back, the orchestra playing 'Only Love Can Break a Heart'. It was their bodies which kept time to the music while their feet barely moved.

It occurred to Francesca that while D'Arcy, Jade and Abigail were more or less sharing Rud equally, it seemed it was always Jade who danced the slow dances with Rud, leaving those dances where the partners didn't touch to the other two. Was there a competition going on for these intimate dances with Rud? If so, then Jade was winning, and how not? In her own way, compared to Jade, D'Arcy was almost as naive as Abigail. In fact, if it came down to it, all three of them – Abigail, D'Arcy *and* Rud, even with his seniority of age and seemingly super sophistication – were hopelessly outclassed by the youngest cousin who seemed to have the wisdom of the ages sewed up.

And interestingly, Judith, who seemed to have forgotten all about her rich, international friends, appeared pleased when Rud danced with Abigail, frowned when he danced with D'Arcy, and positively flushed with irritation when he was cheek to cheek with Jade.

In the end it was Jade, not Jackie Kennedy, who led the Conga the exhibition rhumba as Francesca had planned, thinking D'Arcy would get a kick out of it. Rather, it was Jade again, with Trace, while Bill looked on, with a murderous but faraway look in his eyes.

Finally, when Francesca thought she couldn't bear it any longer, people began to leave. The President nicely thanked his hosts for a fun evening but Bobby commented wryly: 'You *do* know the most interesting people, Governor Sheridan. And when I invite you to *my* house I'm going to remember that, and *you* remember to wear your bathing trunks because you might very well be the first one I push in the pool.'

Everyone within hearing distance laughed at that one, including Bill. And then Tallulah took over the piano on the bandstand to play and sing Noel Coward's 'I went to the Most Marvellous Party'!

Once the crowd in the ballroom was considerably thinned, conspicuous by their absence were Rud and D'Arcy, Jade and Abigail, as well as Judith, Bill and Trace. 'Where is everyone?' Francesca asked herself and went down the stairs to the reception hall where some of the guests had managed to spend the entire night at the bar. Now that they were finally reaching the end of the evening, was the family having a private party down there without her?

Yes, they were all there along with a few late hangers-on, Francesca saw. How nice! The whole family having a friendly drink together. So sweet. So cosy.

Jade was offering to mix a cocktail for Rud while Judith began to voice an objection. But Jade, waving the bartender away, ignored her. First she poured a cocktail glass full of vodka, then raised the bottle of vermouth as if to add a few scant drops, but instead she brought the bottle to her lips, her mouth suggestively rubbing against the mouth of the bottle, tipping the bottle then so that a few drops of the liquid entered her mouth, but then an excess wet her lips, coated them, dripped. Then the tips of her fingers wiped it all away and she took those same fingers and sucked on them, and then placed them to Rud's lips and wiped them with all four of them, finally proffering her pinky for him to suck on, which he did. Then and only then, she handed him the brimming glass of straight vodka. 'Jade's martini,' she announced, whispering throatily, gazing deep into his eyes.

Trace Boudin's laugh rang out as D'Arcy and Abigail gasped – Abigail stunned, and D'Arcy admiring and envious at the same time. *What a performance!*

Judith, seeing her son sucking on the proffered pinkie, his eyes shining, was filled with rage. *Cheap, contemptible theatrics!* It was Carlotta all over again!

Rud, his eyes not leaving Jade's, tasted his drink, nodded, speechless. He had never seen anything like it. He had had many experiences with women several years older than Jade . . . whenever he was able to escape the relentless eye of his mother, but he had never experienced anything like this. It was the most intensely erotic experience of his life.

Bill said nothing, didn't move a muscle. He, like Francesca, was taken back in time to a Christmas Eve party in Boston almost twenty years before when he had witnessed . . . experienced . . . the very same performance. Only then the ingredient had been gin instead of vodka, it had been 'Carlotta's martini,' and the man for whom the cocktail had been mixed was Captain Bill Sheridan, U.S.M.C. . . . .

PART TWO

Before the Party

II
1942

1.

When Francesca Collings first saw Captain Bill Sheridan, magnificently resplendent in his dress uniform at Mimi Appleton's Christmas Eve party for the men of the Armed Forces, her heart did flip-flops. It was the only word she could think for the feeling that came over her.

This is what they must mean by love at first sight, she thought, and picked up her glass of champagne and toasted herself. Not only was it the first time she'd fallen in love at first sight, it was the first time she'd fallen in love . . . period.

He was so big . . . so virile! And that gorgeous smile – it was overwhelming. *He* was overwhelming. He was without a doubt the most attractive man she'd ever laid eyes on. And then when he came limping over to where she was playing bartender at Mimi's insistence, even though she didn't know the first thing about mixing drinks, she feared that she might stop breathing altogether.

'Can you spare a glass of that champagne for a soldier wounded making your world safe for democracy?' He grinned at her, his eyes crinkling at the corners.

She knew he was teasing, of course, but a girl couldn't help feeling guilty. 'You're going to be all right, aren't you? I mean your leg—?'

'They said it was going to mend fine but now that I've seen you I'm not at all sure about the condition of my heart. You'd better hurry up with that champagne to help it keep beating.'

Delighted, Francesca laughed. *He likes me too. He's flirting with me!*

She leaned over the bar confidentially. 'To tell the truth, Captain, this champagne is not of the very best. Mimi – she's our hostess – is chintzy that way. Since her parents are away in Palm Beach for the holidays, she decided to take advantage of their absence by throwing this party. She said the least she could do was to "treat our brave men in uniform to a celebration in one of Beacon Hill's finest homes on this wartorn Christmas Eve . . ."' Francesca giggled. 'That's the way Mimi talks. But the only brave men she invited tonight are officers and gentlemen. She said her parents would be mortified if she filled their home with ordinary enlisted men who might, heaven help us, have "sticky fingers."'

Francesca rolled her eyes for emphasis. 'And then she went out and bought the cheapest champagne she could find and ordered the rest of us to bring the sugar and the coffee and whatever else is rationed!'

Then she asked herself why, for goodness sake, was she rattling on about dumb Mimi and her cheap champagne? Catch Carlotta rambling on about Mimi to the handsomest man ever! What she should be doing was talking about herself. Or better still, she should be asking *him* questions, letting him do the talking. That was what a girl was supposed to. Men liked to talk

51

about themselves and loved a woman who listened. And most of all she should be making herself sound interesting, exciting, fun! The way Carlotta would. . . .

'I know. I'll make you a Zombie. I was just looking it up in this bartender's guide. The Zombie's guaranteed to turn you *into one* in about five seconds. Are you game?'

He laughed. 'I think I'll stick to a martini. Not as exciting but at least I'll know what I'm getting. I *always* like to know what I'm getting.'

Was that a sexual innuendo? Francesca wondered. Uncertain, she just smiled at the Marine with what she hoped was an alluring smile and concentrated on mixing the martini. Three parts gin to one part vermouth. She measured carefully, wanting it to be perfect. 'Olive or a twist?'

'Definitely a twist. I *love* twists,' he said meaningfully and she blushed, aware that 'twist' was old-fashioned slang for a young woman.

But then he tasted the martini and groaned. 'You're cute, lady, but you've got a heavy hand with the vermouth.'

Her heart sank even though she knew that he was kidding around. She was about to offer to make him another with far less vermouth this time when suddenly there was Carlotta, laughing and tossing her red-gold hair, her characteristic gesture. Carlotta, in a strapless bright green party dress in the new length which barely scraped the knees, with matching green ankle-strap high heels that emphasized her shapely calves and slender ankles.

'I'll make you a martini, soldier,' she murmured and as Francesca and Bill Sheridan watched, he as if bewitched, Carlotta did her martini stunt which never failed to mesmerize her audience. The glass full of straight gin, the bottle of vermouth brought to the lips, the lips glistening with the liquid, and then the proffered pinkie to suck on . . . his lips parted and by now dry with anticipation. Then the finale – the throatily whispered, 'Carlotta's martini. . . .'

Francesca, silent and subdued, watched Captain Sheridan taste the martini, his eyes firmly fixed on her sister's face and when he pronounced the martini 'perfect,' she knew that although she had seen him first, Captain Sheridan was now taken. *She* wasn't the only one who had fallen in love at first sight that evening.

Before Bill finished his 'perfect' martini Carlotta dragged him into the middle of the room where the rug had been rolled up and insisted he dance with her, bad leg and all. He didn't protest and while the phonograph played 'Be Careful, It's My Heart', they stood practically motionless, his hands locked in place around her waist, her hands entwined around his neck, he looking down into her eyes, hers gazing up into his.

Was it possible, Francesca wondered sorrowfully, that Carlotta was the *third* person who had just fallen in love? It was unlikely. It was more likely that Carlotta was casually infatuated, perhaps having fallen in love lightly for a few minutes . . . a few hours, even for a few days. But even so, Francesca knew that as far as she herself was concerned, nothing would ever be quite the same again. Then, watching them from behind the bar, Francesca experienced an emotion she'd never felt before – jealousy! *It just wasn't fair!*

Oh, she was used to men preferring Carlotta but it had never bothered her before since she loved Carlotta so much herself, was proud of her beauty, her zest for life, her special sparkle. Besides, she felt protective of Carlotta ever since their parents had died and they'd been left alone in the world except for their niece, Judith, and under the circumstances, Judith hardly counted. No, she'd never minded playing second fiddle to Carlotta before, but then she herself had never been in love before with a man who had fallen under Carlotta's spell. And she had never, never imagined how much it would hurt!

Then she felt guilty. How could she resent her darling Carlotta? It wasn't Carlotta's fault if she was . . . Carlotta . . . irresistible Carlotta. . . .

A lieutenant sat down on a bar stool, called her 'Blondie,' and wanted to know if she could make him a Hurricane. Dispiritedly Francesca advised him to stick to the champagne. 'Frankly, Lieutenant, I'm a lousy bartender. The worst.'

'In that case, how about a dance?'

She shook her head. 'I'm not supposed to leave the bar unattended. Besides, I'm not much better at dancing than I am at mixing drinks. Now my sister – she's the one with the red hair dancing with that Marine with the bad leg – she's a terrific dancer, as you can see. And can she mix a drink! Maybe if you're lucky, you can persuade her to make you a martini. I guarantee you an experience you'll never forget.'

The lieutenant apparently took every word she said literally for he immediately transferred his gaze to the swaying Carlotta, body pressed against the Captain's, eyes closed, his head bent down to meet hers. Her lips were moving – she was crooning along with the recording into the hypnotized Captain's ear.

'Wow! That's your sister? She's beautiful!'

'That's the least of it,' Francesca murmured but the lieutenant didn't hear. 'Deep In the Heart of Texas' was on the phonograph now and he jumped up to claim Carlotta for the number before someone else did since the disabled Marine obviously wasn't up to jitterbugging.

Bill Sheridan didn't want to relinquish Carlotta to the Navy but he had little choice in the matter. She had already switched partners as well as her rhythm and was twirling, her skirt flying high above her legs revealing glimpses of silky thigh. He went back to the bar to pass the time with Carlotta's nice sister. She was pretty and sweet and friendly, and it always helped to have the family on your side if you wanted to make serious time with a girl, and that was exactly what he intended to do with Carlotta. . . .

He launched a barrage of questions at Francesca, eager to know everything there was to know about the Collings sisters. Francesca knew that he was really only interested in Carlotta and only minimally concerned with her, but she'd answer all his questions, being very, very careful to be friendly in an impersonal way . . . the way she was with practically all the soldiers and sailors she met at the different dances and parties for the men in uniform. While it was a girl's patriotic duty to be as obliging as possible within the confines of being a 'nice girl' – these men were sacrificing so much for so many and could be going off to their death – it was important to keep a balance between being friendly and getting involved. Now it was vital not to let Bill Sheridan or Carlotta know that she had so foolishly fallen in love with a man who had just given his heart to another.

Certainly, she'd be polite, the way she'd be to an ordinary mortal who hadn't already broken her heart and so quickly.

He asked where they lived.

'Just a few blocks from here.'

'With your parents?'

'No, our parents died a little over a year ago.'

'And the two of you work?'

'No, we both go to school, I'm a sophomore at Radcliffe and Carlotta's a freshman.'

'Ah, Radcliffe girls. . . .'

'You know some then, I take it?'

'I *have*. I'm a Bostonian myself and just before I went into the service I was graduated from Harvard Law, but not being really toney, nor a member of one of Harvard's proper clubs, I was free to go out with Radcliffe girls, which as you may know, is something really high-class Harvard men never do. A Yalie perhaps, but never a Harvard man.'

In spite of herself, Francesca laughed. 'So far, neither I nor Carlotta have found that a problem. But then there's a war on in case you haven't noticed, and that does change things. I daresay that there isn't a boy at Harvard, toney or not, freshman or upperclassman, who wouldn't give his eyeteeth to date Carlotta.'

'I daresay . . .' he smiled ruefully. 'Then I take it she does date Harvard men . . . college boys, that is?'

'Hardly,' she couldn't resist teasing him. 'As I said, Captain, there *is* a war on, and it's every able-bodied girl's patriotic duty to date our servicemen.'

He nodded, apparently digesting this information. But he said, 'The two of you are lucky then . . . to be able to go to college without working.' He himself had worked ever since his twelfth birthday . . . all through high school, college and Law School. Actually, the Marine Corps had been a breather for him after carrying a double load for so long.

'Yes, I suppose. Not that we're rich but we do have a small trust fund. It's enough if we don't go crazy and buy out the stores. Sometimes I have to crack the whip over Carlotta's head but generally she listens to me . . . *if* she's in the mood.'

'Yes,' he said, turning on his bar stool now to watch Carlotta on the dance floor. 'I thought that's how it is.'

'What do you mean? How do you think it is?'

'That you're the big sister, that you look after Carlotta.'

She bristled, anger cutting through her melancholy, even though his words were no less than the truth. 'Hardly that,' she said. 'There *is* only a year's difference between us. I'm nineteen and Carlotta's eighteen. And by the way, Captain, I have a name too. It's Francesca.'

He crinkled his eyes at her again, ignoring the tartness in her tone. 'Hi, Frankie.' He picked up her hand and kissed it. 'We're going to be good friends so why don't you drop the Captain and start calling me Bill?'

Especially since I won't be a Captain for very long.

They'd given him a choice since his leg was so tricky. It might take a year before he'd see active duty again. He could sit it out at a desk or take an early discharge. He'd been undecided before but tonight . . . in the last few minutes . . . he'd made up his mind. It wouldn't be like he was a shirker – he'd done his duty. It wasn't his fault he'd been put out of action only a year into the fighting, and as it happened, so opportunely. What better time to get started on both his legal career and political one when there was a shortage of able men on the home front? Considering that he'd been awarded the Navy Cross for exceptional heroism in action, why should he leave the field open to the 4-Fs? And a girl like Carlotta. . . . How long would she sit around twiddling her thumbs waiting for a man to come home and marry her?

He had a long way to go and a man didn't get there by not seizing the moment . . . not grabbing at an opportunity when fate thrust it his way. . . .

He reclaimed Carlotta for 'I'm Dreaming of a White Christmas' but it wasn't a white Christmas he was dreaming of at all, but an inauguration – his hand on the Bible swearing to uphold the Constitution and in the background was his First Lady, the most beautiful, sexy, red-haired first lady who felt like a million dollars in a man's arms. . . .

Carlotta sat down at the piano to accompany herself while she sang 'Blues in the Night' and although practically everyone there knew the words – it had been on the hit parade for several weeks – no one sang along. No one would dare break the spell. The song might have been written for Carlotta alone.

One of the servicemen leaning over the piano wanted to know what Carlotta was doing in Boston. Why wasn't she in Hollywood? She had better legs than Gable, she was prettier than Veronica Lake and sexier than Rita. 'Baby, you oughta be in pictures.'

Carlotta tossed her mane of hair and laughed her enigmatic laugh. 'Oh maybe one of these days I will be. . . .' She gave Bill Sheridan a sidelong glance and he thought, over my dead body.

Once they started singing Christmas carols, Carlotta grew restless. 'Let's go someplace more exciting,' she told Bill.

'OK, let's,' he said, thinking, this was more like it. He was eager to be someplace else, along with her.

'Come on, Frankie,' Carlotta beckoned to her sister. 'We're leaving.'

Francesca saw that Bill looked surprised and, sensitive about being a fifth wheel, she said, 'I'll stay. You two go on,' and saw Bill Sheridan draw a breath of relief.

'No,' Carlotta was adamant. 'We came together and we're leaving together. Now be a good girl, Frankie, and get our coats.' 'We're a team,' she told Bill.

He didn't know what to make of it. Was she reluctant to be alone with him or what? Was she just being provocative, a form of playing hard to get? He looked to Francesca as if she might clarify things but she only shrugged. If Carlotta was making an issue of her going along with them, what could she do? Maybe Carlotta simply didn't want to be alone with him. . . .

Then a tiny spark of hope flared up within her. Maybe Carlotta didn't really like him all that much, incredible as that was. Maybe – just maybe – there was still a chance for her with him. It would be humiliating to be second choice but it was better than nothing . . . better than never seeing him again. And sometimes these things worked out. She had heard all kinds of stories. . . . You never could tell, and while there was life, there was hope.

She went to get their coats. In the meantime, Bill spoke to his buddy, Kyle. They'd come to the party together and now Bill asked him if he wanted to come along. They'd hit some of the clubs. Kyle was willing. The blonde wasn't the knockout the redhead was but she was curvy and cute. Actually, she had bigger jugs than her sister.

The foursome spent Christmas Day together and the following three nights as well. On 29 December Kyle couldn't make it and Bill brought along Tommy Hemingway to keep Francesca company, which was all right with her. It couldn't have mattered less. Tommy was as good company as Kyle, maybe even a better conversationalist. It was all the same to her. She was only along because Carlotta insisted on it. She said she wasn't going to have Frankie sitting home alone during the holiday season. For Francesca it was easier to go along with Bill and Carlotta, with whoever Bill brought along, than to sit and wonder what it was they were doing at any given moment: *Were they eating Italian in the North End, drinking red wine and holding hands across the table? Or were they sitting in the back seat of the 1938 Buick Bill had scrounged, necking?*

So far Francesca hadn't been able to elicit anything concrete from Carlotta as to how she really felt about Bill Sheridan, and she was afraid to ask *too* many questions, thereby revealing her own true feelings. And Carlotta was infuriatingly unforthcoming, refusing to be pinned down.

They were dressing to go out on the 30th with Bill and whoever it was he'd show up with – Tommy, Kyle, or someone new. 'Do you *really* like him?' Francesca probed.

'Of course I like him. Would I be going out with him if I didn't like him, silly?'

'How much do you like him?'

'God Almighty, Frankie, how do I know how much I like him? He's really good-looking and you know I like them good-looking. And he's crazy about me and I love them crazy about me,' she giggled.

'I think he's in love with you, Carlotta. *Really* in love.'

'Well, good. That's nice.'

'You wouldn't want to see him get hurt, would you?'

'God Almighty, Frankie! That's his lookout, isn't it? I've got all I can handle worrying about myself. And that's what you should be doing too. Worrying about yourself instead of him. We should all worry about ourselves and just one more thing—'

'Yes? What's that?'

'Well, *two* more things. One is having fun and the other is where are we going to get some more nylons. I've just sprung a run in these and they're my very last pair. I'm really going to cry if I have to wear those horrid rayon stockings.'

Francesca went to her bureau drawer and took out a pair of nylons wrapped in tissue paper and handed them over.

'Are you sure you want to give them to me?' Carlotta asked, already pulling a stocking on. 'I feel bad taking your last pair.'

56

'It's not the last,' Francesca said dryly. 'Only the next to last.'

'Oh, goodie! In that case I accept your sacrifice in the light in which it is offered, my darling Frankie. Do you want to know whom I really love from the bottom of my heart?'

'Who?' Was she going to say Bill?

'*You*, Frankie. Who did you think I meant – Judith?'

And they both went off into a gale of laughter.

While Judith was their niece and almost the same age as Francesca, and all three of them had practically grown up together, there was no love lost there to say the least. There was barely friendship. Judith was probably one of the hardest people in the world to be friends with, much less love.

Still, apparently Judith had indeed found someone to love her, to take her for better or worse, in sickness and in health and all that jazz. In fact, Judith was getting married the very next night, New Year's Eve.

'Just think,' Francesca mused. 'Judith's getting married before either of us and to someone filthy rich! And she's invited us to the wedding even though we've barely spoken to her in over a year. Amazing!'

'Do you want to know what I think is really amazing?' Carlotta asked, while reviewing her appearance in the full-length mirror. 'How Judith ever managed to pull this whole thing off—'

2.

Judith had grown up despising Francesca and Carlotta, even as the three of them played together and eventually went off to school together. For one thing, Judith instinctively knew that she was not pretty and that they were very much so, especially Carlotta. They wore their hair in curls, adorned with bows and ribbons and blossomed forth daily in dresses bestarched and beruffled like two brightly coloured, cultivated spring flowers, and they had winning ways – bubbling laughs and chirpy voices and feet that barely touched the ground.

Judith's toes didn't twinkle, her hair was tightly braided and she hardly ever smiled, much less bubbled. Her dresses were not only unstarched but frequently unpressed as well since Priscilla, her mother, had no time for that nonsense – she was without a husband to put bread on the table and was much too busy earning a living, determined to accept as little help as possible from Hugh Collings – the father she and Francesca and Carlotta shared – and Jane Collings, her half-sisters' mother, the stepmother she detested.

If the winsome Carlotta and Francesca with their fancy dresses, ringlets and huge assortment of toys and dolls weren't by themselves enough to make Judith hate them, there was the added factor of Priscilla's rantings and ravings against them and their mother Jane.

The day Hugh Collings brought the pretty, red-haired green-eyed Jane home to meet the seventeen-year-old daughter of his first marriage, Priscilla knew that she had to leave her father's house. There was no way she could tolerate living with this woman – a slut if ever she saw one, and only a year older than she herself. Jane, the daughter of an immigrant Irish maid, was obviously marrying her father for the material comforts he could provide her as well as the status the Collings name afforded.

Priscilla was poisoned with her jealousy and hatred. Accordingly she married the first man who was available – her father's keeper, a timid man who put up no fight, John Tyler. Then she allowed her father who was secretly and guiltily glad to have her out of his hair, to give them a small house in the South End as a wedding present. But even as she accepted the house, Priscilla resented its size (small) and its location which was not what she thought she deserved – the Back Bay or Beacon Hill. This served to feed further the fires of her hate. The more Jane and Hugh gave her, the more her resentment of them built. By the time she gave birth to Judith, and Jane to Francesca, and Carlotta a year later, Priscilla was half-mad with her rage.

When Priscilla's husband, John, 'a born loser,' as she characterized him, contracted diphtheria and succumbed to it, her father immediately offered his financial support. But now Priscilla refused his 'sanctimonious charity,' preferring instead to feed his guilt by earning her living as a practical nurse which, she pointed out with perverse relish, was no better than being a common scrubwoman.

Then, inexplicably, she turned around and said she'd allow her father and stepmother to care for Judith during those hours she 'slaved to keep body and soul together.' At the same time she decreed that while she couldn't accept anything 'brand-new' for Judith, she would accept Francesca's and Carlotta's hand-me-downs since Judith was smaller than they, and she would also allow Judith to have the toys the girls discarded. 'Brand-new' would only be accepted at Christmas and on Judith's birthday.

It was as if Judith was the instrument Priscilla chose to torment Hugh and Jane with, as if having the unlovely Judith in their lovely home in her limp, washed-out dress and her second-hand doll – one open-and-shut eye malfunctioning – would serve as a reminder of how she and her child were suffering deprivation while they and their privileged daughters enjoyed everything life had to offer.

Following this pattern Priscilla permitted Judith to attend the same day school as Francesca and Carlotta but not to join them in their elocution lessons, singing and piano instruction, and certainly not at dancing school. Judith would be allowed the bare basics but none of the frills.

By this time Priscilla was too irrational to consider what she might be doing to her daughter, so obsessed was she with making her the bane of her father's existence. She succeeded in this only too well and if Judith reacted by behaving in a hateful manner, Priscilla wasn't able to judge since her daughter's disposition and manner was not much different from her own.

Francesca and Carlotta had long given up on 'being nice' to Judith by the time they were in high school, and only included her in their plans and fun when their mother absolutely forced them to. To them, Judith was no more than an irritating pain in the neck.

'You try to be nice to Judith and what do you get?' they complained. 'A slap in the face!' Judith was not only surly and ungrateful, she acted like she was really better than everyone else – smarter and somehow superior.

Still, Hugh and Jane bore the guilt Priscilla had managed to impose upon them heavily and they continued to try and persuade Priscilla to accept their help on Judith's behalf. They were doing just that the night they died along with Priscilla. It was an unseasonably hot evening in June of '41 and they'd taken Priscilla to dinner at an inn in Marblehead in a last-ditch effort to convince her to allow Judith to enter Radcliffe in the fall along with Francesca. So far, Priscilla had refused their offer of tuition maintaining that Judith would go to work since she didn't have a rich father like Francesca, ignoring Hugh and Jane's protestations that it would be criminal if Judith didn't go to college, she being so smart, and doing so much better in her studies than either of their daughters.

The Marblehead Arms was a big, old, wooden barn of a place and once the grease fire started, the building went up like a tinderbox. When it was ascertained later that the three had died from smoke inhalation rather than the more terrible flames, Carlotta and Francesca were able to take some consolation in this. But it was of no consequence to Judith – she had detested her mother almost as much as she detested her young aunts. Certainly she had contempt for Priscilla, who had dissipated both her life and her hatred by whining, ranting and assuming a posture that had netted them both nothing but a penniless, powerless, wretched existence. Her mother had been a stupid woman but she herself was smarter by far and she'd do better. The only true revenge was when you ended up on top while you bested your enemies.

Judith wasn't dismayed when she found out that she'd been left without a dime except for the cramped little house. She had expected no more. Her mother hadn't anything to leave her and her grandfather's will hadn't mentioned her. Rather, he had left everything to his wife, Jane, knowing that she would take care of Priscilla and Judith as well as her own daughters. But since Jane was dead too, everything went to those smug bitches who had nothing on their empty minds but good times and pretty dresses. Well, she'd show them! She'd show everyone! They'd all pay . . . every last person who had mocked her behind her back, but especially those two! She had grown up in the shadow of their charmed existence and now she was going to come out of the shadows and put them there. . . .

Even though their father's estate turned out to be far less than everyone had expected, Francesca told Carlotta that they should talk to the trustees about giving a share to Judith, enough for her to get through college.

'I don't see why we should,' Carlotta responded, not looking up from painting her toenails. 'Judith doesn't deserve anything. She's such a nasty little prig and she acts like she's doing us a favour when she so much as talks to us. She acts like we're little dopes just because we're pretty and she's not. Besides, we hardly have enough money for ourselves.'

'Come on, Carlotta. That's not exactly true—'

'But that's what you said . . . that we had to be careful and not buy anything except maybe a lipstick once a year.'

'Carlotta, you're impossible! That's not what I said at all. All I said was that we have to— Oh, never mind. You know exactly what I meant. And I think it's only right that we help Judith since that was what Mother and Father would have wanted. After all, she *is* Daddy's granddaughter.'

'So what? Who cares? Let her take care of herself if she's so all-fired smart.'

'I just want to give her enough to go to college.'

'Why must she go to college? What's so great about college anyway? All you do is spend four years ruining your posture bending over books, not to mention your eyesight. I'm not at all sure *I* want to go and maybe you should think twice about it too. Just think of all the fun we can have spending our money for the next four . . . five years if neither one of us went.'

'What would we do instead?'

'Oh come on, Frankie, don't be such a stick-in-the-mud. We'd have fun. We'd travel. Go to Europe or even around the world.'

'There's a war in Europe, remember? Besides, Mother and Father wanted us to go to college. And that's what we're going to do.'

'We could go to California and lie in the sun. Get a house on the beach maybe. I've always dreamed of going to Hollywood. Maybe we could both become movie stars. Wouldn't that be fun? At the very least, we'd get wonderful tans. They say the sun shines every day in Hollywood. What do you say, Frankie?'

'I say we go to school and offer to send Judith too.'

'Oh, all right! If we must! The problem with you, Frankie Collings, is that you're too nice for your own good. For *our* good. I only hope we don't live to regret your decision . . . to give all our money away to Judith and not go to Hollywood instead.'

'Thanks but no thanks,' Judith told them when they told her of their decision to give her tuition money. 'I don't need your charity. I have resources you know nothing about.'

'Really?' Francesca was surprised, assuming that Judith was referring to money.

'Yes, really.' Judith tapped her temple. 'Up here. It's called a brain. Did you ever hear of it?'

Carlotta shot Francesca a look that spoke volumes. *You see what you get when you try to be nice to Judith! Insults!*

When they left Judith's house, they had no idea what it was Judith planned to do but Francesca had to admit that it was impossible to be nice to Judith. The best thing they could do was stay away from her. See her once a year maybe. Thanksgiving or Christmas.

'You know what I think we should do now if we really want to use the old noodle?' Carlotta tapped her head as Judith had. 'We should celebrate.'

'Celebrate what?'

'Celebrate all the money Judith just saved us. I think that was lovely of her. Why don't we go to lunch at the Copley, toast Judith, and then go on a shopping spree?'

Francesca laughed. 'Think you're ready for a new party dress, do you?'

'As a matter of fact,' Carlotta said prissily, 'I wasn't thinking about myself at all but about *you*, Miss Smarty Pants. Filene's and Jordan Marsh have all the autumn things in already and I was thinking that if you're going to Radcliffe you should have an entire new college girl wardrobe.' Then her tone changed to one of incredible sweetness. 'Because anyone as nice as you . . . as wonderful as you . . . should have—' She flung out her arms in an expansive gesture, 'the world!'

'Oh, baby, that is *so* sweet!' The tears welled up in Francesca's eyes. They'd lost their parents, their niece Judith was a terrible bitch, but they were wonderfully lucky, they had each other.

'And you know what else, Frankie? I don't care how smart Judith is. I think she's a damn fool that she doesn't appreciate you.'

Francesca wiped away her tears. 'I must say I have to agree with you totally. And now I suggest that we proceed to the Copley and order that champagne, if we can convince them we're old enough to be served. We'll drink to forgetting about Judith and her remarkable brain.'

Carlotta giggled. 'We'll drink to the day she comes crawling on all fours, begging us to forgive her for her arrogance, asking us if we can spare a couple of dollars for old time's sake. . . .'

'And what will we do?'

'I know what *I'd* do but you probably won't let me do it. *You* will undoubtedly forgive her, you old softie, you.'

3.

Even before her mother died, when she was only fifteen, Judith had a plan laid out for her future. By the time she was twenty-one she planned to be rich and powerful. Accordingly, she'd made a list of her own plusses and minuses, being brutally frank. A plus was her cleverness, a minus was her personality. Oddly enough, she listed her general unattractiveness as a plus. That would be her secret weapon – nobody expected a girl so limited in physical beauty to be able to marry for money, and history taught that the most successful military strategy was the surprise attack.

College had never been part of Judith's master plan. Nursing school was, and by the time she was graduated from high school she'd already been accepted for nurse's training at Mass General. By renting out her house she had enough funds for the incidentals, and was free to devote herself to her course of study and her research. She spent a lot of time at the public library, and her research materials were the various *Who's Whos*, the local newspapers – the society columns and the business pages. She read extensively on general finance, accounting, estate management, the law. She even read whatever sex manuals were available.

While she wasn't popular with either the other nurses in training who laughed behind her back for being such an odd ball, or with the young interns with whom the other girls relentlessly flirted, she was a big favourite with the patients, especially the aged. She acted demure, modest and was soft-spoken. She was warm, caring, dedicated, cheerfully performing the most menial and noxious chores that the other girls tried to avoid. All this was part of her exercise in personality modification. Above all, Judith was efficient and trustworthy, and the regular staff knew they could rely on her.

Then, only six months into her training, Judith's plan was accelerated when, fortuitously for her, the Japanese attacked at Pearl Harbour and the country geared up for war. That the United States would be drawn into the fight had been inevitable, and Judith had foreseen an acute shortage of nurses. Now that young men all over the country were rushing to enlist, so would be a great many trained nurses. It all added up – if trained nurses were going to be in

61

short supply, so would practical nurses as well, especially those who were extraordinarily competent as she was. Why waste further time completing her training when, for her purposes, the one profession would do as well as the other? Accordingly, she consulted her files, or dossiers as she liked to think of them, and one name stood out from all the rest.

Judith presented herself at the Dudley Stanton mansion on the 'water side' of Beacon Street in the Back Bay several days before Christmas. The holiday season was always a busy time for everyone, rich and poor, and especially so for the rich, Judith reasoned. They were bound to be shorthanded, more so because there was a sick old man in the house, one who required round-the-clock care.

Judith was lucky, for it happened that she came at the most propitious time possible. Adeline Purvis, the eldest of Dudley Stanton's three nieces, who supervised her ailing uncle's household, was at her wit's end. They were leaving for Palm Beach the very next day and everything was going wrong at the last moment. Rose McCarthy, the nurse who had the midnight shift, had informed her only that morning that she was unable, for personal reasons, to leave the Boston area. On top of that, Adeline had not yet found a cook, their Boston cook having refused to go to Palm Beach from the very beginning.

In fact, at the very moment Judith arrived, Adeline was sitting at the big mahogany desk in the panelled library busy on the phone with an agency in Palm Beach, demanding that they line up several cooks for her to interview the minute she got off the train. As far as Adeline was concerned, a cook took precedence over a night nurse any old time. She was counting on entertaining in Palm Beach and how could one entertain without a cook? Indeed, how did one eat at all? If worse came to worse, she could always make the housekeeper, Mrs Beachum, or even a maid fill in on Dudley's nightshift. How much attention did the old buzzard require in the middle of the night? But they needed a cook *immediately!*

Still, when Mrs Beachum told her that a Judith Tyler was at the door seeking employment as a practical nurse, Adeline took it as an act of Providence. She'd heard that nurses, practical or otherwise, were in short supply and if the woman wasn't a total incompetent, she'd hire her! Why look a gift horse in the mouth? Besides, how much did any nurse have to do on the midnight shift? Smoothe Dudley's pillow when he tossed and turned?

'Nice, quiet-looking girl,' Mrs Beachum observed and Adeline said, 'Show her in.'

Adeline liked it that Judith Tyler was plain and dowdily dressed. The pretty ones were totally unreliable. Some good-loooking rotter beckoned and they were off and flying.

'I am curious as to how it happened that you appeared on our doorstep like some abandoned infant in a basket. We always get our nurses from the agency, or on Dr Phillips's recommendation. Whatever possessed you to knock on our door?'

Judith explained that she'd been talking with some nurses and one of them had heard that the Stanton household was in need of a practical nurse. She wasn't sure whether this was true but since she was looking for employment she thought she'd give it a try. 'You know how it is,' she explained deferentially. 'In every occupation there's always talk about where work is available and which are the *good* places to work . . . where the people are pleasant and fair.'

'Oh?' Adeline preened. 'Is that what they say about us? Well, I'm gratified to learn that there are still employees who appreciate these qualities.'

Judith explained that while she had been enrolled in nurse's training where she was at the top of her class, she was forced to abandon her studies due to financial necessity. 'But I've already learned enough to be a good nursing assistant. If I hadn't needed money so badly—' She looked down in embarrassment.

This girl was sounding better every second, Adeline thought. Since she needed money badly, she could be hired cheap and that would please her husband Wallace, he being such a bear about economical management. He despised it when her sisters occasionally took over the running of Dudley's household. He said that Theodora was a spendthrift and Nancy Lee a fool when it came to money.

The thing that annoyed *her* about her sisters was how they tried to get out of their obligations, always dumping everything on *her* shoulders. And did Wallace care about *that*? Hardly. All Wallace cared about was that Dudley think she herself was the niece most concerned about his welfare . . . that he change his will to favour her. She could understand that but did Wallace care how much she suffered with the problems of Dudley's household? All he had to do was take care of the business affairs and send over those endless streams of paper for Dudley to sign, and of course, keep Theodora's husband Eddy from trying to take over. But that wasn't difficult. Eddy was such a moron. As for Nancy Lee, all she thought about was getting herself another titled husband or one more gigolo to make love to her. That's all Nancy Lee cared about – satisfying her disgusting sexual desires. Where had that hot blood come from? No one else in the family was like that. There *had* been stories about Dudley. But that had been years ago . . . before he had had his first stroke. It had been whispered that he frequented women of dubious reputation, but that wasn't really abnormal considering he had never married. But thank God, that was water under the bridge now. . . .

'You do have recommendations?' Adeline asked even though she'd already decided to hire Judith Tyler.

'You could check with Mass General. I'm sure they'll vouch for me. And I'm a Collings. . . . That is, my mother was a Collings.'

Adeline was familiar with the name. Good family even if there wasn't too much money there. 'Was it your parents who died in that fire at Marblehead?'

'My mother died in that fire, along with my grandfather and his wife.'

'Yes, now I remember. Hugh Collings. He left two daughters, didn't he?'

'Yes, my aunts – Francesca and Carlotta Collings.'

'Yes . . . yes . . . I heard that one of them is *very* pretty *and* fast.'

Judith lowered her lids modestly. 'Well, you know how that is. People tend to gossip when a girl is very attractive.'

'I suppose. And you? Do you have many boyfriends?'

Judith blushed. 'Oh no. Even if—I'm much too busy for that. I don't have *any* boyfriends.'

Marvellous, Adeline thought. The girl was too good to be true. 'If I engage you, you'll have to start immediately. Can you do that? Can you leave for Palm Beach right away?'

'Oh yes, Ma'am. I'm free to do whatever you require.'

'Then it's settled. Good!'

It really was, Adeline thought. The girl seemed very bright. She wouldn't be surprised if she turned out to be more than a practical nurse. Maybe she could be trained to go over the bills with Mrs Beachum so she herself wouldn't have to be bothered. And perhaps she could plan the daily menus with the cook. *Oh dear, the cook!* She had to get back to that problem immediately.

Adeline went over her schedule with her husband. She was leaving the next day with the housekeeper, Mrs Beachum, the butler, Charles; the maid, Clara; and Nurse Higgins who would set up the sick room. Then Dudley would follow the next day with Nurse Woods and the new girl Judith. Walter would help get Dudley on to the train and then he would drive the car down. 'Unless you want me to leave the Rolls and Walter here for you and I can hire a car and driver down there?'

'No, you'd better have Walter with you. Dudley likes the old gaffer and we don't want him bellyaching unnecessarily. The important thing is to keep Dudley happy if it doesn't interfere with anything else.'

'You *will* be down Christmas Day?'

'I'll try. I'll have to be flying back and forth all the time anyway, damn it. Until we get Dudley to sign that power of attorney I have to be a damn errand boy, shuttling the papers around. I want you to remember what it is you're supposed to be doing down there. Try not to forget that *you're* not on vacation. Hammer away at him about the power of attorney, about giving us a bigger share in his will—'

'Really, Wally, do we have to go all over this again?'

'If that's what it takes to get all this through your head. Try to keep Teddy and Eddy away from him as much as possible, and that goes for Nancy Lee too. Don't let her mewl all over him. If she shows up find her a lifeguard or someone with a big dick to keep her busy.'

Adeline tittered. 'Really, Wallace!'

'I wasn't being facetious, Addy. This isn't a laughing matter. Two hundred million dollars is hardly funny.'

Hardly, Adeline thought. But what was really funny was the figure Wallace was quoting her. She had always thought that Dudley was worth more like three hundred million. That's what her own father had always said. Was Wallace trying to put something over on her too? Or was everyone only guessing?

When Walter who had been with him for thirty years carried Dudley Stanton on to the train and deposited him in his car, his employer clung to him. Dudley Stanton's world was vanishing; he felt everything dropping away from him, he who had once ruled supreme if discreetly, without a lot of fanfare and publicity like the old boys, Rockefeller, the Vanderbilts and the old bastard Ford.

Walter was more than a chauffeur, he was an old friend and he no longer had many of those. These days he had only the nieces, Addy, Teddy and Nancy Lee. Nancy Lee was by far his favourite since she was the least greedy and the most amusing. Adeline was the really greedy one, along with Wallace. Teddy would be if she had a brain in her head or if she had a husband like Wallace. As it was, Eddy was no match for Wallace. If he himself didn't dislike Wallace so much it would be amusing to watch Eddy trying to get his toe in the door in the company, and Wallace slamming the door shut on it everytime. He had often thought of leaving his entire fortune – by his own rough estimate he was worth about four hundred million but he had trouble keeping track lately – to Nancy Lee just for the sheer pleasure of thwarting Addy and Teddy and their husbands. But then that thought was encompassed by the painful awareness that Nancy Lee would dissipate the fortune and his company in a few years with her dissolute ways. She'd already gone through three phoney counts with bulging cocks who had taken her for whatever she was worth. And then when it was all gone, what would be left to show that he had lived and accomplished?

Oh, God, now that it was too late, how he regretted never having taken the time to find himself a good woman who would have been a companion to him now, who would have given him children to carry on his name and perpetuate what he had built . . . to have made it all worthwhile.

Every day he reminded himself that he had to do something before it was too late. Establish some kind of a foundation . . . make endowments ensuring that all he had worked for would go to benefit mankind rather than the poor excuses for humanity who were his family . . . so that his name would live on and stand for something. He had to find the strength to do it! But it was so hard. All the sedatives. These days he could barely rely on his own brain, much less his sick body. And he couldn't trust his lawyers anymore, not knowing which ones bore allegiance to Wallace rather than himself. And it was such a drain being on guard all the time against their encroachment . . . they trying to wrench the powers of control from him before his body was cold.

With his good hand, he gripped Walter's arm. 'You'll be down soon, old friend?'

'Of course, Mr Stanton. I'm leaving in the Rolls the minute I get back to the house.'

'Good. I'll rest easier when you get there.'

Poor Mr Stanton, Walter thought. For all his money, he had nobody. Not one of those three nieces gave a toot for him. He saw that new girl, Judith, watching them make their goodbyes and he said to her, 'You take good care of Mr Stanton, young lady, you hear?'

'Oh I will,' Judith assured him, smiling at the sick old man and his old servant, and Walter thought when she smiled like that, so sweetly, she wasn't such a bad looker.

Judith took Mr Stanton's hand in hers and patted it, and the sick man looked up at the face innocent of makeup and guile and into her clear blue gaze and thought that he saw there the essential goodness of the untainted young, and he felt reassured.

Then the other one, Bonnie Woods, bustling about the car briskly told

Walter to leave so that she could get Mr Stanton settled in properly. He'd have an early dinner in his night clothes, then she'd give him a sedative so he'd be sure to get his rest. 'Here,' she told Judith. 'You get him undressed and I'll go find his nightshirt.'

Dudley Stanton's body was so devoid of flesh he seemed only skin and bones and Judith handled him ever so delicately as if, if she weren't careful, he might shatter. He moaned and turned his face away from her, suddenly ashamed in the face of her youth, of his infirm body, his skeletal form, his wrinkled and shrivelled penis.

Intuitively, she guessed what was upsetting him and she murmured soothingly, 'Everything will be just fine.'

Bonnie Woods, back with the nightshirt, laughed in her brusque manner. 'Of course everything will be fine! Why wouldn't it be? I'm going to go to the dining car and see if I can wrestle up a nice bowl of hot cereal and some rice pudding. Maybe a dish of Jello. Something that will go down real easy and stay there. . . .'

Behind Miss Woods's back, Dudley Stanton made a face and when Judith grinned at him secretively and mischievously, he was gladdened and smiled at her in appreciation.

After dinner, and with Mr Stanton apparently dozing off – sometimes he fought the sedatives – Bonnie Woods asked, 'Well, Judy, do you think you can hold down the fort while I get myself a nightcap in the club car?'

'Of course. I'll manage fine. Take your time.'

'You talked me into it. After all, you never know who you can run into in a club car. Maybe I'll even meet Mr Right.'

As soon as the nurse left Dudley Stanton stirred and saw Judith sitting there so placidly, just watching him. 'Talk to me,' he said. It was a plea. No one really talked to him anymore.

'Aren't you sleepy?'

He smiled slyly. 'Sometimes those sedatives don't work and I pretend they do so they won't make them stronger.'

She nodded, understanding. 'What shall I talk about?'

'Tell me all about yourself.'

'Well, I'm an orphan, really alone in the world. I do have two aunts who are about my age but they have each other so they don't think about me much. They think the world belongs only to them because they have some money and they're beautiful and all they want to do is have good times. . . .'

And then *he* understood how it was and he reached out with his good hand but it trembled. Judith took it between her two hands to steady it and he felt their warmth and strength.

'And what is it you want, my dear?'

'Love. To give it and receive it. . . .'

He nodded and she saw that his lips were white with dryness. She poured a little water into a tumbler and held it to his mouth and he sipped.

Hours later, Judith heard Bonnie Woods in the corridor, laughing raucously, talking in a loud drunken voice, heard a male voice respond, heard them both stumble into the adjacent parlour car, even heard the click of the lock.

The train picked up speed the way trains do in the darkness of the night, rocking along violently, and when Dudley Stanton awakened, disoriented and afraid, Judith stilled the tremors of his frail body by climbing into the narrow berth and holding him hard to her.

4.

Almost immediately Judith took on twice the duties expected of her, some of which were thrust upon her. Bonnie Woods had gone off with the Mr Right she'd met on the train and Judith offered to do double duty. Adeline didn't resist too hard in accepting Judith's offer. It was a blessing not to have to try and find someone else when she was already putting up with an inferior staff.

'Are you sure you'll be able to manage?' Adeline asked perfunctorily, not expecting anything but an affirmative answer. 'Of course, Nurse Higgins will do the shots and whatever really medical tasks there are. All you have to do really are the bedpans and changing the bed linen . . . things like that. And I know Walter will be glad to help you with the lifting and all when he's not busy. And then you can sit and read to Uncle Dudley when you don't have anything else to do. That way you can rest even when you're on duty. And of course, you'll find a little something extra in your pay envelope.' (Why not? They'd be saving on a registered nurse, she thought.) 'And don't even thank me. It will just be a gesture of appreciation.'

'Thank you. Do you think we could put some kind of bed for me in Mr Stanton's room? It would be easier, and then I—'

'Don't say another word. Of course we could. That's a wonderful idea. A real timesaver.'

When they moved Judith's cot into Dudley's sickroom he too thought it was a wonderful idea. He remembered how good it felt that night on the train when she had climbed into his berth.

Nurse Higgins certainly didn't mind that Judith would be sleeping in Mr Stanton's room, not feeling at all usurped. She considered herself lucky to have Judith around. She didn't try to get out of a thing, satisfied to do all the dirty work, which was fine with her especially since she was having trouble with her feet. Swollen they were, probably from the change of climate.

Still when she found Judith exercising Mr Stanton's paralyzed leg on Christmas morning when everyone was downstairs unwrapping presents, she was furious with the nerve of the girl. 'And who told you to do that? No doctor ever said one word about doing that. You're overstepping yourself, my girl, not to mention that you may be doing harm to Mr Stanton's whole nervous system. Here—' And she unceremoniously shoved Judith aside with her considerable bulk and began adjusting the covers about Dudley, who protested by flaying out at her with his good arm.

'Oh stop!' Judith begged. 'Please Miss Higgins! You're upsetting Mr Stanton. I never would have done it if I'd thought there'd be this scene. If you'll just stop, I'll leave. I'll quit! Anything if you'll only stop upsetting Mr Stanton!'

'Hold on here,' Nurse Higgins stepped back. 'Who said there's a scene? Who said Mr Stanton's upset? Who asked you to quit?'

'I'm sorry,' Judith said with a quiet dignity, addressing herself to Dudley Stanton. 'I can't stay on in a place where there are scenes, when I've only tried to act on my patient's behalf. And I certainly can't have you upset. I will have to leave.'

Her words struck terror in Dudley's heart. Judith was the first nurse who had ever treated him like a person rather than a body . . . a corpse. Why, she was more angel than girl! He couldn't lose her. He wouldn't! He was still the master of his house, by God! He found his voice. '*You're* staying! It's Miss Higgins who will be leaving!'

Bertha Higgins stepped back, her mouth open in amazement. Somehow, in a matter of a few seconds, she had lost one of the easiest berths she had ever had. And what about her months in Palm Beach? The season in the sun she'd been promised? 'We'll just see what Mrs Purvis has to say about this!'

Adeline, dispensing gifts to the staff, was already distracted and resentful. Nancy Lee was present, as were Teddy and Eddy, but where was Wallace? He had broken his promise to be there and Nancy Lee's gold-tipped cigarette had fallen out of the jade and ivory holder and had burnt a disgusting hole in the pale blue and rose Aubusson. And she didn't give a damn that Nancy Lee had brought her two pairs of nylons as a Christmas present. God knew where they came from or what she'd done to get them. It was ridiculous. Not three weeks into the war and already there was a shortage of nylons. God knew what was next!

Adeline listened to Nurse Higgins for only a few seconds before flying into her own rage. 'Why did you upset Mr Stanton? God, don't I have enough problems?'

Teddy's Eddy thought that since Nurse Higgins was a registered nurse, and Judith only a practical one, Judith should go. 'What do you know about anything?' she turned on him.

The important thing was that Dudley liked Judith and Wallace had told her to please Dudley in all the little things so that he wouldn't make a fuss about the larger issues. Besides, these registered nurses were a pain in the fanny. The minute the clock ticked off their eight hours, they dropped everything, even if it was a bedpan! If they were young, the minute they were finished they were off to meet their boyfriends. if they were older, all they wanted to do was sit around and eat candy. A box of chocolates wasn't safe from destruction around them!

She went upstairs to speak to Dudley, found Judith sitting by the bed reading aloud from a biography of Roosevelt and Dudley chuckling at some observation Judith had just made. It was the picture of tranquility! And as soon as he saw Adeline, Dudley blurted: 'I don't want to see that Higgins woman's face again!'

'Of course not, Uncle Dudley. I quite agree with you.'

The matter was settled.

Adeline was willing to go along with Judith's plan to hire a round of part-time practical nurses to assist her rather than a couple of RNS who were in short supply and posed more problems than they solved. Especially since Judith was willing to do all the interviewing, hiring and take care of all the details. As Judith herself said, the nursing duties required in Dudley's case really only involved keeping Dudley comfortable, plus dispensing a few pills, and Judith was certainly qualified to do that. Dudley's illness, after all, wasn't a life-or-death matter. According to Dr Phillips, it was only a question of time, since Dudley's condition was one of irreversible gradual deterioration, unless he suffered another stroke which could finish him off quickly.

'What about the . . . needles?' Adeline felt it was her duty to inquire about the shots, but she screwed her face up in distaste.

'Oh, the administering of the needles are just a matter of technique,' Judith told her. 'You know, often nurses are better at it than the doctors. Right from the beginning I had a good touch. It's just that. First, you have to get the vein to stick out prominently and then you have to stick—Here, let me give you an idea—' She reached for Adeline's arm.

Adeline backed off in horror. 'That's not necessary. I'm sure you know what you're doing.'

The most wonderful part of it all, as far as Adeline was concerned, was that once Judith arranged for several part-time locals from West Palm Beach to come and go on a revolving schedule to do all the menial duties, Judith was not only free to devote herself completely to making Dudley comfortable, getting him into his wheelchair and out for daily airings, something which he hadn't done much of before, she was finding time to help her, Adeline, by taking care of some of the burdensome details of running the house. She took the initiative as Mrs Beachum, the housekeeper, never did. Thus, she herself was free to go off to the Bath and Tennis Club or the Everglades for some golf. She even had time to go boating on Lake Worth with friends. . . . Even Wallace was pleased since Judith always found some kind of mistake in the various tradesmen's bills, which resulted in the saving of money. Best of all, she, Adeline, now only had to pop in on Dudley for a couple of minutes a day. She *did* hate the smell of the sickroom.

The only fly in the ointment was that Wallace was beginning to experience difficulty in getting fuel for the company's plane which was a damned nuisance since Wallace did have to run back and forth repeatedly. Trust something like that sneak attack on Pearl Harbor to come along and spoil what amounted to the best season she had ever enjoyed in Palm Beach. But she guessed that Wallace would take care of the fuel problem with the right amount of cash slipped to the right person. And if not, she'd ask Judith if she had any bright ideas on the subject, since she was so smart as well as capable. Amazingly so for one so young. Was it possible she was lying about being only eighteen? Then she laughed at herself for being so silly. That one didn't have a touch of guile in her, and she was hardly sophisticated enough either to deceive or conspire to deceive.

Walter had just returned from the pharmacy in town and Judith asked him if he had had any trouble getting any of Dr Phillips' prescriptions filled.

'No, Miss Judith, why would I?'

'Well, I thought perhaps because Dr Phillips is licensed in Massachusetts and not in Florida—'

'Oh, that wouldn't be any problem. We've been doing business with the same pharmacy for twenty years. And every year Dr Phillip's comes down at least once to check up on Mr Stanton. I guess he made some kind of arrangement with the pharmacy as well as with Dr Prouty who sees Mr Stanton here.'

'I'm sure you're right.'

But then rather than ask Dr Prouty for certain drugs she wanted, she asked Dr Phillips for a few blank but signed prescription forms when he did come down to see Dudley. 'I want them just in case . . .' Judith told the doctor. 'Just between you and me, Dr Phillips, there have been times when I've called Dr Prouty and it was days before he got back to me. I guess he's just not as dedicated as you,' she flattered him.

Jonas Phillips had just pronounced Dudley in the best shape he'd seen him in in ten years. He even said that Judith's physical therapy must be doing some good even though he didn't usually put credence in it. And those roses in Dudley's cheeks. It had to be that Judith was getting Dudley out into that fresh sea air. He saw no reason not to give the devoted girl the blank prescription forms she asked for. If she wanted to give Dudley some of those special vitamins she found listed in those medical journals she was so fond of reading, what harm was there in it? The worst thing that could happen was that she'd waste some of the Stanton money and Addy and Wally would end up with a few dollars less. And who knew? The placebo effect couldn't be entirely discounted.

'You've got a little treasure there, Addy,' he told his hostess as she pulled him along to the party at Gloria Biddle's in Manalapan. 'Try and keep her.'

'My God, yes! You should see her giving Dudley a back rub. Thirty minutes, if it's a second. Wasn't it clever of me to find her?'

After Walter left the room, Judith carefully removed the labels from one of the prescription bottles. Vitamins were good for Dudley, but a little stimulant every now and then was going to make him feel even better. Like a boy of eighteen. . . .

Dudley Stanton was convinced that his physical therapy was working . . . that he felt *something* stirring on his paralyzed side. And the massages Judith administered were the best part of his day. All the other nurses had been stingy in the time they allotted for the massage and their touch was brisk and impersonal. But Judith always washed her hands with warm water first, then kneaded every inch of him so tenderly, slowly . . . as if every touch was a caress. He couldn't remember being this happy and satisfied in years.

Then one afternoon as Judith was giving him his massage, she took his old and withered penis – that which was as good as dead for all the pleasure it gave him – in her warm hand and massaged *it*! At first he gasped, his eyes flew open wide and he looked into her face. She was smiling sweetly at him. No, it wasn't a dream, and he closed his eyes again and moaned, savouring the exquisite tremors, the almost forgotten sensations coursing through him. Her fingers were incredibly gentle as they moved up and down and he groaned, praying for climax one second, and postponement of it the next.

Then, he screamed out in exultation as he ejaculated, then moaned again

70

and again as his body shook, then he screamed out again, and wept, reaching for the hand that had provided him this pleasure he hadn't experienced for a decade. He took the hand to his lips and kissed it convulsively until Judith withdrew it, and placed her lips there on his dry, thin ones. And he groaned in exquisite gratification and gratitude.

It was the first time Judith had kissed a man, certainly the first time she had touched a man's genitals. In the ensuing days, she got better at both.

She learned to kiss him first – to brush his lips lingeringly then withdraw before applying pressure, to suck at his bottom lip, to part her own lips and let her tongue do much of the work; to dart it in and out, allowing it to caress every inch of his opened mouth as it reached out as if to swallow her tongue. Then when he was in total frenzy, and only then, did she grasp his member, moving her hand up and down slowly at first, then increasing and decreasing the pressure and speed until he begged for release.

Then one afternoon with the sun streaming into the room, she couldn't bring him to ejaculation no matter how she coaxed his penis manually and he wept in frustration.

'Don't cry,' she whispered. 'Judith will fix it,' and she brought her mouth down to where her hand had been and kissed him there the very same way she kissed his lips – softly, persuasively, licking, flicking, nibbling, even gently biting before taking the phallus into her mouth deeply, hugging it with her lips and sliding them up and down and around until he erupted into her with a scream.

After she had cleaned and was settling him in for his afternoon nap, he said, 'I love you.'

'And I, you. . . .'

He believed her. He wasn't fool enough to think that she loved him in the romantic sense, the way a young girl loved a young man, or the way a strong woman loved a man her equal in age and strength, but he was convinced that she loved him the way a caring sensitive woman might love a good friend, in a warm, affectionate and compassionate manner.

As for the way *he* loved *her*. Ah, that was something else again. One part was gratitude and another appreciation, but a large part, the largest was the unadulterated love of the young boy madly infatuated with the lovely girl in the first throes of romantic enchantment combined with the mature love of the virile, healthy man for his sexual partner, with a sense of giving and receiving, an equal evocation of body and spirit. But whatever the nature of her love, he wasn't prepared to turn it away. By God, he wasn't dead yet! And what was more, Judith had given him a reason to live. . . .

Dudley directed Walter to go to the finest jewellery store on Worth Avenue – he no longer knew which one that might be – and purchase a bracelet for Judith. Since he had to give Walter some guideline, he gave him the only one that made sense to both of them – he told him to spend ten thousand dollars.

'And how shall I pay for it, sir? Shall I charge it?'

'No,' Dudley said grandly. 'I'll give you a signed cheque and you'll fill in the amount. *They* might think I'm as good as dead and have taken over the running of my company but I'm still the master of my personal resources,

Walter old boy. There, in that desk . . . the top drawer. Bring me one of those chequebooks.'

He hadn't signed a cheque in three years and it felt damn good to do it now, using his good hand while Walter held the chequebook in place.

Still, he anticipated some kind of backlash. Most likely, the minute Walter made the purchase, someone – a salesclerk or a chance observer – would call Addy. But he wasn't worried. He could still deal with that greedy bunch! He felt stronger than when he was fifty . . . forty . . . maybe even, thirty-five!

But then Judith surprised him when he presented her with the diamond bracelet with the Ceylon sapphire set in the centre. She burst into tears and refused to accept it. 'How can you think I could accept any gift for what I've done out of love?'

Dudley was further surprised when he was unable to change Judith's mind and she herself returned the bracelet to the store. Then he was sure that she was not only kind and wonderful, but a young woman of complete integrity with loving and generous instincts, so unlike his grasping relatives.

5.

Soon after the return to Boston, Adeline insisted that she needed a vacation on her own, away from all household cares and obligations. She'd received an invitation from her old friend, Lucy Cole, in Atlanta and she wanted to go. 'I'll be gone scarcely four weeks,' she told Wallace who was against her going.

'You got absolutely nowhere in Palm Beach getting the old bastard's power of attorney and there's been nothing from him about changing his will – everything's still divided three equal ways after all we've done for the old man. Suppose while you're gone, he drops dead. Then what?'

'But he won't,' Adeline offered cheerfully. 'Ever since Judith's taken over his care he's positively blossomed.'

'Is that good?'

'Well, it does give us more time, doesn't it? I promise that when I get back I'll keep at him day and night. And with Judith in charge while I'm gone, Teddy and Nancy Lee won't even have to come here at all, and you won't even have to move in here. You can stay where you're comfortable in our house. And then you can just check on things when you come by with your papers or to discuss things with Dudley.'

Judith decided to use the four weeks Adeline would be gone to make a definitive move. First, she ensured the complete allegiance of the staff. She had always addressed all the servants deferentially, asking for rather than commanding their help. Now she went to Dudley and advised him how inadequately his servants were being compensated. Wallace and Addy were so niggardly when it came to the help, and it just wasn't right. It behoved him as one of the more fortunate and privileged persons in America to be more generous than others. 'Let the Stanton name stand for fairness and charity and we all know charity begins at home. Take Walter. And Mrs Beachum. They've been with you for years and they're so loyal to you, far more than—Well, never mind. And their salaries are below standard, salaries are going up what with the war—'

Dudley hadn't even thought about any of this before, concerned as he'd been about his own health and well-being. But now that he was feeling so much stronger, he was ashamed to be called up short by his angel of mercy. 'Of course you're right, Judith, as you always are. You decide what everyone should get and tell the office that's what I want and if Wallace objects, I'll deal with him!'

Judith personally made the announcement of the raises, managing in the process to be modest even as she took the credit. In addition, she told each member of the staff how vociferously she'd defended them, personally vouching for their dedication and honesty whenever Nancy Lee or Teddy cast any aspersions on them. 'I just tell them off, just as I've told Mrs Purvis in the past when she's made the same kind of remarks. I told all three of them that I will not listen to that kind of talk about any of you.'

As a result the help were barely courteous to Nancy Lee or Teddy when, under Judith's instructions, they turned them away at the door with a curt, 'Mr Stanton is sleeping,' or 'Mr Stanton is out for airing with Miss Tyler,' or 'Mr Stanton is having his massage and cannot be disturbed.'

Eddy was as easily turned away when he came on company business, but of course, not Wallace. Judith had to deal with him herself.

'Mr Stanton has just fallen asleep and in all conscience I just can't bring myself to wake him. He had a bad night.'

The bad night had consisted of Judith holding him and covering him with kisses whenever he stirred, but she was hardly about to divulge that. 'Why don't you just leave those papers and when Mr Stanton awakens, I'll give them to him and send them back to you.'

At first Wallace didn't feel that he could insist she wake the old man, but after this happened three or four times, he insisted on seeing his uncle. He had matters to discuss that couldn't be put off. But Judith was prepared for this too. 'If you'll tell me what these matters are exactly, I'll relay that information—'

The impertinence of the girl! She was getting too big for her breeches, and Wallace pushed past her and up the stairs to Dudley's bedroom. Judith raced after him, and followed him into Dudley's room to cry out, 'I told Mr Purvis that you were resting, Mr Stanton. I tried to stop him but he wouldn't listen, he pushed right past me.' Her voice broke and at the same time she rubbed her arm, gasping in pain.

The significance of this wasn't lost on either Wallace or Dudley.

'I didn't touch you!' Wallace cried out.

'I know you didn't *mean* to hurt me—'

'Get out!' Dudley croaked. 'And don't come back here again! From now on, you can leave all your papers at the door.'

'That was very courageous of you, Dudley, but I'll have to leave.'

'No! Never! I won't allow it!'

'Oh, my poor Dudley. They'll make my life miserable but it's you I'm concerned about. I'm afraid of what they'll do to you.'

'What can they do to me? I'm still in charge. They still don't have my power of attorney. I'm still the one who has to sign the papers. They can't do anything without me—'

73

'They'll find a way. You can't win. You're an invalid and they're too strong for you. And they have all the lawyers on their side.'

'I'm getting stronger every day. And I have you. You'll help me!'

'How can I help you? They're too strong for both of us. Who *am* I, after all? I'm barely nineteen and not much more than a servant.'

'Don't say that! I'll marry you! I know I'm old and sick and can only offer you money but at least you'll have that – the name and the position. And then after I'm gone you can have a real man in every sense of the word. Marry me, Judith, and we'll fight them together!'

She had anticipated that Dudley would propose but she couldn't accept . . . not yet. If she married a sick old man only a few months after having gone to work for him, she was too vulnerable to legal attack. She'd be labelled an opportunist, and they'd have Dudley declared incompetent and their marriage invalid.

'Oh, Dudley, as much as I want to marry you and take care of you, I can't. They'd just go to court and have you declared mentally incompetent. As it is Wallace is probably talking to the lawyers this very minute.'

Dudley's heart was palpitating and he grew frightened and the more frightened he became the less he could think of what to do. All he knew was that he couldn't lose Judith. 'Tell me, Judith, tell me what we can do!'

'I think the first thing we must do is find you a legal firm . . . the best in the city . . . one that has nothing to do with Stanton Enterprises or Wallace. One which is above reproach.'

She read a list of the most prestigious law firms in the city to Dudley, then the names of the senior partners in these firms, waiting for a name to ring a bell in Dudley's consciousness. While Wallace and Addy had conspired to keep Dudley shut off from both old friends and business associates, Dudley had once been one of Boston's leading citizens, had known everybody who was anybody and enjoyed the respect of the city's élite. She was hoping that one of these names belonged to someone who remembered Dudley with respect and affection.

When she came to the name Fenton Hardwicke of Hardwicke, Hardwicke and Lindsay and Dudley called out, 'Fenny!' she knew she had found the person she was looking for. 'Fenny? Then you know him?'

'Know him? Fenny and I are old chums. Harvard classmates. We both wore the old green pig-studded tie!'

'What?' Judith cried out impatiently. 'A pig-studded tie?'

'That's the tie of the Porcellians, my club at Harvard. When the club was founded in 1791 they called it the Pig Club because its first members, Francis Cabot Lowell and Robert Paine, loved roasted pig. But later on they decided they needed a more dignified name,' Dudley chuckled.

'And both you and Fenny belonged to the old Pig Club? What fun!' Yes, she thought, Fenny was her man.

Fenton Hardwicke, who had established the law firm of Hardwicke, Hardwicke and Lindsay before serving on the Massachusetts Supreme Court, had gone back to full days at the firm after retiring from the bench, and his name

74

was a hallowed one. Why, even Franklin Delano Roosevelt hadn't been elected to the Porcellian Club! What court in Boston would dare deny former Justice Fenton Hardwicke's client and old friend?

Judith called the firm and made an appointment for Mr Stanton to meet with his old friend in a week's time. Then she had a tailor come to the house to take Dudley's measurements for six new suits, one of which was to be ready within the week. 'It's a disgrace!' she told Dudley. 'A man of your stature not having a new suit in years.' And while she herself had been shaving and trimming Dudley's hair, she arranged for a barber to come to the house every morning to ensure a perfect daily shave, the most fashionable, meticulously trimmed hair styling.

But Dudley was bewildered. 'How can I go to Fenton's office? Why didn't you ask him to come here to see me?'

'Because while you might be in a wheelchair, we want you to appear to be in tip-top condition and the most vigorous health. After all, what significance has a wheelchair?' she asked gaily. 'The President doesn't have any problem conducting a war and leading the country from a wheelchair, does he?'

While Dudley could have pointed out the President was at least twenty years his junior and wasn't actually sick even though crippled, he had never seen Judith so jubilant and excited. He couldn't bear to burst her bubble of enthusiasm and expectation. By God, he wouldn't let her down!

The morning of their appointment, Judith increased the amount of stimulant she administered on a daily basis. Just a tiny bit. Not enough to harm Dudley, just enough to make him feel good, full of energy. And then she had to compliment herself when she wheeled him into Fenton's office. In his new suit, bright tie, massaged to a rosy glow, his hair well barbered, his nails buffed, several pounds heavier than he'd been when she entered his employ, Dudley looked the picture of superb health. Even Walter, who helped her as far as the lift, was impressed. 'You look like a million dollars, Mr Stanton,' And then, 'You too, Miss Tyler. You look right pretty.'

'Why, thank you, Walter,' she dimpled. While she knew that she didn't look exactly pretty, she did appear 'right' in her new black suit, which while decorous, was decidedly not dowdy. And for the first time in her life she wore a hint of lipstick – a pale pink. To wear *none* in this day and age would make her seem a bit *outré*. As it was she now presented the image of a modest young woman but one who was definitely on top of things.

Old Fenny couldn't believe how good his friend looked after all the stories he had heard about him having one foot in the grave. But what was even more extraordinary than Dudley's appearance was his near total recall. Why, the son-of-a-gun remembered an escapade they'd shared back in '88! An adventure he himself hadn't even thought of in at least thirty years . . . forty years, maybe . . . much less remembered in absolute detail.

Dudley reminded Fenny of the time they – two freshmen and fearful of horsing around in Boston where they might be spotted visiting a house of ill repute – had gone down to New York's notorious Tenderloin section and visited the infamous Haymarket, the most brazen bordello of the day, and had actually run into one of their most dignified professors, Jasper Layton. 'Will you ever forget the look on old Jasper's face?' Dudley asked. 'And remember how he ran down the corridor in his longjohns which were as bright red as the Haymarket's velvet walls?'

Fenny was truly astonished. He had no way of knowing that Judith had interrogated Dudley for hours until he had come up with a vague memory of that excursion to New York, and had even suggested to him that the Haymarket's walls were upholstered in red velvet and that the professor had been in his underwear. Once she had gone over all the details with him again and again until he was convinced that everything was indeed fact, he was able to retell the story without a hitch so confidently that Fenton was chagrined that his own memory was not as keen. After all, they were both seventy-two.

What a damned shame Dudley was so inconvenienced by being forced to sit in a wheelchair when he was still as sharp as a tack, Fenton thought. Why, he should be in the forefront of that company of his, still functioning as one of the country's most brilliant financiers. Damn it, the country needed men like him now in wartime! That was why he himself had gone back to work after retiring from the bench. Just because a man was in his seventies didn't mean his abilities were gone . . . that he was to be shunted aside by men who didn't have one-tenth of his wisdom.

'They're so avaricious, I fear for Mr Stanton,' Judith confided to Fenton. 'I don't think they'll stop at anything. I'm convinced that in their attempt to get Mr Stanton's power of attorney, they're prepared to have him declared incompetent.'

Fenton smiled smugly. 'I think I'd actually enjoy seeing them try. Now, let's proceed step by step.'

The first matter to be taken up was Dudley's will. He wanted Addy and Teddy out altogether, with a few bones thrown to Nancy Lee. But Judith, in line with her position as a fair and kind person, suggested that he leave all three nieces something. 'You were fond of them once. . . .'

In the end it was agreed that Addy and Teddy would each get twenty-five thousand, with Nancy Lee getting fifty, in the hope that she'd use the money to start life anew and get herself a respectable husband.

'And the servants,' Judith reminded him. Especially Walter and Mrs Beachum. You must provide for them generously.'

'You think of everyone, Judith but yourself.' But he was going to make sure she was taken care of, in spite of herself. He told Fenton that he wanted to leave half his estate for the establishment of some kind of Foundation and half to Judith who was the best friend a man could hope to have in a lifetime.

But Judith was shocked, aghast. 'It would be wrong. You only know me a few months—'

'A lifetime,' Dudley corrected her.

'No, Dudley, I can't allow you to do this. I wouldn't even know what to do with so much money. It's a terrible responsibility. If you want to leave me a few thousand dollars, I could accept that. I would say that you were being kind and even fair but I don't want to even think about that time when—'

Fenton, thinking that Dudley was fortunate in having found this unusually mature young lady who was so obviously concerned with his welfare, had to agree with Judith. Leaving the bulk of his fortune to charity was one thing, but leaving half of it to Judith wouldn't work out. While he felt reasonably sure that he could beat Dudley's family in a competency hearing, a contesting of a will in which so much money was left to a woman Dudley hadn't known for that long was quite another thing. . . . If Dudley wanted to provide for Judith he certainly should be able to do that . . . there were other ways. He could make her an outright gift now, and he could appoint her as the executor of his will, along with the law firm, as well as making her the trustee of the Foundation which would assure her of a couple of million dollars in fees. . . .

Dudley said he would accept *all* of Fenton's suggestions and alternatives, although Judith still protested – she'd be accepting far too much money, while Dudley thought it still wasn't enough for the woman who had restored him to life and made that life worth living. Personally, he wasn't going to rest until he made her his wife.

And Fenton thought Dudley was a lucky dog, convinced that they were more than employer and employee. What was old Dudley up to? Was he capable of getting off his jollies? He himself hadn't had an erection in seven years.

It was agreed that for the present, Judith would have Dudley's power of attorney, the better to deal with Wallace Purvis until he could be eased out of the company.

After thinking things over Judith decided that the wisest thing to do was get rid of Stanton Enterprises and, at the same time, Wallace and his bunch. Convincing Fenton that Dudley was up to running his company had not been difficult but she knew better. And she wasn't fool enough to think that she could do it either, no matter how many assistants she relied upon to help her. More so, she didn't want to have to rely on anyone except herself for she trusted no one else, and what she was capable of was managing an *invested* fortune, not running a multi-faced company.

Stanton Enterprises was one huge privately-owned holding company that served as an umbrella for many companies involved in shipping, mining, railroads, oil, lumber and manufacturing. Now Judith proposed to Dudley that they sell off everything and invest the proceeds in public corporations where others did all the work and the investors reaped a clean and clear profit. At first Dudley was deeply upset at this idea – his company gone with only a stack of stock certificates to show for it all? His building – the Stanton Building, the tallest building in the city with its thousands of employees – would that be gone too?

'It doesn't have to be. It could be incorporated into the Stanton Center which will house your Stanton Foundation and more . . . so much more! The Stanton Theater for the Performing Arts. . . . Maybe the Stanton Museum or the Stanton Library. . . . Perhaps there can even be a Stanton Hospital. Why should all this wait until after you're gone? Let's do it now . . . or as soon as we can. Let the Stanton name stand for something more than money in your own time, Dudley! It's what you should have done ten years ago . . . twenty years ago. . . . Don't you see? It's a dream which can come true in your lifetime. A dream that can make the dreams of millions come true while you're here to see to it!'

Dudley, tears streaming down his cheeks, could only see Judith. *She* was his dream come true. . . .

Judith got into the bed with him to kiss away the tears and even though, for the sake of conserving his strength, she rationed his sexual gratification to once a week, she thought that this time she would make an exception to celebrate their pact. This time, when she took his organ into her mouth, delicately washing it with her tongue, it took only a few seconds before he erupted into her, his body shuddering and trembling. And he burst into fresh tears. 'Oh God, why can't it be twenty years ago?' he lamented.

She pressed his head to her breast. 'We'll try, Dudley. We'll try to push back the clock.'

But she knew that she had to work fast. Rather than pushing back the clock, she had to beat it.

6.

Judith's first action as the empowered head of Stanton Enterprises was to fire Wallace and his brother-in-law Eddy, their services terminated with 'one hour to vacate the premises.' She did this personally the better to enjoy Wallace's rage. As anticipated the family immediately filed for a sanity hearing for their poor uncle who had fallen under Judith's malevolent spell. The sanity hearing was set for the autumn and in the meantime Judith proceeded with her plan. She fired the handful of executives who were most flagrantly loyal to Wallace, this serving as a reminder to the others as to who was signing their paycheques. Then she brought in a team of experts to keep everything running as she started selling off the various divisions of the company.

In order to facilitate the discreet investment of the proceeds of these sales, she bought a small, dignified brokerage house which arranged for the discreet purchase of huge blocks of the usual blue-chip stocks, in addition to the shares of those industries for which she foresaw a glorious post-war future, companies which would produce television sets and business machines and planes, foreseeing a new era when the general public would jump on a plane as easily as they did a bus. Dudley approved of everything she did, admiring her precocious business acumen as much as he did everything else about her.

And as the country geared up for its battle of survival so did Judith. She got busy on her personal home front. She started a search for the proper site for the proposed Stanton Center, interviewed architects and ordered renderings and blueprints, and taking a leaf from the President, she had an indoor swimming pool built in the basement of the Stanton house and brought in a trainer to supervise Dudley's rehabilitative swimming exercises. No one would be able to stand up in court and accuse her of acting in her own interest.

She instituted two regular evenings a week. One was the Tuesday night salon to which she invited the brightest and the best of Boston's Brahmin society – the theologians, educators, artists and patrons of the arts, as well as those who merely shone at the art of clipping coupons. The Saturday night dinners were reserved for Dudley's old friends and associates from his more active days where the conversation was light and bright.

For these occasions she enjoyed dressing Dudley up as if he were her doll. He wore only pale suits, never dark and sombre; brightly coloured ties or ascots.

Sometimes she decked him out in a silk smoking jacket or one of burgundy velvet. And then sitting at the head of his dinner table, he even drank a few ounces of wine along with his guests, as anyone in good health might. The food served was always splendid and hardly anyone took notice that Dudley ate a somewhat more restricted fare.

The assembled discoursed on everything – the state of the Boston Community Fund, the policies of Harvard's president, perhaps even a bit of gossip about who was seeing whom. . . . Everyone was unfailingly impressed with Judith, especially Dudley's friends' wives who were her senior by at least forty years but not threatened by her youth as they might have been if she'd been sleek and glamorous. Rather, they were sympathetic. 'Such a young girl to have so much responsibility on her shoulders.'

One thing definitely in Judith's favour was that she was always becomingly attired – no short skirts, no exposed cleavage. In fact she was so modestly dressed she didn't even wear the minimal string of pearls that was really mandatory, considering that she was serving as Dudley's hostess. One would have thought that was the least Dudley would have gifted her with, under the circumstances.

While guest lists varied from one Saturday to the next, it almost always included Judge Hardwicke and his wife Alicia, who told Fenton, 'If I had a daughter, I would like her to be very much like Judith Tyler.'

With things going so well, Judith was reluctant to go to Newport for the brief New England summer season, but once there in residence at the Stanton 'cottage,' as the summer homes of the rich were referred to there, she thought that if she never went anywhere else, she'd be content. When she'd done her research on Newport, as thorough as usual, she'd come across the words of the Grand Duke Boris of Russia who had said of Newport, 'I have never dreamed of such luxury . . . such an outpouring of riches. It is like walking on gold!'

Judith agreed. Stanton Halls, standing proud on Bellevue Avenue, that street of golden homes bordering on the Atlantic, did seem more suitable for royalty than mere citizens of democracy – vaulted ceilings, leaded windows, a neo-Gothic extravaganza. She spent hours wandering through the house, touching panelled walls, running her hand over polished wood, sitting in the conservatory lush with greens and its view of the sea, strolling down its art gallery filled with the paintings of Dutch masters. There were Imperial porcelains, museum quality pieces from the factory in Sèvres, marble fireplaces brought intact from chateaux in France, antique carpets from Persia, velvet-soft with age. And Judith became more determined than ever. If this was Stanton's castle, then she would be its reigning queen. And if she would be queen, then she would have to possess, if not a king, then surely a prince. And this would be where he would be born . . . in Stanton Halls, a prince's ancestral home.

She worked harder than ever to make Dudley happy, feeling an affection for him born out of gratitude – it was he who would make all things possible. And even though he felt stronger and happier each succeeding day, he also felt his inadequacy more acutely. A man could give a woman all the money in the world, but he couldn't feel like a man if he was unable to lay with her the way it was intended.

'I only wish I could do for you what you do for me,' he said to her one day as they sat on Stanton Halls' private beach, he having been lifted from his wheelchair to the sand. She knew what he meant – he wanted to take her to the heights of climax. There was one more thing she had to do for Dudley Stanton.

There in the sand, she undressed him and then herself, positioning her body on top of his. At first he was startled, and then afraid. 'But I can't—' he cried out in anguish.

'But you can! Where there's love, everything is possible.'

With her hand she manipulated his shaft against her labia and while he didn't enter her, he wasn't sure and she didn't enlighten him. But he did become excited and his breath grew laboured. Judith, pumping furiously, panted and moaned and within minutes she screamed out in fulfilment, and as she did so, he spewed his meagre semen. Afterwards, he was even more grateful to her than he had been before. He had actually given a woman – his beloved Judith – the kind of pleasure a real man could, and Judith reflected that a little pretence was a small enough gift to make to a man who was going to give her everything!

'Oh, marry me, Judith! Marry me!' he begged and while she fully intended to do just that, it wasn't quite time.

It was only a sanity hearing and not a spectacular murder case but since this was Boston where the public didn't often get a chance to read about such high jinks, the newspapers played the case up to the hilt. The cast of characters was intriguing – the nurse, a mousy nineteen-year-old girl and not even a real nurse; the sick old man, paralyzed, his fortune rumoured to be a half billion dollars; the three nieces – two socially impeccable and the third thrice-married and thrice-divorced from titled Europeans, all seeking control of their uncle's fortune and company which was fast being sold off under their noses, and claiming that the mouse was unduly influencing their poor, senile uncle for her own gain.

While it was Dudley Stanton's diminished mental capacity that was on trial, it was Judith Tyler's reputation that was at stake and her aunt Francesca called, asking if there was anything she could do. If it would help, she and Carlotta would come and testify, attesting to Judith's good character.

But Judith was scornful. 'My good character will speak for itself. Do you really think the court would take anything you and Carlotta said seriously? More likely, anything either one of you said would be more detrimental than helpful since they'd be bound to consider the source.'

Francesca hung up on her and she and Carlotta didn't attend the hearing, but the general public packed the hall of justice, hoping to hear some lurid and juicy details about life among the very rich.

Judith, wearing low-heeled slightly scuffed navy blue pumps and a navy rayon dress with a white peter-pan collar, her drab blond hair in a knot, wheeled her employer into the courtroom. He was nattily attired in pearl gray worsted, an exact match for his sleekly combed hair, his red silk pocket handkerchief matching his red silk tie. He didn't look at his three nieces at all, they all in furs since it was November. Nancy Lee wore a three-quarter length silver fox while Addie wore plain dark brown mink and Teddy was in black Persian lamb since she believed black was her most becoming shade.

The three nieces told similar stories – they'd been dedicated to their uncle for years, seeing to his comfort and seeking to make his last years pleasant until Judith Tyler wormed her way in and proceeded to take advantage of the addled old man. 'Oh, how I rue the day I hired her!' Adeline wept, dabbing at her eyes with an ecru linen handkerchief. 'Uncle Dudley, so befuddled, was just putty in her hands. She turned him against us. . . .'

Wallace Purvis testified that when he ran the business the firm had flourished. He produced charts and graphs and financial statements, and even those who really didn't understand financial statements couldn't help but be impressed by the numbers being thrown around – not mere hundreds of thousands but millions! Wallace asked the court plaintively: Was the man who allowed Judith Tyler to fire the executive responsible for such huge profits in his right mind?

The psychiatrist the nieces brought in spoke mostly in general terms but Dr Prouty of Newport testified on their behalf, saying he found the aged man frequently disoriented and divorced from reality. But Boston's own, Dr Jonas Phillips, emphatically stated that he found Mr Stanton's physical condition vastly improved since Miss Tyler had joined the staff, and his mental outlook considerably brightened. And the psychiatrist giving testimony for Dudley Stanton joked, saying that he wished he himself had Mr Stanton's financial savvy, confessing that while talking with the financier, he had asked him for a tip on the stock market and – he smiled sheepishly – it had proved most lucrative.

Walter the chauffeur testified how he played chess with Mr Stanton at least twice a week, and how Mr Stanton usually beat the pants off him. 'I'd say Mr Stanton's got all his marbles and then some. . . .' Then Walter revealed how he'd been sent to buy a token of gratitude for Miss Tyler – a $10,000 bracelet, and a murmur swept through the courtroom, followed by another when he added, 'And she returned it to the jewellery store herself . . . said she couldn't accept it when she'd only been doing her duty.' Then, gratuitously, he offered: 'Those nieces . . . they ain't a tenth the woman Judith Tyler is. Sure, she's only a young girl but she really cares about Mr Stanton and them others – all they care about is Mr Stanton's money.'

The nieces' attorney objected but the words had been said, and coming from a plain man of the working class and not from one of the very rich, they carried the ring of sincerity, of unbiased truth.

Mrs Beachum the housekeeper testified, 'Miss Tyler is a saint and they – them others, they're a hard bunch.'

The rest of the staff, one after the other, confirmed this sentiment, told of Judith's loving round-the-clock care. Then came several members of the Tuesday night salon to give testimony on how well-informed Dudley was, how he was up on everything from what was happening on the warfront to the state of the arts. And then came some of the old friends who gathered at the Saturday night dinner parties to offer their evaluations: ' . . . Such a charming man . . .' 'Bright . . . so bright!' 'As brilliant as ever.' Alicia Hardwicke, the Judge's wife, said of Judith: ' . . . Always dressed so modestly. I never saw her wear so much as a jewelled pin or a string of pearls. All I ever saw was her total dedication to Dudley.'

Most telling of all was the testimony of Judge Fenton Hardwicke who played golf with the presiding judge, Lucas Safire. Fenton, who had left the actual conducting of the case to junior members of his firm, had himself sworn in to relate how Dudley remembered an escapade they'd shared in colourful detail. ' . . . And this happened in 1888!' Then he told how when Dudley Stanton wanted to leave half his money to Judith Tyler, she had flatly refused.

'In that case she's the one who should have her head examined,' came a loud comment from one of the spectators, and that was the big laugh of the afternoon.

Dudley Stanton was his own best witness. 'It was my intention to leave my fortune to a foundation – all of it since my friend, Judith Tyler, was unwilling to accept anything for herself. But Judith said, 'Why wait? Do it now! Build the Stanton Center now! The people of Boston need it now! She's inspired me with her selflessness. She's having plans for the Center drawn up and what a vision she has! A hospital! A museum! A library! She says she wants Boston to have the biggest and best private library in the whole world! If listening to Judith Tyler's dreams of a better world to live in, if trading off my commercial companies for the purpose of realizing these visions makes me crazy, I guess I am!'

And then he paid tribute to his friend by comparing her to Eleanor Roosevelt, the president's wife who was her husband's legs, as Judith was his, and a hush filled the courtroom. It wasn't even necessary for him to tell how Judith, in trading off Stanton Enterprises to reinvest the proceeds in America's public corporations, had increased his net worth by many millions, making that much more money available to the Stanton Foundation, to be utilized for the public good.

The hearing was not only a total rout of Dudley Stanton's nieces and Wallace Purvis but a tour de force for Judith Tyler, who was now ready to become a bride.

Judith planned her wedding like any nineteen-year-old marrying any young, rich and healthy groom. She'd wear white, certainly. Why should she not? It *was* her first marriage and she was as virginal as any bride should be. And it would be as lovely as any gown any breathless bride would wear. It was her day! The day she'd become one of the richest women in the United States. She ordered her gown and Dudley's wedding suit, paying as much attention to every detail of his attire as she did her own.

They'd be married in the Stanton house on Beach Street on New Year's Day, 1 January, 1943, the ceremony to be performed in the drawing room with all the furniture removed to accommodate the three hundred guests. Judge Hardwicke would give her away and his wife Alicia would be her matron of honour. Who should be best man? Judith pondered over this for a few minutes before she came up with just the right person – Dudley's friend for thirty years – Walter. What a perfect touch! And she would have the Right Reverend Howard Yates Smith, one of the most revered theologians who attended her Tuesday evenings, officiate.

Then she thought about her invitation list. Naturally there'd be no relatives since Dudley had only the nieces and she her two aunts. The staff! Yes, that was a lovely idea. All the staff would be guests and they'd have only hired help for the evening, and she'd be lauded by the other more distinguished guests for her democratic thoughtfulness. Then she selected these distinguished guests from the many who had passed through her doors ever since she had initiated her two evenings a week.

But then, practically at the last minute – only two days before the wedding – she decided to invite Francesca and Carlotta. They'd think it was strange since she hadn't even spoken to them since the time she'd refused their offer to send her to Radcliffe except for the telephone call from Francesca just before the hearing, but so what? She'd say that since it *was* her wedding day as well as the first day of the new year, she wanted to begin anew with them. What would be more natural than in light of her newly found happiness, she wanted to extend the hand of friendship to the only family she had in the whole world, except, of course, for her wonderful new husband?

Actually she couldn't bear it if Francesca and Carlotta weren't there to witness her moment of triumph – her elegant mansion, her distinguished guests, her wedding gown that cost $2500, and her magnificent wedding present from her groom – the twenty-two carat diamond that hung simply from a thin gold chain around her neck. (She had picked it out herself . . . had gone down to New York to attend the auction at Parke Bernet of the estate of a White Russian who had fled to Paris to escape the Reds, then fled the Nazis to land up in New York only to die and leave these fabled jewels of a time gone by. She had also picked up a blood-red ruby at the sale.)

So she called and Carlotta answered which Judith found irritating. She would have preferred to speak with Francesca but she extended the invitation at which point Carlotta laughed. 'You're kidding!'

'Not at all,' Judith said and went into her prepared speech about how she wanted the three of them to be friends.

'Well, I suppose it would be kind of interesting. I guess Frankie and I would love to come but I have a date with this handsome Marine and I can't possibly disappoint one of our men in uniform, can I?'

'By all means, bring him along,' Judith said sweetly. 'How can any celebration these days be complete without a serviceman after all?'

Actually, Judith thought, it rounded out her guest list nicely. One brave man in uniform and her own dear aunts. She sincerely hoped they ate their hearts out!

III
1942–1943

III

1943–1945

Bill Sheridan showed up at eleven to escort Francesca and Carlotta to the Tyler-Stanton nuptials which were to be held at noon. He walked in on a family argument. Francesca, in pale blue crepe, was upset that Carlotta was wearing a cocktail suit of champagne-coloured satin. 'You *can't* wear that colour!'

'Why not?' Carlotta tossed her hair. 'Don't I look nice in this colour?' she asked in a small-girl voice. 'Bill,' she appealed to him. 'Don't you think I look pretty?'

Of course he thought she looked pretty. More than pretty. She looked gorgeous as usual. Gorgeous enough to eat and he said so. Francesca reproached him with a look.

'You know darn well we're not talking about whether you look pretty. We both know one does not wear white satin to someone else's wedding. White and particularly white *satin* is only for the bride. Otherwise you're competing with the bride, which is not nice. Especially today since this bride is not pretty and you are.'

'My suit is not white. The colour's called champagne and it's more cream than white.'

'Same thing and you know it and I want you to take it off this minute.'

'Bossy, bossy, bossy. You're lucky that I love you or otherwise I wouldn't put up with you for a minute. If I go change, Mistress Frankie, we're going to be late and that will be even worse. How will it look if we walk in *after* the ceremony? Niece Judy will be very upset.'

'We'll have to risk it,' Francesca said curtly and then, 'Please, Carlotta. Be a good girl.'

'What do you say, Bill? Shall I change?'

'Oh no, you don't,' Bill grinned. 'You're not getting me into this.'

'Oh, you're just as bad as Frankie,' she sighed. 'Nobody's any fun.' She started to mount the stairs. 'Why do you think I said yes to Judith in the first place? Because I wanted a little fun. Now you're spoiling everything, Frankie. I would have loved to see the look on Judith's face when I walked in in this dress. Spoilsport!'

When she came down again twenty minutes later in another cocktail suit, this one of emerald-green satin with a thigh high side-slit and a deeply plunging neckline, Francesca was almost sorry she had sent her to change. Carlotta in cleavage-revealing green satin was more of a scenestealer than she was in champagne satin.

They *were* late and all the guests were already seated in the drawing room in rows of gilt chairs. They arrived in the middle of the Bach and Handel organ selections preceding the ceremony and an usher quickly seated them in the last row, and all heads turned as if in unison to look at them, and there was a low buzz of speculation and recognition. Francesca ignored it – there was always that kind of response when Carlotta entered a room – but Carlotta smiled charmingly at one and all.

The Reverend Smith was already in place at the improvised altar banked with white flowers – spikes of delphinium, sprays of Madagascar jasmine, bouquets of Easter lilies and pots of pale Christmas poinsettias, ropes of smilax and a *prie-deux* upholstered in satin and filled with orchids and bride's roses. And facing the Reverend was the groom in his wheelchair with best man Walter standing close by. Dudley was very elegant in a continental cutaway with a white double-breasted waistcoat, an opal stickpin in his pearl gray cravat and a white rosebud in his left lapel.

Carlotta, leaning across Bill who sat between them, whispered to Francesca, 'Do you see how he's dressed? Couldn't you just die?'

Francesca put a finger to her lips. 'Sh!'

'Well, I think he looks plain *silly*. Judith just gussied the poor old thing up, trying to gild a tired old lily. After all, this is only a house wedding and he's about as old as Methuselah.'

'Carlotta! People will hear you! Do hush up!'

'Oh, all right. A girl can't even have a little fun,' she pouted and placed her hand on Bill's thigh.

Although the pale white hand just rested there lightly, barely touching, Bill reacted as if it were searing him with its imprint. To his acute embarrassment he went into erection, and brushing her hand away, he quickly crossed his legs before anyone could see. But Carlotta had seen and she was delighted. Dimpling at him, she put her hand back on his thigh, but this time she moved her hand back and forth caressingly, the fingertips lingering here and there.

Francesca couldn't help noting this by-play and, blushing furiously, she averted her eyes. She could have killed Carlotta. It was bad enough for her to be sitting next to Bill Sheridan, wanting him and knowing that he wanted Carlotta, but to sit watching her tease him and he responding so visibly was really too much to bear. Besides, what Carlotta was doing was so cheap and she was only doing it for the same reason she had wanted to wear the ivory satin suit – to amuse herself and shock everyone else.

As Lohengrin's Wedding March pealed out, Alicia Hardwicke walked down the aisle preceding Judith on Judge Hardwicke's arm and Francesca thought that it was a mistake to come here today. She didn't believe for a minute that Judith really wanted to be friends with them. All she wanted was to show off her fancy house, her fancy guests, and just generally crow in their faces about how rich she was now going to be.

But she tried to concentrate on the wedding ritual instead of Carlotta's fingers now creeping up under Bill's jacket. And he, who should have known better, was *letting* her do it even though his face was bright red! Carlotta was acting trashy but he was acting like a damn fool!

Out of the corner of her eye she saw Carlotta's hand move downward, hooking itself into his beltline. She couldn't stand it another second and whispered furiously, 'Carlotta! If you don't behave yourself I'm getting up and leaving this minute!'

Carlotta giggled and Bill got even redder in the face if that was possible, and there was a rustle as everyone turned around to stare at their unruliness.

'What God has joined together, let no man put asunder.'

Judith leaned down and placed her lips on her husband's upturned ones, then proceeded to wheel him back down the aisle as the organ boomed out Mendelssohn's triumphant Wedding March.

The reception line formed in the Red Salon as the waiters circulated with trays of champagne.

'Do we have to get on line?' Carlotta complained. 'I'm starved. I didn't have any breakfast. Can't we sneak into the dining room now and beat everyone else to that buffet? And then we can go and congratulate Judith on a full stomach. That's what it takes, you know, to face her – fornication. Oops, I meant *fortification*.'

Bill howled. He thought Carlotta was terrifically funny as well as gorgeous. And even Francesca had to laugh.

The reception line moved slowly.

'Don't you think Judith's gown is spectacular?' Francesca asked Carlotta. 'She really looks quite lovely.'

'Judith *lovely*? Aren't you going a bit far? I think you're confusing Judith with that rock hanging around her neck. It must be twenty carats, at least. Now *that's* lovely. When I get married, I'm going to insist on one just like it.'

Francesca knew that this was just some more of Carlotta's nonsense, but Bill frowned. As a matter of fact, he looked worried.

'I want to wish you every happiness, Judith,' Francesca kissed her on the cheek. 'And you too, of course, Mr Stanton.'

Judith smiled archly. 'But you have to call him Dudley. If I'm your niece then Dudley is your nephew. But I'm sure you won't insist on him calling you Aunt Frankie, will you?' And everyone laughed politely.

Carlotta, instead of speaking first to Judith, went straight to Dudley, leaning down to kiss his withered cheek. 'But *I* do insist. You *will* call me Auntie Carlotta, won't you?' She looked provocatively at Judith, waiting for a sharp retort but Judith wasn't paying attention. Instead she was practically *staring* at Bill Sheridan.

Judith thought that this had to be the most attractive man she had ever seen, and for the first time in her life she was looking at a man with that special awareness that he was indeed, a male, and she, after all, a female. Never having so much as flirted with a boy it was a shock to feel that peculiar sensation . . . an actual fluttering in her vagina. But having read much clinical material on the subject, she immediately categorized the sensation for what it was – sexual desire. Then she corrected herself. What she was experiencing was more than sexual desire. It was *lust*.

Francesca made the introductions. 'Our niece, Judith Tyler Stanton and her new husband, Dudley . . . Captain William Sheridan of the United States Marine Corps.'

'Yes, Frankie. We can recognize the uniform,' Judith said dryly. But when she spoke to Bill her tone was almost coy. 'They must call you Big Bill Sheridan.'

Francesca and Carlotta looked at each other in amazement. This *was* a new Judith! It almost sounded as if she were flirting!

Bill grinned. 'I have to admit that I've been called that many times.' He moved to shake Dudley's hand. 'A pleasure, sir.' Considering his height and the fact that Dudley was sitting, Bill practically had to bend in half to reach the aged man's hand which only pointed up the physical disparity between the two.

Judith flushed, feeling her old rage against the sisters rising up again. She had invited them this day to flaunt everything she now was, now possessed, but somehow they had turned the tables on her . . . they with their handsome young Adonis and she with her frail, sick, crippled husband. . . .

She forced a smile. 'Now, tell me, Captain Sheridan, whose friend exactly are you – Frankie's or Carlotta's?'

Bill put an arm around both girls. 'I'll fight any man who says I'm not a friend to both the beautiful Collings sisters,' he said gallantly.

'Oh my,' Judith's eyes rolled mischievously. 'That sounds either very sad or very wicked.'

Bill quirked an eyebrow. 'How so?'

'Well, three people does imply a triangle, and that's sad because there's always one who loves and is not loved back, and then, of course, there is the *ménage à trois*, and that *is* wicked!'

Bill merely grinned in answer to her sally, thinking, this niece has sharp teeth. And again Francesca was sorry she had come. How ridiculous to think that Judith would change.

But Carlotta laughed, her derision barely masked. 'Really, Judith! A triangle implies love and a *ménage à trois* – sex. And what would you know about either one?' Francesca gasped but Carlotta laughed again and pinched Judith's cheek. 'Just kidding.'

Judith, eyes narrowed, agreed, 'Of course you are.'

It was time for them to move on to Alicia and Fenton Hardwicke, on the receiving line, and Bill was eager to meet the Judge, seeing as he headed one of the most prestigious law firms in Boston, a valuable contact for a lawyer starting out at the bottom of the ladder.

'I'm so glad that Frankie and Carlotta brought you, Big Bill Sheridan, and we *will* talk later,' Judith promised. 'I want us all to get to know each other better. Right, Dudley dear?'

Dudley blinked. 'Of course. Whatever you say, Judith.' He had just got married and while he did feel exhilarated, he was also feeling the strain.

No matter that Dudley appeared in such brisk good health, after the ordeal of ceremony, receiving congratulations, toasts to his and his bride's future and good wishes for a happy New Year, he was obviously exhausted, Judith decided. He needed to rest.

Dudley protested weakly but Judith was adamant, reminding her husband teasingly that tonight *was* their wedding night and he would need his strength.

But instead of calling on Walter who was celebrating with the rest of the staff — they keeping to themselves naturally enough instead of mingling with the other guests — she sought out Bill Sheridan to help her. 'I need the aid of a strong man to help me get Dudley into his bed and I don't want to ask Walter since he's a guest today. That is, if your bad leg will permit you to –'

'No problem.'

Bill laid Dudley down on the big four-poster and Judith arranged the covers about him. 'Now, close your eyes and try to sleep.' She kissed her husband on the forehead most tenderly and Bill, watching her, wondered what she was all about. Clearly she'd married the old guy for his money and he couldn't really blame her. (As a matter of fact, looking around this house with its magnificent furnishings and treasures, he himself got a hard-on almost as big as the one he had for Carlotta.) Still, Judith acted as if she really cared for the old boy.

They slipped out of the room in silence since as soon as Dudley closed his eyes, he appeared dead to the world. In the hall, Judith said, 'I hope that wasn't a strain on your leg.'

'No, not at all. It's coming along.'

'How long will you be out of action, Captain?'

'Me or my game leg? The leg they give four . . . five months. As for me, I won't be seeing any more action. Fighting, that is. I'll be discharged soon.'

'Really?' The rhythm of her heart accelerated. 'Then you'll be leaving Boston soon? Going home. . . .'

'Boston *is* my home. I was born and raised here. Went to college here. Harvard Law.'

Of course, she thought. She should have realized that from that unmistakeable broad A but she hadn't been paying attention to his accent. She'd been too preoccupied with his overwhelming sexuality . . . her body's reaction to his overwhelming appeal . . . to her – what? Awakening?

'Then you're staying in Boston?'

'Yes.' He wondered why she was being so intense.

'Well, that will be wonderful. We must see more of each other. Dudley and I, you and Frankie and Carlotta. . . .' She laughed softly. 'That is, if you intend to keep up your relationship with them.'

'Oh, I fully intend to do that.' He'd been acquainted with Carlotta for a week but it didn't matter. The week felt like a thousand days. . . .

Yes, of course you intend to keep up the relationship, she thought. And of course it's Carlotta you're really interested in. And it was Carlotta whom she herself detested more than Frankie. More than ever now . . . now that she was committed to spending her nights with Dudley and his withered body, while Carlotta would lie in the arms of this beautiful animal. . . .

Still, there are all kinds of possibilities.

She looked into his magnetic blue eyes. 'Do you realize, Captain Sheridan, you've wished me a long and happy life with Dudley, but you haven't yet wished me a Happy New Year?'

He grinned. 'By all means, Happy New Year, Judith Stanton.'

He was shocked when she put her arms around his neck, pressed her body against his hard one and drew his head down to crush her lips against his. He

91

had no choice but to kiss her back, thinking that Judith Tyler Stanton, prim and proper, was full of surprises.

In the middle of the night Judith had to call Dr Phillips who took one look at Dudley and called for an ambulance. Dudley had suffered another stroke and possibly another heart attack. 'The wedding was probably too much excitement for him. . . .'

Judith broke into uncontrollable sobs. 'It's all my fault. I shouldn't have given in to him but he wouldn't take no for an answer. He was so insistent that we get married and have this big celebration that I thought perhaps it might be best just to let him be happy. . . .'

'And he was. I've never seen a man so overjoyed. And just remember, Judith, if you hadn't taken such good care of him he probably wouldn't be alive now. He never would have been able to survive this latest attack.'

'Then he will survive?'

'I think the odds are with us. God knows we'll try, Judith.'

'Oh yes, we'll try!' Judith cried fervently. 'We'll do it!'

She was convinced that not faith but will and determination could move mountains. How not? She had come this far by exercising will, determination, and her wits, of course.

Thank God she had had the wit to allow Dudley to change his will only a week before, leaving half of everything to his wife-to-be, and only half to the Stanton Foundation, so even if they weren't successful in saving her husband, she'd have that much. She *had* toyed with the idea of having Dudley leave her everything, making him think it was his idea, but in the end, she held back. It was too soon after her protestation that she'd accept nothing. *Everything* would have made even her new-found allies such as the Hardwickes suspicious . . . maybe even given grounds for the contesting of the will. . . .

Seemingly half-hysterical, Judith rode to the hospital in the ambulance with Dudley, begging the unconscious man to live . . . at least for just a while longer.

For the next six weeks she never left her husband's side, sleeping in his hospital room each night. She never even as much as went down to the cafeteria to eat her own meals, spoonfeeding Dudley each mouthful of Jello herself. Everyone at the hospital concurred that never had they witnessed such complete devotion. And even those who had doubted Judith before, were now convinced of the sincerity of her feelings. If she didn't truly love Stanton, why would she now struggle so hard to keep him alive? Dead, he was worth at least three hundred million to her and alive, he was going to be a bigger burden than before, his paralysis more extensive, his speech impaired.

Once Judith took Dudley home, she was no less dedicated. She slept no more than three or four hours a night. She brought in more doctors, speech therapists as well as physical therapists, professionals who could offer more than her own untrained efforts.

Dr Phillips remonstrated with her. 'You're going to get yourself sick, Judith. And all these specialists . . . these therapists. . . . You're beating a dead horse.'

'Don't you dare use the word "dead" to me. Where there's life there's hope, and I, for one, will never say die. I won't rest or stop until Dudley is back to being the man I married.'

She meant that sincerely. It was Dudley who had given her his love . . . who had given her everything. Or to be more precise – *half of everything*. She had to keep Dudley alive and functioning until she had it all.

By the time Bill was ready to be discharged in March, he and Carlotta had an understanding – they were more or less going steady, seeing only each other but with certain exceptions. These exceptions were those Carlotta insisted upon and to which Bill had to agree simply because he had no choice. It was that or nothing.

For one, Carlotta refused to give up hostessing at all the dances to entertain the men of the armed forces. She maintained that it was her patriotic duty to do this, just as it was to go out with old friends in the service who were home on leave and would soon be back in the thick of it, who might even be going to their death. How would she feel if this happened, knowing that she had denied them the pleasure of an innocent date or two? How would Bill himself feel knowing that because of his selfishness, a brave hero had died without the memory of a funfilled, perfect evening?

And then there were the men who did duty on the home front, doing what they could for the war effort. Like Whit Truesdale, who with his punctured eardrum, still wanted to do what he could and he swore that for each date Carlotta gave him, he'd purchase a war bond from her on the night she manned the Bonds for Victory booth. There was a contest to see which girl could sell the most bonds and be named Miss Victory and so far, she was leaving everyone else in the dust. How could she resist Whit's offer?

Bill knew this was all bull – that none of Carlotta's exceptions had anything to do with patriotism but with Carlotta's restlessness . . . her unwillingness to be pinned down . . . her need for constant change and excitement. Or maybe it was just another way of teasing him, the way she teased him with her body, her mouth, her fingers, playing him like a violin, building him up to a crescendo that never quite crested.

But *that*, at least, was some comfort. Since she didn't go all the way with him, he felt reasonably sure that she wasn't going all the way with anyone else. Certainly not with Whit Truesdale, whom Carlotta labelled as a nice kind of sweet jerk. 'Believe me, Bill honey, I wouldn't go out with him at all if he weren't buying war bonds from me.'

On those evenings when Carlotta was otherwise engaged, he fell into the habit of spending the time with Francesca who made sure she was available for him. A little piece of Bill Sheridan was better than nothing. But even as she commiserated with him about Carlotta's temporary defection, she was careful to defend Carlotta too. 'She's only eighteen. And she does want to do her part. It's all I can do to persuade her to stay in school when she's so eager to spend all her time working for the war effort.'

She felt it was her duty to defend Carlotta's capriciousness. As much as she was in love with Bill herself, she knew that men could come and go in a girl's life, but a sister was forever. No matter how she felt about Bill, she owed her first loyalty, her primary love to Carlotta. And if it came to pass that eventually Carlotta did marry Bill, she'd have to force herself to be happy . . . pleased that her sister was wed to a man of substance and high character, a man who loved her deeply, who would take care of her. Carlotta needed that – a man who would take care of her.

But if it *didn't* work out that way . . . if Carlotta tired of Bill, well then, that was another story completely. One that might possibly have a happy ending for herself. *It was possible, wasn't it? Just barely possible. . . .*

In the meantime, Francesca was the one to whom Bill confided his dreams and ambitions. He told her how he'd grown up poor and was determined to be rich and important. He told her all about his political aspirations . . . how he was determined to climb the political ladder, step by step, until he was President of the United States.

At first, Francesca laughed, assuming that he was joking. She knew that all little boys said this when they were young, or maybe it was their mothers who envisioned this for them as they rocked them in their arms. But how many grown men ever made such a statement . . . dared to think it was possible? No one she had ever known. But then when she saw that Bill was dead serious, that he meant every word, she fell even more in love with him and felt anguish for him. She knew only too well how terrible it was to dream an impossible dream . . . one that didn't have much chance of coming true.

'But you're Irish Catholic,' she said gently. 'There's never been a Catholic President. Everyone says there never will be.

He grinned. 'Everyone? You only say that because *you're* Boston Protestant.'

'That's not so. We *are* Protestant but our mother was an Irish Catholic. Carlotta and I are half-Irish. As a matter of fact, when we were little and fought with Judith, she always called us dirty Micks. Of course she got that from her mother, our half-sister, who hated all of us, Carlotta and me as well as our mother. I guess dirty Mick was the worst thing Judith could think of.'

Bill laughed. 'That's the insult they pinned on me too when they were looking for the worst thing they could say. I guess we should shake on it – it's something we have in common.' He held out his hand and she took it and they shook on it, and somehow it was as if they were making a pact, but Francesca wasn't sure what the pact was about. Certainly being called dirty Micks was the least of what they had in common. Foremost was that they both loved Carlotta who didn't believe in impossible dreams. Carlotta, if asked, would most likely say impossible dreams were a waste of time and one made the most of the moment.

'Tell me, Bill, how does one go about getting to be President?'

'Well, if you're rich, you can skip a lot of steps. But if you're me, just an impoverished about-to-be ex marine with a medal for bravery and a Harvard law degree, you make the most of what you have. You push it as far as it will go. You get yourself the best job possible in the best legal firm available, and start working the wards, trying to get a toe in the door, then a foot, then a whole leg, and you hope very hard that you get enough people to believe in you.'

'Oh, *I* do!' she cried out impulsively. 'I believe in you. . . .'

He seized her hand and kissed it. 'I know you do, Frankie. And I wish you'd help me convince your sister to believe in me too.'

She swallowed hard and lowered her eyes, afraid to look into his and betray herself. 'I will,' she promised, 'and I'll also help you in whatever other way I can. I mean, in your career.'

He smiled at her fondly. 'Frankie, you're the best.'

But she knew that he didn't mean that. What he really meant was that she was second best.

'Judith!' Francesca blurted. 'She could probably help you with a job.'

'Two great minds with but a single thought,' Bill grinned. 'Exactly what I've been thinking. A position with her friend, Hardwicke's firm would be a hell of a start.'

'Yes, but we can't count on her too much. I'm not sure that she'll be willing to help. As I've told you, Carlotta and I are two of Judith's least favourite people in the whole world.'

'But she invited you to her wedding.'

'Yeah, but I think that was because she wanted to show off how smart she is, how she had managed to snare such a big, rich fish. It doesn't show she likes us or that she'd be willing to help any friend of ours.'

But Bill, recalling how on her wedding day, Judith had suddenly and inexplicably thrown her arms around him and practically ground her goddamn box against him, thought that, just possibly, she *would* be willing. 'Maybe she won't but then again, maybe she will. Anyhow—'

'It's worth a try,' they said at the same time and shook hands again. 'Two great minds—' Bill laughed and Francesca laughed along. It was good to be Bill's partner plotting his future with him. It drew them that much closer. . . .

'I'll call Judith first thing tomorrow,' Francesca promised. 'And if she won't help, I'll try the lawyer who settled Daddy's estate. And there's always Whitman Truesdale. He's a lawyer too and he'd do just about anything for Carlotta.'

Bill grimaced. 'Thanks a lot.'

As it turned out, it wasn't necessary to call anybody since the morning mail brought an invitation from Judith to Carlotta, Francesca and Bill Sheridan to come to dinner on Friday evening.

'Forget it!' Carlotta told Francesca. 'Judith's wedding was boring enough. Dinner with Judith and Dudley would be stultifying!'

'I doubt that Dudley will be at the dinner table. From what I've heard I don't think he's up to that these days.'

'All the more reason not to go. Judith alone will be completely unbearable.'

'I don't think you understand, Carlotta. I was going to call Judith today to ask her to put in a good word for Bill with Judge Hardwicke about a job with his firm. This dinner will be the perfect opportunity to do that.'

'Oh all right,' Carlotta pouted. 'If I must. My goodness, the things a girl does for a man! It practically amounts to prostitution!'

In the end, Carlotta didn't go. Justin Darsley, with whom she'd gone to dancing school, was home on leave and presented her with an offer she couldn't refuse – a jitterbugging marathon at a hotel on the North Shore. They were raising money for some war cause or other. Just which one Justin wasn't sure but he had a private bet on the side with a buddy who claimed that he and his girlfriend would shut out all competition.

'But the sucker's never seen *us* in action,' Justin crowed. 'What do you say?' Carlotta said yes.

Francesca was furious with her. 'How *could* you? A jitterbugging marathon, of all things. We have important business at Judith's. Bill's future! Don't you care?'

Carlotta rolled a strand of red-gold hair around a finger. 'Of course I care. But I feel sorry for Bill if his future's dependent on Judith. But really, Frankie, the truth is you're better off without me along. Judith merely dislikes you but she *loathes* me. You and Bill will do fine without me. And poor Justin! This contest means so much to him. And he's just finished his officer's training and God knows where they'll be sending him. If we win the marathon just think what a wonderful memory that will be for him to take into battle. Please, Frankie, please! Don't make me disappoint him!'

'Oh, all right,' Frankie gave in as usual to Carlotta's blandishments. Probably she and Bill *would* do better without her. She herself always tried to control the feelings of antagonism Judith evoked in her but Carlotta never did. With Carlotta, it was always full speed ahead.

'Thank you, darling Frankie. And you will wish us luck, won't you? Do you think I should wear my hair up or down?' And she lifted it up with two hands to give Francesca the effect of the upsweep. 'What do you think?'

As it turned out it wasn't dinner with just Judith. Fenton and Alicia Hardwicke were present too, and even as Francesca was wondering how to bring up the matter of Bill's availability for employment, and his wonderful qualifications, she gradually became aware that there was already an ongoing campaign towards this end. It seemed, incredibly, that Judith had already initiated it.

'Judith's been telling me great things about you, Captain,' Fenton Hardwicke told Bill over pre-dinner cocktails and poached oysters. 'That you've been decorated for bravery in action and that you graduated at the top of your class at Harvard.'

Bill was taken aback. It was no secret that he'd been decorated – the medals he wore attested to that, but how did Judith know that he had graduated at the top of his class? He shot her a look but she only smiled at him enigmatically.

Over the *suprême de foie gras en casserole* accompanied by a Chablis Pouilly, Fenton declared, 'There's no one I admire more than a man who has done his bit for God and country. . . .'

The consommé was served along with a Bâtard-Montrachet and savouring the wine, Fenton insisted that there was nothing like a true hero to lend dignity to a legal firm.

Francesca wondered if Fenton was in his cups.

The main course, escalopes of veal, was served with a Mâconnais and Alicia and Fenton pronounced it superb, adding, 'Fenton, you *must* ask this young man to come to work for you.'

By dessert — a simple one of vanilla ice cream and strawberry sauce, accompanied by a New England favourite, a cranberry liqueur, it was *fait accompli*. Fenton had asked Bill to join his firm and Bill had accepted.

Then Judith proposed that they drink a toast to Bill and to Dudley, poor thing, peacefully asleep in his bed. Francesca, lifting her glass of champagne in toast, couldn't believe that it had all been this easy and that Judith had done it all. Perhaps she had, after all, misjudged Judith. . . .

But Bill was older than Francesca by several years and he had been to war. Therefore, he was more sceptical. Why had Judith done what she did? Just to be nice? Or was there something she wanted? Some kind of trade? . . .

Bill was in the tiny office assigned to him at Hardwicke, Hardwicke and Lindsay, going through a stack of files to familiarize himself with the affairs of the firm's most important clients when his phone rang. He reached for it eagerly, hoping it was Carlotta — she'd promised to try and make it for lunch. But it was Judith. She wasted little time on small talk. She said she wanted to meet and discuss some business with him. He checked his watch. It was only eleven-thirty. Carlotta might still call. 'How about tomorrow? Would you like to come to the office?'

'Tomorrow then but not at the office. I want to speak with you privately.'

Privately? Of course. That's why she had placed him here in her lawyer's office. She wanted her own private eyes and ears in the firm, her own man on the inside. It was the trade-off for helping him get the job. Why not? She was entitled to something in return.

'Lunch, then? The Ritz-Carlton?'

'No. The Ritz is hardly private. I own a house that's unoccupied.' She gave him an address. 'One o'clock sharp.'

He studied the address, an unfashionable one. Francesca had told him that Judith still owned the house her mother had left her. He guessed that she had held on to it for meetings just like theirs . . . private meetings. But that really didn't surprise him. He had figured Judith for the kind of woman who played her cards close to the chest.

The house was a small Cape Cod saltbox in the South End. He rang the bell, heard her call, 'Come in,' and he entered. Then her voice issued from upstairs. 'Lock the door and come up.'

He had a funny feeling as he bolted the door, not unlike that which he had experienced in the New Guinea jungles when a sudden rustle in the black night made the hair at the back of the neck stand on end. Slowly he mounted the narrow wooden staircase. At the top of the stairs there was a small hallway opening on to four closed doors. Sizing up the situation in correct military fashion, he figured the four doors meant three bedrooms and a bath.

'In here!' Her voice came from behind the door to his extreme right. *What the hell is she up to?* Was she lurking behind the door to brain him with a baseball bat?

Then he smiled in self-derision. *Hey, Sheridan, you've faced worse and you've got the ribbons to prove it. I guess you can handle one nineteen-year-old self-important squirt half your size. There's nothing in there to scare you.*

He threw open the door and instantly he knew that he was wrong for what he saw scared the hell out of him! . . .

Jesus! Lying on the bed was Judith, stark naked with scrawny breasts and her ribs showing.

This must be some kind of a joke, he thought, only Judith wasn't smiling and God knew, he didn't feel much like laughing. Actually, he felt kind of sick and while the room was cold, he felt the sweat break out in his armpits.

'It's kind of draughty in here and you're hardly dressed for it,' he tried being funny, but it was hardly a laugh . . . certainly not to him.

'It will warm up, I promise you.' Her voice was cold . . . so cold that it was ridiculous to try and play it for laughs.

'What do you want, Judith?'

'What do you think I want?'

'I'm not sure.'

'Trust your instincts.'

'My instincts tell me to get the hell out of here.'

'I thought you were smarter than that. It's to your advantage to stay.'

'How so?' He was playing for time, trying to figure out what to do.

'Come here. I don't like talking across the room,' she said although it was a small room. Only a few feet from where he was to where she was.

He went over and tentatively sat on the edge of the bed. 'What do you want?' he asked again.

'Just what do you think I want? I want you to fuck me.'

They shouldn't have but the words came as a shock. They hit him in the belly like a mighty fist. Still, he tried to keep his voice even. 'I'm in love with Carlotta.'

How dare he bring up her name when I'm lying here waiting? He could love Carlotta to kingdom come but he was still going to fuck her.

She stroked her nipples, circling them with her fingers, flicking the nipples, keeping her eyes on him. She could practically feel him inside her, big, hard. She moved her hands down over her belly to her pubic mound, playing with her labia. Then she inserted two fingers into her vulva and moved them in and out, in and out.

In spite of himself, he watched with an odd fascination.

'You're wasting time. You *are* going to do it. You are going to fuck me.'

'Why should I?' but he began to feel the excitement grow within him.

'For several reasons. Because I got you your enviable position and I can as easily take it away. Because I can introduce you to the people who can help your political career. Because I can raise money for campaigns. So stop wasting time and take off your clothes. Besides, you want me.'

He tried to laugh but the laugh stuck in his throat.

She moved her hips to meet the thrust of her fingers – up . . . down . . . up . . . down. . . .

Watching her, hearing her laboured breathing, the smell of her sex filling his nostrils, he became aroused. But it was crazy. Even her unlovely breasts with the nipples in erection were strangely erotic.

'You do want all the things I can do for you, don't you?'

'I'm not a whore for hire . . .' he muttered.

'Are you sure?'

'Yeah, I'm sure,' he barked, angry now and perversely, the anger fed his arousal.

She was a bitch and he wanted to stick it into the bitch now – hard, up to the hilt. He wanted to jam it into her, ram her. He wanted to split her in two.

She removed the fingers from inside her and reached up to touch his mouth with them. She ran them over his lips and he could taste her saltiness. She watched his swelling grow and she laughed.

'What do you say to five hundred dollars a fuck, once a week? That's a lot of money and you don't have a cent. A man who wants to run for public office needs some money. Call it seed money.'

He seized her hand, holding the two fingers she was rubbing his lips with, a few inches away.

'Once a week for how long?'

'Until I'm no longer buying.'

He opened his mouth and took the two fingers inside, bit them until she gasped in pain, and then she began to rub his swelling with the palm of her other hand.

He thought of new suits, a car, even of Carlotta whose body he hadn't yet possessed but upon whom he was eager to shower presents, and he was hard as a rock.

He stood up abruptly. 'A straight twenty-five hundred a month,' he said, taking off his jacket, discarding it, reaching for his belt buckle.

She laughed again. 'So I was right and you were wrong. You *are* a whore – it's only a question of how much.'

When he was fully stripped, he dragged her off the bed on to the floor, threw himself on top of her, attempting to ram himself into her. He met resistance. And then he realized that the bitch was a virgin!

He thrust again brutally, tearing her hymen. In . . . out . . . raising himself up, then lowering himself down, hammering away, using his penis as a weapon. He'd tear her apart with his cock!

3.

'Marry me, goddamn it!' Bill whispered huskily, his fingers pressing into his beloved's delicate white arm. They were sitting in his newly acquired two-year old Plymouth convertible for which he had paid through the nose since car production was nil and all cars, especially convertibles, were in short supply. They'd been necking for at least an hour with almost no touching except for the lip and now they were swollen and he was half-mad with frustration, both physical and mental.

'You're hurting me. . . .' Carlotta murmured, pulling her arm from his grasp.

'We're getting married' he yelled, having just decided this was the only tack to take with her. He'd tell her, not ask.

'Don't be a silly, Billy,' she laughed, leaning over to kiss his throat, getting him hot again before he had even cooled off.

'I'm much too young to get married.'

'Nineteen isn't too young.' He was prepared to give her statistics on how many girls were marrying at sixteen or seventeen these days when he realized quoting statistics to Carlotta would be the height of inanity.

'I'm not nineteen *yet*. I have another month to go. Besides, if I don't finish college, Frankie will kill me. She has her heart set on us both graduating.'

'She wouldn't care about college if you were happy. And who says you have to quit school if you get married?'

He meant that. He believed in college education for women. Besides, an educated woman made a better wife for a man with serious political aspirations. But what was the use of talking about it anymore tonight? He could see that he wasn't getting anywhere.

The best idea might be to work through Frankie. If he could persuade Frankie that the best thing for Carlotta was to be married . . . that it would settle her down before she did anything really wild or crazy, then Frankie could work on Carlotta, persuade her. Carlotta always listened to her sister in the end. And one thing he knew for sure – Frankie was on his side. They were the best of friends. She approved him. All he had to do was convince her that it was in Carlotta's best interest to marry him and soon.

He reached for Carlotta again but she turned her face to the side so that her mouth eluded his. 'My lips are already bruised. You'd better take me home now. I have an early class tomorrow. You forget I'm a schoolgirl' she said primly.

He decided to buy Carlotta an engagement ring for her forthcoming birthday. A diamond ring. What girl could resist a diamond ring? What girl didn't love a surprise? Especially Carlotta who loved jewellery and the excitement of surprises. . . .

It would work as a surprise. It was one thing to ask a girl to marry you, or even to order her to. But to have the prize in your hand to flash before her provided the added inducement of its sparkle, its beauty, its eternal allure. If she said 'no,' she'd know that the prize would disappear before her eyes – a negative inducement.

He told Frankie that he was going to buy a ring. 'But don't say anything to Carlotta. I want it to be a surprise. I'd like you to help me pick it out and then when she shows it to you, I'd appreciate it if you acted thrilled too . . . show her you're delighted.'

Engagement ring? She had no idea his thinking had gone this far – engagement . . . marriage. Oh, she knew that he was mad about Carlotta, but marriage? Didn't he realize Carlotta wasn't ready for this? Would she still be going out with every Tom, Dick and Harry in uniform if she were? He was a fool, damn him! Didn't he know that Carlotta was as capable of dropping him at this point as marrying him? And she herself was supposed to act thrilled! To *urge* Carlotta to accept his ring, to become engaged, to marry him! It was so unfair that she should be put in this position.

'I think you're being hasty, Bill. I don't think—'

Bill put his arm around Francesca. She trembled but he didn't notice. 'You don't think *what*, Frankie? That I'd make a good husband? That I'd take care of Carlotta? That I love her enough?'

'Of course I think you'll be good to her, that you'd take care of her and that you love her very much, but—'

'But what?'

'It's Carlotta. *She's* not ready to settle down.'

'But she can be,' he said resolutely. 'She would be if *you* told her that she should. . . .'

The arrogance of him! Why should she tell Carlotta that? That it was time for her to settle down when she was only nineteen? Just to accommodate him and his male desires?

As if he read her thoughts, Bill continued: 'Don't do it for me. Do it for Carlotta. The way she's going, she's only going to get into trouble. She's better off marrying me now.'

He was feeding the anxieties she already had about Carlotta. She *was* wild. A *little* wild. But she was young. Didn't a young girl have a right to be a little wild? Carlotta always told her that she, Frankie, wasn't wild enough, that she was too proper, too 'nice.' And maybe Carlotta was right. Carlotta was the one who had more fun.

She was so confused. Maybe Bill was right. Maybe Carlotta would be better off married. Maybe she herself was being selfish and as a result, her darling baby sister would end up having a terrible life. . . . What then? Finally she told Bill that she'd help him pick out a ring and then she'd act properly thrilled, but she wouldn't . . . couldn't actually *urge* Carlotta to accept.

'Why not?' He narrowed his eyes, his voice suddenly steely.

'Because I can't urge Carlotta to marry anyone unless she's desperately in love, and only Carlotta knows whether she loves you enough. . . .'

'Oh, she loves me,' he said confidently. 'She's told me so enough times.' But suddenly, he was unsure. 'Why? What has she told you? Has she told you she *doesn't?*'

Francesca hesitated. She wanted to be absolutely truthful, fair to all three of them, herself as well as Carlotta and Bill. But how could she be absolutely truthful without betraying at least one of them? And she wasn't even sure what was the absolute truth.

'What is it?' Bill demanded. 'Has she told you she doesn't love me?'

'No . . .'

'Has she told you she *does?*'

'Yes. . . .' But he didn't understand that the word love didn't mean the same thing to Carlotta as it did to him . . . to her. . . .

'Well, there you are. I *knew* she loved me.'

She had to let it go at that. Poor Bill. He didn't know there were all kinds of love. . . . Degrees and variables. Or, most of all, that there was a season for love and she seriously doubted that for Carlotta that season had yet arrived. . . . And if she told him, he wouldn't understand. He was too blindly in love to understand certain things about her sister . . . that part of Carlotta's magic was her ability to inspire consummate love in others while she gave only little bits and pieces of her self in return. That was the reason Carlotta was indefatigable, infinitely glowing and never depleted while the others – those who loved her like herself and Bill – rode an emotional see-saw, raised to the heights one minute, sent plummeting the next, leaving them drained and exhausted with their love.

And there were things that Carlotta had told her that she had no right to

101

divulge. . . . Like the confession Carlotta had made to her recently about how she wasn't in the least tempted to give up her virginity, even though she did enjoy necking, even 'light' petting.

'So you don't have to give me any more lectures about the dangers of being "loose," Frankie darling, for I have no intention of being a fallen woman. It's against my religion,' she'd giggled. 'I don't believe in giving so much away for free, even if I wanted to which I don't. And what's more, I don't *have* to go all the way with anyone in order to satisfy my terrible lustful desires. I find it much more exciting to get a guy *hot* . . . real hot . . . red-hot, and then, *not* deliver.'

Francesca had been upset. 'But that makes you a—'

'A c.t.? A cock-teaser?' Carlotta laughed. 'You don't have to be afraid of using the word, Frankie. It won't bite. And sometime you should try being one. It might not be nice, but it sure is fun.' She struck a dramatic pose. 'Just picture it. There he is – whoever – poised on the pinnacle of his desire. His voice ragged with passion. He's pleading for consummation. He's in a frenzy, panting hard. His breathing is so irregular that I'm concerned . . . well, a tiny bit concerned . . . that he might be having a heart attack, or maybe, even thinking of raping me!'

Even though Carlotta was all burlesque, Francesca gasped. 'What do you do then?'

'What do you think I do?' Carlotta drawled. 'Watching him, listening to him, my juices flowing, my little vaggie all aroused by *his* unconsummated passion, *I* come!'

'I don't understand. What do you mean – *you* come?'

'I mean exactly what you think I mean. I come. I have an orgasm without him so much as touching me—' Her voice thickened and her eyes glinted.

Shocked, even frightened by the change in Carlotta's tone – she was so intense! – Francesca told herself that she had heard enough . . . that as the elder sister and the self-appointed guardian of Carlotta's morals, she should cut short this discussion, let Carlotta know that she found the whole subject 'distasteful,' and not one nice girls pursued. But she didn't. The truth was that even as she was relieved to hear that Carlotta's virginity was still intact and that she and Bill were not lovers, she was avid to hear more details.

'And then what do the men do?'

'Oh, they have no idea that I've had a climax. And since they haven't, they're going out of their minds. They don't know what to do with themselves or their erections. Sometimes they *really* lose control. They wrestle with me, trying to force themselves on me, or try to dry hump me. But of course,' she said primly, 'I don't allow that.'

'What does that mean – dry hump?'

'Really, Frankie! In a couple of months you're going to be a Radcliffe junior and you don't know what dry humping is? It seems I've severely neglected your education,' she teased.

'Never mind that business. What is it? It sounds disgusting!'

'It is,' Carlotta laughed. 'It means they try to screw you through your clothes. Or if they've gotten that far, through your panties. That's why it's called dry. Get it? No penetration!'

'That *is* disgusting!' But then she couldn't help herself and asked, 'And if they succeed in this disgusting act, what happens to the–?'

'The jism? That all depends on whether they've got *it* in or out of their pants. If it's in, well— And if it's out, then—'

'Never mind! I don't want to hear.'

'But I told you. I've never permitted that. But once this sailor gave himself a hand job right in front of me. . . .'

'Oh! What did you do?'

'Well, since I had already had my own orgasmic experience—' she seemed proud of her choice of words—'I simply had another without so much as touching myself once! What do you think of that?'

Francesca was speechless, incapable of answering. But then she did ask a question, one she had promised herself never to ask. 'And Bill? – What does he do when he's . . . aroused?'

'Oh, Bill, he's a sweetie. He never does anything absolutely frankly vulgar. And he tries very hard to be the gentleman and not too pushy. But I suspect that after he kisses me goodnight he goes home and masturbates into his toilet. . . .'

'Carlotta!'

'Well, you asked. And as long as you're asking, there's something else I can do—'

Francesca wasn't sure she really wanted to know but on the other hand, she thought she'd expire if she didn't find out. 'What?'

'I'll show you.' She lay down on the living room rug and then Francesca thought that Carlotta was going to masturbate right there and then and she began to protest but Carlotta told her to hush up. 'I am *not* going to touch myself, so you can stop having a fit, you old prude. And you have to be quiet so I can concentrate.'

She closed her eyes, raised her knees and parted her thighs. She lay stiffly for a couple of minutes, silent, then she parted her lips, moaning softly and beginning to breathe heavily. She closed her thighs and opened them, closing again and opening again, as she revolved her hips in a steady rhythm. Her body tensed and she grunted and groaned – the groans and little cries coming louder and louder and faster and faster until she screamed out. Then her body shuddered and trembled until she lay limp, heaving and sucking in air.

'Oh . . .' Francesca uttered, exhausted, and Carlotta smiled smugly. 'You see. I don't really need a man at all. I can teach you how to do it. It's all a matter of concentration and muscular control . . . *inside*. Here, lie down—'

But Francesca, fascinated by what she'd just seen, and repelled at the same time, mumbled, 'Maybe some other time. . . .

Recalling the scene, Francesca wondered if it were only a matter of time until Carlotta tired of making love to herself. She had a feeling that one of these days, it wouldn't be enough. Maybe that would be the test of how deeply Carlotta loved . . . when she discovered that that which she did for herself was no longer sufficient . . . when she felt she had to surrender herself completely to a man. . . .

Bill rejected the first tray of diamond solitaires the jeweller showed them.

Twenty-five points, forty points . . . Carlotta would laugh in his face. 'It has to be at least one carat,' he said.

'That means upward of five hundred dollars, according to the clarity, purity and cut,' the jeweller warned him.

'That's OK.'

Francesca looked at him inquiringly but said nothing.

But then looking at the second tray, Bill rejected those too. 'What do two carats run to?'

'The larger the stone, the more per carat, sir.' But the jeweller was more respectful now. Although sales of wedding and engagement rings had picked up dramatically with the young men getting engaged or married before they left for the services, rarely were these diamonds larger than a half-carat. He brought out two trays, one with rings ranging around two carats and a selection of those hovering around three. Bill, recalling Judith's wedding with Judith wearing a diamond as big as the Ritz around her neck and Carlotta's remark that she would insist on a diamond as big when she got married, instinctively shoved the velvet tray of smaller stones aside and picked up a ring with a square cut stone set in a fishtail setting which made it appear even larger than its three carats.

Francesca gasped. 'That one must cost at least two thousand dollars,' she whispered. She wondered if he was so crazy about Carlotta it was actually affecting his mind.

'Try it on, Frankie, so we can see how it looks.'

Her hand shook as he placed the ring on her third finger, left hand. 'But you can't possibly afford anything like this.'

Bill's face reddened, thinking that all it would take would be about one month of Judith's money. He mumbled something about having money saved up from his time in the services. 'How do you think it would look if Bill Sheridan, Hardwicke, Hardwicke and Lindsay's most brilliant and promising attorney, on his way up the political ladder, allowed his fiancée to go around town with a dinky little diamond?'

'It would look like you were a proper Bostonian who remembered that thrift is a virtue second only to godliness,' she countered tartly.

'Do you like it?' he persisted, ignoring her comment.

She took off the ring as if it burned. 'No, I don't like a fishtail setting.'

'Larger stones *are* beautifully set off in the simplicity of a Tiffany setting,' the jeweller said quickly, picking up a ring Tiffany-set and holding it up to the light. 'See how blue. An excellent stone. Gem quality.'

Finally Bill chose a pear-shaped diamond weighing 3.17 carats and Bill went into the office to settle the bill. He didn't want Francesca to see him hand over three thousand dollars in fifty dollar bills. Accepting the notes, the owner of the store reflected that it was probably black-market money. Who else paid in cash?

On their way out with the little velvet box tucked into his pocket, a tray of pretty rings in the showcase caught Bill's eye. They were of yellow gold set with bursts of diamond chips, tiny rubies, little sapphires and emeralds, or combinations thereof. 'Are those friendship rings?' Bill asked.

'They're called cocktail rings but many people buy them as friendship rings.'

'Let's see them, please.'

'What are you doing?' Francesca whispered. Was he going to buy Carlotta *two* rings? One for day and one for evening wear?

'Picking out a friendship ring for my best friend,' Bill said, smiling at her sweetly. 'It has just occurred to me that since Carlotta's going to be nineteen, her sister's going to be twenty any day now. You never told me the exact date but I think it's all right if I give you your birthday present today, isn't it?'

Tears filled Francesca's eyes. 'But I can't—'

'Of course you can. Otherwise you'd be saying you're *not* my best friend. Would you want to say that?'

She shook her head, unable to speak, and he chose a swirl of yellow gold with emerald chips and picked up her hand to slide it on her finger.

'Oh no, sir,' the jeweller said. 'Friendship rings go on the right hand, not the left.'

'Oops!' Bill dropped Francesca's left hand, picked up her right. As she stood there woodenly, he slid the ring on the third finger. 'Do you like it?' he asked and she nodded. 'Does it fit?'

She found her voice. 'Like a glove.'

While Bill paid for the ring, this time writing a cheque, she raised her hand holding it this way and that. *Emeralds*. It was her ring but Bill had chosen stones the exact colour of Carlotta's eyes.

Bill put away his chequebook. 'Happy birthday, Frankie, my friend.' He leaned down to kiss her.

'Thank you,' and as she raised her face for his kiss, she moved her face a fraction and his mouth found hers. It wasn't the first time he had kissed her but it was the first time their lips touched and even though it was but a brushing, her body reacted so violently, so longingly that she yearned to cling to him . . . never to let go.

So this is how it feels to kiss the man you love! And this is how it happens that good girls get in trouble. . . .

Then she knew for sure that Carlotta didn't really love him, otherwise how could she ever feel his kiss and then let him go? She herself was supposedly the 'good' sister and Carlotta the 'fast' one, but if the situation was reversed – if she was the one Bill loved – then she would never, ever, no matter how well trained her vaginal muscles, do for herself what Bill Sheridan could do for her.

4.

It was one of those nights when Carlotta was out with a 'uniform' and Francesca had made sure to stay home just in case Bill chose to drop by to talk. He always wanted to stay 'just a few minutes more' but she always sent him home by eleven or eleven-thirty at the latest. She knew why he tried to linger – so that he'd be there when Carlotta's date brought her home. But she couldn't allow it . . . couldn't help him spy on Carlotta. Besides, there were times when Carlotta didn't roll in until almost dawn and the idea of she and Bill just sitting there, waiting, was intolerable. Still, she suspected that sometimes after he left, Bill parked his car up the street where she couldn't see in the dark, and kept his vigil.

As it was a lovely evening, warm for early June, they sat in the small garden in the rear of the house, drinking iced tea. Tonight, Bill wanted to talk about a party he planned to give for both Francesca and Carlotta, since their birthdays were only eight days apart. His plan was to have the party on the last Saturday in June since the next day was Carlotta's actual birthdate.

'I want the party to be a surprise for Carlotta. I wish it could have been a surprise party for you too, Frankie, but I need your help to plan it. What do you think? Should I rent a room in a hotel or should we have it here in your house? Then we could use the garden too.'

'It depends on how many guests you're thinking of inviting.'

'Well, we'd invite your and Carlotta's girlfriends, and those who have boyfriends who are still around can bring them. But we're definitely not inviting any of Carlotta's menagerie of fighting heroes.'

Francesca smiled wryly. 'I didn't think we were. But we have to invite *some* men if we're going to have a gaggle of unattached females. . . .'

'Oh, we will. I'll supply them. Some of the guys from the office. A few politicians. A handful from the Democratic Business Men's League. I might as well do myself some good at the same time. But I'm going to handpick each one just to be sure none are the kind to catch my sweetheart's fickle eyes. There won't be a single man in uniform, for sure,' he chuckled, making a joke of it but Francesca knew he was dead serious.

'Well, you can always lock her up or take away her shoes. . . .' Francesca smiled to soften the sarcasm but Bill was deaf to it in any case.

'It's all for her own good, believe me.' But Francesca didn't believe him . . . not completely.

'Whom shall I invite for you, Frankie? You get a choice. Do you prefer a lawyer or a businessman or – well, I guess you wouldn't like any of my politician friends . . . they're mostly too old anyway.'

Suddenly she was mad. *What does he think? That I'm incapable of getting my own date? That no one ever asks me out?* Did he think that just because she had a sister who was irresistible this rendered her so unattractive she couldn't get a date on her own?

'Don't trouble yourself. I have someone in mind whom I'd like to invite if that's OK with you. Or would you like to handpick my date too?'

Again he took no notice of her sarcasm. In fact, he disarmed her by saying, 'I *would* like to handpick him if I could, just to make sure he's good enough for you. You deserve only the best, Frankie.'

Oh, she agreed. She *did* deserve the best. The problem was the best was already taken.

'So who's the lucky guy you're going to invite?'

Since she didn't have the slightest idea, Francesca stuck out her chin. 'That's for me to know and for you to find out,' she said pertly.

They decided it would be better after all to have the party at a hotel so that they could hire a band. 'It would never be a real party for Carlotta unless there's dancing,' Francesca said.

'Yes, I know. But here's what we'll do. I'll tell her I'm taking her out for a very special evening – a round of the best places in town and I'll come by here to pick her up while you wait at the hotel with the others. Then, just before we leave, I'll give her her ring and then as soon as we get to the hotel and everybody yells 'surprise!', we'll announce our engagement.'

There he goes again, Francesca thought. Turning the birthday party into an engagement party. He was so sure of himself. So sure of her – good old Frankie, who was going to help him convince Carlotta to accept his ring and agree to be engaged, even though good old Frankie has told him repeatedly that she couldn't and wouldn't make up Carlotta's mind for her. 'I told you, Bill. You can't be sure Carlotta's going to agree to marry you. Why can't you accept that?'

'I'll never accept it,' he said calmly. 'Just like I wouldn't accept it if someone told me I couldn't ever be the President.'

Then Francesca didn't know whether she wanted to scream at him or cry for him. Or for herself. . . . 'I have a headache,' she said. 'Perhaps you'd better go.'

He looked surprised but quickly agreed to leave, kissing her on the forehead. 'Poor Frankie,' he said tenderly. 'Poor little head.'

Go quickly please. You're killing me with your tenderness.

After Bill was gone she sat on in the dark of the garden with the sweet smell of the rambling roses that climbed up one side of the house. She fingered the ring he had given her which she wore on a chain around her neck. And she daydreamed although it was night.

They were in the jewellery store. He passed right over the ring with the little emerald chips. He chose, instead, one studded with sapphires and slipped it on her finger. 'They match your eyes,' he murmured, gazing into them, 'which are beautiful beyond compare.'

Bill was drenched with perspiration by the time Judith was finished with him – sweaty, hot and exhausted. She was a bitch in heat but she fucked like a tigress, claws and all, raking his back with her nails, biting his mouth, grabbing at his balls.

He always meant to get it over with quickly – in-out, bim-bam, thank you ma'am, and out the door. Each week he swore to himself that was how it would be, hating himself for selling himself, hating her for buying, just plain hating her, period, but it was never that simple or over that fast.

Each week making his way to her house, he thought that maybe this time he wouldn't even be able to get it up because he hated her so much, or because she was so unappealing. Each week he dreaded the day, the hour, when he'd walk into the house, the routine always the same – the door unlocked, he locking it after him, mounting the stairs to find her lying on the bed, nude, waiting . . . he undressing in silence as she watched.

Sometimes the routine varied in that she was fingering herself when he walked into the room . . . warming it up. No matter, either way, by the time his pants were off, his cock was hard, engorged, ready to slam into her . . . he himself as hot to get at it as he had ever been in his life. What was it about her that made him want to ram into her? To give her the fucking she demanded? What was the turn-on? Was it the adversarial relationship they shared? Or was it that each one wanted to make the other submit? Beg for it . . . ask for quarter. Or was it only how hot she was for him? So hot she could have torn his prick right out of him. . . .

Maybe it was all his pent-up frustration from dealing with Carlotta. Maybe he was doing to Judith only what he yearned to do to the elusiva Carlotta – she who figured both in his wet dreams and his idealized vision of the future.

He took his shower quickly, eager now to get the hell out of there, eager to erase from his mind what had just taken place for another week. When he went back into the room to take his money from the top drawer of the bureau, part of the routine too, Judith, still lying in bed, told him that since she'd be going to Newport the first of July and since she'd promised to introduce him to the right people who could help him, she was going to host a reception for him on the last Saturday night in June, the 26th.

'Can't make it,' he said. 'I'm giving a birthday party for Francesca and Carlotta at the Ritz on that night.'

'At the Ritz!' she taunted. 'You must be rolling in money.'

'Well, it's a big occasion. Francesca turns twenty on the nineteenth, and Carlotta will be nineteen on the 27th.'

'Yes, how well I know. This month is my twentieth birthday too. I tell you what we'll do. You cancel your party and we'll make the party at my house a triple celebration. At the same time I'll introduce you to all those people who can help you.'

He considered. He *had to* meet Judith's people. He hadn't been fucking her brains out just for the money. And the people he'd been cultivating on his own were hardly in the same class with the ones Judith could produce. On the other hand, Carlotta would bite his head off if he told her that her birthday celebration would be held at Judith's house instead of making the rounds of the most exciting places in town as he'd promised her. And Francesca wouldn't like it any better. She'd chew him out too.

'The plans are already made. Couldn't you have your reception the following week?'

'No. Dudley and I will be in Newport the following weekend. And most people will be out of town anyway for the fourth of July.'

'What about the Saturday night before the 26th? The nineteenth?'

'Afraid not.' She was enjoying giving him the business, he thought. 'The people I want to invite on your behalf are not the sort you invite at the last minute. It's the 26th or nothing.'

He made up his mind quickly. After the 26th, he'd be engaged to Carlotta and finished with Judith. Once he and Carlotta were formally engaged, he wouldn't dream of continuing with Judith, much as he had enjoyed, for the first time in his life, having money to burn.

But he wasn't about to tell Judith that now . . . that he didn't intend to keep on with her. First he had to meet her influential friends.

When Francesca, in off-the-shoulder pink satin and tulle, opened the door to Bill she thought she might faint. Bill Sheridan in ordinary every-day clothes was handsomer than any man had a right to be, Bill Sheridan in uniform had been overwhelming, but Bill Sheridan, tanned, in a white dinner jacket, his yellow hair smoothly swept back, was so beautiful it was enough to break a girl's heart.

'You look wonderful,' she breathed. But he didn't even hear her.

'Where's Carlotta?' he whispered. 'I want to give her her ring before we leave for Judith's.'

'She's still upstairs,' she said dully. He might have said I looked pretty, she thought.

'Is she dressed?'

She gave him a funny look and he smiled sheepishly. 'I just wanted to know if she was decent. I was thinking of going upstairs and giving her the ring right away.'

'I believe she's decent but if I were you, I wouldn't be in any hurry to give her that ring. She's still mad at you, you know, for making us go to Judith's tonight.'

'You think I should wait until tomorrow then? Take her out to dinner and then give it to her?'

Oh, he wants too much of me, and he never stops! Maybe he'll want me to go along on their wedding night too, to escort Carlotta to her bridal bed.

Still, she nodded. 'That probably would be better. Dinner for two with candlelight and roses.'

'You're right. And her birthday isn't until tomorrow. It's just that the damn ring is burning a hole in my pocket. I won't be able to relax until I see it on her finger, you know?' He smiled at her, expecting her understanding. She forced herself to smile to let him know that he had it.

'And you *do* understand about the party tonight, don't you, Frankie? That it was really important for me to be there.'

'Yes, I understand.' *And I did talk Carlotta into going. But that's all I'm going to talk her into. Now you're on your own. . . .*

Then Carlotta came down the stairs in a white strapless gown, the red hair cascading over white shoulders, and his heart stopped. He didn't think that he could wait until tomorrow to give her the ring, to seal their future together. . . .

As soon as they were admitted into Judith's house ablaze with lights and its rooms filled with flowers, Bill's pulse quickened. He didn't know where to look first. Or more accurately, at *whom* to look first. Wherever his glance fell he saw a person of prominence whose face was well-known enough for him to recognize.

'Over there . . .' he whispered to the girls. 'That's the president of the second largest insurance company in the country. And there—' he pointed, 'that's Congressman Curley.'

'Well, I saw *that* woman's picture in the paper today – the stout one in black with the long string of pearls. She's Patricia Chase. Her club just raised over a million dollars for the USO!' Francesca told him. 'And that man over there – the one talking to Mr Cabot. Isn't he the president of the Tradesmen's First National, Carlotta? Remember we met him when—'

Carlotta wasn't interested; she wouldn't look. Her dark crimson mouth pouted. 'I don't think there's even going to be any dancing. All I see is a string quartet. Some birthday party this is!'

Bill didn't hear. He was preoccupied with tying a name to a face. Unless he was mistaken, the man standing all alone in the corner was the owner of the

109

Globe. What a party! Who in influential Boston wasn't here? If just twenty-five percent of these people . . . twenty percent even, threw their support behind him, he wouldn't have to start on a local level in the City Council or the State Senate. He'd be able to skip all that, save several years and leap right into the big time. It made him dizzy just to think about it. He couldn't even think Republican or Democrat. Did it really matter? You went where the support was and the money.

'Lookie, lookie, lookie, here comes cookie,' Carlotta said out of the corner of her mouth. 'It's Judy in gray, of all things. Twenty years old and she's wearing *gray!*'

'Well, you finally got here,' Judith said to Bill, ignoring Carlotta and Francesca. 'We have no time to lose if you're to meet everybody. Come, I want to introduce you to Governor Saltonstall.'

'The governor's here?' Francesca was impressed.

'Of course,' Judith replied smugly.

'What about Eleanor?' Carlotta asked wide-eyed. 'Did the President send her in his place or is he here himself?' Then she sniggered at her own jibe.

'While I take Bill around, Francesca, why don't you take your amusing little sister up to see Dudley? He's feeling a little depressed that he couldn't quite make it downstairs tonight and I'm sure Carlotta, with that wonderful wit of hers, will cheer him up.' And she took Bill's arm, leading him away.

Bill did look apologetically over his shoulder just in time to catch Carlotta sticking out her tongue at him. 'Great work, Frankie. This is a great party you talked me into . . . I must commend you.'

Francesca sighed. 'Well, we really came for Bill's sake not to have a good time. And it *is* supposed to be our birthday party too.'

'Sure. And do you know what we're getting for a birthday present from Judith? A knife in the back.'

'Just try and remember, it's for Bill's sake. And now shall we go upstairs and say hello to Dudley? It would be the nice thing to do.'

Carlotta tossed her hair. 'No, I don't think so. Why don't you go by yourself since you're the nice one in the family? As for me, I think I'll just meander over to the bar and get myself a drink. A daiquiri, I think, since the *yanguis* who invented the cocktail while working the Daiquiri iron mines in Cuba, attributed medicinal qualities to the drink, and that's what I need right now. Strong medicine. And then I'm going to see if I can find a man here under thirty who wants to have a little fun.'

Francesca, wondering where that story about the daiquiri came from, watched her sister snake her way through the throng, undulating her hips in exaggerated fashion. There wasn't a male in her wake who didn't stop mid-conversation to stare at her. This might be an older, conservative crowd but that didn't mean Carlotta wasn't a show-stopper. She always was, whatever the milieu.

I'd better stick with her, Francesca decided. The mood she was in, God knew what she'd be up to. The more conservative the crowd and the more important the people, the more Carlotta felt challenged, and wanted to shock. She might even end up drunk, sitting on the bar and singing, 'Pistol-packin' Mama.'

Francesca went scurrying after Carlotta.

'Put the top up!' Carlotta ordered Bill when they got into the car.

'But you always want it down.'

'I don't want it down tonight. Tonight, I'm cold. *Very* cold,' she said ominously. And then she turned her body away from him and Bill got the message.

Carlotta didn't much enjoy not being the centre of attention, his as well as everyone else's. And while she *had* created a little sensation of her own this evening – how not when she had looked more desirable than he had ever seen her – he hadn't spent much time with her . . . had, in fact, scarcely spoken to her all night.

Still, even with Carlotta mad at him, he felt exhilarated, heady with the success of his evening. Practically everyone he'd been introduced to seemed to like him, was impressed with him – his war record, the fact that he was working for Judge Hardwicke's firm. He had even received invitations to be a guest speaker at lots of organizations – the Veterans of Foreign Wars, the Woman's Club, the Holy Name Society, and a labour leader had asked him to address a group of longshoremen. Everyone was interested in hearing a returned war hero speak.

He wondered then, if he was going to be able to end it with Judith quite yet, speculating whether the contacts he'd made this evening were enough to do it for him, or if he'd have to continue screwing her for a little while longer. . . .

Could he risk *not* going on with Judith? On the other hand, could he risk Carlotta finding out? Suppose she did accept his ring, vowed to marry him, stopped seeing all the others, and then found out? He wouldn't put it past Judith to be the one who told her all about it. No, of the two choices, he couldn't risk losing Carlotta. He could make it without Judith if he had to . . . he couldn't make it without Carlotta.

He reached out to touch her arm as she looked out the window of the car into the night. She pulled her arm away and he saw that she was not only pouting but surly. This was something new, he thought. She often pouted, but he had never seen her really sullen. *Goddamn it! Just when he was about to give her the goddamn ring!* 'You didn't have a good time tonight?' he asked lamely.

'Oh, was I supposed to? Did you hear that, Frankie?' She turned to Francesca in the back seat. 'Bill wants to know if I had a good time? Did *you* have a good time? Or do you think that only Judith and Bill had a good time tonight?'

Francesca didn't answer. *Why, Carlotta's not just mad at Bill – she's jealous! She's jealous of him and Judith!* She couldn't remember Carlotta being jealous of anybody before. She'd always had far too much self-confidence for that. Did this mean that she was really in love with Bill, far more than she herself rationalized?

Bill had just come to the same conclusion. Carlotta is jealous! he exulted. And if a girl was jealous, it meant only one thing! She cared, even if she wouldn't admit it!

Maybe the fact that he'd been busy with Judith tonight instead of mooning over her as usual, was working to his advantage. Maybe tonight was to be his night on all fronts. Maybe he'd do well, after all, to give her the ring tonight . . . when she was hot with jealousy.

Francesca said goodnight and went upstairs leaving Carlotta and Bill alone in the living room. She was more than depressed. She was disturbed.

She took off her party dress which she had thought so becoming but which Bill had never complimented her on. But that didn't matter now. All she could think of was Carlotta. She'd begun the evening making something of a spectacle of herself, drinking and flirting with men much too old for her, and married besides. And just last night she'd come home at four in the morning more than a little tipsy after a date with some kid in the Merchant Marine. And she had scraped through her college year, skipping a lot of classes in the last couple of months of the term. What *was* going to become of her if she didn't settle down soon? And while by her own admission, she didn't 'go all the way' with anyone, that was probably the only thing she didn't do. She did need a steadying influence, someone stable and dependable to straighten her out.

Francesca brushed her teeth, creamed her face clean, put out the lights and got into bed, but she doubted that, tired as she was, she'd be able to sleep.

Tonight, looking around, she'd seen several women only a few years older than she and Carlotta, women who were married to the successful, steady, reliable men who filled the room – women who didn't have to worry about their futures and who enjoyed the good life of the respectable and the secure. She had thought if Carlotta were married to one of these men, she too would be respectable and secure. There'd be no more coming home in the middle of the night drunk. There would be no more sailors pawing at her, trying to 'dry hump' her or giving themselves 'hand jobs' right in front of her. She'd be safe . . . even from herself.

And she, Francesca, had to face it – Bill was such a man. He might well end up being even more successful than all those men at the party, a man who would protect and nurture Carlotta, and most of all, keep her safe. He loved her enough to do that. . . . And she herself had to love Carlotta enough to do what she had to – help Bill save her from herself. She had to urge her baby sister to accept Bill's proposal to be engaged to be wed, no matter at what pain to herself. It was the only right thing to do. It was the only thing she could do.

They were standing up. Carlotta was waiting for him to leave. He tried to put his arms around her but she pushed him away. 'Go kiss Judith.'

Bill tried to laugh, the remark being too close to the truth. 'Why would I want to do that? I don't even like Judith and I'm crazy about you.'

'Oh, really? One would never know it. I could have sworn you were crazy about Judith.'

'Come on, Carlotta. Judith's just trying to help me with my career.'

'If you ask me Judith's trying to help herself . . . to *you*.'

'Judith? Frigid Judith? That's a laugh.'

'I have a feeling that's all an act. After all, that old rooster she married can't do anything even if she wanted him to – I think she's got hot pants and what's more, I think she's got them for you. Why wouldn't she? Look at her husband and look at you!'

He moved closer to put his arms around her. 'Think there's a difference, do you?'

She started to smile now. 'You might say that. I bet every time Judith looks at you she get's a hard-on.'

He kissed the back of her neck, behind her ear. 'Don't be silly,' he murmured. 'Girls don't get hard-on.'

'Don't they?' She threw her head back, letting him press against her hard, let him put his hands on her breasts without a struggle.

Even as the blood rushed to his head, roared in his ears, he realized that talking about Judith having the 'hots' for him was acting as a sexual stimulus for Carlotta . . . giving his usually elusive love the 'hots.'

He eased her down on to the sofa, his hands going crazy now, one even slipping under the fabric of her strapless bodice, something she had never allowed before. When he felt the silky skin of her breast, he moaned softly and then she removed his hand. *Damn!*

But she wasn't withdrawing. Rather, her eyes were glittering and the beautiful lips were parted in a smile. 'I have the most fabulous idea! You must make love to Judith!'

'What?' He mustn't have heard her right.

But she was excited, her breath coming fast; he could practically hear her heart beating against his. 'Yes, you have to do it! And then she'll really put herself out for you! Don't you see? If you make love to Judith, she'll be your puppet, she'll go out of her mind and really break her back for you!'

She kissed him and then reached down, touched him *there*, and his head reeled. The idea of him fucking Judith had brought Carlotta to a point months of wooing never had!

He made an instant decision. He'd take the chance! He bent over her again and whispered in her ear.

When he was finally leaving, he was happier than he could remember ever being before. While they hadn't gone all the way, he was almost fully content with how far they had gone. She had allowed him to kiss her there and it had been incredibly sweet, and she had touched him repeatedly, almost as if she couldn't keep her hands off him. But best of all, she was wearing his ring!

They kissed again at the door, their tongues entwining.

'I think the best part of it is that she's actually paying you to make love to her, you sexy prostitute you,' she giggled. 'Oh, how I wish we could tell Frankie but we mustn't. Frankie wouldn't think it was funny. You know how Frankie is. She's so idealistic and she thinks you're the soul of morality. We can't disillusion her. Swear you'll never tell. I'd hate for Frankie to disapprove of our engagement.'

He was more than willing to swear. His fucking Judith turned Carlotta on but it would probably turn Frankie against him for life. And while, more than anything, he yearned for Carlotta's love, he still wanted her sister's respect.

When Bill left Carlotta on Saturday night he was floating on a cloud. But by Tuesday afternoon his euphoric state had slowly dissipated and now on his way to see Judith for the last time before she left for Newport, he was shrouded in gloom. Filled with self-disgust at what he was doing with Judith, he realized that he'd been looking forward to his engagement forcing him to call it quits with her. But the way things stood now, he had to continue with her for at least a few months more. What Judith had done for his career on Saturday night had made her more indispensible to him rather than less. And now he himself had made her that much more indispensible by using his affair with her to fuel the fires of Carlotta's love . . . *if he could call that love.* . . .

He was no longer sure that it was. How could it be love when the girl who supposedly loved him wanted to hear all the details of him making love to another girl? That sure as hell wasn't the way it was in the movies. . . . If it was love, it sure was a strange kind of love, needing all the dirty little details of his screwing Judith to titillate her. . . . And telling himself that Carlotta was just a kid didn't help. Francesca was only a year older and he couldn't imagine her loving a man and getting kicks out of this situation. Rather, she would be filled with revulsion, heartbroken. She would cease loving that man and she would be right. . . .

But of course, Frankie was an unusually mature young woman. Maybe that was it, he told himself. Maybe Carlotta still had to grow up. But then it occurred to him, that if she did grow up . . . matured, would she still love him, or would that love turn to revulsion for him too?

He no longer knew all the answers. And who was to say what love was really all about? Who said it had to be moonlight and roses? Maybe love was just different things to different people. . . .

Well, with Judith in Newport for eight weeks, he was going to have a reprieve from the situation. . . . Anything could happen in two months. Maybe the situation would resolve itself.

Ready to leave, he took his money out of the top drawer of the bureau. As always, now that it was over, he was anxious to get out quickly. He had really earned his money today. Judith had been hell on wheels, insisting on taking the upper position, riding *him*, whipping him on with snapped-out commands, setting the pace. But now it was over for eight weeks. . . .

Then he heard her say, 'So I'll see you in Newport next Tuesday afternoon.'

He swung around to face her as she lay half-covered by the tangle of sheets, one dark-brown-nippled breast staring obscenely at him. 'I can't go to Newport!'

'Why can't you?'

'Getting there and coming back will take the whole day. I've got a job, remember?'

'I could hardly forget considering that it was I who got it for you. But I've taken care of that. I told Fenton that I'll require your services every Tuesday . . . so many legal technicalities to be discussed. . . .'

He was flabbergasted. If he refused, it might even cost him his job. Then he thought of something she couldn't possibly dispute. He wouldn't have enough gas to go back and forth to Newport every week. 'Can't do it. There's a war on, remember? Gas rationing?'

She snickered. 'I'll get you all the gas you need.'

'Where? How?'

'Really, you amaze me! I hardly took you for naive.'

Then he was furious. Hadn't she ever seen the war bond poster showing a dying GI and the legend – 'He gives his life – you only loan your money.' And she was willing for that bleeding GI to die a little faster by patronizing the black market for her own obscene, selfish reasons? And she thought he'd be willing too? It was the worst kind of insult. 'I fought at Guadalcanal, damn you! I saw men dying all around me. Do you really think I'd undermine those guys dying for the fat cats here? Maybe if you'd seen them bleeding their guts out you wouldn't be offering me black market fuel.'

She only smiled. 'So you still have some standards left? That's good to know. I thought perhaps you were *all* whore.'

He thought then that he really would hit her, beat her up, slap her silly, blacken her eyes, rip her cheek open with the flat of his hand, break her jaw with his fist, flatten her nose into a bloody pulp. . . .

Maybe that's what she really wants even more than she wants her pussy rammed! . . .

But then he was only tired, and filled with the old self-loathing. She was right. He was a whore as much as any tramp who sold her ass for two bucks. And he was worse than she was. 'You're right,' he said. 'I am a whore but you're the whoremonger. But I have my limits and I won't take your black market gas.'

She laughed. 'Then take the train.'

After he was gone, Judith thought that Bill Sheridan was more fool than whore. He still had no idea that while she enjoyed . . . relished . . . the pleasures of his beautiful strong body . . . indeed, lusted for it, what she was really buying was the services of an impregnating stud, one with certain genetic advantages. Bill Sheridan was all the things she wanted her son to be – bright, dynamic, ambitious . . . even heroic under certain circumstances, majestically tall and handsome, virile and healthy . . . a winner, a champion. With the Stanton money and name behind him, her son would be even more – he'd be a prince.

She never doubted for a moment that she would bear a son. A son was what she wanted and a son was what she would get. She believed in her own will and determination the way some people believed in God.

Her big problem was time. She doubted that Dudley would last another year although she was doing everything that could possibly be done for him, and no longer doing those things that only made him feel better – the stimulants, the sex. She had to be extraordinarily careful not to overtax him now that he was almost completely paralyzed . . . almost completely spent. Still, she could not let him give up hope. Each day the speech therapist still came and each day the physical therapist still visited. She would need whatever faltering speech she could elicit from him, and while she didn't absolutely have to have his faltering signature, it would be better to have it than not. How much more impressive that, upon learning he was to be a father, Dudley himself asked the lawyers to draw up a new will, leaving the same half she was willed now, to her, and the other half – that which was to have gone to the Foundation yet to be established – in trust for his heir, his miracle-producing wife to be the sole trustee. And how much more inspiring if he were to sign it himself in his trembling hand in front of witnesses rather than she did it for him. . . .

Then she would be in control of it all, and who would be able to challenge any part of it? It would all be airtight and she would be home safe. As for the Foundation, the Stanton Center, she would unselfishly endow that herself, in her own time, in her own way, spending only as much as she chose. It would certainly wait until after the war was over. . . .

All she needed was the pregnancy. How ironical life was. In novels and in films, a good girl only had to be betrayed by her passion once to find herself 'in trouble.' And here she was, married to a husband with a great fortune to harbour her child, and she hadn't conceived after repeated opportunities. There was only one thing to do – step up the schedule before her time ran out. She'd have to have Bill come to Newport twice a week which would make her life that much more enjoyable, and as a side benefit would also take him away that much more from Carlotta.

She hadn't forgotten how jealous Carlotta had been the night of her party. Oh, how she wished that she could let Carlotta know that she and Bill were lovers. But the satisfaction of telling Carlotta wasn't great enough to jeopardize her position. Once her child was born, she couldn't afford to have speculations over who his father was. Only she herself could know for sure, and there was only Bill to draw his own conclusions. But she wasn't worried about his guessing, speculating, *knowing*. By the time her son was born, Bill Sheridan would be in so deep, he would have as much to lose as she if the truth came out. The more important Bill became, the higher he rose in station, the more he, too, would need to keep their secret . . . the secret that would bind them together for the rest of their lives. . . .

Bill Sheridan would always belong to her more than Carlotta.

When Judith told Bill that he was to come twice a week to Newport, he was enraged. 'Are you crazy? I'll be doing nothing else except riding that damn train!'

'You can always sleep over. We have wonderful accommodation for guests,' she teased. 'There's swimming, tennis. . . . You *do* play tennis, don't you?'

'No, I can't do it!'

'Let's see. You're getting what now? Twenty-five hundred a month? That's a lot of money, a fortune really. But we'll raise it. Let's see. Do you think four thousand sounds fair?'

Four thousand dollars a month! It was insane! Some people didn't make that in a year. Why was she willing to pay it? He couldn't be *that* good. And other than the money, she treated him like dirt, talked to him as if he were shit. She couldn't possibly be in love with him. But even knowing that he was going to hate himself that much more, he couldn't turn down four thousand a month! How could he? And he had become accustomed to having the money. He *needed* it!

Still he hesitated, torn. He *knew* it was the classic case of selling his soul to the devil, that he was only getting in deeper. He'd never be free of her. It was bad enough that each time he screwed her, he found his own excitement growing, almost as if he couldn't screw her hard enough, almost as if he wanted to screw her to death!

'And I've been thinking,' Judith said carefully, watching his face. 'Maurice Tobin is going to run for Governor next year. He's going to need a lieutenant-governor to run on his ticket. Wouldn't that be a wonderful start for you? A wonderful beginning to a lustrous career. . . .'

Bill felt the remainder of his defences crumbling. 'You're saying that you can do that? Get me that place on the ticket?'

'Oh, I can't guarantee it. If I guaranteed it . . . promised you that, I'd be lying and I wouldn't want to do that. But you do have my promise that I'll do all I can and I do have influence. You know that. In the meantime I think you should have a headquarters and a full time staff working for you, looking ahead. You'll find that you'll be asked to speak more and more to different groups and organizations as the months go by . . . all over the state and that's what you want to do – gain statewide recognition. You're definitely going to need a staff. And then there's the business of public relations. Yes, it's time to get you launched . . . see to it that a day doesn't go by without your name in the papers. And your picture too. Women are going to find that face of yours irresistable. And when we can't get you in the papers for free, there's always a form of paid advertising discreetly called "in the public interest" to push your image.'

'But the lieutenant-governor thing is a couple of years away. How do I know you won't lose interest once you start to lose interest in—'

'In your particular talents?' She cupped his testicles so that there'd be no mistake as to which talents they were talking about. He flushed but he didn't move away and she knew that she had him. 'I'll put it in writing since you don't trust me completely,' she said, amused. 'But you won't mind if we don't refer to services rendered? You understand. Let's see. How shall we put it? "In view of my sincere and abiding interest in that which our great country has to offer, I hereby pledge—" Well, you're the lawyer. You write it up. . . .'

'But why? *Why* are you willing to do all this for me? There are a thousand guys who—'

'Yes, there are but *they're* not Big Bill Sheridan. Let's just say you've caught my fancy and I can afford to indulge my fancies.'

But he still didn't get it no matter what she said. He thought about it all the way back to Boston on the train. He wondered if it had anything to do with his loving Carlotta . . . with their engagement. He knew that Judith didn't like her aunts. Was she just getting her kicks fucking the man who was in love with Carlotta? Getting him to betray Carlotta and participating in that betrayal?

He laughed bitterly. If that was the case, considering how much Carlotta was enjoying the situation, the joke was on Judith. . . . Or was it?

The summer went by quickly for Bill. Between spending two days a week in Newport and travelling across the state making speeches to men's organizations, women's clubs, Gold Star mothers, labour groups, in addition to his appearances at bond rallies and war plants, he was barely able to put in any time at the law office. Fortunately, Fenton Hardwicke was pleased just to have him taking care of the Stantons' affairs and to have it mentioned in the papers that Bill Sheridan was a member of his firm. It was a splendid association for them both.

On weekends, Bill served as a judge at county fairs, attended politically sponsored boatrides and picnics, block parties and church affairs. The only way he had much time for Carlotta was to drag her along whenever he could, which didn't exactly thrill her, especially since she wasn't seeing anyone else or going to any of the places she really enjoyed. She complained to Francesca, 'It's all so boring. Watching Bill pin a blue ribbon on a pig isn't my idea of a good time.'

But Francesca who was now committed to Bill and Carlotta's engagement and marriage in order to save Carlotta from herself, gave her pep talks. 'Think of the wonderful future you and Bill will share when he's a senator or maybe the governor!' She didn't dare mention the word *president* because Carlotta, being Carlotta, would have only scoffed and Francesca wanted her to take all this seriously, take it to heart.

'Just envision it, Carlotta. Think of the honour. Just think of Bill as Senator Sheridan, and you sitting in the gallery of the United States Senate. You'll be wearing furs of course, and a suit by the latest designer and a wonderful hat, and the other women will be whispering, "Oh, that's Senator Sheridan's beautiful wife. Don't they make a gorgeous couple?"'

'Oh God! That sounds even more boring than standing by while Bill makes his big decision as to which pig gets the blue ribbon. Even though I must say, the pigs *are* cuter than most of Bill's ward heelers.'

Francesca smothered the urge to giggle. She didn't dare encourage Carlotta by laughing. 'You mustn't talk that way. Your job is to help Bill. *You* have to be nice to everybody too. Bill's going to be a great man and then you'll reap your rewards. You'll go to Washington and go to all the teas and luncheons and those wonderful balls we're always reading about. Why, you'll probably dance with the President, whoever he is at the time, wearing the most fabulous ballgown Washington's ever seen!'

But Carlotta shook her head, looking as if she might cry, 'But I don't want to dance with the President,' she said piteously.

'Why not, for God's sake?'

'Because I'd much rather go to the dance at the USO wearing just what I'm wearing right now.' She touched the skinny shoulder strap of the bare-backed sundress she was wearing.

Francesca was losing her patience. 'But why, Carlotta? Any girl would be thrilled to be the woman I just described. . . .' Francesca knew she herself would be. 'Why wouldn't you be happy?'

Carlotta ran her fingers through her hair. 'Because . . . because it all sounds so set and stuffy . . . no surprises. It sounds *nice* but dull. It sounds like nothing exciting would ever happen to me again.'

'And going to a noisy USO dance with the music blaring and dancing with one stranger after the other in a hot, airless room – *that's* exciting?'

'Yes, it is. I don't know why exactly but I hear the music playing and my feet want to dance and the night's like one of those birthday cakes with all the little charms inside. You don't know what you'll find, but you want to bite into each

118

and every piece just to make sure you're not missing the best one. I see all the boys . . . all the different ones, all the different faces and my heart starts to beat fast and I wonder, what's special about this *one*, and I want to dance with him and find out. . . .'

Francesca was sceptical. 'And how often *is* there something special about him, whoever he is?'

'Oh . . .' Carlotta smiled vaguely. 'Almost never. But that's not the point. That's the fun of it. It's like Russian roulette. You spin the cylinder and you never know what will turn up. . . .'

'And Bill? You don't find him exciting?' She herself did. Exciting enough for ten lifetimes.

'Oh, Bill is sweet and I do love him, truly I do . . . but it's always the same.'

No surprises, no excitement. Even the idea of his screwing Judith for money, which *had* been exciting, had lost its appeal. Even Bill's recounting of all the little details—*he touched her there . . . she bit his shoulder . . . he mouthed her nipple . . . she screamed out, 'faster'. . . .* It was all beginning to wear thin, no longer giving her the same tingle it had in the beginning. She even suspected that Bill was beginning to make things up to please her.

Somewhere, somehow, there had to be more. . . .

'You know, Frankie darling, *you* could talk Bill into letting me go only to the dances and parties. He has the utmost respect for your opinion. He thinks I'm a scatterbrain and that you have your head screwed on right. And I swear, I wouldn't even flirt with anybody. I wouldn't do anything except dance. Believe me, I wouldn't even dream of going out with anyone but Bill. I know how much he loves me and I value that, really. But just dancing and a little bit of talking and a few laughs – how could that possibly hurt? All I'd be doing would be entertaining our servicemen for a couple of hours. And you know how Bill feels about our boys in uniform. When he gives those speeches, all he talks about is how much we owe them . . . that nothing is too good for them, no sacrifice too big.'

Besides, all she wanted to do was dance with them, not fuck them! He should talk, the hypocrite . . . screwing Judith for money and his stupid old big chance! He wanted her to be pure but he himself was hardly the Virgin Mary! But she couldn't tell Frankie all that.

'But what about your accompanying Bill when he makes speeches? Your place *is* at his side.'

'Oh shoot! Why don't *you* go with him instead of me? You're so much better at this kind of thing than I am. People always like you and you take notes on everything – what Bill said that pleased the audience. What didn't go over that big. I've *heard* you and Bill analyze these things for hours on end. You've even broken up the crowds into ethnic groups and percentages – ten percent Jews, twenty-five percent WASPS, thirty percent Irish Catholics. Really! It's amazing! I don't know how you do it. You're really great at politics! And you like it and I don't. So why can't we all do the things we like and then we'll all be happy?'

Well, that did make sense, Francesca thought. And she supposed it couldn't hurt if she went along with Bill instead of Carlotta. And later on when there was politicizing to do, Carlotta would be older and might even enjoy campaigning . . . see it as a challenge. She did like challenges. And certainly, with her beauty and personality she'd be an asset to Bill. Of course, she'd never be another Eleanor Roosevelt, but then would Bill want her to be?

Finally, Bill agreed to what Francesca proposed. As she said, what harm was there in Carlotta attending a few dances for the men in uniform? It *was* patriotic. Maybe it would help to get all that nonsense out of her system. He was just grateful that she had lost interest in his affair with Judith. Not that it had done him any good in the end. She still went so far and then no further. She let him get all hot and bothered and she herself seemed to be poised on the pinnacle of uncontrollable passion and then pfft. . . . She withdrew and it was all over for her even as he himself was still groaning for fulfillment, still trying to figure out how she could be so passionate one moment and cold the next. . . .

At least with Judith you knew what was what. She was hot as a pistol until she came in a screaming climax. One thing he was grateful for . . . that the summer was coming to an end. How he hated making love to Judith in Newport under her husband's roof, locked up in her study while Dudley lay but a few doors down the hall, sick, paralyzed, dying. . . . It made him feel like the biggest prick that ever lived. . . .

Judith and Dudley returned to Boston the first week in September, she suspecting that she was, at last, pregnant. A week later, it was confirmed. Now she had to convince Dudley that however ill, and almost completely paralyzed, he had fathered a child. It wouldn't be too difficult – poor Dudley's senses were dulled from intensive medication and prolonged bedstay, from dozing and awakening at odd hours so that he almost didn't know day from night. He only knew that it was day when he ate and when his therapist came, and it was night when Judith lay down beside him. So when she came to him that afternoon to undress before him – something she hadn't done since his last attack – he couldn't fathom why the sun was streaming in through the window, illuminating her in such a way that she appeared to be an angel. Had he died and gone to heaven without being aware of it?

No, he couldn't be dead, he decided, since he could feel her weight upon him. 'Wh-what?' he cried.

'There, there . . .' she kissed his dry lips. 'We're going to make love, Dudley darling, just as we did before—'

'Bu-but . . . can't . . .' he uttered, in his stilted speech.

'Oh yes you can. Oh, my sweet Dudley, I want you to give me a baby . . . a son to carry on your name.'

Then he again thought he must be dreaming. How could he give Judith a baby? He couldn't. . . .

But Judith was so alive . . . so persistent. She persuaded him that he wasn't dreaming. That if he wanted a son, he had to try . . . to feel . . . to harden . . . to ejaculate . . . that his sperm was as potent as he was himself. 'You don't have to do anything, Dudley darling. All you have to do is let Judith help you. . . .'

She was promising him everything. She was promising him immortality and he believed in her.

She kissed him down there. He could see her head moving. And then she moved up on him and pushed his flaccid organ into the right place, made the right motions. She pushed and ground, she sighed and groaned, she shivered for him and screamed and writhed. If he didn't quite *feel* what was happening – or did he? – he could see and hear and it was almost as good. . . .Sometimes, he told himself dreamily, the dream was better than the reality. Or was it the other way around? . . .

Dr Phillips was as excited as if he had fathered Judith's child himself. He had witnessed a miracle . . . a triumph of the spirit over the state of the body. He had no doubt that it was Judith's indomitable will, her unflagging dedication that had caused this miracle.

Fenton Hardwicke, called in to draw up Dudley's new will was full of admiration for Dudley. 'That sly old dog . . .' he told his wife Alicia and she wondered what was wrong with Fenton. He and Dudley were the same age and Dudley was sick, physically incapacitated, yet Dudley *could* and Fenton couldn't, and she wasn't thinking about fathering a child.

When Bill went to take his money from the drawer, he found an extra $4,000. Quickly he looked over at Judith, still reposing, watching him with a sober expression.

'Your severance pay,' she said.

So it was over, at last, and he was filled with both relief and regret. And the regret wasn't only for the money. Their relationship had been an adversarial one but there had been a certain quality present in their coming together that he knew he'd never find again . . . a certain intensity of passion that would make all other relationships saltless to the taste.

'But not to worry. You'll still have your headquarters and your staff. . . .'

He knew what he should have said. Stuff it, or forget it, or words to that effect. But he didn't. He said nothing. He didn't even ask her why. Rather, he raised his hand to his forehead in a salute and was off. . . .

And a sense of desolation filled her. It was a bitter moment, not at all what she'd expected. Already, she wanted him again and it was almost unbearable to think that she would never have him again . . . never feel his body again, never feel him inside her again, never again have all that which Carlotta was going to have. She could have continued but it would have been a risk . . . one that she could not afford to take. She couldn't put her future and that of her child at risk.

She admired him for not asking questions, not asking her why. But he'd know . . . guess . . . soon enough, and then he too wouldn't be willing to take the risk, she was sure. Both of them had a healthy regard for priorities, that was one of the things that made them a match. As for Carlotta, she didn't deserve him, and she, Judith, was going to make it a priority that she didn't have him. If she herself couldn't, why should Carlotta whom she detested?

The day Dudley was to sign the new document, Judith again, and for the last time, gave Dudley one of her special shots, spruced him and had him brought downstairs and placed in his wheelchair. Then she wheeled him into the library

121

where Fenton waited along with a male secretary and Bill Sheridan, who *was*, after all, the member of the firm in charge of the Stantons' affairs.

Dudley, flushed with pride over his almost unique accomplishment and the benzedrine coursing through his veins, rallied sufficiently from his reverie to sign his name to his last will and testament. Still, the efforts of the therapist notwithstanding, this took several minutes to accomplish during which time Judith's eyes met Bill's squarely, her gaze clear and open, offering no answers. But then, his eyes asked no questions. He knew and she knew and there was nothing to be discussed.

After the signing there was a small dinner party: Judith and Dudley, Fenton and Alicia, Francesca and Bill and Carlotta. Naturally Judith wanted her only family to share in her and Dudley's happiness.

Dudley ate porridge and rice pudding while the rest of them dined on *foie gras* with truffles and mushrooms and rare roast beef. Dudley was permitted a few sips of the champagne, since there were toasts to the anticipated Stanton heir.

Francesca thought Bill was unnaturally quiet and repeatedly asked him if he was all right.

Carlotta drank too much wine and draped herself all over Bill to tease Judith, knowing, of course, what she knew.

Judith took note of Francesca's unusual concern for her sister's fiancé's well-being and could hardly *not* take note of Carlotta's public display of affection for the father of *her* child. Well, she could still call the tune.

She kissed Dudley in a burst of spontaneous affection and everyone at the table applauded, led off by Alicia Hardwicke, and Judith again vowed to herself that since she couldn't have Bill Sheridan, neither would her niece.

IV
1943–1944

1.

The house was decked with ropes of holly and huge poinsettias, both red and white, were banked in every nook and cranny. Great wreaths tied with red and green satin ribbon were mounted on every door, on every mantle, and sprigs of mistletoe hung suspended in the doorways and from every chandelier. In the reception hall stood an enormously tall Christmas tree, its boughs laden with red and white balls and candy canes, with a beautiful frosted angel on top, and in the drawing room was an even taller tree, this one dressed with only silver ornaments and perky red velvet bows, topped with a silver star.

In the dining room, the oversized table groaned with the traditional turkeys stuffed with chestnut dressing, and honey-glazed hams decorated with cherries carved into tiny stars.

Outside, the rows of evergreens were decorated with lights, each one all of a different colour – one all blue, the next all red, and the one after that, all green. And as a final touch of whimsy, Judith had had the most enormous Santa Claus erected while his reindeer pranced across the lawn.

Judith wanted it to be a Christmas Eve party to be talked about by all for many years to come and one that Dudley would remember for all his remaining days. Her private hope for him was that he would last her pregnancy . . . endure to see the birth of their child. The fact was that he was the only person in the world for whom she had true, altruistic affection since he was the only person who had ever truly loved her.

And she intended that this Christmas Eve party would be one Bill Sheridan would never forget . . . he and Carlotta and Francesca. And if everything went as she planned, then that was exactly what it would be. . . .

Judith in her bright red velvet gown (never before in her life had she worn bright red) which accommodated her pregnancy, gave out the presents, all wrapped in silver paper and tied in magenta satin ribbon, one for each guest, all one hundred-and-fifty of them, each gift thoughtfully selected with its recipient in mind. For Bill there was a gold key which would open the door of his new headquarters, fully staffed, and for Francesca, there was a ring, of all things, one with a cluster of sapphires. Francesca was dumbfounded. An expensive ring when Judith didn't even like her?

'I noticed that that ring you wear on your right hand . . . the one Bill gave you for your birthday, was set with emeralds and I thought that wasn't right. I thought you should have one with sapphires to match your eyes.'

And then Francesca thought that Judith was not only observant, but sensitive. And she herself always underestimated Judith, thinking only of her less attractive characteristics, instead of giving her credit for her better qualities. *Or is Judith softening?* Was this what happened when a woman was going to have a baby?

Francesca fingered the ring, thinking she should put it on since Judith was waiting for her to do just that, but the ring was sized for the third finger and it would seem odd to put a ring from her niece on her fourth finger, left hand.

Judith apparently guessed what she was thinking. 'Here . . . Why don't you put that emerald ring on your left hand?' She did it for Francesca. 'And now you can put my ring on your right hand in friendship for we are that now, aren't we? Friends?'

'Of course,' Francesca murmured, looking down at her hands. It felt so strange to have Bill's ring on her left hand, but she had to say it did look right. . . .

Carlotta, in a short evening dress of bottle green velvet cut low in front to display the swell of creamy breasts, tapped her silver sandal impatiently. *Where's my present?* She didn't have a doubt that Judith had left her present for last just to be mean. She wouldn't be such a wise guy, Carlotta thought, if she knew that I know who the father of her baby is. . . . And Frankie wouldn't be so damn pleased with her new ring either, if she knew what Judith had made Bill do. . . .

Carlotta watched the stack of presents dwindle . . . dwindle . . . dwindle, as Judith handed them all out to her guests, one by one, until they were all gone and Carlotta was still empty-handed.

'Oh Carlotta!' Judith called out. 'I must apologize. I forgot all about you!'

I just bet you did, you pregnant bitch! Then she laughed. *I got your number, Judith, and it's the same old one you've always had.*

She went over to tease Bill about his impending fatherhood and his nice new gold key. But she would be careful not to let Frankie hear, and Judith watched her saunter off. *Oh, I haven't forgotten you, Carlotta dear.* No, she had a Christmas present for Carlotta, all right, only he was late.

Trust Trace Boudin to make a delayed entrance, Judith reflected. Deliberately, no doubt. Most likely to make a dramatic entrance. But one couldn't be sure. Men like Trace Boudin were notoriously unreliable. It was part of their charm and Trace Boudin was undeniably charming. That was part of his stock in trade.

She'd come upon Trace Boudin through word of mouth, in a manner of speaking. Looking ahead to that time when the war was over and she erected the Stanton Center, she occasionally bought a few paintings which would eventually grace the Center. She wanted *names*, she told the gallery owners. She didn't know anything about art but she knew a name when she heard one, or more accurately, saw one on a painting . . . names like Van Gogh, or Renoir, Picasso or a Dutch master. If anything should come up – something not outrageously expensive since she wouldn't be played for a fool – she'd be interested in hearing from them.

And then she received a call, a cautiously worded call. Would she be interested in a few paintings that had made their way to America from France . . . the Netherlands? Paintings that had been *liberated* by the German occupation, as it was artfully stated. There was a certain gentleman, lately arrived in Boston, who might be able to put the right art lover together with the right painting for a price. . . . But she had to remember that Rembrandts,

126

for instance, didn't come cheap no matter what the circumstances, and the circumstances were a bit risky.

Risky, yes, Judith thought, as risky for the buyer as for the seller. The cost of such a painting would be exorbitant, and considering the source, there'd be no way of properly authenticating such works. And where could such pictures be displayed? Only in Germany and only if the Germans were victorious. These were pictures, if bought by an American, which could only be enjoyed in the secrecy of a special, locked room.

No, she wouldn't be interested, but she *was* interested in meeting the gentleman with the audacity to push such a scam. Maybe he and she could do business. There was an incredible amount of money to be made during the war. The clever person who didn't have a penny before a war could end up a millionaire, and the millionaire a billionaire. And while she did control several hundred million (she was still trying to estimate the fortune to the last dollar) a billion was such a nice, round, comfortable figure.

Judith met Trace Boudin for tea at the Copley. All around them there were properly hatted and gloved matrons sedately sipping their Earl Gray ... English tea from a bomb-strafed country. Remarkable, Judith thought. Sometimes it was hard to tell that there was a war going on. And it was no less remarkable that she was sitting at a linen-covered table across from a man with luxuriant, black, wavy hair, a black moustache, a swarthy complexion, and gleaming white teeth fixed in a non-stop smile ... a man, despite his meticulously fitted, chalk-striped gray suit with a ruptured duck in his lapel – the sign of the discharged veteran – who most closely resembled a nineteenth-century riverboat gambler straight out of a Hollywood film. And they were discussing paintings that had been stripped off the museum walls of war ravaged nations by Nazis, no less. Most remarkable.

And even more remarkably, she was enjoying herself. Trace Boudin, while not as classically handsome as Bill Sheridan, possessed at least as much sexual magnetism, more, she supposed, pure animal appeal. And while there was no possibility that she would ever know this man in the biblical sense – only a damned fool, a moon-calf of a girl, or a reckless, feckless woman would ever get mixed up with a man like Trace Boudin – there was a certain titillation in their verbal exchange.

'Where did you get hold of these paintings? Or should I say, *how?*' she asked, even though she wasn't buying.

The black eyes narrowed trying to gauge her interest.

'Oh, they're not in my possession. They're with friends ... friends whose interests I represent. Just call me a sales representative,' he grinned sardonically and she saw the smile which didn't quite reach his eyes.

'And these friends? Where are they?'

'On the Coast. California.'

'Los Angeles?'

'Definitely.'

'And what do your friends do? Besides offering stolen paintings for sale?'

He smiled at her use of the word *stolen* but again the eyes didn't smile. There was a certain cold steeliness instead. 'All kinds of things,' he said vaguely.

127

Judith didn't press. She knew she wouldn't get a more comprehensive answer at this time. Then again, she didn't need one. She got the drift.

'And how did your friends get hold of these paintings?' she asked, more to test him.

'The new owners of the paintings sent them over to be sold.'

'But how? Hardly through the mail.'

'Hardly.'

'But why?'

'Because they need the dollars. It's expensive to wage a war against half the world. I'm sure you understand.'

'And they expect to raise the money *here*? In America? While they're at war with us?'

His coal-black eyes glistened. 'For everything that's for sale there's always a buyer. Interested?'

'Me? Certainly not. I'm a good American. I would never do business with the enemy.'

He laughed. 'Of course, you wouldn't.' Then he asked the waitress what they had in the way of imported scotch. 'You'd be surprised how difficult it is to get good scotch these days, Mrs Stanton. Now if I were in Los Angeles I wouldn't have any problem. I can get *anything* I want in Los Angeles.'

Judith was sure that he could. Maybe even in Boston. She felt it to her very fingertips and she always trusted her intuition. She found Trace Boudin more than interesting – she found him fascinating, as fascinating as a cobra and easily more attractive. And while snakes were repellent to most people, there were those who were quite taken with them, especially those who had a taste for danger. Yes, she and Trace Boudin, whoever he was – Mississippi riverboat gambler . . . imitation Clark Gable . . . smooth operator with connections – she and he would be able to do business. . . .

There was dancing in the marble-floored conservatory for those who were of that inclination. Carlotta was so inclined and she went to find Bill. While Bill didn't do a good Lindy – maybe he was too tall or maybe even too conscious of his position in the stream of things to perform the necessary gyrations – he did do a mean rhumba. So she was in the drawing room when Trace Boudin made his entrance, incredibly suave in his tuxedo, somehow different from the roomful of pale, proper Bostonians. And the second she saw him she thought, he could have played Rhett Butler! *Gorgeous, sexy Rhett!* And she felt a stirring somewhere . . . she guessed that it was in her loins. . . .

She had never understood why Scarlett preferred pale, proper Ashley to the sexy, saturnine Rhett. That was the big flaw in the movie. And she believed in movies. She always told herself that one of these days, *if* she didn't marry Bill Sheridan, she'd go to Hollywood and be a star. . . .

Judith took Bill aside in a corner of the drawing room for a private talk with her and Fenton. She was thinking about buying a winery in upstate New York and she wanted Bill to go there and look things over. He'd have to be gone for a few days. Fenton was agreeable but Bill wasn't. The last thing he wanted was to leave town, especially during the holiday week. It would be a chance for him and Carlotta to spend some time together, something they hadn't been able to do much of lately.

'Why me? I'm a lawyer, not a vintner, and I don't know a thing about wine.'

Judith smiled complacently. 'I hardly want you to go there to taste the wine or inspect the vats, or whatever they are.'

'Well, what do you want me to do – check the books? I'm not a bookkeeper either.'

Judith chuckled appreciatively. 'You'll take an accountant with you. It's their corporate structure I'm interested in – the distribution of stock and that sort of thing. I want to make sure everything is as it appears to be. I don't want to buy a pig in a poke. I want every detail checked and double-checked. I want to know that everything is legal and in order. And then I want you to negotiate for me. It will be easier if you stay there until all the papers are drawn up. We'll stay in touch by phone.'

'Stay until all the papers are drawn up? That would take me into next year and then some!'

'Well, that shouldn't be a problem,' Judith said as if talking to a perverse child. Nothing happens between Christmas and New Year. I'm sure you don't have any appointments or speeches. . . .'

'I have *other* commitments.'

Judith's face tightened, a warning that she was tiring of his objections. 'Oh, we'll let you come home for your New Year's celebration if that's what's worrying you. And then you can go back.'

Fenton spoke up. 'Oh, I'm sure you'll be able to wind things up quickly. We all know how efficient you are, my boy.'

Bill shook his head, giving up. He looked around for Carlotta. She was going to be mad as hell about this but what could he do? He noticed that the drawing room was emptying . . . the guests drifting towards the adjoining conservatory. It must be the music, he thought. He could hear it in here. The band was beating out a dramatic Ravel's 'Bolero' and it had a magnetic appeal, a kind of magic.

'Well, that's settled,' Judith smiled. 'Now shall we go see what everyone is up to in the conservatory? The music *is* exciting, isn't it?'

Except for the music, there wasn't a sound in the room and no one was dancing except for Carlotta and Judith's stranger, Trace Boudin. It might have been an exhibition tango . . . Boudin's hand on Carlotta's waist, an electric tension between them as, unsmiling, they looked into each other's eyes, dipped and moved . . . as he bent her backwards in a graceful arc. They might have been alone in the room as they danced, immersed in a mysterious intimacy for there were no intimate embraces in the tango.

Bill didn't like it. 'He looks like he might be a professional tango dancer,' he said with contempt, as if he were using the word 'gigolo,' or even *pimp*. He looked at Judith. Between them there was a mysterious intimacy too, even an electric tension.

'You know, now that you mention it, I think Trace did mention something about his having been exactly *that* . . . a professional tango dancer . . . at some point in his career.'

'Oh yes?' Bill asked. 'And what career is that?'

'Oh, he's a businessman now.'

'What kind of business?'

Judith giggled, an uncommon thing for her. 'I'm not really sure. Probably monkey business. . . .' Then she shrugged. 'But it's only a dance, what matter?' And her eyes said, 'We've shared so much more.'

Seeing how upset Bill was, Francesca tried to engage him in trivial conversation. He was *very* upset. First, there was that business about going out of town and now, Carlotta was still dancing with that Boudin person . . . one dance after the other. She herself had spoken sharply to Carlotta about it but Carlotta only smiled dreamily, then ignored her completely.

Bill and Francesca approached the bar to ask for a plain glass of soda water for Francesca. Tension always left her mouth dry. Then, spotting Carlotta sitting on a bar stool with Trace Boudin standing, leaning over her, she stopped dead in her tracks, said to Bill, 'Oh, let's forget it, I'm not thirsty anymore.'

But Bill too had seen them, Carlotta with her lovely legs crossed, holding out a full cocktail glass to Trace as she ran her vermouth-moistened finger over his full sensual lips, her head thrown back, her eyes fixed on his, his eyes sparkling, his teeth gleaming in his dark face.

Oh no! Francesca cried silently. Carlotta's martini stunt and it was heady business. Carlotta only performed it when she meant business . . . was intent on making an intense impression.

Francesca automatically turned to Bill. He was rigid and his usually ruddy complexion was drained of all colour . . . he was as pale as Carlotta herself.

Francesca looked around, trying to locate Judith. Judith must be furious at this exhibition if she was witnessing it. It was exactly the dramatic sort of display she detested. Then Francesca sighted Judith and indeed she was watching. But the funny thing was Judith was *smiling!*

Carlotta was nowhere in sight and Bill had had enough. 'We're leaving!' he told Francesca. 'I'll get our coats. You go find your sister!' he snapped.

Francesca searched from conservatory to library to dining room and back to the drawing room again, even waiting in vain in front of the two locked powder room doors hoping that Carlotta would emerge. She even checked the pantry and the kitchen to be sure. But she didn't spy Carlotta, or Boudin either.

She considered trying upstairs. Maybe Carlotta had needed to powder her nose urgently and the downstairs powder rooms had been occupied? But then she decided against it, half afraid she *would* find Carlotta up there.

'I don't know,' Francesca smiled apologetically at Bill. 'I can't seem to find her. Maybe she's using an upstairs bathroom . . .' her voice trailed off.

'No, she's gone.'

'Oh? Why do you say that?' She didn't know what else to say.

'Because her coat is gone.'

As they went out the door the orchestra was playing, 'I'm Dreaming of a White Christmas', and outside, as if on cue, tiny snowflakes like little stars, started to drift down slowly. 'Oh look, Bill, the snow's beginning to fall,' she cried, trying to sound enthusiastic. 'I guess it will be a white Christmas after all.'

'Great.'

They drove in tense silence. *Please dear God, don't let him insist on coming in with me to wait for Carlotta.* She didn't think she could endure that. And then there might be a terrible scene . . . a scene from which there would be no going back.

She switched on the radio. 'Silent night, holy night . . .'

Bill switched the radio off.

When they pulled up to the curb Francesca hastily threw her door open. 'Don't bother to get out, Bill. I want you to get home before the snow gets heavy.'

He smiled at her gently then. 'I thought maybe you were going to tell me not to come in because Carlotta was probably in bed asleep and you didn't want me to wake her . . .'

'Oh . . .' She hadn't thought of *that*. 'Well, she probably is. She did have a lot of champagne and champagne always makes her sleepy and—'

'That's funny, I could have sworn she was drinking martinis.'

'Oh? Really?' She got out, ready to close the door. 'Well, Merry Christmas, Bill. You *are* going to church with us in the morning?'

'I'll be by. Unless you think Carlotta will still be sleeping off all that champagne?'

'Oh no, I'm sure she'll be fine – as good as new,' Francesca said brightly, hoping it could be true.

But Bill shook his head. 'We're never as good as new from the moment we're born. Never again. Except maybe for you, Frankie. If anybody can swing it, it's you.'

She watched him drive away. Yes, the snow flakes were getting bigger and they were falling with an increasing rapidity.

She went upstairs to check although she knew full well that Carlotta wouldn't be in bed. Then she went downstairs again to sit by the living room window which overlooked the street. As if she weren't nervous enough – sick at heart, really – the snow's density increased by the hour, fuelling her sense of impending doom.

What was it Bill had said? *We're never as good as new from the moment we're born.*

Deep inside she had this feeling that from this moment on – or maybe from that moment Trace Boudin had walked into Judith's house – *nothing* would ever be as good as new again. Nor the same again. And when she'd seen Carlotta mixing her martini for Trace, she felt Carlotta would never be safe again. . . .

2.

At five a.m. a dark Packard pulled up to the curb and Carlotta alighted. She ran up the stairs, turned around and blew a kiss. She didn't have to use her key

131

because Francesca flung the door open before Carlotta even fumbled in her bag.

'Oh, Frankie darling!' She threw her arms around her sister. 'Merry Christmas!'

'Don't Merry Christmas me. How *could* you? How could you do this to Bill?'

'Please, Frankie, don't scold me. Don't spoil this wonderful evening for me. . . .'

Francesca wanted to shake her. 'For you? There are other people in this world beside you. You're a selfish, spoiled brat, that's what you are. How could you do this to Bill?'

'Bill! Bill! Bill! That's all you ever think about. I can't do this because Bill wouldn't like it. I can't do *that* because it would be bad for Bill's public image. What about *me*? Don't you care about me? What *I* want? You're forever taking his side against mine . . . always defending him, always telling me how wonderful he is, how lucky I am to have him, how good-looking he is. . . .'

'Well, he is! He's the best looking man I've ever seen but that's the least of it. He's an honourable man and—'

Carlotta stared at her. 'Why, Frankie, you're in love with him! You are! And I've been a selfish, spoiled brat not to have realized it before!'

Francesca's face flamed and she started to protest but Carlotta wouldn't listen. 'Oh, Frankie, why didn't you ever say anything? Good God, do you think I'd have ever started up with him if I had known? All you had to do was say something and I would never have— You know that, darling Frankie, don't you? That if only you'd said something, I would have— Frankie! Why are you looking at me like that?'

Francesca just shook her head. What was Carlotta going to say? That if she'd known that Frankie Collings, sister of the irresistible Carlotta Collings, was in love with the man to whom Carlotta was engaged, she, Carlotta, would have handed him over like a piece of bitten-into apple pie? How could she explain to Carlotta that it wasn't done that way. You just didn't hand a man over to a sister like a discarded dress, like second-hand goods. It was something you couldn't explain if the other person didn't understand it in the first place.

And Francesca was flooded with shame for all three of them – for Carlotta who didn't understand something so basic, for Bill who so desired a woman who was incapable of understanding real love and for herself who, knowing that indigestion might well follow, would gladly eat of that piece of leftover pie, even in its nibbled-at stage. . . .

Carlotta yawned, ran her fingers through her hair. 'I guess we can talk about this tomorrow, can't we? I really have to go to bed this minute. It's been a monumental evening. . . .' She started up the stairs.

'Carlotta!' Francesca called after her. 'What do you mean – a monumental evening?'

'Oh, Frankie, you *know* what I mean!'

'Carlotta, you didn't—?'

Carlotta just ran up the stairs, not answering. And Francesca did know what she meant even as she didn't want to know. Carlotta, who had got her thrills and satisfaction from men wanting her, had finally met that one man to whom she had finally surrendered her body. *Trace Boudin!* Just his name was enough to send a chill through Francesca, and she was frightened for Carlotta.

The first thing Francesca did when she woke in the morning was to run to the window the way she and Carlotta had when they were children and it had snowed through the night. It had been so exciting when the drifts were several feet high. And then if the storm had passed and the sun was even threatening to come out, they'd bundled up in galoshes and scarves and mittens even before they'd eaten their breakfast and ran out to build a snowman.

A picture flashed through her mind: Carlotta in a one-piece green snowsuit, the buckles of her galoshes flapping, her knitted hat covering almost all her hair but for several bright red tendrils escaping that matched her red, red cheeks, laughing in delight as she pranced and danced in the fresh, dazzling whiteness, her spirit as pure as the driven snow. . . .

Oh, Carlotta!

Why didn't they do that this morning? Not wait to eat breakfast. Just bundle up and run out and build a snowman? What a wonderful surprise it would be for Bill when he got there. He'd told her that when he was a kid, there'd been no front yard, only the narrow, bleak street, and before a kid could get out there, the snow had already been dirtied, sullied, and that had spoiled it for him. He had never even wanted to build a snowman. Rather, he and his friends had filled a wagonful of snowballs, packed wet and hard . . . more ice than snow . . . and went out looking for victims.

Yes, they'd build a snowman for Bill. Two pieces of coal for eyes, a carrot for his nose, a piece of red pepper for his mouth. He'd be adorable.

She ran to wake Carlotta. Carlotta wouldn't care that she had had only four hours of sleep. Carlotta was always game for anything, that was one of the wonderful things about her.

But when Francesca flung open Carlotta's door she saw that Carlotta was gone. Gone at nine in the morning on Christmas Day. Where had she gone? And why? *Oh, God, why?*

It was a room in a rather run-down-at-the-heels hotel named ironically enough, The Sunnyside. Carlotta, in a tight sweater and an equally tight skirt, was awaiting her instructions as Trace Boudin called down to the desk for extra ashtrays and glasses. He already had several bottles of liquor. He knew better than to try and get whisky on Christmas Day in Boston.

He hung up and told her, 'All you have to do is walk around a lot, keep pouring the drinks without waiting to be asked.'

How could he miss with a looker like Carlotta?

'It wouldn't hurt if when you're filling the glasses, you brush up against them. . . . You know, baby. You know how to do that, don't you?' He winked at her.

'Is that all I get to do?' Carlotta asked petulantly. 'I thought I was going to stand behind them, look at their cards and give you signals and things like that. . . .'

Trace laughed. He couldn't believe that a girl who looked like Carlotta was that naive. 'You're hardly ready for that, baby. You don't even know how to play Poker.'

She tossed her head. 'But I do know suits – spades, hearts. . . .' She smiled, showing dimples. 'I know War, Old Maid, Hearts. . . .'

His eyes became slits. 'I just bet you know how to play hearts. . . .' He pulled her to him, ground his lips into hers. She could feel his teeth. When she came up for air, she traced the sliver of that thin white scar that snaked across his cheek with her fingertip, and a delicious shiver of excitement coursed through her.

Trace pulled her to him again and then pushed her down on the bed.

'Do we have time?' she whispered. 'Before your friends come?'

He checked his watch. His lip curled. 'A half-hour. If that isn't enough time, we'll let them pound on the door.'

Bill arrived at eleven o'clock, right on time. Francesca was still in her robe, too nervous to even think about getting dressed. She'd been trying to think up some plausible explanation for Carlotta's absence. Not that Bill would believe her. He wouldn't even believe that Carlotta had come home last night at all.

'You're not dressed,' Bill said.

'I never thought you'd get here on time what with the snow so heavy.'

'I left a half-hour early and I skidded all the way over. You'd be surprised how much time skidding can save.' He looked around. 'Is Carlotta up?'

'Oh yes. Bright and early. You were right, you know. Carlotta *was* home when I got in last night, fast asleep.'

'Is that so?'

'Oh yes. She left me a note not to wake her. It seems she had a headache and as Mr Boudin offered her a ride home she took it since she didn't want to make . . . us . . . leave the party early.'

He nodded, too polite to call her a liar, she guessed. While she was sure Bill didn't believe her she would still have to get to Carlotta first and brief her on the story.

'Well, where is she?'

'Carlotta?'

'Of course, Carlotta. You said she was up. . . .'

'Oh yes. She said she was going to skip church. It seems she promised to help out at a Christmas party the Junior League was giving over at St Elizabeth's in the children's ward.'

'Really? That's funny? She never mentioned that to me.'

'Oh, you know Carlotta. Everything slips her mind.'

'That's true,' he said evenly. 'But what about Christmas dinner? I was going to take you both out, remember? And then we were going to that party at the Veterans' Hospital and on to the McWilliams Orphanage to give out presents—'

'Of course I remember,' Francesca said testily. 'And now if you'll excuse me, I'll go get dressed for church. Probably by the time we come back Carlotta will be here waiting for us.'

When they came out of church, Bill suggested that they go on to midday dinner and phone Carlotta from the restaurant. 'I guess she'll be able to get to the restaurant under her power. She seems to be getting around fine, snow and all.'

Francesca sat down again after phoning her house. 'Not home yet. I guess she couldn't get away.'

'I guess.' He hoisted his glass. 'Well, here's to you, Frankie. Merry Christmas. Drink up. We'll just have to finish off this bottle of wine by ourselves.'

It was nine o'clock by the time they were finished with the orphanage and the Veterans, and arrived to an empty house. 'I guess I'll be taking off,' Bill said, not taking off his overcoat. 'I'm leaving for New York at six in the morning.'

'I wish you didn't have to go,' Francesca said, then burst into tears. It had been a day of incredible tension. 'And you're going to be away for several days. . . .' She was frightened.

He smiled tiredly, his eyes not crinkling as they usually did when he smiled. This time his smile didn't even reach his eyes. 'Does it matter . . . really matter, how long I'll be gone?'

'Of course it matters,' she said through sobs. 'Carlotta will feel terrible that she missed you. And we haven't even opened our presents.' She gestured at the pile of presents under the tree, Bill's presents for the sisters having been added to theirs.

'Well, why don't you and I open ours right now?'

'Oh no! We have to wait for Carlotta.'

'All right. Whatever you say. We'll open them on New Year's Day. Assuming Carlotta's back by then. . . .'

'Don't say that!' Francesca forgot all her pretences. 'Oh, Bill, fight for her!'

'I don't know that I really want to.'

'But you love her! You love her so much!'

'Yes, and that's why it's so hard. It's hard to love somebody who doesn't love you back.'

Oh tell me about it, Bill Sheridan! It was the hardest thing in the world. 'She loves you . . .' Francesca cried as he walked out the door.

Again, Carlotta didn't come home until the early hours of morning and again Francesca was waiting up for her. 'Bill's gone, you know,' she blurted out when Carlotta walked in. 'He had to go to New York on business for Judith and he won't be back until New Year's Eve.'

'Oh darn!' Carlotta pouted deliberately, her insincerity obvious. 'He didn't even tell me he was going.'

'He didn't have much chance to tell you anything, did he? Judith only told him about it at the party.'

Carlotta shook her head. 'Isn't that just like Judith? To send him out of town without notice.'

'Let's not talk about Judith. Let's talk about *you.*'

'Can't we do this tomorrow? I'm dead on my feet.'

'We didn't even get to open the presents. . . .'

'Why didn't you? You and Bill should have.'

'We were waiting for you.'

'That was silly.'

'Obviously it was since you don't give a damn. OK, where were you? I won't even ask with whom you were but I would like to know what you were doing that was so important to keep you away all of Christmas Day.' She was trying to keep her voice down.

But Carlotta's voice rose. 'You know, Frankie, there's something you seem to have forgotten. I'm only a year younger than you and you're my sister, not my mother. And you're not my keeper either! And now I'm going to bed!' She pushed her tangle of hair back with two hands . . . two *ringless* hands.

'Your engagement ring!' Francesca cried. 'You've taken off your engagement ring! Where is it?'

'Oh . . . in my purse. I hit my finger and it swelled up—' She turned to the stairs.

But Francesca could always tell when her sister was lying. She snatched Carlotta's bag from the hall table, opened it, turned it upside down, its contents falling on the floor. There were her keys, her compact, her comb, her lipstick, a handkerchief, a crushed package of Lucky Strikes, a cigarette lighter, some loose change and a crumpled dollar bill. No ring.

'Where is it?'

Carlotta laughed nervously. 'Now, you're not going to believe this but it's the truth. We . . . Trace and I . . . went to this lovely party and some people started a card game. Poker. . . . And just for fun I sat down. I mean, I thought it was just for fun. And since I didn't have any money, for a joke . . . I mean, I thought it was a joke, I said I'd put up my engagement ring for collateral.'

She talked faster and faster, until her words were falling out of her mouth over each other. 'I never dreamed they were taking me seriously. I never dreamed they'd really keep my ring. . . .'

Francesca's hand whipped out and cracked Carlotta across the face. Carlotta's hand flew up to her cheek, her mouth dropped open, her eyes grew huge before she burst into tears. Francesca was just as shocked as Carlotta. Never in her life had she struck another person.

Carlotta turned and ran up the stairs. She'd never forgive Frankie! Never! Frankie cared more about Bill and his damned ring than she did about her own sister! And she felt bad enough about the damned ring! She felt terrible! Trace had sworn that he only needed it for about five minutes to call the hand . . . that he'd win the hand and then they'd have the ring back and ten thousand dollars besides.

At the top of the stairs Carlotta turned around, said piteously, 'Trace said he's going to get the ring back. Truly. He will, Frankie, he will!'

Then only did Francesca fully realize what happened. '*You* didn't lose Bill's ring, did you? *He* lost it. You gave *him* Bill's ring and he lost it? *He* lost Bill's ring, and you gave it to him!' Her voice kept rising until it was a scream.

Carlotta covered her ears and ran for her room. *Bill's ring! Bill's ring! Bill's ring!* That was all Frankie cared about. That it was Bill's ring. Maybe if she told Frankie how her precious Bill had earned the money to pay for that ring, she wouldn't be worrying about him so damned much!

But she knew she couldn't do that. She couldn't do that to Frankie. Frankie loved Bill as she herself never had, never would. She loved only Trace Boudin! She'd love him forever!

Francesca never went up to bed that night. She sat in the chair by the window, the streetlight falling on the now filthy snow.

Carlotta had not only surrendered her body to Trace Boudin . . . she had surrendered her very soul.

3.

Bill couldn't figure it out at first. Judith had instructed him to investigate the Green Haven Winery's corporate structure but there was no corporate structure, only a mess of papers that took him a whole day just to go through and assemble, to find that five per cent of the company belonged to Cousin Howard, seven per cent to Cousin Joshua, twelve per cent to Uncle Peter, only it seemed Uncle Peter had sold five per cent to Aunt Gertrude who then, it appeared, owned twenty-two per cent. Uncle Harry had owned ten per cent but had passed on, and it wasn't clear who had inherited his share. A mess, and why Judith, who was as sharp as a tack, would want to get involved in all this crap was a mystery. Negotiating for this company with twenty or so family members voting their percentages would take a year.

And then after two days, Julian Winthrop, the accountant who had accompanied him, complained: 'I can't figure it out. The books are a jumble, I don't think anyone's really kept them for years. I just found bills which have gone unpaid for five years. And that cousin Hattie Winker who's supposed to be the bookkeeper can't or won't give me any answers. As for assets, a winery should have an inventory – you know, wine that's aging in the barrel, or bottled, ready for shipment. Well, frankly, Bill, I don't think there *is* any . . . I don't think any *exists!*' He seemed awed by this possibility. 'I think we should just go and take a look for ourselves!'

'What – into the barrels. No, I don't think so. What I think we should do is pack and go home. Julian, my pal, what I think is, we've been *had*.'

'You mean they tried to put one over on Mrs Stanton? But I don't get it. How did they think they were going to get away with that?'

'It's a puzzle all right.' But of course it wasn't. The only puzzle was *why* Judith had wasted his time.

He went straight from the train station to Judith's. He had no sooner sounded the brass knocker than the door opened. It was Judith herself standing there and next to her was Trace Boudin, obviously ready to leave since he was wearing his overcoat, a wraparound belted cashmere with a slouch fedora to match. His black eyes glistened with amusement, his teeth gleamed, as he tipped his hat to Bill. 'Attorney Sheridan. . . .' He bowed slightly.

Bill thought of giving him one to the jaw – his arm ached with the impulse. But of course it wouldn't have helped and his argument wasn't really with Boudin. He was only an instrument and it was people who killed people. . . .

'What are you doing here, Bill?' Judith asked, but not at all surprised to see him. 'I thought you'd be burning the midnight oil at Green Haven. But come in. Mr Boudin was just leaving.'

Before they even reached the library, Bill asked: 'What kind of business exactly are you doing with Boudin?'

'Oh not very much. He's getting me a little of this, a little of that . . . whatever's in short supply. He's nothing more than a small-time chiseller,' she said with contempt. 'Anyone who'd get mixed up with the likes of him on a serious basis is a damn fool and *I'm* not a fool. But I have to say he's *very* attractive in a purely physical way. He must be *very* good in bed. But I wouldn't be so foolish as to fuck him,' she said, choosing her words deliberately.

'Oh? Why not? You've been known to fuck every now and then.'

She laughed. 'But even when one fucks, one should pick and choose. If one's smart, that is. His kind always tries to get his hooks into a woman . . . use her, sell her, whatever. And *I*, unlike some others, don't like being used. I'm a user myself . . .' she smiled tauntingly. 'And I know enough to use people like Boudin, just as his employer uses him.'

'Who's his employer?'

'Have you ever heard of Ross Scott?'

'No, I don't think so.'

'Really, Bill, you're so provincial. If you want to be somebody on a national scale, you'll have to broaden your scope. You should know what's going on all over the country in every field of endeavour. Ross Scott is the California arm of you know what.'

He was stung. 'If I'm so provincial maybe you'd better spell it out for me. The arm of what?' By now he knew but he had the need for her to say it.

'Let's just say Ross Scott is connected. I believe that's the expression. Ross Scott even does business with the Nazis!' She raised her eyebrows. 'Can you imagine?'

The Nazis? Judith was right – he *was* a provincial and compared to her, an innocent. He had a lot to learn. He had come to Judith to ask her why she'd sent him on a fool's errand but the moment he saw Boudin, he had known. She had never had any interest in the winery. She had simply wanted to get him out of town for two, three days, while Boudin got his hooks into Carlotta.

And she was making no bones about it! So confident that she had everyone where she wanted them, she was laying all her cards on the table. She was using Boudin who was also being used by Scott, and Boudin in turn was using Carlotta, just as Judith had used him, Bill Sheridan, who had been the biggest patsy of them all. He had let Judith get her hooks into him . . . made him her slave. As for Carlotta, Judith, the master schemer of all times, had gauged her weak spot, her Achilles heel, just as she recognized his – his ambition. And she exploited weak spots.

Judith knew that Carlotta liked living on the edge, and that the smell of danger was an aphrodisiac beyond reason. And Trace Boudin reeked of danger.

Bill looked at Judith's belly burgeoning with his seed. He had betrayed himself and in a sense, it was he who had betrayed Carlotta. Perhaps, most of all, he had betrayed the child Judith was carrying – his child. And for the first time the child within her became real to him.

He couldn't even denounce Judith. He had boxed himself into a corner. He

138

had boxed *all* of them into a corner. It was probably too late for him to save Carlotta whom he loved, and he certainly couldn't save the unborn baby from the woman who would be its mother, but maybe he could still save himself and then later . . . sometime when he was stronger . . . he could try to rescue all of them. . . . He had to try. 'Go fuck yourself!' he said and spat at her feet, his spittle showing on the dark Persian carpet.

Once outside in the dark cold night, he turned up the collar of his coat and headed into the wind.

He found Francesca sitting on the brick steps in front of the house, huddling into her jacket, a navy peaked cap on her head.

'What are you doing out here? It's nearly midnight and it's colder than a witch's—' He let the last word go. She didn't answer him and he gingerly sat down next to her. 'Jesus! These steps feel like solid ice.' He saw that as a matter of fact there were still patches of ice here and there, glistening like crystal in the dark. 'So what *are* you doing out here?'

'I couldn't stay inside. *He* came over just a while ago.'

'I see.' He did indeed see. After seeing that he was back in town, Boudin had hustled over from Judith's.

He scooped up some hardened snow from the side of the stairs, packed a snowball and hurled it. He aimed at the street lamp, but he missed. He didn't even clear the lawn.

'What are you doing back in town? I thought you were going to be away for several days.'

'Wild goose chase.'

'I don't understand.'

He gathered some more snow, rounded it into a ball and threw again. This time he hit the pole and a resounding smack echoed in the still of the night. 'Judith sent me on a wild goose chase just to get me out of town.'

A look of horrified comprehension crossed Francesca's face. 'You mean this was all deliberate, planned? Boudin—?'

'Yep.'

But how could Judith have known Carlotta would fall for Boudin like a ton of bricks?'

'She *knew*. You might say she had Carlotta's number.'

'Oh my God! She's so clever. So diabolically clever. But why? Why would she want to do that?'

He couldn't tell her that in some way he himself was at least partly responsible. 'You always said she hated you and Carlotta, especially Carlotta. . . .'

'Yes. She's always hated us, and especially Carlotta. She wants to destroy her, doesn't she? But not you. She's helping you. She just opened that headquarters for you . . . staffed it. Why?'

'I guess she wants me in her pocket.' Then he stood up, reached into his pocket and came up with the gold key to his new headquarters that had been his Christmas present from Judith and tossed it. It didn't make a sound as it fell, just disappeared into the snow.

'Carlotta's engagement ring—' Francesca spoke falteringly. 'It's out there too. We were shovelling a path on the sidewalk . . . and she lost it. . . .'

'Uh-huh. Well, who knows? Maybe she'll find it again when the snow melts.'

'Do you really think so?'

Bill shrugged. 'There's always a possibility. And now, how about us going into the house? I could use a cup of hot chocolate. I'm freezing my ba—' He stopped. He didn't talk that way in front of Francesca. She was a lady.

He held out a hand. She took it and he pulled her up from the stairs. She stumbled and he caught her, steadied her against him.

'Oh Bill. . . .' She buried her face in his chest.

He wrapped his arms around her, trying to comfort her. 'My father told me something when he was on his deathbed. He said, "Remember, laddie, the fight's not over until the last battle's fought. . . ."'

'And—?'

'And then he died.'

'Oh . . . Oh!' She wasn't sure what Bill was trying to say.

They went inside. There was no music playing. It was *very* quiet. They looked into the softly lit living room. A small fire burned in the hearth but Carlotta and Trace weren't there. They looked in the dining room to the right of the centre hall. It was empty too.

'Maybe they're in the back,' Francesca said. 'In the sun room.' But then they heard the voices floating down the stairs . . . Carlotta's high-pitched, bell-like laugh . . . his deeper one.

Francesca and Bill snapped around to look up the stairway. On the first step was one of Carlotta's penny loafers. Her other shoe was on the third step. Then, near the top of the stairs, lay Carlotta's discarded hunter green sweater. And then they couldn't see anything else for the top landing was shrouded in darkness.

Francesca turned to look at Bill. His mouth was a tight, straight line. She couldn't see into his eyes. She herself was sickened. More, she was ashamed for her sister, who was shameless. *In their very own house and knowing that she, Francesca, was bound to come in from the outside in a few minutes. . . .*

'What about my hot chocolate?' Bill asked evenly.

'I think you should leave,' she murmured.

'You're going to send me out into the cold, cruel night without my hot chocolate? Shame on you! Come on,' he pulled her along into the kitchen, pushed her down in a chair. 'I'll make it,' he said, taking off his coat. 'Where do you keep the cocoa?'

'In the cupboard to your right.'

'OK. Why don't you take off your jacket and stay a while?'

'Bill, what are we going to do?'

He opened the refrigerator, took out a bottle of milk. 'There's an old saying: "When the going gets tough, the tough get going." What are we, a couple of sissies?'

'But what about your career? Judith was going to back you . . . you were going to run for lieutenant-governor next year. . . .'

'Hell! I was beginning to think that was a mistake anyway. I'd rather go for Congress. . . .'

'Will you be able to, without Judith's support?'

140

They had to keep talking, to go on making conversation, Francesca thought feverishly. They couldn't stop to think about what was going on upstairs.

'You bet I'll be able to. You forget I made up my mind to be President of the United States long before I even knew there was a Judith. From the time I was a little boy. . . .'

He sounds all right, Francesca thought. But then when he poured the chocolate she saw the furrows in his brow. Oh, he was in terrible pain. . . .

'Do you want a cookie?'

'What do you take me for? Of course I want a cookie.'

She got up to get the tin of cookies and through the window she saw that the snow was beginning to fall again. 'Oh look,' she wailed. 'It's snowing again and the old snow hasn't even melted yet.'

'Well, the old snow was dirty. In the morning it will all be covered up by a nice, brand-new white blanket.'

She looked at him. It was he who had told her that nothing was ever brand-new ever again, especially people.

4.

Carlotta wanted all four of them – she and the only three people in the whole world she really loved – to be friends. She proposed that the two couples – she and Trace, Bill and Francesca – see the New Year in together. There was a party at the Ritz . . . a benefit . . . and there'd be dancing, champagne and noisemakers. She and Trace had already bought four tickets. 'Please, Frankie!'

What could she say? Francesca wondered. That she no longer would be friends with her sister? That she had crossed her off for good? She asked Bill if he would be willing to go along.

'Why not?' Maybe it would be better if they at least kept an eye on the guy.

What else was there to do? Still, he did some checking on his own. It was always possible, he knew, that Judith was misrepresenting the facts. But the phone calls he made confirmed that Ross Scott, gentleman hood, was Boudin's employer, and that Boudin was really no more than a small-time hoodlum who supplemented his earnings by gambling and preying on women who didn't see past his racy good looks, his flashy smile, the nipped-in Savile Row suits.

Even the benefit was formal. Boudin wore his discharge pin in his dinner jacket lapel, which struck Bill as odd. Was Boudin, in spite of his fancy tailoring, just a clod who didn't know better, or did he have something to prove?

They sat clinking glasses around, Carlotta's hand on Boudin's thigh, when Bill gestured toward Boudin's pin. 'When did you get out?'

'September . . .'

'Infantry?'

'Yeah, sure.'

'Purple heart?'

'Yeah, I got a Purple Heart,' Boudin's eyes became cold steel. 'What is this – the Inquisition?'

Bill shrugged. 'Just asking as a fellow combat man.'

'Is that so? I could have sworn you were a 4-F . . .' Boudin grinned, smoothing his black moustache. Carlotta laughed and Boudin said, 'No offence, friend. Just kidding.' He lit up a cigar.

Bill smiled tightly. 'It's OK, I'm laughing too. Where did you get it?'

'In the chest . . . missed my heart by a half-inch they tell me.'

'Oh, poor little heart!' Carlotta cooed.

'No, I mean location . . . geography,' Bill persisted.

'Africa . . . Tunisia.'

'Pretty rough there, hmmm?'

'You bet. I got it in June . . .' he clutched his heart, warming up. 'June fifth to be precise. And they couldn't even get us out of the area for fifteen days. We just lay there in a field hospital set up a few yards from the fighting.'

'Now, *that's* funny,' Bill said grimly. 'They must be lying like hell to us over here. They told us all fighting ceased in North Africa in May. The bad guys surrendered on 12th May to be *precise!*'

Francesca held her breath but instead of being embarrassed or even angry at being caught, Trace only put out his cigar and laughed. And after a few seconds, Carlotta joined in. Then she stood up, her white chiffon skirts swirling. 'Let's dance. They're playing my favourite.'

'What's that?' Francesca asked. '"Smoke gets in my Eyes?"'

'Oh, Frankie,' Carlotta squealed. 'You're terrible when it comes to recognizing songs. It's "People Will Say We're in Love". . . .'

They moved out on to the dance floor; her hands locked behind his neck, her lower body pressed against him. She thought she had never been this happy in her entire life.

'What do you think, Bill?' Francesca asked, biting a nail. 'That he never was in the service at all? That he's the 4-F? He certainly looks healthy enough,' she shook her head. 'Look at that tan in the middle of winter!'

'I think it's much more likely that what he is, is a draft dodger.'

'Oh!' Francesca was shocked, then indignant. 'Don't you think we should tell Carlotta?'

He smiled at her sadly. 'Would it do any good? You heard her laugh when I just as good as called him a lying-son-of-a-bitch. She doesn't care what the hell the bastard is.'

'But what can we do?'

'Nothing. Just hope she gets that smoke out of her eyes, and we can't do that for her. She has to do it for herself.'

Then, watching, they saw Carlotta break out of Trace's embrace, and crack him across the face.

'Oh my God! They're having a fight! In public!'

Bill was pleased. 'It could be worse.' But then Trace slapped Carlotta back, much harder than she had slapped him, and much louder.

There was a communal, shocked silence on the dance floor as the other couples watched and the orchestra played, 'As Time Goes by'. Bill sprang from his chair. He'd kill that son-of-a-bitch! But Trace left the dance floor swiftly and disappeared into the lobby. Bill ran after him but Boudin was gone. So then he returned to the ballroom, attempted to help Francesca comfort Carlotta but Carlotta lashed out at both of them, frantic. They tried to hold her back but she tore from the room, wailing, 'Trace, Trace!. . . .'

Francesca started after her but Bill held her back. 'But she doesn't have her coat. . . .'

'I guess she'll manage. Sit!' he commanded. 'You and I are going to sit here and drink to the New Year, goddamn it!'

He picked up the magnum of champagne that sat in the silver cooler and filled both their glasses. 'Happy New Year, Frankie!'

But it wasn't yet 1 January, 1944. There was still a half-hour to go until midnight.

Carlotta never got dressed that day. Rather, she wandered from room to room in her housecoat and refused to go out to dinner with Francesca and Bill. 'Are you going to mope around for the rest of your life because you had a fight with that sleazy—?' Francesca demanded.

'I'm warning you, Frankie! Don't you *dare* say a word about Trace!'

'What are you going to do? Slap me the way he slapped you in front of all those people?'

'What do I care about them? Less than nothing. It's you, Frankie, who's so concerned with what other people think. *This* is what I give for what they think!' She snapped her fingers.

'I don't think that's the issue. The issue is, he hit you! Where's your pride?'

'I hit him first. It was just a reflex action on his part. I can understand that!'

'I don't know what's gotten into you, Carlotta. You know a man a week and you're completely crazy. It's as if you've fallen under his spell. Don't you realize what he is?'

'Yes, of course I do. He's a businessman who—'

'Oh, really! What business is he in?'

Carlotta elevated her nose. 'He has various interests – race horses, a night club, an import and export firm—'

'And where are these businesses located? And what does he import and export during a war? Bombers? Machine guns?'

'His business interests are in California if you must know. And that's why he isn't here today. He had to leave for Los Angeles this morning. That's what we fought about actually. I wanted to go with him and he said it wouldn't be opportune—'

'Opportune, is it? I'll say it wouldn't be opportune. I know all about those business interests in Los Angeles. These so-called interests are his involvement with a gangster . . . a racketeer! And these imports. They've got something to do with the Nazis! The Nazis, for God's sake! . . .'

'Oh, that's a lie! That's the biggest lie I ever heard! Who said that? Bill? Of course, Bill. He's jealous, that's what he is. Otherwise, why would he make up such a ridiculous story? Really, Frankie, how can you believe all this drivel? And jealous or not, I would have thought better of Bill. He should be ashamed of himself!'

'No, Carlotta, it's *you* who should be ashamed of *yourself!* To carry on about a man who's been hired to make love to you. . . .'

Carlotta stared at her unbelievingly. 'What are you saying? Are you out of your mind?'

'It's not I who's out of her mind. I know this is hard to believe, but Judith's done exactly that. . . .'

'Oh, this is insane! Why would Judith do such a thing?'

'Because she's jealous of you, I guess. And she doesn't want you to be happy with—'

'With Bill?' Carlotta laughed bitterly. 'And that's the story Bill told you? And you believed it?'

The nerve of him! Carlotta raged. *He should talk . . . after he sold himself to Judith! Oh, how she wished she could tell Frankie the real truth!*

'It's ridiculous, Frankie. And the reason I know how ridiculous it is, is because I *know* Trace loves me desperately!'

'And how do you know that?'

'Because he told me so, that's how!'

'Oh? And men haven't been known to lie to a girl, I suppose?'

Carlotta shook her head smugly. 'I know it's true.'

'How? How do you know for sure?'

'Because I feel it in every fibre of my body . . . in every nerve. My head tells me it's true and so does my heart. Every beat of my heart says, "Carlotta loves Trace! Trace loves Carlotta!"'

'Then your heart lies.'

'No, it doesn't!'

'Then your heart is mistaken.'

'Oh no. When I look into his eyes I see the truth, Frankie,' she said resolutely. 'I see love!'

But Francesca knew what it was Carlotta saw in those coal-black eyes that spoke to her . . . that aroused her to this passion. It was the message: *I am dangerous! Proceed at your own risk! I dare you to fall in love with me!*

And she had. Carlotta had never been one to refuse a dare. Rather, she had always found danger and risk-taking irresistible . . . fatally irresistible. And Francesca was in a state of despair. Her baby sister was only a beautiful moth drawn to Trace Boudin's perilously flickering flame!

But nothing was going to help. Not now, anyway. Maybe in time Carlotta would find this out for herself, and she herself could only hope that it would happen before Carlotta was too severely burned at Trace Boudin's flame to survive. . . .

'And you know what else, Frankie? Trace said that next time maybe he'll be able to take me along with him when he goes to L.A. He says he has a friend in the movie business and when this friend sees him, he'll want to make me a star! Isn't that wonderful?'

Maybe Bill was right, Francesca tried to console herself. Maybe things had to get worse before they got better.

Trace was gone for several days and didn't call once. By the sixth day Carlotta was in a rage. 'I'll fix him!'

Francesca saw her go to the telephone, then heard her giggling. But she didn't know to whom Carlotta was talking and she didn't want to ask. But then when Carlotta hung up and started up the stairs singing, 'That Old Black Magic', Francesca asked, 'Any reason for this pleasant change in mood?'

'Got a date. And you'll be so pleased to hear who I'm going out with. None other than Whit Truesdale, one of our most eligible bachelors.'

Francesca *was* pleased but puzzled too. Although she had dated Whit to get him to buy war bonds from her before she had become engaged to Bill, and he'd been crazy about her since she was fourteen, Whit had never been one of her favourite dates. If she was stepping out on Trace Boudin, as the expression went, why Whit? Carlotta had always said he was as dull as dishwater.

'And you know what else, Frankie? Little old Whit's going to get the surprise of his life.'

When Carlotta came downstairs dressed for her date she had never looked more seductive. She wore a clinging black jersey with a plunging neckline and her new black ankle-strapped sandals which had cost her a year's worth of ration stamps. And then when Whit called for her, he acted as if he'd been presented with a great big frosted birthday cake baked especially for him and he couldn't quite believe his luck.

Hours later when Carlotta came home, her hair in spectacular disarray, she told Francesca, 'Whit thinks he received the present of his life and he doesn't even know why.'

'You're talking in riddles. What happened?'

'Well, first we had dinner at the Goose and then I asked him if he had reserved a hotel room. . . .'

Francesca frowned. 'I don't understand.'

Carlotta's laugh tinkled. 'Neither did Whit at first. But eventually he figured it out. And then he practically fell over himself running to the phone to call the Copley.'

'Do you mean what I think you mean?'

'I do indeed.'

'But why? Why did you do it? And with Whit Truesdale, of all people.'

'Can you think of anybody better to drive Tracy crazy? Except maybe for— Well, he's out of the question.'

'Who's out of the question? Bill?'

'Well, yes. I wouldn't dream of going to bed with Bill.'

'Oh, really? And why not, now that you're going to bed with every other man in town?'

Carlotta laughed. 'Oh, Frankie, you *are* funny! Every other man in town? So far I've only gone to bed with Whit Truesdale.'

'And Trace Boudin.'

'Well, Trace is different. With Trace, I didn't go to bed. With Trace, I made love.' She made it sound as if it were something holy.

'So there *is* a difference?'

'Oh yes,' Carlotta said dreamily. 'And once you get your feet wet, you'll see what I mean.'

'I doubt very much that I'll ever *go to bed* with anybody according to your definition. I expect that I'll just make love . . . with one man.' And then she *had* to ask. 'And why wouldn't you go to bed with Bill?'

Carlotta smiled sweetly. 'I do have standards even if you don't think so. I don't go to bed with men who are taken.'

145

'Oh?' Francesca pretended not to know what Carlotta was talking about. 'Bill's taken? You've only been *not engaged* to him for about two weeks.'

'Oh, he's taken all right, even if neither one of us will admit it, you little devil you.'

Francesca didn't want to discuss it. It was too delicate a matter, too tenuous, and much too soon. And Bill hadn't even kissed her. Not a real kiss. No, he was still in mourning for his lost love, no matter how stoically he appeared to be taking Carlotta's defection.

'I still don't understand why you chose to go to bed with Whit.'

'But I told you. When Trace gets back and hears what I've done, he'll go clear out of his mind.'

'You're going to tell him?' Francesca was astounded.

'Of course. Silly Frankie. That's the whole point. . . .'

Oh, she told him all right. The doorbell rang at almost midnight and she was downstairs alone, Francesca having gone to bed. She had a new Frank Sinatra record and she was playing it over and over . . . dancing around the room. She ran to get the door and there he was and her heart stood still. At first he was all smooth charm, kissing her here and there, her neck, her shoulders, her lips. His hands were all over her, and she threw her head back and her hair hung down, reaching almost to her waist.

'Oh, I missed you, baby,' he said into her throat. 'Did you miss me?'

'A little,' she teased.

'Oh, just a little?' he laughed, not believing that.

And then, eyes gleaming, she told him, and before her eyes he turned from suave, debonair Trace into a raging, jealous monster, and the exquisite tremors shook her. . . .

Francesca, in bed but not asleep, had heard the doorbell and then Trace's voice. At first it was low . . . no more than a persuasive, melodic drawl. And then it was quiet. She imagined them kissing, he perhaps pushing Carlotta down on the couch. In spite of herself – she was ashamed of herself to eavesdrop – she got out of bed and went to the door and opened it to hear better. And then she was sorry that she had.

Trace's voice was very loud: 'You two-bit whore! You slut!'

And then she heard the sounds of violence. Slaps. Crashes. Something smashing . . . a plate, an ashtray, a vase? And then there was a louder but duller sound. Oh God, what was that sound?

Then there was silence and Francesca grew even more frightened. Had that bastard hurt Carlotta, *really* hurt her? Had that noise been Carlotta falling? She had to find out. She tiptoed down the hall to the landing. Still, there was silence, punctuated only by . . . what – heavy-breathing? Was Boudin standing over her beautiful sister's body with a knife in his hand? *What, dear God?*

She had to see. She crept down half the flight of stairs from where she could look into the living room. And then she saw why there was only silence except for the breathing. There were Trace and Carlotta, nude, their bodies entwined and moving in the rhythm of love on the rug in front of the fire, the room dark except for the firelight. But it was a strange kind of love, for now she *could* hear sounds – little cries of exultation from Carlotta, and a stream of obscenities from Trace Boudin – *whore, slut, bitch, cunt!*

Feeling faint, her senses reeling, Francesca turned to creep back up the stairs and then to run down the hallway, back to her bed where she pulled the covers over her head.

Carlotta never returned to school after the holidays. 'It's just not for me, Frankie. I never wanted to go to college in the first place. It's what you wanted for me.'

'And what *is* for you? Besides trash like Trace?'

'I'll pretend you never said that, Frankie, because I refuse to fight with you, or with Bill. You're my darling sister and Bill's my friend, and no matter what either one of you do or say, that's the way it's going to remain. But I'd like to say one thing more, if you'll let me. I'm very happy that you and Bill are what the gossip columns call "an item."'

Francesca was cold. 'We're not living in a gossip column and Bill and I are not an item.'

'Oh, yes you are!' And Carlotta ran over to Francesca and kissed her several times, then tickled her, and in spite of herself, Francesca started to laugh and protest: 'Stop that! You're impossible!'

Finally Carlotta did stop. 'Oh, Frankie, try and be happy for me because I'm so happy.'

But of course Francesca wasn't happy for her. How could she be? A pattern had been established, one that she found abhorrent. Every time Trace Boudin disappeared on Carlotta – which happened more and more frequently – Carlotta responded by going out with other men – soldiers, sailors, Marines, and Whit Truesdale, and she not only went to bed with all of them but told Trace all about it and in detail. This one touched her breast in a certain way, that one stuck his tongue in her navel, or licked her armpits, her toes, *there*. . . . And always Trace responded violently, driven by anger one moment, and to sexual excess the next.

And the reason Francesca knew all this was because Carlotta insisted on telling her all about it, although Francesca didn't want to hear, covered her ears, fled from the room. But no matter what, she never repeated any of it to Bill. But then again she didn't have to. . . . Somehow, Bill knew.

Francesca pleaded with Carlotta. 'Don't you see what this is doing to you? You're soiling yourself, cheapening yourself. . . . He's dragging you down to his level. More and more you're becoming like him. Soon there will be nothing left of you. Why can't you see it and walk away from him?'

'I can't! I *need* him!' Carlotta's eyes were big and she was more anguished than not.

'Need him? Why do you need him?'

Then she smiled a strange, crooked smile. 'Because we're two halves of the same being. Without him, I'd be incomplete. . . .'

'No! I don't accept that! I never will! It's just part of this terrible obsession of yours. And if you don't get rid of it . . . of him . . . it will destroy you.'

Then, Carlotta's mood swung again and she shook her head and laughed. 'Destroy me? Trace loves me and he's going to take me to Hollywood and I'm

147

going to be a star and we're going to live happily ever after just as if we were in a fairytale. . . . You'll see, Frankie, you'll see.'

An obsession . . . a horrible obsession. She's on a collision course and there's nothing to be done. Maybe there never was. . . .

But then she thought of Judith who had known that Carlotta would be drawn to Trace Boudin, and was now, most probably, obscenely gloating, and she thought if she herself was a different kind of person, she would surely kill her and then not feel sorry at all. . . .

5.

Bill sat alone in a back pew that Sunday in June since he hadn't been invited to Rudyard Tyler Stanton's christening, as Carlotta and Francesca hadn't been invited either, since all communication between them and Judith had ceased. Francesca would have accompanied him if he had told her he had planned on coming today, but she certainly would have thought it was strange, and who could have blamed her for that?

But he was sorry he had taken a seat so far in the back. He had come here to get a look at his son and he couldn't see anything but a small bundle in a long white lace robe. He had an urge to run up there and take a closer look!

Judith spotted him at once. *How dare he come here today?* What was he doing here? Trying to frighten her with his presence as a form of revenge? Or was it a subtle threat? A bid for blackmail money? The idea of paying blackmail was more disturbing than just the mere handing over of money. The idea of being in Bill Sheridan's power was intolerable. It was bad enough that she had never ceased thinking of him, of the incredible high, the excitement, the passion, the feel of him. . . . That too, was a form of bondage . . . of being in his power.

She seethed through the ceremony, angrier with herself than with him. She had executed a carefully planned scheme and then she had slipped up. She had made a mistake. She should never have brought Trace Boudin into it and set him on Carlotta. If she hadn't indulged herself in that nonsense, allowing herself to be jealous of Carlotta possessing Bill, then Bill wouldn't have thrown everything she was doing for him back at her. Then he would have been further along in his career and would therefore have had too much to lose personally to threaten her. And she had calculated in error. She had underestimated how much he cared for Carlotta. Or was it his integrity she had underestimated? Or had she over-estimated his ambition? Or had she allowed his attraction for her to muddy her thinking? It was a deadly attraction and she had allowed it to place her and her son and her plans for their future in jeopardy.

And what was more, she had placed herself in a dangerous position with Boudin. She hadn't followed her own rule; she had, after all, let that offal get his hooks into her. Simply by hiring him to go after Carlotta, she had inadvertently let him know too much about her affairs. One of these days he would put two and two together and then he would have her if she weren't careful. . . .

She took her son in her arms. Oh, how she loved him! Her beautiful, sweet prince! And she could allow no one to cast aspersion on him! She was going to keep him all to herself and would allow no one to threaten him or her in any way . . . taint their lives with gossip or scandal . . . hold either one of them in his power.

She would deal with anyone who even hinted at making waves. She'd do whatever was necessary.

Bill's fingers gripped the pew in front of him, his knuckles white from the pressure. He *had* to take a closer look at his son, gaze into his face and see if he saw anything of himself there. If only he could hold him in his arms just once! It would make up for everything he didn't have . . . had had and lost. Carlotta and this election year of '44. He could have been running this year, would have been running if he hadn't wasted valuable time counting on Judith's support, counting on her to do for him what he should have been doing for himself. Now he'd have to wait for '46. *In '46, my son will be two years old, and in effect, fatherless.*

He got up and left, not sure he would be able to control himself, not sure that he could keep himself from running up there and grabbing his son just so that he could hold him just once!

In September Dudley Stanton, after spending the summer with his wife and son in Newport, succumbed. Carlotta saw the death notice in the newspaper. 'Anyone for a funeral?' she quipped and Francesca gave her a reproachful look. Naturally, they wouldn't attend the funeral but still, death was no joking matter, and Dudley had seemed to be a nice man.

But Bill did attend the funeral in the hope that Judith would bring their child along to pay his last respects to his 'father.' He was disappointed, but Judith made it a point to speak to him, wanting to settle things with him . . . to get it over with. 'So good of you to come, Bill. Dudley always liked you.'

'He hardly knew me.'

'So then why did you come?'

'I thought that—' He would come right out with it. 'I thought that maybe you'd bring the baby with you. I wanted to see the baby.'

'You just wanted to see the baby?' She looked at him suspiciously. Was it that simple? Not blackmail? Not wanting to scare her with his presence in order to take revenge for the coupling of Trace and Carlotta?

'That's all Judith, I swear it. I just wanted to see my son. Surely you can understand that urge? A father's natural desire. . . .'

But what Judith saw was that Bill's paternal desire to see his son was even more dangerous than the motives she had attributed to his presence. When and where would this paternal craving end? Would it *ever* end, or would Bill just get greedier and greedier?

'Forget it! You had a job to do and you got paid for it. I was willing to do more but you chose not to accept my largesse, although you still have the job I got for you. So, our books are balanced. Now stay out of our lives. There's no place in them for you—'

There were other people pressing in, waiting to offer their condolences to the bereaved widow.

'We can't talk here. Come to my house next week. Tuesday. Three o'clock.'

He counted the days, the hours, the minutes. But when the time finally came and he was admitted into the library where Judith was waiting for him, the first thing she said was, 'Rudyard is not here so don't count on seeing him. . . .'

'But—'

'But nothing. Now listen to me. I'm still willing to help you if you forget this nonsense about Rudyard. James Curley from the 11th District is going to run for Mayor next year which means that his seat in the House will be up for grabs in '46. I'll help you get that seat. Will that satisfy you?'

'You still don't get it. I don't *want* your help after what you did – setting that scumbag on Carlotta. . . .'

So, it isn't only Rud! It's still Carlotta! She sneered. 'Do you really think I could have done that if Carlotta wasn't hot for scumbags in the first place?'

For that he wanted to hit her! How he yearned to! But what would it accomplish? 'I don't want anything from you except to see my son! Is that so much to ask? Just once?'

'There isn't any such thing as once with greedy people and we've already established that you're greedy. And he's not *your* son. He's my son and the son of the late Dudley Stanton. And nothing's going to change that. Where's your proof? Only *I* know for sure. And don't think you're going to lurk around in the shadows waiting for a glimpse of the boy. I won't hesitate to have you arrested as a pervert or possible kidnapper. Try that on for size as a vote-getter.'

Oh, she's tough, he thought. Tough and heartless. But he knew that before. 'I'm not afraid of you.'

'But you *should be*! Boudin tells me Carlotta is after him to marry her . . . to take her to California. And if you think things are bad now, you haven't seen bad compared to what marriage with Boudin would mean. And all it would take would be a high sign from me. . . .'

She could see him wince at that.

'The best thing you can do for everyone concerned – you with your political future to think of . . . Carlotta . . . Rud – is stay clear of my son. If you persist in your efforts, all you're going to do is raise speculation. Suppose Boudin catches on to our little secret? Then neither you nor the son for whom you profess these strong paternal feelings would be able to draw another really free breath again!'

He left without another word. As he was getting into his car, he saw a nanny wheeling a carriage down the street. His son? He didn't wait to find out. . . .

From a window, Judith watched him drive away. Which of the three reasons she had given him to stay away had been the most persuasive – his own future, Carlotta's, his son's? . . . Did Bill Sheridan himself know?

She herself wasn't sure that if Bill Sheridan had said the right words . . . persuasive words . . . there couldn't have been a future for the three of them together . . . she, Bill and their son. . . .

Witch . . . bitch . . . whatever or whoever she was, Bill had to hand it to her. She was *something* all right. He didn't have a doubt that if he had her in his corner, he would have walked up in that '46 contest for the House seat from the 11th District and would have undoubtedly ended up in the White House. . . .

And she was probably right about everything. . . . He could only hurt his son if he hung around, persisted. . . . And Carlotta. . . . He didn't doubt for a moment that Judith could call the tune for her. But with whom did the ultimate decision for *her* future really rest? With himself? With Boudin? Or only with Carlotta herself? As for Boudin being a threat to his son's future, Judith had posed that threat, but she hadn't seemed overly concerned. There could only be one answer. One way or another, Judith had Boudin in her pocket and not only on her payroll.

Yes, she was something! . . . And she had given him something to think about. Why shouldn't he run for the 11th District seat – Boston, Charlestown, Somerville and Cambridge? They knew him, they'd applauded him, they liked him. He'd intensify his efforts in those areas, gather a staff of volunteers around him who'd work without pay. And in his corner he would have the best, the most selfless, tireless worker he knew – Frankie!

And who knew? Maybe by that time he might even get Carlotta back in his corner. Maybe by that time the spell Boudin had cast over her would be broken. But whatever happened with Carlotta . . . even if she was gone for good, he'd still make it to the White House. He could still have that. Without Carlotta, without any hope of ever having a relationship with his son, he could still have that and Frankie. He knew that he could always count on her.

'Please, Frankie, please! Let's have a family Christmas Day dinner at home like we used to . . . Just the four of us. . . .'

'It's out of the question. I won't sit down at the table with Trace Boudin and neither will Bill. Why should we pretend that we're all friends when we despise him? As for calling it a family dinner, that's some more of your ridiculous fantasizing. If you ever do marry him – that is, if you manage to talk him into it,' she said contemptuously, 'you can count me out as family.'

Carlotta burst into tears. 'That has to be the meanest thing you ever said to me! That if I marry the man I love, you're not going to be my sister any more. How can you say that to me? No matter what you ever did . . . even if you cut off my arm . . . I wouldn't say such a thing to you!'

In the end, Francesca couldn't withstand Carlotta's tears, her wan face and dispirited moping and she gave in. They'd have Christmas dinner for the four of them if Bill agreed. And then Bill did although it made him physically ill to see Boudin and Carlotta together, but Frankie's argument, that if they were all together occasionally they could better keep tabs on the situation, convinced him.

Francesca and Carlotta had cooked for days and every possible dish that could be considered traditional for Christmas would be on their holiday table. They hadn't been able to decide on having turkey, a ham, or a goose, so Carlotta had come up with all three. 'But where did you get the ration stamps for all this?' Francesca asked, amazed.

'Oh, I didn't have to use any stamps. Trace picked it all up without taking one stamp from me. Isn't he wonderful?'

151

'You sound like a simpleton. Wonderful to be dealing in the black market? Wonderful is hardly the word. Try slimy, or crooked, or unpatriotic—'

Carlotta began to cry again. 'It's not really unpatriotic. Everyone says the war will be over soon. . . .'

'But it's not over yet!' Oh, what was the use? she thought. And if she said that neither she nor Bill would eat any of the tainted food, Carlotta would only cry some more and she couldn't bear any more of Carlotta's tears. That's all Carlotta did lately. She was a bundle of nerves – her beautiful, formerly insouciant sister who could shake anything off.

When Bill arrived, he was jumpy. He told Frankie, 'Don't get mad if I don't eat much. Between our black market specialities and watching that slimeball mauling your sister right in front of us, I'm more likely to throw up than eat.'

'You promised you'd make an effort to be pleasant,' Francesca reminded him.

And then when Trace Boudin arrived in his vicuna coat and his slouch-brimmed fedora tilted rakishly over one eye, he too seemed edgy. But when he shook hands with Bill, he was in cool command, grinning, eyebrow cocked à la Gable. Insolent, Francesca decided. *Challenging*. And she was sorry she had ever agreed to this dinner. She should have had her head examined.

No sooner did Carlotta take his coat than Trace, in a silver gray slightly too-tight silk mohair suit, looking more Hollywood than Boston, went to the phone. Then, over pre-dinner cocktails and goose liver pâté, he went to the phone again. They had only got through the fruit compote when the phone rang and the call was for Trace. He came back to say, 'Gotta go, business calls.'

'Business on Christmas Day?' Francesca queried.

Boudin flashed his teeth. 'Business is business.'

'What kind of business?' Bill asked politely enough.

'A couple of truckloads of cigarettes just moved into town. Luckies, Chesterfields, Pall Malls. All the brands that are in short supply. Only paper and tobacco but worth a small fortune.'

Carlotta ran from the table and in a couple of minutes she reappeared in her silver fox jacket, her Christmas present from Trace. 'I'm going with you.'

'Natch. I was counting on you to help with the distribution.'

'Carlotta! Our Christmas dinner!' Francesca protested.

'You and Bill have your dinner and then we'll all have leftovers tomorrow.'

'What's your brand, Sheridan?' Boudin asked. 'Camels? I'll bring you back a carton or two. A Christmas present.'

'Thanks but no thanks. I don't mind smoking my Wings. I'm glad to let the guys at the front have the Camels.'

'Those suckers? Let *them* smoke the Wings.'

With that, Bill slapped Boudin across the cheek. Not a hard slap, hardly more than a rap, but it was telling. Boudin's hand slipped into the inside of his jacket, almost as if he were going for – what? But he changed his mind. Instead, he winked. 'Every man to his own poison, I always say.'

After they left, Bill put his arms around Francesca to try and comfort her. 'What do you say we throw all this crap in the garbage and go out and get some decent food?'

'OK. Let's go out to eat but why don't we pack this stuff up and leave it somewhere where they're feeding the needy today? We'll just keep it our secret that it's Trace Boudin's crap. . . .'

Bill laughed. That was one of the things he loved about Francesca. All her secrets were such innocent ones. . . .

6.

Francesca and Bill were going to the New Year's Eve party the Teamsters were throwing at the Sly Dog over in Somerville. Francesca didn't know what Carlotta's plans were since she and Carlotta had hardly spoken since Christmas. But watching Carlotta pace all day in her housecoat, making herself one martini after the other, alternating between singing along with her Sinatra records and crying, she perceived that something upsetting had occurred between Carlotta and Trace – either they had had another of their frequent battles or Trace had once again left town on one of his mysterious trips, leaving Carlotta to spend New Year's Eve alone.

When Bill came by to pick her up, Francesca urged that they take Carlotta along. 'She's been in the house all day crying. I don't think we should leave her alone.'

'Sure,' Bill agreed without inflection and then it took Carlotta only about twenty minutes to dress as if she were loaded for bear. Her red hair had been thrown into an upsweep with curls escaping here and there and her dress was black satin which clung to every curve.

Carlotta danced with practically every man there, then left the private room where the party was taking place and went into the main room of the club where the public was drinking in the New Year. When she didn't come back after a while, Francesca went to look for her. She found her at the bar, focusing her attention on a dangerous-looking character with a shaven head and slitted eyes.

'Come on Carlotta, it will be 1945 soon and Bill and I want to welcome in the New Year with you. We're going to make a special toast. We're drinking to the war being over really soon.'

Francesca tried to get her off the barstool without making a fuss but Carlotta resisted. Instead, she draped herself over the character with the shaved skull. 'I'm drinking with friends,' she slurred, kissing the man full on the lips. 'Blade's a friend of Trace's, aren't you, Blade dear, and any friend of Trace's is a friend of mine. . . .'

Francesca went to get Bill. Maybe he could get Carlotta to come back to their party, away from this awful-looking man. But by the time Francesca came back with Bill, Carlotta, her silver fox jacket thrown over her shoulders, was going out the door with Blade.

'Oh, Bill, she's leaving with him! And did you see him? Did you see what he looks like? She said he was a friend of Trace's!'

'Yes, I saw him,' Bill said grimly. 'He has a reputation in this neighbourhood— The word is he's a killer for hire.'

'What?'

'He's a hit man. He kills for a price.'

'Oh my God! What shall we do?'

153

'There's only one thing to do. You get a cab and go home. I'm going after her.'

Francesca went home and waited. She put on the radio to make the waiting more bearable. She didn't know for whose safety she was more concerned – Bill's or Carlotta's, the sister she wanted to protect, or the man whom she loved more than she could put into words. When the clock struck twelve, and the radio announcer asked that everyone join in in a prayer for peace in 1945, Francesca prayed that both Carlotta and Bill would return safe, unharmed.

Later, when Bill brought Carlotta home, dishevelled but apparently none the worse for wear, Francesca put her to bed, grateful that her prayers had been answered. Then she went back downstairs to Bill. 'You must have had a terrible time . . . you were gone so long.'

'No, it wasn't so bad. I followed them to a rooming house but I managed to get her away from him before . . . well, before anything really happened.'

'But how did you do that? You said he was a—Did he have a gun?'

Bill laughed shortly. 'No, only a knife. I guess that's why he's called Blade.'

'Oh, my God, he could have killed you—'

'Neh. He turned out to be nothing but mush. But I am beat. I'll say goodnight.'

'OK, but are you sure that that was all there was to it? It was that easy? He didn't put up a fight?'

'Oh, a little bit of a fight. There was a *little* skirmish. That's what took us so long actually. We got a little messy and I didn't want to upset you unnecessarily so I took Carlotta back to my place to clean up. . . .'

She knew it! There was more to it than Bill was telling her. But she wouldn't press him. As he himself said, he was beat. She'd get all the details from Carlotta in the morning. She kissed him goodnight and he left. Then she saw that he had dropped his handkerchief. She picked it up to see that it was *stained. Bloodied!* It was Bill's blood which he had shed saving Carlotta from that monster Blade . . . blood shed saving Carlotta from herself!

Then she began to get angry, very angry. Bill's blood had been shed, he could have been killed, all for Carlotta . . . because she couldn't keep away from trash. And for the first time she really, seriously questioned whether Carlotta was worth it . . . risking one's life and happiness.

In the morning Francesca grilled Carlotta for details but while she was sheepish and ashamed – as well she should be, Francesca thought – she was remarkably short on answers. 'I'm sorry, Frankie, but I just don't remember much about what happened,' she giggled. 'I guess I had one too many. . . .'

'One too many? I'd say you had several too many. Do you realize you could have been killed? That Bill could have been killed? I saw the blood on Bill's handkerchief. How bad was his wound?'

'I really don't remember. I think it was only a scratch on the shoulder. But Bill didn't want you to know. He said you'd only be upset. I do remember promising him I wouldn't tell you so don't say anything to him. It *was* only a scratch. . . .'

'I thought you didn't remember.'

'Well, I remember *that*. But please don't say anything to Bill. I did promise. And don't be mad at me. I can't stand when you're mad at me. I promise you it won't ever happen again. That is my resolution for the New Year. I'm never going to bed with another man just to make that rat, Trace, jealous.'

'But I thought you didn't go to bed with Blade. . . . I thought Bill said that—'

'I didn't. What I meant is I'm never going to start up with trash again just to make Trace jealous.'

'Does that mean you're through with him? You're through with Trace?'

Carlotta laughed. 'Will you stop jumping to conclusions? I love Trace. My resolution means just what I said – that I'm through going to bed with anyone but him. From now on, I'm going to be as pure as the driven—I'm going to be as pure as you, Frankie darling. Now give me a big kiss for the New Year and tell me you love me . . .'

Francesca never could stay mad at her baby sister for long. She kissed her. 'I'll tell you one thing, Carlotta, I bet I love you a lot more than Trace Boudin does.'

When Trace phoned Carlotta several days later to meet him at the Drexell, a downtown hotel with an unsavoury reputation, she was off and running, forgetting that she was going to play mad at him for deserting her on New Year's Eve without a word. Francesca was furious but it didn't help. Carlotta was hopeless.

She came home several hours later, intending to sneak up the stairs without being seen but Francesca was coming down the stairs at the same time and screamed 'Oh, my God!' when she saw her sister's face. It was a mass of bruises, her lip was split, and one eye was almost closed, swollen and purple. Her beautiful sister!

'That monster! I'm going to have him arrested!'

'It wasn't Trace's fault,' Carlotta said defensively through her bruised lip, trying to push past Francesca who blocked her path.

'Oh my God! I don't believe this! You're defending him!'

'It *wasn't* his fault, I tell you. It was mine!' Her mouth was so damaged, so puffy, that her words came out slurred.

'Tell me, then. What did you do to warrant this beating?'

'I told him . . . I told him that I went to bed with Blade. Now, will you let me pass? I want to take a bath and go to bed.'

'But you *didn't* go to bed with Blade. That's what Bill said. And that's what you told me.'

'So I made it up. I said that I did. I lied. I made up details. Even the size of his—'

'Stop! Spare me! So you told Trace that you went to bed with Blade. Then what?'

'Then he went out of his mind and he did this—'

'And then what? Did you tell him you were through with him forever?'

'Oh, Frankie, you simply refuse to understand,' Carlotta said wearily. 'Afterwards we made love like we always do. . . .'

155

'How do you go on living with yourself?' Francesca asked almost dispassionately. 'Don't you disgust yourself? You disgust *me*.'

Carlotta burst into tears. 'Oh, Frankie, you *really* don't understand. I can't help myself. . . .'

Francesca stood aside to let her pass. 'Then no one else can either. One more thing. When Bill comes over I want you to stay out of sight. I don't want him to see you until your face goes back to normal. If it ever does. If Bill were to see you like this, he'd go after Trace and then he might get hurt, really hurt this time. And frankly, Carlotta, you're just not worth it.'

'Oh, Frankie, how can you be so hard?'

'Hard? It's you who don't understand, Carlotta. You're breaking my heart!'

Carlotta shook her head. 'But you're not crying. Why aren't you crying for me?'

'Oh, you want me to cry, do you? Well, I'm not going to cry for you ever again. I'm not going to cry for *anybody* ever again, except maybe for myself.'

But she did. She cried when Franklin Roosevelt died on 12th April. She cried for him and for the nation. And then on the 13th she cried for Eleanor Roosevelt who had lost a giant of a man, a great hero. On the 14th, she cried again for Eleanor when she learned that Franklin had died in the arms of another woman.

On 7th May she cried tears of joy when Germany surrendered and it appeared that the war in the Pacific would soon be over too. She cried too in early June. These times her tears were for herself and her tears were ones of joy when in cap and gown, she graduated, and Bill and Carlotta were in the audience cheering her on. Most of her fellow graduates would be seeking jobs but not she. She already had her job cut out for her, helping Bill get that seat in the House in '46.

She cried again in August . . . the 6th, when they dropped the terrible bomb on Hiroshima. This time she was thinking of the children and the terrible destructive force that had been set loose upon the world for all time to come. Bill tried to comfort her. He told her to think of the good that would come out of it . . . how it would shorten the war and save thousands and thousands of lives, and how maybe the threat of such a bomb might keep the world safe from war in the future.

Later that month, when the Japanese surrendered, she cried in relief. The war was finally over, the world was at peace and they could all get on with their lives. Bill would launch his campaign for Congress, and hopefully Trace Boudin would disappear into the woodwork along with the other slime now that the black market would be no more. . . .

And then in September Francesca cried for Bill when he told her he'd have to abandon his campaign in the 11th District. 'Joe Kennedy's boy Jack is back in town and word has it that he's going to make a run for that seat.'

'You mean you're going to give up before you even start?'

'I'm not giving up. I'm just giving up on the 11th. I'll have to pick another district.'

'But it's not fair. You've done so much work there already. You're so well liked in the district.'

'They'll love Jack. He's loaded with charm.'

'But you're a war hero.'

He smiled sadly at her. 'So is Jack.'

'But most of the district is made up of the working class and it's what you come from – they can identify with you and you with them. And John Kennedy has only had the best money can buy. He probably never worked a day in his life outside of the service.'

'Any good politician knows how to overcome that problem and Jack is one of the brightest.'

'All I can see is that you're both fairly equal, except that *you're* better looking.'

'Oh, I don't know,' he smiled at her affectionately. 'People love his hair, I've heard.'

'Oh you! I'll match your pretty yellow hair against his unruly mop any old day. I say, "Give him a fight!"'

Bill stopped smiling. 'No. I can't afford a fight in which I'm so outmatched from the start.'

'But how are you outmatched? We just established that—'

'I'm outmatched by his father's money. Outdistanced by his father's influence. And John is both a Kennedy and a Fitzgerald. I won't stand a chance. I'm not giving up. I'm just beating a strategic retreat to another district. . . .'

She understood. Still, she cried bitterly.

But Francesca never shed a tear when, a week before Christmas, Carlotta told her she was pregnant.

'Are you sure?'

'Yes. You have to help me, Frankie.' Her voice was unimpassioned, dull.

'Of course I'll help you,' Francesca reassured her. But she knew it was already too late. Now there was no longer any way Carlotta could be saved from Boudin. 'Let me think— I guess we'll have to have a wedding right away. How far along are you?'

'I don't know . . . eight . . . nine weeks. . . .'

'Then we have no time to lose. We'll say premature babies run in our family. I guess we'll have to have the wedding next week— Just get Trace over here and we'll start making the arrangements. I think just to make everything seem normal we should have a formal wedding with a small reception. Maybe twenty . . . thirty guests. . . .'

She couldn't really believe she was doing this – *marrying Carlotta off to Trace Boudin with a formal wedding.* . . .

'I'll talk to Dr Hewitt right away about his officiating. Of course I won't tell him you're pregnant. I'll just say that the groom has to go away on business and you want to go with him so that's why we're having a quick wedding. . . .'

'There's not going to be any wedding,' Carlotta said in a listless voice.

'But there has to be a wedding, Carlotta . . .' she said gently. 'If you're pregnant. . . .'

'I need an abortion, Frankie, and you have to help me. You have to help me get rid of the baby!'

Francesca couldn't believe her ears. 'But that's a sin, Carlotta! A sin against God! Besides, you could die! No, I can't let you.'

She was thinking that Carlotta had finally come to her senses, had realized how awful Trace Boudin was, and didn't, after all, want to marry him. Poor Carlotta. But she had to marry him now.

'Listen to me, Carlotta. You'll marry him and then after the baby's born, you'll get a divorce,' she was talking fast in her urgency. 'I promise you it will be all right. And then after the divorce, you'll remarry. Everybody . . . anybody . . . will still want you. Just you remember that you're the beautiful Carlotta Collings who no man can resist!' She laughed shrilly in a kind of hysterical desperation.

She was sure she spoke the truth . . . that Carlotta would be able to live Trace down and come out of this mess practically unscathed. But first they had to get her married, get the baby born, divorced and then they'd see. . . . 'I want you to know, Carlotta, that no matter what, I'll stand by you. I'll help you get through this— I'll help you take care of the baby.'

Carlotta didn't respond and Francesca wondered if she was in shock. 'Carlotta—' She touched her on the shoulder as Carlotta just sat there, staring into the fire.

'You don't understand, Frankie. I have to have an abortion. Trace is gone!'

It couldn't be true but it was. She'd assumed that Carlotta was so devastated because she was pregnant and *had* to marry Trace when she didn't really want to any longer. But the simple truth was only that Trace Boudin had flown the coop. . . .

'Where is he?'

'I don't know. California, I guess. All he said when I told him that I was pregnant was that I was a slut, a whore and that I wasn't going to stick him with some other man's bastard. Oh, Frankie,' she wailed, suddenly come to life. 'I'm never going to see him again.'

'Tell me the truth, Carlotta. *Is* the baby his? There's no chance that—? You haven't slept with anyone else in the past two . . . three months?'

'Don't you believe me either?' Carlotta demanded angrily. 'My own sister?'

'Please, Carlotta. I'm not saying I don't believe you. I'm just trying to find out if Boudin has any reason to doubt you. . . .'

'I told you no. I haven't gone to bed with anyone else in a year . . . ever since last New Year's Eve. . . .'

At first, it didn't register.

'Well, then, it doesn't really matter *what* Trace believes, does it? It's just as well, really. I must have been crazy to think that you should marry him anyway. Don't worry. We'll think what to do and we'll work it out. I'll help you. We'll—'

Then it hit her. 'Look at me, Carlotta.' But Carlotta, who was standing next to the fireplace, turned her face away, slumped to the floor where she half-sat, half-lay.

'Look at me, Carlotta!'

'No, I don't want to— You're frightening me and I'm half out of my mind already . . .'

'What was it you just said? You didn't go to bed with anyone else since last

New Year's Eve? But you *didn't* then either. Bill and you both said that Bill rescued you before anything happened. Isn't that so?'

But then they didn't come home for a long, long time. They went to Bill's apartment to clean up. . . .

'Why am I frightening you, Carlotta. Because I know the truth? Is it the truth that's so scary?'

'What truth? I don't know what you're talking about.'

'Don't you?'

Carlotta began to sob. 'Oh, Frankie . . . Oh Frankie, we didn't mean for it to happen. . . .'

At first, Frankie's voice was quiet. 'Oh no, of course you didn't.' Then it began to rise. 'But it did, didn't it? Didn't it?'

'Oh, but we didn't want it to—'

Her voice was deceptively sweet. 'Of course not. You couldn't help yourself. Isn't that it?'

'Oh, Frankie, I knew you'd understand. That's what I told Bill. That Frankie would understand. He was so upset. . . . But you know, it just happened. It was just that he was so brave . . . he was my hero. He came after me to rescue me and he fought with Blade. He wasn't afraid of Blade. Blade was so scary and Bill wasn't afraid. And then when I threw my arms around him to thank him, then I saw the blood! It got all over me and then we had to go to his place to wash up. . . . You see, we didn't want you to know that Bill was hurt because we didn't want to upset you. . . .'

'Of course you didn't. So you didn't tell me *anything* . . . nothing that would upset me. But you told Trace. Like you've always done. So, naturally, he didn't believe you now when you told him that only he could be your baby's father.'

She paused in order to keep control of herself, to keep herself from screaming.

'That was a mistake, Carlotta. Always telling Trace about the men with whom you made love. Tell me, how did you describe Bill's lovemaking?'

Carlotta was bewildered by the turn in the conversation. 'I told him the truth. That making love with him was like a storm – all thunder and lightning. But that making love with Bill . . . well, it was like a soft summer rain.'

'Oh, Carlotta, you talk like a poet, do you know that? Still, it was a mistake, you know. You should never tell someone you love that you've made love with another. A bad mistake.'

'But I had to! I had to tell him all about it. Every touch, every cry of love!'

'Love? Well, perhaps. How would *I* know?' Her tone was light, as if what she said was inconsequential, but she felt as if her voice were separate from her body, as if her body were disconnected from her heart. 'But you made *two* mistakes, Carlotta. Telling Trace and telling me. Telling me that making love with Bill was like a soft, summer rain. . . .'

'Oh, Frankie, I didn't want to tell you— Really, it's as if it never happened.'

Francesca spoke ever so softly. 'But it did happen, Carlotta. It happened and nothing can change that.' She walked out of the room, into the hall, started for the stairs.

'Where are you going?' Carlotta cried out.

'Away from you. Just like Trace.'

'But you have to help me! You can't leave me alone!'

She crawled across the floor on her hands and knees to clutch Francesca's legs. 'You're blaming me but you shouldn't. . . .'

'Who shall I blame? Bill?'

Carlotta wanted to scream out, 'Yes, Bill. Blame Bill!' But she couldn't. 'No, not Bill. He didn't want to— It was me. I had to take my dress off to try and wash out the blood, and I . . . I was drunk and there was Bill . . . so strong and brave. I put my arms around him. I kissed him.' She was quiet now. 'Don't blame Bill, but forgive me!'

Francesca thought of Bill confronted with a nude Carlotta, grateful and kissing him . . . seducing him with the very love he'd carried around in his heart for so long. No, she couldn't blame Bill.

'I don't blame Bill,' Francesca said dispassionately. 'It was you, Carlotta, you. Bill always wanted you and he had never had you, not really. He *had* an excuse . . . the best – he loved you. But you? You have no excuse. You didn't love him, you don't love him, but you knew how much I loved him . . . how much I loved you. . . . It was only you, Carlotta, who betrayed me. You didn't love Bill and yet you still betrayed me. And for what?'

Carlotta was confused. 'For what? For love!'

Francesca laughed. 'What love? Love of Trace? Do you really call that animal rutting you shared love?' She pulled away from her sister and mounted the stairs.

'But you can't desert me, Frankie!' Carlotta called out piteously, 'What will I do?'

'Oh, you'll think of something. Your kind always does.'

'But what about Trace? How will I get him back?'

'Oh, I wouldn't worry. They say that true love always finds a way, and Trace is that, isn't he? Your true love?'

Carlotta married Whit Truesdale the day before Christmas. They eloped, since Whit's aunt and uncle, who had raised him, didn't approve of Carlotta. And then when Bill heard the news, he knew that it was ended, finally, for good. He proposed to Francesca, or rather he said, 'Marry me!' as if it were an order, and she said she would.

And so they were married, only a few days after Carlotta was, just before the New Year rang itself in, with each one of them hoarding a secret. Francesca didn't know that Bill had fathered Judith's son, and he didn't know that Francesca knew that he had made love to Carlotta . . . that Carlotta had been first with him once again.

It was Carlotta who knew it all, even why she had chosen Whit Truesdale over Bill when she had needed a father for her child. . . .

PART
THREE

After The Party

V
1962

The final 'one for the road' had definitely been drunk and each of the indefatigable hangers-on who lingered on to the last minute had been escorted to his car by the security people. The party was finally over when one of the governor's aides rushed into the room. 'What is it Mort?' Bill asked dryly. 'Another cross-burning on our front lawn?'

'No, sir, it's an advisory from the Coast Guard. They're expecting the hurricane to hit the Keys before dawn and the eye of the storm to be passing over us around noon.'

Wrong! Francesca thought. The hurricane had already hit and the eye of the storm would be a week in passing. . . . She turned to her guests. 'Nothing to be concerned about, really. All we have to do is batten down the shutters. There are two auxiliary generators and we always keep a large supply of candles on hand.'

'I must say, you and Bill certainly live an exciting life down here,' Judith drawled.

'Well, I think it's very exciting. I've never been in a hurricane before. All we get in California are earthquakes, and they're over in a couple of minutes.' Jade said.

Trace laughed. 'But then we do have the aftershocks.'

Jade thought about that for a second. 'Yes we do, don't we? And sometimes they go on for a long time afterwards, don't they, Father?' She looked him straight in the eye and finally it was he who looked away.

It was another hour or so before the household was bedded down – Jade and Abigail sharing the room next to D'Arcy's and Trace assigned the third bedroom in the wing off the North Hall, along with Judith and Rud.

Francesca had been waiting for this moment all night, eager to be alone with Bill, to ask him all those questions that were scurrying around in her mind like so many mice. *Why* had he danced with Judith so often? *What* had they talked about? What did he think of the changes in Judith's physical appearance and what about Jade? Did he think she resembled Carlotta in more ways than just the physical? Didn't he think her brazen? More like Trace in that way than Carlotta?

But then when she finally slipped into bed after brushing her teeth and cleaning her face, Bill was already asleep. Or was he only pretending, she wondered, not wanting to talk?

But Bill was half-asleep, half-dreaming, a state of being in which images, both conscious and semi-conscious, were conjured up. In this half-dream he was standing between his son, Rud, who was extending both hands to him, and Jade in her green party dress, she holding out her arms – slim, white, supplicating arms. But he wasn't sure whether the apparition was really

Jade . . . or Carlotta. But did it really matter? Weren't they really one and the same? And then Judith appeared from out of nowhere, her arms folded across her chest, as if she were just waiting and watching. . . .

D'Arcy had planned to sneak next door to Abigail's and Jade's room as soon as her mother, who had forbidden any more visiting tonight, was safely asleep. She was dying for some girl talk, wanting to find out how Jade felt about Rud, whether there was going to be competition there. But then, lying in bed waiting, she fell fast asleep.

Rud lay in bed, unable to sleep, and amused himself by making up rhymes. Abigail.

> She's very sweet and very nice
> But truth be told, she's bland as rice . . .

He thought that was pretty good and went on to D'Arcy:

> She's cute and blond and très, très hot
> But hard to get? Definitely, not!

And then there was Jade. But even as he tried to think of words to describe her that would end in a rhyme, he couldn't force his brain to perform. All he could do was visualize her, his body remembering how she felt in his arms when they'd danced, his senses recalling how she'd wet her lips from the bottle of vermouth, wiped the lips with her fingers, sucked on them, given him her pinkie to suck on, and his brain went crazy. What he had wanted to do at that moment was push her off the bar stool on to the floor, and then throw himself down on her, to pound away at her until they were both exhausted and senseless. . . .

At first he touched himself without being aware but then he was hot at it, and quick, furious with it. Then, within a minute, he buried his scream of ejaculation into his pillow and fell asleep almost immediately, spent.

Jade had assumed that once she and Abigail were alone, her sister would besiege her with questions about Carlotta. And she'd been prepared. The simple questions she'd answer directly, and the harder ones, she'd try to work out as they went along. Her number one priority was to impress Abigail with how Carlotta had talked about her constantly, always saying how she adored her. . . . Tell her how Carlotta was always figuring out how to fight the Truesdales for her but then fate had intervened in the shape of a red Rolls-Royce and a certain tree, a giant ancient redwood.

Carlotta was coming home from a party at the beach when she smashed into the redwood. The Rolls and the redwood apparently led charmed lives – both were relatively unhurt. Only Carlotta was severly damaged – her lovely white neck had snapped. It was as simple as that.

The papers made a big thing out of the tree being a redwood. Nobody, it seemed, had ever taken particular notice that redwoods grew in Southern California and not only in the northern part of the state.

The newspaper accounts also related how Carlotta Boudin, who had been as famed for her escapades as her beauty, once attended a masquerade ball at the Palm Grotto, the Sunset Strip Club owned by her husband, sportsman and entrepreneur, Trace Boudin, posed as Lady Godiva, and rode a great white horse through the club's elegant lobby.

The Grotto's demise predated Carlotta's by only a couple of years but the story was one people liked to recall and retell endlessly about the days when Hollywood was really Hollywood and Carlotta Boudin one of its most glittering stars.

Yes, she was ready with pretty much all the answers, and then as a climaxing gesture, she was going to unfasten the diamond and emerald necklace from her throat and hand it over to Abigail. *This is for you, Abby, from our mother. She always said she wanted you to have it. Diamonds and emeralds from Carlotta . . . to Abby with love. So much love, Abby!*

But no sooner had Jade turned to get her toothbrush from her vanity case, than Abigail, still in her too-pink party dress, was asleep, lying on top of the pale pink satin spread on one of the twin beds.

Poor Abby, Jade thought. She was probably exhausted from her trip, the party, and all the emotional turmoil. . . . She went to the other twin bed, pulled off its spread and covered her sister with it, tenderly tucking it about her.

Don't worry, Mother, I'll try and take care of her.

It was a repeat of the promise she'd made the day she found Carlotta's diaries a few months after her mother's death. That day she'd not only vowed to love her sister and watch out for her, but to avenge her mother's death, for beautiful glorious Carlotta Collings Truesdale Boudin was prematurely dead at thirty-five and someone had to be held accountable!

Once Jade had read that guns didn't kill people – people did. Well, red Rolls-Royces didn't kill people either, nor did giant ancient redwoods. People killed people, even beautiful glorious redheads, and after reading the diaries, Jade knew exactly who those people were – Frankie, Judith, Trace, and Ross Scott, and not necessarily in that order. But they all were going to be made to pay. . . .

Unable to sleep, Francesca got out of bed and went into the adjoining sitting room so as not to disturb Bill who finally slept peacefully after much fitful tossing and turning. She went to a window and unfastened the shutters. It had been raining but now it had stopped, and the wind was now only a soft breeze, but she had experienced many hurricanes since she'd been in Florida and she knew this was but a lull before the storm.

She thought she saw someone on the beach but it was too far away to tell for sure without binoculars. *Who'd be so foolhardy as to brave the angry forces of nature about to strike? Only a fool who didn't know enough to get in out of the rain. Carlotta. . . .*

There'd she'd been, married to Whit, finally as safe and sound and secure as a girl could get. Mrs Whitman Truesdale, society matron, mother and wife, living in the Truesdale brick townhouse. Now, any smart Boston girl knew that there was nothing as safe as a Boston brick house and only a total fool would leave such a haven to step out into the rain. . . .

But Trace Boudin had beckoned from California and Carlotta was gone, never looking over her shoulder, her back to the wind, headed straight into the storm. She'd been a damn little fool who had ended up dead. . . .

She had never forgiven Carlotta, but God knows, she had never wished her dead . . . never wished for her to be the poor broken sparrow who hadn't been strong enough to withstand the storm.

As a shaft of remembered pain pierced her heart, a bolt of lightning streaked across the sky and the rain fell again, so dense the sea was vanished from sight, and Francesca quickly closed the window and then the shutters.

No, she had never seen Carlotta again after that terrible night when she'd learned how Carlotta had betrayed her, and no, she had never forgiven her, but she had heard from Carlotta, and oh how she wished she hadn't. If she hadn't received all those letters from Carlotta – letters begging for forgiveness, pleading for advice and direction, pleading for news of the baby she'd left behind – letters she'd never answered, maybe she wouldn't have taken her sister's death so hard, wouldn't feel so damned guilty. . . .

And worst of all to bear, even now she couldn't find it in her heart to forgive Carlotta!

Trace Boudin didn't fall asleep for a long time either. He didn't feel nearly as insouciant as he made it his business to appear. His mind seethed and churned overtime. When Ross Scott had ordered him to accompany Jade to Sheridan's party in order to press the Outfit's offer on him, he hadn't thought about how he could reap some personal advantage out of it, but now he was here, he could see that the situation was fraught with all kinds of possibilities. Not that he hadn't always held the key, had it ever since Carlotta had told him that Sheridan was Judith's kid's real father. The problem was which was the right, safe keyhole in which to turn that key? Sometimes a guy could unlock a door only to have the ceiling fall on him or the floor open up and swallow him.

He had considered blackmailing Sheridan for a long time only the Boys had always had their own eye on him to use for their own advantage and he couldn't afford to screw up any of their plans. That wouldn't be healthy.

As for Judith, he had always thought of how he could separate her from some of her millions, but he'd always been wary of her, especially since she'd become Scotty's business partner – a secret one – in Scotty's so-called 'legit' ventures – the Jade Hotel in Vegas, the movie studio. . . . When she'd become Scotty's partner she'd almost as good as bought him. She had certainly bought his silence.

But now the picture was changed. Judith was no longer Scotty's business associate. Once Carlotta hit the dust, Judith seemed to lose all interest in Ross Scott Enterprises. And now with that little bastard of hers all grown up and ready to fly, she probably wouldn't want anyone to find out that she'd been the notorious Ross Scott's silent partner. Any more than she'd want it known that Sheridan was her kid's father.

God knew, he needed the money now, more than he had ever needed it before. And besides the money, how sweet it would be to even the score with her for all the shit she'd made him swallow. Boy, would he enjoy nailing her ass to the wall! But the question was, was the bitch ripe for plucking or wasn't she? That's what he had to find out in the next few days. The problem with Judith Stanton was that just when you thought you had her in a corner, she always managed to pull a rabbit out of a hat which not only floored you but knocked you silly!

And he had other things to think about. Jade, for one. He didn't like the way she was looking at him ever since they arrived. What was that all about? He had to keep her in line, at least until she was twenty-one when she'd get the jewellery collection Carlotta had left her. Jesus! The collection had to be worth at least a couple of million. He was afraid to try and grab the few pieces she already had in her possession which she always carried around with her, as if guarding them with her life. Suppose she went squealing to Scotty that he'd taken them? Scotty had given Carlotta most of the jewellery himself, and he had a soft spot in his heart for Jade, probably the only soft spot he possessed, the son-of-a-bitch!

And there was his daughter, Abigail Truesdale, to think about. He had never really doubted for a moment that she was his daughter but who had needed her? She was only excess baggage, and even Carlotta had changed her mind about trying to get the kid away from the Truesdales once she got to California. And it was no wonder. Compared to Jade, she was a dog. Not one tiny bit like Carlotta. And say what you would about Carlotta, there was never anyone like her. Maybe not even Jade. Sometimes he still dreamed about Carlotta. Sometimes he even dreamed about her with Ross Scott. . . . He'd been right about that all right. He had known that once Scotty saw her, they'd be in like Flynn. . . .

But it was funny how he could look at Abigail and not feel a thing. He had thought that maybe there'd be something. A twinge of recognition . . . but, nothing! And as far as he could see, he had nothing to gain by telling her he was her flesh-and-blood. Carlotta had told him that Whit Truesdale hadn't had a nickel of his own, so when he'd kicked off, he hadn't left her a thing. Now, when those guardians went, it would be a different story since they were convinced that she was Whit's kid. Then she'd be in for a bundle. . . .

Judith usually fell asleep within seconds of laying her head to the pillow since she was a firm believer in self-discipline. One resolved one's problems during the daylight hours when the mind was sharp and the thought processes unmuddled. But tonight, despite the self-discipline and the lateness of the hour, she wasn't able to will herself into the arms of Morpheus.

Rather she thrashed about, disturbed and feeling vaguely threatened, not completely sure by what or by whom. But she did know it wasn't Trace Boudin in the room next to hers who disturbed her tranquility. One false move, one false word and he would have had it. One word to Ross Scott about Boudin's extracurricular activities at the Jade . . . about how he had been skimming off the top at the casino for years, and he was as good as dead!

Was it Jade, then, who threatened her feeling of well-being? Was that even reasonable? Jade was only a child. But Jade had hinted that she was going to get at her, Judith, by sinking her hooks into Rud, and she *was* alluring, even if she was but a child. Still, hadn't she dealt with this particular problem before . . . with all the predatory females who wanted to get their hooks into her son? Well, she'd deal with it again. . . .

One thing she knew was that in order to maintain her control over Rud, she

169

had to keep him bound close. She had to pick and choose his companions, especially the females, and she had to keep on doing that even though it became increasingly more difficult as time went by. It had been easier when he'd been a child. There'd been no boarding schools. He'd been tutored at home until he was fourteen and then he had attended a day school so that he could still live at home. Then she had allowed him a tiny bit more freedom so that he wouldn't chafe at the leash. And now that he was eighteen – that age when a young man was at the height of his sexual power and desire but still emotionally immature – keeping control demanded the finest touch, the most exacting balancing act: letting the reins out a little, then pulling back; cracking down, then bestowing a special favour; alternating between magnanimity and strict discipline; mixing small doses of freedom with larger doses of domination.

Even so, maintaining control in the past summer had been extremely difficult, especially when it came to women, for in addition to being at that dangerous sexual age, Rud had achieved a possibly new standard of male beauty. He had surpassed even her expectations. And in addition to his manly beauty, there was that easy charm, that grace, that slightly rakish air that drew the girls to him like moths to a flame and as if that weren't enough, there was the Stanton fortune to attract the avaricious. But she certainly hadn't raised her son to be any woman's plaything. She had no intention of allowing the focus of his existence to centre on women.

But women weren't the only things that could trip up a rich, handsome Adonis with marvellous manners and engaging ways, one who was cultured and superbly educated. Dillettantism was another, as was the playboy syndrome which afflicted many rich men. The symptoms were a predeliction for excessive drinking and partying, an addiction to fast cars and hard drugs, an excessive lust for polo ponies and big yachts, and companions of a dissolute bent. And the prognosis for this playboy syndrome: a life of small achievement, lack of glory, even failure. . . . Not at all the future she envisioned for her son . . . what she had in mind even before she conceived him . . . when she had only dreamed of him and all the splendours that would be his . . . and hers.

And there was also the reality that she was jealous of his time and company, that she wanted it all, or a least most of it for herself. And one big problem was that as much as Rud was a target for every female under fifty in his radius, he seemed to like the women as much as they liked him.

Yes, control was all and as a young man got older and the enticements without became increasingly more alluring, and the discipline within harder to enforce, there was only one answer – the money! Especially so since Rud had had an expensive upbringing and had developed lavish tastes . . . especially since he was going to devote his life to public service, a notoriously low-paying way of life, and since, unfortunately for Rud, every cent left to him by his father's will was in trust for him . . . with his mother having the complete say. Any monies Rud would receive during her lifetime would only be his by her dispensation, which meant that he'd be dependent upon her until the day she died. . . .

Unless he married a woman with a fortune of her own. And eventually he *would* marry. The question was *who*. . . . As Judith saw it, the decision would

170

have to be hers. Any man who would be President needed the right kind of wife, and she herself knew better than Rud what qualities constituted the right kind. . . .

Jade? Hardly. Still, Jade, even though she was only fifteen, did have a *special* allure. After all, Rud was his father's son, and Jade, her mother's daughter. . . . But in the end she would chew Jade up and spit her out.

No, it wasn't the spectre of Jade who was destroying her peace of mind tonight. It was Bill Sheridan . . . still. . . . And it wasn't that she was afraid of him, afraid of what he was going to demand from her. Rather it was the memory of them together that made her blood surge too wildly to let her find rest.

She had sent him away, putting over a thousand miles of distance between them, yet the memory and the desire had lingered on. Bill Sheridan, big and blonde and virile, in her bed. . . . The two of them, breast to breast, belly to belly, his thick phallus plunged deeply into her. Oh, she'd wanted him, still wanted him, and one way or another, she'd have him again. She had bought him once . . . she could do it again, using a different kind of tender. Actually, she had already bought him twice . . . once his presence, and then his absence. . . .

It had been 1950 and Carlotta had been gone from Boston since '46. Only Bill had been left in Boston to threaten her and Rud's existence. Not that she had thought that Bill would ever knowingly reveal that Rud was his son. Even if he hadn't wanted to protect Rud, he would have wanted to protect his career – he *was* a Congressman, and he would want to protect Frankie and his daughter from scandal. But his very presence in Boston was a threat. Bill, with that telltale gleam in his eye whenever he accidentally bumped into Rud, the desire and the longing all too evident to the sharply observant. And how could she know for sure how Rud would grow up? Even at six he had resembled Bill in certain ways. Maybe, with each passing year, he'd resemble Bill more and more until the resemblance would be impossible to ignore. . . . She had to get Bill out of Rud's proximity. . . .

'Get out of town,' she told him. 'Out of Boston . . . out of Massachusetts. . . .'

'Are you out of your mind? I'm a United States Representative from this state. Why would I leave when this is what I've worked toward all these years? Just for your peace of mind?' he asked derisively. 'No way. . . .'

'You'll go,' she said complacently.

'Like hell I will!'

'For one million dollars?'

'What can I buy for a million dollars that will mean more to me than what I already have?'

'Two million dollars . . .' she said.

'Where would I go?'

She considered. 'How about Florida? There's a land boom going on there. The state's in a flurry of development. With two million dollars and your abilities, you could end up owning half the state. And then, with so large a financial base, why – the sky's the limit.' She laughed. 'Who knows? Maybe you'll end up the mayor of Miami Beach.'

171

He wanted to crack her face. She always did that to him, brought out the violence in him. He always ended up wanting to beat her into a bloody pulp.

'What will I tell Frankie?'

'Tell her that I'm blocking your way with my money and influence. That just for the hell of it, just because I hate the sight of both of you, I want you both out of Boston. That I'm prepared to make it impossible for you to continue here politically.'

'Three million,' he said.

She laughed heartily. 'I always said you were a whore, Bill Sheridan. Three million it is. . . .'

Although it was dark in the room, almost pitch black with the windows shuttered, it was well past dawn by now. She got out of bed, went to the windows and opened the shutters. It was like a madhouse out there – the winds raging at who knew what velocity, trees uprooted, great palm leaves flying by, large staves of wood, a shutter, pink tiles from the roof. . . .

Excited by the violence of the storm, Judith was more determined than ever to have Bill Sheridan again. There had been other men in her life since Bill, but none of them his equal.

They'd cut a deal before, and they'd cut a deal again. And Frankie and D'Arcy, Trace and Jade, had nothing to do with it. It was, after all, a matter only between her and Bill and their son Rud.

2.

When Abigail woke that morning it took her several seconds to realize where she was and it was dark in the room because the windows had been shuttered in anticipation of the hurricane. Abigail peered through the gloom to see Jade's bare shoulders outlined by the sheet covering her. And then she saw that she herself was still wearing her party dress. She'd fallen asleep without getting undressed, without even saying goodnight to Jade. Should she wake Jade, she wondered, eager to do exactly that. But then she decided to wait. In the meantime, she'd get undressed, take a shower, and then get redressed. Maybe by then, Jade would be awake and they'd be able to talk a while before going downstairs. That's why she'd been absolutely desperate to come to Florida, to have that private time with her sister. In fact, she'd been so desperate to come, she'd been ready to run away if it had come down to it. . . .

She'd been home alone when her invitation to the Sweet Sixteen had arrived and for a few seconds she'd been thrilled. Her Sheridan relatives hadn't forgotten that she existed after all! But then, a moment later, she was filled with despair. Her Aunt and Uncle would never let her go. They'd always forbidden any contact with the Sheridans or Jade, just as her father had done before them.

They'd made their position clear on that right after her father's funeral, which had come straight on the heels of Carlotta's death. Her father, it seemed, had been able to survive his wife's desertion but not her death. Seven days after Carlotta was laid in the warm Southern California earth, he'd gone up to the attic of his Uncle George's brick house in Louisburg Square and hanged himself.

They'd just returned to the house after the funeral when Aunt Selena intoned,

'Carlotta was evil in life and her evil lived on after her in death. She as good as reached out from the grave and put that noose around Whitman's neck herself.'

Abigail, thirteen, had shivered at her words. She wanted to cry out, 'No. it isn't like that at all! It's like in *Wuthering Heights* . . . Cathy and Heathcliff – her spirit calling out to his until they were reunited in death!' But she hadn't. To speak of Heathcliff and Cathy to Aunt Selena? Impossible. Besides, she really didn't believe that herself. She knew the truth – Carlotta had of her own free will abandoned them both – her husband and her infant daughter, and there was no way to twist that ugly fact into anything romantic.

And the other reason she didn't speak out was that she never disputed anything her grandaunt said. How could she? The truth was she'd always been a little bit afraid of her Aunt Selena and her forbidding manner. Maybe her mother had been too.

Sometimes, she played the game of *What if.* What if her mother and father hadn't gone to live with George and Selena after they eloped? What if her mother and father hadn't been dependent on Uncle George and Aunt Selena? Her mother must have detested living with them. How could she not? *What if?* Would the story have had a different ending?

A week after the funeral there'd been a cremation in the back garden. Cleaning out her nephew's room, Selena had discovered a cache of movie magazines and studio stills featuring the enticing Carlotta. There was also a pile of small items Carlotta had left when she'd fled – a paisley scarf, a rhinestone pin, a silk gardenia attached to a hair clip, a white silk blouse with a lipstick smear on the collar, a half empty bottle of Jungle Orchid, its scent long gone off. There was even a pair of lace-trimmed pink silk panties.

Abigail had watched all these remnants of her mother's past going up in smoke and had wanted to snatch something from the flames for herself, if nothing more than a copy of *Silver Screen*. But it had been impossible under Selena's watchful, vengeful eye.

No, it was highly unlikely she'd ever be permitted to go to Palm Peach for the party. Two years before, she had wanted to send Christmas cards to the Sheridans in Florida and to her sister in California, more as a reminder to them that she existed than anything else, but she'd been so foolish as to ask Selena for help in obtaining the proper addresses. While she knew Selena would never countenance letters, she had mistakenly assumed that she would find the sending of Christmas cards innocent enough. But then Selena had told her exactly what she thought of the Christmas cards idea and her words had been seared in Abigail's heart forever.

'I can see that you really don't understand the situation, Abigail,' Selena had said in her usual clipped tone. 'But you're old enough. It's high time you did. Your mother who abandoned you was nothing more than a harlot. I know this is a harsh term but the Bible uses the word, and like the Bible, I don't believe in mincing words. And her sister Francesca couldn't have been much better. They were both wild and common and their conduct after their parents died often bordered on the scandalous. We begged your father not to have anything to do with them . . . especially Carlotta, even before she took up with Trace Boudin.

173

But your poor father was obsessed with her. If he hadn't been, he'd still be alive today. Just keep that in mind. As for Francesca, whom did she marry but the same Irish opportunist your mother discarded? As for your sister Jade, she's not only the daughter of a harlot, but of a notorious gambler, a criminal. So I ask you, are these the people to whom you propose to send Christmas cards? I should think not. Rather, I should think that since you and Jade share the same bad blood on your mother's side, you'd do well to thank God every day that *you*, at least, have the Truesdale blood to countermand it. And you must strive each day to see that it prevails.'

It occurred to Abigail that as they had had the burning of her father's souvenirs of Carlotta in the backyard, maybe Selena would yet call for public bloodletting to exorcise her of her bad blood. At that point, Abigail was more than eager to forget about the Christmas cards and never mention the names of her sister or her Sheridan relatives again, or for that matter the names of her cousins, the Stantons, who only lived a short distance away.

While Selena didn't find Judith Stanton or her son quite as objectionable as Jade or the Sheridans, they didn't get a clean bill of health either. For in addition to her tainted bloodlines, Judith had made what the Truesdales considered a too-flamboyant marriage – Dudley Stanton having been too old and too rich, and Judith too young and too poor. And worst of all, Judith didn't mind spending the Stanton money too ostentatiously for their taste.

No, there was no power strong enough to make George and Selena let her go, and she sat down and cried. She knew she was too old to cry like a baby and should have been, by now, able to accept the way things were. But it was so hard not to be disappointed, so hard not to long for the impossible . . . like love. Certainly George and Selena didn't love her. She was a duty to them, not a person to be loved. And probably her father hadn't loved her either. Probably he'd been too crippled in spirit by Carlotta's betrayal to love the fruit of his disastrous union. Oh yes, she could understand them not loving her, but understanding was one thing, and happiness another, and how could anyone be happy without love? That's why she'd clung to the illusion that her mother must have loved her a little, that maybe Aunt Francesca would too, and maybe even Jade.

She might as well just rip the invitation up, Abigail thought. It was her one chance to see her aunt and her cousin D'Arcy, but it was no use! She picked up the invitation again and its envelope and then she saw that there was a train ticket inside too, and a handwritten note!

My dear Abigail,
While we've never met, I hope that the occasion of D'Arcy's sixteenth birthday party will rectify this unhappy situation. I do hope you can prevail upon your grandaunt and granduncle to allow you to come celebrate with us.
Accordingly, I've included a round trip train ticket and I wish to extend to you an invitation to visit with us for a few days following the party. I do hope you'll be able to join us, especially since we're

also extending an invitation to your sister, Jade, and your cousins Judith and Rudyard Stanton.

Jade was going to be there! Her sister Jade! How could she not go? she asked herself. She was so excited about the possibility of seeing her sister, she didn't stop to think that her aunt's note was curiously stilted and formal, considering that she was only sixteen and her aunt's own dead sister's daughter. Or maybe it was that she'd lived so long in a formal, stilted household, she saw nothing amiss in the tone of her aunt's note. But whatever, all Abigail could think of now that she knew Jade was going to be there too, she wasn't going to give up so easily.

Francesca had sent her a train ticket and no matter what George and Selena said, she'd go. Oh, she'd ask, she'd beg on her knees but failing all that, she'd just run away and go! What could they do to her? Lock her up? Send her to jail? She was tired of being a scared little mouse. Yes, if it came down to it, she'd sneak away and go! Finally she'd get to see her sister, and then, just maybe, she'd find out, once and for all, if the mother who had left her behind had ever loved her even just the tiniest bit. . . .

She made a list of promises, all the things she'd do if just once they'd make an exception and let her go visit the Sheridans. (She wouldn't even tell them that Jade was going to be there.)

She'd spend twice as much time on her homework.

She'd never again let her attention stray in church and she'd volunteer to assist at Sunday School every week instead of every other week.

She would never again complain about making Sunday calls with them, and she'd never again try *not to* sit next to old Mr Pearson when he joined them for tea. (He had a problem with catarrh and spat every few seconds into a tissue from the box he always carried with him, which he then deposited into a brown paper sack which he also carried with him.)

She'd give up watching television for six months, or if they preferred, she'd give up only her programmes, and would watch the shows of which they approved.

She would *not* go to the Joan Baez concert for which she already had her ticket. Instead, she'd sell the ticket to Jaynie Truman who was desperate to go and had been unable to get a ticket, and she'd donate the money to charity instead. . . .

Before she was done, her list was three pages long, and then she decided to wait until morning to present it, which would give her the whole night to gather up her courage. She went to bed clutching her invitation to her breast, praying: 'Oh, please, God, let things work out for me just this once.' There *was* that round trip train ticket. That should help since George and Selena wouldn't have to lay out any money. How did Aunt Francesca know that the cost of the ticket would have been reason enough for them not to allow her to go – that to them cleanliness wasn't next to godliness – thrift was?

Abigail went down to breakfast, her invitation in one hand, the train ticket and the list of promises in the other, and her heart in her stomach. Then, eager to get it over with, she showed them the invitation immediately, even before she gulped down her juice.

'When did this invitation arrive?' George asked.

'Yesterday. While you and Aunt Selena were out.'

They exchanged significant looks. Then Abigail showed them the train ticket.

'Why didn't you tell us about this invitation immediately?' Selena asked.

'Because I wanted to prepare this—' She held out the list of promises. 'I promise I'll never again ask to go anywhere if—'

They took turns reading her list and she was encouraged by the fact that they hadn't immediately refused permission. And she'd been careful to keep her voice modulated and not to plead. Pleading would have been deadly. Tears, even worse. Abigail knew that to George and Selena tears were an abomination, the worst breach of good taste, a sign of deficient character, and would have meant an automatic refusal.

Now, unbelievably George said, 'An impressive list . . .' and Selena said. 'Yes, you've made some good choices. What do you think, George?'

'Well, there is the train ticket.'

'Yes, and travel *is* broadening. And I suppose Francesca and that governor husband of hers can't do too much damage in a weekend since we have raised Abigail with standards. As for their daughter, she really can't be held responsible for her parents anymore than we can hold Abigail responsible for *her* mother.

'You're right,' George observed. 'Right as usual.'

Abigail couldn't believe her ears. While she'd been hoping and praying, she hadn't really believed that they'd let her go and now it looked as if they were! What she didn't know was that only the evening before, Selena had reminded her husband that the Labor Day weekend would be the last opportunity they'd have of getting away to the shore. And it would be heaven, for once, to be relieved of the responsibility . . . of dragging Abigail along, worrying about her table manners or with whom she was spending her time. The matter of companions was a special worry these days. And there was the matter of expenses. The long weekend would be four days. One less room for four days plus twelve meals added up to a not inconsequential sum.

Selena nodded to George and then he actually said: 'Very well, Abigail, you may go!'

'Oh, thank you, Uncle George! Thank you, Aunt Selena! You won't regret it, I promise!'

Selena held up a hand. 'I hope not. And we *will* expect you to live up to all your promises. As soon as you've finished eating you may go to your room and write your letter of acceptance. But I must say it wasn't very thoughtful of your aunt not to specify when you are to arrive or—'

But she did! She invited me to stay for a whole week!'

'I see no mention—'

'There was a note included—' She had flushed the note down the toilet so that they wouldn't know Jade was invited too.

'Oh, may I see this note?' Selena held out her hand.

'I can't find it. I must have thrown it away in the trash by accident. . . .' *Oh, God! Don't let her search the trash!*

'Hmmm. . . . That *was* careless of you, wasn't it?'

'Yes, Aunt Selena. I'll try and be more careful in the future.'

'Yes. . . . Well, you must bring your cousin a nice present. A book, or perhaps a box of linen handkerchiefs with an embroidered initial. You can buy it out of your allowance.'

'Yes, Aunt Selena,' she murmured.

Selena leaned back in her chair, pleased with the way she and George had handled the situation, although they would have to get the girl a new party dress, she supposed. One that would do service for a couple of years until she debuted. And she'd allow Abigail to buy herself a pair of shoes out of her allowance to go with the dress. Perhaps a pair with those little spool heels. . . .

3.

Jade came awake slowly, finally focusing her eyes on Abigail. 'Oh Abby, I had the most wonderful dream.'

Abigail sat down on the edge of the bed. This was what she'd come to Palm Beach for – to share these intimate moments with her sister. 'What was the dream about?'

'About Mother. It was such a nice dream. We were in her bedroom. It's the most beautiful room. I've kept it just the way it was when she was alive. All mirrors and satin and white carpeting and a vanity table with every kind of lotions and creams . . . cosmetics in every possible shade.'

Abigail nodded. She knew all about her mother's bedroom. She'd haunted the used-book stores looking for old movie magazines and had found one which featured an interview with Carlotta in which her bedroom was described down to the last detail, even to the forty-foot long mirrored wardrobe that occupied a whole wall.

The dazzling Carlotta prefers to stay close to the hearth of her beautiful villa which nestles against the lush hills of Bel-Air, to spend all her free time with attractive hubby, Trace Boudin, owner of the fabled Palm Grotto on the Sunset Strip. Always in attendance is Carlotta's darling little girl, Jade, who's a miniature copy of her stunning mother.

There were several candid shots accompanying the article. One of them was a picture of the portrait of Carlotta that hung above the bed – she in a white ball gown, the long hair falling about her shoulders, the tilted green eyes come-hither, the red mouth glistening. Portrait of a movie star who for a short, magical time reigned as queen of the ball.

'That painting? Does it still hang above the bed?'

'You know about the portrait?'

'I saw a picture of it in a magazine from the early fifties. I never forgot it. . . .'

Then Jade decided to fib a little, to change her dream to include Abby, 'Well, in my dream you and I were just sitting around . . . talking to Mother.'

Abigail leaned forward. 'I was in the dream too? What were we talking about?'

'Nothing special. You know, just about life and poetry.'

'Poetry! I love poetry! Which poem was it?'

177

'Oh, I don't remember. But we were eating vanilla ice cream and little white iced cakes and we were just talking and laughing. Everything was all in white. The three of us were dressed in white, flimsy summer dresses and white curtains were stirring in the breeze at the windows. . . .'

'Oh . . .' Abigail sighed. 'It sounds . . . wonderful. . . . Oh, I wish we were all there now . . . in your dream. Oh, I wish. . . .'

'I know, I know,' Jade drew her sister's head to her bosom, glad that she had told her little white lie to Abby, including her in the fantasy. 'I wish we were both there now, too. But you know what? Sometimes we can just sit, you and I, and talk about it . . . as if it were real. The three of us, just sitting around and talking and eating ice cream. That way Mother will still be real for both of us.'

Abigail nodded her head dreamily. Somehow, she had known that it would be like this between her sister and herself. As if they'd known each other always. And she wished she had something to share with Jade, something lovely and romantic, just as Jade had just shared her dream. It didn't matter what, as long as it was some kind of romantic confidence.

'I had a dream last night too,' Abigail lied.

'Yes? What did you dream about?' Jade asked eagerly.

'Why . . . Rud!' He was the first thing that came into her mind.

Jade was startled. 'Rud?' Abby hadn't seemed all that interested in him last night. She seemed to like him well enough, but not romantically . . . not in a sexual way. Not in the way she herself had been drawn to him. 'But what did you dream about? What were the two of you doing in the dream?'

Abigail didn't know what to say, wasn't prepared to give details. And Jade seemed so interested. She'd be disappointed to hear that they'd only been talking or laughing. 'We were kissing. A real movie kiss. Our mouths were open!'

'Open?' Jade was surprised and Abigail, encouraged, decided to be even more audacious. 'Yes. His tongue was practically in my throat. And then he told me he loved me!'

Jade's eyes widened. 'Really?' Abby had to have very strong feelings about Rud to dream all this. 'And what did you say?'

'What do you think I said? That I loved him too.' That was obviously the answer Jade wanted . . . a romantic one.

'And do you really?' Jade's eyes were fastened on Abigail's. If Abigail had a crush on Rud, it was clear to her what she had to do . . . not even flirt with him herself. She'd just have to forget that she had ever been drawn to him. And it didn't matter that she'd planned on flirting with him just to drive Judith crazy, if for no other reason. The important thing was that Abby, who had never known her mother's love, should have what she wanted. It was the least she could do for her sister. 'Do you think you're really in love with him?'

Abigail was sorry she'd ever started the whole thing. That was the trouble with a lie, no matter how innocent. You just kept getting in deeper and deeper. What could she say to Jade now after telling her that Rud had been kissing her in the sexiest way and that they had told each other they were in love? That she thought he was really nice? She'd sound so silly . . . and *dull*. No, she had to tell Jade what she was waiting to hear, what she'd think was exciting . . . their very own secret.

178

'Oh, yes, I really think I'm in love!'

Jade looked away so that Abigail wouldn't be able to see her sinking heart in her eyes. She'd have to help Abby get him! 'We'll have to get to work on this. If he's not in love with you already, he's going to be by the time he leaves! And then when you both go back to Boston, you'll have it made!'

'But D'Arcy—' Abigail protested. 'I think she's really knocked out by him and— And she's prettier than I am!'

Jade was indignant. 'You're every bit as pretty as she is! Prettier. . . .'

Besides, D'Arcy can't have him. She's his sister!

The problem with Abby was that she had no self-confidence. It probably had to do with her upbringing by those stuffy Truesdales. She'd just have to instil some confidence in her. She hopped out of bed and went to her suitcase, pulled out a pink cashmere sweater with a deep V-neckline. 'Take off that shirt and put on this sweater. *Without a bra . . .*'

'No bra?' Abigail was shocked.

'You heard me. You're going to give D'Arcy a run for the money.' Her sister Abby was going to give everyone a run for the money – D'Arcy, Judith, even she herself.

Abigail laughed, excited by the idea of suddenly becoming a *femme fatale*. 'Oh, Jade, I love you! I love you more than anybody in the whole world!'

'Well, you'd better! Because I love you more than anybody in the whole wide world!'

'Really? What about your father? He seems so wonderful!'

'Oh, sure. I love him too.' She could hardly tell Abby that while she had once adored Trace . . . before she'd discovered Carlotta's diaries . . . she now wished him dead. She couldn't very well do that without giving the whole story away and she wasn't ready to do that.

Jade was barely twelve, still she sensed that something was wrong just months before Carlotta died.

It was a winter twilight, and while the sun had been shining brightly but a half-hour before, suddenly it was nearly dark. Carlotta, wearing something long and white that seemed to float on the air, was loath to put on the lights. Instead, she lit a candle that flamed bravely in the dusk of the room. 'There, isn't that lovely?' she asked Jade. And recited softly,

> My candle burns at both ends;
> It will not last the night;
> But ah, my foes, and oh, my friends –
> It gives a lovely light!

Without really understanding the poem, Jade sensed that it really wasn't about a candle at all and that her mother didn't think so either. And then, frightened, not wanting to allow the candle to burn out prematurely, she ran to blow it out. But Carlotta only relit it. 'Candles are meant to burn brightly, Jade, and only for a brief time. It's the nature of things.'

179

And then Jade knew that her mother was but ' . . . a beautiful little fool' – a phrase from a novel she was reading. In many ways, the book's heroine reminded her of her mother. They were both exquisite flowers who couldn't always manage to hold up their heads, their stems being too fragile. . . . But then Carlotta died of a snapped neck . . . her stem severed, and Jade realized that they – Gatsby's beloved Daisy and Carlotta – weren't really alike at all. In the end, Daisy was relatively untouched by the lives of the people she herself broke in her careless fashion, and Carlotta? It was Carlotta who broke while the others survived.

But it wasn't until Jade discovered the diaries that she understood almost everything. Then she knew that once upon a time Carlotta had been, if not wise, then strong, her flame almost inextinguishable. But that was before certain people entered her life and certain events broke her heart and placed her inside the red Rolls to smash against the redwood . . . to snuff out her life . . . a candle burned at both ends. Accidents? Or a death wish, or only Carlotta's heartbroken answer to a puzzle for which she couldn't find an answer?

There'd been an investigation in to what really happened on the last day of Carlotta's life . . . a coroner's report. It mentioned considerable traces of 'controlled substances' in the bloodstream along with alcohol. Lots of alcohol. The official verdict had been: death by accident from driving under the influence. . . .

To Jade the alcohol made no sense. Only a few months earlier Carlotta had stopped drinking altogether. She'd been to one of those places in Palm Springs where film stars and rich people went to dry out when their drinking was becoming a real problem. Had Carlotta gone off the wagon that day at the party in Malibu? All Jade knew for sure was that her mother was serious about having stopped drinking . . . she seemed to have developed an aversion to liquor. She wouldn't taste a drop of anything, not even the champagne she'd adored. Hadn't she knocked that glass of champagne out of Trace's hand when he held it out to her a couple of weeks after she had come home 'dry'. '*Come on, baby,*' *Trace urged.* '*It's only champagne, not hard stuff.*'

Carlotta, smiling. '*No, I don't think so.*'

'*Just a sip. A sip won't hurt you.*' *He holding the glass only an inch from her mouth.*

Carlotta trying to laugh. '*But it won't help me either. Please, Trace, I don't want it.*'

'*The fuck it won't help you.*' *He, not laughing, not even smiling.* '*Maybe it'll help put you in a better mood. The truth of it, Carlotta, is – you're no fucking fun when you don't drink. And if you're not fun, who the fuck wants you around? Not me. Not Scotty.*'

She no longer smiling. '*Well, in that case, I can just pick myself up and go someplace else— Jade and I. . . .*'

Now he was laughing. '*It's not that easy, baby. And that's not the way the scenario goes. The scenario says you stick around and you be fun . . . the way you used to be. . . .*'

She, pushing his hand with the champagne glass away. '*Who's writing the scenario? You? Scotty? Who?*'

180

'You know who's writing the script. You damned well better know it.'

He brought the glass to her lips and grimaced, trying to force her lips apart with its rim.

She lashed out and the glass went flying out of Trace's hand and crashed against a wall, glass and pale liquid falling to the floor.

He grabbed her arm and bent it back, she gasping. Then Ross Scott came into the room. He, sizing up the situation, told Trace to cool it, his pale eyes twin cubes of ice.

Scott, turning to Jade, who was watching everything, silent and frightened, laughed: 'Your mother and father play funny games, don't they, sweetheart?'

Jade, anxious, knowing that it wasn't a game she was watching – more like a movie, maybe – laughed along with her godfather, Scotty. It was a relief to laugh, especially since seconds before when her father was twisting her mother's arm, she had wanted to cry.

The legitimate newspapers only said that Carlotta had been at a Malibu party and gave the essence of the coroner's report. The scandal sheets gave different versions, even had different guest lists, but all agreed that Marilyn Monroe had been present at the beach house with an unnamed visitor from the East, a famous politician. And Ross Scott, a close friend of the Boudin family, had been there too, along with J.C. Hunt, the popular TV talk show host with his latest, a six-foot Dane with enormous breasts who spoke no English.

Reportedly, Trace had broken down when he heard the news. He blamed producer Charles Dryer for the tragedy. Carlotta had been in the jacuzzi with Chuck and they'd been drinking vodka straight from the bottle, sifted through a mouthful of ice cubes and a wedge of lime. 'Chuck, that stupid son-of-a-bitch, dared Carlotta to chug-a-lug that bottle of vodka and everyone knew Carlotta couldn't refuse a dare!'

Then it appeared that after Carlotta had passed out in the jacuzzi, and they'd dragged her out, she'd insisted she was going home and driving there herself.

Chuck Dryer said he had no accurate recall since he'd been pretty well smashed himself. He did have a vague recollection of Carlotta finishing off a bottle of something but he doubted that it was vodka since Harry Prince – the agent whose beach house it was – was a cheap bastard who only stocked what he drank and vodka wasn't his drink. Unless of course it was some imported stuff Carlotta's former boss at Majestic Studios had brought along. Scotty – Ross Scott – did have connections, and he never drank anything but the best. 'Say what you will about those guys, they *always* have the best, whether it's liquor, women or dope.'

A local socialite from the Colony, a well-groomed blonde whose main occupation was giving fundraising parties for politicians of both parties (that way, whoever won, she had the inside track), said that after Carlotta had been pulled from the jacuzzi, someone had given her a little red pill just to 'wake her up.' She could swear, although she didn't want to be quoted, that it was MM who gave her the upper. The woman also reported that the politician who had accompanied Marilyn was tickled to death at being at a real Hollywood party in Malibu and had spent the afternoon going around asking when the orgy would be starting. . . .

The same lady's husband who was in Texas oil thought that it was Boudin himself who had dared his wife to toss the vodka off in one throw. In fact, he distinctly remembered him holding the bottle to Carlotta's lips even as it ran down her chin. A lot of it spilled into the jacuzzi, which was OK, since the alcohol served as a disinfectant which didn't hurt since there'd been a lot of activity going on in the jacuzzi that day. . . .

After Jade read everything she realized one thing – she'd never *really* know what happened that day. Even if she'd wanted to question Chuck Dryer herself, it wasn't possible since only a couple of weeks after Carlotta's crack-up, Chuck, attending a film festival on the Riviera, went to a party aboard a yacht, fell overboard and drowned even though the yacht wasn't at sea.

That was right after Carlotta died and *before* Jade discovered the diaries, and there were a lot of things she didn't understand. She'd look up at the portrait of her mother hanging over the bed and ask: 'Well, Mother was it worth it? The sunny, reckless days . . . the sparkling, crazy nights? Life lived at a dizzying speed?'

Tell me, Mother! Send me a sign. Was it better to have lived life as you did, then leave it before it had a chance to turn into something sad and dreary? Or had it already turned?

That was before she discovered the diaries, but she already suspected that her mother had made a lousy trade.

She looked into the mirror, knew that the face she saw there was her mother's face as it would be forever transfixed in time, and for everyone who had ever known her mother, loved her, she would remain forever young, forever beautiful. But she herself would grow old and then she wouldn't look like her mother anymore. Unless she didn't grow old either. Unless she too was doomed to end up burning her candle at both ends. . . . But then she discovered the diaries and she determined that she would grow old, that she wasn't going to end up like her mother at all. She might look like Carlotta now, and love like Carlotta once had, but she wasn't going *to be* like Carlotta. . . . Carlotta had been like the emerald – beautiful, glittering but soft . . . easily cracked . . . easily broken. She intended to be much smarter . . . more like the diamond. Everyone knew diamonds were hard.

After she'd discovered the diaries, Jade knew many more answers. The problem was, they also posed new questions.

'Anyone for riding?' Jade came out of the bathroom dressed in a creamy satin blouse, white jodphurs and shiny black riding boots.

Abigail laughed. 'I don't think anyone's going horseback riding today even though I think the hurricane's over. You haven't looked outside yet. You have to see all the damage.'

'Oh, I didn't expect to go riding. I just felt like wearing this. How do I look?'

'Gorgeous.'

'And so do you in my sweater. Only you haven't followed my instructions, Miss Truesdale. . . .' She went over and gave Abigail's breasts a little squeeze. I distinctly told you *no bra!*'

'But—'

'No buts. Off with that bra before I take it off you myself. And I warn you. You won't stand a chance with me.'

'OK, you asked for it –' She went for Abigail who threw up her hands, laughing. 'OK . . . OK . . . I give up.'

'Wise move. Start stripping!'

Abigail, blushing, pulled off the pink sweater and turned around, away from Jade, to unfasten her bra.

'Oh, how sweet she is. How modest,' Jade teased and danced around to face Abigail. 'And what lovely sweet titties. Oh, how Ruddy boy is going to love them. . . .'

Abigail hastily pulled the pink sweater on again to cover her bare breasts. 'There! Are you satisfied?'

'Very much so. Very nice. Now just walk around a little and let me see how you jiggle.'

'Oh, you *are* impossible!'

'I know,' Jade said complacently. 'And you know what else? I think your jeans aren't tight enough. You forget this is all-out war. D'Arcy's bound to fight dirty. So I think you'd better wear *my* jeans which will be a little bit tighter. With tight little bum and tits jiggling, little old Rud isn't going to have eyes for anyone but you.'

And much as it hurts, that's the way it has to be.

She pulled a pair of jeans out of her suitcase and handed them over. 'Hurry. Put them on. If we don't eat breakfast soon we're going to miss lunch.'

4.

Rud was drinking coffee in the dining room, smoking a cigarette, hoping Jade would appear for breakfast without Abby. It was going to be a problem to get time alone with Jade if Abby was going to be forever tagging along. As if getting away from Judith wasn't difficult enough.

He remembered the day just three weeks ago in Newport when they'd received the invitation to D'Arcy's party. He remembered the day exactly since it was the same day Judith screwed him out of screwing DeeDee Clayton.

His strategy had been to get out of the house early before Judith caught him . . . before she had a chance to go over his complete schedule for the day and inserted herself into the middle of his activities the way she had a habit of doing. He had even decided to skip breakfast in order to get clean away but he didn't quite make it. Just as he was almost out the door, Beatrice Ewing, Judith's secretary, nabbed him. 'Oh, Rud, your mother would like to see you before you leave.'

'Tell her I'll see her when I get back. I have an early tennis date.'

'But she said to be sure and tell you that she has to discuss an invitation with you. It's one she has to respond to right away. And she also wants to talk to you about that boat—'

Crap! Judith'd been dangling that boat over his head all summer. What he'd really like to do was tell her to take that boat and stuff it!

'She's in the library waiting for you.'

He bent down and kissed the top of her head. 'So what's this terribly urgent invitation, Judy my love?'

Judith passed him the invitation and the accompanying note inviting them to stay the week at the Sheridans. 'Great! I've always wanted to meet the relatives. Let's go.'

'Well, if you think so, maybe we will. You're the boss.'

Rud smiled wryly. Judith liked to play the game that he was the cock of the roost, but both he and she knew better. But he always played along. Sometimes, in order to beguile her, he even resorted to a kind of subtle flirtation that implied that even though she was his mother, he found her delightfully, even sexually, attractive.

'Don't you want to go?' He had no idea what it was his mother had against her relatives but then, the labyrinth of her mind often puzzled him. 'I think it will be fun.'

'You!' Judith accused playfully, 'You think *everything's* fun.'

'What's wrong with a little fun? And who knows? Maybe we'll all become great pals. I for one would like to meet my cousins—D'Arcy and the two sisters. What are their names again?'

'Abigail Truesdale and Jade Boudin.'

'Right. They do have different fathers, don't they? Which one is the pretty one?'

'I have no idea. Why do you assume one is and the other isn't?'

He shrugged. 'You know how it is when two sisters have a different parent. One's invariably pretty and the other, a bow-wow.' And he barked, expecting his mother to laugh.

But she didn't. Rather her tone was caustic. 'And do you have statistics to support this scientific theory?'

Oh no . . . I must have hit a raw spot there.

'Well, I vote we go. And now I must be off. I have a date on the courts.'

'Whom are you playing?'

'DeeDee Clayton and I are playing doubles with Hutch and Lauren.'

'DeeDee's your partner?' Judith hooted. 'I didn't know she had the mental capacity to tie a pair of tennis shoes. . . .'

Ah, but it's not her ability to tie a pair of sneakers that intrigues me, Mother, but her ability to give head. Still, he laughed obligingly and edged towards the door, but Judith was too quick for him. 'I tell you what, Rud. Why don't you ask your friends to join us for lunch?'

He stiffened. '*Us?*'

'Yes. I thought I'd meet you a little after one at the Casino and then after lunch you and I could take a drive over to Kelsey's and have a look at that boat you've been talking so much about.'

Damn! He had nearly pulled it off. But now he had no choice but to throw in the towel for this afternoon. From experience he knew that there was no way of getting around her. And the hell of it was she probably had no intention of buying that sloop he'd coveted all summer. No, she'd wait until next summer now and would dangle the boat in front of his nose all year.

He forced himself to smile. 'Swell, Judy. See you around one then, and for God's sake, don't wear a dress with a low neckline. Hutch is taken with you and we don't want to give him a heart attack.'

Judith giggled. She wasn't taken in by this kind of flattery but she enjoyed it when Rud teased her, pretending she was one of those older women who fascinated young men.

'And do accept that invitation. It might be useful to get friendly with old King Sheridan. I could think of a worse association for a brilliant young man with his eye on the White House.'

This remark too was part of the game he played with her. Secretly he pictured the various ways in which he could throttle her – with a boat line, a tennis racket string, maybe one of DeeDee's tennis shoe laces. . . . But in the meantime, she had managed to screw up his fucking DeeDee today. . . .

When Abigail and Jade walked into the dining room, he scrambled to his feet, mindful of his manners, but inwardly groaning. Damn! Abigail *was* going to be hanging around all the time. And with this damn weather he couldn't even ask Jade to go for a walk on the beach. And she looked so sexy in those riding clothes even though he wondered why she was wearing them.

'You don't expect to go riding today, do you?'

'Don't be ridiculous,' she sneered, having decided to take this tack with him to discourage him from being interested in her. 'Who would go riding on a day like this? Where is everybody?'

'Well, Francesca finished her breakfast about fifteen minutes ago. She had to go see about some housekeeping stuff. She said that since they were short on staff this morning because of the hurricane, everyone was to help themselves.' He indicated the sideboard where there was an assortment of the usual breakfast items in addition to several silver chafing dishes. 'And it seems Uncle Bill was up really early as was your father, Jade. Up and out—'

Jade gave a short, disbelieving laugh. 'My father up so early in the morning and in the middle of a hurricane?'

'We are now in the *aftermath* of the hurricane and the storm is on its way north. Aunt Francesca said it was just part of Bill's duties as governor to assess the damage and decide what has to be done. So that's where Uncle Bill and your father went.'

'Well, aren't you up on things?' she marvelled dryly, puzzled as to why Trace had gone with Bill, and Rud was puzzled as to why she was being so bitchy. Last night she'd been so friendly . . . more than friendly.

'Why don't you two sit down and let me wait on you?' He draped his white napkin over his arm with a flourish and bowed from the waist. 'Ladies, I await your orders. There are scrambled eggs, sausages, bacon, cereal both hot and cold, rolls, toast, Danish pastries and preserves of all kinds.'

Abigail laughed and sat down. 'I want eggs with bacon and toast with peach marmalade.' But Jade rolled her eyes to indicate that she found Rud's performance juvenile. 'Don't bother yourself about me. I'm just going to have coffee and I'll get it myself.'

She poured the cup of coffee and sat down across the table from Abigail but

Rud, fixing Abigail's plate, persisted. 'I think that if you ate something, maybe you'd put yourself in a better mood.'

'Really?' Jade drawled. 'Is that what you were thinking? I was thinking about where was Judith, and how come she let her little boy out of his room all by his little self. . . .'

Abigail gasped. Jade had been more than rude, she'd been cruel, and why? While she didn't really have a crush on Rud, she thought he was very sweet.

And Rud recoiled as if Jade had slapped his face. *What a bitch!* Well, if that was the way she wanted to play it, it was OK with him. She could just go screw herself!

Jade stared into her black coffee. She supposed that she'd gone too far. She didn't have to be *that* mean. But it was too late now. But the important thing was that Rud should forget about her and concentrate on Abby, and now he seemed to be doing just that. He was setting Abby's plate down in front of her and talking to her in so low a murmur she couldn't even hear what he was saying. Well, good, she thought dispiritedly. That was exactly what she wanted. Rud and Abigail!

Even whispering some pointless nonsense in Abigail's ear, and looking down the V of her sweater, Rud couldn't help wondering what had happened between last night and this morning to make Jade act that way. Suddenly he realized that Abigail wasn't wearing a bra. Now that was interesting! He hardly thought her the type. And then D'Arcy came running in, breathless, and it was obvious from all the movement going on under *her* sweater that she too, was braless. And *her* jeans were easily as tight. In spite of Jade, things were warming up!

D'Arcy went up to Rud, pouting prettily, 'I can't believe no one woke me up and the three of you are having a good old time without me!'

By all means, join the party,' Rud said cheerfully, throwing Jade a look.

So she was right about D'Arcy having eyes for Rud, Jade thought. She was practically shaking her boobies in his face! Well, she hoped for D'Arcy's sake, as well as for Abby's, that nothing came of it. It was terrible to think about the consequences if they were attracted to each other without knowing that they were brother and sister.

As for Rud, he was thinking that it would be a hell lot more fun trying to make Jade jealous with D'Arcy than it would be with Abby. But the trick of it was to get started before Judith came down to breakfast and messed things up. . . .

5.

Judith awoke in a foul mood. She hadn't fallen asleep until well after dawn and now it was past noon. She hated starting the day after it was half gone. She went to the windows and opened the shutters to see that it was only drizzling now and it looked like there was an army of ants out there working to erase all signs of the destruction. She only hoped that the hurricane wore itself out before it hit New England. Newport, to be specific.

Before going downstairs, she knocked on Rud's door to see if he were still in bed. She hoped so. That way, she'd know he hadn't been up to anything he shouldn't, like carrying on with that redheaded cousin of his, or talking with Bill. *She* intended to have a talk with Bill before there was any conversation between the two of them. When Rud didn't answer her knock, she opened the door and found the room empty and went downstairs to find him.

The housekeeper was starting to clear the sideboard when Judith entered the dining room. 'Good morning, Mrs Stanton. I was just taking away the breakfast things but I'll be glad to get you whatever you'd like. An omelette?'

'No thank you. Juice, tea and toast will be sufficient. Where is everybody?'

'The Governor is out checking on the damage. The hurricane you know. Mr Boudin went with him. Mrs Sheridan is in the kitchen seeing to some things. We're short-handed today. Most of our staff comes in by the day from West Palm Beach and what with the storm, hardly anyone showed up. And then when we lost the power, it seemed only one of the two auxiliary generators was working, and the freezer's on—'

'Please! Spare me the details. Where are the young people?'

'Oh, they're all upstairs. Since we are short-handed, Mrs Sheridan suggested that the young people make up their own rooms. . . .'

'An excellent idea.' She sat down and the housekeeper set a place in front of her. 'Do you think I could have some *fresh* toast? And how long has that tea been sitting?'

'I'll fetch a fresh pot of tea, Mrs Stanton.'

'Good, and chilled juice, please. You *can* chill the juice?'

'As I said, the freezer's out but I'll try my best.'

'Do. And do you have a morning paper?'

'No ma'am. The storm, you know,' she said and made a fast getaway, while it occurred to Judith that if the kids were upstairs making up their rooms, why was Rud's room empty? What was he up to? And with whom? She decided to go back upstairs and see what was doing. . . .

She went in the direction of the sound of voices, laughter and music which led her to the room the sisters were sharing. She flung open the door to see Rud lying on one twin bed with Abigail and D'Arcy pushing and tugging at him, all of them laughing and red in the face. On the radio Sammy Davis was plaintively asking, 'What Kind Of a Fool Am I?' Rud, seeing her, leaped to his feet, D'Arcy pulled down on her sweater, and Jade came out of the bathroom.

'Aunt Frankie sent us up to make our rooms,' Rud explained lamely, and D'Arcy further elucidated. 'We decided we'd all work on one room at a time. . . .'

'Yes, I see. A team effort.'

'So we're making the beds while Jade does the bathroom,' Abigail said earnestly, 'and when we're through here we're going to do D'Arcy's room and then Rud's.'

'And it takes only one person in riding clothes to straighten up a bathroom but three to make a bed?' Judith marvelled dryly.

'I'll say it does,' D'Arcy giggled, 'when one of the three refuses to get out of the bed and the other two have to work around him.'

'Yes, I can see that that would make the job more difficult,' Judith laughed.

She couldn't believe that Rud was indulging in this juvenile horseplay but it all seemed innocent enough. 'Well, I'll leave you children to your work. But Rud dear, do try and be more cooperative. You must stay out of that bed!' she mocked him.

Abigail ran after her. 'Oh, Judith, they really don't need me in here. May I make up your room for you?'

Judith beamed at her. 'Why, I think that would be very sweet of you, dear. And very thoughtful. Thank you.'

As soon as Judith was gone D'Arcy immediately started pushing Rud down on the bed again, as Jade, leaning against the door of the bathroom, drawled. 'Oh dear me, Rudyard, *do* be a good boy and stay out of that bed!'

Rud picked up a pillow and hurled it at her.

It was Francesca who brought Judith her breakfast. 'I hope the juice is chilled sufficiently for you, Judith. I would have nestled it in a bowl of shaved ice but I'm afraid we lost all our ice before we got the generator going.'

'Oh, I am sorry to be so much trouble, Frankie. Perhaps in view of all these difficulties, we should leave—'

'That's out of the question right now. The airports are closed and the trains aren't running either. The hurricane is following a path right up the coast.'

'Oh? And have you heard from Bill?'

'No but I'm sure he'll be back by evening.'

'And I heard Trace went with him. How odd! Hurricanes hardly seem his cup of tea. Why did he go?'

'I thought maybe you'd tell me.'

'I, Frankie? How would I know?'

'Because as I recall, you and Trace always talked things over.'

'Hardly, Frankie, hardly. Anyhow, it appears now that it's Bill and Trace who are talking things over, doesn't it?'

What's she hinting at now? Well, she wasn't going to stand here bantering with her. 'You'll have to excuse me, Judith. There are things I have to see to—'

Then she noticed Abby standing in the doorway. 'Did you want something, Abby?'

'Well, I just finished making up Judith's room and I thought that maybe there was something I could do for you down here. They really don't need my help upstairs and I could dust, or do dishes—'

'Thank you for the offer,' Francesca said curtly, 'but it's not necessary. We're managing. Now, if you'll both excuse me—'

How curious, Judith thought. She could understand Francesca being short with her, but why this poor sweet child? One would think she'd be much warmer to Carlotta's daughter. She smiled at Abigail who looked as if she felt rather foolish.

Abigail raised her shoulders in embarrassment. 'I only meant to help—'

'Of course you did. And that was lovely of you. Why don't you join me in a cup of tea? There's an extra cup and saucer and I'll share my toast with you.'

Abigail was delighted and ran to sit down next to Judith. Judith poured the tea. 'Cream or lemon?'

'Which do you take?'

188

'Lemon.'

'Then I'll have lemon too.' And seeing that Judith didn't take sugar, she didn't either.

'Do you help out at home?' Judith asked.

'Oh yes. I have my regular chores, and of course I keep my own room and bath. Aunt Selena keeps only one maid and she can't do everything.'

'I should think not.' Yes, little Abby was a very nice girl. It was a wonder that she was Carlotta's and Trace's love child. Now, Jade – no one would ever doubt that she was Carlotta and Trace's daughter, even without the startling resemblance to Carlotta. It was a matter of character. She wondered how many of the others knew for a fact that Abby was Trace's daughter. Francesca and Bill probably. And she guessed from the conversation she'd had with Jade, that Jade knew. Obviously the Truesdales didn't know. They wouldn't have kept the girl for a minute if they knew. But who would ever reveal? Not Francesca nor Bill. And she didn't think Jade would either. Only Trace would – *if* he had something to gain, and *if* someone didn't have the power to stop him.

Of course, she herself had that power.

'Are you having a good time in Palm Beach in spite of the hurricane, Abby?'

'Oh yes. As a matter of fact, I'm having a good time right now, having tea with you. There's only one thing I feel bad about – that we both live in Boston and we've never met before.'

'You know, I was thinking exactly the same thing. When we get back to Boston we'll have to rectify matters. You'll have to come to dinner, or at least tea, once a week. How does that sound?'

'Oh, it sounds really neat.' And she moved her chair even closer to Judith's, sighing contentedly. Judith was being so nice to her, so warm . . . much more so than her Aunt Francesca. Judith was acting like she was her aunt rather than just her cousin. She really liked her a lot. . . .

'But I don't want to keep you from having fun with your cousins. I'm sure you'd rather be upstairs with them—'

'Oh no! I'm enjoying myself really. . . .'

And Judith realized that she was really enjoying herself too, basking in this girl's obvious admiration. Why the girl was acting practically starry-eyed! And how many people felt that way about her? Not even her son Rud. . . .

After a while Judith and Abigail went upstairs to see what the others were doing. They found them in Rud's room. Once again Jade was in the bathroom, and Rud and D'Arcy were ostensibly making the bed, again laughing uproariously, and again Rud was lying in the bed, only this time, D'Arcy was lying on top of him.

Seeing Judith, D'Arcy rolled off Rud, breathing hard and giggling. Rud sat up and Jade came out of the bathroom. She was glad that Judith had turned up to break up the action between Rud and D'Arcy. She'd been thinking about how to do that herself without making Rud think she was jealous. Not that she wasn't, but what really pissed her off was that while she had stepped aside for Abby . . . had deliberately antagonized Rud so that Abby could have a clear field with him, Abby had gone off, had left the field open to D'Arcy, who was moving in on Rud like an armoured tank. What was wrong with Abby? She wasn't even giving D'Arcy a good fight.

Well, now that Judith was here, she'd take care of them, and well she should, considering. . . .

But Judith, while annoyed, had no intention of building this up into a major incident. That was the worst thing she could do, she decided. Still, she had to say something, and it was best delivered in an amused, condescending fashion.

'Really, Rud, what would your friends at Harvard say about your behaviour? That you retrogressed to the age of twelve?'

Rud's face darkened with anger. How did Judith always manage to make him look the fool, no matter what he did? And this time she'd done it in front of not only D'Arcy, but Jade. As for Abby, he didn't give a damn what *she* thought. The way she was toadying up to Judith made him sick!

'As for you, D'Arcy,' Judith went on, 'what do you think your mother and father would say to your behaviour?'

'D'Arcy got to her feet. 'Oh, big deal! If you must know, my father would probably laugh. As for my mother, well, sometimes she *is* hopelessly old-fashioned. But, God, we were just fooling around. . . . Are you going to tell her?'

'No, I don't think so,' she said kindly. 'Why upset her over a little "fooling around", as you said?'

The truth was, she didn't want to tell Francesca anything. It was only Bill to whom she wanted to speak. In fact, she was eagerly awaiting his return. She was dying to learn what and he and Trace had found to talk about all day. . . .

6.

Bill and Trace hadn't really been alone the whole time as they moved around by jeep and helicopter viewing the damage. When Trace had insisted on accompanying him that morning, Bill knew that Boudin had only been looking for a chance to talk to him without chancing any intrusion. Now, on their way back, exhausted and wet, dirty and hungry, they were finally alone except for the trooper who was doing the driving. But he wouldn't be able to hear anything and Bill said, 'Well, spit it out, Boudin. What is it you want?'

'It can wait. We've got all week.' He had decided that after the gruelling day, maybe the timing was off. The time to hit Sheridan with an offer he couldn't refuse was when he was feeling good, sated with rich food and fine liquor, and when he himself was feeling on top of things.

'Don't count on the week, Boudin. I might send you packing before the week's out.'

'That wouldn't be so smart, Sheridan. And Scotty, my business associate, says you're smart.'

'Associate, my ass. He's your boss and you're nothing more than a flunky in a fancy silk suit.'

You're also the scumbag who stole Carlotta away and most probably put her in the cold, cold ground where the California sun doesn't shine.

He remembered Carlotta dreamily fantasizing on a gray, snow day. *If only we could be in California today . . . lying in the sun. Oh, Bill, wouldn't it be wonderful to make love in the sun?'* He wondered if Trace and Carlotta had made love in the sun. . . .

190

'You know what's wrong with you, Sheridan? You've got an attitude problem. You always did. And a man who wants to be President shouldn't have an attitude.'

'Are you threatening me, flunky?'

'No, we don't threaten people. Sometimes we just give them a little nudge, a warning, you might say.'

'You stupid son-of-a-bitch,' Bill said, bringing his face within an inch of Boudin's. 'Do you know who you're talking to with your warnings? They don't call me the King down here for nothing. You're on my territory now, and on my territory you could wake up dead, and no one would ask any questions.'

For a moment Boudin's eyes shifted uncertainly but then he recovered, smiled his icy smile. 'I know how that is. We work that way too.'

'Shit!' Bill said. 'But since your boss has sent a punk to do a man's job, let's hear it and be through with it.'

What the hell? He would spit it out. The important thing was to keep his own cool. 'Sure. This is it in a nutshell, and whatever you decide to do, it's your ass, *King*. The Kennedy people are making things hot for Scotty and his friends, if you get my drift, Bobby doesn't know when to pull his punches. He's stepping on too many toes and the boys don't want Bobby in the attorney-general's office no more and that means they don't want Jack in the Oval Office come '65.'

'So they don't want! So what?'

'So the people Scotty represents figure that if Kennedy loses the South in '64, he might well lose the election. They also figure that you control a big block of Southern votes and that if you *withdrew* your support from Kennedy, well there goes the election. And my people know how to return a favour. They know how the game is played.'

'Meaning?'

'Meaning you play ball with us and we'll play ball with you. Everyone knows you plan on throwing your hat in the ring sooner or later. When you do, you'll be our boy. Our people will throw their support, which is considerable, behind you.'

'I see.' Bill's voice was controlled, without inflection which made Trace feel more confident now, more relaxed. He was thinking that Bill was going to go for it and he wasn't going to have to squander his hole card in a last ditch attempt to lean on him. He much preferred to save that hole card – that he knew Rud was Bill's son – for his own personal gain, and not Scotty's.

'And if I don't play ball?' Bill asked.

'Then you might just find out that there are dangerous enemies out there, much more dangerous than your strictly political ones.'

'Your threats don't scare me.'

Boudin laughed. 'They should. Even Presidents get knocked off. . . .'

Bill reached over and grabbed Boudin by the testicles and squeezed. 'Listen to me good, Boudin. You go back to that hole you crawled out of and tell your friends that Bill Sheridan says they should go fuck themselves. Nobody tells me whom to support. You got the message straight, shithead? If you do, just say yes.'

Boudin's eyes bulged. His hand grasped Bill's wrist trying to pry his hand loose from him, but he was unable to do so and finally he had to groan, 'Yes,' and Bill released him.

For that, King Sheridan, one day I'm going to kill you!

'If it weren't for Jade . . . if I didn't want to screw the week up for all the kids, you'd be out on your ass this minute. So just keep that in mind and keep your filthy mouth buttoned and stay out of my way!'

Boudin decided he'd do just that for the time being. But he had a couple more irons in the fire and right at this minute they were both inside the big bastard's house.

Francesca came to the door to greet Bill. 'How does everything look out there?' She ignored Trace.

'It could be worse,' Bill said, and then Jade came rushing up and she too ignored Trace, putting her arms around her uncle. 'Oh, Uncle Bill, you poor thing! You look like you've had a terrible day.'

Francesca took Bill's arm and practically pulled him away from Jade, feeling ridiculous at the role she was being forced to play — physically removing her husband from her niece's embrace. 'I'm sure your father's wet and tired too, Jade,' she said. 'Why don't you make him one of your famous martinis?' She and Bill left the two of them, Jade and her father, standing there.

Trace scrutinized Jade speculatively. What's she up to? The way she rubbed up against Sheridan you'd think she had a case on him. She's a little fool just like her mother, he thought grimly. Carlotta too never seemed to know which side her bread was buttered on. Instead of wasting her time on Sheridan, why the hell wasn't Jade making those goo-goo eyes and rubbing herself up against her rich and very eligible cousin? Last night, he was like a fish caught on her hook, for sure. Now, there was a situation that could eventually pay off in really big bucks. Of course there was Judith to contend with. There was no way she was going to stand by and let her prize fall into Jade's lap. Then again, maybe he could help Jade out with Judith and then Jade could help Daddy in turn. . . .

He draped an arm around Jade's shoulder but she shook it off violently. Today really wasn't his day. But he stayed cool. 'What's wrong, baby?'

Jade looked into his eyes. For nearly three years she had held it all in, waiting to let it all out, to vent the hatred and rage that had been building up until she thought she might burst with it. Oh, once she had loved him so . . . once, when she had still believed in the fabled love story of Trace and Carlotta. That had been before she discovered the diaries. . . .

But this was the week of revelation.

'If anybody knows what's wrong, it should be you.'

It had been a tough day and he was losing his patience. 'What are you talking about? Spit it out.'

'I'm talking about my mother's diaries.'

He was startled. 'Your mother kept diaries?'

'Yes. And I found them and now I know everything.'

He seized her arm, twisted it behind her back. 'What do you think you know?'

'I know that you murdered my mother!'

He let go of her arm, and laughed. 'You stupid little fool. She was tanked and she smashed herself up. . . .'

'That was only one day . . . one hour. You were killing her for years. You sold her.'

He laughed again. 'Who did I sell her to – white slavers?'

'Maybe. Maybe that's the right term. You sold her to Ross Scott.'

His hand whipped out and slapped her across the face. She didn't utter a sound, only placed her palm against her cheek. 'How dare you talk that way to your father?'

'My father? Are you sure exactly who *is* my father?'

And then, even though there was really nothing very funny in what she'd just said or in the look that crept over Trace's face, she laughed and laughed, and kept on laughing, unable to stop. But when she had read those pages in Carlotta's diaries, she hadn't laughed at all. . . .

Carlotta had taken the train to California. She, who was afraid of almost nothing, had been afraid to fly. It wasn't so much the fear of crashing as the scary feeling that you had no control over your own life when you were up there above the clouds. Somebody else was in charge of the controls . . . of your life . . . and it was a feeling she couldn't bear.

She didn't enjoy the trip. How could she? For three full nights and two full days it was hard not to constantly think of the sweet little baby she'd left behind. Tiny Abigail, scarcely three months old. But she consoled herself. It would hardly be any time at all before she went back to get little Abby – the visual proof of her and Trace's great love. *A great love!* She told herself that over and over. Otherwise, why would he have finally sent for her?

He'd sent for her because he couldn't live without her. And once he saw Abigail he was bound to love her as much as she herself did. She couldn't wait until he saw how sweet Abby was. How her eyes were the same colour as his, how her hair curled in the same way his did, how darling she was when she smiled and cooed. Oh, she couldn't wait until he saw little Abby.

Together they'd laugh over the name Abigail – such a prim and proper name for such a tiny baby! George and Selena had insisted on calling her Abigail, wanting her to be named after the second First Lady, who George claimed as an ancestor on his mother's side. After all, Abigail Adams had not only been a *First* Lady but the quintessence of a lady in every sense of the word. And Whit of course wouldn't argue with them. He hadn't had the backbone to stand up to them even when he'd brought her to their house to live after they'd been married and they treated her like some dread and foul plague that had invaded their home.

Now, she'd never have to look at them again – never have them look down their snooty Boston noses at her. Now she was on her way to Trace and soon he'd hold her in his arms again, tell her how he couldn't live without her, tell her that she was his, only his, forever. . . .

Trace Boudin . . . Trace Boudin . . . Trace Boudin . . . the train's wheels sang chugging across America. Trace loves Carlotta . . . Trace loves Carlotta. . . . The music rang in her ears.

She'd hated him when first he had walked out on her. For weeks, and even for months. But then, after a while, she hadn't blamed him. How could she, really? Hadn't she herself told him in detail of how she went to bed with other men? Could she blame him for not believing her when she'd told him that she was pregnant and that there hadn't been anybody else in months? But now he believed her. He had even told her that he was sorry for not believing her immediately, for not marrying her then. And after a little while, they were going to get Abby and then it would be the three of them. . . .

She'd *tried* with Whit. She never meant to hurt him. She had turned to him and he had jumped at the chance to marry her. He couldn't wait to marry her! But then, after, he couldn't wait to get back at her, lashing out at her constantly, wanting to hurt her. Poor Whit! He just couldn't find it in his heart to forgive her. All he really cared about was that no one else knew that he'd married a woman with another man's child growing inside her. Especially Selena and George. . . .

But now that was all water under the bridge. Once she got to California and Trace, everything was going to be wonderful! It would be almost like a fairytale. It would be like a real Hollywood movie with everyone living happily ever after.

She stepped off the train into the California sunshine and practically fell into his arms. But then, over his shoulder, she saw that there was someone else with him – a slim, elegant man with a smoothly-shaven head and strange almost colourless eyes . . . frightening eyes, that glittered in the sunlight. He had a severe slash of a mouth and an immaculately trimmed Vandyke. Trace introduced her. Ross Scott! *Just call him Scotty.* But Trace's awed tone almost shouted. *Be nice! This is no ordinary man!*

Back in Boston, Trace had spoken of Ross Scott as if he were his friend, his associate. But now she instantly and instinctively knew that Trace was afraid of him. Who then was Ross Scott if no ordinary man? And although that southern California sun warmed her skin, she shivered and she knew that she was afraid too.

They whisked her away in a black Bentley and took her to the pink villa nestling in the hills that would be her home. She couldn't believe her eyes. There were terraces and gardens, fountains, a pool inlaid with mosaics, tennis courts, even stables! How had Trace managed to produce this miracle? Inside the house was as splendid as the outside, decorated with an arrogant, knowledgeable disregard for period or rule of style, a magnificent mélange of pastel *bergères* standing next to chairs upholstered in patent leather, alongside sofas adorned with winged arms of gilded wood. White Art Deco ladies and crystal gleamed on lucite tables and leather *objets d'art* were reflected in mirrored cabinets and a Venetian bowl reposed on a modern, lacquered, ebony pedestal. She was stunned. How had Trace accomplished all this? Chosen and designed and selected? *Paid* for it all? And how had he acquired the Palm Grotto, the chic club on the Sunset Strip he'd told her about?

And then it came to her. Trace hadn't wrought any of this. It was all Ross Scott. *Scotty!* He owned it all! It would be his home in which she would live. And then when they took her upstairs to her bedroom – all white velvet and satin and mirrors, she knew whose bed it was that she'd sleep in. Ross Scott owned it all . . . owned Trace . . . owned *her*. She was lost!

For a moment she thought about running. But to where? Was there a haven for her any place? Could she run to Bill whose strong arms had once held her? No, he was Frankie's now and Frankie had already turned her back on her. Back to Whit, who really despised her even as he wanted to possess her? Back to Boston where her baby lay in her crib? No, it was too late for all that. The bridges that could take her back were already burned to a crisp.

Trace held her fast and murmured in her ear, his voice as sweet as any siren's: 'You *have* to do it! For us . . . for our love. Do it for our baby. Think of the great life we'll be able to give little Abby when we bring her out here. If you truly love me, Carlotta, you have to prove it!'

And she slept that night with both of them. First with Trace's false terrible god and then with Trace, he who had sent her a false message: *I love you.* . . .

She was broken and shamed, but Trace was proud. He'd promised his god a sacrifice of such beauty as he'd never seen before and he delivered!

Within the month she was pregnant again and whose baby it was — Scotty's or Trace's — didn't much matter to her. But Trace was ecstatic. 'Scotty's real pleased. He wants us to go down to Mexico and get you a quickie divorce and then the same day, we can get married there. If it's a girl, Scotty wants us to name her Jade after the hotel we're building in Vegas . . . a jewel in the desert. How about that?'

When her response was less than enthusiastic, he shook her by the shoulders. 'Let's see some of that old Carlotta sparkle. We don't want any long-faced deadheads around here.'

Jade? Why not? Did it really matter any more than it did who of the two was her father? It was Abigail, after all, who was the lucky one. Abigail, who was named for a First Lady, who would grow up in Boston and never get up in the morning and feel that false warmth of a California sun, never listen to Trace Boudin's lying lips, never look into Ross Scott's almost colourless, terrifying eyes. Oh, lucky Abigail and poor little Jade. Abigail Truesdale was safe!

When Jade finally was able to stop laughing, she looked at Trace and said evenly. 'So you see, I do know everything. Everything and more. I even know all about yours and Scotty's various activities . . . everything written down in my mother's diaries in black and white.'

Oh, he believed her now! She could see it in his eyes.

'For your sake, Jade, I hope you're one smart canary. Sometimes when canaries sing too much or too loud, they can get on your nerves. And then—' He placed his hands around her neck then withdrew them.

She didn't want him to think she was afraid of him even though of course, she was. How could she not be when she knew of what he was capable? She mocked him: 'You wouldn't really want to do that, would you? I just *might* be your daughter, after all.'

'Well, you might and you might not. But there's always Abigail. I know for sure whose daughter *she* is. If I were you, I'd think about that before I did any running off at the mouth.'

She did think about it – all through the evening and then, intermittently, all through the night between dream and nightmare.

7.

Bill was up with the morning sun, big and orange-pink as it came up over the Atlantic. Today he was going to check on the destruction the hurricane had wrought in the northern part of the state, and he wanted a chance to talk with Judith before he left, while the rest of the household was still asleep.

He knocked on her door softly, loud enough to wake her, he hoped, but not loud enough to wake Rud or Trace in the adjoining rooms. But she must have been up since she opened the door to him within seconds, and then seeing her, he wondered if she'd been anticipating a visitor. She was wearing a black satin nightgown with the breasts outlined in lace. Did she always go to bed dressed like this, even though she had no man lying beside her? The thing of it was that her hair was perfectly arranged, her make-up as if freshly applied. *Had* she been expecting him, or had it been Trace just next door? Nothing was impossible, he'd learned, and Judith was a woman with a healthy sexual appetite.

'You're up bright and early.' She sat on the edge of the bed.

'I'm leaving in a few minutes and I wanted to talk to you.' He outlined the gist of his and Trace's conversation.

Judith chuckled. 'Is that why you got me up at this ungodly hour? To tell me that you told Boudin to go fuck himself?'

'I wanted to warn you. . . . I think he knows that Rud's—Carlotta knew. To be on the safe side, we should assume she told Boudin.'

'If that's so, why didn't he use that as part of his threat to pressure you into doing what he and his friends want?'

'Maybe he wants to keep that separate. He might be planning on blackmailing you with that.'

'Yes, that makes sense. He threatened you on behalf of his friend. Me, he'd blackmail for money. He *does* need money.'

'Everyone needs money.'

She laughed. 'Some people need it more than others. Boudin needs it just to stay alive.'

'If he comes to you with this, are you going to give him the money he needs to stay alive?'

'I don't have to—I have some information too and what I know about Mr Boudin could get him dead in a hurry. The other way, his demise is a matter of time. He'll stay alive until he's found out. Unless, of course, he finds that money elsewhere.'

Bill was satisfied. He didn't have to know the details. All that concerned him was protecting his and Judith's secret. But now it was time to discuss their other business – why he had invited her and Rud to Florida, and suddenly he was unsure. He had marshalled all the reasons Judith should allow him to see his son, but what he'd assumed were convincing reasons now seemed inadequate. His big point was that when she'd paid him off to get out of Massachusetts, he'd been too powerless to be of any use to her or Rud, but all that had changed. Now, he *could* be of use, and if he didn't pose any threat to her—? But could he convince Judith? He was suddenly mute.

196

But then smiling, Judith helped him out. 'You want to see Rud. You want to be friends with him. You want to have some kind of a role in his life. . . . Is that it?'

'Yes,' he breathed, grateful that she'd found the words for him. 'Believe me, I don't want to make waves. As much as you want to maintain the status quo, so do I. What I propose is a trade-off. You let me have only a small part of Rud . . . allow me to be his mentor, his patron, his friend and then in time, maybe his sponsor, and in return I'll help you mould him into a President.'

'So far you haven't moulded yourself into the presidency.'

'But I will! I will be President! You can count on it.'

'When? It's Kennedy for sure in '64.'

'I'm planning on '68.'

She thought about it. 'Maybe . . .'

'No maybe about it. And then there will be so much I'll be able to do for Rud.'

She seemed more amused than impressed. 'I don't know how much you can do for Rud. After all, his chances for the presidency are about thirty years away. God knows where you'll be then . . . what you'll be doing. . . . And even so, I don't think we need your help.'

He was losing her and he began to speak more urgently. 'You're banking on your money and money alone can't do it.'

'Money is power. You know that.'

'But knowledge is power too. Savvy is power. Toughness is power. The world's changing, Judith. Money isn't enough anymore.'

'Is this more of your "man of the people" rhetoric, King Sheridan?'

'Listen to me, Judith! I can do it for me and then I can do it for him!'

His eyes blazed and a current of electricity coursed through her, starting in her head and working its way down. No wonder Bill Sheridan had swept the South like a plague, she thought. He *was* convincing and it wasn't his words. It was the sheer force of his personality, his charisma. He *was* mesmerizing and her son was his son. No wonder women fell under Rud's spell like so many zombies. It was more than his physical beauty. He had all of his father's magnetism and it was as much sexual as it was anything else. She felt it as strongly now as she had felt it almost twenty years before.

'You propose then to make my son a king too?'

He laughed then, thinking he had convinced her. 'The first obligation of royalty is to provide a succession to the throne.'

'Perhaps . . .' she said thoughtfully. 'We can give it a try, I suppose. Discreetly. I still have my house down here. I could open it up for the season. . . . A trial period, shall we say?'

'Then it's a deal?' He stuck out his hand, trying not to yell in his exultation. What he wanted to do was climb to the rooftops and shout his joy to the skies!

But then to his surprise — and he'd thought he was beyond surprise, especially with Judith who had always been full of surprises — she released the straps of her nightgown and let it fall to the floor. 'Lock the door,' she commanded him and it could have been twenty years before. . . . Only Judith's body was much improved.

Was he tempted? He wasn't sure. She had always fascinated him in that perverse manner. Whatever. . . . He was the consummate politician and he knew that often, to close a deal, you had to sweeten the pot.

He began to take off the clothes he had put on less than a half-hour before and she lay down on the bed and opened her thighs for him. He mounted her. 'If I remember correctly,' he said, feeling the excitement come to life within him, 'that first time we *intimed*, you'd been married for a time and yet you were a virgin, which led to certain conclusions being drawn about Dudley Stanton. So, tell me, Judith, how *did* you convince Dudley that he was the father of your son?'

'Like this—' She rolled out from under him and mounted him. 'When one's on top, it's all that much easier to be convincing.'

She'd been beneath that first time with Bill. She'd been on top when she persuaded Dudley that he was inside her. By far she preferred the upper position and that was where she planned to remain with Bill Sheridan – on top of things, on top of him. Later on, they'd see. But for now, riding him, feeling him inside her, was good.

Not even an hour after Bill left her, Trace knocked surreptitiously on her door. Dressed for the day now in a two-piece turquoise silk dress, Judith admitted him without any fanfare. She had been expecting him, sooner or later.

Trace was not at his best, she saw. He was trying to be his usual cool self, but he was sweating. She could see the tiny beads of perspiration on his forehead. She was the cool one. She wasn't even concerned that Rud might overhear anything – she'd allowed Bill to waken him, to take him along on his excursion.

'Well, Trace, what can I do for you today?'

'You can give me a million bucks,' he said with a crooked grin, trying for the light touch.

'That's a lot of money. What do you propose to do for that money?' She knew how the conversation was going to go and how it was going to end so well, she was already bored with it.

'It's more what I'm *not* going to do. For a million bucks, I'm *not* going to divulge that Sheridan's your kid's father.'

'You have no proof so all you can do is slander. But *I* do have proof – of how you've been skimming money from the casino at the Jade for years. Proof. Not that Scotty would require proof. He'd take my word for it.'

Boudin paled under his perennial tan. *How did she know? How could she know that for every dollar the casino took in, he'd be taking————off the top?* That was why he needed the money. He was getting edgy that he was under suspicion. He needed to throw some money back in. . . .

There was only one way she could have proof. She had people on the inside spying on him!

'Your accounts as of 31 July, 1962 are short almost two million dollars. But you're only asking for one. What were you going to do? Come back next month for more? Frankly, Boudin, I couldn't care less how much money you've been stealing from Scotty and the boys. All I care is that you don't step on *my* toes, and that includes keeping your mouth shut about my ever having dealings with Scott. You make a wide circle around me, my greedy friend. Get

198

even just a little bit close and I divulge, and you're a dead man. Quick! This way, going on the way you are, you might last another couple of years. Who knows?'

Oh God, if only I could kill her right here and now! If only I could put my hands around that neck and squeeze all the breath out of her! But what good would it do? It won't get me clear with Scotty.

'I can see you have a clear grasp of the situation, Trace, so would you mind clearing the hell out of my room? I've brought some work with me and I have to get at it. And there are already enough damn insects in here buzzing around. That's Florida for you in September, especially with the wet weather we've been having.'

Again, he thought about choking her. He should have known that he wasn't going to win with her. She'd always outfoxed him. And then laughed at him. There had to be a better way. Maybe right from the start . . . in the very beginning . . . he'd been going about doing business with her in the wrong way. Maybe the right way to approach Judith was the same way he'd been dealing with other women all his life. She was a woman, wasn't she? She had a cunt, didn't she? And one way or another, all any woman wanted was to have her cunt filled. . . .

He tried to compose himself. Instead of leaving he sat down in the lounge chair, carefully adjusting his trousers so that their perfect crease wasn't disturbed, and he consciously placed his devil-may-care grin back in place. 'You're tough, Judith. You're a lady and you're tough as hell. It gets me every time. It really turns me on.'

She looked up from the paper she had already started to read. 'Really?' she asked as if intrigued.

'Yeah. Nothing gets me as hot as a tough lady.'

'That's very interesting.' Her eyes took on a new sparkle. 'Tell me more.'

He sprung from the chair then like a cat sighting an object of prey and was all over her, pulling her to him, his hands moving down her back over her buttocks, pressing her against his swelling organ, rubbing and revolving it into her. 'Feel that, Judith?' he whispered. '*That's* what you do to me!'

'Mmmm . . . that feels good . . . so good. Oh, I like that!' she breathed, and he thought he had her. Probably she hadn't had a good fuck in years!

He pushed her down on the bed, covered her lips with his wet ones, put his tongue into her mouth. And she let him. She sucked on his tongue, let him unbutton her blouse, bury his face in her breasts. She let him ease down her panties and kiss her there, insert his tongue there . . . in, out, licking, flicking. He lifted his head a moment to murmur, 'Does Judith's tough, hot little pussy like that?'

'Mmmm, Judith's tough, hot little pussy *loves* that!'

She waited until his penis emerged swollen and excited before she began to laugh. She laughed so hard she could barely stop long enough to say, 'That's what I said about Palm Beach in September. So many pesky little things flying around. I wouldn't be at all surprised if there weren't a lot of vermin crawling around too. Maybe you'd better put Trace's hot little, tough little prick back where it came from before an even larger rodent comes along and bites it off!' She snapped her teeth at him and began to laugh all over again.

Back in his room, Trace swore to himself that he'd kill her. Definitely. One of these days he'd kill both Judith and Sheridan. He'd have to figure out how to do it. But right now he had to plan what he was going to do next. He had struck out twice and in addition, there was Jade threatening to spill her guts about what she knew about his and Scotty's activities. Once she'd said that, he knew the damn diaries existed. Damn Carlotta for writing it all down! If only he could get his hands on those diaries! Maybe there was more information in there that he could somehow use! Maybe when the girls were out of the room he could search it. There were only so many places in one guest room where Jade could hide them.

But first things first, which meant coming up with some hard cash. Even a little would help. Keep the mob off his back for a while longer. Well, at least the goddamn sun was out today. Maybe he'd wait until he was able to search Jade's room for the diaries, and then he'd head to Miami and look up some old buddies. See what was cooking there. The place was hopping with drugs. If nothing else, he'd find himself a game. And if he was lucky, a set-up. It was too bad about Carlotta. When'd she'd been around, just having her draped on his arm was enough to open a lot of doors that he couldn't get through by himself. He'd been hoping that Jade would serve the same purpose but she was a lot tougher than Carlotta had been. . . .

'I can't believe Daddy did this to me! How could he go off with Rud and leave me behind? It was so mean!' D'Arcy complained to her mother as they sat having breakfast by themselves.

'I wasn't up when your father left this morning but I imagine he thought that he was being nice when he took Rud with him.'

D'Arcy savagely stabbed a sausage with her fork. 'I'm not saying he shouldn't have taken Rud. But why didn't he take me along too?'

Francesca didn't know if D'Arcy was feeling put out because she'd been deprived of Rud's company or her father's. She always had been jealous of her father's attention. 'I guess your father assumed you'd want to spend the day with Abigail and Jade.'

'Oh, I do,' D'Arcy took a healthy bite out of her buttered toast, 'but if I had had a choice, I would have picked Rud over them.'

So it *was* the lack of Rud's company she was bewailing. Well, she should have known, and it was natural enough, considering Rud's attractions. She'd been hoping that D'Arcy wouldn't get a crush on Rud – she pitied the girl who got involved with Judith's prize cub. But there was no point in making a fuss. He'd be gone in a few days and that was the wonderful thing about being sixteen . . . falling in and out of love a hundred times.

'You *do* like Abby and Jade then?'

'Sure, but between you and me, I think they're both a bit strange. At first Abby practically hung on me until Jade arrived, then she fell all over Jade, and then she acted like she had a case on Rud and then suddenly all she did was follow Judith around. What girl in her right mind would prefer Judith to Rud?'

Francesca sighed. *Maybe a girl in search of a mother.* 'And Jade? What do you find strange about her?'

'Well, when I first saw them together, I thought she was taken with Rud too, and frankly, I was worried. I mean she is spectacularly beautiful and all and I thought that she was going to beat my time with Rud for sure. But then yesterday, she was really snippy with him for no reason at all . . . like she

200

couldn't stand the sight of him which is just fine with me. But I don't think Rud understood it any more than I did.'

Francesca thought she understood it. Jade was more interested in staring into her Uncle Bill's baby blues than she was an eighteen-year-old's. Obviously, she found Rud's attractions paling in comparison whith those of an older, powerful man of the world. Carlotta always preferred the men to the boys. But then again, could one really call Trace a man?

'Look, D'Arcy, why can't all four of you just have fun together without all this romantic competition? After all, you're all cousins.'

'That would be fine,' D'Arcy giggled, 'if we were all girl cousins. But when one is a gorgeous male and he's only a *second* cousin, well, there is nature to be considered, Mother dear.' Then she grew serious again. 'And do you know what else is strange about Abby and Jade? They're so different. Abby is such a little goody-goody and Jade's . . . well, Jade's dynamite.'

'That's not strange. They had very different upbringings and different fathers.'

'I guess Jade must take after her mother and Abby doesn't. Aunt Carlotta was dynamite, wasn't she?'

The last thing Francesca wanted to discuss now was Carlotta. 'I suppose you could say that. Maybe that was the problem. . . .'

'Problem? Why do you say that? I'd say she had an absolutely fantastic life. She married Trace Boudin who looks just like Clark Gable and she herself was a fabulous movie star. I think she had a wonderful life.'

How wonderful could a life so brief be? 'I hope so, D'Arcy. I hope it was wonderful.' That was true enough. She had never forgiven Carlotta but she had never wished her an unhappy life.

'Mother, how come you never saw Aunt Carlotta again after she went to California?'

This wasn't the first time D'Arcy had asked this question, and it probably wouldn't be the last. But what was she to say? How did you tell a young girl that the sister you'd adored had betrayed you by making love with the very same man who was your husband and *her* father? You didn't. 'I'd rather not talk about that, D'Arcy. It's still much too painful for me. Carlotta's death is still much too fresh for me to talk about her.' That at least was the truth.

'And now, shall we plan our day? I want you to entertain the girls while I do my best to entertain Judith, if it kills me and it probably will.'

'Why don't you like Judith, Mother?'

'Oh, that's a long story, D'Arcy and I'm not up to it.'

'I wish you'd try and like her for my sake because I really like Rud and it would be wonderful if both our families got to see more of each other. They own a house here, you know, practically next door to the Kennedys. Wouldn't it be great if they started coming down every year?'

'Look, D'Arcy, you have a crush on Rud, but it's not going to last. I know it's a wonderful feeling to *think* you're in love and it's easy to be infatuated with a boy as good-looking as Rud, but you're going to be in love a hundred times before you're through.'

D'Arcy shook her head. 'I *know* it's the real thing.'

With all her heart Francesca hoped that it wasn't. She had the feeling that, even without Judith Stanton, Rud was the kind of boy who might very well break a girl's heart. As some girls were born to fall in love too easily, some boys were born to break girls' hearts. And if the boy had Judith Stanton for a mother, then double the poor girl's chances for a shattered heart.

Trace walked soundlessly down the hall to the girls' room. If he were lucky they'd be downstairs and he could duck in fast, find the damn diaries and be on his way to Miami in no time. He listened at the door. Damn! They were still in there. He could hear Jade's voice and then he realized that it wasn't a conversation he was listening to but a reading. Jade was reading to Abigail from Carlotta's diary.

> I look at Jade in her crib and I want to cry. It's not that she isn't darling or that I don't love her. Of course I do. But every time I look at her I can't help thinking of my darling Abigail back in Boston. I'll never be truly happy without her. Still, I know that she's better off where she is. That's what I must always remember. But all of me yearns for her. I think of her every day. No matter where I am I always see her sweet face before me and I hear her name floating on the breeze. Abigail!

Jade's voice broke and Abigail cried, 'But if she loved me so much why didn't she take me with her?'

'But I read you that passage when she's on the train and she wrote that she intended to send for you.'

'But she didn't!'

'No. She changed her mind once she got to California. You just heard me read that she knew you were better off in Boston.'

But Abigail wasn't mollified. Rather, the tears staining her cheeks, she practically shouted, 'Better off? What does that mean?'

Jade could barely keep back her own tears. 'I told you, Abby. Whenever I asked about you she always said the same thing – that you were with your father and his aunt and uncle and that they were very respected people in Boston, and that in order to understand what that meant I'd have to understand how Boston was. She said that it wasn't like California where everything was new and everyone came from other places. That Boston was a *real* place, with values and standards. She said you'd have the right kind of life and she had no right to disrupt that life just because she wanted you with her. That that would be very selfish of her.'

Selfish? That was a funny word to use, Abigail thought. All these years she'd assumed that if she knew her mother really loved her, it would be enough to make up for everything. But it wasn't true. It wasn't enough. Now that she had heard the actual words read to her from the diary, she knew that they were only words and words didn't make up for never having a mother.

What was it that Jade had said – that Boston was a real place with values and standards ... that she'd have the right kind of life ... therefore she,

Carlotta, had no right to disrupt it? . . . *That's bull! Just plain old bull!* Had her mother really believed that having a proper kind of life made up for a life without love? Did Jade believe it?

But she herself would act as if she believed it for Jade's sake. At least Jade acted as if she loved her.

'Let's go eat now, OK,' and while Abigail went to wash her face, Jade stuffed the diaries into a big leather duffel bag, and then added the few pieces of jewellery she'd brought with her. She wouldn't put it past Trace to try and steal the diaries or the jewellery either. She'd just have to tote the big bag along with her wherever she went.

They walked down the hall, arm in arm. 'Now you listen to me,' Jade said. 'Yesterday you left the Rud field completely open to D'Arcy while you went running after Judith. That's no way to get a guy, by running after his mother. You have to slug it out with D'Arcy, watch her every minute. She's pretty clever even if she acts like a scatterbrain – that's just an act – and if you're not careful, she'll leave you in the dust.'

'But—' She wanted to tell Jade the truth . . . that while she liked Rud, she didn't have a real crush on him.

'No buts. You saw what D'Arcy was doing yesterday. Lying all over him when they were making the beds. . . .'

'But I just *can't* do these things. I just wish that you—'

I wish you were in love with Rud and then I wouldn't have to go on with this charade!

But she couldn't admit to Jade that she had told her a lie. 'I wish it was you who had to do all this stuff. At least you'd know how to do it,' Abigail said ruefully and Jade forced herself to laugh. *Oh, Abby, how I wish it was me too!*

8.

'How nice!' Judith chirped as she entered the dining room. 'Just we ladies. . . .'

'We were just about finished,' Francesca said, 'but we'll be glad to keep you company while you have your breakfast.'

'Let me help you from the sideboard,' Abigail said, jumping to her feet. 'There's French toast—'

'I'll just have juice, toast and tea, dear.' She sat down. 'Jade, how pretty you look today. Do you always wear your pyjamas to breakfast?'

D'Arcy tittered but Jade in pink satin, just smiled. 'Aren't you familiar with lounging pyjamas, Judy? Everybody wears them to breakfast where I come from. I guess it's a Hollywood custom.'

'Ah yes, Hollywood,' Judith nodded. 'Where they make those images schoolgirls everywhere die to emulate. Is that your ambition, Jade – to be in films like your mother?'

'Maybe. What do you think of my chances? *You* must know all about the movie business.' Jade fixed Judith with a knowing stare.

'I? Why should I know anything about the film business?' Her tone was faintly amused but kind as if she were humouring a not-quite-bright child.

'Because you were part owner of Majestic Studios. . . .'

'*I* an owner of a movie studio? Hardly the type of investment I'd consider. Majestic Studios?' she repeated, as if mulling the name over in her mind. 'Isn't that the studio your mother was working for when she retired from the screen?'

Jade fought for control, trying not to scream. *Retired* was hardly the word. *Forced off the screen* was more like it.

It's all over. Now my career is gone too. The only thing that was really mine, besides Jade. Scotty says I'm through in films. I begged him. I got down on my hands and knees and begged. Even Trace begged. Of course he only wants the money and the reflected glory. Wants to show me off – his movie star wife. . . .

But not that it did any good. Even doing all the debasing, humiliating things I've always done for Scotty didn't help. He says there's nothing he can do. It's Judith who wants me out and Majestic is her baby. He says when it comes to the Studio, she's the boss. Judith! I knew she hated me but I didn't know she hated me enough to destroy me!

I don't know what I'll do with the rest of my life now. Just wait until those buzzards, Trace and Scott, devour me until there's nothing left? If only I could die . . . just cease to be! But then what will happen to Jade? I see Trace looking at her sometimes and I know what he's thinking. . . . How can he use her in the same way he's used me?

No, I won't let him! Jade vowed again, sitting there. *I won't let him and not Ross Scott and not you, Judith! I'll expose all of you!*

'Yes, Majestic was my mother's studio and I could have sworn that she said that *you*, Judith, had the controlling financial interest.'

'Well, I'm afraid your mother was in error.' Judith turned to Francesca. 'I can't imagine where anyone got the ridiculous idea that I would invest in the film industry.' She sipped the juice Abigail set before her. 'Some of Trace Boudin's nonsense, I suppose.' She laughed. 'Oh, I *am* sorry, Jade, but sometimes your father does get some fanciful ideas. Right, Frankie?'

Francesca didn't respond and Judith turned back to Jade. 'As a matter of fact, I don't have much interest in films altogether. I must confess I've never even seen any of your mother's pictures.'

The truth was she'd seen each and every one of them, some twice. She'd sat in the darkened theatre and watched Carlotta's image on the screen, as beautiful and glamorous as she'd been in life, as alluring as when Bill Sheridan had desired her above all else, and had determined to wipe that flawless face off the screen forever. It hadn't been difficult. Ross Scott was no less a whore than the two-buck hustler, Boudin, or Bill, the only difference being their price.

Wanting to change the subject, Francesca asked, 'Did Rud leave a note for you? He went off with Bill this morning, you know, to inspect the hurricane damage up north. . . .'

'Yes, I know. I told Rud that it didn't sound like fun to me, but if that was what he wanted to do—'

Francesca was surprised. 'You were up when they left?'

'Oh yes. I was catching up on some paper work. But speaking of the hurricane, how is it doing? Has it blown itself out yet?'

'I'm afraid not. It's hitting the New York and Jersey coastlines now and it's increased in velocity considerably but they're hoping it will dissipate itself before it reaches New England.'

'I certainly hope so,' Judith said as if the hurricane were a personal affront directed at her. 'But I'm so glad the sun is shining here. It does make all the difference.'

Jade went upstairs to change into something more appropriate since she, D'Arcy and Abby had agreed they'd go over to the Bath and Tennis Club and see what was happening there. D'Arcy thought a lot of her friends would be there.

She could tell immediately that someone had been in the room rummaging around since she had made sure that the spreads on the beds were just so before they'd gone down to breakfast, and the pillows perfectly plumped and aligned. Now one spread hung crookedly and the pillows were no longer perfect.

It was Trace. She really didn't think it was Judith's style to go sneaking around in bedrooms and it was Trace's. Still she wanted to make sure, and there was nothing like bearding the lions in their respective dens. Still toting her big leather bag, she made her way down the hall to the wing where Judith and Trace were staying.

Trace's door stood open and there was a maid making up the bed. 'Hi,' Jade said. 'My father's staying in this room. Have you seen him?'

'No ma'am. Haven't seen anybody.'

If he wasn't here and he hadn't come downstairs, where was he? Smiling a bit sheepishly at the maid, Jade went to the wardrobe to see if Trace's clothes were still there. They were. Most of them, anyway. Wherever he was, he planned on returning.

Then she knocked on Judith's door and heard a brisk, 'Enter.' Judith had already changed into yellow silk since she was going off with Francesca for the day. Bridge, lunch, cocktails.

Deciding she had nothing to lose at this stage, Jade launched a frontal attack. 'You searched my room.' An accusation, not a question. 'But of course you didn't find the diaries because I had them with me.'

Judith laughed. 'Oh, so that's the reason you're lugging that obscenely overlarge thing. So your diaries really do exist. But no, Jade, I didn't search your room. Sneaking in and out . . . opening drawers, peeking and peering . . . so messy and inefficient. Hardly. Besides, your diaries are of no interest to me.'

'They should be. I can expose you with them.'

Judith looked at Jade for a few seconds before saying, 'Sit down, Jade, and let's get this over with once and for all because, frankly, you're getting to be a terrible bore.'

Jade trembled with anger. 'When I'm done, you won't be bored, I promise you!' Still she sat down on the edge of the bed.

Judith remained standing, looming over Jade, having found this a psychologically effective tactic. 'So you want to drag out all my secrets. Why?'

'Why?' Was Judith crazy? 'To expose you! To everyone . . . to the world! To Rud!'

'But why do you want to do that?'

Is she so stupid? 'Revenge, that's why! For destroying my mother's life!'

Judith gave a short laugh. 'You're being very melodramatic and that's a mistake. Melodrama distorts everything out of perspective. I hadn't even seen your mother for years before she died.'

'But you didn't have to *see* her, did you? All you had to do was pull strings. *You* destroyed her, all right, with Ross Scott's and Trace's help. The three of you did it.'

And Francesca. I mustn't forget Francesca.

In spite of herself, the tears began to flow. 'Why did you do it? She never did anything to you!'

'Since we're letting our hair down I'll be completely honest with you, Jade. I always despised your mother from the time we were little girls. She was such a smug little girl, so arrogant. She didn't give a damn about anyone else. And she was such a little show-off with her red curls and pretty dresses, her dancing and singing. And she was greedy. Always wanting everything for herself – all the attention, all the admiration, all the love. And then when she grew up, it was still the same. Then she wanted all the men, whether she loved them or not. Oh yes, I hated Carlotta, but destroy her? I didn't have to. She destroyed herself.'

'No! It was you! Without you there wouldn't have been a Trace or a Scotty. You threw her to those vultures who sucked her dry. You handed her over to them like a piece of bloody meat!'

'Keep your voice down, Jade. Do you want everyone to hear you? The servants? Do you want everyone to know that the glamorous, legendary Carlotta Boudin was nothing more than a gangster's slut?'

Jade lunged at her with long painted fingernails, but Judith, cool, managed to sidestep the assault and Jade fell back on the bed in a crumpled heap.

'Now listen to me, Jade, because I'm sick of this conversation. If your mother hadn't been a tramp to start with, I couldn't have touched her. What was the title of her last movie – *Born to be Bad?* Well, that about sums up Carlotta. Nobody *makes* a bad woman. I didn't even introduce your mother to Trace. He simply came to my party as did your mother and they flew to each other, like birds of a feather. A deadly attraction.'

'No, she wasn't bad,' Jade cried. 'She was . . . foolish, that's all. Lots of girls fall for the wrong men. She was just foolish and you took advantage of that.'

'I didn't stand behind the bed with a whip and force her to submit to Ross Scott, did I? I didn't tie her hands or force her thighs apart or spread her cheeks or pry her lips open to receive him. . . .'

'Stop!' Jade covered her ears but Judith was deliberately relentless. '*I* didn't turn her into a whore and a slut.'

'No,' Jade sobbed. 'Not a whore, not a slut!'

'Then why didn't she resist?'

'She couldn't. . . . She was afraid. She had nowhere to turn.'

'Other women find a way when they really want to. And that movie business? Yes, I ordered her contract to be terminated, but what of it? Other stars have had their contracts terminated and they turned around and went to other studios, or formed their own production companies, went into television. Why didn't she?'

'She couldn't,' Jade said piteously. 'She was too tired, too weak. She was a wounded spirit. . . .'

She was a beautiful bird with brilliant plumage but her wings were damaged. She could only fall. . . .

'And why did she abandon her daughter? What kind of a mother does that? You hold me responsible but did I force her to abandon her child because Trace crooked his nasty little finger?'

'She never *meant* to abandon Abby. When she went to California, she intended to get her back.'

'Intended? But she never did, did she?'

Jade could feel her strength returning. 'No, she didn't, but then, she couldn't, could she, if she were really a good mother? Any good mother would protect her daughter from Trace Boudin . . . keep her from knowing that Trace was her real father. But of course for a different reason than you yourself want to keep your son from knowing that Bill Sheridan is his father.'

Seeing the muscle twitch in Judith's cheek, Jade knew she was on the right track. 'He . . . Bill . . . is the real reason you wanted to destroy Mother, isn't he? I'm right, aren't I? Bill fathered your son . . . maybe you even loved him. I don't know about that. I don't even know if you're capable of love. But since you yourself couldn't have him, you wanted to make damn sure Mother didn't have him either. Right?'

When Judith didn't answer her, Jade took that as an affirmation. 'But why Mother and not Francesca? I'm sure you don't like her either and she's the one who ended up with him . . . who married him. Why Carlotta and not Francesca?'

Judith smiled oddly. She could be completely honest with Jade. She had nothing to lose. 'Because Francesca doesn't matter. She never did. Carlotta was the one Bill always loved. There was nothing he wouldn't have done for her. He would have even thrown his career away for her.'

But it was time to wrap this conversation up. She sat down on the bed next to Jade. 'I think you're a lot smarter than your mother, so I'm going to summarize this for you and I hope you get it straight. All that stuff in your diary about my having done business with Ross Scott doesn't amount to anything. There's no proof anywhere. It's what they call "hearsay," and in this case only the doubtful declarations of an unstable woman. So the only real revelation that has any substance to it is that Bill is Rud's father. So let us consider. Again there's no proof and Bill will hardly substantiate it. Carlotta is dead and all he could do now would be to lose what he has – his wife, his daughter, possibly his career. And Rud, in the end, will believe me because he *has to* – you see, without me, he has nothing. So what will you have accomplished?' She paused for emphasis.

'I'll tell you what. You will have forced me to retaliate by telling your secret – yours and Carlotta's – that Trace Boudin is really Abigail's father. And then what will you have done but *undo* the one and only good thing your mother ever did in her life – protect Abigail from Trace as a father? Poor Carlotta! She made a choice for little Abby, and gave her Whit Truesdale, a wise choice but all in vain. . . .

'So actually now you have to make the choice for Abigail all over again. Trace Boudin or the Truesdales? Because I assure you, if you tell I tell, and if I tell, the Truesdales will most surely disown her, and then where will Abby be?

In badman's land, just like you. I guess you're really the unlucky one. You never did have much of a choice, did you?'

Checkmate!

Judith was right. The decision was hers. Revenge on Judith, or protecting Abby from the awful truth? Did she have a choice?

And then Jade perceived Judith's real strength — the ability to read people . . . to know what they'd do under a given circumstance. She had known what Carlotta would do when she laid eyes on Trace . . . fall under his spell. And she'd known what Carlotta would do when confronted with the other devil, in the form of Ross Scott. As she knew that she, Jade, would back off, and choose her sister's salvation over revenge. . . .

She picked up her duffel bag, ready to leave. 'I might be making a poor bargain. Trace himself might lower the boom on Abby.'

'He won't. Trust me. I can take care of Boudin.'

Jade believed her. Judith could probably take care of anybody. She was the devil, and she herself had just made a pact with her. But she'd done the best she could.

'And if I were you, Jade, I'd just burn those diaries. As I told you, I'll watch out for your sister, and time will take care of Scott and Trace. . . .'

What about you, Judith? Who or what will take care of you?

But all she said was, 'Why, Judith? Why will you take care of Abby?'

Judith looked surprised. 'Because that's part of the deal we just made. We have made a deal, haven't we? Besides, I like Abby. I like her a lot. She's everything I would wish for in a daughter. She's a lady, she's sweet, innocent and docile.'

Docile! Was that the key word then? Jade wondered.

She went to the door and Judith called after her. 'One more thing, Jade. Stay away from my son.'

Jade turned around. 'Since you have your son completely under your control, wouldn't it be simpler to tell him to stay away from me?'

'I'm not sure. After all you *are* Carlotta's daughter and he *is* Bill's son. It might be difficult.'

'If I were you, Judith, I think I'd be more concerned about D'Arcy. After all, *she's* her father's daughter just like Rud is his father's son. . . .'

And Judith thought, yes, this one's a lot smarter than her mother ever was. . . .

9.

Rud had had a wonderful day with Bill who had treated him like a man, not a boy. He'd asked his opinion on everything, and had evaluated each and every answer. What a difference from the way his mother treated him, the difference being one mainly of respect. Still, all day he hadn't been able to get Jade off his mind. Why had she suddenly done an about-face? Why, after Saturday night, when she'd clearly made love to him with her eyes, had she treated him with derision on Sunday?

By the time they returned to La Casa del Presidente, he was so worked up, he was ready to make a grab for her the moment he saw her, and demand to know why. But it was almost seven by then, and time to change for dinner. It seemed

208

Francesca had invited two couples for dinner, Pamela and Steven Boch and Ginny and Seth Mars.

All through the first course, Rud tried to catch Jade's eye, but she concentrated on her curried oysters, sipping continuously on her wine, and didn't glance his way even once.

He thought she looked especially spectacular in a one-shouldered sweep of pleated white chiffon and her hair piled on her head in a seemingly careless profusion of curls, wisps and tendrils with a jewelled band encircling her forehead. Like some mysterious, sexy Egyptian princess, he mused, who had somehow materialized at their twentieth-century dinner party.

Ginny Mars must have been on the receiving end of his thought waves because she asked Jade if her dress was one of Neil Chapman's 'Daughters of the Nile' collection she'd seen recently in New York. 'I swear, honey, you look like you just jumped off some Egyptian barge to join us.'

Jade laughed. 'If that's the case, who's my Mark Antony?' She made a show of looking from one man to the other, deliberately bypassing Rud and allowing her gaze to linger on Bill. 'But no, my gown isn't from any recent collection. It was my mother's. She wore it to the opening of the Jade in Las Vegas. I know because I have a picture of her wearing it that night. . . .'

She knew every detail of the picture by heart. Carlotta in the Egyptian-style gown, hanging on to Ross Scott's arm, he unsmiling, Carlotta laughing into the camera. A couple of steps behind was Trace, carrying Carlotta's white fur, bringing up the rear although he was supposedly the owner of the hotel and casino. Carlotta always laughed for the cameras, or at least smiled brilliantly, a smile brilliant as diamonds, as brilliant as tears, Jade reflected, sipping her consommé and signalling the butler to refill her glass.

'And that dress you wore Saturday night?' Pamela Boch asked. 'That was your mother's too?'

D'Arcy, the film expert, answered for Jade. 'That was the dress from the movie, *Born to be Bad*,' and now she signalled the butler to refill *her* wine glass and Francesca frowned. She really didn't like any underage youngster having wine at dinner but Bill always said that a civilized glass of wine never hurt anyone. But while D'Arcy was her concern, Jade wasn't. She was Trace's and she couldn't see him objecting to his daughter drinking wine. And where had he disappeared to without a word to anyone? How nice if he'd just picked himself up and gone back to California. It was just too bad he hadn't taken Jade with him and then everyone would stop talking about Carlotta.

But it seemed like they weren't going to do that. Now Ginny Mars wanted to know if Jade still had all her mother's dresses. 'From all her movies?'

'Most of them. Usually the Studio gave her the dresses to keep. I'm going to give half the collection to Abby.'

Abigail's cheeks flamed red. 'But they won't fit me, Jade. I'm taller. You might as well keep them all since they fit you so well.'

Rud accepted more wine as Andrew the butler walked about the table, unobtrusively refilling the glasses. Jade was probably just putting on an act, pretending she was put out with him. It was an act with which he wasn't unfamiliar. The younger girls frequently pulled it, thinking it got a guy crazy so that he'd end up begging them to forgive him for some imaginary slight.

Then, finally, inadvertently, their eyes met for a second, and it was a shock to Rud to see in Jade's eyes an intense longing. But then, quickly, a veil came down over those green eyes, shutting him out again, so thick a veil that he could almost touch it.

He heard Judith ask Jade a question . . . an innocuous one, but her tone was most pleasant. And he'd thought she didn't like Jade. And then he heard Jade answer her in an even pleasanter tone. What was going on here? Was there something he had missed? He could have sworn that Jade hated his mother.

Jade, sipping the Cabernet Sauvignon served with the breast of duck in a blackcurrant sauce, reflected on the situation too. *Here we are acting like the best of friends . . . me and one of the two women who ruined my mother's life. Incredible!*

I'm sorry, Mother, but I think I did the right thing, the only thing I could do . . . taking care of Abby, even if I had to make a pact with the devil to do it. Just like you did.

As for Rud Stanton, I'm sure I'll get over him one of these days, won't I?

The conversation over *demi-tasse* and liqueurs centred on the hurricane. Bill said that the damage on the Southern seaboard had been minimal compared with the havoc wrought in New Jersey, New York and Connecticut.

'Have you heard anything about Newport?' Judith asked, concerned about her house there.

'No, not Newport *per se*, but all the beaches in Massachusetts are taking a terrific beating.'

'Oh, I hope Aunt Selena and Uncle George went home before the storm hit! They were vacationing on the North Shore. Have you heard anything about the North Shore, Uncle Bill?' Abigail asked, worried.

'I'm afraid not, honey. The reports just aren't that specific.'

'Your aunt and uncle are very responsible, Abby,' Judith reassured her. 'I'm sure the moment they heard the storm was on its way, they packed up and went home to their nice, safe brick house. And you know what everyone says about a good brick house in Boston – it's impervious to both storm and man. Isn't that so, Frankie?'

Francesca smiled thinly. 'I really don't remember. It's been such a long time since I was in Boston.'

She suggested a game of bridge for the older set after dinner, leaving the young people to entertain themselves. She was figuring on two tables until she realized that without the children, they were only seven.

'Oh, Rud will make an eight,' Judith offered. 'He's an excellent player.'

Now he was really going to choke her, Rud thought. What was she trying to do? Sabotage him? Now he was going to be stuck with the fogies all night instead of having a little fun with the girls. Just before they'd sat down to dinner, D'Arcy had whispered that she had managed to score a few joints at the club that afternoon, enough for a real party. 'Say what you will about the area being invaded by Cubans, I can see a vast improvement in many areas,' she'd giggled.

But then Abby begged, 'Oh, let me play instead of Rud. I can be your partner, Judith. I often make up a fourth for Aunt Selena and Uncle George. They say I'm quite good.'

'To tell the truth, Judy, you'll be better off with Abby. I'm really pooped.' He could kiss Abby, he thought, and then he did and she turned pink with pleasure. It was going to be a great evening. She was going to be Judith's partner, and then later, when it was time for bed, she'd be alone with Jade again. A really perfect evening!

'You two just sit here while I get the goods,' D'Arcy whispered when the three of them were in the upstairs library, while she stood at the door waiting for the two patrolling State troopers to move on down the corridor. 'You wouldn't *believe* where I've stashed the merchandise,' she giggled, 'and I'll spare you the grisly details. Believe me, it's like living with a bunch of bloodhounds between my mother and these Nazis outside. I'll be right back. Just don't start without me,' she leered.

Once she was out the door, Rud grinned at Jade. 'What do you think she meant by don't start without her?'

Jade shrugged. She was uncomfortable with Rud sitting so close to her on the sofa. She was too warm and she'd had too much wine. Her head was swimming. She closed her eyes, leaned her head back against the cool leather. Perhaps she should just go to bed, she thought, as Rud moved closer to her, his arm beginning to encircle her shoulder, his fingers caressing her skin.

'Don't. . . .' What was wrong with him? Hadn't she discouraged him? Hadn't he taken the hint? She edged an inch or so away from him but he moved closer again, keeping his arm where it was .' I want to and you want me to, don't you?' His lips went to her shoulder. 'Don't you like me?'

'I do. I did— I mean—'

He kissed her closed eyelids. 'Then why do you act like you don't?'

'I don't know.' Her head was reeling. 'You have to stop—'

'Why? Why do I have to stop?' His lips travelled down the contours of her face toward her throat.

'Because we mustn't. . . .' But when his lips reached the hollow of her throat her neck arched the better to receive them.

'Why mustn't we?' he breathed against her skin as his lips travelled towards her mouth. His mouth found hers and he exulted over how perfectly they fitted each other, his lips and hers. He opened his mouth and his tongue prised her lips open and they parted to let his tongue enter, to take possession as if that were its divine right.

Then his mouth began moving down. 'I love you,' he murmured.

'No, you can't!'

'But I do! Why can't I?' One hand pulled the gown off her shoulder and then down, while his mouth pushed the material from her breast and his other hand reached up to caress it.

'Stop!' she cried, but she didn't move, didn't push either his mouth or his hand away.

'Say it . . .' he said, lifting his head for a moment. 'Say you love me too. I know you do! I felt it the minute I saw you. I felt it . . . that you loved me and that I loved you. You felt it too. Say you did!' And his mouth went back to her exposed breast, encircling her nipple, sucking and licking.

Her hands moved to fondle his bent head, his hair, the back of his neck. And she forgot everything – Judith . . . Abby. She even forgot the reason she'd come to Palm Beach in the first place. 'I love you too . . .' she whispered.

They had a few seconds of warning since they could hear D'Arcy exchanging remarks with one of the security men right outside the library door. They jumped to opposite sides of the sofa, and Jade adjusted her gown. And then suddenly, she was clear-headed and sober, and furious with herself. How could she have so forgotten herself? In a few ridiculous minutes she'd chanced endangering Abby's whole future, undoing all she'd done to discourage Rud. Now she'd just have to do it all over again. And now it was going to be twice as hard. He had told her he loved her and she had told him that she loved him back. . . . Twice as hard, twice as painful.

D'Arcy barged in holding up a little paper sack triumphantly and locked the door behind her. She put a stack of records on the stereo without taking the time to choose and pick. Then she laid out the joints on the coffee table in front of the sofa along with a couple of matchboxes, and sat herself down in the middle of the sofa between them.

Sneaking a look at Jade, Rud saw that her mouth was set in a hard line and she appeared angry. *God! What was she mad about now? Because D'Arcy sat herself down between us? What does she want me to do?* Was he supposed to say something to D'Arcy? Tell her that he wanted to sit next to Jade? But then she'd probably be mad about that too. He began to suspect that she was the kind of girl who was never satisfied no matter what a guy did. He'd met that kind before. But he was stuck with her no matter what. He loved her! God, he loved her! And she'd told him she loved him too. And the joy of that filled him so, he thought he'd burst.

If only they could be alone. . . . Maybe later, he consoled himself. Maybe the pot would make D'Arcy sleepy and she'd go to bed and leave them alone. . . . 'What are you waiting for? Fire up!' he told D'Arcy.

Jade got to her feet a little unsteadily. 'By all means, D'Arcy, fire up! Children must play. But personally, I'm going to bed. Or maybe I'll read a good book.'

Rud's mouth hung open. *What is it with her?*

'Great balls of fire, Jade, I never took you for one of these mealy-mouthed moralistic goody-goodies,' D'Arcy shook her head in disgust.

Jade smiled. 'But it has nothing to do with morals. It just has to do with plain old boredom. I can't think of anything more boring than trying to get high with a couple of refugees from the playpen. It's all so juvenile. But do be careful not to get caught, kiddies. Your mother, D'Arcy, would probably be disappointed in you since she seems to be a moralistic, high-minded type. And you Rud, you don't want Mommy to rap you across your little baby-boy knuckles? Now, nighty-night to you both. Do have fun but don't get carried away. I hear tell that marijuana sometimes has some pretty weird effects on children.'

She closed the door gently behind her, but then once out in the hall, she ran for her room trying to hold back her tears until she found cover.

'Did you *ever*?' D'Arcy rolled her eyes at Rud. 'What's wrong with her, you think? What got into her?'

He knew what was wrong with her! She was just a bitch, a class A bitch! But he felt like crying. 'Nothing got into her. She's just a bitch. There are a lot of girls like her.'

'I'm not.'

He was full of rage but he turned his luminous smile on D'Arcy. 'I know you're not.' He leaned over and kissed her. 'And what do we really care about her? It just means no pot for her and more for us. . . . So let's light up!'

'In a minute. . . . First I have to even the score.' She put her arms around his neck and kissed him, first softly and then more intensely.

The Bochs and the Marses had gone home, the security men were locking up downstairs after having made their routine check of the grounds, and Abigail, Judith, Francesca and Bill all went upstairs together. 'It's quiet as a graveyard up here,' Bill said. 'The kids must have gone to bed.'

'But it's not like Rud not to say goodnight to me first,' Judith observed, mildly annoyed over this lapse.

'I guess they were pretty well knocked out—' Francesca offered, but she was surprised. It usually took about two hours of arguing and a derrick to get D'Arcy into bed, no matter what. 'I'll just check to make sure. D'Arcy always forgets to turn off the lights.'

'The men will do that—' Bill said impatiently, eager to get to bed. It had been a particularly long, exhausting day. 'Besides, the world won't come to an end if the lights are left on one night.'

'But I'm right here. I might as well—'

OK, OK, if you must.' Bill turned to Judith and Abigail with a tired smile. 'Frankie thinks her daughter is physically incapable of turning off the lights, the TV, even a faucet. . . .'

'Oh, hush.' Francesca opened the library door as Bill, Judith and Abigail stood by as if it really was a matter of suspense if the lights had been left on or not. But the room was in complete darkness.

'Satisfied?' Bill asked.

'Not quite, Mr Smarty-Pants. The stereo's making a noise. It wasn't turned off. And what's that funny smell in here?' Her hand groped for the wall switch which flooded the room with an overhead light and then she gasped.

Bill and Judith with Abigail bringing up the rear came rushing up to see Rud, his length stretched out on the sofa, awaken slowly, blinking into the strong light. His body half-covered the still sleeping D'Arcy, one of his legs wedged between her two.

'D'Arcy!' Bill cried out.

'Amazing!' Judith drawled.

'What's so amazing?' Francesca snapped, already feeling defensive about D'Arcy.

'That it's your daughter lying there and not Carlotta's.'

Abigail, who knew what the strange smell in the room was, fled down the hall towards her room. She was only grateful that it *was* D'Arcy lying there, and not Carlotta's daughter Jade. Judith looked really mad and she didn't want Judith, no matter what, to be mad at her sister Jade.

10.

Bill was the first one up the next morning. Actually he'd never fallen asleep, and then after a couple of hours of futile tossing and turning, he'd gone into the sitting room adjoining his and Francesca's bedroom, poured himself about three inches of bourbon and eventually watched the sun come up over the ocean. He was mad at everybody – Rud and Frankie and Judith, but mostly he was furious with his daughter. How could she have done this to him? While he didn't blame Frankie for resenting Judith's implication that D'Arcy was a tramp, Judith wasn't far off. Under the circumstances, he himself was shocked and revolted by his daughter's behaviour and it didn't help to tell himself that she didn't know Rud was her brother. Mostly, he was embarrassed before Judith. He'd never dreamed that this would happen!

D'Arcy had ruined everything for everybody by her behaviour and to top it off, Frankie was mad at him for giving her a tongue-lashing, instead of being angry with D'Arcy as she should have been. But worse than Frankie's anger was Judith's. She'd served notice that she was packing up and going home. He wished he could just say *good riddance*, but he couldn't! Not when she was taking Rud with her.

At least Rud had done the right thing. He'd acted like a man, taking all the blame on his shoulders, even for the pot, insisting he'd brought it with him from Boston. Not that anyone believed him. And how could anyone really blame the boy? It was up to the girl to set the pace.

And where did Frankie get off being mad at him? None of this would have happened if she'd raised D'Arcy to be a little more strait-laced. Like Abigail! Shit, even Trace Boudin's daughter could be raised to act like a lady, but not his own!

Still, Frankie was right about one thing, even if she didn't have all the facts – Judith *was* making too much of a big thing out of it. Sure, the threat of incest was there, but nothing happened! Rud swore that nothing happened and he for one believed him even if he wouldn't take D'Arcy's word for it. The kids had had a glass or two of wine too many at the dinner table, and then on top of it, the pot, and then they'd been left alone. So they fooled around a little. Hell, it could happen with any two kids under the same circumstances. He just had to convince Judith that it wouldn't ever happen again.

If only Jade hadn't gone to bed and left them alone! Actually, he, too, like Judith, would have thought it would be Jade and not D'Arcy lying there. He could have sworn that the boy had a yen for Jade. For God's sake, D'Arcy was like a baby compared to Jade.

He checked his watch. It was nearly seven. He had to go talk to Judith before anyone else was up. Certainly before Frankie awakened. He peered out the door to make sure that his security men weren't anywhere around.

'All bets are off,' Judith told him. 'I must have been insane to think this would work out.'

'You're acting on impulse. Think it over.'

214

'I have . . . all through the night. I acted on impulse when I decided to come. That's when I made a mistake.'

He tried cajoling her, putting his arms around her, pressing himself against her, whispering into her ear.

'It won't work. The situation is untenable.' It was, and she had to keep that in mind. She'd allowed her own desires to colour her good judgement, and she couldn't afford to do that. She'd done without Bill Sheridan for all these years, she'd have to discipline herself to continue doing just that. Too much was at stake.

'Nothing happened. I'm sure of it.'

'It doesn't matter. The situation is potential dynamite. Sooner or later Rud and D'Arcy would see each other again. For God's sake, they're brother and sister! I don't care how far they did or didn't go. The risk is there and I will not take the risk. I'm leaving today!'

'You won't be able to get on a plane today.'

'We arrived by private plane. It's standing ready.'

'They won't let it take off. All the airports north of Washington are closed straight up to Maine.'

'In that case, I'll take the train.'

'You can't. They're not even running as far north as Washington.'

'Then I'll hire a car and driver. Even if I kept Rud in quarantine until we left, the situation with Frankie is impossible. It's too bad she found my remarks about D'Arcy so offensive but what did she think I'd say? She really should have taught her daughter better . . . to keep her skirts down, or at the very least, to keep her thighs together.'

Ordinarily, hearing these words about his daughter from anyone – man or woman – he would have lashed out. But he himself was mad at D'Arcy for doing this to him, and this was Judith in whose power he was . . . would be for a long time, so he only mumbled. 'Come on, Judith . . . they both said nothing happened.'

'Maybe nothing did, but then again, who can believe either one of them? Rud is being a gentleman trying to protect a girl whose honour is questionable in the first place,' she snapped. 'As for D'Arcy, what *would* she say? What did Carlotta ever say that convinced you her honour was intact?'

Bill's intention was to slip back quietly into his bedroom but Francesca was up, sitting at her dressing table, brushing her hair hard. 'And where were you visiting at this hour?' she demanded. 'Don't tell me. Let me guess. You were talking to Judith, apologizing for your daughter being a whore?'

'Hold on, Frankie! No one used that word—'

'So you weren't doing that? I know. You had a change of heart and decided to act like any other father would who had found his daughter with an older, more sophisticated man? You were in Rud's room then, reading him the riot act?'

'No, I wasn't apologizing to Judith and no, I wasn't reading the riot act to Rud. As far as I'm concerned, this whole thing is a tempest in a teapot!' God, how he wished it were!

'Good. I couldn't agree with you more. If both you and Judith didn't start putting all the blame on D'Arcy, I would have thought nothing of the whole thing. So a couple of kids were making out a little and then they fell asleep. Big deal! They should have both been called on the carpet for smoking marijuana and that should have been the end of it. I would have grounded D'Arcy on that score and Judith could have done whatever she damned pleased. But to make this whole thing filthy with obscene implications— And then to have you back up Judith! Why was it D'Arcy's fault and not Rud's? Why is it always the girl's fault?' As soon as the words were out of her mouth, she was hit with a pain . . . a memory. . . .

I don't blame Bill. It was you, Carlotta, you!

Carlotta replying: It was me. . . . Don't blame Bill but forgive me!

She, too, had blamed the girl, and not forgiven.

Her tone was softer now. 'So where were you so early this morning? Apologizing to D'Arcy for how you spoke to her?'

'No, I don't think I'm quite ready to go that far. I *was* talking to Judith. I was just trying to talk her out of leaving . . . to just give it a chance to cool down around here.'

'I see. That's what I said in the first place. You were with Judith, begging her to stay, apologizing for D'Arcy's behaviour.'

Oh God, Frankie! You just don't know the half of it.

Francesca called down to the kitchen, ordered a pot of coffee, told the housekeeper not to bother setting up the breakfast buffet – whoever showed up for breakfast this morning could just ask for whatever it was they wanted. Then she went into the sitting room where Bill sat staring dejectedly out the window, not dressed or shaved, and she found that old habits died hard. 'You should have something to eat. I'll have the kitchen send up a tray.'

Don't bother. I have my breakfast.' He held up a glass half full of bourbon. This answer only refuelled her anger and she swept out of the room. There had to be something more here than met the eye. Why was he so despondent? In the course of his career, he'd been up, he'd been down, he'd suffered major setbacks and immediately came back fighting. And now to be crushed over . . . *what?* Two kids making out and smoking a little pot? Judith going home before the week was over?

Why, she hadn't seen him taking anything so badly in years . . . not since Carlotta had taken up with Trace Boudin.

Judith called down to the kitchen to have her breakfast sent up on a tray, along with a copy of the Yellow Pages. She'd find a car and driver to take them to Boston if it was the last thing she did. Then she went to Rud's room, to tell him to pack his bags. After one sharp rap she walked in to find him still asleep. She walked over to the bed fully intending to wake him but looking at him asleep, his hair rumpled, the long eyelashes curling on his cheek, she could feel herself soften. She'd let him sleep. She still had to find a car and driver.

When he heard Judith leave the room, Rud's eyes flew open. She was the last person he was in the mood to see this morning. Although it was Bill who had lost his cool last night, it had been Judith who had precipitated the whole fuss.

Christ! You would have thought he'd been found in bed with the Virgin Mary. Correction: it was more like he was the virgin who'd been raped by the whore Magdalene. Actually it was poor D'Arcy who had caught all the fire even though his mother had still managed, as usual, to make him look like a real asshole.

And the fuck of it was there hadn't even been a fuck! Not that there might not have been if he'd been more into it. D'Arcy had been hot to trot, he guessed, but he himself had been hotter under the collar about the way Jade had acted, than he'd been hot for D'Arcy's body. The whole goddamn thing was really her fault – Jade's! If she hadn't suddenly iced up on him, walked out on him after he'd told her he loved her and she had said she loved him, he wouldn't have been there on that couch diddling around with D'Arcy. The poor kid. She hadn't cried when his mother had cast her aspersion, or even when Bill had really dressed her down. But then when Judith said she was going home, she'd burst into tears, making him feel even guiltier than he already did. She really had feelings for him.

But as far as leaving was concerned, that was fine with him. He'd just as soon go home and forget that Jade even existed!

Abigail couldn't wait for Jade to awaken. As soon as she saw Jade stir, she sat down on the bed and blurted: 'You missed it!'

Jade stretched. 'What did I miss?'

'D'Arcy and Rud being caught sleeping on the couch together.'

Jade sat up straight, fully, sickeningly awake. 'Last night?'

'Yes. We all went upstairs together after Aunt Francesca's friends went home. Me and Judith and Aunt Frankie and Uncle Bill. It was very quiet when we got upstairs but Aunt Frankie wanted to check and she opened the library door and it was dark so she put on the light and there they were there— On the couch, asleep and the room smelled like a druggie's paradise and his leg was in between her legs.'

Jade closed her eyes. She wanted to ask Abby if D'Arcy was wearing panties, if Rud's fly was open, but she couldn't bring herself to do it. She thought maybe she was going to throw up. She concentrated on fighting down her nausea, wished she could pull the covers over her head and go back to sleep. She had had all kinds of crazy dreams, but now the reality was the nightmare. 'Then what happened?' she asked dully.

'Uncle Bill yelled out, "D'Arcy!" and Judith said, "Amazing"'

'Amazing? What did she mean by that?'

'She said it was amazing that it was D'Arcy who was lying there and not Carlotta's daughter, and I guess she didn't mean *me*.'

'No,' Jade laughed bitterly. 'I guess she didn't.'

This was all her fault. She'd driven Rud to it. She'd pushed him into it. She should have seen what was going to happen and done something to stop it instead of pushing Rud into doing to D'Arcy what she really wanted him to do to her. *If only*— But what the use of thinking about *if*. . . . She'd done the only thing she could. Abby was in love with Rud and Judith had ordered her to stay away from Rud if she wanted her help in protecting Abby from Trace.

'You mustn't be too upset about all this, Abby. Sometimes these things just happen. You know how it is. They just got carried away, went further than they intended. It doesn't mean anything necessarily. . . .'

'Oh, I know and I'm not upset. Not *that* upset. I mean if he's the kind of boy who's only interested in sex, well— To tell you the truth, Jade, when Judith said that – you know – about how she was amazed that it was D'Arcy with Rud instead of you, the only thing I really felt was relief. Relief that it was D'Arcy and not *you!* I wouldn't want Judith to think that you were that kind of a girl. After all, D'Arcy's only my cousin but you're my sister. You're the one I really love!'

'And I love you.' But as she hugged Abby, she thought how she still wished it was she herself who had felt Rud Stanton's loving arms around her . . . had felt his love inside her.

'But you haven't told me what happened after that. After Judith said it was amazing. . . . What did Rud and D'Arcy have to say for themselves?'

'Oh, I didn't wait to see. I just ran to bed.'

And then Jade thought that poor Abby was just putting on an act about not being that concerned. She *had* been terribly hurt. Otherwise why would she have run off to bed? . . .

Rud quickly donned a pair of jeans and a sweatshirt. The least he could do before he went home was to try and square things for D'Arcy. He doubted that either Bill and Francesca were convinced that nothing had really happened. Or Judith. But all Judith really cared about was not that he had allegedly screwed D'Arcy but that he had screwed at all. If Judith had her way, he'd be celibate until he was forty at which time he could go for it – once – just to produce an heir. Then, that way, she'd have another poor turkey to sink her hooks into. . . .

Besides squaring things for D'Arcy, he wanted to apologize to Bill and Francesca. He didn't want them to think he was just another rich kid who took advantage of a young, infatuated girl . . . a selfish bastard who thought only of his cock.

Francesca wasn't pleased to see Rud at her door. While she hadn't disliked him on sight, she'd been nervous about him from the start, apprehensive about his startling good looks and almost professional charm, knowing somehow that being Judith's son, he would be trouble. And as it turned out, she'd been right. While she was satisfied that nothing really monumental had transpired between him and D'Arcy, the fact remained that something disturbing *had* happened, something that had disrupted the harmony of her home, something ugly.

'I came to apologize to you, Aunt Frankie.'

'It's not necessary,' she said stiffly.

'But it's necessary for me. While the whole thing was nothing more than a few kisses, I still feel responsible in that—'

'You don't have to say anything more, Rud. I'm convinced nothing happened so there's nothing you have to feel responsible for. A few kisses . . . nothing really so earthshattering.' She forced herself to smile.

'But I didn't want anyone to think badly of D'Arcy. I should have acted in a more responsible fashion. It was up to me to remember that I was a guest in your house and that I shouldn't be kissing your daughter no matter how pretty she is or how tempting the kisses. . . .' He smiled ingenuously. 'As for the marijuana . . . what can I say except that it was a stupid, immature act on my part to bring it with me in the first place and then share it with D'Arcy? Please don't blame her. Blame me and please forgive me.'

Ah, but forgiveness is not my strong suit, Mr Stanton. Still, she felt her position towards Rud softening. He sounded sincere. Warm. In all fairness, was he to be held accountable for being Judith's son? And to blame him? For what? For kissing a pretty girl? Even a little *more* than kissing which it probably had been? The marijuana was something else again but somehow, she felt sure it was D'Arcy who had supplied it. But even that wasn't so terrible either. All the kids tried it, sooner or later, at least once. An experiment of youth. So what was his crime? Being too charming, too good-looking?

Poor D'Arcy. No wonder she was attracted to him. What red-blooded girl could resist him? No more than she could have resisted Bill Sheridan. . . . And then she felt a wave of sadness. Not that the incident had occurred, but only how it had all turned out. It could have been a sweet little interlude for D'Arcy . . . a brief, romantic flirtation with love that she could have looked back on later with fond remembrance. . . .

'I'm sorry that it all ended like this . . .'

'I am too, Rud,' and impulsively she kissed him on the cheek.

Francesca knocked on D'Arcy's door.

'Go away, whoever you are.'

'It's your mother, D'Arcy.' She tried the door. It was locked. 'Come on honey, let me in. I didn't come to scold you.'

At least her mother had stuck up for her last night. D'Arcy unlocked the door and then ran back to bed. When Francesca saw her face, red and swollen from crying, she cried out, 'Oh, D'Arcy!'

'I just want you to know one thing, Mother. I'm never going to forgive your husband for the things he said to me. And in front of Rud!'

Francesca hugged her. 'He really didn't mean them. He was just upset. And you don't have to call him my husband. He's still your father.'

'Don't defend him! You always defend him no matter what he does and I hate that. Why can't you once say he's wrong? Say I love him but say he's wrong!'

'All right. I love him but he was wrong this time.'

'Then you believe me? That we barely made out?'

'Yes, I believe you.'

'What was the big deal all about?'

'I think it was about Judith . . . that your father was embarrassed in front of her.'

'So he cares more about what Judith thinks than how I feel?'

'Well, sometimes we do worry more about what outsiders think than we should . . . foolishly. But that doesn't mean that—'

'Oh, Mother!' D'Arcy broke in. 'He's going home today and I love him. What am I going to do? Judith hates me and now she'll never let me see him again. I know it!'

219

D'Arcy was right about that. That was Judith's style all right. *Hate my sister, hate me. Hate me, hate my daughter.* It was a cycle that would never end in Judith's and her lifetime. And what a waste it was. What could have been loving relationships that could have brought joy to them all were now only festering sores, never to be healed, even as her own memory of Carlotta was a festering sore, a crippling disease from which she'd never recover. . . .

'Mother, will you help me see Rud again?'

How could she say yes, knowing what kind of difficulties with Judith lay ahead? She had no idea if Rud even felt anything more than a friendly kind of affection towards D'Arcy. He had spoken of her with fondness, but love? Tempetuous, passionate, all-consuming love that would not be denied, no matter what? Hardly. Perhaps it might have been but it was already too late for that. There was a right season for love to bloom between two people, and who knew if there would ever have been one for them? But how could she say no to D'Arcy in her time of anguish?

'We'll see, D'Arcy.'

'No, don't say "we'll see." When people say that it just means they don't want to say no flat out. Say *you will!*'

'All right, *I will*! I'll try anyway.'

'You'd better believe I'm going to hold you to that.'

'All right, but now I want you to do something for me. I want you to wash your face, get dressed and go talk to your father. I want you two to make up.'

D'Arcy's voice went dead again. 'No! I may talk to him again but I'm never going to forgive him. He betrayed me last night. Instead of saying, "She's my daughter and my daughter doesn't do anything wrong!" he denounced me as if I were some terrible person, and in front of Rud and his nasty mother! No, I'm never going to forgive him!'

'You're upset now, D'Arcy, but you don't mean it. You must forgive him. It's better for *you* to forgive.'

You're a fine one to talk, Frankie Sheridan. You didn't forgive and it has soured your life.

'Try, D'Arcy. Tell me you'll try.'

'Oh, all right, I'll try!'

She'd just made a decision. She herself was going to try too and there was only one way she could do that now. Carlotta was dead but her daughters were very much alive and while she couldn't be a mother to them, she *could be* a loving aunt, a good friend. Actually, it wouldn't be so difficult to be a friend to Abby – Jade would be the problem. Still, she suspected that of the two, Jade was the one who really needed a friend.

Rud was amazed to find Bill drunk so early in the morning and still drinking. What time had he started, he wondered, and why? Just because of that dumb incident last night? It was hard to believe. But more than amazed, he was embarrassed for his uncle. He had had a different impression of Bill Sheridan. He'd thought he was tough, strong, even hard, a man of the world certainly, not a man to drown himself in liquor.

Rud quickly made his apologies for the scene last night, again assuming all responsibility, eager in his embarrassment to get it over with and leave. But Bill wouldn't let him go that easily. Instead, he got up and put his arms around Rud, telling him he understood perfectly, reassuring that if anyone was to blame, it was D'Arcy. He hugged him tightly, told him how sorry he was that his mother was so determined to leave. 'But we'll see each other again, Rud, I swear it!'

Rud was shocked to see tears in his uncle's eyes.

When he was finally able to tear himself away from Bill, Rud wondered what to do with himself. He wasn't ready to face Judith yet. He wasn't really in the mood to face anyone. Maybe he would just go take a long walk.

Well, it was a beautiful day, if nothing else, he thought, as he walked down the beach. Hard to believe that there'd been a hurricane. Hard to believe that this was only Tuesday and they'd only got there Saturday night. Then he spied D'Arcy, sitting on the sand and staring out to sea. He didn't want to see her now, talk to her, and he turned back towards the house. But just then she stood up and saw him. 'Rud!' She waved frantically and he had no choice but to go towards her. She broke into a run to meet him and threw herself against him. 'Oh, Rud!'

He pushed her away gently. This was all he needed now . . . all *they* needed. Who'd believe they hadn't planned to meet on the beach to pick up where they'd left off last night, after all the protestations of innocence and the apologies?

'Oh, Rud, I thought maybe I'd never see you again.'

'Look, D'Arcy, it's not such a hot idea for us to be seen together this morning. They'll be convinced that we're really having a thing.'

'I don't care what they think! Do you?' Tears welled up in her heavily made up black-lined eyes.

She obviously was in an emotional state and he hesitated to tell her in so many words that he *did* care . . . cared a lot more about what certain people thought than he actually cared about her. 'We have to care, D'Arcy,' he said kindly. 'For now, anyway.'

His words were a mistake. The 'we' made her think that it was the two of them against the world and the 'for now' implied that there was a future for them.

'Oh, Rud, I do love you! Do you love me too?'

God! There was that question again. 'Do you love me?'

How many times had he been asked that question? He'd lost count. Sometimes, it was a command. 'Tell me that you love me!' And the girls weren't always as young as D'Arcy. Why did they ask? Someone should have told them to wait until they were told. And it was always hard for him to say no. Almost impossible.

'You do, don't you?' she pleaded.

'Of course I do!'

Well, what else could he say? She was on the edge of hysteria. Maybe if he said no she'd walk straight into the Atlantic until the surf covered her head. And he *did* love her, in a way. She was family and she was sweet. Besides, how could it hurt to say that he loved her?

'But now you'd better go back to the house and let me take my walk by myself.'

'But you're leaving today,' she said mournfully, rubbing at her already reddened eyes. 'Your mother said so. . . .'

'Yes, but I'm not sure she'll be able to pull it off with travelling conditions the way they are.'

'But we will see each other again, no matter what?'

He ruffled her hair affectionately. 'Of course we will.' She *was* sweet. 'See ya.'

'See ya,' she smiled bravely.

She stood there watching his figure disappear down the beach before she turned back towards the house. He had said they would see each other again, she consoled herself, and her mother had said she would help. What did she care what Judith thought or her father said?

11.

'Let's go down and have some breakfast,' Abigail said. 'I'm starving, aren't you?'

'Kind of. . . .' But Jade was more interested in finding out what happened last night after Rud and D'Arcy had been discovered, rather than bacon and eggs. She had a feeling that as a result of last night, the week in Palm Beach was going to be considerably foreshortened, and if she still planned to settle her score with her aunt, she had better get cracking. It looked like that score was going to be the only one she was going to be able to settle for the time being since she'd been forced to make a deal with Judith and she was too afraid to push Trace too hard right now. Judith said she'd take care of Trace but then while Judith was very clever and strong, she still didn't know Trace and Scotty like she herself did. She knew enough to be afraid . . . knew that someone dear to her could still get hurt in some terrible way.

Once upon a time there'd been a man in Carlotta's life, a man other than Trace and Scotty. Peter Weiss. He'd been Carlotta's director, a very nice man of whom Carlotta, it seemed, had been fond.

He's so sweet to me on the set. And so careful not to hurt my feelings when he has to tell me I'm doing a scene wrong. He talks to me like I was some very precious, very delicate doll who might fall apart, break into little tiny pieces if he even looked at me sternly. (He doesn't know that having already been broken, I am a doll who is on intimate terms with the glue pot.) But of course he never does look at me sternly. Those liquid brown eyes are too soft, too full of understanding – and more. They're brimming over with everything . . . and more. I want to tell him that he mustn't look at me that way. His eyes are too expressive. They say too much. I read them and I'm afraid. For myself and even more for him. How does the song go? 'People will say we're in love . . . ?' And the people I know are all too knowing, too alert to danger and too dangerous when they're aroused.

Several weeks later:

I've told Peter that he cannot . . . must not . . . ever try to be alone with me. He must never even rehearse me in private. Nowhere. Not

222

in my dressing room, not in my home, not even on the set unless it's in front of everyone.

I'm so afraid that his eyes, or even his smile, even the warmth in his voice will give him away. People might say we're in love. . . .

I've told him repeatedly to be careful . . . cautioned him a million times even though he has never so much as touched my hand. But today, even as I told him again, he shook his head at me and then he did touch my hand. That was all but I snatched it away quickly, as if his touch burned, but it is he whom I fear for . . . that he will feel the heat.

Three weeks later, there was another entry in the diary concerning Peter Weiss.

I've told Scotty that I don't want Peter Weiss on my next picture, that I find him insufferable. I told Scotty they must get me another director. Now people won't think we're in love!

But then only a few days later:

I will have another director on my next picture. (The next line was illegible since the ink had run.) *They tell me that Peter is paralyzed for life . . . will be confined to a wheelchair forever. I wonder how long is for ever. Peter was found severly beaten – certainly severely is not severe enough a word – almost to death. Left for dead probably, in a vacant lot on the south side of Beverly Hills.*

People might have said we were in love but we had never so much as exchanged a kiss.

Rud let the sand run through his fingers. Jade was the most coldblooded bitch he'd ever met, Rud brooded, but at least she hadn't asked, 'Do you love me?' She at least had waited until she was told and only then whispered, 'I love you. . . .'

But so what? She was a bitch with a heart sculptured out of ice, with lips that lied.

He stood up. He had to go back to the house, find out if they were leaving for home. And he had to face Jade. She was probably convinced that he had screwed D'Arcy too. But what did he care? Let her be convinced. Let her eat her heart out. But a voice in his head said, *you wish!*

Judith intercepted him. 'Would you believe I can't find a chauffeur willing to drive us to Boston today? They're all whining about rivers flooding and collapsed bridges and fallen wires. I can't believe no one is even tempted by a thousand dollar bonus! I don't know what this country is coming to—'

'I'll do it for a thousand dollars. We'll rent a car,' he offered, his face blank of expression.

Judith was annoyed, suspecting that he was baiting her. 'Why would you need a thousand dollars? I don't know what point you're trying to make, but you're being absurd. I doubt your driving skills are up to the job.'

Predictable, he thought. Didn't she always think he was inept when it came to practical matters? Madame Stanton's son was super handsome and extremely bright – she'd be *terribly, terribly* disappointed if he didn't bring home a perfect point average – and when the time came, he'd make a brilliant President, but when it came to the nitty-gritty of life's little challenges such as changing a tyre or opening a bulky bottle of ketchup, to Judith he was a zero, an idiot, a washout. And possibly, she was right.

'So be it, Judith. So I take it we're not leaving today. Tomorrow then?'

'Possibly. In the meantime, the less time we spend in this house the better. Let us say you've indulged in quite enough activity under this roof to last us for quite a spell.'

He ignored her cheap shot. 'A hotel then? We're moving to a hotel?'

'Possibly. We'll see. In the meantime I want to take a look at our house here. I might be putting it up for sale. I want you to go with me and then we've been invited to Mar-A-Lago for lunch with the Duke and Duchess. It seems they too have been stranded here by the hurricane. Why don't you go and change into something more appropriate?'

'What would you suggest? A Tux? Tails?'

She managed a smile. 'Really, Rud. Is this what passes for humour at Harvard these days?'

'Sorry. It's the best I can do on an empty stomach. You don't mind if I have a little breakfast first, do you?'

'Haven't you eaten yet? We'll be eating lunch soon.'

'Well, just a bite then to tide me over. I am a growing boy. I don't even drive a car really well yet.'

Judith decided it was time to make up. 'Don't be sensitive, darling. All I meant was that the men I spoke with were professional drivers and if they didn't want to chance the trip, why should you? Now go and have your bite to tide you over. In fact, I'll keep you company while you eat. I could stand another cup of tea. I believe they're serving in the breakfast room this morning.'

By the time he saw Abby and Jade seated at the table it was already too late for him to back out, especially since Judith sailed in in front of him with a cheerful 'Good morning.' He nodded in their general direction, held a chair for his mother, and thought he'd sit himself down at the foot of the table, away from them. But that would appear childish, as if he'd been wounded and was pouting. And he didn't want to give Jade that satisfaction.

He sat down next to Judith, facing the girls. Then, inexplicably, as he whipped open his napkin with a flourish, he said, 'And just in case anyone is wondering, let it be known to one and all that no, I did *not* seduce D'Arcy Sheridan last night, and she did not seduce me. What transpired was little more than an affectionate kiss or so between cousins, at which point we discovered that we were really very tired and decided to take a little snooze.'

He turned to the maid who entered the room and asked for a glass of orange juice – a double, on the rocks. Then he looked directly at Jade who looked back at him just as directly, neither frowning nor disbelieving. If he had to describe her expression he would have to say that it was only kind of . . . *sad*. And then he was aware that she'd done it to him again – made him sad . . . sad, upset, bothered and bewildered.

He found that he wasn't very hungry after all and he went upstairs to change while Judith stayed on to talk to the girls. 'I have an idea,' she said as if suddenly inspired. 'Rud and I are going to lunch with the Duke and Duchess of Windsor after we take a look at my house here. Why don't you come along, Abby? It will be interesting for you and it's always good to meet important people. I'd ask you to come too, Jade, but I don't think it would be fitting to bring *two* uninvited guests.'

'That's OK. I understand perfectly.'

Abigail was torn. 'I'd love to go with you but I don't think I can leave—'

'Yes, you can,' Jade told her. 'Really. It's fine. You go and have a good time. I want to stay and wait for my father anyway.'

'Oh, that's right,' Judith said as if remembering that Jade did have a father. 'Where *is* Trace? I just realized that he wasn't here for dinner last night.'

It *was* funny that while Trace had just disappeared yesterday, Judith was the first and only person who had asked where he was, Jade thought. 'I think he'll be back today. I'll just wait for him. They've finished cleaning out the pool and I'll go for a swim and catch some rays. Maybe I'll talk D'Arcy into hanging out with me.'

'Are you sure?' Abigail asked. 'You're sure you don't mind—?'

'I'm sure. Come on. I'll keep you company while you change.'

She couldn't have been more pleased that Judith, Rud and Abby would be away from the house. Now all she had to do was find out what Francesca, D'Arcy and Bill were doing.

'Now hold still and you'll be done in a sec.' Jade gave a final flick of mascara to Abby's lashes. She stood back to view her artistry. 'Mmm . . . gorgeous! Even the Duke is bound to succumb to your charms, never mind Rud.'

Abigail giggled. 'You don't think I'm over made up? I mean, three coats of mascara? What would Aunt Selena say?'

'Maybe *she'd* say that you look gorgeous. . . .'

'Fat chance!' she giggled again, excited that she was going to spend the afternoon with both Judith and the Windsors. Nobody at school would believe that she'd actually lunched with the Duke and Duchess! When there was a knock at the door she jumped. 'Oh, that must be Rud or Judith to see if I'm ready.'

But it was Francesca who took a deep breath. This was her very first effort to be a friend to her nieces and she found herself actually nervous. *Ridiculous!*

'D'Arcy and I are going to lunch at La Petite Marmite and then shopping on Worth Avenue. There's a lot of sales and I thought it was time everyone got a present. I mean, you two and D'Arcy. D'Arcy's feeling a bit gloomy and I thought maybe you two would help me cheer her up. How about it?'

'Oh, I'd love to but I can't,' Abigail said smugly. 'Judith's invited me to lunch with her and Rud and the *Windsors!*'

'I see. What about you, Jade? You're not going?'

'No, I wasn't invited.'

'Well, *I'm* inviting you. Will you come with me and D'Arcy?'

'Thank you, but I think I'll wait around for my father.' *You're a little late, Aunt Frankie. I already have other things in mind. . . .*

'Oh yes, your father. I was wondering what happened to him. Is he coming back today?'

'Possibly.'

'Well, if it's only possibly, why don't you come with us? We'll have fun,' she urged.

'No thanks. I'll just work on my tan. Is Uncle Bill going with you?'

'No, he's feeling a little under the weather. He's just going to take it easy in his room. . . . Oh by the way, we're all invited to a party tonight across the Sound. But we'll talk about that later. We'll be back around four.'

Well, at least she had tried, Francesca thought. Neither girl had hardly been wildly enthusiastic about her invitation, but at least she had tried.

Jade sat by the pool in a white bikini with the radio tuned to a station playing golden oldies . . . 'If I Loved You' . . . 'I'm Just a Prisoner of Love'. . . . Their mood was her mood. She painted her toenails bright red even though pale, frosted shades were the vogue. She flipped herself every ten minutes by the clock to make sure she didn't burn. When the clock showed three-thirty she went inside the house and up the stairs and down the hall, keeping an eye out for security guards. She didn't want anyone to see her slip into Bill Sheridan's bedroom. She checked her wristwatch. Twenty-five minutes to four. Just right. Francesca had said she'd be back by four.

The door was unlocked and she walked in without knocking to find the room in almost total darkness, illuminated only by the TV set facing the bed. The sound was mute but a baseball game was being played out in living colour. She realized then that the room was shuttered with only the barest of slits of sunshine filtering through. But by the light of the TV she could see Bill sprawled across the bed, dead to the world . . . a drunken stupor from the looks of it – an almost empty quart of bourbon on the nightstand, an overturned glass in the bed, a wet stain beneath it infusing the air with the pervasive smell of alcohol.

He was already nude which pleased her. It would have been difficult to undress him in his state, his body would have been dead weight. She quickly stripped herself of the two wisps of bathing suit and lay beside him thinking that he might be too drunk to awaken, too sodden for her to arouse. But it didn't really matter – it would be enough for Frankie to find them in bed together, naked.

Still, he would have to be conscious. She worked her body against his, running her hands down the length of him – his shoulders, his back, his buttocks, the inner part of his thighs until he began to stir. Then she kissed him – his closed eyelids, his mouth, his throat, moving down to his shoulders, lingering now and then to nibble. When she got to his breasts she sucked while her hands cupped his testicles first gently and then more persuasively, and then his body began to move against her. His arms came up to embrace her and she abandoned his nipples to put her mouth against his, and his mouth opened as if to suck in great gulps of air but it was her lips he was trying to devour . . . her tongue he was seeking to swallow, and she began to do instinctively what she had started out doing mechanically.

His eyelids fluttered open and when he saw who it was, he was amazed. 'Carlotta!' he breathed. 'You've come back to me,' and then she almost forgot that she wasn't her mother, never had been. . . .

He looked into her face. Oh yes, Carlotta! Her green eyes glittering up at him . . . her long red hair spread out on the sheet . . . her white skin glowing in the near dark, glowing and inviting.

His hands reached for her now, wanting to feel the softness of her skin, his lips sought again to take possession of hers, and he moved to mount her.

And then for a moment she panicked, not knowing who she really was – her mother or her mother's daughter. And who was this virile handsome man – the father or the son? Perhaps it didn't matter? But then she knew it did. Everything you did mattered, and she changed her mind, and she pulled away. . . .

The first thing Francesca noticed as she walked into the bedroom was that the television was on with the sound off, and only then did she become aware of the figures in the bed. She didn't cry out; she didn't yell. She simply snapped off the television leaving the room in almost total darkness, and then went into the adjoining sitting room and locked the door.

Bill, the blood pounding in his head, found himself cold sober and wished that he wasn't. For a little while he'd been somewhere else – someplace far back in time – but now he was definitely in the present, and Francesca was locked in the sitting room, and it was Jade in the room with him, and not Carlotta. And he didn't even know what the hell to say to her. Why had she done this?

She was putting her bikini back on, and then she was going out the door without a word. 'Why?' he asked her.

'Why not? I am Carlotta's daughter,' she answered as if that explained everything, and then she was gone, and he still didn't know why she'd done it. She was like Carlotta in many ways but she was not Carlotta. There'd never be another like her. Carlotta had been more than long red hair and green eyes, more than pale glowing skin and red lips . . . more than just mere flesh and blood. Carlotta had been something of the spirit, a dream maybe . . . and more in the head of the dreamer than real. For him, she had never been quite real, never really within his grasp any more than she had been in this room this afternoon. And now he pitied himself that for a few minutes he had been deceived again . . . to fantasize that she existed and loved him.

Still, he was glad that nothing had actually happened, that the act of love, if that was what it was, had not been consummated. He wasn't really sure but even before Frankie walked in, he thought he felt Jade pull back, away from him, even as Carlotta had always done except for that once. . . . But how was he ever going to convince Frankie that nothing had happened? Why should she believe him when he hadn't even believed D'Arcy on much less incriminating evidence?

He went to the sitting room door and started pounding. 'Frankie! Frankie, let me in! Let me explain!' But after a while he gave up, went down the hall to his study and locked himself in, not sure who he wanted to lock out.

Jade went to her room to wait for Francesca so that they could finally finish up the settling of their account. She was sure she would come and she got ready to receive her. She took the diaries out of the duffle bag and placed them on the desk, open to certain pages. Then she went and sat at the window overlooking the water, waiting for Frankie, waiting for the sun to go down. She thought of how this afternoon had been the closest she would ever come to being Carlotta, and even so, she hadn't quite made it. . . .

Francesca thought about how she'd rushed home to get to Bill that afternoon. The urge to go home to see him had come over her at the Hangout where she and D'Arcy had stopped for a coke after their shopping. She'd been sorry that she had left Bill when he'd been so upset. She didn't know what was upsetting him, still she should have been more sympathetic, more understanding, been there for him. That was what made a marriage a good one, being there for the other person. So she had left D'Arcy sitting with some friends, to follow later, and she'd gone tearing out of there to get home to him and . . . *this*.

Maybe it was all her own fault. Perhaps the problem was that the only ground rules in her marriage and in her life had been Bill's. Whatever rights she had held as a person she'd given up years before when they'd first met. Maybe she had already abdicated before that, when she had first started putting Carlotta's needs before her own. That had been a mistake. On the one hand, she'd made Carlotta a weaker person by doing that, and had started the slow killing off of Frankie Collings, person. Between the two, Carlotta and Bill, there wasn't a whole person left who was Frankie Collings Sheridan, but only a shell.

If she hadn't wanted Jade and Abigail in her home in the first place, they shouldn't have been there. Ditto for Judith and Rud. She should have demanded that Bill recognize that what she wanted, counted as well . . . was important too. Then, none of this would have happened. Still, the time to take a stand had been years before when she should have been strong enough not to marry a man desperately in love with another woman, no matter how much she loved him.

Her secretary knocked on the door and Francesca just called out, 'Yes?' not wanting to unlock it.

'D'Arcy called, Frankie. She said she was going home with Eloise Andelson and would call back later. And Abigail called to say that she and the Stantons wouldn't be back for dinner or the evening, and asked that I tell you and her sister. And Mrs Hubble wants to know what to do about dinner.'

'Tell Mrs Hubble to forget about dinner and call D'Arcy. Tell her that the Stantons aren't going to be here tonight and she can spend the night at the Andelson's if she wants to. Then you can go home, Bess.'

'Frankie, are you all right?'

'Yes, of course I'm all right.'

If she wasn't, she was going to be. She was going to make sure of that. And no matter what else she did, she was going to tell Judith to get out the first thing in the morning. And she would tell Jade to get out now. She might not have a husband after tonight, but this was still her home and she would no longer tolerate bitches, witches or harlots under its roof. And not ghosts, either.

She got the key and unlocked the drawer which held Carlotta's letters – all those letters begging for her forgiveness. Why had she kept them? To make herself feel guilty, or just sad? She should have freed herself of their hold a long time ago. She lit the gas jet in the fireplace, threw them in and watched them burn. It was, if nothing else, a beginning. A symbol of a beginning, anyway.

'I want you to pack up and get out,' Francesca told Jade.

'But my father isn't here.'

'When he comes back, I'm going to send him packing too. He won't have any trouble catching up with you. You and your father are two of a kind.'

That was as good a starting point as any, Jade thought. 'You know I'm not even sure he *is* my father. What do you think of that?'

Francesca was startled but then she shrugged. Why should that surprise her? Why should Carlotta have changed her spots once she settled in Hollywood? 'What I think is that once a whore, always a whore. And you're one just like your mother.'

Then she sat down, as if the weight of her words had weakened her. 'Carlotta went to bed with men at the drop of a hat. What Carlotta wanted, Carlotta took . . . *did. Just like you.*'

Jade realized then that Francesca was getting this whole thing wrong. She was assuming that she had almost gone to bed with Bill because she wanted him, wanted his body. She didn't even know that this whole thing was about revenge, about getting her back for what she'd done to Carlotta. And she had to know.

'You've got it all wrong, Frankie! I didn't want him. I wasn't *hot* for him. That's not why I did it at all!'

Francesca smiled sourly. 'Of course not. I should have known. You did it for the same reason your mother did exactly the same thing. *Not* because she really wanted him, *not* because she loved him. She just did it for the hell of it – because she was just a bitch in heat and didn't care who the man was or whom she hurt. Yes, your mother went to bed with Bill. Did you know that?'

'Yes, I knew that. It's in the diaries. I told you I had my mother's diaries. It's all in there! Everything!' She ran to the desk, picked up one of the notebooks and flourished it in the air. 'Everything is here! How you wouldn't help her! How you turned your back on her! How she wrote you letter after letter, begging you to forgive her, begging you to be her friend. How you never answered her! Not once! How you helped to kill her!'

'Kill her? I didn't see your mother for years before she died. I wasn't even there!'

'That's the point,' Jade's voice dropped. 'You weren't there for her. You turned your back on her, let them destroy her by bits and pieces. She had nobody to go to, nowhere to turn and you never answered her letters. . . .'

'Let *them* destroy her? Who are *they*?'

'Trace and Scotty. Scotty is the man Trace sold her to . . . he's the one who might be my father.'

229

'But I didn't send her running after Trace. No, first she betrayed me and then she betrayed herself.' She was determined not to lose her control. 'So that's why you seduced my husband? To get even for what you *think* I did to your mother?'

'First of all I didn't seduce him. *It didn't happen.* But even if it did, what makes you so sure *I* had to seduce *him*? And what did *she* do to you that your husband didn't? He did it, and you married him. She did it and you turned your back on her, left her to die. . . .' Then suddenly the defiance was gone and her voice was piteous. 'She had always counted on you. She had no one else.'

Francesca saw then that the main thing about Jade was that she was in terrible pain. She was, in the end, only a fifteen-year-old girl who had loved her mother and was caught up in a situation not of her making which was just too ugly for her to bear and she was trying to fight back, to wipe it all out. And her own anger was dissipated, and what was left in its place was despair. No matter what had happened or hadn't happened between Jade and Bill, she had to make Jade understand. . . .

'Yes, Bill betrayed me with Carlotta and yes, I married him just the same. But there was a difference between his betrayal and Carlotta's. He had always loved her, wanted her, and had never had her. I was devastated but I could understand that, his love for her. But Carlotta never loved him, had never wanted him. For her to make love to him and have him make love to her was *nothing* to her. It broke my heart but it was *nothing* to her. A whim. . . . And Carlotta knew how much I loved Bill . . . loved her. Do you know that at first even though *I* loved Bill, I encouraged her to marry him because I knew he would protect her? I was willing to give him up then, willing to help him win her over, and believe me, that was a terribly hard thing to do—

'So hard . . . but a person has to draw a line somewhere. I could forgive Bill for loving but not Carlotta for her selfish callousness . . . for not loving *me* enough. . . .'

'Oh but she did! In the end she loved you so much. In the end she made a supreme sacrifice for you even when you wouldn't talk to her any more.' Jade turned the pages of the diary hunting for the right entry. 'Here . . . here it is – 23 December, 1945. It was the day before she married Whit Truesdale. Here, read it!'

Francesca turned her head away. 'No! I don't want to—.'

'You must. Then you'll understand what she did for you.'

When Francesca wouldn't take the diary from her, Jade said, 'Then I'll read it to you. . . .'

'No!' but Jade read:

> *'I went to see Bill today, to ask him what to do. There's no one else to ask since Frankie won't talk to me. They're the only two people I have. My only friends. They've always loved me and forgiven me . . . even when I've been bad. But this time I've hurt Frankie too badly. She can't forgive me and I don't blame her.*

*What I did was hateful and having had too much to drink is no real
excuse . . .'*

Francesca, crying, said, 'I don't want to hear any more.'

'But you must. You have to know the truth!' And then, Francesca silent, she
went on:

*'And Bill. I've been awful to him too. And yet he still loves me.
Loves me enough to forgive me. When I told him about the baby
and how Trace had left me, he asked me to marry him! He swore
he'd love me and the baby forever. Trace's baby! He said he'd take
care of us both. Oh, God, how I am tempted! But God, give me the
strength to resist Bill and his safe, loving harbour. I can't marry
him! He's Frankie's now and I've hurt her enough. Even if I never
saw either Bill or her again, at least I will have done that for
her. . . .'*

Jade finished in a whisper and closed the book. 'So you see, Aunt Frankie, she
loved you quite a lot . . . enough to give up her safe, loving harbour.'

Neither one of them spoke, Jade thought that she could read more . . . could
read to Francesca of how Whit Truesdale, to whom Carlotta had also told the
truth, had married her but had been unable to forgive her and had made her
life a purgatory until she ran away to Trace and Scotty and found . . . hell. But
seeing the stricken look on her aunt's face, she knew that she had already read
enough.

'So you see, Aunt Frankie, my mother was foolish and she was weak. She
made bad mistakes but she herself wasn't bad. Not really bad. She didn't
deserve to be destroyed, did she?' And finally her voice broke and the tears
came.

'No, she didn't, she didn't.' Francesca wanted to cry too but it was too late
for her tears. 'I was foolish and weak too. Maybe if I had been stronger and
able to forgive her I could have saved her. But I'm not sure about that. I think
Trace's pull was too strong for her, and no matter what, nothing could have
kept her from him. . . . But I too am punished . . . in a way, destroyed.'

Then the full impact of what she'd done hit Jade. She had helped destroy
Frankie who was, in the end, no guiltier than Carlotta. Maybe less so. . . . 'But
you must believe me, Aunt Frankie. Nothing happened in that room today. At
the last minute I changed my mind. I wasn't going to go through with it. And
Bill, he didn't even know what was happening . . . he was drunk. He thought it
was all a dream. He thought I was Carlotta. . . . You mustn't blame him. It was
all my fault. Oh, Aunt Frankie, forgive me.'

*The same words! Don't blame Bill. Forgive me! Is the nightmare destined to
go on forever?*

Did she explain to Jade that it didn't really matter whether the act had been
consummated that afternoon? That the important thing was, drunk or sober,

231

dreaming or awake, Bill had been ready to be seduced by the girl he thought was Carlotta . . . and that the worst betrayal of all was that Bill, already committed to her, and knowing how much she loved him, had offered Carlotta marriage only a few days before he married her, good old Frankie, a *persona* completely *non grata*. . . .

No, she couldn't inflict any more burdens on this child.

'No, Jade, I can't forgive you because I don't blame you. I see now that none of us are to blame, not really. Not you and not Carlotta and not me. We're all victims . . . life's victims, and I don't even know why. But I think it's you who have been victimized the most. To carry all this around in your heart! Forget it all, Jade, if you can! Burn those damn diaries and save yourself!'

'But I can't. There's stuff in there about Trace and Scotty and Judith—'

'Judith? I know she deliberately brought Carlotta and Trace together but what else did she do?'

'It doesn't matter now. But I have to save those diaries so that eventually I can get revenge on them for what they did. I can't do it now because I have to keep Abby from knowing that Trace is her real father and Judith has some information that will keep Trace quiet. That's more important now than getting even with her. . . .'

Francesca nodded. One of Carlotta's daughters already knew far too much . . . more than a young girl should.

'Burn the diaries,' Francesca said again. 'Leave them to God to deal with. . . .'

Still, Jade felt guilty for what she'd done. Maybe she had even wrecked Frankie's marriage. 'Please, Aunt Frankie, you won't blame Uncle Bill, will you? I told you. He really didn't know who I was. He thought I was Carlotta,' she said again.

To cover up how much those words hurt, Francesca made a feeble joke. 'Well, that's something, isn't it? He could have thought you were Judith.'

Oh my God! Jade thought. She doesn't know! She doesn't know about Judith and Bill! She doesn't know Rud is Bill's son. If she did, she wouldn't be making jokes about Judith.

And I can't be the one to tell her! I've already done enough! And this is the one thing I can do for her . . . withhold the last straw that would most certainly destroy their marriage!

12.

When Abigail awoke she was dismayed to find Jade packing. 'What are you doing?'

'I want to be ready to leave as soon as my father gets back.'

'Oh no! Not you too! I might as well go home too. With you gone, and Judith and Rud going today too, if they can, there doesn't seem much point in my staying,' she wailed.

'That's silly. You can still have a good time with D'Arcy and Frankie and—'

'No, I can't. D'Arcy doesn't even like me and Aunt Frankie's been cold to me ever since I got here.'

'I think they both like you a lot. It's just that D'Arcy thinks of you as competition for Rud and Aunt Frankie— Well, I think it's just that she has some personal problems on her mind that don't have anything to do with you.'

'Oh, I don't care about them. Do you really have to go?'

'Yes. I think the reason my father's gone off like this is because he had a fight with Uncle Bill and it will . . . well, it will be better all around for everyone if we cleared out.'

'But when will I see you again? It doesn't seem fair. We were just getting to know each other and we've hardly had any time together. . . .'

Jade hugged her. 'I know. I'm heartbroken about it too. But we'll get to see each other again soon.'

'When? How?'

'I don't know right now but we'll work something out.'

'I know! Maybe you could visit in Boston at Christmas. You couldn't stay with us because Aunt Selena wouldn't allow it but I bet if I asked Judith, she'd let you stay at her house and then I could come over there and that way we'd all be together.'

'That sounds great,' Jade said although she knew it would never happen.

'I just know Judith will do it. You can't believe how wonderful she was to me last night, making sure I wasn't left out of the conversation and she kept telling me how she was going to make sure we saw a lot of each other once we got back to Boston.'

'Good. And in the meantime, since my father isn't back yet, why don't you and I spend at least part of this day together alone, just the two of us? We'll go out for breakfast and just hang out, walk around the town. Neither of us have seen anything of Palm Beach and this might be our last chance. . . .' *To be alone together for a long, long time. . . .*

'Wonderful! But first I want to say goodbye to Judith just in case she's gone by the time we come back.'

'And Rud,' Jade reminded her coyly. 'Don't forget Rud.'

'I won't but if you ask me he's more interested in *you* than me . . .'

'Don't be silly. Why do you say that?'

'Because last night when we were alone *you* were the main topic of conversation. All he did was ask me questions about you.'

Jade made a face. 'That's only because he thinks I'm some kind of a freak. He's Boston and I'm Hollywood so that makes me exotic which is another word for weird. Admit it, you think I'm weird too?' And she pounced on Abigail, tickling her until they were both red in the face and laughing hysterically.

While Abigail went to find Judith, Jade found Francesca conferring with the housekeeper and cook about a last-minute dinner party for that night – a farewell party for Judith and Rud who were now scheduled to leave first thing the following morning – Logan Airport in Boston was resuming operations at 6 a.m. the next day.

'But why, Aunt Frankie? You told me that you were going to ask Judith to leave your house today regardless of anything else. That you'd made up your mind not to put up with her anymore no matter what.'

'I changed my mind for D'Arcy's sake. It means a lot to her to have things end this way – outwardly pleasant, if nothing else. My main reason for doing this is if D'Arcy sees this whole situation with Judith and Rud somewhat rectified, she won't be so full of rage towards her father. Regardless of what happens between me and Bill, it's not good for a young girl to carry around that kind of rage against her father. It leads to her committing all kinds of self-destructive acts in order to vent that anger.'

Jade gathered that her aunt wasn't merely talking about D'Arcy and that she meant well, but how could D'Arcy's situation possibly apply to her own?

'And D'Arcy's so delighted that Rud is staying this extra day and that there's a possibility now that they might see each other again, she's not even mad at Judith any more which is just as well. As for Judith, apparently she's decided too that it's better to end things neatly and pleasantly – she's behaving quite well. She's even acting friendly to D'Arcy.'

'Is that good?'

Francesca laughed. 'It can't hurt. D'Arcy thinks she's in love with Rud. The best thing is to let her find out for sure for herself since the best way to drive a girl into a man's arms is to forbid her to see him. And D'Arcy is a very headstrong girl. While I hope this *is* only an infatuation, I don't want to see D'Arcy spend her life with an unfulfilled obsession.'

Jade could understand Frankie wanting to give D'Arcy her head, using the appeal of the forbidden fruit principle. *She* didn't know what the actual facts were. But what was Judith, who knew the facts better than anyone, thinking of? Well, maybe she too was thinking of the forbidden fruit principle, didn't want to make D'Arcy too attractive by denying Rud access to her.

'Well, I hope you're right, Aunt Frankie. All I know is I sure pity the girl who has Judith for a mother-in-law.' She made a joke of it, rolling her eyes expressively.

Francesca laughed but then looked at Jade curiously, 'Maybe I'm reading the signals wrong, but I received the impression that you were pushing Abby in Judith and Rud's direction.'

Then Jade opened her eyes wide. 'But I thought you understood about that. Abby *needs* Judith. Judith's the only one who can protect her from Trace!'

They were assembled in the living room awaiting the dinner guests and possibly the reappearance of Trace Boudin. Jade thought how they all looked like a movie in living technicolour – she herself in bright orange, liking the shock of colour against her red hair; Abby wore pale blue and D'Arcy hot pink. Frankie was in bright red and Judith wore black, as if she, somehow, knew something the others didn't. Bill, in a navy blue blazer and white trousers, commented that the ladies resembled a bouquet of spring flowers, and then Rud commented, 'Except for Judith, of course. Unless we call her the Black Dahlia,' and laughed.

'My, that has an ominous ring,' Judith forced a smile.

'Not at all,' Bill said quickly. 'It makes you sound glamorous, like a lady of mystery.'

Judith arched an eyebrow. 'Me? I'm an open book,' at which Rud laughed again and this time his mother gave him a dirty look.

Rud, reflecting the inverse of Bill's colour scheme – white blazer with navy blue slacks, looked particularly handsome tonight, Jade thought. He had spent the afternoon hours playing tennis and the time in the sun had lent a fresh overlay of golden bronze to the tan he'd brought with him from Newport. She was avoiding eye contact with him, as she was with Bill – she was too embarrassed to look at Bill – but when she did sneak a look at Rud and saw that he was looking at her with intense resentment she could have burst into tears.

Then when the waiter, who was taking orders for drinks, asked him what he would like, Rud drawled, 'I think I'd like a martini' and then, loudly and challengingly he demanded, 'What about it, Jade? Will you mix me one of your very special martinis?'

He spoke with so much hostility that everyone turned to look at her to see what she would answer, and without hesitation, she responded, 'No, I don't think so. I've decided you're not man enough for one of *my* cocktails.'

Jade had thought it would come out as *sort* of a joke but from all the shocked faces and Rud's burning one, she knew she had gone too far. I am just like my mother, she thought, managing to burn all my bridges behind me. . . .

And then Trace came rushing into the room, as if he were eager not to be late for the party. He was grinning and wearing narrow black trousers, an incredibly white shirt unbuttoned almost to the waist, exposing a lot of black chest hair. The shirt had an exaggeratedly wide collar and its sleeves were very full and caught tightly at the wrists. Again Francesca thought how he looked like a riverboat gambler, and Bill thought as he had in the long ago past, how much the slimy bastard resembled a tangodancer, gigolo or pimp – take your pick. And as Jade trembled with revulsion, D'Arcy sang out just as she had at her party, 'Oh, Uncle Trace, you really do look just like Rhett Butler!'

And then Jade noticed what Trace was carrying – it was a little yellow bird.

'What have you got there?' Bill asked, his eyes narrowed.

'What does it look like?' He held it up. 'It's a canary, you know, the kind of birds that sing. I found it on your doorstep. The little fellow is dead, unless, of course, it's a girl. Somehow, it managed to snap its little head. Isn't that a damn shame?'

'Where were you all this time?' Abigail asked. 'Jade was worried about you.'

He laughed. 'Oh, she shouldn't have done that. Since I didn't want to get in the way, all you being family, I just lit out for Miami for a couple of days.'

'Oh, how nice,' Abigail said politely, secretly sorry that he was back since it meant Jade would be leaving too. 'And did you have a good time?'

'Nice of you to ask, love. Yes, thank you, I had a very good time.'

Actually, he had had more than a good time. He had struck gold in Miami . . . you might call it, Cuban gold, and he'd come back with a cool hundred thou which would help tide things over for a while. As for the rest of the money, he felt like he was on a roll!

The TV had been on in Bill's dressing room while he'd been getting ready for the evening, and the latest hurricane report was that the storm, which had finally blown itself out, had hit Boston's North Shore particularly hard. Bill remembered then that Abby had said her aunt and uncle were staying at the Dory Inn there and before he went downstairs, he'd instructed an aide to place a couple of calls to see if they could get some more pertinent information.

Now with the guests having barely arrived, having hardly tasted their drinks or eaten any of the tiny potatoes stuffed with caviar, the aide came into the room and whispered in Bill's ear. Bill left and after ten minutes or so returned to whisper in Francesca's ear, and while Francesca went around and spoke to all the guests, explaining why it would be better that they leave, Bill took Abigail aside, to prepare her for the bad news.

When Abigail came to, she was on the sofa in the drawing room, with Judith on one side of her, and Jade on the other, and Francesca was saying, 'I think I'd better call the doctor to give her a sedative.'

'Nonsense,' Judith said. 'Abigail is a strong girl. She's going to be just fine, aren't you?' And she spoke to Abby in an undertone, sympathetically but firmly.

Then Francesca suggested that perhaps Abby should go upstairs to lie down for a while but Abby protested, 'Oh no, I don't want to lie down! I don't want to be alone!'

'Of course you don't,' Judith soothed.

'But you won't be alone,' Jade said. 'I'll go up and stay with you.'

'And I will too,' D'Arcy spoke up, although somewhat reluctantly. She wanted to do the right thing yet at the same time she wanted to spend whatever time was left with Rud. But maybe Rud would go upstairs with them too. 'Why don't the three of us go up with Abby? You Jade, and me, and Rud?'

'No!' Abigail protested again. 'I'd rather stay here with everybody.' She was frightened and bereft and Judith was being so comforting.

'Let the child be,' Judith took Abigail's hand in hers, and Jade murmured meaningless words only meant to be consoling.

'Oh,' Abigail said pathetically. 'I'm really an orphan now.'

'But you're not alone,' Jade said quickly. 'You have me.'

'And me . . . us . . . now and always,' Francesca said. And she meant it. This time, she wouldn't fail. This time she'd be there for Carlotta's daughter. Abby would make her home with them, with her and Bill and D'Arcy. Whatever arrangements she made with Bill to keep their marriage going had nothing to do with taking Abby in . . . wouldn't affect that. 'Isn't that right, Bill? D'Arcy?' She looked to them to back her up, to reaffirm what she was saying.

Bill, eager to say and do whatever Francesca wanted at this point, hastily said, 'Of course,' and D'Arcy echoed, 'Of course. After all, we're kissin' cousins.'

But Abigail didn't acknowledge their words. She didn't look at them. Rather, she looked from Judith to Jade. These were the only two people who cared about her, and while she *was* griefstricken about Aunt Selena and Uncle George, she was already worried about what was going to become of her now. There were no other Truesdales to take her in, and no matter what Frankie was saying, she didn't want her, hadn't liked her the minute she saw her. What did happen to a girl who was orphaned when she was not quite an adult, but not a child either?

When Abigail didn't respond to what she had just said, Francesca understood that it was a rejection of her and her family. And why wouldn't Abigail reject her? Hadn't she rejected Abigail all these years with her silence? It was too late for her to be a substitute mother to her niece, or even a real aunt. Still, Abby would come and live with them, by default if not by choice.

Rud and Trace were the only ones to have nothing to say. Rud was deep in thought. Abby didn't realize it yet but she needed no consoling. It was more like congratulations were in order. There she was with all those Truesdale millions and no strings attached, no aunt or uncle or mother sitting on her neck, dictating her every move. She was free! Or she would be in a couple of years or so when she came into her own.

Trace was thinking along the same lines. His daughter, the heiress, was up for grabs, fortune and all. All he had to do was come up with the right approach. Nothing so gauche or blatant as suddenly declaring his parental claims – Judith would nail him for that, blow the whistle on him. Or Jade would, with her fucking diaries. No, something very clever, inspired even, was in order. He had to make an offer so artless no one could refuse.

Abigail remembered that she didn't know *how* her aunt and uncle had died, only that they were dead. 'I can't understand why, when they must have known the hurricane was on its way, they didn't go home. That was so unlike Aunt Selena. She always said to be forewarned is to be forearmed. What happened exactly, Uncle Bill?'

'I don't know, honey. I couldn't get any details. All that's clear is that they were at the shore when the storm hit and. . . . Well, actually all they really said was that the bodies had been recovered. But once you're back in Boston I'm sure you'll learn more.'

Yes, Francesca thought. Regardless of anything else, Abby would have to go back to Boston for the funeral. And she'd go with her, of course.

'Perhaps it would be best – if you have room for us on your plane, Judith – if Abby and I fly back to Boston with you in the morning. There will be arrangements to be made and Abby and I can stay in the Truesdale house until— And maybe you can come with us too, Jade?' Yes, it would be good if Jade came too. Jade would be a real comfort to Abby in the next few days, more so than she herself.

'Of course I'll come,' Jade said quickly. 'I want to be with Abby.'

'And I'll come too,' D'Arcy said in a rush. 'Abby should have as much family as possible with her at a time like this. Besides how would it look if she had hardly any family with her at the funeral?' What a stroke of luck! To get to go on Judith's and Rud's private plane with them and to get to spend a few days in Boston before she had to start boring old school!

But then Judith spoke up. 'I understand that all of you want to stand by Abby in her hour of need but it's really not necessary. There's no need to disrupt all of your lives. I know how Bill relies on you, Frankie. He probably can't spare you. As for the arrangements, my staff and trustees of the Truesdale estate can take care of everything. Routine. And I wouldn't dream of allowing Abby to stay in that house just now. Too depressing. She'll stay with us . . . with me and Rud.'

Unconsciously, Abigail rubbed her cheek against Judith's arm and Francesca thought, Judith is probably right. It would be depressing for Abby to stay in that house, and obviously Abby wanted to stay with Judith. And as Judith said, all the arrangements and legal tape would be easily and routinely handled by staff. She herself would fly up once the funeral was set and she'd stay in a hotel. Then she could take Abigail back to Florida with her.

'Could Jade come with us?' Abigail asked Judith eagerly. 'For a few days?' And Rud's pulse quickened as he waited for his mother's answer.

'Well, she *could*,' Judith said judiciously. 'But we mustn't be selfish, dear. Jade's school is probably starting next week. . . .'

'I could miss a few days. It doesn't matter.'

'But it's not necessary. The funeral is over in a couple of hours. It makes much more sense if you saved your visit for Christmas when Abby will be feeling more cheerful and you'll be able to stay for at least a week and everyone will be more in the mood to enjoy each other's company. And until then, Abby will be just fine with us, and no one has to concern themselves about her.'

Abigail looked at Judith with big eyes. Was Judith saying what she thought she was saying? That she'd go home with her tomorrow and stay with her? *Live with her?*

Jade was startled. She had assumed that Frankie would take Abby in, even with the trouble between her and Bill. And even with their problems, the Sheridan household was where Abby belonged. Frankie wanted to be a friend to them now, especially to Abby who was so completely innocent, who only wanted love and nothing more.

Francesca put it into words. 'What are you saying, Judith? That you want Abby to stay with you, live with you?'

'Exactly. Abby and I have become very close these past few days. Isn't that so, Abby?'

'Oh yes,' she breathed. 'Oh yes!'

And Francesca realized that it really was too late for her and Abby. Too late in every way. She had thought that Abby would come and live with them because she really wanted her niece with her, and because Abby had no other choice. But now it appeared that Abby did have a choice and had already chosen – Judith.

'Well, you can see Abby feels the same way I do,' Judith said reasonably. 'Oh, I know you have a prior claim, Frankie, but you and Bill are so – what shall I say – preoccupied. Political life *is* demanding. And it's the really practical thing if you think about it. This way, there will be almost no disruption in Abby's life. She can attend the same school, have the same friends, and then, when she graduates she can attend Radcliffe. Please, be assured that Abby will have a very good life with me . . . us, that she'll have everything she should, and . . . I've always wanted a daughter. . . .'

'Oh . . .' Abby sighed blissfully.

Francesca shot a quick look at Jade. She wasn't objecting. She appeared what – satisfied? What Judith was saying appeared to be making sense to Jade although she despised Judith as much as she herself did. Jade, at fifteen, seemed to know that which she herself was still struggling with – that in real life one had to settle . . . to compromise, and that always, there were priorities. And most obviously, this was what Abby wanted. . . . What more was there to be said?

But then Trace did have something to say. 'Hold on here a minute. I think everyone is overlooking something I, in good conscience, can't. Abby is Jade's sister. My own baby's flesh and blood. These two girls belong together. Jesus! If I didn't take Abby into our home so these girls can be together what would I be able to say to Carlotta when I meet her at those golden gates? I know damn well what she'd say—' Here he paused for a second to wipe at his eyes. 'She'd say, "Trace honey, why didn't you take my baby to live with you so that my two precious girls could be together? You know that was what I always wanted. . . ."'

Now, how can any of these turkeys jump on me for this?

238

'Hell, I don't want Carlotta to have to say that to me and Jade doesn't either, do you Princess?'

Jade was staring at him unbelievingly, unable to answer.

'No, these girls belong together and I'd be false to Carlotta's memory if I didn't insist that Abby come live with her sister Jade.'

He turned to Abby. 'You *do* want to live with your sister, don't you sweetheart?' He was sure that Abby wouldn't choose *him*, but she would choose Jade.

Jade wanted to scream out, 'No, she doesn't want to come live with me!' but how could she? What would Abby think then?

She looked desperately to Francesca . . . to Judith. *What do I do now? Help me! Help me save Abby from Trace!*

Abby looked from Judith to Jade. She knew what she wanted . . . she wanted them both. Judith, the mother, and Jade her sister. And Francesca and Bill looked at each other. They knew what Boudin was up to but what could they do about it? Trace had outsmarted them all, even Judith. Why didn't Judith say something?

But no one spoke until D'Arcy said, 'I do declare, Uncle Trace, I think what you just said about meeting up with Aunt Carlotta at the golden gates and all, is just about the most beautiful thing I ever heard. Oh, Abby, how lucky you are that out of this terrible tragedy there's this wonderful benefit – that you and Jade can be together!'

Amen, Rud thought. *Yes, Abby, do us all a favour and go to live with your bitch of a sister and her crap artist of a father.* But then he thought, if Abby came to live with them, that might take some of the pressure off him, and that wouldn't be bad at all.

Still, Jade hadn't said anything and neither had Abigail.

'What about it, Princess?' Trace prompted. 'Do we want Abby to come live with us?'

Abigail's eyes were fixed on Jade's waiting for her answer.

Why doesn't Judith say something? Finally she said the only thing she could say, 'Of course I want Abby to live with us!'

Desperate, Francesca said, 'Why don't we all sleep on this? In the morning, we'll all be able to sort things out more clearly.'

'Good idea,' Judith said. 'Then I'm sure we'll all make the right decisions.' But she looked at Jade when she said this and Jade interpreted her look: 'I've done my part. Now it's up to you. You're a clever girl. You figure it out!'

And what was there to figure out? Abby was torn between her, her sister and Judith, not knowing which way to turn, unable to make the choice for herself. And the turns? Trace the vulture, to the right, and Judith and Rud to the left . . . respectability, a privileged life, a golden future. Possibly the golden boy himself. No choice was needed, only the push in the right direction was required.

In the morning, Jade was gone! At first Abby was hysterical and then bewildered. Why had Jade pretended to love her, and then, just like Carlotta, abandoned her? And the note she had left – 'I love you. I'll write.' What did those words mean in the face of her abandonment? And the necklace she had left for her, Carlotta's necklace, all sparkling diamonds and glittering emeralds. . . . What did *that* mean in the face of Jade's betrayal? It was just like Jade, all flash but in the end, just hard and cold. . . . She threw the necklace down. 'I don't want Carlotta's jewellery. I don't want anything from either one of them!'

Judith picked up the necklace. If Abby didn't take it, Trace would. There'd come a time when Abby would appreciate it, would accept it for what it was – a lovely, costly piece of jewellery, without a name, without a face, and without a memory.

Francesca watched Judith enfold Abby in her arms, comforting her. Did Judith really love her? But did it really matter? Abigail would *feel* loved, and that was what counted.

Actually she was more concerned about Jade. Where did she go? She was so young and so alone. She tried to appear hard and tough, but how tough could she be to have made this kind of decision? It was a decision made out of love and a willingness to sacrifice. And if one loved like that, it made one very vulnerable. Jade was Carlotta's vulnerable daughter and there were Trace Boudins everywhere.

Bill understood why Jade had run away and he could see how that might have appeared to be the only answer to her. But Christ, she was only fifteen, a baby really, despite her seductive charms, and he had this terrible feeling that maybe, like Carlotta, she was doomed, bad news for herself as well as for anyone who fell in love with her. For a while he'd thought Rud was drawn to her, and who could blame him if he were? Least of all himself. . . . But she was out of bounds for Rud. With her connections Jade was sudden death for any man with a political future. But he'd try and keep an eye out for her once he found out where she'd gone. But one thing he wouldn't do when and if he located her was bring her back. Wherever she lighted, whatever she did, she was far, far better off distanced from Trace Boudin . . . as much as Carlotta herself would have been.

D'Arcy couldn't figure out why that crazy Jade had disappeared in the middle of the night. Well, she had thought she was weird right from the start. And now, Abby, that lucky duck, was going to be living in the same house with Rud!

As was usual by now, Rud couldn't figure Jade out. She was probably the most irrational human being he had ever met. First hot, then cold. But in between he'd felt *something* emanating from her. And that one time they'd been alone on the library couch – kissing, embracing, caressing – he could have sworn that– Oh, screw it! Screw her! Still, he was filled with this terrible sense of loss.

Trace called for a plane reservation. That vicious little cunt had spoiled what might have been his biggest score ever, what could have pulled him out of the hole for good. And besides that, she'd made a fool of him – she'd sneaked into his room and lifted several thousand dollars off the roll he'd brought back from Miami! She was a nasty little cunt, but she was a smart one . . . she knew that a gambler always carried his stake on him in cash. But one of these days he'd catch up with her and take it out of her ass! But he'd wait until she turned twenty-one, when she took possession legally of her mother's jewellery collection. . . . In the meantime he would have to explain Jade's disappearance to Scotty. He was going to be mad as hell. He had that soft spot for Jade. And on top of that, there was Bill Sheridan's refusal to go along with their plan to get Kennedy out of the '64 race. Boy! He sure would like to put Sheridan's nuts in the grinder.

Bill, Francesca and D'Arcy came out to wave goodbye to Judith, Rud and Abigail as they were leaving for the airport in the governor's limousine. Bill wanted to put his arms around Rud but didn't dare to in front of Francesca and Judith. But he'd figure out some way he'd get to see the boy again. He would! And in the meantime he had to find a way to deal with Frankie.

Francesca kissed Abigail but her niece barely responded. Then Francesca thought that she probably *wouldn't* fly up to Boston for the funeral, after all. What was the point? Besides, she had a lot of thinking to do about her own future. She had married a man who she had thought was a hero, and while she loved him no less, she had to, at least, deal with the fact that he was at best, a flawed hero.

Judith shook hands with Francesca and then with Bill. Things hadn't worked out quite as she had planned. But if she didn't have Bill all wrapped up in ribbons and coloured cellophane, she did have Abby. As for Bill, she wasn't through with him yet either. 'Until we meet again,' she smiled into Bill's eyes, causing his blood to surge with hope.

Then Trace came bounding out of the house, with a big grin on his face. 'How about giving a lift to the airport to this poor Angeleno just trying to get home? Say what you will, there's no place like a man's home turf to relax and at the same time flex his muscles, if you know what I mean?' He thanked Francesca for her hospitality and as he got into the limousine, he said to Bill, 'For God's sake, man, let's keep in touch, and let us know if you change your mind.' He winked.

D'Arcy kissed everyone, Rud lingeringly. And then when they were all in the car, Abigail snuggled up against Judith. A wave of gratitude, stronger than love, engulfed her. Judith wanted to be a mother to her! And Jade? Jade was just like Carlotta and who needed another Carlotta? Not she, certainly. Not anymore. . . .

The Sheridan family watched the limousine pull away, go down the driveway and out the gates. D'Arcy waved and waved until the car was out of sight. Frankie was surprised by D'Arcy's good spirits. She had expected her to be desolate at Rud's leaving, despairing and tearful. But instead, D'Arcy's lips were smiling and her eyes were sparkling. What was she thinking? Francesca wondered. If she had thought about it, maybe she would have guessed.

More or less in the memorable words of her favourite heroine, D'Arcy was thinking: 'I'll think of it all tomorrow. Tomorrow, I'll think of some way to get him back. After all, tomorrow is another day.'

PART
FOUR

Into The Future

VI
1963–1964

1.

The Sheridans were in Palm Beach on November 22nd, having arrived the day before. D'Arcy was expected the next day and the whole family would stay through the Thanksgiving weekend the following week. Bill was in his upstairs study that afternoon going over a list of possible candidates for the gubernatorial race in '64, since according to state law he couldn't succeed himself. He needed someone to run who would take orders well, who wouldn't allow his, Bill's, power to wane while he was sitting out the years until '68, when Kennedy would be through with *his* turn in the barrel. At the same time he needed an attractive figurehead who would always publicly turn to him – the *real* governor – for leadership and advice. Suddenly, his hand whipped out to crush the list of prospective names. It had just occurred to him who the perfect candidate would be when his assistant, John Lee Conrony, broke in, turned on the TV set and cried, 'The President's been shot!'

Bill and John Lee watched as a distressed Walter Cronkite reported that the President had been shot three times, then added that the first reports indicated that Kennedy had been seriously wounded. 'Get Frankie in here!' Bill barked and gripped a pencil so hard, it snapped in two.

In minutes, John Lee was back with Francesca's secretary Bess. 'Frankie's up in Jacksonville speaking on a forum on civil rights.'

'Well, get her the hell back here! Then pour me a drink and then the two of you go find yourselves another TV!'

'Yes sir,' Bess said, 'but are you sure you want to be alone at a time like this?'

He was sure.

Some time later, it was announced that the President was dead. Bill was so engrossed in what was transpiring on the TV screen, he wasn't even aware of the time when Francesca came rushing in. 'Oh, Bill, how horrible! What a terrible thing for the country! Poor Jackie and those two darling children!'

Bill looked at her dumbly. Didn't she realize what had happened? He had just lost his chance for the presidency in '68! Johnson had just taken the oath of office on *Air Force One* and what voter would ever forget he had taken the oath standing next to the brave, bloodstained widow? And whom would the Party run in '68 but the incumbent – the man who took over the reins from a martyred and already legendary president?

Bill told his assistant he wouldn't be taking any calls and he and Francesca retired to their bedroom to watch the proceedings . . . for starters, Lyndon making his first televised speech as President from Andrew Field.

Francesca couldn't stop crying and after a while, Bill patted her hand. 'Don't you cry, I'll work everything out. I'm still going to be President. It'll just take a bit longer. Lyndon will probably only be elected to one term – he's bound to screw up in the next five years.'

Francesca stared at him. 'What are you saying? The President is dead and you're only thinking about—'

'Uh-uh, Frankie, the President's not dead. The President just walked into the White House and that's a mighty big chair Lyndon has to fill – a martyred hero's chair, who, dead only a couple of hours ago, is already a thousand times bigger than he could have hoped to be in life. And is Lyndon really up to it? There's Khrushchev and Vietnam and the Civil Rights mess and there's that Irish Mafia who look on Lyndon as some big shitkickin' buffoon and they're not going to make it any easier for him. Nope, old LBJ might very well trip over his own big feet. . . .'

He patted her hand. 'Dry your tears, Frankie, there are big things in store for us. I'm going to run for president in '68, and next year you're going to run for governor of the great state of Florida.'

It was late into the evening and they were still watching television when Francesca realized that D'Arcy hadn't telephoned. She had only missed making that daily call once or twice in the three months she'd been away at school in Boston and its absence on this day when people were reaching out to each other in pain and shock disturbed Francesca. Was something wrong? Was D'Arcy sick?

'Good God!' Bill was exasperated. 'She's due home tomorrow. I guess she figured that whatever she had to say to you could wait until then. I'd think you'd be glad she skipped a call for a change. All the calls only mean that she's homesick and lonely.'

The truth was, he was pleased that D'Arcy was homesick and lonely in Boston. That's what she deserved for going against his wishes and enrolling in college there. Maybe if she was miserable enough, she'd come back to Florida where she belonged.

When D'Arcy first proposed going to college in Boston he'd hit the ceiling. The Florida governor's daughter belonged in a Florida school! He didn't expect D'Arcy to choose Florida State right there in Tallahassee. No girl with D'Arcy's juice would want to attend a school in the same town where her mother and father spent much of the year. But she could have picked the University of Florida in Gainesville or the University of Miami in Coral Gables. But Boston? 'Out of the question!'

The real reason he didn't want D'Arcy in Boston was Rud. It was also the reason, he knew, that D'Arcy insisted on Boston. Francesca knew it too but when Bill and D'Arcy crossed swords over this only a few weeks after D'Arcy's party when she was starting to send in her college applications for the following year, Frankie had to take D'Arcy's side. She'd promised that she would help D'Arcy see Rud again and one way or another, D'Arcy had to resolve her passion for Rud . . . to work it out of her system.

Besides, she still nursed so much resentment against her husband, she took a perverse pleasure in siding with D'Arcy against him.

In the end, Bill had had to accede to Francesca's demand that D'Arcy be permitted to go to school where she wanted. That was part of his penance for having been found in bed with Jade and it didn't matter that the actual act had never come to pass, or that Jade had instituted the encounter. He still had to

248

pay the piper for a while anyway. So he'd backed off while D'Arcy made out applications to two schools in Boston with Radcliffe her first choice. If Abby went there, why shouldn't she? And then she only applied to Boston University because her guidance counsellor said she had to have a safety school in case Radcliffe rejected her.

D'Arcy was positive that they wouldn't dare. Her mother was an alumna and her father was the governor. Would any school dare turn down a governor's daughter?

But then apparently Radcliffe dared and Francesca herself was properly furious. She somehow suspected Judith's fine hand had intervened and demanded that Bill call Harvard's president personally. He was reluctant since he didn't want D'Arcy there in the first place but Frankie was a raging tiger and he had to give in again. But the powers that be at Radcliffe held their ground and still wouldn't admit D'Arcy for the very simple reason that she didn't even come close to meeting their requirements.

While Bill's own ego was somewhat deflated to hear that his daughter couldn't cut it scholastically, he was delighted. Maybe this was the end of the Boston madness. Still, he tried to soothe Frankie. 'You knew that D'Arcy's SATs were low and she's never got good grades. It doesn't mean that she isn't bright, it just means she'd rather be cutting a rug than cracking a book.'

But Frankie wasn't mollified. 'Cutting a rug is an expression that hasn't been used in fifteen years,' she snapped. 'Try twisting the night away, or rocking out. Really, you date yourself, you sound out of touch. Would Jack Kennedy be caught saying, "cutting a rug" in this day and age?'

He recoiled as if she had slapped him. She was going too far. 'Don't feel so bad, Frankie,' he retaliated. 'Your brainy daughter can still go to the University of Miami and major in scuba diving. That should be about her speed.'

It was only a retaliatory crack, made in the course of a personal argument between husband and wife, but D'Arcy, walking in on their conversation at just that point, didn't know that. And it was a new resentment against her father, added to the one she'd almost but not quite forgotten when he'd turned against her in the Rud/Judith/library couch fiasco.

When the letter of admittance from Boston University arrived, mother and daughter both were determined that D'Arcy would go off to Boston and show them all. Francesca had visions of D'Arcy doing so brilliantly in school that her father would be ashamed that he had ever cast aspersions on her daughter's scholastic abilities, and the people at Radcliffe apologizing for having turned her down, and D'Arcy had visions of her own. One was of her father, Judith and Abby being amazed at her scholastice achievement, but the more vivid one was of her and Rud in a torrid clinch, but this time it was the *real* thing!

If anything, she was more determined than ever to make it with Rud, and through the months of waiting until it was time for her to enter college the following autumn, her vision grew, fed on dreams and nourished with imagination. Rud became even more handsome, sweeter, larger than life. His remembered kisses of that night on the couch grew more ardent, every word that he had uttered became more urgent, ever more passionate. Like Topsy, Rud just grew until he was more than a young man . . . until he was full-blown young god.

In the months following the party, D'Arcy had written to both Abby and

Rud. He answered her first letter right away, but then he didn't answer the next one for weeks, and after that, not at all. Abby, on the other hand, answered all D'Arcy's letters through spring. It was Abby who, answering for both herself and Rud, apologetically turned down D'Arcy's and Francesca's invitation to join them in Palm Springs for the Christmas vacation, extended without consulting Bill. Judith was taking them to Paris! Abby wrote. Perhaps, instead, D'Arcy would come up to Boston for spring vacation. But then, several weeks later, Abby wrote regretfully to withdraw the invitation for D'Arcy to visit on the Easter vacation – since they had had such a wonderful time in Paris, Judith had decided that they'd go to London for the spring break!

Then there'd been a picture post card from London which depicted the changing of the guard at Buckingham Palace, with a message written in Abby's handwriting and signed by both Abby and Rud. After that there were no more communications and D'Arcy steeled herself to wait until September when her first year of college would begin, and she'd see Rud again.

2.

Francesca accompanied D'arcy to Boston in September to help her get settled in. She also wanted to see Abby, to see how she was getting on. D'Arcy could barely wait for the moment when they went calling on the Stantons, but then she was crushed the moment they were shown into the drawing room.

'I am so sorry Rud couldn't be here,' Judith told them. 'He planned on it but then this terrible nuisance with the house in Newport came up, and I had to send him down there to see to it. But, of course, Abby is here—'

Abby took Francesca's breath away. Under Judith's care, the immature rose-bud's petals had opened to reveal a flower of a whole new colour. The dark hair that had just *hung* was now flatteringly blunt cut to shoulder length with deep bangs and waved forward on the cheeks, and she was collegiately fashionable in high leather boots, a cashmere sweater, a camel's hair jacket and a correct single strand of unmistakably real pearls. She looked like the perfect 'Cliffie,' Francesca thought, exuding an air of self-confidence which was awesome.

Abby poured the tea, mixed the cocktails, and directed the maid as if she'd been doing exactly that all her life. She talked about Paris and London and the wonderful shopping while Judith looked on with pride and affection. And why shouldn't she? Francesca asked herself. The present Abby was Judith's own creation, almost as if she had borne her, and there had never been a Carlotta.

Everyone said the right thing. Judith promised Francesca that she'd keep an eye on D'Arcy, have her to dinner and that sort of thing, and Abby promised D'Arcy that the two of them would get together all the time, at least once a week, to talk about college and clothes and boys . . . girl stuff. . . .

At first there were telephone calls from both Judith and Abby while D'Arcy waited to hear from Rud. And Judith did invite D'Arcy to dinner and to tea but then had to break the engagements for one valid reason or other. And Abby was always too busy to see D'Arcy, mostly with her schoolwork. 'All I do is study, study, study,' she complained on the phone. 'I had no idea college was going to be this hard, did you?'

Then D'Arcy started calling the Stanton house almost every day, asking to speak to Rud but never, not even *once*, did she manage to reach him. It didn't matter when she called – morning, noon or night. He was always unavailable for whatever reason, and it didn't help to leave messages since he never called back. Finally, it was D'Arcy who got the message – Rud wasn't getting hers. It was the only reasonable explanation.

She began to spend most of her time plotting how to get through to Rud, how to circumvent Judith and Abby who were trying to keep them apart. When she wasn't plotting she was busy hating – Judith; Abby, who lived in the same house with him; and then her father; and only after that, the gray relentless New England weather. She couldn't concentrate on her classes, found little time to study, or even to make friends. Certainly she wasn't interested in any of the boys who asked her out for a beer, or to share a doobie. Even her roommate didn't know what to make of her. At first she had thought she had acquired a lively, cute, pretty Southern belle of a friend who would be ready for a good time at the drop of a hat, and here was D'Arcy Sheridan, formerly known as the Sunshine Girl, a bitter, nervous wreck who was getting thinner by the day, because she was often too preoccupied to remember to eat.

The only things D'Arcy did consistently was call her mother, scheme how to outfox Judith and contact Rud, and speculate as to why he wasn't calling her. Even if he didn't get her messages, why wasn't he calling under his own initiative? It got so she was afraid to leave her room because she might miss the call that never came. Then it occurred to her Rud probably didn't have her phone number, didn't even know which dorm she was in since neither Judith nor Abby had ever given him this information.

There has to be another way, she thought, and going to the Stanton house and demanding to see him wouldn't work either. The servants probably had their orders and she'd be told that he wasn't at home, and no one knew when he would be. So she started walking the streets of Harvard Square endlessly, looking into bookstores, coffee shops, the hangouts, peering into doorways and up and down alleys. She haunted Harvard Yard, loitering in front of those buildings he might enter, searching lounges and cafeterias, in this Hall, out that Commons.

And then finally, when she least expected to see him – it was a cold, raw, windy November day and she was just taking a lonely, morose walk down by the River, there he was! He was walking fast, just as any ordinary mortal might be, any nondescript college man or everyday Cambridge resident. But it wasn't any of these – it was her Rud!

She called out his name but he couldn't hear her. He was on the other side of Memorial Drive and the expanse between them was too great, and if the noise of the wind blowing off the Charles didn't drown everything out, the sound of the cars speeding down the Drive did. She dashed out, unmindful of the traffic, effortlessly dodging cars with the expertise of an old urban dweller. If state of mind had been a factor, she could easily have floated high over the cars.

'Rud!' she screamed out again and he turned and after a few seconds realized who it was. 'D'Arcy!' He started back towards her. Still she kept running and in a few seconds she hurled herself at him. 'Oh Rud!'

He was shocked to see how different she was from the D'Arcy he remembered. She'd been cute and round and her hair had been a smooth, blond cap. Now she appeared to be startlingly thin, this evident even though she was wearing a too-large quilted parka, and her hair was long and straight and slightly greasy, hanging limply from a middle parting. He remembered her in a brightly coloured summer dress which showed off her large and pretty breasts. Now her face was pinched and in addition to the big parka, she wore a woollen scarf wrapped around her throat several times and heavy boots.

'D'Arcy,' he laughed uncertainly. 'What's happened to my Sunshine girl?' It was just something to say.

'I guess she's disappeared into your terrible winter but she'll be back!' *Oh, I will now that I've found you again!*

'So what brings you to Boston?' he asked while he looked around, his eyes darting down the Drive. He was already late!

'What am I doing here? I'm going to school here. I'm at B.U. Didn't you know?'

It was really too much that no one had ever breathed even a word about her being in Boston but she couldn't waste time on that now. 'Are you just taking a walk? Don't you have a car? Can't we go some place warm to talk? I've been calling you forever. I can't believe I've been in Boston *three* months and we haven't even seen each other once!' She tugged at his arm. 'Let's go some place warm!'

'I'm sorry, D'Arcy, but I'm meeting someone.' He looked down the street again nervously.

'But I've got to see you. We have a million things to talk about. Do you absolutely have to meet someone this minute?'

'I'm afraid so and I'm already late. Look, I'll call you and we'll get together.' He was late, goddamn it! And if he didn't get going Barbara would just get uptight and drive away. She wasn't one to sit in her car playing with herself while she waited for him! 'I'll call you tomorrow, OK?' He tried to gently disengage his arm from her grasp.

'But you don't have my number. Can't we meet tonight?'

'No, not tonight. I'm busy. Why don't you give me your number and —'

'Can't you break your date?'

'No, D'Arcy. I'm sorry.' He *was*. He was glad to see D'Arcy but he wasn't about to break his date with Barbara Beddings for her. Between his mother and Barbara's husband, the state senator, the opportunity to bang Barbara didn't come around often enough to suit him.

'Well, when *can* we meet?'

'Tomorrow,' he said quickly. 'How about tomorrow?'

Damn it! Barbara will drive away for sure! She was always jumpy as hell waiting in her car for him. Afraid she'd be spotted. 'We'll meet for lunch. The Midget? OK? Twelve o'clock.'

But she didn't want to see him, really see him, for the first time in some sandwich shop! She wanted to be alone with him! She *needed* to be alone with him! 'No!' she cried.

He had had enough. 'I have to go. Call me.'

'No, wait!' She caught his arm, desperate. The name of a little hotel she'd seen in the Square flashed into her head. 'Meet me at the Liberty Hotel in Harvard Square tomorrow.' She'd go there right now and reserve a room.

'At twelve, OK? Just ask for me at the desk. Do you know where the Liberty is?'

'Yes,' and he rushed off.

D'Arcy considered following him to see where he was going and whom he was meeting, but then abandoned the idea. He might catch her spying on him and he'd be mad, and that was the last thing in the world she wanted.

The young but world-weary desk clerk took her money. 'You got it. One double room for tomorrow, the 22nd. Check-out time is eleven sharp the next day. Will you be needing anything else?'

'Like what?'

He winked. 'You know, the stuff that grows on people's lawns.'

She stared at him for a second. 'You mean *grass?*'

'You got it.'

She looked into her wallet, figuring. 'How much?'

When she arrived at the Liberty at eleven, her arms full of packages, the desk clerk smirked. 'Check-in isn't till twelve o'clock. I can't let you go up yet.'

'Oh, give me a break, will you? I'm not even staying until tomorrow.'

He winked. 'I didn't think you were.'

She took the fruit out of the paper bags, polished the apples and pears until they glowed, arranged it all in the cornflower-blue bowl she'd bought for $2.98. Two apples, two pears, two bananas, two oranges. She was sorry she hadn't bought grapes. Grapes were a natural for lovers. She could have peeled them one by one, fed them to Rud, placing each one carefully into his perfect mouth as he reposed in bed like an ancient emperor, nude and beautiful. She, of course, would be the nude and nubile temptress.

She opened the box of chocolates, placed it on the nightstand, resisting the temptation to pop one in her mouth. She wanted even the box of candy to be perfect, pristine. She had a bottle of champagne too. It cost only $2.49 and she'd been amazed to discover that one could buy champagne so cheaply. But how was she going to chill it? She wasn't about to ask that slimy worm downstairs if he had a plastic bucket of ice for her, much less a silver wine cooler. She went into the small bathroom and turned on the cold water tap. Yes, the water was icy-cold, just as she had thought it might be.

Humming, she removed the green oiled paper from the small bunch of flowers she'd bought at the stand on the corner. She would have preferred red roses which said, 'I love you,' but their cost had been prohibitive. As it was the green vase for the flowers had cost another three dollars, and she was running out of money. Since she was going home the next day, her mother hadn't bothered to send her a cheque this week.

Still, she was enjoying her enforced thrift. Somehow it made her and Rud's meeting more romantic – as if they were impoverished lovers embracing in a garret, enduring all kinds of economic hardship in the name of love.

She put a stick of the incense called Nocturnal Delight into the little burner and lit it, inhaling the fragrance. It was more than spicy and sexy, she thought. It was sweet too, and as she stripped herself of her clothes and stepped into the shower, she sang, 'Sugar, sex and spice, oh, my baby's very nice. . . .'

She soaped herself all over, caressing her own skin that soon *he* would be caressing.

He was late and she went through ten, fifteen minutes of hell. Why was he late? Wasn't he coming? Had he been hit by a car? Or was it *his* car that was wrapped around a telephone pole, smashed up in his haste to get to her?

And then, finally, there was a knock on the door and she flung open the door and then the smile on his lips faltered when he saw that she was naked, her arms outstretched, her freshly-washed hair falling over her still beautiful breasts. . . .

When he was poised over her, ready to enter, and only then he remembered to inquire softly, 'You're wearing something?' Used to women who took precautions, he hadn't brought a condom. She, unable to wait another minute, another second, breathed, 'Oh yes! Yes!'

But then he couldn't help but realize that it was the first time for her, and that she couldn't be wearing an IUD or a diaphragm. But he was beyond asking any more questions and D'Arcy was gasping, begging him to thrust and push and be inside her!

Only afterwards, he said 'This was your first time—'

'Oh yes,' she breathed, glad that she had come to him untouched, unspoiled. 'Are you pleased?'

She thought surely he would be. In all the books she'd ever read the man was always thrilled when the girl was still a virgin, that no other man had been there first.

'Yes, of course,' he said, 'but you said you . . . had protection. How could you when—?'

'Great balls of fire, Rud, didn't you ever hear of the Pill?'

Of course, the Pill! But then he wondered why a girl who was still a virgin would put herelf on the Pill. All the women he knew who were on it complained that it made them feel sick, that it made them fat. And D'Arcy was more than slim. It seemed to him that she would have waited for the Pill until that time at least when she was no longer a— But then, D'Arcy was up and out of the bed, her eyes sparkling, pulling on his arm. 'Come on, let's take a shower together. First I'll wash you and then you'll wash me and then. . . .'

He laughed and was out of bed in a flash, following her into the shower, and laughing all the way. Say what you would about older women like Barbara Beddings – they were expert, their touch was sure, and there was an intensity that was exciting – but the sex lacked a certain freshness, an air of spontaneity, the feeling of a shared passion, that sex with girls like D'Arcy had. It was more fun, less an act of desperation. And there *was* something to be said for the relaxed atmosphere of sex games with an unmarried woman – the heady feeling that you could do it again and again, take a few hits, maybe eat a few chocolates, and then do it again!

With Barbara it was always: *For God's sake, we can't waste time with that!* (Whatever it was he was doing that wasn't strictly business.) *Let's do it, let's get it done, I have to be home in an hour. . . .*

As the afternoon wore away he had another revelation. With Barbara and women like her, it was always *me, me, me!* Selfish sex! With D'Arcy, it was more like *you . . . you . . . you! Always he!*

When he left around six it was dark and usually at that hour on a cold and dark November evening, the Harvard Square streets were quiet, nearly deserted until the kids started drifting out again, an hour or two later. But tonight there were people in the streets, an excitement in the air, a tension. He didn't go a block, walking quickly to his car, before he learned why the streets were busy that night – the President had been shot, was lying dead for several hours already . . . all the time he'd been lying with D'Arcy. Years later when someone recalled what he been doing at that exact point in time when John Kennedy was assassinated, Rud would remember, embarrassed, that he had been with D'Arcy Sheridan, fucking his brains out!

Judith, he thought, would be wondering where he was, why he wasn't with her, digesting this historical event with her. She'd be mad as hell, probably, but in the end it would be all right. Abby would placate her. Abby was good at that, taking a hell of a lot of the pressure off him.

Rud had said he'd be back tomorrow at four. Of course the creep at his desk would want her to pay for the room in advance and she was almost broke. She had to get some more cash. She'd have to cash in her aeroplane ticket first thing in the morning before the eleven o'clock check-out time. Then she'd do some more shopping. She'd buy more fruit. Grapes, and something . . . more *esoteric* like figs. Oh yes, figs. They were like a woman's lower lips, shaped like a freshly opened flower. And she'd buy perfume too, lots of perfume – to spray her body, the sheets, the whole room! It was only a crummy room, the crummiest, but she'd make it smell like heaven. She'd make it smell like paradise.

At ten o'clock, Francesca couldn't stand it anymore and picked up the phone to call D'Arcy. It was probably only minutes but to Francesca it seemed like an eternity as the phone rang and rang and no one answered

'See, something *is* wrong,' she told Bill. 'They're not answering.'

'So no one is standing guard by the phone. Everyone in the dorm is probably watching television like everyone else in America tonight.'

'But someone's supposed to be on telephone duty. . . .'

'Tonight is a special night. Tonight the rules don't apply.'

Finally a girl did pick up and when Francesca asked for D'Arcy, the girl said she'd look around for her. She sounded disoriented, and then after a while she came back to say 'I can't find her.'

'But where is she?' Francesca asked foolishly.

'I don't know. The President is dead,' the bodiless voice said as if that was the answer, as if that changed all the rules and how could anyone know anything.

3.

When D'Arcy awoke the next morning it took her a few seconds to orient herself, and then she panicked. What time was it? She had to pay the room clerk before eleven. She looked at her watch but it said twenty past three. It had stopped! She threw on her clothes and ran downstairs. There was nobody at the desk but the wall clock told her it was almost eight o'clock. She ran outside, not even noticing that it was cold and grey, that the streets were strangely deserted, that there was no hustle and bustle as there usually was on

255

a Saturday morning in Harvard Square with a lot of the students on their way to have breakfast out.

She pulled her plane ticket out of her desk drawer and went over to the bed where her roommate Leslie lay asleep and shook her until she rolled over and groaned, 'I didn't get to bed till four.'

'I need a few dollars to get to the airport. I'll pay you back when I get back from Florida after Thanksgiving.'

'In my bag. Have a good Thanksgiving if anybody can this year.' She turned over and went back to sleep.

'Oh, I'm going to.' She was going to have the best Thanksgiving of her entire life. But what did Leslie mean by that *if anybody can this year*. Oh, well, what did it matter?

She dickered with the desk clerk about getting a rate for the week. He was extra surly this morning and wouldn't budge an inch. 'What do you think we run? A flop house for busted-out students?' But D'Arcy was feeling too good to react other than to call him a disgusting animal.

After that she went and bought goodies. Since Rud was coming at four, they'd have dinner in the room, or if they were otherwise engaged at that time, they could always have a late supper. She bought olives and nuts, cheeses and pâtés, and long skinny French bread. She thought about buying an Italian salami but decided against it as not elegant enough. Instead she bought paper thin slices of prosciutto and a small jar of caviar, the golden kind, and a tin of smoked oysters. After all, oysters were supposed to be an aphrodisiac . . . as if she needed *that!* She also bought two bottles of French wine.

And then, since she'd be spending the whole week in the hotel, she decided to invest in a clock radio. And then she thought: 'Suppose he spends the night?' which of course was exactly what she wanted and she raced back to the grocery store for a carton of orange juice and a jar of instant coffee, little packets of sugar and a jar of powdered cream substitute, and then back to the appliance store to buy one of the little pots that boiled water instantly.

She stopped at a shop that displayed lotions in the window – the kind that were edible and came in different delicious flavours. She chose Strawberry Rapture, and hoped Rud loved the taste of strawberries. Then into the little store that sold oriental stuff to buy a kimono. In a week's time you could only spend so much time absolutely in the raw, she thought, and bought a black satin robe with a golden dragon emblazoned on the back. Blondes looked wonderful in black. And just to dress the room up and to fill in odd minutes, she bought a few magazines. Besides, on those nights Rud wouldn't be able to sleep over, she'd need something to fill in the hours until he returned. A *Time* for him and a *Mademoiselle* for her, and *Playboy* for those times when their energies flagged. She thought that was cute of her to get the inspirational reading matter. And then for a touch of class, she bought a French fashion magazine, *La Femme*. She could just about make out a sentence if she skipped a few words here and there but Rud was bound to be impressed.

Then and only then did she remember that she was supposed to be on a plane heading for home and she ran to a pay telephone and put in a collect call, hoping that her mother hadn't left for the airport yet. She hadn't, and she didn't get mad when D'Arcy said she wasn't coming home at all . . . that she was going home with Leslie to Teaneck, New Jersey since Leslie wanted her to meet her brother, Burt, who'd be home from the University of Wisconsin for the holidays. In fact, Francesca was only relieved that D'Arcy was all right and was even willing to think about another boy, one who wasn't Rud Stanton.

'Call me from Leslie's, D'Arcy. Collect. And if you need money I can wire you some at Leslie's.'

'Oh no, Mummy, I'm fine.' She did feel a shade guilty at her deception, and was unable to resist a little embroidery. 'I'll let you know how it turns out with Burt. Leslie says he's a hunk.'

'OK, sweetie, I hope he is. I was just so worried when I couldn't reach you last night. I thought that maybe you were taking the President's death very hard and—'

'What? What did you just say about the President?'

'That I was worried about how you took his assassination. . . .'

'Oh yeah. Right. Yeah, I did feel simply terrible!'

Rud was fifteen minutes late but D'Arcy had steeled herself against that possibility and she didn't nag him about it. She knew men didn't like to be held accountable for every second, and that the surest way to lose a man was to hold him too tight. She had to play it cool, at least as cool as she could manage.

He thought she looked adorable in her Japanese kimono, her pale blond hair pinned high in an upsweep, her cheeks pink, and he told her so. Her cheeks flushed even pinker and he drew her into his arms and kissed her lingeringly. Then when he released her, he started to undress quickly. She was startled at first by this haste but then she laughed, thinking that he couldn't wait, and she had no argument with that. He was no more impatient than she. Still, she thought she'd slow him down some, to heighten his excitement and her own.

She let her robe drop to the floor, touched his erection delicately, teasingly. 'Let's take a shower.' But he pulled her to him. 'Sounds wonderful but I don't have the time.'

'Why not?'

He lifted her off her feet and carried her to the bed. 'I only have an hour.' He laid her down and was lowering himself to the bed when he caught sight of her new clock radio. 'No. Not even an hour. About forty-five minutes.'

He put his lips to her breast but she couldn't concentrate. 'Why do you have to leave?'

'We're going to Washington.'

'Who's we?'

His lips trailed from breast to belly, back again to her breasts. 'Judith, Abby and me. Mother wants to pay her respects to the Kennedys. And then Sunday . . . tomorrow, his body's going to be carried up Pennsylvania Avenue by cassion. You know, the riderless horse business with the boots reversed in the stirrups. . . .'

No she didn't know. All she knew was that he was leaving Boston. 'But why do you have to go?' she persisted.

He raised himself for his entering thrust. 'Because Mother thinks we should.'

He groaned. In. Out. All around.

Her breathing was laboured. 'I thought she didn't like Joe Kennedy.'

'She doesn't.' *Why didn't she shut up?* He hated it when women talked their way through it. 'But she said it's the right thing to do. That we're all Massachusetts people, kind of like family. Besides, she admires Jackie.'

He accelerated his movement, priming himself for his climax.

'When will you be back?' she asked frantically.

He didn't answer for a full minute, concentrating only on the shuddering of his body. Then, still inside her, he said, 'I guess we'll be back on Tuesday. Monday's the funeral with a mass at St Matthew's and the burial at Arlington. Mother wouldn't miss this historic occasion. World leaders from over ninety countries will be there, including de Gaulle. And there will be receptions afterwards. . . .' He looked at the clock again. It was a quarter to five. If he wasn't out of here by five, he was dead. He wanted to pull out. He *had to* pull out. As gently as possible he asked, 'Did you?' He didn't think she had. In fact, he was sure she hadn't.

He pulled out, rolled over on his side, rubbed his hand over her, inserted two fingers into her and manipulated them, making sure he made contact with her clitoris. It took less than a minute before she screamed out. He knew it wouldn't take long. The really young ones were ultrasensitive to finger-fucking. The older they got, the longer it took.

D'Arcy had climaxed but she was so distraught, it was anticlimactic.

He was leaving and she didn't think she could bear it. 'When will you be back?' she asked again.

His tone was gentle. 'I told you. Probably Tuesday.'

'Will you come here the second you're back?'

He groaned silently. *They're all the same!* 'I'll try.' His voice was soft but he had half a leg out the door.

'I'll be here. I'll be waiting,' she called after him as he dashed down the hall toward the stairs.

She didn't know what to do with herself. Scream? Run out into the street naked? There was this feeling of bereftness, of emptiness, a long tunnel of emptiness. This was only Saturday. How could she last until Tuesday? Where could she dump this block of frustration? She wished that it was a thing of substance – a sackful of something she could put down in a corner and order it, 'Stay there!' She had to do *something*. She took the bottle of Strawberry Rapture, that which he was supposed to lick off her and she off him – a procedure which should have taken long, delightful hours – and smashed it into the chipped porcelain sink and watched as its lovely pink creaminess slithered down the drain.

She opened one of the bottles of wine, congratulating herself that she had remembered to buy a corkscrew. If only he was there to commend her on her efficiency. After she finished off the first bottle she intended to open the second but she fell asleep. When she awoke around twelve o'clock she had a blinding headache but luckily she had a tiny bottle of aspirins in her handbag and she swallowed four of them and fell asleep again.

When she awoke Sunday morning she felt terrible. She'd call her mother, she thought. That would make her feel better. She'd pretend she was calling from

Teaneck, New Jersey and having a marvellous time. She'd tell her mother that she and Leslie's brother Burt, who *was* an absolute hunk, had really hit it off!

She had to place the call through the desk. She picked up the phone and gave the creep the number. 'It's the Governor's house,' she told him with a measure of arrogance. 'Do you think you can manage to place it?'

He snickered. 'Yeah, I can place it. The question, baby face, is – can you pay for it?'

'Yes, I can pay for it, turkey. Come up and get the money!'

He laughed and put the call through. Bess answered the phone. 'D'Arcy! How's Teaneck?'

'Great. Just great. New Jersey's sensational. Is my mother there?'

'Oh, they went to Washington for the funeral, hon. Isn't it just awful? But you try and have a good time.'

'Yeah. Sure.'

'I'll tell her you called. I'm sure she'll call you the minute she comes back. Let me have your number there. . . .'

'Never mind. I'll call her. When are they coming back?'

'I think Tuesday.'

D'Arcy opened the second bottle of wine and unwrapped all the food she'd bought for her and Rud's romantic dinner – the cheeses and the pâtés, the prosciutto and the caviar, and ate it all, along with the olives and the nuts and the long French bread. She stuffed it all into her mouth, barely waiting to swallow before she stuffed in more. And then when she thought she couldn't swallow another bite, she opened the tin of smoked oysters and stuffed them into her mouth with her fingers, oily as they were. And then she sucked her fingers clean before she ran to the toilet to heave, after which she collapsed on the bed, exhausted.

There was a knock on the door. *He's back. He's come back!* She ran to the door, threw it open, and saw that it was the acne-scarred slimeball of a desk clerk. He leered at her naked body. 'I've got the charges on your call.'

'What call?'

'Your call to the governor,' he laughed mockingly. 'It's $2.75 but if—'

'If what, you pathetic nerd?'

He ignored the name-calling. 'I can get away from the desk for a half-hour or so. . . .'

'Isn't that wonderful? Why don't you use the time to go fuck yourself?'

She went to her bag, took out three singles. 'Keep the change.'

He took it, smirked. 'Let me know if you change your mind.'

She went out to get some wine. When she couldn't find a liquor store open, she came back to ask Creepo what he had in the way of alcoholic beverages. He was in the back room behind the office and she rang the desk bell until he came out.

'You won't believe what I just saw on TV!'

'All right,' she sighed. 'Tell me.'

'Lee Harvey Oswald being shot! Right on camera!'

'Well, I do declare! Isn't that fascinating? And who's Lee Harvey Oswald?' She didn't wait for an answer. 'I want something to drink. What do you have?'

'Whadda you mean? What do I have? This is a hotel, not a fucking liquor store.'

'So what do you have and how much?'

'I got a half gallon of guineau red but it will cost you ten bucks.'

'And how much did it cost you – two?'

'Hey, I'm busy. You want it or not?'

She still had a ten dollar bill and she slapped it down on the counter. He pocketed it and went into the back room and brought out the jug. 'If you want to come back and watch the TV, you can.'

'Now, why would I want to do that? But if you see anybody else getting shot, give my room a buzz.'

The half-gallon lasted her through the night until she passed out in a stupor. In the morning she awoke nauseated and with a terrific headache and the first thing she did was throw up. She told herself what she needed was some food and she went down and out on to the street. It was Monday, she calculated after a little deliberation, but the streets were totally deserted. What was going on? And then she found that most of the stores were closed. Something strange was going on in Cambridge. Had the whole town gone out of business? She had no idea that the whole nation was attending a funeral that day via the television. Still, she too was in mourning but it was all very personal.

The pizza shop was open and she ordered three large pies with everything to go but when they were ready, she found she had only enough money to pay for two. In the end, the proprietor let her have all three. What was he going to do with a pie that already had an overbaked crust? She took the pies back to her room and wolfed them down, swallowing as rapidly as she could. Then she ran to the bathroom to eject everything, which took more time than it had to swallow it all. She had two aspirins left and she downed them with the dregs from the jug of wine and hoped she'd be able to sleep again.

That was the end of that – the aspirins, the wine, her money. She had run out of everything but time. She still had plenty of that to kill until tomorrow. After a while she realized she wasn't going to be able to sleep and she thought about that awhile and dispiritedly got out of bed, washed her face, brushed her hair, put on a quick application of mascara and went downstairs again.

She smiled at the room clerk. 'Ah never did find your name,' she began, forcing her dimples.

Suspiciously he grunted. 'It's Dom. Dominick. Why do you want to know?'

'Well ah don't want to keep calling you *hey you*, Dom.'

'Hey, whadda you want? You want something?'

'As a matter of fact ah do. Something to make me feel real good, you know?'

'Hey, I don't have no hard stuff.'

'Ah didn't think you all would.' She batted her lashes. 'But I bet you all have somethin', right?'

'You got no bread, right?'

She was relieved that he got her message and she shook her head prettily. 'No bread.'

He rubbed his mouth with his hand while he considered. 'I got some good grass.'

She giggled coyly. 'No grass. It gives me the munchies and I'm not in the mood for nibblin'.'

'That's too bad. I could give you something to nibble on,' he leered. 'You want uppers or downers?'

'Both.'

He gestured to the back room. 'Come into my parlour. . . .'

But then she didn't move.

'Now what's your problem?'

'I'm not a fly.'

Who the hell did she think she was? Besides, she didn't look so good as she did when she came in. 'If you're no fly then *you* don't fly. So stop wasting my time.'

D'Arcy considered. She was sure her mother would rather she gave up the gold wristwatch which had been her seventeenth birthday present to Creepo rather than her body. She took off the watch and laid it on the counter. He eyed it while he said, 'I'm not a pawnbroker.'

'Believe me, asshole, I know all the things you're *not*.'

That was going to cost her. 'So now it's asshole? What happened to the Scarlett O'Hara routine?'

She smiled nastily. 'I guess Scarlett took a good look at you and decided it was gone with the wind. Do you want the watch or not? It's real gold.'

He picked it up to examine. 'OK. Six of each.'

'A dozen of each. That watch is worth a lot of money.'

They settled on eight of each, plus a jug of wine.

The routine was simple. She took a downer with a half glass of wine to sleep and when she awoke, she took an upper with a quarter glass of wine. When she was up, she read the magazines she'd bought that first day. She went through them all until she got to the French magazine. She studied the picture on the cover. It was of a stunningly beautiful girl with heavily black-rimmed eyes, an ink-black geometric hairdo that didn't quite cover the ears and came to points on the cheeks, and she had a big, luscious petunia-pink mouth. But why did she look so familiar, she wondered. Was it the mouth or the expression in the eyes? She laughed. She was really going nuts. She could have sworn that if not for the slight Oriental lift to the eyes and that black, black hair the model could have been Jade!

She decided it was time for one of the yellows and she clicked on the radio. What was so awful really? A yellow, a little wine, and some good music. . . .

By the time Tuesday came and went without a word from Rud, she still had half her supply of pills and the wits to call her mother so that Francesca wouldn't try to call her at Leslie's in Teaneck. She begged Dominick over the phone to put in the call to Florida, promising him she'd get the money for the call the next day when her boyfriend came. He refused and then she remembered that all she had to do was find a dime and then she could go to a pay phone and make a collect call. She found the dime after she emptied her purse and then she was on her way once she took another pill.

She told Francesca that things were going hot and heavy with her and Burt and Francesca told her how sweet little John-John had saluted his father's coffin. 'It was enough to break one's heart.'

'Did you run into Rud and Judith?'

'No. What makes you think they were in Washington?'

'No reason. A guess.'

'You sound funny, D'Arcy. Are you all right?'

'Sure. I gotta go. He's calling me. Rud. I meant Burt.'

'Did you say Rud at first?'

'No. Bad connection. . . .'

When Rud called on Wednesday, Dominick put the call through since he hadn't connected him to the bitch's room when he called the day before. When the phone rang, D'Arcy pounced on it, thinking wildly, I have to take a shower! I have to wash my hair! I have to pull myself together!

'Oh Rud, I've been going crazy waiting to hear from you!'

She had to get Creepo to send up the maid. She hadn't seen hide or hair of a maid since she got here. *What a fleabag! Don't they ever change the sheets?*

'When are you coming over?' And then, 'Tonight? Not until tonight?' How was she going to stand waiting until tonight?

'I said I'll *try* and get over there tonight.'

She couldn't argue with him. If she made a fuss he'd think she was being clingy and men hated clingy women. She'd be all right now that she knew he was coming. And she'd have time to do all the things she had to . . . maybe she'd even try a new hair style. She'd certainly get the sheets changed. She remembered she hadn't eaten anything since the pizzas. When was that? Yesterday or the day before? No wonder she was so lightheaded. Maybe after they made love tonight they could go out to dinner like any in-love couple might. A real dinner in a nice restaurant with candlelight and flowers.

At eight Rud called again. 'I'm sorry as hell, D'Arcy, but I can't get away. We're having a big Thanksgiving party here tomorrow and Judith's put me and Abby in charge of the decorations. And it's a big job. We've got the living room to do, the dining room, the front hall and—'

D'Arcy was confused. He wasn't coming because of decorations. 'What kind of decorations?'

He laughed. 'Oh, Judith's got it into her head to have the whole house Thanksgivingey this year. She has cardboard cut outs of turkeys and Pilgrims and Indians, and bunches of Indian corn and these huge pumpkins and squashes. You know – the works. It's really out of character for old Judy but Abby and I are humouring her. You understand?'

No, she didn't! He was fooling around with cardboard turkeys and pumpkins and Abby, when he was supposed to be here with her!

'I'll come over to your house right now. I'll help! I'm really good at decorating. Everyone always says that. I'll help!'

'No, D'Arcy,' he said firmly. 'I don't think that would work out.' Didn't she know that just the sound of her name was anathema to Judith?

'Oh . . .' she wailed like a wounded animal. 'You're going to come tomorrow then? Tomorrow morning?'

'No, that's impossible, D'Arcy. The party's tomorrow. The Thanksgiving party. I won't be able to get away. Friday, maybe. Will you still be there Friday?' He had to get off the phone. 'D'Arcy, will you still be there Friday?'

He hadn't understood why D'Arcy had holed up in that godawful place in the first place, but he hadn't gone into it with her. He'd assumed that for her own reasons she hadn't wanted to go home or spend the holiday in a deserted dormitory.

'Can't I come to the party?' she pleaded. She'd go back to the dorm and get something to wear, she thought. Something absolutely gorgeous that would knock their eyes out, something that would leave Abby in the dust. 'OK? I'll come? Right?'

'Oh hell, D'Arcy, that's impossible. Mother's got all the seating arrangements made. She just wouldn't— Look, I have to go. I'll call you Friday, OK?'

He hung up but for a few moments D'Arcy talked into the dead phone. 'But Rud darling, of course your mother will want me there. I'm family! As much family as Abby! We're kissin' cousins, remember? Please let me come! Pretty please!'

But then there was a dial tone and she said, 'Sorry, I guess I have the wrong number,' and hung up.

She took the last of her pills, two of each kind. Then she finished off the wine. She was kind of disappointed in the results. She *was* seeing double but that was about all. Then she giggled. She was seeing two Ruds and two were better than one . . . better than none.

On Thursday, Dominick was off duty for a change. In this crummy job, it really was a national holiday when they gave him a day off, the fuckers. He'd decided to spend the day in his crummy room on the third floor, smoking dope and sleeping. But then he got to thinking about the bitch, Miss D'Arcy Sheridan, who claimed she was the daughter of the governor of Florida. Not that he believed her. If she was the governor's daughter what was she doing in a joint like this?

He realized that he hadn't seen her in the flesh since Monday when he'd traded her the pills for the watch. On Tuesday he hadn't seen her or spoken to her on the phone. On Wednesday he had put the jock's call through to her and she'd called down to demand a maid be sent up but he had put her in her place. But now he was worried. He decided she was trouble. As far as he could figure out she hadn't been out of that room since Monday which meant she hadn't eaten since Monday at least. And she had those pills, *his* pills. Maybe even though it was his day off he should go down and check on her. Better still, he should get rid of her. Just throw her out, even if he had to give her back the extra two days money. If she made a stink. The more he thought about it the more he knew he wanted her out before there was some trouble which he didn't need.

He went down to the desk, shook the old man who was on duty but nodding off, told him to stay alert, for God's sake, and got the key to the bitch's room.

He knocked once and when he didn't get an answer, he used his key and walked in. First thing he realized that the radio was on. It was Peter, Paul and Mary singing Dylan's 'Blowing in the Wind.' Then he saw her. *Jesus!*

The lousy broad was sitting straight up in the bed, her back against the headboard, stark naked, eyes shut, and the sheets were covered with blood. Her blood! It looked like the blood was running out of her in twenty . . . thirty places! *Holy shit!* He thought he was going to piss in his pants, but all he did was run for the toilet to throw up.

4.

Why should he be the one to call the ambulance or the pigs? Dominick sweated. The guy who called the pigs was the one who got it in the ass. Let that fucking jock who balled her report it! Averting his eyes from the body, his eyes swept the room. What was here to incriminate him? No container from the pills – he'd given them to her loose. He spotted the empty wine bottle and decided to wipe it gingerly with his handkerchief just to make sure his prints weren't on it, then he sprinted downstairs and told the relief man to go take a nap in the back room and he prepared to make his call. He had the guy's name – Rud Stanton. 'Send up the maid,' she'd said. 'Rud Stanton, one of *the* Stantons, is coming over and he's not used to pigsties.' Yeah, he knew who the Stantons were – you could hardly walk through Boston and not see the fucking name all over.

He got a faggot butler and the son-of-a-bitch wouldn't call Mr Stanton to the phone until he told him if he didn't get Stanton to the phone, they were all going to be fucking sorry.

'Oh, D'Arcy! D'Arcy!' Rud hugged her body to him and for those brief terrible seconds his love knew no bounds. And then he realized that she wasn't cold, and that all the blood on her was not rivers of blood but many, many tiny rivulets. Stained with the blood, he turned to Dominick hovering in the doorway. 'How long is it since you called the ambulance? Why aren't they here yet?'

When Dominick confessed that he hadn't called for any ambulance, Rud thought that he would kill him, but then he remembered that it was more important to get D'Arcy to a hospital while she was still alive. She was still alive! And if she lived, he'd make it all up to her. *God, just let her live and I'll love her always!*

He made a direct call to Stanton Memorial because he wanted to make sure D'Arcy would get the fastest service, and the very best in care. But Judith, when she arrived at the hospital and conferred with her administrator who, too, had been called away from his Thanksgiving dinner, thought he had called Stanton Memorial for another reason. 'At least you knew where to take her so that none of this leaks out.' Rud started to protest but Judith cut him short. 'You're certain they didn't call the police at that hotel?'

Rud nodded mutely.

'Well, thank God for small favours.' She looked at his bloodstained suit with disgust. 'I've sent for a clean suit for you – for heaven's sake, you look like a male Jackie Kennedy with all that blood all over you.'

He thought that was a pretty tasteless remark but he said nothing. Who was he to talk about anything?

'Once you change, I want you to go to that place and remove all of D'Arcy's personal effects. The reason I'm sending you personally is that we want this

264

thing contained, and the fewer people know about it, the less chance there is for scandal. My God, this time you've really done it!'

Then, realizing how she sounded, she smiled at him. 'You must forgive me if I sound harsh, but what I'm trying to do is protect D'Arcy. One whisper to the police and she'll be detained. Who knows? They might even insist that she be sent to a mental institution for observation and who knows for how long. In a case of attempted suicide – if indeed that was what it was . . .' her voice trailed off.

Sensitive to every one of Judith's nuances, he asked: 'What are you trying to say, Mother, that it *wasn't* an attempted suicide, that it was some kind of a trick to impress me?'

'Well, one mustn't be naive,' she drawled. 'If she were really serious about killing herself employing a razor, there are much more effective ways than making dozens of tiny nicks that barely cut the flesh. One deep slash in the neck or a couple of serious strokes at the wrist would have been much more to the point, wouldn't you say?'

He could feel his own blood draining from his head and he sat down to lower his head between his legs. *Sweet, loving D'Arcy and all that blood!*

He himself was totally to blame, but his mother's callousness revolted him.

'Of course, even if it wasn't really suicide, it *does* show a sick mind. But then I always did think she was unstable. Really, Rud, what ever were you thinking of when you launched this sordid, pathetic affair?'

He saw red then, but he didn't know which of Judith's words stung the worst? *Pathetic?* D'Arcy really loved him. Was that pathetic? As for sordid, he himself was the one who was sordid. And it had hardly been an affair. They had made love on only two occasions, and the second time he had given her the rush act. But what was the use of arguing with Judith. She was a bitch but he was the son of the bitch who had acted like a real bastard.

He just wished he could cry. 'Those cuts. . . . Will she be scarred?'

'Those cuts are so superficial the scabbing won't even last but two or three days. Scratches. If you stop to think about it, it was all very clever of D'Arcy. So much blood and so little damage. I imagine she figured she'd scare the living daylights out of you and I guess she did, at that. I hope it scared you enough to make you think twice before you have another romantic misadventure, such as your affair with Barbara Beddings. . . .'

Barbara? But how did Judith—?

'Yes, I know all about Ms Beddings. Her husband came to see me. He's outraged, as well he might be. I told him you'd never see her again. But what are we going to do with you, Rud?' Her tone was playful but there was a note of underlying steel. 'How *are* we to keep you out of trouble until you're elected President? That *is* our goal, remember? I'm doing my part but are you doing yours?'

It was a strange day, Rud mused. He had rushed D'Arcy to the hospital, praying that there was still time to save her, and now Judith was talking about keeping him out of trouble until he was old enough to be elected President. They had managed to cover a lot of ground in one day . . . in the matter of a couple of hours. Maybe he should preserve his bloodstained suit just to show himself some day how far he had come. . . .

Rud found D'Arcy's room at the Liberty spotless, the bed freshly made up, not a speck of blood anywhere.

'The police? Are they going to come around snooping?' Dominick asked, sweating. 'Do they know about the pills?'

Rud, wanting to get even with this prick for not calling an ambulance, for not asking how D'Arcy was, nodded. 'Yes to both questions. As for the pills, they asked me if I knew where she got them,' he said, which was a lie.

'Did you tell them?'

'I thought I'd leave that to Miss Sheridan. I guess if you were nice to her, she won't tell on you. But if you weren't, well, who knows? Where are her things?'

'Oh, I have them right here, Mr Stanton. Everything's here. I even saved her magazines. You'll tell her that I asked about how she was? Tell her I was really worried. Everything's in the suitcase – her clothes, the clock radio, even her bowl and a vase. . . . And there's her magazines, stacked next to the suitcase.'

'You can throw those away,' Rud said, picking up the suitcase. Then he noticed that the magazine on top was a French one and he smiled a sad little smile. *A French magazine, of all things. What a sweet, funny girl D'Arcy was.* He picked up the magazine. There was something strangely familiar about the cover girl. She looked very French, he supposed, with that hair-do. Then it struck him whom the girl resembled even without the long, red-gold hair. Jade! He tore off the cover, folded it carefully and slipped it into his pocket as Dominick watched him.

Snotty jock! Lousy preppie! How he wished he could blow the whistle on him, him with his fancy Harvard accent and his fancy cashmere coat.

Rud went back to the hospital where he intended to stay until D'Arcy awakened. The first face he wanted her to see was his own, to let her know that he was there for her. No matter what his true feelings for her – love or friendly affection – she had suffered at his hands. It didn't really matter to him whether his mother was right about it being a fake suicide attempt, which he doubted. What mattered was that she'd been driven to desperate measures and his hands weren't all that clean.

But Judith insisted he go home. 'I've been talking to our staff psychiatrists and they say the worst thing in the world for D'Arcy would be to see you at this time,' she lied. 'She needs a recovery period completely without your presence. She did this . . . this thing because of you and if she's to get well she has to do it without you. As it is they wanted to hospitalize her in the psychiatric ward, but I've talked them into letting her go back to school, providing she undergoes outpatient treatment. So I've assured them that she would and that you'd stay away for the time being. . . .'

He didn't want to agree but what could he do? He certainly didn't want to see D'Arcy locked up in the psychiatric ward. If she could go back to school while undergoing therapy, then her life would take on some normality and he owed her that – a life as normal as possible.

When D'Arcy awoke the first thing she thought of was that she was alive!

And she was glad! Glad she was alive and still living in the same world with Rud! And then she wondered where she was. It wasn't the Liberty Hotel for sure. This was a very clean place, the walls were stark white and she was in a bed with rails on either side. Then she saw the women in their starchy white uniforms and those little caps and she knew she was in a hospital. And then she fell asleep again. When she awoke again, she saw Judith. *What's she doing here?*

'D'Arcy dear! I'm so glad you're going to be all right and that there's not going to be any scarring. *That* was my first concern. You're such a young, beautiful girl with a wonderful life ahead of you.'

D'Arcy felt her face, her chest, her arms, remembering that she had cut herself in dozens of places. But there were no bandages! ' . . . superficial wounds,' she heard Judith say. 'And then I thought to myself, why say anything to Bill and Frankie? Why upset them needlessly? Don't you agree?'

D'Arcy was confused and she didn't feel good certainly, but she agreed. Oh, God, she agreed. The last thing in the world she wanted was for her mother and father to know about this. 'Where am I? I know it's a hospital but—'

'You're at Stanton Memorial. I like to call it *our* hospital, mine and Rud's. . . .'

'But how did I get here?'

'Chance. A fortuitous chance. The people at that hotel called for an ambulance and all the hospitals get their share of emergencies. Luckily when it was *your* turn it was also Stanton Memorial's and the ambulance brought you here. And then when someone in admittance heard the name Sheridan, it rang a bell. They knew that there were Sheridans related to the Stantons. God moves in mysterious ways.'

'Rud! Does Rud know I'm here?'

'Of course. As soon as the hospital called me, I told Rud.'

'Then why isn't he here? Didn't he want to come?'

'Of course he *wanted* to. . . . But he couldn't make it.'

'Why?' The word was torn out of her. *Doesn't he care? I took those goddamn pills because of him. I cut myself all over because of him. I bled. . . .* 'Why couldn't he make it?'

'He was busy, dear. We all have our priorities but they don't necessarily mesh with one another's. It's unfortunate but true. This is the day after Thanksgiving. Classes will be starting again Monday, so there's studying and preparation and Abby needed help with a project.'

Oh my God, D'Arcy thought. She closed her eyes in pain. She had almost died and Abby needed help with a project. . . .

The next time she awoke, Judith was still there. Or she had left and come back again. It didn't matter. 'I want to see Rud,' she told Judith. 'Can I see Rud?'

'Not now, D'Arcy dear. Rud's very busy but he and Abby send you their best wishes. They both wish you a speedy recovery. I've spoken to your mother and father. It seems they thought you were in New Jersey so I said you had returned from your visit there with the flu and that you had called me. But I reassured them, told them I had the situation under control.

Frankie said the minute you're feeling better you're to call her. Perhaps you'll do that tomorrow. . . .'

D'Arcy's head was perfectly clear the next morning and as soon as Judith appeared she told her firmly, 'I have to see Rud. Today!'

Judith sat down by the bed. 'I think it's time we got a few things settled. You tried to kill yourself and that, in case you don't know it, is a criminal offence. While they might not arrest you for it, you can be remanded to an institution for the mentally disturbed. So far, I've used my influence to keep that from happening. But ultimately, it's all up to you. You can make up your mind to overcome this fixation with Rud, or face the consequences. Now, Rud is concerned about you, naturally, and he wants what is best for you. And what we all feel is best for you is that you forget about him and go on with your life.'

'And that's what Rud said? That's what he wants? Why doesn't he come here and tell me that himself?'

'He's too busy.'

Oh God, how can I believe all this? 'And you expect me to take *your* word for this, Judith?'

Judith smiled as if she felt sorry for D'Arcy. 'Do you have any choice? Rud isn't here to tell you differently, is he? And he *hasn't* been here. You're a smart girl. You figure it out. I'd say that was the bottom line, wouldn't you?'

D'Arcy couldn't argue with that. Rud certainly wasn't there and hadn't been . . . ever. And that *was* the bottom line.

'Now, pay close attention, D'Arcy. I've vouched for you personally and you're going to be released this afternoon. And that's the end of it. Otherwise, I might be forced to re-evaluate my position. And what will you have accomplished? You'll make your mother unhappy, and you'll embarrass your father publicly, and he'll never forgive you for that. And what's more, you'll be an embarrassment to Rud, and I daresay he wouldn't think you were worth that either.'

Judith was right, D'Arcy thought. Judith was terrific at bottom lines, and so was her son. She had nothing more to say to Judith and she turned her face to the wall.

Judith talked to her back. 'So it's all settled. You'll go back to school and forget all about . . . us, and we'll all forget that this ugly incident ever happened. . . .'

5.

D'Arcy had mixed emotions when she found out she was pregnant a week before Christmas. Maybe something wonderful was going to come out of this nightmare after all! For a couple of days she was excited, thrilled, imagined she *felt* the baby inside her even though she knew that it was impossible, and for a couple of days she laughed and fooled around and even sang, a turnaround for her. One girl in the dorm even asked, 'What happened, D'Arcy, have you fallen in love?'

It wasn't that far from the truth. For a couple of days, her hate for Rud Stanton was suspended. She told herself it must have been some kind of misunderstanding that he never came to the hospital. Maybe Judith had been lying from the very start. *Maybe Rud never knew I was there!*

It was a hunch that took her back to the Liberty Hotel. She told Dominick she had come for the things she'd left in her room even though she'd taken her packed suitcase with her when she'd left the hospital. No longer worried about the police coming to question him – it had already been almost a month – Dominick snarled, 'What are you trying to pull? Your jock boyfriend picked up your things on Thanksgiving Day. After he went in the ambulance with you he came back and got them so don't you start with me. You'd better ask him . . . if he's still around, which I take it he ain't.'

No, he ain't! Even Dominick knew a bottom line when he saw one.

Still, who knew? Maybe it was Judith who had prevented him from coming to the hospital. . . . And once he heard she was pregnant with his baby, he'd be thrilled. He'd say, 'To hell with everything and everybody! Let's get married!' And they would and then the three of them would live happily forever after.

But then, she had her doubts about that too. She had to face it. Rud wasn't a baby. How could his mother keep him away from the hospital if he really wanted to see her . . . if he wanted her even one-half as much as she wanted him? How could she go on kidding herself? If he wanted to see her, what stopped him from coming over to her dorm? If he was concerned about her, why didn't he at least call? And then she began to hate him again. And she began to get really mad.

Like it or not, love her or not, this baby was *his*. He'd just have to marry her. She'd tell him about the baby and if he didn't offer marriage, she'd just tell him that he had to . . . marry her, or face the consequences. And if *that* didn't work, she'd just go to Judith and tell her that she was pregnant. Then, wouldn't Judith make him marry her since the last thing in the world Judith would want would be for her darling son to be known as the unwed father of Bill Sheridan's darling little daughter's darling little baby? After all, that could prove very, very embarrassing when it came time for Mr Rud Stanton to run for public office.

Yes, she'd make him marry her. If worse came to worse, they could do something about that later. At least, this way she could keep her baby and the baby would have a legitimate father, one with a respected name. In this world, wasn't that what counted – a respected name? And for the sake of her child, she wouldn't even teach it to hate his father. No, most likely the poor kid would learn to do that on its own. . . .

Then D'Arcy did another turnaround, and was sure that she was wrong . . . she wouldn't have to force Rud . . . threaten him. . . . He would do all the right things on his own because, in the end, he really did love her . . . would love his baby as much as she already did. . . .

She knew better than to try and call Rud. The surest way to nab him was to hang around the Stanton house, waiting for him to go in or out.

It was only two days before Christmas. It was cold but sunny and it had snowed the night before and people were outside digging their way out, laughing and making light of what was a commonplace Boston winter routine. D'Arcy lingered across the street behind a parked car where she wouldn't be noticed, but from where she had a perfect view of the huge iron gates guarding the Stanton property.

And then she saw him emerge from the house and he appeared as splendid as ever. Why had she imagined he would have changed in four weeks, his golden image somehow gone or tarnished? He was wearing a big quilted jacket, a muffler and woollen gloves but no hat, and when the sun lit his yellow hair in a certain, magical way, it appeared that he was wearing a halo, or maybe even a crown. And she almost ran out then, across the street, to yell to him, to have him look up, see her, run to her. . . .

But then Abby came running out of the house laughing. And D'Arcy thought bitterly, 'Why shouldn't she laugh? What did she have to worry about?' Abby too was wearing a jacket, muffler and gloves, and her jacket was the same colour as his – bright red. Funny, D'Arcy thought. She didn't recall Abby laughing that way even once during the days they'd all spent together. The most you got out of Abby then was a sad little smile, or maybe a wistful one.

It was like they'd all been different people then even though it was only a little more than a year ago. And maybe they *had* been different people. How innocently she had kissed Rud on that library couch that day, and oh, how she had loved him when she'd been sixteen. And now she was only seventeen but with a baby growing inside her and she knew she'd never be really young again. Nor the same. And Abby, from the looks of her, wouldn't ever be the same again either. . . .

Abby and Rud were starting to build something in the fresh new snow behind their gates. A snowman? Then D'Arcy saw Abby pick up some of that fresh, new snow and pack it into a snowball, hurl it at Rud, hitting him in the face and he chased her . . . little Abby, who a little over a year ago hadn't even known how to flirt.

Abby fell in the snow and then he was on top of her, picking up handfuls of snow and squishing them inside delighted Abby's collar. Even from across the street, D'Arcy could hear Abby's ecstatic squeals. Then Judith came to stand in the opened doorway . . . to laugh and enjoy the antics of her two precious darlings.

Then D'Arcy knew she wasn't going to approach Rud with her news of the imminent Stanton heir. She wanted no part of him. It was what – four weeks? – since she had been in the hospital recovering from the love of him, and here he was – laughing in the snow, playing with Abby with Judith looking on . . . all three of them happy and pleased with life, he acting as if he didn't have a care in the world, as if she had never existed for him . . . she with wounds that didn't show but which would never really heal.

They could all go to hell, the three of them. To hell!

She went home for Christmas the next day, thinking she'd tell her mother but not her father that she was pregnant and between them, they'd figure out what she was to do. She wanted to keep the baby if she could. She hated the baby's father but she loved her baby.

But then D'Arcy didn't confide in Francesca either. Francesca was upset enough when she saw her daughter for the first time since she'd entered college in September. D'Arcy was so thin; D'Arcy was so pale; so pallid, so listless, so subdued. And D'Arcy wondered what her mother had expected – for her to stay round and giggly and silly forever? Still, D'Arcy couldn't bring herself to upset her mother further, especially since she had so many other things on her mind. She was actually planning to be running for governor the coming year!

'But you haven't done *anything*, Mother. Why do you think people will vote for you?'

'Well, one reason is that your father will tell them to,' she laughed, 'and you know how popular your father is. The voters of Florida will do practically anything he wants.'

'You mean they're all his stooges as much as you will be?'

'D'Arcy!' Francesca was hurt.

'I'm sorry, Mother, I didn't mean to hurt your feelings but it's the truth, isn't it? He's just running you because he can't succeed himself, and then you'll just do whatever he tells you to.'

'Well, maybe I'll just surprise everybody and have some ideas of my own . . .'

Her mother doing what she believed in rather than what her father did? D'Arcy doubted that. Still, she knew that things weren't the same between them as they had been . . . not since her Sweet Sixteen party. She just felt it.

'Tell me about some of your ideas.'

'Do you really want to hear?' This really *was* a new, changed D'Arcy.

'Yes, I want to hear.' Was it possible that her mother had changed so much that she actually had ideas that weren't her husband's?

'Well, I've already been travelling around the state, talking about Planned Parenthood. . . .'

Planned Parenthood? Under the circumstances, that was almost funny.

'And what does Dad have to say about that?'

'Well, he thinks that the issue is a hot potato but I'm not sure how seriously he's taking it all. But I *am* quite serious about it and I intend to campaign on the issue just the same. What do you think of this as a slogan? A vote for Frankie Sheridan is a vote for the Pill. . . .'

'What?' D'Arcy laughed. It was the first time she'd laughed in weeks. 'How about diaphragms? Or IUDs? Are you leaving them out in preference for the Pill?'

'Actually, I don't prefer one over the other. What I'm for is Planned Parenthood . . . Birth Control, and my idea is to see that information and the options of birth control are available to every woman in the state, no matter how poor she is, or how uneducated.'

'You *are* serious,' and then she couldn't help but test the waters. 'And how do you feel about abortion, Mother? Do you consider it a sin against God?'

Francesca was startled by her daughter's question. But the words had a familiar ring. Weren't those the words she herself had used when Carlotta had asked for her help in obtaining an abortion?

That's a sin, Carlotta. A sin against God.

At that point in their conversation, she'd actually been urging Carlotta to marry Trace, divorce him later rather than undergo an abortion. How naive she'd been. Childish. Foolish. Had she cut the conversation short there, had helped Carlotta to obtain her illegal abortion, how much all-around unhappiness would have been avoided. The only sin had been what followed. . . .

271

'I'm for abortion, D'Arcy. Legal abortion. . . .'

'Oh . . . and you don't think it's murder?'

'Murder? Such a dramatic word. First of all, D'Arcy, I'm of the school that doesn't believe that in the first stages of pregnancy there is a life. There's only an embryo. Second, I most definitely believe it's a woman's decision. Her body, her choice. I really don't think it's the Church's business, and it's certainly not the business of a bunch of lawmakers who are, with only a very few exceptions, *males*. Maybe some day when the Pope is a woman and a woman sits in the White House, and not only as a First Lady, I'll change my mind about that. But until then, I think a lot of unhappiness is perpetrated in the name of anti-abortion. If a woman who already has more children than she can properly care for, or if a young girl is going to spend the rest of her life never being able to overcome a youthful mistake because of an unwanted pregnancy, those are the sins.'

'But if a young girl *chooses* to have her illegitimate child?'

'Then that certainly is her choice and I would wish her the best of luck. But I imagine it's very hard on both mother and child in today's world. Maybe in the future. . . . Or the girl could have her baby and then give it out for adoption. That certainly is an alternative but that's a hard decision too. You have to be very strong to live with knowing that you have a child out there whom you'll never know. Now, wouldn't it be better to avoid all these terrible decisions by teaching young women and older, ignorant women to practise birth control and see that they have its tools?'

'You know, Mother, I *really* hope you win. I think you're going to make a wonderful governor. And then the next time out I bet you'll be able to make it all on your own, and not as Daddy's stand-in.'

Yes, her mother was going to be a very convincing candidate, to the women especially, and her father was in for a lot of surprises.

D'Arcy's old friends called and came over, urged her to go with them to Fort Lauderdale where the boys were, where, during Christmas vacation, youth reigned supreme. But D'Arcy would have none of it. The time had passed.

Francesca urged her to see her friends, to loosen up, to have some fun.

'I'm no longer in the mood, Mother. It all seems so juvenile to me now.'

'But why, D'Arcy? You're only seventeen. You have a right to be juvenile.'

D'Arcy smiled sadly. 'But you've changed, Mother. You've grown and matured. Give me that option too. Don't you want me to mature, to improve with age like you?'

'Of course,' Francesca told her. Still, she missed the old D'Arcy terribly . . . the D'Arcy who had laughed all the time, the D'Arcy who had thought she was Scarlett, even the D'Arcy who had thought she was in love with Rud the golden boy. . . .

What her mother didn't know, D'Arcy thought, was that it was she herself, the future governor of the state of Florida, who had helped her mature, to realize what she had to do.

After D'Arcy went back to Boston, Bill asked in an offhand manner, 'Did D'Arcy mention Rud to you at all? Does she still have a crush on him?'

'She didn't mention him and I thought it was best not to ask. I think D'Arcy has really grown up, changed a lot.'

'I'll say she has. She barely spoke to me.'

Yes, D'Arcy was still angry with her father, Francesca knew. But she'd get over it, just as she had apparently got over Rud.

6.

After she had the abortion, D'Arcy was filled with a feeling of emptiness, sorely missing the baby who had been inside her for so short a time. It was as if part of her had been annihilated. It might have been only an embryo and not a life, as her mother believed, but as far as she was concerned, it was murder, and she herself wasn't the murderer, nor was the doctor who had performed the act – the murderers were Judith and her son.

She tried buckling down to her studies. She attended her classes faithfully and she studied every night, trying to concentrate on the positive. But it all seemed purposeless to her now. She felt as if she were adrift, without an anchor.

When it was spring break, she decided not to go home to Florida but to go take a look at this farm in New Hampshire she'd heard about, a commune where everyone supposedly was mellow and the women cooked and sewed and minded each other's children and the men practised carpentry and made brooms to sell and everyone took turns tending the vegetable gardens.

No one asked her for anything, assuming she'd share whatever she had and that she'd work like everyone else for the common good. When she made up her mind to stay she gladly turned over whatever she did have – a little cash, two gold bangle bracelets, a pinky ring fashioned of tiny garnets, a locket on a chain, an ankle bracelet which she had worn to the beach with her bikini. She was only sorry she no longer had the expensive watch she had traded for the coloured pills, the 'red birds' and the 'yellow jackets.' She wouldn't have had need of the watch at the commune, no one kept track of the time.

When spring turned to summer, D'Arcy, in the long cotton skirt she'd sewn by hand – the very first thing she had ever made all by herself – tucked wild flowers behind her ears and wore her hair in one long braid, and when her sandals wore out, she went barefoot. She sowed and hoed and weeded and when she reaped she was filled if not with joy, at least with pride, and she made soup with her bounty and was extremely pleased when everyone said it was good. At night those who could played their guitars and everyone sang, and D'Arcy was content.

But then a new arrival brought a few capfuls of d-lysergic acid deithylamide as his contribution to the group and some of the group who had already dropped out, turned on, and an eighteen-year-old boy who saw a 'multihued, fantastic and metamorphizing image' – was it God? – beckoning to him from the middle of Dundee Lake, he jumped in to find out and never came out.

And then after one member of the group accused another of stealing his stash, it wasn't too long before two mothers with children started fighting over one bottle of milk which had already turned sour from lack of refrigeration. It was then that D'Arcy suspected that it all might be beginning to fall apart.

It was late in August when she took the unwed, pregnant Patty to town to find a doctor. Patty was in her seventh month, and while there were a few women at the commune who practiced midwifery, no one seemed to know what to do about the pains Patty was experiencing which didn't seem at all like labour pains. While they waited for the doctor to see Patty, D'Arcy couldn't help but be aware of the lifted eyebrows of the other women sitting in the waiting room. She became acutely conscious of her long skirt soiled with the dust from the walk into town, and her bare, dirty feet, and her braid which hadn't been touched in three days. She found herself wishing she'd taken the time that morning to at least brush and rebraid her hair, but it hadn't seemed important. Nothing at the commune seemed *that* important. And then when the nurse, with her nose in the air as if she smelled something bad, led Patty away to the bathroom with a big bar of kitchen soap, a washcloth and a towel *before* she was admitted into the doctor's presence, it was D'Arcy who was ashamed. What was it her mother had said? Pride in one's appearance wasn't a matter of vanity, it was a measure of one's self-esteem.

Patty recovered but the baby inside her had already been dead. They said she should have seen a doctor long before, and D'Arcy was forced to wonder if that too had been another form of murder?

The water pump in the kitchen broke down and no one knew how to fix it. And then D'Arcy became aware of how cold the early mornings were. Fall came early to New Hampshire, and it occurred to D'Arcy that the winters probably came early too, and that they should all be busy laying in a supply of firewood, especially since quite a few of them were sleeping on thin mattresses on the bare floor. She considered herself lucky that she had a bed, and that she had had enough sense to bring her all-weather boots and her quilted parka with her when she had come in early spring.

She tried to organize the others into daily wood-gathering forays, and knitting on a regular basis, so that they'd have a product to sell now that there were no more vegetables and the carpentry production seemed to have come to a standstill. The only thing that seemed to raise a spark of interest in anyone were the few marijuana plants which they were harvesting.

She begged and pleaded for everyone to have some gumption, some pick up and go – one of her father's pet phrases – until she looked around and realized that all the ones with any gumption had done exactly that – had picked up and gone, and the ones who remained were the ones who didn't think anything much counted, much less themselves.

But she counted! D'Arcy Sheridan still counted!

For several days, D'Arcy wandered the streets of Boston, hardly conscious of the areas she covered or the parks where she spent the nights, all her belongings in one big shoulder bag, trying to figure out what to do. From time to time while on the commune, she'd called her mother – she had always made sure she kept a dime to place the collect call – so that Francesca wouldn't worry too much about her, and she knew that all she had to do now to get help was to call and ask for it. But she couldn't bring herself to do it, mostly because she didn't want to admit to her father that she had screwed up. She was eighteen now, an adult, and she could make it on her own. All she had to do was get her act together.

She stayed alive by panhandling, finding a place to flop every now and then.

Then she met a girl who invited her to stay at her place, one which she shared with maybe twelve or fourteen people at any one time. It was a commune of sorts, a city one, and being city dwellers, the members were more affluent and enterprising than their country counterparts. They were able to beg for money on the streets, sell a pint of blood, offer their services for laboratory experimentation, or deal in drugs.

They slept on cots, in sleeping bags, on mattresses, sometimes on the bare floor itself. But at least the apartment had steam heat and the walls were decorated – on one wall was a huge mural of someone's psychedelic trip, on another, painted in huge black dripping letters, the legend – *Jesus lives!*

D'Arcy stayed there for a few weeks, thinking that any day soon she'd have enough money to get herself some decent clothes so that she could get herself some kind of a job . . . so then her life would make sense, might even make a difference in the grand scheme of things. Then one morning, she awoke on a grimy blanket next to an equally grimy partner. Then she remembered that she had actually chosen this partner after ingesting a couple of goofballs, and filled with self-disgust, she cursed herself. She saw the couple who were supposedly so in love arguing over who would get first use of the hypodermic needle they were sharing.

Will that be me a year from now? She'd only be nineteen then, and that meant so many damn dreary years to get through . . . unless or until the needle did the trick better than that razor she'd played with in her previous incarnation.

God! Maybe her father wouldn't care, but her mother would! How could she do that to Francesca who, the last time they had spoken on the phone, had sobbed through the whole conversation, knowing only that her D'Arcy was one of the kids who hadn't made it, who had chosen to 'drop out' instead. . . .

She had given her child up to abortion, D'Arcy thought, but she still had reasons enough to drop back in. She could still make a difference, maybe even make the world a better place to live for other children if she tried. She could still make her mother proud, if not her father. And she could still even up the score – she could 'get' Rud Stanton for what he had done to her.

Super reasons, all!

She went to the pay phone on the corner. You put your dime in, you placed your collect call, and then hopefully, you got your dime back. She always had. But this time it wouldn't matter since she was going home. . . .

D'Arcy Sheridan lives!

VII
1964

Francesca met D'Arcy's plane and it was something of a shock to see her this first time in almost a year. It wasn't that D'Arcy was too thin or too fat or that she was messy like some of the kids – the ones they used to call beatniks who were now referred to as hippies. Actually, D'Arcy looked like any nice, pretty college girl in her black tights, flat shoes, short skirt and turtleneck sweater, and while her hair was extremely long, it was also smooth and neat. Finally, Francesca realized what the difference was – D'Arcy's eye's had lost that special sparkle of youth . . . her eyes were old.

'Oh, D'Arcy,' she hugged her close in the limousine. 'It's so good to see you. And I must say, you've come home just in the nick of time.'

D'Arcy forced a smile. She *wanted* to be warm and gay and loving for her mother and maybe she would be . . . in time. But right now it was so hard to make believe that everything was as ever. 'Why am I just in the nick of time?'

'Well, the election is only three weeks away and I have to step up my campaigning. I don't have that big a staff that I can't use your help. You will help me, won't you?'

'Sure. To tell you the truth, I forgot that this is a big election year. I haven't watched any TV or read any papers lately.'

'Well, then you wouldn't know what's happened . . . that your father is supporting Senator Goldwater for President.'

For the first time Francesca saw a flicker of interest in D'Arcy's eyes. 'You mean Barry Goldwater, the arch-conservative Republican from Arizona?' She was incredulous.

'The very same.'

'Oh, this is too funny!' D'Arcy began to laugh which annoyed Francesca. 'What's so funny?'

'The situation. And you, Mother? Which ticket are you running on? The Democratic or the Republican?'

'I'm running as a Democrat, naturally.'

'And you don't find all this funny? Father *was* the Democratic Governor of Florida and he's sponsoring you to succeed him, and at the same time he's supporting the Republican nominee for President? It's more than funny, it's crazy time!'

The truth was that Francesca had been as aghast as D'Arcy was now amused by Bill's decision to throw his considerable support behind the Republican candidate.

Everyone knew that right from the start Johnson was having a hard time dealing with the Kennedy ghost, aggravated by the fact that Bobby Kennedy was building what amounted to a government in exile composed of New Frontiersmen who all felt a hostility towards LBJ. Still, these same people wanted the vice-presidency for Bobby, and LBJ had to tell Kennedy no way. Then, to make sure that the Kennedyites wouldn't come to the convention and nominate him regardless, Lyndon issued the statement that ' . . . it would be inadvisable for me to recommend to the convention any member of my Cabinet. . . .'

When Bill heard that statement he knew what the vengeful and powerful Kennedy faction of the party would do – they'd challenge Johnson for the presidency in '68, and where would that leave him? Definitely on the outside.

He had to go after the vice-presidency himself. If he got that, then *he'd* be the one on the inside track in '68 if for any reason Lyndon didn't run, but most definitely in '72 either way. Lyndon had to give him the nod for the V-P slot. After all, he was the man . . . the man who could deliver the South whose citizens were beginning to wonder if the Democratic Party was indeed their party what with the Civil Rights Bill LBJ had practically bulled through Congress.

It was a self-confident, cool and collected Southern statesman who went to a hot and steamy Washington in early August, after making sure to leave whatever remained of his Harvard accent at home – Harvard accents were anathema to Johnson. It was a raging, frothing tiger who returned. 'The son-of-a-bitch turned me down! The bastard said he didn't want me . . . didn't need me!'

'How dare he?' Francesca was almost as enraged as Bill himself. Although she was no longer committed to acting as Bill's straight man she still had tremendous respect for his abilities, and while she had not forgiven him his perfidy, none of her strong feelings for him as a man had been eradicated. She loved him no less than she ever had. 'Doesn't he realize what an asset you'd be as V-P? Doesn't he know how many votes you control?'

'He said I was a damn fool. He said that if I were as astute a politician as I thought I was, I'd realize that since he himself was from Texas, anybody from the South was out of the question . . . that he needed a Northerner. Then he even questioned my ability to bring in the votes. He told me that "things are a-changin'," ' Bill mimicked the President. 'That "kings are going out of style . . ." He said I should just go home and tend to my Cubans and my crackers and that if I got lucky, maybe one day I'd get my chance in the barrel.'

'Oh!' Francesca cried. 'How crude! What are you going to do?'

'As Lyndon would put it himself, "I'm going to sit on it a spell." '

That night Francesca allowed Bill to make love to her for the first time since the week that followed D'Arcy's momentous party. He was crushed, she still loved him, and it had been so long, and love was a restorative. And Bill went to sleep that night thinking that if nothing else, at least Frankie was back in his corner.

By morning, Bill had decided to throw in his lot with the Kennedyites who wouldn't actively oppose Johnson but wouldn't support him either. If he did for them, they'd do for him, when the time came.

'But will they?' Francesca demanded. 'They've never liked you nor you them. And you'll have alienated LBJ forever, and to what end? And what about Trace Boudin's threat? That it would be unhealthy for you to back a Kennedy?'

'Screw Boudin and his friends and screw Johnson. I'm not afraid of *them*, and I don't need Lyndon.'

'Please, Bill! Think about it!'

'There's no more time. The election is only three months away.'

But then almost immediately, Bill had his answer. The Kennedy forces said thank you but no thank you. Bobby didn't want any part of anyone who had connections to the mob. Considering that Bill's niece was Trace Boudin's daughter and Ross Scott's godchild, Bill would be more of an embarrassment than anything else.

While he was madder than hell, Bill had to admit to himself that there was a certain amount of irony in that – he had thought the same thing about Jade but in regard to Rud. Things did have a way of coming back to haunt you. But the important thing to consider now was that he had been rejected by both Johnson and the Kennedy people, and the answer to him was like handwriting on the wall. You weren't supposed to get mad, you were supposed to get even and he'd do just that. He was going to throw all his voting weight behind the Republicans and their choice, Goldwater!

'But that's insane!' Francesca was appalled. 'You can't suddenly become a Republican. No one will know what to make of it. They'll think you've—'

'Lost my marbles?'

'Yes, or that you're a turncoat, a defector, that sour grapes have affected your good judgement. Bill, you cannot support Goldwater! He stands for entirely different things than you do!'

'I don't care. My mind's made up. We're both going to support Goldwater!'

Me? I'm running for governor on the Democratic ticket!'

'Yes, Frankie. I know that. I'm the man who put you on the ticket, remember? And while you're campaigning for governor on the Democratic ticket, you're still going to speak out for Goldwater!'

'No, Bill, I can't do it!'

He looked at her disbelievingly.

'I can't do it and I don't think *you* should do it. In the past Goldwater has come out against rural electrification and a large segment of our voters are rural. And he voted against the nuclear test ban treaty and he voted against the Civil Rights Bill. I've always been so proud of you that you're one of the very few Southern governors that took a stand for Civil Rights, and *I* will not deviate from that position! If I'm going to be governor then I will not ever give voice to anything I don't believe in nor will I *not* speak out for things I do believe in. Do you want me to withdraw from the race?'

He looked at her coldly. 'I wouldn't dream of asking you to do that. You're going to make a great governor, Frankie. You've done your homework, and you're very well prepared. But I have to tell you how I feel too and that is, anyone who's not for me, is against me.'

Their lines were drawn.

'Now, I want you to help me in these last weeks of the campaign, D'Arcy, but one thing I don't want is for you to get drawn into your father's and my division on this.'

'But, Mother, I feel the way you do.'

'The issues are one thing, D'Arcy, but personal relationships are another, and you're *our* daughter. No matter how things stand politically, I want you to remember that. I realize what it may take hoeing a fine line but you're a big girl now. I'm sure you can manage it.'

The problem was her mother didn't understand how much she already resented her father, not on a political basis but on a personal one.

More than anything, Bill was relieved when he saw D'Arcy. He had worried about her living on that hippie commune. Frankie, despite all her nonsense about distributing the Pill to every girl over twelve, didn't know what was going on. She thought that all there were to hippies was long hair, bare feet, and maybe listening to the Beatles. She didn't acknowledge the underside, how some kids dropped out, never to return.

But D'Arcy was back, safe, and if she were a hell of a lot more serious now, that was all to the good. And if she were concerned about issues, so much the better. Better than turning your back on the world and doing nothing. And thank God, there wasn't one word about Rud out of her.

And she was full of beans, and he was glad of that too. When he put his arm around her and asked if she'd like to accompany him on a tour of pro-Goldwater speeches he was making in several Southern cities, she almost tore his head off: 'Are you *serious?* Do you really think I'd go with you while you talk up a man who is just dying to get us into a real war in Vietnam?'

He tried reasoning. 'Barry didn't put our boys in Vietnam in the first place, did he?'

'Do you deny he's militaristic? Or that he's for nuclear weapons? Or that he voted against the Civil Rights Bill? Or is it, Father, that you yourself are just like him?'

He was taken aback by her vehemence. It sounded to him like she was more against him personally than she was against Senator Goldwater and he backed off. But while D'Arcy had expressed her own sentiments, politically speaking, Francesca couldn't condone the tone D'Arcy had taken with her father.

'I think you owe your father an apology, D'Arcy.'

'I think he owes us one, for the stands he's taking.'

'D'Arcy!' Francesca protested.

'It's OK. Forget it. Contrary to popular opinion, every one in this family is entitled to his beliefs and the freedom to express them. I'm all for free speech even if my daughter thinks I'm a fascist dictator.' Bill smiled tightly.

It was a joke but D'Arcy quickly retorted, 'You said it, I didn't!' and Francesca remembered what Bill had said to her, ' . . . anyone who's not for me, is against me.'

The truth was that despite the jocular tone he was taking, Bill was worried. The more he evaluated the situation, the more he recognized that Goldwater, an essentially charming, bright man of personal integrity, had lost the election the day he was nominated in San Francisco. And having his wife, and now his daughter, going around the state, pushing LBJ as much as they were pushing Frankie herself, was making him look like a damn fool. And Frankie had been supposedly only his stand-in! Even his own new party, the Republicans of Florida, was using her candidacy to ridicule them both:

282

'Frankie's running to let Bill do it!' and 'A vote for Frankie Sheridan is a vote for the King! Vote against the monarchy for Florida!' It had become a farce, a fiasco.

D'Arcy, campaigning with Frankie, did make a fool of him. God damn it, if a man wasn't a king in his own castle, how could he expect to be king anywhere else? And then there was that demonstration in Miami, with whites and blacks marching together, a supposedly peaceful demonstration which turned ugly. Several of the more truculent demonstrators were arrested and that night, right there on national television for the whole country to see, was the Governor's daughter being dragged away by one of his own state troopers, still carrying her sign: 'Down with the man who opposes equality for all!'

The question was, as Bill saw it, against whom was the Governor's daughter protesting? Goldwater, or her father?

Francesca ordered a plane to stand ready.

'Where are you going?'

'To Miami. To get those kids out of jail. Come with me, Bill. It will be good for you,' she said, not explaining whether it would be good for his soul or his image.

He shook his head and she said, 'Oh, Bill. I'm sorry. I really am!'

He smiled coolly, in an impersonal sort of way. 'Are you? You shouldn't be. My pollsters tell me you're going to be elected for sure. The women in the state adore you. And why wouldn't they? You're the first person who's ever told them they can spit in their husband's eye and get away with it. They're loving it . . . they're eating it up.'

2.

When the smoke cleared, Lyndon Johnson was President by a landslide, Hubert Humphrey was the Vice-President, Robert Kennedy was the new senator from New York and Frankie Sheridan was the new governor of Florida, and Bill Sheridan was out in a political no-man's-land from which there was no coming back. He was of neither party now and his base of power was gone. The Republican candidate had carried only six states, one of which was his own. As for the remaining five Southern states, Bill was accorded no credit for bringing those in. With the bitter segregation wars being fought in these states, *no* Democrat, not even a Kennedy, could have carried them. And the fact that Bill Sheridan couldn't even deliver his own state, Florida, destroyed his credibility as a power broker.

One thing was clear, Bill Sheridan was no longer a viable contender for the presidency in *any* year.

Oh, he could probably be governor of Florida again after Frankie's special two year term was up. According to the changes in Florida's constitution, Frankie's two year term was a transitory one, after which either he or Frankie could run again. But without his power, and the brass ring of the presidency forever out of his reach, it had all lost its flavour. Besides, with the sweet taste of victory in her mouth, with the pungent after taste of power, would Frankie be willing to step aside for him? He was hardly sure. She had shown him where she stood.

But Francesca didn't find her victory all that sweet. After two years of Bill

283

being the penitent, she had allowed him to find comfort, love and possibly forgiveness in her arms . . . *once*. But now their roles were reversed again. She was the one who had sinned against him, and he was the sinned-against. Now it was his life that was a shambles, and it was she who was the governor, who was in the awesome situation which any love-crazed teenager might find herself in – pregnant, and in effect, without a husband, the only difference between her and that teenager being one of age and position. She *was* the self-appointed advocate of birth control, and *she* should have known better.

And the worst of it was that she still loved him so and it was hard to bear that it was she who had helped bring this great warrior to his knees.

She tried appeasing words. 'I begged you not to desert the Party—'

'So you did. And how does it feel to be so completely vindicated?'

'I had to do what I felt was right, didn't I?'

'Absolutely. You had the courage of your convictions, and now you're Ms Governor and your conscience is clear. You must be very happy.'

'Bill, don't do this to us.'

'Us? Is there an us?'

'It was you who wanted me to be governor. You said you'd be there by my side and—'

'Yes, I wanted you to be governor but I never wanted you to cut off my balls in the process.'

Then Frankie didn't know which one of them had perpetrated the greater sin? Which sin was more sinful than the other? For him to have loved another woman more than he had loved her, or for her to have been instrumental in his castration?

'But you said that if I were governor, you'd help me—'

'Ah. . . .' He held up his tumbler half full of bourbon as if in a toast. 'But that was before I knew exactly how self-sufficient you were, how capable. Not to fear, Frankie. You're going to make a great governor!'

But she had never wanted to be governor. She had only wanted to be his wife, to love him, to have him love her back, to have him love her first and utmost.

She urged D'Arcy to make it up with her father, to try and console him in his hour of despair, even to tell him she was sorry.

'But *I* didn't do anything wrong. He did. He backed a candidate for personal reasons.' Not to mention what he had done to her on a personal basis. . . .

'Being in the right isn't always the most important thing, D'Arcy. Loving is.'

D'Arcy shook her head. Governor or not, her mother was still a sentimental fool. But for her mother's sake, she'd make a conciliatory move in her father's direction.

The funny thing was her father wasn't angry with her for having campaigned with her mother against his candidate. Certainly not as resentful as she was towards him.

'What are your plans, D'Arcy?'

'To go back to school.'

'A wise decision.'

'I thought that I'd major in political science.'

He smiled. 'Thinking of going into politics like your mother?'

284

D'Arcy flushed. 'Not necessarily. There are other things a political science major can do, relevant things.'

'I'm sure. So where do you want to go? Which school?'

'I'd thought I'd go back to B.U. if they'll have me.'

There was only the most minute fluttering of his eyelids. He was no longer worried about D'Arcy and Rud getting together. He could see where Rud might have been attracted to the old D'Arcy, full of fun and with her Southern belle ways, but not this new D'Arcy, any more than the new D'Arcy would find Rud relevant enough.

'And what are you going to do now, Father?'

He chuckled. The old D'Arcy had always called him Daddy. 'I'll come up with something. But what will you do until the new term starts next year?'

'I thought that if it was all right with you and Mother, I'd like to go to Europe for a few weeks.'

'Any place in particular or do you just want to travel around?'

'I want to go to Paris. I know this might sound silly but I have a feeling Jade is there. About a year ago I saw a picture on a magazine cover – a model. The girl had very black, short hair but . . . I think the model was Jade!'

'It was. While we haven't been in touch, your mother and I have kept an eye on her. And we haven't been in touch because if Jade wanted to be in touch with us, she knows where we are. We thought we should respect her desire to keep her distance, let her have her space. Isn't that what the young people want? Their space? But why this sudden urge to see Jade after all this time?'

'Because I've been thinking about her. I realize I never got a chance to know her. And I think now that I'd like to . . . that we could be friends.'

'Why not?'

When D'Arcy left him she had the feeling that not much of what they'd discussed mattered much to him – that his mind was on other things.

D'Arcy prepared for her trip, Francesca prepared for her inaugural day and pondered her dilemma, and Bill pondered his. He pondered and brooded and drank and wondered what he was going to do with the rest of his life. He was only in his forties and there were a lot of years to fill in. But there was something he could do! *If he himself couldn't be President, his son still could!* And he could be there with him, the power behind the throne! And to hell with what he promised Judith! Besides that promise to stay away from Rud no longer had any more relevance since there was no longer any danger of Rud and D'Arcy being attracted to one another – that time had come and gone. The last thing the new D'Arcy would want to be was some politician's selfless and docile wife, the kind Frankie had been before she turned on him.

And in the meantime, he'd move to Boston and get to know his son. Why shouldn't he move back to Boston? What was left for him in Florida? His wife the governor? That was a laugh. She'd shown him where he stood with her.

In Boston he'd feel alive again. He'd have a resurrection! To keep himself viable as a king maker he'd launch a movement, a forum, a platform that would be his very own, a chance for him to be visible, to be heard loud and clear. He could do it! He still had a lot of favours to call in, important people he could call on to get the national exposure he'd need. But he had to pick an issue, one that would be his alone. Something that would be very close to people's hearts, more than Vietnam, more than the Cold War, the Black question, the feminist movement, the nuclear arms race, or campus unrest. *Law and Order!* He'd declare war on crime in the streets, on drugs and violence, on the Mob who was behind every vice known to man. His cry would be to clean up America so that every law-abiding citizen could enjoy what he had worked so hard to build and preserve.

The only words Francesca heard were, ' . . . go back to Boston.'

'But why? Why would you want to go back there?'

'Why not? It's my home town, and it's a city full of vitality. It's in the thick of things. And what's here for me in Florida anymore?'

Me! her heart shouted. But she said softly, 'I'm here, Bill, and I'm for you.'

He laughed as if she had made a joke. 'I can't stay here. There's a time and place for everything and my time in Florida is over.'

'But what about me?' she cried, 'What about us?'

'*Us?* Come on, Frankie. Is there an us any more?'

'But there has to be an *us*. Oh, Bill, I love you! This political stuff, it has nothing to do with us as man and wife.' She was desperate. 'Maybe I was wrong in what I did, but—'

'But what? If you really feel you were wrong then you still have an option. . . . You can come with me . . . go back to Boston with me.'

But that wasn't what she had in mind. Besides, she really didn't believe that she had been wrong in what she had done. 'But, Bill, I've just been elected governor. I have a responsibility to the people who voted for me. And there's so much I'm planning to accomplish – the Planned Parenthood Centers, the housing legislations, civil rights— You want me to resign before I've even begun?'

He shrugged. 'It's your decision, Frankie. Your choice.' He knew what her decision would have been before. . . .

'Face it, Frankie. You can't have it both ways. You can't have it all.'

How dare he? 'Why do I have to choose between being governor and our marriage? You didn't have to make that choice. And now, why must you choose Boston over Florida? You can launch your movement from here just as well as you can do it from Boston. In fact, I'll help you—'

No, his face was set. She knew that look. Was it simply a matter of choosing between Florida and Boston? Or was it that he wanted her to have to choose, making what she wanted a miserable second to what he wanted? 'Is going to Boston so important that you're willing to leave your wife for it?'

'Isn't that the point?' he taunted her. 'A *wife* would come with me, but a politician who's more interested in her career than her marriage would stay. *Will* stay?'

'Why?' she raged. 'Why must you go back to Boston?' And then she gasped. 'Oh my God, it's Judith! It's Judith, isn't it? You want to be close to Judith! Oh, I wondered why you had that compulsion to see Judith again, why you insisted on inviting her to that damn party! What a fool I was! I thought you were lusting after Jade, but it was Judith all the time, wasn't it?'

She began to laugh but it was a laugh verging on the hysterical.

'Don't be a fool!' he lashed out. 'Of course it's not Judith I want! It's her son! *My* son!'

And then she stopped laughing. She thought that just maybe she might not ever, never, laugh again.

There was some more conversation between them, more or less relevant, but insignificant to that which had just been said.

She rambled on, talking now as she had laughed before, unable to stop. 'And all this time I thought it was Carlotta you loved. I knew you went to bed with Carlotta. . . .'

'You *knew?*' he asked, but she ignored him and went on, 'I thought I wouldn't recover from that, but I did. And then I found out you actually asked Carlotta to marry you when she was pregnant with Trace's child and that even though we already had an understanding, you forgot about me, pushed me aside as if I were nothing but an old dish rag. Still I pretended that it didn't hurt. I went on, standing by you, and now I find out that it wasn't just Carlotta all along. . . .'

Still, he was incredulous that she knew that he had indeed made love to Carlotta, had indeed proposed marriage to her. 'You knew and you didn't say anything? You didn't care?'

'Oh, you fool!' She flayed out at him with her fists. 'Didn't care? I could kill you for that. I cared so much I was ashamed to let you know that I knew! Can you understand that? I thought that if you knew that I knew and did nothing about it, you'd think that I was a worthless, shameful creature who had no dignity, no self-worth. And I wanted you to love me, almost as much as I loved you, almost as much as you loved Carlotta. And even then I didn't blame you. Oh no! Blame the hero? Never! I excused you. I said to myself, he loves . . . loved . . . Carlotta so much, and love is its own excuse. You see, I know what it is to love shamelessly, to an excess beyond the ordinary. And then you almost made love to Jade, and still I excused. Still I stayed. Jade, after all, was part of Carlotta. And now I find out that it wasn't Carlotta who was your great love, after all. No, it was Judith whom you always loved, Judith, the mother of your son!'

'No,' he cried. 'I never loved Judith. I never cared about Judith! I only screwed Judith for the money! She needed a man to impregnate her and I needed the money!'

Oh my God! All this pain for money? She didn't know which was worse – loving Judith, impregnating her out of love, or doing it all just for money. . . .

'But we came here to Florida. We left Boston. . . . Did we come here with Judith's money too? She never *forced* you out of Massachusetts then, did she? She bought you out?'

He nodded.

'Oh, I *am* a fool. I always wondered how you made so much money so fast. I told myself that I was a dummy . . . that I didn't understand finance. Whatever you told me, I believed. I thought you were a financial genius. Oh, sometimes I wondered, but I never asked. But how could I question King Sheridan? He could do no wrong and whatever he told me, I believed. Believed because I loved you.' She shook her head, bemused. 'All these years . . . and it wasn't Carlotta who came first in your heart. It was Judith and her money and her son. Your son, Rud, and again I was second. Me and D'Arcy were second to all

287

this—' And then she realized. 'Oh, my God, D'Arcy! *He's her brother!* And she thought she was in love with him! And you and your Judith made her feel like she'd done something terrible— And— Oh, my God, how could you? You bastard! How could you expose her like that? She was your daughter and you just put her out there to hang in the wind!'

He was mumbling words of contrition now, words of sorrow but she didn't hear them, had no interest in hearing them. She wanted to beat him with her fists but she was too spent. Instead, she poured a glass of whisky from the decanter and lifted it to her lips. Then, she changed her mind, and tossed the liquid in his face. 'Bastard!'

He took out his handkerchief and mopped at his face. 'I'm sorry, Frankie.'

It was the first time in their lives he had ever said those bald, simple words – *I'm sorry.* But it was so late . . . so very, very late.

'Well, this time it's you who can't have it all. *You* choose.' But of course it wasn't a place she was talking about at all, and again he said, 'I'm sorry, Frankie.'

They both went to the airport to see D'Arcy off and after her plane was aloft, Bill asked Francesca if she was going to tell D'Arcy about Rud.

'No, not I. How can I tell my daughter that all these years she really didn't have a father . . . not in the true sense of the word. Not a father with whom she came first.'

The next day Bill flew north and Francesca did not see him off at the airport. Rather, she put into practice what she had preached, and had an abortion. There were all kinds of sins, she reflected, and some sins were worse than others. Sometimes you had to choose and it was not always a really free choice.

VIII
1964–1965

1.

The blue door swung open and there she was – not the girl from the magazine cover with the short, precisely carved black hair and the black-lined doe eyes, but Jade with her own long red hair and unpainted face and wearing a flannel nightshirt. Nervous, not sure of how welcome she would be, D'Arcy's mouth went dry.

But Jade's mouth made a great big O, and then she smacked her head and rolled her eyes, jumped up and down and whirled around as if she'd gone beserk at the sight of D'Arcy. 'Great balls of fire and I do declare, if it isn't my little old cousin from the United States! Aren't you a sight for sore eyes!' And she reached out, pulled D'Arcy inside and slammed the door.

She threw her arms around D'Arcy. 'Oh, I can't begin to tell you how good it is to see you!' And then in the same breath, 'How did you find me?'

'Will you stay here with me?'

D'Arcy had been there for almost half an hour but she first looked around. 'Is there room for me?' It was one large plain room with but a few pieces of very basic furniture and a single bed, covered with a rose satin and lace bedspread, the only really pretty thing in the room.

'We'll make room. I'll sleep on the floor. It *is* pretty plain, isn't it?'

D'Arcy decided to be honest. She was *only* going to be honest with her cousin. That was the only way to be real friends. She walked into the kitchen that was no more than a cupboard really but which also housed the bathtub. 'It's the *plainest!*'

Jade was unoffended. 'I like it. It pleases me. It suits my mood.'

And then D'Arcy knew what she meant and thought that perhaps the apartment suited her mood too. 'But that single bed? No lovers?'

Jade laughed. 'Hey, D'Arcy, you've been here only a few minutes. Give me a break!'

'If I give you a break now will you break down later and reveal all?'

'Who knows?' Jade teased but she was just so glad to see D'Arcy she thought that maybe she would break down and bare her very soul.

After they'd eaten what D'Arcy considered a *très, très,* French meal – a long skinny loaf of *pain,* slices of *rosbif* from the *charcuterie,* a wonderful cheese Jade called *Fleur de Decauville,* and a marvellous wine that Jade dismissed as a *très vin ordinaire* – D'Arcy suggested that since her mother had made a reservation for her at the Ritz, Jade and she should take advantage, have fun experiencing the *luxe* life together.

'The Ritz? You sure rate with your mother.'

'I told her I didn't deserve it . . . that I hadn't done anything so great, but she insisted. She told me, "D'Arcy, you deserve it. In this life, you deserve everything you can get!" So what do you say?'

'I say, "Why not?" *We* deserve everything we can get!' And they both giggled. 'But give me a couple of minutes to put on my mask.'

Sitting at her improvised dressing table, Jade transformed herself with a few quick strokes – a pale, matte face, a very red mouth, deeply shadowed eyes and silvered brow bones. Then she threw on a dark fur coat over the flannel nightshirt and said, '*Voilà,*' and D'Arcy thought she was very *voilà* indeed.

'Isn't this lovely?' D'Arcy declared of the Ritz's pale silk walls, the real linen sheets, the golden tasselled draperies, the gilt wall sconces. 'I thought this is how I would find you living.' They were ensconced in the big double bed eating another meal of caviar, toast points, oysters and champagne.

'*Moi?*' Jade laughed. 'I'm only a poor working girl. *You're* the rich American princess.'

'Not really,' D'Arcy said, suddenly sober. 'Once upon a time . . . a million years ago, I was. But my days of wine and roses are over.'

Jade didn't want them to be sad. 'Ah, but you're wrong. Here we are drinking champagne and here is our rose!' She picked up the silver bud vase from their supper tray which held a single perfect deep pink rose.

D'Arcy shook her head. 'This is but a fling. But what about you? Are your days ones of wine and roses?'

'Hardly,' Jade said, sad then too. But then she grimaced exaggeratedly, making fun. 'I work terribly hard, you know. And they push me here and shove me there and pull my hair. Sometimes they yell at me and even beat me! Modelling is not all what it's cracked up to be.'

But D'Arcy remained in a serious mood. 'But everyone must adore you and tell you day and night that you're beautiful, and you must go to exciting parties all the time. Don't you?'

'Sometimes. When I get lonely. When the loneliness gets bad.'

'But you must have lots of friends.'

'Not really. Not *real* friends. I haven't had a real friend since my mother died.'

D'Arcy reached out a tentative hand. 'Jade, I want to be your friend. Your *real* friend. Will you have me?'

First Jade took the hand and squeezed it and then she laughed through tears. 'Only if you promise to love, honour and obey.'

'D'Arcy's eyes filled with tears too. 'I might have trouble with the obey. . . . Obedience isn't my strong suit.'

'I know. It isn't mine either.'

D'Arcy ran a finger around the tiny bowl of caviar to get the last tiny egg and then sucked on it. 'If you were lonely, why didn't you ever write?'

'Oh, a couple of times I wrote a letter to your mother. But then I tore them up. And several times I wrote to Abby but she never answered me. I think my sister must be very angry with me.'

D'Arcy wanted to say something nasty about Abby, something about her being too selfishly busy with a certain party to bother about writing to her sister, but she sensed that this would upset Jade and would only serve to come between them.

'Why would she be angry with you?'

'I *did* run away and she probably thought I was running away from her . . . that I didn't want her to come and live with me and Trace.'

'Why *did* you disappear that night?'

'Because I *didn't* want her to live with me and Trace. She was right about that. It was the reason she probably didn't understand. I didn't want her to live with us because I didn't trust Trace. I was afraid he'd try and get his hands on her inheritance.'

292

D'Arcy was shocked. '*Your* father would have done something like that?'

Jade looked deep into D'Arcy's eyes. 'No, not *my* father for sure. *Abby's* father was very likely to try and do something like that.'

'Oh!' But D'Arcy wasn't sure she understood what Jade was saying. 'You *do* mean that Trace is really Abby's father?'

'Yes. But I'm not sure he's mine. My real father might be the man he works for who's no better than Trace, maybe far worse.'

'Oh!' And then because Jade had told her the most telling kind of revelation, she knew she had to tell one in return to seal their friendship forever, and she blurted, 'I was pregnant and had an abortion!' Then she began to cry.

'Oh, D'Arcy . . .' Jade put her arms around her. 'How terrible for you. Didn't your mother want to help you keep the baby?' It seemed to her that Francesca might have wanted to do that.

'She never knew. I never told her. You're the only one I've told. You won't tell her, will you?'

'Of course not. And you won't tell Abby what I told you?'

'No. Never.' Then D'Arcy knew that they were indeed friends forever. 'I'm so sorry that we didn't become friends right away when we first met.'

'That was my fault,' Jade said. 'I couldn't think of anything else but my own problems . . . of anyone else but Abby and me.'

'No, it was me. All I had on my mind was Rud. What's wrong with us girls? Why do boys always come first? And friendship with other girls a poor second? I was afraid of you. You were . . . are . . . so beautiful and I felt so threatened. I thought surely he was going to go for you instead of me. I guess I was just plain jealous of you. It never even occurred to me at the time that it was possible that you weren't even interested in him. . . .'

What was the point now, Jade thought, in telling D'Arcy that she had been very much interested but had passed in favour of Abby. It was no longer pertinent to anything.

They sat in bed silent for a while, each lost in their own thoughts. Then, suddenly, Jade asked, 'The father of your baby? Did you consider marrying him and having the baby?'

'I considered it. God, how I considered it! But I never told him about the baby. To tell the truth, I never got the chance.'

'Why? Did he go away?'

'You might say that. Actually he went running back to his mother and that was that.'

Running back to his mother? The words rang a bell and Jade leaned back and sucked in her breath. She didn't want D'Arcy to say another word. But D'Arcy did. 'He went running back to his mother and your sister Abby.'

And then Jade wished D'Arcy had never come to see her, had never told her her secret. But now it was too late. In a way it was too late for both of them.

The next morning the first thing D'Arcy said was, 'I'm going to scratch the rest of my trip. I want to spend the whole time with you,' and Jade knew she had to put all the unwanted, terrible images D'Arcy had placed in her mind on hold. She had to make this a happy time for them both.

'I'm all yours.'

'But what about your modelling?'

Jade shrugged. 'I'm pretty successful. I can work when I want to, and not work when I don't want to. To tell you the truth I work only when they yell at me a lot or I really need the money. Since I don't spend a lot of money I don't need it all that much and that gives me a degree of independence.'

'You're lucky.'

Really? Tell me about it. 'Why do you say that?'

'You're lucky that you're so beautiful and you're in demand as a model. Suppose you weren't? What would you do?'

'Starve to death, probably.' *A joke.*

'You could have asked my mother for money, you know.' *No joke.* But Jade knew, even if D'Arcy didn't, that she had already taken enough from Francesca – her trust in her husband, if nothing else. But she didn't want to think about that. At least, not during D'Arcy's stay in Paris. 'Actually I didn't need money at first. I stole some money from Trace before I left Palm Beach and then I had a few pieces of my mother's jewellery with me—'

'And you sold it?'

'Yes. In New York. Before I came to Paris.'

'I wondered how you managed.'

'Yes. There was a man in New York who helped me sell the jewellery and get a passport.'

'Aha. *Cherchez le man!*'

Jade giggled. Despite the bad time she had had, D'Arcy still managed to be funny which was wonderful of her. 'It wasn't like *that*. He was an old friend of my mother's.'

'Her lover?'

'Oh, D'Arcy, you're impossible! You have a one-track mind.'

No, not lover. All they ever did was look into each other's eyes and he ended up in a wheelchair after being beaten half to death with a baseball bat. No, not lover! Only a poor, crippled friend. . . .

'And then you came to Paris and got work as a model?'

'Not at first. First, I was a photographer's assistant. Armand's assistant. He's the photographer I do most of my modelling for now.'

'Is *he* your lover?'

'D'Arcy, will you stop? Of course he isn't my lover. He's a homosexual.'

'Well, don't get mad. I understand that even homosexuals can do it with women.'

'Armand doesn't. Not with this woman, anyway. Besides, even if *he* wanted to, why would I?'

'D'Arcy considered. 'If you put it that way, I don't know why you would. I mean, I'm sure you have all kinds of more *desirable* opportunities, shall we say?'

Jade laughed. 'Yes, shall we say . . .' she said enigmatically.

'Oh, come on, Jade, you can tell me. *Do* you have lots of lovers?'

'Oh, all right, I'll tell you, if you promise not to bring the subject up again.'

'I promise. Now, what's the answer.'

'No.'

'What do you mean, no?'

'I answered you and the answer is still *no*. I do *not* have lots of lovers.'

'That's not fair. I have to ask one more question.'

'Yes?'

'Do you have a *few*?'

'The answer is still no, and you are *not* permitted any more questions.'

She had told D'Arcy the truth. She did not have lots of lovers, not even a few. When she had first come to Paris, there had been many men but no lovers. There'd been only faceless men with whom she had had sex, not made love. It had been easier that way – to submit, not to resist. She had been lonely. She'd been lonely in Los Angeles but never as desperately as after she'd run away from Palm Beach, leaving the only two people in the world she really cared about. There was a song she always thought of – 'I Left my Heart in San Francisco'. Only the way she sang it, the words came out: 'I left my heart in Palm Beach . . .' which of course, sounded terrible . . . so unmelodic. Then one day she had awakened in a strange bed and the bed linen wasn't clean and the face on the other pillow was alien and unbeautiful and she'd been filled with self-revulsion. She had thought it was the men *she* was using, holding cheaply, but it was she herself whom she was using, demeaning, deadening, just like Trace and Scott had used, demeaned and deadened Carlotta. And there had been all those men to whom Carlotta had given herself so carelessly, to get back at Trace. Carelessly and foolishly. And she, Jade, wanted to be the best part of her mother, not the most foolish, not the most self-destructive. . . . And after that, there had been no more faceless men, certainly not lovers.

Jade couldn't help asking, 'And you? Have you had lovers other than—?' She couldn't bring herself to say his name.

'Other than Rud? No. Rud was the first and only.'

Jade closed her eyes. Even though it was terrible of her, considering the terrible circumstances, she envied D'Arcy. How she wished she could say those words – Rud was my first and only. . . .

D'Arcy wanted to order breakfast from room service but Jade insisted they go out and see Paris. They decided to start on the Left Bank and so they took a taxi down the Place de la Concorde to go over the bridge. D'Arcy was amused when she saw how the drivers seemed in a contest with each other rather than just trying to get somewhere. 'The driving here is almost as wild as it is in Boston.'

'Or in Los Angeles. I guess things are the same all over the world no matter where you are,' Jade said.

But both she and D'Arcy knew that in a certain way neither Paris nor Los Angeles could ever be the same as Boston.

Although it was really too cold, they had their *café au lait* and croissant at a pavement café.

'So what do you do when you aren't working?'

'I take classes in French.'

'But your French is terrific. You ordered from room service last night and you just ordered our breakfast. You even conversed with our cranky taxi driver.'

Jade laughed. 'But what did I say to that cranky taxi driver? *Bonjour?* Believe me, some of my worst times speaking French have been with taxi drivers. When I first arrived here and went shopping for a mattress, I made the most terrific gaffe. I mixed up *matelot* and *matelas* and I ended up telling the taxi driver to take me where I could buy a sailor.'

She made D'Arcy laugh and that was good. 'I just don't want to speak French like a displaced American. I want to learn to speak it like a native and I want to be able to read French in the original. . . .'

Seemingly inexplicably, D'Arcy burst into tears and Jade was at a loss. 'Why are you crying?'

'If you want to learn to speak French like a native, it means you have no intention of ever going back to America and I'll probably never see you again!'

'Of course you will. You'll come back to Paris and some day . . . sometime, I'll go home again.'

'When?'

'Well, I'm not sure.'

'Soon?'

'Maybe. . . .'

'Why can't you come back now?'

'I thought you understood about that, D'Arcy. It's Trace and my godfather, Ross Scott. I want to stay on the other side of the world, far away from them.'

And because I can't trust myself to be in the same hemisphere with Rud, and because, like you, I don't know if I can trust myself to resist him. And Abby loves him . . . I can't do anything to endanger that love.

To distract D'Arcy by changing the subject she added shyly, 'I'm also taking lessons in writing.'

'You are? What kind of writing?'

'It's a course in creative writing. Short stories, mostly.'

'That's really neat, but what I want to know is in which language are you taking this course? In French or in English, to write in which – English or French?'

They sat under the trees at the Place Furstemberg. 'I saw your picture on the cover of a fashion magazine you know,' D'Arcy told Jade, even though this was a painful reminder of that time at the Liberty Hotel. 'But your hair was short and black. What was that all about?'

'It was a wig. At first I always wore that wig. I wanted a disguise. I thought no one would recognize me if I changed the colour and the style of my hair.'

'But who were you hiding from?'

'I just wanted to take precautions in case someone in America saw my picture like you did.'

'But you weren't hiding from *me*?'

'No, of course not. I was hiding from Trace and Scotty. I didn't want them to know where I was. But then I realized that I was being silly, that if they wanted to find me they would. They can always find anybody if they want to. They have their ways.'

'But they never did?'

'No. I guess I exaggerated my own importance to them.'

What she had done was to make copies of those pages in the diaries that referred to Trace and Scotty's criminal activities and had burned the rest.

Someday, she had figured, she would use the pages to get them, to even the score but then she had realized that the pages were more than incriminating evidence – they were an insurance policy and she had sent copies to Ross and Scotty with the advice that additional copies were also in the hands of different people who would turn them over to the authorities if anything happened to her. It was a lie but they didn't know that and she had specifically said *different people* so they wouldn't know where to begin searching.

'I'm surprised that considering you were afraid that they might be looking for you, you decided to be a model at all.'

'Well, at first I was a photographer's assistant as I said, but it was such a bore. I had to make up the models and fix their hair. The ones that weren't top of the line, that is. The really big ones have specialists, of course. And I'd have to hold the fan to make their hair blow if that was the look. And I ran errands. Getting props, searching all over Paris for the right accessories. And unless I had to get something that weighed a ton, I wasn't given cab fares. I had to take the métro and I hated that. After all, I'm an L.A. girl and there we don't even have a subway.

'Then one day an account executive took a look at me and said, "My God, she's another Carlotta Boudin!" I wasn't using the name Boudin so they had no idea I was really her daughter. But they adore American movie stars so Armand took another look and said, "*Oui, il y a la ressemblance. . . .*" And then they wouldn't take no for an answer and I finally agreed to model but only if I could wear the black wig. To tell the truth, I was just glad not to have to chase all over Paris on the métro.'

They were back on the Right Bank strolling along the Rue de la Paix, looking at all the beautiful things there were to buy – crocodile belts and alligator purses, silk blouses and cashmere sweaters and ropes of pearls. 'Mother says I'm to buy lots of wonderful French dresses for myself, but I really want to bring her back something spectacularly special.'

'I'll take you to all the houses and get you a discount.' Yes, Jade thought, Francesca did deserve something very special. And she thought that maybe she could send Abby something special with D'Arcy. D'Arcy could meet her somewhere and give her the present with all her sister's love.

'Did you ever get to see Abby?' She'd been waiting to ask that question, but hadn't before because of the Rud-Abby connection.

'Once. When I first arrived in Boston. My mother and I went calling on them. Mother wanted to see how Abby was getting along, and I, of course, was hoping to see Rud.'

Twice. Actually I saw Abby twice . . . the second time when she and Rud were playing in the snow, happy as two cooing doves.

'And you never got together with her again?'

'Don't you get it, Jade? She didn't want to see me or Judith didn't want her to see me. Either way it amounts to the same thing. They didn't even invite me for Thanksgiving even though I was family and didn't go home for Thanksgiving.'

Instead she had spent Thanksgiving in the hospital, bleeding with Judith at her side instead of Rud. But what was the use of laying *that* on Jade?

Jade could see the hurt expression on D'Arcy's face reflected in the shop window as they stood looking at a black party dress without really seeing the dress at all. Still, she persisted, she had to know: 'That one time you did see Abby, how did she look?'

'Marvellous. Much, much prettier than when you saw her in Palm Beach. She was beautifully dressed and brimming with self-confidence. She was glowing.' Yes, that was the word for Abby. She was glowing the day when she had seen her romping in the snow with Rud. 'Positively glowing.'

Jade nodded, satisfied that she had done the right thing when she had run away, leaving Abby in Judith's care. But she had made D'Arcy unhappy with her questions. 'I know. How would you like to go to a party tonight?'

'I thought you didn't go to parties.'

'Oh, I do sometimes. On special occasions. And this *is* a special occasion, having my very own cousin visiting from across the sea.'

'OK, you're on.' Why not? It would be the first party for her too in a very long time.

D'Arcy bought the dress they were looking at in the shop window, and insisted that Jade pick out a dress too on Francesca's credit card.

'Oh no, I couldn't do that. Besides, I can buy my own. I earn lots of money.'

'You don't understand. Mother will be so happy when I tell her she bought you a dress. Make it a really groovy one, something to write home about.'

'Well, if you put it that way.' She tried on a gold lamé mini, tight and at least three inches shorter than what was being worn in the United States and D'Arcy pronounced it the grooviest! Then they taxied over to the Rue du Faubourg St Honoré to have their hair done at Alexandre's who, Jade told D'Arcy, was the only stylist to whom the *crème de la crème* entrusted their heads.

'But will he take us without an appointment?'

'That *crème de la crème* I was talking about? Well, you're looking at the *crèmiest*. I am, after all, a very hot cover girl.'

D'Arcy saw exactly what Jade meant. Once they entered the hairdresser's august environs consisting of many rooms designated by colour, Jade ignored the receptionists' protestations that they didn't have anything down in the book for her with icy hauteur, and raised her voice only slightly. Yet there were many whispered consultations among the help with a great running back and forth and then they were shown into the great Alexandre's presence in the Blue Room (also known as the Throne Room). He kissed Jade, murmured something about an '*enfant terrible*,' and D'Arcy gathered that he was telling Jade fondly that she was a naughty girl, and she knew that Jade was indeed, *hot*.

Three hours later as they swept past the still waiting smocked countesses, ambassadresses, vicomtesses in triumphant twin hairdos, hair piled high with escaping tendrils at the nape and curling wisps on forehead and cheeks, D'Arcy reflected that Jade was as much a reigning queen of the current Parisian scene as her mother had been in Hollywood in her day.

'Now, *this* is elegant,' D'Arcy whispered to Jade as they entered the apartment near the Bois, decorated with crystal chandeliers, hanging tapestries and satin upholstered furniture. 'This is how you should live.'

'*Moi?*' Jade mocked. 'Oh, this is much too elegant for me. This is decadence.'

D'Arcy looked around. There was a woman old enough to know better who was wearing a dress which exposed most of her breasts, and there was a gentleman with rouged cheeks, and another in black tie, who sported a shoulder-length coiffure with curls on his cheeks kept in check with diamond studded hairpins, but that was about as decadent as it got as far as she could see, disappointed. 'Whose apartment is this? Who's giving the party?'

'Marcella. She's a model, definitely the hottest. Over there,' Jade pointed. 'With the young boy in the kaftan.'

D'Arcy saw a woman about forty with orange lips and a dead-white skin, with features seemingly carved out of marble. She was rapier-thin with platinum waves lying close to her skull. 'If she's a model and the hottest, you're in trouble, Jade. You're never going to make it. Whew! She's weird!' Then she saw Marcella turn to a woman and kiss her lingeringly on the lips and D'Arcy gasped.

Jade laughed. '*C'est la vie!*' She indicated a pink-marbled table about three feet in diameter which stood in the middle of the room. 'See that table? The first time I came to a party here I drank six glasses of wine and danced on it.'

'Really? Do it now for me!'

'Afraid not. I don't do that sort of thing any more.'

A woman with heavy breasts in a white satin dress undulated past and D'Arcy, noting the white-blond hair, whispered: 'I think she's doing Marilyn Monroe.'

Jade nodded. 'She is, but she's a *he*.'

D'Arcy was impressed. 'I guess this *is* decadence but I don't see anyone doing drugs.'

'Of course not! This is *elegant* decadence. Marcella never allows it in the salon. If you're interested, try the kitchen. There's probably a full menu set out in silver bowls, even the Thai stick.'

D'Arcy shook her head. 'No thanks. *I* don't do that sort of thing any more.'

As the hour grew late Jade looked around for her Cinderella to tell her it was time to go back to the Ritz where the elegance was merely elegant. She found D'Arcy in the master bedroom sitting on the bed next to Marcella whose orange-tipped long white fingers were making a trail down D'Arcy's black taffeta

'D'Arcy!' Jade cried out and D'Arcy snapped to attention and Marcella, annoyed, said, 'You Americans! So gauche!'

Jade handed D'Arcy her coat. 'Really, D'Arcy. What did you think you were doing? Can't take you any place.'

'Great balls of fire! I wasn't going to do anything!'

'You sure seemed on the verge of *something*.'

'I still had my dress on, didn't I?'

'Yeah, but for how long?'

'I wasn't going to do anything. I was just curious to see how it worked.'

'When were you going to stop?'

'At the moment of truth,' she giggled and Jade did too.

'Your moment of truth might have come a little late and then what would you have done?'

They stepped out into the cold, clear night. D'Arcy giggled again and said,

'Then I guess I might have had an interesting Parisian experience to take home with me. Well, come to think of it, that party in itself was an interesting Parisian experience, interesting enough.'

'Do you know what a real French experience would be? A little affair of the heart. No Parisian woman worth her salt doesn't believe in at least one affair of the heart. An interlude . . . I'll think about it and maybe I'll come up with someone exactly right for you. . . .'

'A love affair?'

'Just a short one,' Jade laughed. 'Just for the length of time you'll be here.'

'Don't bother. Long or short, I don't do that sort of thing any more.'

Then Jade sighed softly. 'I know. I don't do that sort of thing any more either. . . .'

'Let's not go back to the Ritz, Jade. I think I've had enough of elegance. Let's go back to your apartment. It's kind of homey there.'

'OK. Let's,' and they set off down the street, arm in arm.

'Are you sure you won't stay over for Christmas? The Windsors are giving a party at their home in the Bois de Boulogne and I have an invitation. People would kill for an invitation.' It was so hard for Jade to let go of D'Arcy.

'Oh, Jade, I wish I could, but for you and not the Windsors. After all, I've done the Windsors – they were at my Sweet Sixteen, remember? – and I really don't have to do them anymore,' she said, trying to make Jade laugh. When Jade didn't, D'Arcy pleaded, 'I must go home for Christmas. My father's gone and my mother's all alone.'

'I know. I feel terrible that your mother and father have split.'

And guilty, Jade thought, wondering how much she herself had contributed to their break-up.

D'Arcy shrugged. 'I guess it was inevitable. He just couldn't take Mother having a mind of her own after all these years.'

'Why do you think he chose Boston to live?' To be near Rud, she thought, even as she asked the question.

'Well, it was his home town. Mother says he plans on organizing a movement that will focus on declaring war on crime. You know, organized crime and all that. Who knows what he's thinking of? Maybe he intends to use that as a springboard to launch a third party. . . .'

'Oh, no, D'Arcy! He can't do that!'

'What, start a third party? It does seem pretty futile.'

Jade didn't care whether it was futile or not. All she knew was that it was dangerous to start up with organized crime and the likes of Ross Scott. 'Don't let him focus on crime!'

D'Arcy laughed. 'Do you think he's going to listen to me? Besides, what does it matter which issue he picks? To a politician one issue is as good as another. You just try and grab one for yourself that someone else hasn't already beaten to death.'

'But I'm not talking about war on crime as a political issue. I mean he shouldn't start up with mobsters. They get you! They always get you!'

'But that's politics, Jade. Someone is always out to get you and it doesn't have to be a mobster.'

'Oh, D'Arcy, you don't understand and you're so cynical.'

'Maybe you're right. Maybe I am cynical. Maybe I should go in for politics myself. Who knows? Maybe I could be the first woman President of the United States.'

Jade could see that she was going to get nowhere with trying to get D'Arcy to see how dangerous the situation was. She just refused to take it all seriously. 'Well, I'd rather see you with a lovely sweet husband and a house full of babies than as President.'

Then she realized she had said the wrong thing because they both thought about the baby D'Arcy had been forced to abort and they grew sad and pensive. But D'Arcy recovered with a pout. 'Thanks a lot. Here I'm dreaming of the presidency and you have me playing housekeeper and nursemaid.'

Jade laughed. 'Well, maybe you can be one of the lucky ones who has it all . . . the husband, the babies, and the presidency!'

And then D'Arcy grew pensive again. 'Maybe I can have it all at that. All I'd need would be the right husband, right? I mean, if I chose right, I could have a President all my own even if I couldn't be one myself. Isn't that so?'

Then Jade didn't know if D'Arcy was kidding or whether, despite her hard words about Rud, she was still having romantic dreams centring around him. But how could she ask her that? There were places in the heart where even the closest friend couldn't trespass.

When they arrived at Orly, they discovered that D'Arcy's plane wouldn't be taking off for at least another hour.

'Let's have a glass of wine while we're waiting,' Jade said, leading D'Arcy to a lounge. Then they sat across the little table, so full of emotion that they could barely speak.

'You'll write faithfully, you promise?' D'Arcy asked tearfully.

'Yes, and you're going to answer just as faithfully. And you will give Abby that present for me and try to see her once in a while?'

'Jade, I told you. She's not interested in seeing me.'

'But you'll try, for me? I'm sure Abby can use a friend too.'

'Why? She has Judith and Rud. She doesn't want anyone else. But all right, Jade, I'll try. For you. As long as I don't have to go near her precious Stantons.'

Jade squeezed her hand. 'Thank you. I know it's difficult for you.'

And then because their time together was nearly up and if she didn't ask the question now she might never have another opportunity, D'Arcy said, 'You know . . . that week in Palm Beach. I was convinced that you and Rud were interested in each other. Was I right?'

They were friends now . . . friends forever, and while Jade knew there shouldn't be lies between friends, she couldn't bring herself to tell D'Arcy the truth in light of what had happened between her and Rud. 'You were wrong, plain and simple. Why, we hit it off like oil and water. Don't you remember?' And then because she wanted to say something, anything that could possibly help D'Arcy accept what could never be, she said, 'And D'Arcy, even then I had a feeling that it wasn't in the stars for you and Rud. I had a feeling then that it was meant to be that Rud and Abby— Well, I had a feeling they were meant for each other.'

'That's just the most awful bull I ever heard,' D'Arcy said harshly.

'I'm sorry. It was just a feeling—'

'Well, feelings suck!' she said savagely.

And then Jade had to laugh, and reluctantly, D'Arcy decided to shelve her bitterness and laugh along. She couldn't go away mad.

They walked slowly to the gate. 'Jade, when *will* you come home?'

'I'm not sure *where* my home is. My mother once told me home is where the heart was, and I wasn't even sure which place *she* was talking about. But I had a feeling it was Boston and not L.A. but I couldn't ask her because she sounded so sad. But one thing I do know, my home certainly isn't in L.A. where Trace and Scotty are. At least you don't have that problem. You know where your heart is. In Florida with your mother. I still don't understand why when your mother's alone now you still want to go back to school in Boston. Is it because you want to make up with your father and he's there?'

'No. And it's not because I want to start up with Rud again if that's what you're really thinking. It's simply what I said – I started at B.U. and I might still be able to squeeze a few credits out of them. And it's a good school for Political Science.'

And what better place to be than where the object of one's hoped-for revenge resides?

'But Jade, I still don't know what you're going to do.'

'What do you mean, what will I do? Tomorrow I'll call Armand and tell him I'm ready to go back to work and he'll yell at me and swear that if I ever take so much time off again I'll never work for him again.'

'And then what?'

'And then I'll take my French lesson and the day after that I may write a story. Or rather, I'll try and write a story. And then Christmas, I'll go to the Duke and Duchess's party. . . .'

'And then—'

'You don't have to worry about me, D'Arcy. I have a lot of invitations for New Year. I even have one to attend a party at Noel Coward's chalet in Switzerland. . . .'

D'Arcy shook her head impatiently. 'I mean, what are you going to do with the rest of your life?' She was so apprehensive for Jade. She seemed so alone.

But it was time for D'Arcy to board. Jade kissed her. 'Don't worry about me. I'll do what everyone else does. Live each day as it comes. . . . But I'll be thinking of you every day, I can promise you that.'

And all D'Arcy could manage was a whispered, 'You all take care of yourself, you hear?'

And then she was gone, but Jade didn't leave until she saw D'Arcy's plane in the sky.

2.

There was an eclectic group of guests at the Windors' Christmas party – an Italian film maker, a celebrated hairdresser, several renowned fashion designers, an assortment of arriviste Americans, as well as Europe's restless aristocracy, all of whom babbled on about where they'd most recently been – Mexico, the Greek Islands, London – and where they were going – Biarritz, Rome, the Costa del Sol. The second most popular subject of conversation was about other parties they'd gone to – who was there, what they wore, and what was served.

The Duchess was mostly into fashion, since she was almost as famous for her fantastic wardrobe and jewels as she was for being the American divorcée who toppled England's throne. She asked Jade what kind of stockings she wore to which Jade replied that she no longer wore stockings, only pantyhose and tights. Wallis then confided that she still wore stockings and that she imported them from the United States at $1.95. 'Isn't that a fantastic bargain?' she asked proudly.

'Wow!' Jade said. 'Really?'

Then Wallis called the Duke over and ordered him to tell Jade how proud he was that she was so clever as to get her stockings from the United States at $1.95 the pair.

'Oh, dear, yes, very proud,' he said enthusiastically and Jade smiled glassily, taking a large swallow of her wine. Then the Duchess, who reputedly possessed the largest privately-held jewellery collection in the world, inquired about what had ever happened to Carlotta Boudin's jewellery collection, and Jade asked for a little something stronger to drink before she answered that one. Then she explained that she had sold a few pieces but that the bulk was in a bank vault until she was twenty-one. When that day came to pass and if she was of a mind to sell any of it, she promised she'd be in touch.

'Do you model the mini?' the Duke asked.

'If that's my assignment, sure. Do you like the mini?'

'I think it's fine if the young lady in question has good underpinnings. For myself, I like double-breasted suits, and I'm not keen on women wearing trousers. What do you like?'

'Oh goodness, gracious,' Jade giggled, 'if you really want to know, I *love* the Rudi Gernreich look. You know – topless. . . .'

The Duke coughed, then reddened, then giggled too. And Wally's Mr Chu, one of her five pug dogs, who was sitting on the Duchess's pink satin Dior lap, peed, making a small puddle which naturally enough seeped through to Wally's thighs. 'Oh!' Wally cried out, then scolded not Mr Chu but the Duke. 'You didn't walk him! It's the one thing I ask of you and you didn't do it!'

At this the Duke burst into tears and pouted, 'Oh, Wallis, you've made me weep again!' and he went upstairs to bed. And Jade asked for her coat and went home.

Then for New Year she went to Noel Coward's pink and white chalet in the Alps. She had never met Mr Coward but she knew that his crowd liked to have a few pretty girls in attendance to dress up the party, and it didn't make any difference to her. It was just a place to go.

The elegant Mr Coward, wearing needlepoint slippers which he said Merle Oberon had worked for him, was delighted when he discovered that she was a carbon copy of the legendary Carlotta.

'She was absolutely charming. You must have some of these sweet little raspberries that I've had flown in from Israel since you seem every bit as sweet as your adorable mother.'

Everything about Noel and his house was a blaze of colour, Jade couldn't help but notice. The road leading to his villa was lined with tubs of pink and white petunias even though it was the middle of winter, and Noel himself wore a bright purple smoking jacket which matched his purple sofa, and his green ascot matched the covering of his coffee table, and everywhere there were multi-coloured needlepoint pillows. 'Mary Martin did this one, and Dorothy Hammerstein that one. Do you know Dorothy? Sweet, sweet, sweet!'

Jade was introduced to Bill Holden who wanted to know if Audrey was coming.

'Audrey?' Jade wondered.

'Yes, Audrey *Hepburn*,' Bill said, as if there were no other Audreys worth discussing.

Orson Welles was there, an imposing figure, and Jade was suitably impressed. Mr Welles told her she was the picture of her mother, which, of course, wasn't exactly news to Jade, but then Orson told her in a confidential tone that even though he had married a legendary redhead – Rita – Carlotta Boudin had been the most beautiful redhead in the world.

James Mason, who now joined in the conversation, added that he had regarded Carlotta as the epitome of Hollywood glamour, at which point Noel came up from behind and uttered, 'When Gertie . . . Gertrude Lawrence, you know,' he explained, thinking that perhaps Jade was too young to know who Gertie was. 'When Gertie and I danced, people said that *we* were the very *definition* of glamour!'

David Niven, another Swiss habitué, told Jade how tragic it was that her so talented mother had been so tragically short-lived, then introduced her to Charlie Chaplin who was sitting by himself, more or less lost in thought. Mr Chaplin had nothing to say to Jade about Carlotta since Carlotta's heyday had been well past his own, for which Jade was grateful. She hadn't come to Switzerland to hold a memorial service for her late and lamented mother. With her fourth glass of champagne in hand, Jade went to the window to stare unseeing at the imposing rise of Mont Blanc.

Noel came up from behind to ask if she were enjoying his Southern view. 'Sweet, isn't it?'

She turned and said, 'Not really,' and Noel shook a finger in her face. 'Naughty! Naughty! Just like your sweet, sweet mother. . . .'

Someone said Irwin Shaw was expected and Jade thought, good, she could talk to *him* since she admired his short stories and maybe he had never known her mother. But then she never found out if he showed up or not, because she went off with a prince something-or-other from a principality she never heard of only because he had violet-blue eyes fringed with incredibly long lashes which reminded her of someone she had once known.

The Prince wanted her to see his chalet which was up the hill above Noel's, and wasn't that what one came to Switzerland for? – the taxes, the skiing, the banks, and the chalets?

But in the morning, she was filled with remorse. She decided she didn't like chalets at all, and was sorry she'd seen this one. After all, that was one of the things she had promised herself she wouldn't do any more – go up to see a prince's chalet. . . .

Here it was, the first day of the New Year – 1965, and she hadn't even made a new resolution. All she had done was break an old one.

3.

It was as if D'Arcy's coming and leaving had left her restless. Her whole life seemed pointless and unrewarding, and she kept asking herself the same question D'Arcy had: 'Well, Jade, what are you going to do next? What are you going to do with the rest of your life?'

And then in the spring, she began to have the feeling that she was being followed. She'd be walking down a boulevard and become conscious that there was someone behind her somewhere, with eyes glued to her back. But then it always turned out to be no one at all. Or was it a ghost? She wasn't sure. And she began to think about moving on . . . to London maybe. She could always get work there as a model and she did have a reputation. And everyone said that London was where it was happening. She'd think about it in the autumn, she thought. She had a strong feeling that she should wait for autumn.

And then one day in June, she knew why she had that hunch . . . about waiting till autumn. One day she just opened her door and there he was and she wasn't surprised. It was as if she'd been expecting him, knew that he would show up. One day she just opened her door and he filled her doorway, taller than before and broader, and just as beautiful! And she forgot that the last time she had seen him she was playing the game of rejecting him with every look. This time, she forgot everything and just about fell into Rud's arms.

Oh, there were a hundred questions she wanted to ask him and there were maybe a million words to be said, but it all waited, all the words that had been stored up for so many months, while their bodies clung together and their lips. Ah, Rud's lips, she exulted. At first they were dry and soft and closed and then they were open and his tongue was sweetly wet. At first his hands were soft and gentle and then they were fast and urgent. She tore her body from his only by sheer will to remove the thin white nightshift she was wearing and he sucked in his breath at the sight of her, more beautiful than he had dreamed, and he had been dreaming of her, imagining her like this, all white skin and pink-tipped nipples, burnished red silky triangle for what – one thousand and one nights? At first he had kept count and then had stopped counting. It had been so long. . . .

He started to tear at his own clothing, flinging his jacket to the floor, then his tie. 'Let me,' she said as he fumbled with his shirt buttons and her fingers were fast and deft, more so than his.

She unbuckled his belt, he pulled down his zipper, she pulled his trousers down his legs and he kicked them aside. Then he picked her up again, rubbing her body against his – up, down, up, down – teasing them both until the tension grew unbearable.

He carried her over to the single bed where D'Arcy had thought there wasn't room for a lover, but she was wrong. There was room only for lovers.

He wanted to wait, he wanted to make love to her body first with his mouth and his tongue and his hands but not this time. This first time there wasn't enough time for slow and leisurely love – he couldn't wait, neither could she.

She threw herself on her back and opened her legs and he positioned himself between them. One hand cupped her breast, the other hand glided down her stomach to find her wetness. She arched towards him and then he moved between her legs and she eagerly reached out to guide him into her. A mutual effort and then she thrust up to meet him with a soft cry. She lifted her knees high to take in more of him, her hands pressing convulsively on his buttocks. This was her own sweet love at last and she climaxed almost immediately with a lingering shudder, and then he did too, the blood roaring in his head.

After the act and only then the foreplay began, the kissing of each other's parts, the petting, the caressing and the murmured endearments.

'How did you find me?'

He was lying on his back, arms folded under his head. She lay on her side, facing him. As she talked, her lips grazed his smooth, tan chest.

'It wasn't difficult.' He told her about seeing her picture on the cover of the French magazine. 'Did you think that black hair would keep anyone from recognizing you, especially someone like me who carried your face in his heart?'

'Oh, don't say things like that to me, she thought. *I'm too vulnerable.* And then, even as her lips brushed the taut skin of his abdomen, she began to feel guilty. *Oh, Abby, I'm betraying you! And what about D'Arcy? Aren't I betraying her too?*

'I can't believe you're here, in Paris, alone. Without anyone.'

For a moment his face darkened. Was she taunting him as she had before? Implying that he was still Judith's little boy? But that was what he was . . . in Paris now only by Judith's dispensation. Then he decided to level with Jade. If you loved someone you honoured them with the truth. Otherwise, it was only the ordinary woman and the usual pack of lies.

'I'm here in Paris alone because I struck a deal. My mother is one of the great deal makers of the world. Did you know that?'

Oh, didn't she? *All* too well.

'When I told Judith that I was going to get my own place next autumn when I entered law school whether she liked it or not, that I'd get a job to pay for it, she offered me ten weeks in Europe as a graduation present if I agreed to live at home. And I grabbed at her offer. I know I should have stuck to my guns and thrown her deal in her face, but when I thought of coming to Paris, of finding you, I couldn't think of anything else. I *had* to come . . . to find you, be with you.'

Jade nodded. She knew. It was only for ten weeks. Ten weeks out of a lifetime. It wasn't so much to ask . . . to take. . . .

They didn't leave her apartment for three days, except for the times Jade went down to buy some food, to make her call to Armand and her agency to cancel all her bookings, to phone her service for messages. He was amazed that she lived without a phone in the apartment.

'But it's simpler that way. To make calls but not receive them. There are no intrusions.'

And there weren't but it wasn't so simple to escape the intrusions of the past. She *had* to ask about Abby.

'She's terrific. And she'd make the best sister in the world if she wasn't so damn committed to Judith?'

Sister? That wasn't what she wanted! Or was it? She was so confused, torn as ever. What *did* she want? She knew she couldn't have it both ways, have Rud both as a brother-in-law and a lover.

306

'Is that the way you care for Abby? As a sister? Surely you care for her in a more . . . you know— Not the way you would as sister. . . .'

He was surprised as if that thought had never entered his mind. 'How could I? Ever since I met you there's been no room to care about anyone else that way.'

Oh how she ached to hear him say just that. *But Abby! And what about D'Arcy?* Obviously he had felt something other than brotherly love for her!

'Are you telling me that there haven't been others?' she teased gently.

'I'm not going to lie to you. Sure, I've had sex with girls . . . women, if that's what you mean. But sex is not necessarily an act of love.'

Well, she couldn't argue with that. She'd had sex with many faceless men, and none of it had been an act of love. 'I know.'

But the 'I know' upset him. 'How many have there been?'

And then she was angry. She hadn't asked him for numbers. 'I didn't count. Did you?'

She would never have asked about D'Arcy since that would have been a deep betrayal of D'Arcy's confidence but he told her about D'Arcy just the same . . . told her about finding D'Arcy that Thanksgiving Day with her multitude of self-inflicted cuts, and she was filled with horror and remorse. D'Arcy had told her about being pregnant, about her abortion, but not about this . . . not about how she had loved so much she'd been driven in desperation to so terrible an act . . . a terrifying act of love. Or about being hospitalized with only Judith by her side.

'Was it only sex?' she demanded. 'Didn't you love D'Arcy at all?' She wanted to hear that he did. She had to know that D'Arcy, after all, hadn't loved and suffered entirely in vain. And she wanted to hear it for his sake too. She wanted him to *care* so that he would be a whole person.

'It's hard to explain. I felt affection for D'Arcy, so much affection that I never would have made love to her in the first place, not caring for her in *that* way. But then I had so much affection for her I couldn't turn away when she was offering me herself as a gift, if you can understand that. But then when I found her bleeding and realized how *very* much she cared, and I thought she might be dead or dying because of me, I would have done anything to save her – loved her, married her, cherished her forever.

'But then when she was in the hospital, Judith said the psychiatrists thought it would be better not to see me so I stayed away, and then Judith said D'Arcy told her she never wanted to see me again, and I thought I had to respect that. And when I never heard from her, I assumed Judith had told me the truth. But then later, thinking about it, I wondered if Judith had manipulated us both. She never did like D'Arcy. So I went to look for her but she was gone, someone said she was on a commune somewhere. . . .'

'What would you have done if you found her?'

'I'm not sure but I think I would have asked her to marry me.'

And then Jade knew that D'Arcy hadn't loved entirely in vain; she had, at least, loved a caring, tender man, as she herself did. But she was grateful, too, that Judith had been not loving to D'Arcy, but cruel. Cruel but absolutely correct under the circumstances.

He asked why she had run away that night. He never understood that.

'But I thought you realized— I thought everyone must have figured that one out. I thought everyone knew what Trace was . . . that when he asked Abby to come live with us . . . with me . . . he was only interested in her inheritance. I had to save Abby from him! If I was gone then she couldn't very well come home with *us*.'

'And you ran away, went out on your own at fifteen, just to save Abby? And Abby didn't know that. She thought you were running away *from* her, not for her.'

'I know. I've written to her but she hasn't anwered. I guess she doesn't accept my explanation and the only thing that would convince her is something I can never tell her, something she mustn't ever know . . . that Trace is really her father.'

'Oh, my God! Who would ever—? Poor Abby. It would be a shock to her but you have to tell her so she'll understand why you—'

'No. I can't do that to her. She never had a mother, and I can't take away the father she did have, the image she has of him and give her Trace Boudin instead. Then she'd have *nothing!*'

'She'd have you.'

'But she really doesn't know me. I'm not part of her past. She needs a past . . . to lean on, that's part of her, that she can be proud of, to know who she is. Like you. No matter how you feel about your mother, you're Dudley Stanton's son and he stood for something. He was a man to be proud of, and the Stanton name is a name to be proud of. You'll always have that.'

He was moved by her understanding, by her wisdom. 'And you, Jade? What do you have? Who? How do you know who you are?'

She smiled at him. 'I'm OK. I may not have much in the way of a father, but I had a wonderful mother, and I know who and what she was, and while not everyone knows how great she really was, *I* know, and the best part of her will always be with me.'

'Good. I'm glad. But if you don't tell Abby who her father really is, how do you know Trace won't?'

'Because your mother won't let him.'

'What? My mother knows that Trace is Abby's father and she took Abby in? She's willing to protect her?' It was mind-boggling.

Jade nodded. 'And I'm satisfied that she *will* protect Abby from him. Say what you will, your mother *is* a very strong woman.'

He could scarcely deny that. And maybe she was something more. Was it possible he had misjudged her? Was it possible that she was *kind*? Why else would she take Abby into her home and her heart and guarantee her protection?

Suddenly, in the middle of the night, he turned to her even as she slept and shook her awake. 'What is it?' she asked, afraid.

But he propped himself up on one elbow and only wanted to know why she had been such an impossible bitch when she was but fifteen and he eighteen, giving him such a hard time. 'Hot one minute, and cold the next.'

'You woke me up to ask me that? How do I know? I *was* only fifteen as you've just reminded me, as if I didn't know. I was confused. I liked you one moment, and was afraid of you the next. And I had my mind on other things – on Abby and on Trace.'

Could she tell him that Abby had a crush on him and she wanted Abby to have him? If anything would make him turn away from Abby, that would be it! And she was sending him back. . . . She *was* sending him back! 'Besides,' she giggled disarmingly. 'I was playing hard to get.'

'I'll say you were. You played so hard to get you made it impossible!'

'Now, can we go back to sleep?'

'Only if you promise never to do it again. Play hard to get.'

She couldn't promise so she did the next best thing. She said, 'If you try me now, you'll see exactly how hard I'm not . . . to get.'

He tried and she wasn't . . . not at all.

When he fell asleep finally, he dreamed of not Jade but Judith.

Be very good, my sweet boy, and always listen to your mother. And then when you grow up, you'll be the President. . . .

He woke up wondering whether he had always really wanted to be the President. Or was it that Judith had convinced him that he wanted it? Had it simply become a habit thinking that? A habit carried over from little boyhood when it had been easy for Judith to brainwash him?

He saw that Jade was up, putting on a pot of coffee, concentrating on measuring out the required amount. Looking at her as she stood at the stove nude, her exquisite profile in relief, he thought he'd trade being President in a snap if he could spend the rest of his time with her. 'Marry me!' he shouted.

She looked up from the coffee pot and laughed. What else could she do? She couldn't take him seriously or let him think she did either. He leaped out of bed, tore across the room into the tiny kitchen, picked her up in his arms and crushed her to him. 'Laugh at me, will you? I'll have to punish you for that!'

'Oh, do!' she cried. 'Punish me with kisses!'

They had to go out into the world, she thought. Ten weeks had been all they had, and it was slipping by, and it had to last a lifetime. But if they stayed in too much and made love too much, they were bound to get too serious, and that was something they couldn't do. *Abby, Abby, Abby!* She said the name over and over, so as not to forget that he was only on loan to her, and when the loan was called in, she had to return him with interest. Return him convinced that the better woman resided in Boston.

They tramped all over Paris together, Jade seeing the city in an entirely new light. *City of Light?* No, she thought, City of Love. They did all the things that lovers did – strolled the boulevards hand in hand, breakfasted on croissants and *café au lait* at dawn before they went to bed, watched the sun come up from behind Notre Dame, and sipped calvados on a terrace on the Champs Elysées in the shadow of the Arc de Triomphe. And always she talked of Abby, how sweet she was, and how good she remembered her to be, and how she must be so well-educated, now that she had already completed her second year at Radcliffe, and was probably still as innocent as ever. All this in pointed contrast to herself.

But he wasn't impressed. When they threw coins into the fountain at the Place St Michel and made a wish, he wished aloud that they were married. And then he cried, 'Quick! Say you'll marry me or I'll jump in and drown myself!'

'Go ahead and jump,' she replied but then when he did, she had no choice but to follow him in.

She took him to a party so that he could see a different side of Paris. But then he was disturbed by the way the men looked at her and kissed her in salutation, wondering if these were the men who had slept with her. At first she protested and tried to assuage his anxieties but then remembering that soon she would have to send him home, she encouraged his jealousy and his anger. Inevitably they fought and he stormed out into the street but then, feeling desperate without her, he turned around to go back only to bump into her as she came rushing out, prepared to run after him, to beg him to come back.

He told her how much he loved her then and she told him how much she loved him, didn't tell him that theirs was only an interlude. Then, not able to wait until they returned to her apartment, they checked into a little hotel nearby.

But their time together was drawing to an end and she knew she had to figure out a way to send him back to Boston, to Abby, and his destiny. Her own? Only to get through life from day to day and wait for that time when she could go home again, once she discovered where that home was.

He has a one-track mind, she thought wearily as he said, 'It's simple, we get married here, then you go home with me as my wife.' It was at least the tenth time he had said just that.

'What have you been smoking?' she asked curtly.

He laughed. 'I'm on to you this time. You can forget that hard-to-get routine.'

'You're acting like a child, you know that.'

'And you can forget that snippy routine too. I'm all yours.'

She tried being dead serious. 'Don't you know we're no good as a team? That I'm poison for any man who's interested in politics.'

Still he wouldn't take her seriously. 'You're too pretty for anyone to think of as poison.'

'Will you stop fooling around and listen to me? With my connections to Trace and Ross Scott, I spell sudden death to any candidate for any office from dog catcher up. . . .'

Suddenly, he *was* serious. 'I'm willing to take the risk.'

'You might be but Judith won't.'

'Judith! I'm sick to death of Judith!'

'You better not be. If ever a son needed his mother, it's you!'

She was up to her old tricks again, he thought, taunting him that he was a mama's boy. But why? She had told him she loved him, why was she back to that old refrain?

They fought all day but by night they made up. Their time was drawing to a close and after he was gone, Jade knew that there would only be sleepless, lonely nights.

The next day he had a new approach. 'I've been thinking— I *want* to make it on my own. I think I want that almost as much as I want you. I want to go home married to you and I want to tell Judith to stick it – everything, her support, her money. I want *us* to do it together.'

She turned away from him. 'Maybe you have the wrong girl in mind. I'm not

310

the kind of girl who would enjoy that kind of struggle. To tell you the truth, it really doesn't sound much like fun to me. I guess I'm just my mother's daughter, after all.'

'Now what does that mean?'

'Didn't your mother ever tell you the story about Bill and Carlotta and Frankie? Bill was very ambitious and Frankie loved him, but Bill loved Carlotta. But Carlotta was hardly the type to stand by Bill's side, be the selfless little wife who'd do anything to help her husband. She wanted fun and excitement and thrills so she chose Trace Boudin instead. And then and only then did he choose Frankie who did all the right things. Well, *I'm* Carlotta's daughter.'

He thought about what she said for a couple of minutes and then he shook his head. 'It won't work. When we talked about your mother you told me that she was really a wonderful person no matter what anyone thought of her, and that the best part of her would always be with you. . . .'

She shrugged. 'That's true but I guess I got the worst part too. You know, the bad with the good. That's the way these things go.'

'Sorry. I don't buy it.'

'What about buying that I simply don't love you enough?'

'Still, no deal. You gave yourself away yesterday when you said that you were poison for any man in politics because of your connections to Trace and Ross Scott. You're only saying that you don't love me because you want to save me and my career just like you ran away to save Abby from Trace.'

'What a colossal ego you have! You just can't accept the truth.'

'Oh, I can accept the truth all right. It's your lies that I can't accept. When you told me you loved me you were telling me the truth.'

'Oh, you. . . . How can you tell the lies from the truth?'

'My heart can tell. My heart tells me you love me.'

'Well, it's your heart that lies.'

Nothing she said mattered. Nothing worked. But she had to find a way to convince him. And the question was not whether she loved him, but did she love him enough to do what she had to do?

There were only four days left before he was to leave and she didn't have the heart to spend them fighting. But then when he said he was going out to buy his love a present, a token of his love, she knew she had to let him go even though she couldn't bear it that they were going to be cheated of those last four days. She kissed him goodbye, desperate to keep him close. And then when he was going out the door, she called out, 'Rud!' And he turned around, 'Yes?' And then she said, 'Oh, I just wanted to say hurry back . . .'

'Oh, I see, it's starting already, you acting like a ball and chain—' She could see that he was pleased and he blew her a kiss. . . . 'Au revoir . . .'

'Au revoir, my love . . .' she whispered.

But then she ran around frantically, throwing things into a suitcase, not knowing what or which. Where would she go? She'd think about that later. Right now she had to hurry so that she'd be gone before he came back.

But it was no good! When he realized that she was gone, that she had fled, he still wouldn't be convinced that she didn't love him – he would think only that she had done exactly what she had done almost three years before, that she had fled in the name of love ... of sacrifice, and he would go searching for her. And even if he didn't find her, he would never be free of her ... free to love someone else ... someone who would be good for him to love ... Abby!

There was only one thing that would positively work ... that would surely work. She glanced at the clock. If she hurried, the timing would be right. She went downstairs to the café on the corner, a neighbourhood kind of place where she was on nodding terms with a few of the regulars. She looked around and saw a young artist from Chicago. His name was Cliff. She didn't know his last name but then she didn't need to. ...

When Rud came through the door the room was in semi-darkness, the shades pulled down against the afternoon sun. But he didn't have to see – the sounds coming from the bed where two faceless forms moved and grappled were unmistakable, and then once his eyes adjusted to the amount of light in the room, he could easily make out that the tangle of hair lying across the pillow was golden red.

When Rud came through the gate at Logan Airport, the only familiar face he saw was Robert the chauffeur's. He was surprised. He would have thought his mother would have come to the airport herself to welcome him home after he'd been gone almost ten weeks, or at the very least, sent Abby. And Abby would have been a reassuring sight right now – her wholesomeness, her proper Boston manners, and her basic all-American good looks. It would have been like coming out of a long, dark tunnel into the light, into the fresh air.

'Where's everybody, Robert?'

'They're in Newport, Sir.'

It always made Rud wince when the elderly Robert called him sir. Rud had told him repeatedly to call him Rud as he had when he'd been a boy but Robert didn't think Mrs Stanton would care for that now that Rud was a grown man.

'What are they doing in Newport?' Rud asked irritably.

'Well, it's not Labor Day yet. The family always stays in Newport until after Labor Day.'

Of course. It was as if he had lost all track of time, forgotten that it was still the last cry of August. He was only aware that it had been spring, and now, suddenly, it was winter, despite the heat of the day.

He had always made it a point when he rode in the limousine alone with Robert to sit up front with him, continuing the habit of boyhood. But when Robert held the rear door open for him after stowing his bags in the boot, he automatically stepped in. 'There's no point in stopping at the house, Robert. Let's just head down to Newport.'

'Yes, Sir, that's what Mrs Stanton suggested. She and Miss Truesdale are planning on a big party for the weekend and Governor Sheridan is already there. He's been back and forth quite a bit this summer.'

That was no surprise to Rud. Ever since Bill had come back to Boston, he'd been a frequent visitor at the house.

312

He shivered, realizing that the car was overly chilled. Obviously Robert, thinking of his comfort, had left the motor running and the air conditioning turned on high all the while he'd been inside waiting at the gate. And now Rud, instead of telling Robert to turn down the air conditioning, turned up his collar and leaned forward to get himself a drink from the limousine's bar.

IX
1968

1.

It was the middle of March and there was snow on the ground but Judith wanted to discuss Rud's twenty-fourth birthday party with Abby as they sat in the library having afternoon tea. 'Isn't it a little early to be planning a party for June?'

'But I want Rud's party to be special this year since he's graduating too.'

'Well, if you combine the two, his birthday and the graduation, into one great big party, that would be pretty special, wouldn't it? And instead of having the party in June, we could have it the 4th of July and have fireworks too. . . .'

'That's a wonderful idea, Abby! You do have such good ideas.' And Judith gave her one of her biggest smiles, and Abby relaxed. Judith had all kinds of smiles in her repertoire, and not all of them were pleasant.

'Yes, this party is very important. The twenty-fourth birthday is such a milestone in a young man's life since it comes before his twenty-fifth.'

Abby laughed uneasily. She could tell that Judith was leading up to something with that simplistic remark. 'Yes, I can count. Twenty-four definitely comes before twenty-five.'

'Yes, of course, but did you know that since twenty-five is the earliest age one can be taken seriously in politics, twenty-four is the last year in which a politically minded young man must get his life in order?'

'What do you mean?' Abby asked even though she now knew where this conversation was headed and she was beginning to feel the first dull throbs of a serious headache.

'I mean that twenty-four is the age that a man in politics should be getting married, thinking of starting his family. People do have so much more respect for a family man, especially these days when so many young people seem to have forgotten all the real values. Yes, the voting public does take a married man that much more seriously and would especially in Rud's case because of his appearance. As it is they'll take one look at him and think he should be testing for the movies, not running for public office. And people always associate good looks with a man being a chaser. . . .'

Wishing only that she could get out of this conversation, Abby tried appeasing Judith with, 'But John Kennedy was already a senator and into his thirties before he got married.' She knew how impressed Judith was with how aptly the Kennedys had always managed their political fortunes. 'And no one seemed to mind that he was very much the bachelor-about-town before he married.'

'But those were different times. And Jack was fresh off his PT boat, a war hero. A hero doesn't need a wife to be taken seriously. And the country was coming out of the war into a time of prosperity so the public didn't mind a glamorous bachelor war hero raising a little hell. It suited their mood. But they feel differently these days with American boys dying in Vietnam and the nuclear threat and young people either taking a psychedelic trip or rioting in the streets. They want stability in their politicians. Look at Bobby Kennedy. Do you think all those children are going to hurt his candidacy for the presidency? I should say not! People know *he* has a stake in the future!'

Now, in addition to the throbbing in her head, Abby was beginning to feel a gnawing in her stomach. This was not an unfamiliar conversation. Oh, she knew Judith wanted her to marry Rud, wanted her to be the perfect political wife, but she'd been trying her best, had done every last thing Judith wanted her to ever since she'd come to live with them. . . .

She'd taken the dancing lessons, the speech lessons, had even gone to a charm school to learn how to put on make-up correctly. She dressed the way Judith decreed, wore her hair the way Judith thought the most attractive, even took the courses at Radcliffe Judith prescribed. And then when she was graduated, she had agreed to take Business Administration at Harvard even though she herself had wanted to take her Master's in Education. 'It's such a benefit for a man in political office to have a wife who knows how to handle money,' Judith had told her. 'You can see the advantages in that, can't you? It frees him from all that worry and one really can't rely on outsiders.' And as usual, she had had her examples ready – Jack Kennedy had had his huge family machine to do it for him, as did Bobby now, and Nelson Rockefeller had his David, and Franklin Roosevelt had had his mother Sara. Mothers, of course, were fine but one couldn't rely on them to be around forever. (This remark had sent Abby flying to Judith's side to protest.) Even Lyndon had had his Ladybird who, say what you will, had a shrewd business head on her shoulders. 'Everyone knew that Lyndon could rely on Bird.'

Judith's remarks had been so pointed, Abby could scarcely refrain from crying, 'Touché,' and racing down to the registrar's that very moment to shout, 'I want my Master's in Money!' And the funny thing was that she had her own money and never gave it a thought – there were people taking care of it for her.

She had cultivated those friends Judith thought suitable, and eschewed the rest. She hadn't bothered with D'Arcy because Judith said, 'She's really not our sort,' and that said it all. And even when D'Arcy had come back from Paris with a present from Jade, and a really reasonable explanation of why Jade had run away, she hadn't written to Jade because Judith said that some things were better left as they were. Jade's father *was* Trace Boudin, and that association wasn't going to do anyone any good.

Yes, she had done *everything!* She had shamelessly flirted with Rud, even submitted to the humiliation of having him escort her to parties, knowing he was only acting under Judith's orders too. She'd done it all for Judith! And she was willing to even marry Rud because it was what Judith wanted . . . her two darlings united forever. Although when she was being very honest with herself, Abby had to admit that Rud was not the man she would have chosen for herself, but what did she know? Judith knew best.

It wasn't that she didn't like Rud. She did. He was wonderful, full of fun, and he had the most wonderful manners, and he would never hurt anyone's feelings if it could be helped. But sometimes when she allowed herself to think about the man she would have chosen, Abby thought she would never pick anyone nearly as handsome as Rud. His good looks made her own mere prettiness seem inadequate. Actually, Rud himself made her feel inadequate and ordinary. Rud's very essence was self-assurance, glamour, a specialness, and how wonderful it would be to have someone who would make *her* feel special. He'd make her feel special and she'd make him feel special. And Rud didn't need *anyone* to make him feel that way – all his life he'd been made to think that he was.

There was a boy she had met in the reading room at the library. He had the warmest, steadiest, brown eyes and a certain tender manner. His speech was slow and when he stated his beliefs, he had such an intensity about him, she knew he was sincere. And she remembered how, when he had described the conditions in a third world country, his warm brown eyes had glowed with compassion. Then, later, when they'd gone for coffee, those same warm eyes had told her he thought that she was very special.

She had seen Noel a few times, for coffee . . . a beer. But she had never invited him home or really gone out with him. Judith would have given him the freeze treatment and Rud would have shaken his hand with a firm grasp but would never have asked him who he knew at Harvard, or tell him how he had crewed in the race at Newport which had brought the America's Cup back home where it belonged. But then again, Noel would probably have never told Rud how he was planning on joining the Peace Corps.

But the important thing wasn't the boys she didn't go out with, or the people she wasn't friends with. The important thing was pleasing Judith, who had taken her into her home and heart, had given her the love she'd never had. And wasn't she the ridiculous one? she mocked herself. What girl in her right mind wouldn't want Rud, so rich and beautiful and with the golden future? It didn't even matter that she had money of her own, or that his beauty really didn't move her, that she had never yearned to touch those incredibly long curling lashes. . . . (A girl had once told her that she was just dying to have Rud's lashes flutter on her cheek and Abby had been bemused, wondering what was wrong with her, Abby Truesdale, that she didn't have this urge.) No, the heart of the matter was who could reject the Golden Boy who had Judith for a mother?

She was just damned lucky that Judith wanted her as a daughter-in-law. The problem was much as she wanted to fulfil Judith's expectations, she couldn't manage, no matter how hard she tried, to pull it off, and she was literally exhausted from the stress and anxiety of the struggle.

'What can I do?' Abby pleaded with Judith now. 'Rud simply doesn't want me . . . not as a wife and not in *that* way.'

For a while after Rud had returned from Paris almost three years ago, she had thought . . . possibly . . . maybe, but then he had pulled back. 'Obviously he wants a different kind of girl.'

She was hoping that Judith would drop it, for the time being anyway, but today Judith seemed determined to pursue it. 'Let's try to analyze it. What do these girls whom Rud seems to *think* he wants have that you don't?'

Abby blushed. 'I— I guess he finds them sexy,' she blurted 'and he doesn't think of me in that way.'

Judith was not disconcerted. 'Well, then, there's only one thing to be done. We must help him discover that you are – *sexy*.'

Abby wished that she could drop through the floor. 'But I'm *not*. You know it and I know it and *Rud* knows it and nothing I do is going to change that.'

'But you *must* change it, Abby.'

Must? Abby was frightened. And then Judith said, 'I *want* to think of you as my daughter, Abby, and it appals me to think of someone else living in this house as Rud's wife and *my* daughter, because whoever the woman Rud chooses as his wife will have to come first with me in all things. You can understand that?'

And then Abby was terrified as Judith knew she would be. She knew this as well as she'd known three years earlier that if she gave Rud his head, allowed him to go off to Europe by himself, he would head straight for Jade. But she had also known that in the end Jade would do the right thing by Abby, by Rud and his career . . . would send Rud back where he belonged.

It was all a matter of reading people, and no matter how recklessly foolhardy Carlotta herself had been, both her daughters knew what a woman was supposed to do and they would do it, once you pointed them in the right direction.

Now listen to me carefully, Abby darling, and if all goes well, perhaps we can make that party we were talking about a particularly auspicious occasion. . . .

Judith was going out that night to one of her numerous charity events. This one was for the benefit of Stanton Memorial and since it was *their* hospital, Abby and Rud had been scheduled to accompany her. But Abby showed signs of coming down with something – the flu, probably, since it was going around, and Judith insisted Abby stay at home, put herself to bed, and drink lots of fluids, and she suggested that Rud stay home with her and see to it that she followed orders. She could ask some member of the staff to stay on duty to take care of Abby's needs, but Abby wouldn't feel bound to listen to them.

Abby protested, saying Rud didn't have to stay home just to take care of her but Rud insisted. God knew, he had had charity affairs up to his neck. 'Oh no, you don't get rid of me so easily,' he teased Abby. 'You're too eager. You're just dying to be here all by your lonesome, aren't you? Whom were you planning on having join you? The professor I saw you holding hands with at Ziggy's?'

Abby played along, pretending great indignation. 'I was *not* holding hands with Professor Martin. If you must know we were discussing— Oh, never mind! It's none of your business what we were discussing, Rud Stanton, and you always did have a dirty mind.'

'Sure, sure. Well, I'm planning on staying right here and seeing to it that you stay in bed without Professor Martin to keep you warm. Or should I say, *hot*?'

'Judith, make him stop!'

Judith laughed. 'Really! Both of you are acting like children. I'm leaving now and you two try to behave yourselves. Why don't you play Scrabble or something? And you, Rud, make sure that Abby stays in bed, takes aspirin and drinks lots of hot tea. I told Mrs Seymour that everyone else could retire early so Abby's completely in your hands. Just make sure she stays in bed.'

'Oh, am I ever going to keep her in bed!' He winked broadly and Abby had a sinking feeling in the pit of her stomach but she forced herself to react to Rud's wink by sticking out her tongue at him.

Why had she agreed to this ridiculous, vulgar charade? And she wasn't even sure what she was supposed to do or how to do it. Her experience at this sort of thing was nil. According to Judith, all she had to do was start things humming and her woman's natural instinct would take over. And Rud would do the rest. . . .

Abby put on her nightgown and robe and Rud insisted on tucking her in, then made a big to-do about bringing her aspirin and a glass of hot lemonade. 'My own secret recipe,' he told her. If she hadn't been nervous she would have laughed at his grave pomposity and made a little fun of him and his secret recipe. As it was she thought he was very sweet to make this fuss over her.

But then, when they were playing Scrabble, she wanted to kill him! She was so distracted she couldn't even think straight and was playing very badly, and his naturally strong competitve streak which always came to the surface whenever they played any kind of parlour game, emerged full-force and he became completely, unbearably obnoxious. He offered to give her hints which was the ultimate condescension, and he prodded her into challenging him when he knew for certain he was right, and she did it even though she knew she was walking straight into his trap. Then when he offered patronizingly to allow her a generous handicap, it was the final straw and she sent the little lettered squares flying.

'Tut, tut,' he admonished, laughing. 'Is Baby Abby having herself a wittle tantwum?'

Then she threw the board at him. 'I don't believe you! Here you are going on twenty-four, graduating from law school, and you're acting like the most immature jerk I've ever seen! You're acting like a kid of ten whose biggest thrill in life is to pick up all the marbles.'

And then she berated herself! *Oh, fine, Abby, you're doing just great!* Any minute he was going to wash his hands of her and walk out, and then what would Judith say?

But he kept right on as he picked up all the little letters and put the game back in its box, humming an infuriating little tune, feeling her forehead. 'You're burning up. But it's all your own fault, getting mad just because you were losing. And you shouldn't get so upset. If you're terrible at the game it doesn't mean you're stupid necessarily, it just means you don't have any aptitude. But the least you could do is be a good sport!'

'Get out!' she screamed and then was contrite. What would she do if he really went and didn't come back? She leaned back against the pillows then and, lowering her eyes, apologized for losing her temper. 'It's just that I'm not feeling well . . . and you *were* gloating. . . .'

'It's OK,' he said graciously. 'I understand. Not everyone can be a good loser. It's an art.' Then she wanted to scream at him again but this time refrained.

'Now, I think it's time for another aspirin and that cup of tea. I'm going downstairs to make it and if you're really sweet when I come back I'm going to allow you two cookies to go with it. Maybe three. Now, how's that?'

'That would be very nice,' she said demurely.

He opened the door with one hand, balancing the heavily laden tea tray with the other, only to find a flushed and naked Abby.

'Oh, Rud!' Abby cried out in confusion and embarrassment. 'I was just changing my nightgown—'

'So I see,' he said huskily, setting the tray down on the nearest flat surface. He had no idea that Abby had such a lovely body, possibly because he had never even thought about it. Her breasts were full and heavy, much fuller than he would have imagined, with large darkish-pink nipples, and her triangle was so thickly covered. He had never seen a woman so heavily bushed and he found that profusion exciting without consciously thinking about it. And he found his breath coming faster, his eyes moving to her face. Her mouth was slightly open and he could see her tongue delicately wetting her lips. His own were very dry.

'Oh, Rud!' And she ran to him as if overcome by desire, her passion stronger than her natural reticence, the notion of her own nakedness being revealed to him igniting that passion, prompting her to abandon all reason.

He trembled as her desire triggered his own and he took her in his arms, kissed her soft lips, felt her tongue enter his mouth and his own entwined with hers.

As she felt his hardness press against her, throbbing with energy and lust, she moaned, pressing herself to him the more, as if she wanted him only to tear through the cloth of his trousers, to thrust against and into her. She moaned and threw her head back and his hand caught in her hair and pulled her head farther back still as his lips ravaged her throat, consumed her breasts.

Even as she cried, 'We mustn't—' she knew that Judith was right – her feminine instincts were all there and working, and she wondered why she had ever thought she wouldn't know what to do. . . . 'Quick!' she whispered. 'Take off your clothes!'

But now Rud was on his home ground and he knew the turf far better than she. 'Slow, sweetheart, slow. It's better when you take your time!' He picked her up and gently placed her on the bed.

'Rud! Abby! What's going on here?' Judith was still in the doorway, and her question a rhetorical one. What was going on was patently clear with Rud's bare back and buttocks exposed to her as he moved over Abby, her hands clawing his shoulders, clutchingly convulsively.

Rud rolled off Abby, snatching at the sheet to cover his nudity, while Abby began to cry, vainly searching for something to cover hers.

'I can't believe my eyes!' Judith sounded truly startled. 'And will you please stop that crying, Abby? And you, Rud, hand her that quilt.'

Rud, covering Abby with the quilt, thought that Judith didn't sound very angry. More dismayed. At least Judith wasn't one of those biddies who was shocked out of her pants so easily. She *was*, after all, a sophisticated woman and wouldn't make a big deal out of what was really an unextraordinary happening. But he sure as hell wished Abby would stop crying. The more she cried the worse it made it all appear.

Judith went over to sit down on the bed, the three forming an incongruous picture – Judith in her Yves St Laurent black velvet and chiffon, Rud in his pale yellow sheet, and Abby cowering under the multicoloured quilt.

Judith smoothed Abby's tousled hair. 'Now, stop crying, Abby. Everything is going to be all right.' She turned to Rud who was working up the energy to explain that it was all his fault, maybe even apologize to Abby for taking advantage of the situation. Yes, that would sound good. He opened his mouth to speak but Judith held up her hand. 'As for you, Rudyard, I have to place the responsibility for this on your shoulders since you are the man, the elder, and certainly the more experienced—'

Rud sighed, wanting to tell Judith to cool it, that while he was sorry he had lost his head, nothing so major had taken place. He should have known from past experience that Judith, no matter how she felt about something, didn't let anything go.

'But I suppose I must excuse your behaviour this time, Rud. I know how difficult it is to control one's physical feelings when two young healthy people are in love and one would have to be deaf, dumb and blind not to know how you and Abby feel about each other.'

At that, Abby began to cry even harder, not protesting, and Rud looked at her in surprise. If she didn't protest Judith's words, how could he? Under the circumstances, he'd look like a callous, selfish bastard. What the hell was he supposed to say to that?

He asked Abby not to cry. He even mopped at her cheeks with a corner of the yellow sheet. *Shit!* He wished there was some way he could get up and get the hell out of here. . . .

Abby's sobs began to subside and she was only sniffling. *Good! Now she can speak up and set Judith straight, that yes, we were carried away but not because we're in love.* But she was silent, smiling at him gratefully, her eyes glistening with unshed tears . . . or was it . . . *love?*

Judith was smiling at both of them. 'Perhaps you aren't to blame, Rud, as much as *I* am. I should have anticipated this. I knew you were waiting until after you were graduated to speak of marriage which really is most admirable of you. A real man does wait until he's ready to take care of a wife. But then . . . tonight . . . you found out that passion . . . physical love . . . is not as patient as you might wish. *I*, seeing how much the two of you were in love, should have stepped in before. . . .'

'Oh, Judith,' Abby spoke up for the first time, 'You're so wonderful, so understanding. And I do love Rud so much!'

Later, Rud would think it was strange that Abby had said this to Judith, instead of saying it to him— 'I do love you, Rud!' But at the moment he was overwhelmed, stricken with guilt.

She loved him and not as a brother or a cousin. She loved him and loving him, she had given him the gift of her body, her passionate innocence. And at that second loved her back, as he had loved D'Arcy when he found her unconscious and bleeding out of her love for him. He knew too many women who loved too easily and too expertly, not to value this pure, trusting love. And he knew the pain of rejection when one offered all one's love to another who placed no value on it at all. . . .

He kissed Abby on the forehead, his silence eloquent. And Judith clapped her hands as if she were not too old nor too cynical to appreciate the beauty of young love. 'So it's all settled – my two children are engaged! But of course it won't be official until we make a formal announcement. And in the meantime I want you two to behave yourselves! We can't have the bride walking down the aisle with the evidence of her love showing, can we?' she joked, and sent Rud down to the kitchen to find a bottle of champagne.

As he brought his glass to his lips, Rud suddenly wondered. He had always imagined that Abby was still a virgin and had marvelled over this – she had to be the only virgin in the world over sixteen. He had never hesitated to tease her about it, and she had always flushed and blushed, but had never denied it. And yet tonight he had entered her so easily. He shrugged, taking a large swallow of his champagne. These days, who knew? All the girls engaged in violent exercise. You couldn't tell the virgins from the heavily initiated.

He had no way of knowing that Judith had taken Abby to the gynecologist for a hymenotomy so recently, telling Abby that there was no sense in her suffering any discomfort. And as Abby sipped her wine, it didn't occur to her that the hymenotomy hadn't been for her sake but for Rud's – that Judith had simply done for her son what she had always done – removing the stones from his path, picking out the thorns, smoothing his way. . . .

2.

Judith had one more thing she wanted to do before she went to sleep. She had to call Bill, share this news with him. He'd be as relieved as she was that the matter was settled. She picked up the phone and dialled, was infuriated to hear a busy tone. Who was he talking to at this late hour? Waiting perhaps five seconds, she dialled again and again heard the busy tone. She slammed the receiver down and thought of having the operator cut into his call, saying it was an emergency. But then she thought better of it. She didn't want Bill to think that she was *that* eager to talk to him. She didn't want him to know *how* important he had become to her in the last three years now that they were both free to enjoy each other's company and maturity, a relationship which had evolved naturally enough, without giving any cause for gossip or speculation. She didn't even have to worry about any striking resemblance between Bill and Rud. Rud had a much softer cast of feature, especially now that Bill was middle-aged. Certainly a similarity of colouring and size was no cause for indictment – a preponderance of white American men were big, blond and blue-eyed.

No, there were no more threats to their having a relationship. D'Arcy had ceased being a threat long ago. Even now when Bill was a frequent guest in her home, D'Arcy showed no inclination to insinuate herself into their lives. Besides, Bill who saw D'Arcy only infrequently, said she was involved with a young man.

Not even the most vicious busybody could find fault with their friendship. She had no other commitment and Bill and Francesca's separation had been legalized. It was quite seemly that they, living in the same city and free of other attachment, would find each other's company both interesting and comforting. They were, as far as anyone could see, old friends, and old friends were usually the best friends. And there was the additional bond of family ties – close but not too close since she herself was the cousin to his daughter.

The only stumbling blocks possible were Francesca, Jade and Trace, and she had Trace where she wanted him, Jade had already proven her reliability by sending Rud back where he belonged, and as for Francesca, she could always outmatch her if the occasion should arise that they had to lock horns. No, none of the three posed any real danger to her as much as she herself did if she allowed herself to become too dependent on the presence of Bill Sheridan in her life, for the more dependent she became, the weaker she grew. And if Bill *knew* that she was dependent on him, then she was no longer invincible but vulnerable.

But how wonderful it was, at last, to have a confidant, someone who knew who she was and what she was, and was neither critical nor judgemental. How utterly delicious it was to be with someone who not only knew her secrets but also her truths! And how delightful it was to have him at her side to revel in the glories of their son, to argue back and forth as to the best way to exalt him. And how good, at last, to have someone who appreciated her mind, to applaud a coup, compliment an astute move, or even to occasionally tell her that a dress was becoming, or that she looked particularly well. He had even on one occasion said she looked pretty! She, Judith, pretty of all things! In many ways, pretty was a word more telling than 'beautiful', 'handsome', or even 'stunning'. 'Pretty' spoke somehow of youth and innocence and romance, of spring days, of a boy and girl walking down a lane doing nothing more earthshaking than simply holding and swinging hands, a nostalgic backward glance at a sweet past she had never known. . . .

And then there was the ultimate bonus, the pleasures of his body for which she had yearned all those years, those joys she had scarcely known, of which, even now, she was never sated. But, as she revelled in his presence, she knew that Bill Sheridan still posed the largest challenge she had ever faced. She had to proceed with caution so that she could stay on top of it, on top of Bill Sheridan, so that he didn't consume her.

She wouldn't call him after all. A call so late at night could be interpreted as a call of great urgency, of great need, could give the caller away.

3.

Bill hung up the phone, the call from Florida leaving him exhausted . . . despondent, and he poured himself another drink – not sure whether it was his sixth drink of the day or the twelfth. All in all, 31 March 1968 might go down in his personal history as the – he counted – as the third worst day of his entire life.

It had started with Johnson's announcement that he wouldn't seek or accept his party's nomination for another term. And the realization of what he had done to himself when he had deserted the Party and gone over to Goldwater washed over him afresh. *This could have been his year!*

But who knew Lyndon would fall apart this close to the election? That the situation in Vietnam, compounded by Bobby entering the race after all, and the anticipation that Gene McCarthy was going to skunk him in Wisconsin after almost beating him out in the New Hampshire primary, would crack that tough old bastard in half?

And now, with LBJ out of the picture, the nomination was truly up for grabs.

325

Even Bobby's tremendous popularity would be undermined by McCarthy's great showing in the early primaries, with Humphrey most probably entering the race with Johnson's enforced endorsement and George Wallace's third party drawing off a considerable block of votes. . . . God damn it, it was an open field and he could have been part of it, a favoured contender!

Here he'd been travelling around the country with his law and order cause, and making an impression, gathering adherents, but what good was it going to do him now after all? Where could he go with it? The country was in such a fucking ferment over Vietnam, it was really the only issue that mattered. The pros and cons of that issue was all this election hinged on – hit them hard, hit them sexy, bomb the hell out of them or get out of where we didn't belong in the first place. . . .

The only thing he could do at this point was switch back to the Democrats, offer his support for whatever it was worth to one of the viable candidates, and just pray that he could latch on to something. Since the Kennedy people had rejected him once, McCarthy was his next obvious choice, and he made the call. He never even got to talk to McCarthy personally. So he made a call to the Vice-President's office and was called back two hours later – since the Vice-President hadn't yet declared, any decision was premature, but it was suggested that he contact George Wallace. Possibly, his and Governor Wallace's concerns were more in tune. . . . He hit the ceiling! How dare they? He had always stood up for the Blacks! And why would he want to waste his time with a third party?

Then he thought it was time to think about the Republican party. He and Nelson were old friends, and Rocky was expected to announce at any moment. God damn it, he and Nelson would make a terrific team! Nelson was from New York and with some of the good old boys from the South, they'd beat the shit out of McCarthy, out of Kennedy, out of anybody! Surely Rocky would see the sense in giving him the second spot on the ticket! And then, since the Democrats were so divided, and if the Republicans had the good sense to come up with a moderate like Nelson and not go for the hard-liners like Goldwater or Nixon, they . . . he . . . would be a shoo-in!

Rocky called back only an hour later, and in person and it was a pleasure to hear his hearty 'Good to hear from you, Governor Sheridan,' and Bill said quickly, 'Got a dynamite proposition for you, Governor Rockefeller,' and he spit it out. How would Rocky feel about having an ex-king who could still call in a following as his running mate come November?

'Frankly, Bill, I don't think you and I could make it as a team since we both have a similar problem. I've been divorced and you're half-way there. And I have the feeling that if all those hardshell buddies of yours down South are in the mood to make a switch in parties they're more likely to switch to George than to an old Northern liberal like me.

'Incidentally, I saw Frankie at a Governors' Conference a few weeks ago. She was one of the key speakers, and let me tell you she was *good*. When she told the fellows that they had better start addressing themselves to a forgotten minority – women – if they wanted to continue in office, let me tell you they sat up and took notice! Even the good old boys who see red everytime they look at a woman in office.

'Yeah, even though you two have been having personal problems, you must be very proud of her. . . .'

'I surely am.'

'Well, be seeing you around, Governor Sheridan.'

'Sure. See you around, Governor Rockefeller.' But his heart was hardly in their little game of good fellowship and respectful salutation.

Then, depressed and half-drunk, he wondered if he *should* throw in with George and his third party. After all, his law and order movement was in line with George's line that ' . . . if policemen could run this country for about two years, they'd straighten it out.'

Maybe he'd discuss it with Judith. Say what you would about Judith, she could cut away the fat and get to the bare bones of a matter quicker than anyone else he knew. In a way, Judith's cynicism was a pleasant contrast to Frankie's eternally bleeding heart which had often been a drag.

It was really funny when he stopped to think about it – after hating Judith most of his adult life, he had gravitated towards her the minute he returned to Boston. Sure, there'd been Rud but Rud wasn't all of it and he damn well knew it. Maybe it was that they were really two of a kind and that they understood each other, craved each other's company. Maybe it was that they were comfortable with each other, at home, you might say.

Had Carlotta ever really known who he was? Had Frankie, even though she'd been loyal all through the years? But Judith knew him all right, even knew what kind of sex he relished most of all – the kind where the kick lay more in the contest of who ended up on top. . . .

Just thinking about it made him hot and he thought about calling her – if nothing else they could discuss the merits of his throwing in his lot with Wallace – when the phone rang. He thought then that the caller was probably Judith since they often had the same thought at the same time, and also because Judith was one of the few people he knew who had the nerve to call so late.

But it was Frankie! Suddenly there was a little flicker of a flame of hope in the core of his misery. And maybe he wouldn't call Judith, after all, because sometimes, at times like this, he only wanted to go home again, back to his castle, back to the time and place where and when he'd been king, and only Frankie truly had the key that would open the castle's doors.

After all, it had been Frankie, back in '66, when it was time for her to make up her mind whether to run for the governship again after her special two-year term was up, who had called him even though they'd been separated, to ask him if he wanted to run for governor, before she agreed to run herself. That had meant only one thing to him, that she had cared enough to be willing to back off for him!

Now she asked him how he was and he said fine, and he passed on Rocky's compliment. Then she asked him if he'd seen D'Arcy lately, and he said yes, that he had taken her and her boyfriend to dinner, and Frankie said that she'd met him at Christmas and had liked him a lot, and Bill had agreed that he seemed like the genuine article.

There was a pause, and then Bill asked her if she had heard that Lyndon wasn't running after all, and she said yes, that she had heard, and then she said, 'I'm so sorry, Bill,' and he thought she might be crying.

And then she said, 'Bill, I'm filing for divorce.' And after a silence he remembered that the fight wasn't over until it was over. And he mumbled, 'But Frankie, we're Catholics.'

But she said, 'Oh but Bill, I only converted. Maybe that makes the difference.'

Probably he *had* drunk too much because he couldn't make sense of the conversation. He wasn't even sure if they were talking about religion or about something else entirely different, and there was another pause in the conversation.

After a while she said, 'Oh, Bill, what's the difference anyway between a legal separation and a divorce, except that the divorce is cleaner? It gives us both a fresh new slate.'

Then he knew for a fact she *was* crying and he couldn't argue with her because they both knew, in fact, that the fight *was* over, but maybe neither of them knew exactly which blow had been the fateful one. . . .

He dialled Judith's number and she answered with a 'Bill?' instead of a hello.

'Yes. How did you know?'

'I knew.'

'Come over.'

'But I'm in bed. In my nightgown.'

'So much the better. We won't have to start from scratch.'

Abby, too excited to sleep, thought she heard a door close down the hall. She got out of bed to take a look and when she saw Judith going down the stairs in a fur coat, it didn't occur to her to ask Judith where she was going at this hour. She assumed that Judith, unable to sleep, was going for a drive. She'd gotten into that habit lately. She said driving around while the whole town slept soothed her nerves.

She got back into bed, and thought about what had happened in her bed tonight . . . her first time and it had ended up with her being engaged, just like Judith had told her it would. A trick and that did disturb her. Still, wasn't all life a trick? And wasn't that the way nature planned it? Even when the couple involved were madly in love, weren't they tricked by sex too, into marriage and procreation.

She remembered that time in Palm Beach when Jade had made her wear a sweater without a bra in order to excite Rud. That was a trick too, using or trying to use feminine wiles, although on a much more innocent level. . . . Maybe she *would* write to Jade if she could find out Jade's current address without Judith finding out. Let Jade know how it all turned out. Then she was filled with regret. It would have been so great if she and Jade could have had a relationship. She *did* have Judith, but she could hardly say to Judith, 'Well, tonight I had sex for the first time but for the life of me, I don't know what all the fuss is about. . . .'

Rud couldn't sleep either although he was exhausted. He felt like he had been run over by a steamroller and maybe he had. But what difference did it make? Since he knew he was never going to marry the one girl he still dreamed about although he cursed himself for a fool when he did, Abby would do as well as anybody else. Better than most. At least she was sweet and uncomplicated, easy to deal with. And she did have her own money. If she helped him to be more independent of Judith, that was no small thing.

It was at that moment that it was firmly resolved in his own mind that he *would* be President of the United States. What else was left now to dream about, to desire more than anything else in the world? His future was as much sealed as if he had signed it away on the dotted line. There was something to be said about marrying a woman for whom one's passion was only lukewarm – it certainly freed a guy to feel passionately about his career.

4.

The following evening Judith and Bill, not having had much time for talking the previous night, were discussing things over a pre-dinner cocktail.

'If you want to be of any use to Rud in the future, you'd better forget all these half-baked ideas about hitching your wagon to George Wallace's dubious star. Really, Bill, his third party is the hopeless cause of the disgruntled loser!'

Bill had to laugh despite his own disgruntled mood. Judith was dismissing old George as if he were no more than a pesky mosquito – squashing him with her trusty but ruthless swatter.

'What do you suggest I do instead? I've been rejected by every candidate in the race except for this little old lady in Bloomington, Indiana who's running under the slogan, "A vote for Gertie Garters is a vote against girdles."'

Judith didn't humour him with even the beginning of a chuckle. Instead, she sighed and drummed her fingernails on the arm of her chair.

'Well, what *do* you propose I do? The only candidate I haven't approached is Nixon and he's a total enigma to me. I can't figure the man.'

'You *can* figure that he'll get his party's nomination. I can't imagine why you bothered calling Nelson Rockefeller.'

He laughed. She was doing it again – dismissing Rocky as nothing but another bug on the wall. She was better than insecticide. Maybe that was why he found her fascinating. 'Then you think I should go with Nixon and pray that the Republicans will give me a bone?'

'I didn't say that. Not if you want to help Rud more than you wish to persist in holding on to your worn-out dream of personal glory . . .'

He managed a smile even though it hurt now that she was turning her spray gun on him. 'Do go on,' he said.

'Let's face it, Bill. No matter *what* you do, you're going to come up with egg on your face. Once a politician loses his credibility that's it! There's no second chance. But you can still help Rud if you come back to the Democratic fold. If Rud's going to get his start in Boston which he is, of course, he has to go the Democratic route. And that's where I've been piling up my sandbags all these years. And if Rud's a Boston . . . a Massachusetts Democrat, then he'd damn well better start off being a Kennedy Democrat because Massachusetts is going to be a Kennedy state until it's time for Rud to challenge Teddy and then hopefully it will be a Stanton state.'

She was making his head spin. 'Hold on. I thought we were talking about this year's election. How did we get to Teddy and Rud's challenging him?'

Sometimes she thought she overestimated Bill's political astuteness. 'Well,

'60 was John's turn in the barrel and now it's Bobby's. How many years will it be until it's Ted Kennedy's turn? Eight? Twelve? They're going to sneak in a Republican somewhere along the line. So we might be talking about sixteen years . . . twenty years from now. It's not inconceivable that Rud and Teddy will some day be pitted against one another. . . .'

Her thoroughness in analyzing a situation never failed to amaze Bill. 'So your idea is that we both support Kennedy this year — Rud and me?'

She nodded.

'But he turned me down four years ago. I hate his guts!'

'What does that mean? Everyone in politics hates everyone else's guts. All you have to do is come out publicly and *say* you support him and then do nothing else, just like Johnson will probably endorse Humphrey but do nothing else for him. It's Rud who will actively work for his campaign. It will be an excellent way for him to get his feet wet. It's fortuitous that Rud's graduation and the election year coincide so he will have the time. As for you, after you declare yourself for Kennedy, you can keep on doing your thing. Your war on crime. Your stand on that will serve Rud well later. It's pertinent, and it's safe. What responsible person could ever take an opposite view except for the criminals themselves? I mean, who could be *for* crime? Besides, this does seem to be a good year for violence.'

Bill might have laughed at that statement — it was so typically Judith — but it was Rud, standing in the doorway who did, beating him to it. Bill and Judith exchanged quick glances. *How long had Rud been standing there, listening? Had they said anything that compromised them?*

'Well Rud, just don't stand there,' Judith said. 'Come and join us in a drink. Where have you been all afternoon?'

'Oh, out. Not doing much. Just enlisting, volunteering to go to Vietnam. I figured that there was nothing like being a war hero to start off a political career with a bang.'

Judith gasped. 'Are you out of your mind?'

'April Fool's Day, Mother,' Rud said triumphantly. 'Gottcha, didn't I?'

He poured himself a couple of inches of Wild Turkey, which was Bill's drink and was now always included on their liquor tray. 'But it's not such a bad idea. After all, you do want me to do my duty by God and country, don't you?'

'It's your duty to serve your country where you can do the most good, and with your superior education—'

'What's the matter, Mother? Is the war too violent for you, Mother, although violence is in this year? You just said that, didn't you? And you're right. I was just reading about a Black who was killed in Memphis during a peaceful demonstration. . . . Even the peaceful demonstrations are becoming stylishly violent.'

'What's got into you, Rud? You're not amusing, you know.'

'I think I know what's really bothering Rud,' Bill said. 'I think that he overheard *us* discussing *his* career and who he should support in the upcoming election and he's annoyed and rightfully so. He's going to be twenty-four soon, he's graduating from law school and he's just become engaged. He's right to resent it. When I was your age, Rud, I would have been mad as hell if anyone dared to tell me what I should be for, or whose star I should follow. So tell us,

Rud, which candidate *do* you believe in and what issues do you think take priority?'

Rud was taken aback and blushed in embarrassment. Here'd he been making this big stink and he didn't even know whom he really believed in, or which issues he thought were the most important. He had never really taken the time to think it all out. He was a joke, even to himself. He was twenty-four years old and he had decided he was going to be President simply because his mother had told him so . . . because they were rich and the living was easy, because he was handsome and could charm the pants off practically anyone with only one really notable exception.

Even that business about teasing Judith with his enlistment. What had that been all about? Laying off his own feelings of guilt about not doing his fair share on her? At one time he had thought about quitting school to go fight but if he had been sincere, could anybody have talked him out of it? What *did* he believe in? Had he ever taken a real stand on anything? He hadn't gone to fight, but he hadn't burned his draft card publicly either. He believed in the cause of the Blacks, but where had he demonstrated this belief? On what streets in which city for what cause had he marched like so many of his generation?

'I think that before I answer you, Bill, I had better do some more soul-searching.'

And from what he had heard, Bill Sheridan could stand to do some soul-searching of his own. Once he had stood for something. When he'd been governor of Florida, he had dared to take unpopular stands because he knew that he'd been right. What had happened to him that he could talk so easily of switching from one man to another, without regard for what each man stood for? What had been his undoing? Ambition, or what? Judith? These past three years they'd been constant companions. Maybe that's what his mother did to men. Stole their manhood. Maybe with his mother there were no half measures. Maybe in order to be one's own man, one had to get away from her completely, not stand and slug it out with her.

After dinner Rud asked Abby if she'd like to do something . . . take in a movie maybe, or go listen to some music. There was a new group, the Riot Squad, playing at the Harp that was supposed to be pretty good. What would she like to do? And then he saw her look quickly at Judith for direction, and he said grimly, 'What's the matter, Abby? Don't you know what you'd prefer? Judith can't help you. She hardly ever goes to the movies and she doesn't know Rock from Rachmaninoff.'

'I was just wondering if Judith had other plans. Plans that included the four of us,' Abby said stiffly.

'What about it Judith? *Do* you have some great master plan for the evening?'

'No,' Judith laughed, pretending that he was being amusing.

'Wonderful! We're beginning to get somewhere. Now that that's settled, which is it going to be? The movie or the Riot Squd? Or do you have something racier to suggest?'

At that Abby burst into tears. 'You're being horrid.'

'Oh my, I see we have an even tougher decision to be made than I thought.

331

Shall we call a council meeting or shall I just make the decision for us? Hell, I'll do it! I cast my vote for the movie unless someone else casts a dissenting vote? Judith? Bill? Anyone?'

Abby's flow of tears increased and Judith said, 'Really, Rud, you should be ashamed, picking on Abby for nothing.'

The truth he was. Only, goddamn it, did Abby have to look at Judith everytime he opened his mouth? 'Here,' he gave Abby his handkerchief. 'No more crying. Can't anyone take a joke around here? Where's your collective sense of humour? Come on, Abby,' he held out his hand, 'let's take a look in the papers and see what's playing.'

At least he had made the right decision, he thought, by choosing to go to the movies. At this point, he'd much prefer sitting in the dark where all that would be required of him was that he hold Abby's hand.

'This time I think you made a mistake, Judith,' Bill said after they were gone. 'She's never going to be able to cope with him.'

'She'll manage. She'll have me to help her.'

'That's what he resents. That's the problem.'

'Don't be ridiculous, that's the solution.'

'You're used to dealing with Rud the boy. Rud the man is going to be a whole other thing and he's his father's son.'

'Meaning?'

'Meaning at his age I wouldn't have knuckled down to anyone.'

'Oh? Wouldn't you have? And then, *didn't* you?'

'I don't follow you,' he said.

'You *would* have knuckled down to Carlotta if you had had the chance, and then you *did* knuckle down to me and my money.'

'Go to hell!'

She laughed. 'Gladly if you'll come along with me.'

Afterward, as they lay in her bed, Judith said, 'You know, I think it's foolish to wait with the engagement party until after Rud's graduation. I think we'll have it right away in two . . . three weeks, and then instead of bothering with a graduation- birthday party, we'll have the wedding in June in Newport.'

'Why the rush? Afraid one of the two people concerned is going to change their mind?

'Don't be absurd. No one's changing his mind. But this is going to be such an exciting year with the election we might as well get a leap on it. This way Rud and Abby will be back from their honeymoon in time for the national conventions.'

He didn't believe her. It was that youth was rebelling all over the world and Judith was afraid that it was a disease that was catching . . . one that might even spread to her corner of the world.

But she was probably right in her thinking. She usually was. So much so that sometimes he wondered what would have happened if she had been on his team in the beginning, that if somehow, to stretch the imagination, he had married *her* instead of Frankie, would he be sitting in the White House now?

It was late when Rud and Abby got home and they went directly upstairs. Abby saw that Judith's door was closed. Usually, whenever she and Rud went out together for an evening, when they came home Judith's door was open which meant she wanted them to come in and talk for a while. Tonight the closed door meant only one thing to Abby. . . .

When Rud bent to bestow a perfunctory goodnight kiss on the forehead, Abby reached up and put her arms around his neck and kissed him as she had the night before. 'Aren't you coming in?' she whispered.

That had not been his intention. But he gave a mental shrug. She expected it and he never liked to disappoint a lady.

5.

'I thought it would mean more to Abby to have a ring that's been in the family,' Judith told Rud, showing him the five-carat solitaire. 'It's the diamond your father gave me when I agreed to marry him.'

Rud laughed. 'He might have paid for it but I can guess who picked it out.'

He was right. The diamond ring was one of several pieces which Judith herself had purchased at the time of her marriage and was in fact, one of the 'smaller' pieces.

'It's the sentiment that counts. Isn't that what they say?'

'Right you are.' Rud closed his fist around the ring and shook it, as if taking its weight. 'I guess that's as good as it gets.'

Judith sighed. Rud was becoming increasingly difficult. '*What* is as good as it gets?'

He threw the ring up in the air and caught it again. 'I mean even if I went out and bought my fiancée a ring it would have been your money I bought it with.'

She forced a smile. 'My money is your money.'

'That sounds nice, Mother, but strictly speaking, it isn't true. If your money was my money, then I'd have it, wouldn't I? I wouldn't have to beg for it or wait until you dole it out.'

'You're being silly, Rud. Of course you don't have to beg for it and it isn't doled out. You've always received an adequate allowance according to your age and needs and now you'll have a larger one commensurate with your married status and general station in life. Now, take this ring and give it to Abby tonight as an expression of your eternal love.'

'Yes, ma'am, mine and yours. Isn't that right?'

'Absolutely. And if you weren't a fool you'd be delighted that I love the girl who's going to be your wife.'

'Oh, I am – a fool. A delighted fool.'

She pursed her lips. 'Really, Rud, I must tell you that this nasty, ironic air you've developed lately is hardly becoming.'

'You're right. But tell me true. If I'm a *very* good boy how much money exactly will I get in the way of an allowance?'

He loved it when she threw her hairbrush at him. In fact, one of the things he enjoyed most in the world, he thought, was seeing Judith blow her cool.

Rud took the ring out of his pocket just after the butler served the chocolate mousse, and smiling slightly, he kissed her and placed the ring on her third finger, left hand. 'Oh! It's beautiful!' Abby exclaimed and jumped up, kissing him, and then running to the head of the table to kiss Judith. In her delighted excitement, she then ran down to the foot of the table to kiss Bill.

333

Well, it's nice that she's so happy and pleased, Rud thought, as he watched her. Once, a long time ago in Paris, he had gone out to buy his love a present and when he came back with a little bit of a ring – gold tied in a lover's knot – he had found his love in bed with another man. At least *this* girl wanted him and his mother's ring, and say what you will, that had to be an improvement.

Since there was so little time to prepare for the engagement party, Judith insisted that everyone make up their guest list immediately, and then they'd send out the invitations by telegram which had a certain amount of cachet and would still allow for people to get their invitations a few weeks in advance. She was giving everyone, including Bill, more or less carte blanche to invite whomever they thought should be there.

But only a few days after he completed his list, Bill called and said he wanted to invite D'Arcy.

From the timbre of his voice Judith deduced that he'd been drinking. 'Now, Bill, do you really think that's wise?'

'It's OK. She's married. She married that boyfriend of hers last weekend.'

'Really! Did she elope?'

'Not exactly. She and Noel went down to Palm Beach and they were married there. They had a small wedding.'

'And Frankie didn't invite you? How cruel! Frankie has her faults but I never thought she was cruel.'

'It wasn't Frankie. I think it was D'Arcy who didn't want me there. After all, she left Boston to go down there to get married and didn't say a word to me. I can't kid myself. Lately I haven't been much of a father to her.'

'Well, D'Arcy has hardly been a model daughter. She hasn't made any effort to stay close.'

'No, it wasn't D'Arcy who didn't stay close. It was me. I didn't stay close. I only cared about myself . . . and . . . my son.'

She was growing impatient with this maudlin behaviour. 'Well, that's no crime either . . . to care about your son.'

'It is when he really doesn't belong to me and my daughter does . . . did.'

He began to cry now and Judith thought he must have had quite a lot to drink to behave so mawkishly. But it wasn't a bad idea to have D'Arcy and her husband at the engagement party and later at the wedding, now that D'Arcy *was* married. It would put everything into perspective for everyone concerned, a beginning and an end.

'By all means invite D'Arcy and her new husband. If it weren't for the engagement party and the wedding, I would arrange a little reception for them myself. Well, perhaps in the autumn. What does D'Arcy's young man do?'

'I believe he's getting his Master's in American History. I think he wants to go for his Doctorate and then teach at the college level.'

'Isn't that nice? That sounds lovely.'

He chuckled sadly. 'I don't know if D'Arcy would agree with you. I think she has other plans for him.'

'Well, she was always a strong-minded girl.'

The more she thought about it, the more pleased she was that D'Arcy was coming to the party. It would be good for D'Arcy to see Rud and Abby together. And then she thought of Jade. She, too, should know that things were settled, that Abby and Rud were a pair.

'I was thinking, Abby, that you should write to your sister and tell her about your engagement. I imagine she'll be so pleased and will certainly want to extend to you her best wishes.'

Abby was amazed that Judith should think of Jade now, especially since it had been on her mind to write to Jade without Judith's knowledge. 'Oh, Judith, I'm so glad you thought of it. I was thinking the same thing myself. Only I don't have her address.'

'Here it is.' Judith handed her a slip of paper. 'She's in London now, working as a model there and quite successfully.'

'London! I wonder why she left Paris.'

Judith chuckled. 'I don't wonder. I understand that London is, as they say, really jumping these days. More fun for young people. In Paris the students are striking and all that business but in London the young people are having a good time with the mod revolution – the Beatles and the mini and all those rock stars. I guess London is where it's happening and you know your sister.'

No, she didn't know her sister really, Abby thought. What had they had together? A few days out of a lifetime? Judith seemed to know more about her sister than she did.

'What should I know about my sister?'

'Come now, Abby. She's just like your mother. Carlotta was always restless. Carlotta always wanted to be some place else other than where she was . . . where there was dancing and where the music played. Where the action was! Why do you think she left your father and you to run away to California and Trace Boudin? Now, I think Jade is a lovely girl in her own way but no one could deny that she's Carlotta all over again!'

And then Abby wasn't sure if she really wanted to write to Jade after all. Well, there was time to think about that. After the engagement party and the wedding. . . . Now she was much too busy. Then it occurred to her to ask how it was that Judith had Jade's address and knew all about what she was doing.

'Really, Abby. Don't you think that I would keep an eye on your sister even if she chooses to keep herself a stranger? No matter what else she is, Jade is *your* family and therefore I want to know where she is and what she's doing just in case she should ever need my assistance.'

Abby was overwhelmed. 'You're such a great person, Judith!'

Judith shrugged modestly and said, 'Now that you're really going to be my daughter, don't you think it's time you started calling me Mother?'

6.

All the yearly income from Abby's trust fund had been piling up in the bank unspent since Judith had paid for absolutely everything since she'd come to live with her, and it had been earning interest, and then the interest had earned interest, so Abby had a large amount of money to draw on when she decided to give Rud an engagement present, saying nothing to anyone. It would be the first major purchase of her life, and the first time she bought anything at all with her own money, so she wanted it to be very special and she wanted it to be something Rud wanted very much. And she knew what that was because he had talked about it often enough.

She was almost as excited as he was when she pulled him outside to the driveway to see the shiny, bright red, low-slung Ferrari. At first he was speechless! He was overwhelmed by the beauty of the car and then by Abby's generosity and sweet thoughtfulness. It was exactly what he'd wanted for years! He hugged her harder than he ever had and jumped into the driver's seat. 'Come on, let's go,' he yelled to Abby. 'Let's take this baby for a drive!'

Abby was about to get in when she saw Judith appear in the doorway, beckoning to her so she told Rud to go ahead, she'd go for a drive later in the day.

'What is that car all about, Abby?' Judith asked unsmiling and Abby had a sinking feeling in her stomach.

'I bought it for Rud as an engagement present. I wanted to give him something he wanted very much.' *Did I make a mistake?* 'Why? Are you upset? Are you angry?'

'Yes, I'm upset, but perhaps angry isn't the word. Let's say I'm depressed.'

'But why?'

'Don't you think you should have consulted me first?'

'But I wanted to do it as a surprise. You know, all on my own.'

'Don't you think that if I wanted Rud to have a Ferrari I would have bought him one a long time ago? God knows, he's been nagging for one for quite some time.'

'But I didn't think—'

'Exactly. If you had thought about it, you would have asked me first and I would have told you that I consider a Ferrari much too dangerous for anyone as reckless as Rud. It's too easy for a reckless, young man to forget himself in a car that's built for speed. And it's much too showy a car for a man in public service. Much too ostentatious. And above all else, no young man should have *everything* he wants. Instant gratification is *not* the way to lifelong satisfaction and a life of achievement. That's what a good mother knows and a good wife has to learn. And you *do* want to be a good wife?'

'Oh, of course I do! You know that. And I'm so sorry that—'

Judith held up her hand. 'I know you meant well, Abby and it's only that you were thoughtless. It's too late to do anything about the car now. You can't very well take it back but I hope that in the future you'll consult with me before you do anything so drastic, and you'll remember that you're not doing Rud any favour when you indulge him in his every whim and fancy.'

'Oh, absolutely, Mother! I promise!'

Speeding out of town to get to the open road, Rud thought that it wasn't so bad to be marrying a girl with her own money. Money bought so many things . . . even freedom. But every time he thought of freedom, for some dumb reason he thought of Jade, and he had no idea why he equated the two. Then he stepped on the accelerator and went even faster.

When he returned he wanted to take Abby for her ride but she begged off, saying she and Judith were going shopping. She still didn't have her dress for the party. So then Rud offered to take both of them for a ride in the new car after which he'd deposit them downtown for their shopping. But then both

Abby and his mother were cool to this suggestion, and he got the drift – he realized which way the wind was blowing.

The party preparations went on about Rud as if he were not a major participant. And he kept himself at a distance from the household in general, giving his final exams coming up as an excuse. The truth was he was brooding more than he was studying. He read something about the male midlife crisis and wondered if that was what he was experiencing although he was only twenty-four. Mostly, he pondered his future and the fate of the world, and wondered how the two were meant to intertwine.

He thought a lot about Abby, wondering just how strong she was. Was she strong enough to break away from Judith? More, was she strong enough for the two of them to break away from Judith? Was it possible that he was strong enough to make Abby strong enough, and then he had to laugh to himself. He was going round in circles. And how could he hope to be a leader of men if he went around in circles, if he couldn't cope with one young woman and one older one?

And then he thought about what Judith had said about violence being big that year, and even though it was a funny concept that violence might be a fad, like fashion, he could see that Judith wasn't far off base. Violence *was* the fashion that year and the month of April the most fashionable. Martin Luther King had been slain and racial violence had erupted in several cities immediately afterwards, necessitating the presence of Federal troops. And in West Germany, police action had been taken against students protesting the attempted assassination of a student leader. In New York City, police had forcibly removed students from Columbia University after they had taken over several buildings and held them for several days, and in Vietnam, troops 100,000 men strong drawn from five countries launched a new offensive they called the largest since the 'action' had begun. Violence!

He read an article about a study which drew the conclusion that hunger and malnutrition were rampant in the nation and he thought that hunger and poverty were forms of violence too. Violence upon violence and any man who aspired to the presidency had to be strong enough to cope with it! If he had trouble coping with two women how could he possibly hope to cope with the problems of the nation? He was a fool and even worse, he was an arrogant fool. . . .

7.

The engagement party was elaborate enough to have been the wedding. 'Don't you think this is the loveliest party you've ever seen?' Abby asked Rud who appeared somewhat less than joyous.

He focused on the spring flowers that were everywhere – yellow and red and orange, purple and pink and white. 'Lovely,' he assured her and then he saw D'Arcy and felt sick. No one had told him that D'Arcy was coming today!

He had known that she was in Boston attending school but he had never tried to see her – it had been too late for that. And he had never asked Bill about her since it would have been painful and what was the use? It had been easier not to think about her at all. But here she was in the flesh and he could

337

hardly ignore her presence! He only wished he had been prepared so he would have had something ready to say to her. . . .

Then he saw that she looked so *well* . . . so pretty in a bright yellow dress just like one of the spring flowers, and he was relieved, and then he discovered he *was* glad to see her. He rushed over. 'D'Arcy! God, it's good to see you!'

'Is it?' she asked, smiling coolly. She'd practised that cool smile all morning.

'You look wonderful!'

She laughed. 'Well, don't sound so surprised. What did you expect? That I'd look the way I did when you took me to the hospital?' she challenged him.

He was taken aback. This was a different D'Arcy than he remembered. But what *did* he expect? It was what – four and a half years since that Thanksgiving? He thought about explaining . . . trying to explain, anyway . . . how he had gone looking for her after she'd been released from the hospital, but it was hardly the time or the place. 'I'd like to talk to you sometime about . . . that time – to explain why I—'

'Oh, I don't think I care to dwell on the past . . .' she said, looking away. 'What's the point?'

'I'd like us to be friends,' he said, trying to take her hand but it evaded his.

'Why not?' But there was that look in her eyes that belied her words. 'So, after all this time it's you and Abby, after all, just like Jade said.'

'Jade said that? But when?'

'When? Let me think. It was in Paris just before Christmas back in '64. Yes, that's right. Just about a year after – well, you remember,' she drawled. 'She was wonderful . . . as beautiful as ever.' *She was more than beautiful. She was my friend.*

He was shaken. He had seen Jade *after* that, the summer after that, and he had told her about D'Arcy but she had never told him that D'Arcy had been there. *Well, there was quite a lot she never told me!* And then he didn't tell D'Arcy that he had been to Paris too, had seen Jade too.

'We keep in touch,' she said. 'She lives in London now, you know.'

No, he didn't know. There was so much he didn't know. But it was hard to talk to D'Arcy. She had quite the attitude. He looked around for Abby and waved her over.

'Abby, look who's here,' he said enthusiastically. 'Did you know she was coming to our party?'

Abby kissed the air around D'Arcy's cheek. 'Of course I knew D'Arcy was coming today, and I'm sure someone told you that too. Don't you ever listen to anything anyone says?' she scolded, sounding almost like Judith, he thought.

'It's so good to see you, D'Arcy. I always meant to get in touch with you after that time when you brought me that present from Jade, but you know how it is. . . .'

'Of course,' D'Arcy said. 'I know.'

But this was something else Rud *didn't* know – that Abby had seen D'Arcy . . . that D'Arcy had brought her a present from Jade.

'But where's your husband, D'Arcy?' Abby asked.

'Husband? You're married?' Rud marvelled.

And D'Arcy laughed at him. 'Yes, I am and I bet someone told you. Don't you ever listen to anything anyone says?' she teased with a bit of malice, using

Abby's words. 'Or did you think *no one* would ever want to marry me?' She pointed. 'There he is – my sweet, new husband. Talking with my father.'

Both Rud and Abby turned to look and this time it was Abby's turn to be surprised. D'Arcy's new, sweet husband was her old and sweet friend, Noel . . . the boy she met at the library a long time ago. . . .

'Noel told me you and he used to be friends, Abby. Now, isn't this nice? Here we are, the four of us, and all old good friends. . . .'

Noel, smiling widely, kissed a slightly rattled Abby on the cheek and shook a bemused Rud's hand. Everyone was cheerful and said the right things and Bill was pleased. How terrific it would be if Rud and Abby and D'Arcy and her husband would be friends and they could all be together often – the four of them and he and Judith. Kind of like a real family!

He left the kids together to really become acquainted and went to find Judith to tell her how great the four of them were getting along.

At first there'd been a small stabbing wrench of jealousy in Abby's heart when she saw who D'Arcy's husband was. Her Noel of the warm brown eyes and the kind, caring heart. But now she examined him more closely. His hair was long and unkempt, really. And he was wearing a rather ill-fitting blue suit which must have been several years old from the way the cuffs of the jacket were at least two inches short of his bony wrists. And while he was as tall as Rud he wasn't nearly as broad, more on the gaunt side. Awkward, really. There was a certain lack of grace. And the way he spoke! She used to think that that slow, deliberate speech was a sign of sincerity, which, perhaps it was, but one could grow old waiting for him to get all the words out.

Then she looked at Rud, resplendent in his beautiful cream-coloured suit which was just right and complemented the beautifully cut blond crest and his violet-blue eyes. And the way Rud moved was really extraordinary as was his manner. Just right! And while he didn't give *her* butterflies, she was filled with pride. The truth was that beside Rud, Noel Rankin was a – she searched for the right word – a primitive, a kind of country bumpkin. And then she wondered why she had ever thought him so attractive. Nice, oh yes, but attractive? He couldn't hold a candle to Rud.

And then feeling good about coming to that conclusion, and relieved, she also felt generous, and she turned to D'Arcy. 'I know this is kind of late notice, but my friend Lacey Horton, who was going to be my maid of honour, just told me she's leaving for Europe the first of June, so I'd be so pleased if you would be my matron of honour, D'Arcy. We *are* family and it would be simply marvellous to have a member of my family as my attendant.'

D'Arcy looked at Rud with a half-smile. 'I'd love it. I can't think of anybody's wedding I'd rather be part of—' She kissed D'Arcy and then Rud. 'What fun!' But then she became very serious. 'Still, I can't imagine why you haven't asked Jade to fly over and be your maid of honour. It seems to me she would be your natural choice.'

'To tell you the truth I never even thought of it,' Abby told her. 'I haven't been in touch with her and she's so far away. You know how it is.'

'But I told you why she— Well, I explained everything to you and you said you understood. And Jade would be so happy for you, Abby. She loves you very much.' And that was the first really sincere thing she'd said the whole afternoon.

'Yes. So you told me. And I have no reason to doubt it. And I really am going to write to her and tell her all about my engagement the very second I get a minute. . . . And now you'll have to excuse me. I really do have to go around and talk to all our guests. Coming Rud?'

'In a minute.' He wanted to talk to Noel and when Bill came to take D'Arcy away – there were people he wanted to introduce her to who didn't even know he had a daughter – they were left alone. 'What's your field, Noel?'

'I'm planning on teaching after I get my doctorate but first D'Arcy and I are going into the Peace Corps. We're leaving for Mozambique in a few weeks.'

'Really? Wow!'

Noel laughed. 'You sound so shocked.'

'No. Not at all. It's just that I know a lot of people who talk about it but I don't know anyone who's actually doing that. But I think it's great. It should be very interesting.'

'Yes, and very rewarding. While we'll be the ones who are teaching we'll also be the ones who are learning, and in the end we'll be the ones to reap the most benefits. It's an opportunity and a privilege to serve others, if you'll forgive my pomposity.'

'No, I don't think it's pompous. I think the people of Mozambique will be very lucky to have you.'

'Well, D'Arcy and I think we're the lucky ones. She's really looking forward to working with those children. She's a nut on kids, you know.'

'No, I didn't know.' Rud glanced over at D'Arcy now who was laughing and talking enthusiastically to someone and he remembered the girl who had been a junior Scarlett and then the sad girl who had loved not wisely at all. Now this same D'Arcy was off to the third world for the privilege of working for its children, and he felt like crying.

He put an arm around Noel Rankin's shoulders. 'I think you're right. I think you and D'Arcy are the lucky ones.'

It was crazy. Noel Rankin didn't have a suit that fitted him and probably didn't care, and yet he envied him more than anyone he had ever known.

Later as Rud, Abby and Judith sat among the ruins of the party as the staff cleaned up, they analyzed it all – the food, the guests, what everyone said, but Rud mostly listened.

'What did you think of D'Arcy's husband?' Abby asked Judith.

'Nice enough but a strange choice for D'Arcy I would think. He seems so serious . . . so earnest. Not at all like D'Arcy. I've always thought of her as frivolous but I suppose people do change.'

'I'll say they do!' Abby popped a salted almond into her mouth. 'Imagine going to Mozambique of all places. Who'd want to be caught dead there with all the heat and flies and no indoor plumbing?'

'Someone not in their right mind?' Judith laughed and Abby joined in.

Rud studied his nails. No, his mother hadn't changed even if D'Arcy had. And D'Arcy wasn't the only one. Abby was changing right in front of his eyes. But then she was in training and Judith was a bitch of a trainer.

8.

Violence seemed to be as fashionable in May as it was in April, and Rud brooded some more. He asked Bill what he thought was going to happen in Vietnam now that all the peace talks had come to naught.

'You don't have to worry about Vietnam now, or even the problems of the nation. Right now all you have to do is concentrate on the matter at hand – Boston . . . Massachusetts.'

'It's hard to close your eyes to everything else. Look at you – you're flying all over the country with your war on crime.'

'But I'm not going to be running for office *here*. You are. But believe me when I go into any particular city, I've done my homework and I talk about their particular problems with crime . . . about the people in that particular area who are the culprits.'

'That's a little dangerous, isn't it? Getting into specifics? Naming names?'

Bill laughed. 'If you're afraid of the heat, don't go into the kitchen, as old Harry said. Besides, all these supposedly tough guys are full of crap. Their threats don't keep me up at night. If they're really tough, you just have to be tougher.'

Rud hoped that it was all that simple. But Bill was right – he had his own problems. He had to be tough enough to get through his wedding.

But the assassination of Robert Kennedy cast a shadow of violence that no one in the country could ignore, and when President Johnson proclaimed Sunday, June the 9th as a national day of mourning, Rud thought they should cancel the wedding, postpone it. Abby thought they should have the ceremony but eliminate the reception. Bill, who was to give the bride away, agreed with Abby. Wining, dining and dancing on this day of mourning would seem callous, possibly damage Rud's image, especially since he would have been working for Kennedy's election as soon as he returned from his honeymoon. Judith had the final word. 'We have over six hundred guests coming from all over the country. We can't possibly cancel now. We have a responsibility to our guests who have made their plans. And you know what good troupers say – the show must go on.'

'Why?' Rud asked. 'Why must the show go on? I never understood that. It's only a show, not something that's going to affect the state of the world.'

'My dear Rud, haven't I taught you that it's not the big things in life that count. It's all the little things.'

'Tell that to Ethel and Rode and Bobby's kids . . . that it's the little things that count. Tell that to all the people who believed in Kennedy.'

Judith was losing her patience. 'Is it *our* fault that some nut got it into his head to kill the man?'

Despite the pall cast over the day, June the 9th dawned bright and clear and only about one hundred of the more prominent guests did not show up. And regardless of everything else it was a spectacular affair with nothing left to chance, not even the natural flowering of nature which normally took place in June. Huge pots of pink and white roses were brought in to dot the landscape all the way down to the shore in the rear of the 'cottage,' and imported tropical plants formed a backdrop for the thousands and thousands of roses. There was a pink and white tent and all the round tables were draped in pink with centrepieces of bride's roses. A string quartet played by the pool along with strolling violinists and there was a rock group besides the usual society orchestra.

341

D'Arcy, the matron of honour, wore pale pink, and Judith a deep pink, and the bridesmaids a medley of the same colour. The bride wore white, Judith's wedding gown which needed only minor adjustments. It had a high Empire bodice, long, tapered sleeves, and the skirt had a slight flare in the back. The train of matching lace was edged in scallops, encrusted with seed pearls, and the veil was fastened to a Juliet cap fashioned of miniature roses, and fell in three layers – nine feet, five feet and three, each layer edged in more tiny pearls.

Abby had planned on wearing the diamond and emerald necklace which Jade had left for her when she had run away, Carlotta's necklace, but then at the last minute she changed her mind. She asked Judith if instead she could wear *her* necklace of sapphires and diamonds, which would take care of the something borrowed, something blue, and something old at the same time. D'Arcy, standing by, solemnly watching the exchange of necklaces, asked, 'And what's new?'

Abby, in high spirits, answered, 'My Dior underpants. They're white silk and definitely brand new.'

As the organ pealed out the strains of the wedding march, Rud, in a grey cutaway so pale it was almost white, reflected that bright red hair would have been a discordant note in this sea of pink and white. But then he felt somewhat better when the clergyman, before beginning the words that would join him and Abby together, offered up words of prayer for Robert Kennedy, the slain warrior.

When the festivities were nearly over, a dark cloud appeared overhead, the first discordant note of the day. It looked like it might rain and everyone glanced uneasily at the increasingly grey skies, wondering whether it was time to depart, and Rud mused that perhaps this was going to be their punishment from the heavens for prematurely dancing on Robert Kennedy's grave.

Bill looked towards the ocean, to the horizon, to try to determine from which direction the threatening clouds were coming and he thought he saw someone on the beach. *Hell!* Where were all the security people they hired? Why weren't a couple of them stationed down there where the grounds sloped to meet the sand? That was the most likely place any gate-crashers would come from, any intruder. He cursed himself for not having instructed the security guards himself. He looked around for a couple of the guards to send down there but he didn't spot one. *What the hell!* Were they all in the house stuffing their mouths? He'd have to go down there himself to check it out. . . .

By the time he was able to make out clearly that the man in the black suit was holding a rifle, it was too late, and as the shot rang out, the thunder roared, and the storm broke.

Pandemonium erupted and everyone ran for cover, crowding under the tent and running inside the house. For about twenty minutes the thunder continued to crack and the rain poured down and then suddenly, it was over. The sun came out again and it was almost as if it had never rained at all, except that the grass was soaked and the garden chairs were too wet to sit on. And then it wasn't until almost all the guests were gone, that Bill was discovered down near the water's edge lying in a red stain of blood, unconscious but still breathing.

9.

Judith, trusting only her own resources, insisted that Bill be flown to Stanton Memorial, and D'Arcy, Noel, and Abby went with her and Bill, while Rud stayed behind with the police. It was well into the early hours of the next day before he arrived at Stanton Memorial to find Noel and Abby trying to console the almost hysterical D'Arcy. 'The bullet missed his heart but it's lodged in his spine,' Abby told Rud. 'He's still comatose and Mother's in there with him and the doctors.'

When Judith appeared, Rud told her that the police thought it was an attempted assassination by a professional killer.'

'I never thought it was anything else,' she said, and Rud was amazed at how calm she appeared, her dead-white face startling against her deep pink gown, the only indication that she was disturbed. 'Don't they know anything else? No one saw anything? What about our own security people, those clods?'

'No one saw anything but of course the police have a lot of people to question yet . . . neighbours. It's a mess. I think we should call the FBI. I don't know if they'd consider this under their jurisdiction but you could do it, Judith, get them to come in on the case. . . .'

'We'll see. We'll wait at least until Bill's conscious. Perhaps he'll be able to make an identification.'

'They expect him to come out of the coma, then? . . . He *is* going to make it?'

'Of course!' It was as if she would stand for nothing less.

But several hours later, Bill was still not conscious and the doctors still weren't able to commit themselves as to whether he was going to make it, and Rud brought up the matter of the FBI again. 'We're losing valuable time, Mother. The earlier they're brought into the case, the better. Why don't you want them?'

'I didn't say I didn't want them. All I'm saying is we'll wait. Perhaps we won't need them. Sometimes things resolve themselves.'

Rud desisted. Maybe Judith knew something he didn't. Somehow she always managed to know a little bit more than anyone else.

Judith proposed that everyone go home and change their clothes and get some rest while she held down the fort.

'No!' D'Arcy cried. 'I'll stay. He's my father.' She was feeling guilty about all the bad feelings she'd harboured against him. Now in the face of what had happened, his transgressions against her seemed like nothing, more like a figment of her imagination. And even Noel's reassurance that she'd been a good daughter didn't seem to help.

'Don't be foolish, D'Arcy,' Judith told her. 'When your father opens his eyes you'll want to be rested and calm so that he won't have to worry about you.'

'And what about you, Judith?' D'Arcy's tone was accusatory. 'Don't *you* have to change your clothes? Don't *you* have to rest so that when Father opens his eyes he'll see a calm and rested Judith?'

'It's good of you to worry about me, D'Arcy, but I've sent for a change of clothes and I've arranged for a room where I can get some rest.' Her tone was that of one talking to a mentally disturbed child. 'Really, Noel, you must take D'Arcy home and see that she gets some rest.'

But D'Arcy would not be appeased. 'Why should I be the one to leave? He's *my* father and what are you to him? I've never gotten that straight.'

'Why, I'm his good friend and often good friends are . . . well, let's just say that they're as concerned as family,' and she turned away, terminating the conversation.

But D'Arcy called after her, 'My mother's coming. She's on her way. I called her. *She* belongs here, not you.' She turned to the others. 'Make *her* leave! She shouldn't be here when my mother comes!'

Rud shook his head helplessly and Abby said, 'D'Arcy, don't! Judith knows best, really she does!' and Noel just tried to lead his wife away. What could he do? Judith was in charge, she was taking care of everything. How could he make her leave? It was her hospital.

It was a pale, grave Judith who greeted Francesca in a gracious manner when she arrived, despite the terrible circumstances. 'I'm sorry, Frankie, that D'Arcy thought it necessary to summon you. I was planning on calling you myself once we had some good news to tell you.'

'Really, Judith, I'm not a child who—'

'Of course not,' Judith soothed. 'You're the governor of a state and as such I know you have to deal with many vital but distressing situations. That's exactly why I didn't want you troubled with *this*.' She gave Francesca a sad, little smile.

But Francesca wasn't up to playing the role Judith was trying to assign her. She'd been up since five in the morning, had been alternately praying and crying, had flown over a thousand miles to be with the man she loved who was lying almost dead, and it was too much that Judith, who had bought her husband, lain with him, given birth to his child, was trying to engage her in this playacting. 'Stop it, Judith! Stop this bullshit! Of course D'Arcy called me! I'm Bill's wife! My place is here!'

'But the divorce—' Judith murmured.

'It's not final yet. And even if it were, it's only a piece of paper. You don't wipe out twenty-five years of your life with a piece of paper!'

'Yes, of course. There *are* things between a man and a woman that are so irreversible, it would take another lifetime to undo them.' Judith's delivery was pregnant with all the things she wasn't saying.

'What's the latest on Bill's condition?'

'The doctors are beginning to be much more optimistic. They say there are signs that he's coming out of the coma, and then of course everything will be all right.'

'I want to see Bill.'

'Of course you do and so you shall. Let me talk to the doctors.' And then she went home for a while, telling Rud that she didn't want to intrude, and he was pleased at her sensitivity.

When she came back to the hospital Judith was wearing a bright red dress as if she was expecting only good news when she got there, and there was – Bill had indeed come out of the coma and the doctors were sure that he was going to pull through. There *was* the bullet still to be dealt with – there would have to be surgery as soon as he was strong enough, maybe more than one operation. There was no telling at this time how much damage had been done to the nervous system . . . whether or not there'd be partial paralysis. Still, he was alive and that was the important thing. Judith ordered champagne so that they could all rejoice.

Then she extended an invitation to Francesca to stay at her home for the time she was going to be in Boston, and Francesca told her that she planned on spending the night with D'Arcy and Noel, and would be returning to Florida the next day or so, now that she knew Bill was going to be all right.

'I understand,' Judith nodded. 'You must have pressing business in Florida. I've heard so much about all that you're accomplishing there – all those programmes for women. It's amazing what you've accomplished. That programme for abused wives! And I read how when that Negro singer—'

'*Black* singer, Judith. That's the term we use now. . . .'

'Of course. Well, anyway, I read how you brought her into the governor's mansion to sing when she wasn't allowed to sing at the reception in Miami, well, I thought that was simply wonderful of you. . . .'

'Not really,' Francesca murmured. She knew when she was being patronized but what was the point in arguing with Judith after all these years.

'Well, I think it was. But anyway, I think everyone should go about their lives as usual now, especially since Bill will be hospitalized for so indefinite a time. I told Rud there's no reason for him and Abby not to go on their honeymoon, and I assume D'Arcy and Noel will still be leaving for Mozambique as planned?'

'Yes. I told D'Arcy that there's nothing she can do for Bill right now that the nurses and the doctors can't do better, and she and Noel do have a responsibility to honour their commitment.'

Then, after she was able to talk to Bill alone, Judith went home again to take care of some more unfinished business.

Ross Scott sounded as if he was pleasantly surprised to hear from her. 'So sorry to hear about your friend, that ex-governor from Florida, Judith. The one who was so vocal in his beliefs. Sometimes it's a big mistake to shoot off your mouth.'

'I'm sure but I didn't call to talk about my friend but yours. . . .'

When she was through talking, Ross Scott said, 'I don't know how to thank you enough, Judith,' and Judith said, 'Oh, you'll think of something.'

She wondered how long would it take. A day? Two? Three, at the most. One thing you had to say about the Outfit – their retribution was much swifter than the Law's.

Then as she stuffed the dossier on her old friend Scott into an envelope and addressed it to the United States Commission on Crime, she reflected that yes, their retribution would take a whole lot longer, months or maybe even years. But then again, retribution and justice were not always the same thing.

Three days later, as Rud and Abby were getting ready to leave on their honeymoon – a tour of Central and South America which Bill had thought would be beneficial for Rud, give him a sense of the country's southern neighbours, the newspapers carried the story of the assassination of Trace Boudin, purported owner of the Jade Hotel and Casino in Las Vegas. Boudin had been gunned down as he sat in the living room of his longtime companion, Debby Gallagher, in her house on the outskirts of Las Vegas. (The account stated that Ms Gallagher was currently facing charges on an unrelated matter – running a house of prostitution.) Pending further investigation, the authorities believed Boudin's death was a mob-related killing, since they had unsubstantiated reports from unnamed sources that Boudin had been skimming money from the casino's cash intake.

Reading the account, Rud no longer wondered why his mother hadn't called in the FBI but he was astonished to discover how far his mother's arms could reach. He knew she was a remarkable woman in many ways but this time she took his breath away. It didn't make her any more lovable to him but it *was* difficult not to admire her capabilities, her deadly efficiency.

When Judith read the account in the paper, her only comment was, 'I never understood why the police waste their time investigating these matters. You'd think they'd just be glad that these people knock each other off, sparing everyone a lot of grief and saving the taxpayers money, disposing of their own garbage, so to say.'

So to say indeed, Rud thought.

Abby stared at the pictures that accompanied the newspaper account in horror. One was a picture of the dead man in palmier days with his actress wife hanging on his arm, another was of the shattered picture window of Madam Gallagher's house, and the third was of Trace Boudin splayed on a sofa, his face grotesquely shattered. 'What an awful business. I guess Jade was right about him all the time. He was a terrible man,' she told Rud, and then she quickly scanned the article to see if Jade's name was mentioned, and was relieved to see that it wasn't. This kind of publicity was bad for everyone, and if they mentioned Jade's name, it could reflect on her – Mrs Rudyard Stanton, and that would be an embarrassment!

Francesca, back in Tallahassee, was inundated with work and would have never noticed the article about Boudin's death if one of her staff hadn't brought it to her attention, and then she was unable to work for hours. She couldn't help but think back to those days in Boston – there had been five of them then, their lives intertwined. Now Carlotta was dead, and Trace, and Bill lay in a hospital bed waiting to see if he would be a whole man again, and she herself sat in Bill's governor's chair and Judith was the one sitting by the hospital bed.

Judith wanted Jade to know she was a woman who paid her debts, so she clipped out the pictures and the story from the newspaper and mailed them to Jade along with the immortal words of the late Martin Luther King crayoned in red letters – *FREE AT LAST!* And because she was aware that Abby had never written to Jade, she included the account of the Truesdale-Stanton wedding cut from the society pages.

Then, several weeks later, she mailed Jade the newspaper accounts which reported the investigation into the alleged criminal dealings of Ross Scott, who, it was believed, was the kingpin of the West Coast branch of mob activity in the United States.

X
1968

Jade had reluctantly allowed Bruno to talk her into coming to Brighton to shoot the last sequence of his art film, *Death On A Beach*, and was regretting it. Accompanying them was a very limited crew and a sleazy rock group who called themselves *The Moss*. It wasn't hard to figure out that they had taken their name from the *Rolling Stones*, who gathered none. They were in Brighton, and not on the Riviera where Bruno would have preferred to be, because the whole movie had been made on a shoestring. But when Jade had finally agreed to come she hadn't known that Bruno intended to shoot the scene with her lying on the sand, completely nude, while her body was picked at and over by shadowy scavengers represented by The Moss.

'Look, Bruno, I am not taking off my clothes so that this scuzzy band of grubs can ravage my pristine body.'

Bruno told her what he always told her when she balked at what he suggested – that his picture was Art and he was going to make her a great star.

They were still arguing about it when Joe Goodman showed up with his trusty Leica. 'What are you doing here?' she demanded. 'What did you think you were going to do? Exploit Bruno's exploitation film by taking pictures so you can have something juicy to peddle? To the pornos, perhaps? Or just one of the rags?'

Joe laughed. Joe laughed a lot, which was nice. Bruno hardly ever laughed since he took himself very seriously. But then Bruno was her lover and Joe was not.

'Believe me, the furthest thing from my mind was shooting you in the buff being violated by a bunch of cockney cretins straight out of a Bunuel film. What I had in mind actually was capturing a day in the life of a budding actress, fully clothed, and it occurred to me that maybe the actress herself would like to do the text.'

'You mean you want *me* to write the words to go with the pictures?'

'Amazing The girl can not only talk, walk and look beautiful – she can actually figure out my intentions which are to make an honest writer out of her, if not an honest woman, or a particularly honest actress. Well, what do you say?'

She said yes, and she and Bruno compromised. They did the ravage scene with her dressed in a mini which was severely tattered.

She had met Joe after she'd been in London about a year. She'd been an instant success as a model and she had been determined to have fun and London *was* fun – the clubs, the parties, the whole scene, the rock stars, and best of all, she was a star! Everyone said so, even the columnists who kept track of these things. They said Twiggy was an embodiment of the times but that Jade Boudin was gorgeous as well as a classic beauty, and that was timeless.

Even Joe Goodman said she was beautiful and she was impressed when he said it – he was a *serious* photographer, not just one who took pictures of girls who looked good in clothes, or out of them for that matter. Joe was a photographer who took pictures of that which was of 'social consequence' as a freelancer and that which was 'newsworthy' as an employee of a newsbureau. And even though he laughed a lot, often wryly, Jade decided that he was a serious person as well as a serious photographer, which was a pleasant change from the others . . . all those she just had fun with.

She invited him to her flat after she told him that she wrote in her spare time (mostly short stories) – when she wasn't either modelling or having fun – and he said he'd very much like to see her writings. He was the first person in London she allowed inside her door. When it came to lovers, she always went to their place.

She'd read that serious writers often gave readings so while Joe sat, listening intently, she read him her most recent story of a girl who came to Paris from the wine country. It was when she came to a passage when the girl stood in her little bit of a kitchen peeling beets that he started to laugh.

She was indignant. 'What are you laughing at?'

'That girl in your story . . . *peeling* beets. How many girls do you know who stand around peeling beets?'

'Any number . . .' she countered coldly. 'Not in London but certainly in Paris.'

'You're a liar,' he said, laughing some more. 'If you knew anything about beets, you'd know that you don't *peel* them – you *scrape* them.'

'How do you know what you do to beets?'

'I'm a country boy from Iowa. I watched my mother scrape them.'

'What's your point, Goodman?'

'My point is that maybe you'd do better if you wrote about something you knew. Maybe about an American girl who came to Paris to—'

'Do go on. To *what*?'

'You tell me. Or better still, put it in your story.'

The trouble with Joe, she decided, was that he probably remembered there had been a Carlotta Boudin, movie star. Maybe back there in Iowa, he had even gone down to the local movie house as a kid and had seen Carlotta up on the screen and knew that *her* mother had never peeled or scraped a beet in her life, had probably never eaten one, beets not being the most glamorous vegetable in the world.

'Oh, go soak your negatives. What do you know about writing anyway?'

She and Joe had remained friends, her only real friend in London, and she couldn't bear it if she lost her friend. Lovers came and went, but a good friend was a friend forever.

Bruno was never her friend. He was younger than Joe and not an American. He wasn't even aware that there had been a Carlotta Boudin. But young as he was, as a 'film maker' who considered himself an artist, he knew Garbo, had seen her films. He told her she was 'Garboesque' and no one had ever told her that before. He also told her that a model was nothing – a body and a face which soon became passé. But a great actress with a Garboesque face, with a body which was better, could live on forever.

She didn't believe Bruno Cerruti. She knew better. An actress ended up dead, the life crushed out of her, by trees, cars, liquor and maybe drugs, but certainly by men. She didn't want to be an actress but Bruno was attractive and not her friend, and he had no idea that she was far more Carlotta than Garbo. Then again, maybe that was part of Bruno's charm – his *not* knowing. That, and his olive-skinned body and his liquid Mediterranean eyes. So different from . . . anyone else she knew. Different was a key word.

Gradually, he wore her down. Modelling was boring and maybe he was right . . . maybe it would be more soul-satisfying to be an actress. At least it was a way to go . . . a way to kill time while she waited . . . waited to go home again. Of course, Joe had been sceptical right from the start. Bruno called *Death on a Beach* experimental art, Joe called it pretentious junk, but she laughed. Joe was a cynic and while he knew a lot, he didn't know that in her heart she didn't much care what it was – that it was just killing time, and Bruno was an accomplished lover. But by the time they were ready to film that last sequence, she knew of course, that Joe had been right. What she was doing wasn't any more soul-satisfying than modelling.

As they sat having dinner that night, Jade discovered that Joe had had more in mind when he came down to Brighton than just their doing a day in the life of a budding actress together. He had brought with him a clipping from a Boston newspaper – an account of the wedding of her sister to her cousin which had culminated in the shooting of the former governor of Florida.

'I thought you should know and I thought it would be better if—'

She looked at him through her tears. 'If it was a friend who broke the news to me? You were right,' and she gripped his hand hard. It wasn't till later that she wondered if Joe knew that her tears had been only partially for Bill Sheridan. Sometimes friends knew more than they should.

2.

When, a week later, Bruno insisted he was taking Jade to Monte Carlo for a few days of rest and celebration, she was puzzled. 'You barely had enough money to shoot that last scene and now you want to waste time and money going to the Riviera when you should be editing the film?'

Bruno gestured impatiently. 'There's plenty of time to edit the picture once I've sold it.'

'But I thought you edit a movie *before* you try to sell it. I'd think you'd be able to make a much better deal once you had a finished product.'

'Deal! Product! You Americans! A film is not a product, it's Art.'

Jade shrugged. Coming from Hollywood, she knew far better than he did what a movie was but if he wanted to think his movie was Art, why should she disillusion him? 'OK, so it's Art. Wouldn't you do better if you had a finished piece of Art to show a potential distributor than—?'

Bruno was properly scornful. 'You shouldn't concern yourself with things you're incapable of understanding. It's my concern.'

So be it, she thought. As far as *she* was concerned, she was just as willing that the picture never got edited, sold, distributed or exhibited. She wasn't exactly proud of it. And if Bruno wanted to take her to Monte Carlo for a few days in the sun, why not? She didn't have anything better to do. But then when she told Joe she was going, *he* was concerned. 'It just doesn't make sense. I never heard of *any* filmmaker, no matter how big or unknown he might be, who'd be willing to sell his picture before he edited it. This way, he's likely to lose all say on the final cut and Bruno thinks of himself as a great artist – he'd never give that up. It just doesn't smell right.'

'Bruno's young and inexperienced. He probably doesn't understand the pitfalls of the business.'

'You're young too. Maybe it's you who doesn't understand the pitfalls.'

'Ah, I might be young but I'm hardly inexperienced.'

'Hardly . . .' he agreed and then she was annoyed and turned it around on him. 'What are you trying to say? That I'm no innocent. Well, I guess I'm not. But why should *that* be your concern? You're not my lover.'

'You're right. I'm most definitely not your lover and it is not my concern if you want to throw yourself and your life away on the likes of Bruno.'

They were fighting, and Jade didn't want to fight with her good friend Joe, so she said, 'Oh, what's the big deal? I'm only going for a few days and I'm not going to do anything more than lie in the sun.'

'But with whom are you going to lie? That is the question.'

Ah, so that's it. He was jealous of Bruno and he shouldn't have been. Bruno was a nothing, a no person, and Joe – he was her dear sweet friend and a great person. Didn't Joe understand that you had to keep the lovers separated from the friends, or otherwise you end up losing your friend? Besides, she was just winding things up with Bruno.

The minute Jade stepped into Bruno's friend's pink chateau in the hills above the city – a palace, really, with its Savonnerie rugs and marbled mosaic floors and its plethora of *objets d'art* – and their host, an enormously fat man with a name she couldn't pronounce (she was to call him Alex) rushed forward to greet them and she felt his greedy eyes poring over her as if she were but one more art object, Jade got an uneasy feeling. Maybe Bruno understood the film business far better than she had thought . . . knew that editing was a long, time-consuming process and that time was money, and that the movie itself was not always the product for sale. And from the way Alex was eyeing her, she could see that it wouldn't take much of a hard sell. But then again, there *was* such a thing as sales resistance, and it didn't have to be on the part of the buyer.

She and Bruno and Alex had dinner that night at an outdoor restaurant in St Jean-Cap-Ferrat which was an informal kind of a place with barechested waiters and wild flamenco guitarists singing gutsy Spanish songs. Bruno, encouraging Jade to sing along, boasted to Alex that she had a beautiful voice. Running his pudgy hand down her bare arm, Alex murmured that her voice surely couldn't be the most beautiful thing about her. Jade, who had had several brandies by then, pulled away from him and ran to the middle of the flowered courtyard, kicked off her high-heeled sandals and began to dance to the music, snapping her fingers, throwing her head back and closing her eyes. She couldn't have cared less that with her abandoned dancing, she was becoming with every passing moment, more irresistible to her host. She danced only for herself.

Soon she was joined by other revellers – a world famous American car manufacturer, his wife and her sister who was married to a Greek shipping magnate, and an Italian car manufacturer, who not only danced but who were throwing food at one another in a spirit of friendly competition. At that point, Jade stopped dancing to wonder what she was doing there. Then at the entrance she saw Joe just standing there, watching her! And never had she been so glad to see anybody. Well, almost never.

She ran over to him and pulled him towards their table, insisting that he join them even though Bruno and Alex were visibly annoyed. They got up, excusing themselves to go to talk a little business, at which point Jade accused Joe of coming down to the Riviera to protect her, which was unnecessary. 'I can take care of myself, you know.'

'From the looks of things I'm not so sure about that. But you're wrong. I just came down to take some pictures of the people who play on the sunny, funny Riviera and I had to eat just like anybody else and I happened to chance on this delightful place.'

'Sure you did. You were going to do one of your pieces of social relevance?' She gestured at one of the revellers who was now balancing a basket of bread on his head as he danced. 'Now that's really relevant.'

'Well, it could be if handled properly. A slice of life among the decadent rich. Interested in doing the text?'

'Oh, Joe, you're too much.'

'I know but before your vulturine pals come back, there's something I want to show you.'

'Gee, I wish you would. I bet it's a whole lot nicer than fat old Alex's. . . .' She put her hand on his thigh.

He removed her hand gently. 'I think you're a little tipsy and . . . maybe I'd better wait to show you—'

'No, I was just being silly. Now that you've started I have to know what it is. Please!' And, suddenly sober, she knew that what he had come to show her . . . tell her, wasn't pleasant. 'It's OK. . . .'

He handed her the teletype. 'It came into the office and I didn't know if they were going to print the story here but I thought it would be better if you were prepared.'

She read the teletype . . . all about how Trace Boudin had been gunned down in his girlfriend's house on the outskirts of Las Vegas. This time there were no tears, only a funny feeling in her stomach. 'He wasn't much, you know, by way of a father. I don't even know for sure if he was my father, you know. . . .'

'I know, I know . . .'

'How can you know, Joe?'

'Because I care about you. Caring gives people a special insight, I guess.'

She saw Alex and Bruno returning, Bruno talking fast, using his hands. 'You want to know something else Joe? There are Trace Boudins everywhere, some a little better, some a little worse. All kinds . . . everywhere, you know?'

'As long as you know.'

'Oh, I do. And I only wish that my mother had known that. And that she had had a friend like you.'

3.

Jade moved that night to the Hôtel de Paris where Joe had taken a room. 'This

353

hotel is old but very expensive. Are you sure you don't want to save some money by sharing a room, Joe?'

'There's a time and a place to save money. I don't think this is either the time or the place.'

Then she knew that Joe was as wise as she about keeping the lovers separated from the friends.

They stayed for several days, having decided to do the essay on Life on the Riviera since Joe had already placed the piece on the budding actress with a magazine. It was a lot of fun and Joe kept giving her tips on being a professional. One of them was to take off her oversized, very dark sunglasses once in a while to get a better view of the terrain. 'I think if you wear them all the time, they tend to distort your impression of how things really are.'

She laughed. 'I'm an L.A. girl, remember? In Hollywood, shades are a way of life . . . an addiction, and I guess I'm still addicted even though I've been away *so long*. . . .'

'You said that so long so longingly. Maybe it's time to go home?'

'No. L.A.'s no longer my home and I don't long for it.' How could she long for a place where Scotty still lived even if Trace didn't? 'Besides, I'm not ready to go home to America, period.'

'I guess I knew that.'

'*You knew! You know*! Joe Goodman, you know entirely too much, do you know that? *That's* your problem.'

'Really? I didn't know I had any problems. I thought I was just about perfect.'

She threw a gambling chip, a chip she hadn't cashed in when they had left the Casino which was going to figure in their story. Otherwise she would never have ventured inside. One thing *she* knew was to stay out of gambling casinos.

When she returned to London she found Judith's newspaper clippings which she put away into a drawer, barely looking at them. She already knew the facts, and the pictures of Trace, the *before* with Carlotta, and the *after* . . . with his face destroyed by the bullets, were too upsetting no matter what. . . .

Then several weeks later, when she received the article about the investigation into Scotty's criminal activities, she thought, piece by piece, all the pieces were falling into place, and maybe someday she would be able to go back to America to find out where her home was.

When Joe sold their piece on Riviera lifestyles to *Harper's Bazaar*, they celebrated. But when Joe suggested they do another on the high jinks of life in Paris, Jade laughingly declined. 'No thanks, I've *been* there.'

'What about one entitled *Antics in the Alps*? Maybe we could even get into one of those clinics where they inject monkey glands into rich butts?'

Jade laughed again. 'Sorry, I've been to the Alps too and I don't even ski.'

'OK, OK, we'll do one here in London. Let's see what we can use for a title? What do you say to: *The Class System Is Still Classy*?'

'Pretty piss-poor. It's a good thing you're a photographer and not a writer.'

'That's what I have you for. You think of another title. But is it a deal?'

'How can I resist your blandishments?'

For a beginning, they went to a party in Belgrave Square, which, as it turned out, was also the end of the article and their professional association, since at

354

that party Jade met Paul Frizon, a film director of considerable reputation, no Bruno Cerruti, he. Paul Frizon took one look at Jade and exclaimed 'Carlotta Boudin!'

It didn't matter when Joe warned her that Paul Frizon, no matter how great a director and how big his reputation, was but a cool, smart hipster who would only exploit her, even as Bruno had. He was just that much older, that much smoother, that much more successful, but essentially they were one and the same.

Joe just didn't understand this time, Jade thought. That Bruno had never heard of Carlotta, and that Paul Frizon had. Joe didn't understand that it was important that Carlotta would live on, not really dead at all.

XI
1969–1970

1.

Rud was ready to go househunting now that their baby was born. It was spring, a perfect time to pick out the perfect house for the perfect family, Mommy and Daddy and Baby Billy. He had thought that Abby would want to name their son after her father – Whitman Truesdale Stanton had a substantial ring, but Abby thought they should name the baby after Rud's father. Then, Judith had suggested that it would be an inspiration to Bill if they named the baby after him, especially since he was coming to their home to recuperate from his surgery, to convalesce and wait for his second bout with the surgeon's knife. It would be a tribute to a man of a courage who had been shot down in his prime defending that which he fearlessly believed in. Neither Rud nor Abby could argue with that, and so it was William Sheridan Stanton.

But then Judith asked if Rud couldn't wait just a bit longer to get his own home since it would be so good for Bill to have Rud, Abby and his namesake right there in the house to cheer him up, to keep him from dwelling on his frailty, the surgery that still awaited him. Rud did understand, didn't he, how depressing it was for Bill, used to being so active, to be tied down to a wheelchair, partially paralyzed? And it would be beneficial to both Rud and Bill to be able to confer on the state of the nation in general, and on Rud's run for the House the following year. And in the meantime, it would also give Abby a chance to get back on her feet, get accustomed to her new role as mother.

'It's really not so much for Judith to ask,' Abby told Rud. 'All it means is a few months more.'

But then spring turned into summer and that meant Newport, and in the autumn they operated on Bill again, his last operation the doctors said. Sending him home again, they were optimistic about his making a full recovery but warned that it would take time, possibly a very long time, and he would need extensive physical therapy, as well as lots of determination and will, coupled with a cheerful outlook.

Then Judith told Rud, 'Now I must *insist* you and Abby and Billy stay on a while longer. Bill's going to require so much more attention now, more than before. I have to see to his physical therapy as well as keeping him occupied and entertained. And if I had my hands full before, what with a million things to take care of, how am I going to manage now without your and Abby's help? If nothing else, I need Abby to help run the house, to see to financial matters, to take care of all the little details. . . .'

'This is absurd, Judith! You're one of the richest women in the country. You can hire all the housekeepers, executives, managers, nurses, physical therapists and secretaries you need. You can hire them by the thousands!'

'You still don't understand, do you, Rud? Of course I can hire people, as you say, by the thousands. As a matter of fact, we do employ hundreds of people as it is, but all that means supervision, and the more people we hire only means that much more supervision, and supervision is the biggest time-killer of all. And at the top level whom can one really count on except blood? Whom can *I* better count on to take care of my top level financial matters than my own daughter? In these past few months, I've come to really depend on Abby. Certainly there are people who know more about finances than she does, more experienced people, but no one I can trust more. I can trust Abby with my life just the way Bill is trusting me with his. Of course I can hire physical therapists, the best, but which of them will work with more dedication than I? It was I, after all, who practically single-handedly kept your own father alive far longer than any one expected.

'And besides everything else, what about Bill's morale? At this crucial time in his life, do you propose to take away the comfort little Billy gives him? Or the satisfaction it gives him to advise you, to talk things over with you, not to mention the help this is going to be to you next year when you're running for the House? Bill's still the same old warhorse he's always been – it's not his brain that's paralyzed.'

Rud was not convinced by Judith's eloquence. He could dish it out himself just as eloquently. But as usual Abby sided with Judith. 'All your life and for the best part of mine, she's been there for us. I can't believe you'd be so selfish as to turn her down when she needs us.' Together, they were too much for him.

And what the hell? he thought. A few months more wouldn't make that much difference.

And then it was the new year, and there was no time for looking for a house. After marking time for so long, he was finally running for his first elected office, and there was no time for anything else!

2.

'I can't even *think* about running for Senator this year. I can't afford the time,' Francesca told the committee who had come to urge her to get into the senatorial race. 'It means at least nine months of intensive campaigning, first for the nomination and then the actual race. You all know how much work it would take to convince people to vote for a woman for the United States Senate, twice as much work as getting them to vote for me as governor, and I'm too busy being governor right now.'

'What if I said you won't have to campaign all that much?' Ralph Higgins, the head of the committee asked. 'I don't see that you'd have to — The facts are, Frankie, that your record stands for itself. All you have to do is declare and go on doing your thing as governor. The most you'd have to do as far as campaigning goes would be to go on television a few times, maybe. But you do that anyway. You just don't realize how popular you are. Every Democrat in the state of Florida loves you, Frankie.'

'Sure, they love me as the governor of Florida. But to love me as a United States Senator is a whole other thing.'

'You *have* to do it,' Jeannie Peterson told her. 'Your record as an advocate for women's rights is unequalled in the South and it's time for you to go national with it. We *need* you in the Senate, Frankie, to do for women on a national level what you've done for women here in Florida!'

And then when the Reverend Harris Clemens laughed and said, 'I'll be satisfied if Frankie does half of what she's done here in Florida for civil rights once she gets to Washington,' she didn't think she had much of a choice. There were too many wonderful people rooting for her, and there was a lot she thought she could do in the Senate . . . wanted very much to do.

'All right. I'll run. But remember what you said, Ralph. I won't have to campaign.'

'Well, now,' he drawled, 'what I said was you won't have to campaign all that much. . . .'

In the ensuing days, Francesca couldn't stop thinking about Bill. How useless he must feel, sitting in his wheelchair in Judith's house, out of things, out of the fray. What would he think about her running for the Senate? Would he be pleased? Would he be proud? Would he want to be at her side, helping her, planning? She never would have been governor if it weren't for him. She would never have had this chance to be Senator if it weren't for him. Oh, if only he could be with her now. . . . He could help her, she could help him . . . sustain him in his hour of need. Sometimes she so yearned to speak to him she had to will herself not to call him. . . .

3.

Every time Rud got fed up with Abby and Judith and even Bill, he would console himself. In a couple of months everyone would be departing for Newport and except for weekends, he wouldn't be with them. And then there'd be Billy to help him get through those. After all, a man in the midst of a first-time campaign with an election only a few months away, could hardly afford to pass much of his time at a seaside resort with wife and mother.

And then he was glad he'd secretly rented an apartment as a kind of getaway. There'd be no sense in going home every night to the big house with the whole family in Newport. Then they'd have to keep a staff and who needed the whole staff keeping an eye on his comings and goings?

Abigail complained to Judith when Rud didn't get down to Newport as frequently as she had expected even though Rud always seemed to have a perfectly reasonable explanation – speechmaking, handshaking and meetings with his election staff didn't always end at five o'clock on a Friday afternoon. 'You'd think he'd be eager to get out of the city and come down here and be with us.'

Judith was not as sympathetic as Abigail expected. 'Perhaps you're not making it as entertaining to be here as you might.'

'Oh, once he *does* get down here, he doesn't seem to lack for entertainment,' Abigail replied querulously. 'He spends more time playing tennis and sailing than he does with me and Billy. And then when he is here, he spends most of his time with Bill.'

'When I speak of entertainment, Abby, I'm not referring to tennis or sailing.'

'Well, then, what *are* you referring to? He hasn't missed a party either, for that matter.'

361

'I'm referring to a very big word, Abby. S-E-X.'

'Mother!'

'No, not *mother*, Abby. Sex! When's the last time you and Rud have had sex?'

Abby was embarrassed. 'I'm not sure. Before we came to Newport.'

'Well, we came here the end of June. And now it's the end of July. That's a month. And before we came here how long was it?'

'I don't remember.'

'*I don't remember* is a long time, Abby, for a man to go without sex.'

'*If* he is!'

'What does that mean, Abby? Do you think that there are other women?'

'I don't have proof but I'm not stupid. We've never talked about this, Mother, but we both know what Rud's reputation was before we got married. They used to call him the Oiled Zipper Kid. It was a joke that Rud put salad oil on his zipper fly so that he could get it up and down that much faster.'

'Please, Abby! That's only a vulgarism. But it *is* true that men who are powerful and dynamic have a stronger sex drive than ordinary men. That's why it's up to you to make sure that he gets enough sex at home. . . .'

Abby didn't like the implication that she wasn't doing her part. 'But Rud hasn't approached me. He hasn't so much as kissed me . . . touched me . . .'

'And what about you? Have you tried to initiate things?'

'I refuse to make a fool of myself. It's the man's place to make the first moves.'

'If I were you, Abby, I wouldn't worry about who makes the first moves. While you're concerned with these niceties, there are plenty of women out there who have no compunctions about making the overtures and are not concerned with whether the man in question is married or not. I think you should better be thinking about your priorities.'

'What would you have me do? Go after my own husband like some cheap slut?'

'When it comes to sex, Abby, behaving like a slut may have its own virtues.'

Abby was speechless. Never before had Judith spoken to her so harshly and it was more upsetting than Rud's dereliction. 'What do you want me to do?'

'Whatever you have to— Whatever it takes. Do I have to spell everything out for you? My God, you're a child of the sixties! The age of women's liberation. Do anything and everything! And you can begin by going into town and getting yourself some of that sexy lingerie even the best stores are pushing. You have to do your part, Abby. *I* expect that of you.'

Now Abby was really scared. 'And suppose I do *everything* and Rud is still more interested in other women?'

'Then my advice to you is forget everything you ever heard about birth control and start making lots of babies. There's nothing more attractive to voters than a bunch of charming children and nothing more effective in keeping a man tied to you even in this day and age.'

Judith believed in practising what she preached when it came to sex, and she was already well experienced in the art of making love to a disabled man. It was, after all, how she had climbed her ladder of success. But there was a difference between then and now. Wheelchair or not, Bill was the man she had always wanted, the only man she had ever desired, the man she was determined to keep as securely bound to her as her son.

Physical therapy? What kind of physical therapy would do for Bill, a man in the prime of his life, his sexual appetites not at all diminished by his handicapped body? Only a physical therapy which included sexual fulfilment. As she might have told Abby, that part of the body not exercised soon atrophied. As they used to say when she was a young girl, *use it or lose it.* Judith was determined above all else that Bill didn't lose it. Sex, to be sure, was not only for the young.

4.

When Frankie showed up in Newport at the end of August, Judith was cordial and the afternoon started out amicably enough. The three of them sat out on the terrace overlooking the ocean, having tea. At first the conversation was stilted but once Francesca started talking about her senatorial race, things picked up, Bill warming to the conversation. 'You've done a great job as governor, Frankie, and the voters know it. You're way ahead of those other dodos running. Don't forget what you've got working for you. They can't touch you for name and face recognition and that counts for a lot. I'm goddamn proud of you, Frankie!' He told the hovering butler to get him a bourbon.

'Yes, we're all proud of you, Frankie!' Judith told her. 'Would you like a drink?'

Francesca said no, the tea was fine, and then watched as Judith took Bill's glass of bourbon from the butler and held it out to him, first playfully putting it to his lips then withdrawing it, teasing him, before she let him have it.

'Are you allowed to drink, Bill?' Francesca asked.

Bill laughed, waved a scornful hand as if his drinking was of no consequence and Judith laughed along. 'I know better than to try and separate a Southern gentleman from his bourbon.'

Abby came out on to the terrace, holding the toddling Billy by the hand. Then the boy broke away from Abby, ran to Bill, crying, 'Par-par!' Judith laughed in delight while Abby explained to Francesca that at only sixteen months, little Billy was confused about his relationships.

Francesca smiled stiffly while Bill lifted his namesake to his lap with Judith's help. Then she could no longer contain herself, 'Oh, Bill!' she blurted. 'I forget to tell you. D'Arcy's pregnant!'

Bill, busy with making a face that he knew would make Billy laugh, barely looked up. 'Is that so? That's wonderful. You're going to make a great looking grandma, Frankie!'

'And you, Bill! You're going to be a grandfather!' She was careful to look directly at Bill, over the head of the small child he held in his lap.

Abby congratulated her and Judith said, 'You must tell D'Arcy how happy we are for her.'

'D'Arcy and Noel are coming home, you know, Bill.'

'No, I didn't know. I haven't heard from D'Arcy in months.' He pretended to snap at Billy's finger with big teeth which sent the little boy into a fit of laughter.

'Yes, it's been two years and D'Arcy wants her baby to be born here, and naturally I'm glad . . . to have them all home. . . .' Her voice trailed off and then suddenly she cried out, 'Bill, I want you to come home!'

Bill stopped tickling Billy to stare unbelievingly at her and Judith gestured sharply to Abby to take Billy and go inside the house. Abby quickly snatched the boy up. 'It's time for his nap.'

'Would you mind leaving us too?' Francesca asked Judith.' 'I want to speak to Bill alone.'

Judith didn't move. 'That's up to Bill. If he wants me to leave—'

Bill squirmed. 'I think Judith has a right to stay. She's been taking care of me for two years and. . . .' Then quietly, 'You've caught me off base, Frankie. I don't know what to say. . . .'

'Say what's in your heart,' she pleaded. 'D'Arcy's coming home and I want her and Noel and *our* grandchild to live with us. Noel can get his doctorate in Florida. I want to make a home for them . . . for *you*. This is all I've ever wanted since you were shot but I never said anything before because you had your doctors in Boston and you needed surgery. Well, now I want to take care of you.'

'But Frankie,' Judith interjected very reasonably, 'You're running for senator. Everyone says you'll be elected. How can you take care of Bill? How can you make a real home for him?'

'This is not your business, Judith. This is between me and Bill. If you come home with me, Bill, I'll drop out of the race. I'll take care of you. I just want us to be together – you, me, D'Arcy, Noel and our grandchild.'

'I can't let you give up being Senator for me, Frankie. I couldn't sit still for that.'

'OK, then don't. Then help me. Finish the campaign with me! By my side! And then help me be the best senator I can possibly be! The two of us can't miss, Bill! We'll be a team again! We'll forget the past, the mistakes. We'll remember only the good part, the wonderful part. We'll just go into the future together and we'll make it a wonderful future!'

Tears ran down her cheeks and Bill's. He loved Frankie. He always had. How could he not love a woman so good, so right, one who loved a man more than she loved herself? But was it enough? *Did* they really belong together? Maybe they never had. He had loved Carlotta, but was that ever right? And now, did he deserve Frankie's love? Had he ever? And Judith? He and she were a pair. They had always understood each other. . . . He looked at Judith now.

Judith was smiling at him. He was tallying up the score, she thought. And he'd come up with the right sum. Help Frankie be senator or help his son be President? Whom did he love more – Rud or D'Arcy? That was an easy one. What grandchild could possibly mean more to him than Billy who bore his name? And who could ever take care of all his needs the way she did? Who understood him? Oh, they were a match, she and Bill. She knew it; Bill knew it. Only Frankie didn't know it.

After a few minutes had passed without his answering, he rolled his chair to the edge of the terrace to stare out to sea. And still he didn't speak. And Francesca knew she had her answer. She got to her feet and so did Judith. 'His place has always been with me, Frankie. He *always* belonged to me, almost from the beginning.'

Francesca brought up her hand and cracked Judith's face and almost immediately a bright red welt suffused the surface. But Judith only put her hand gently to Francesca's cheek and said, 'Poor Frankie! You just never understood. . . .'

5.

'This has to be the best surprise in the world!' Jade hugged D'Arcy as best she could what with D'Arcy's pregnant belly getting in the way. She patted the belly. 'And that's a wonderful surprise too. The best!' She turned to Noel. 'I know it's a cliché but I really do feel as if I know you after D'Arcy's letters all these years.'

'All these years?' D'Arcy scoffed. 'We're only married about two and a half years.'

'I know,' Jade sighed, 'but sometimes I lose all trace of time living here in the hinterlands.'

D'Arcy hooted. 'London's the hinterlands?'

'Well, you know what I mean. Not in America.'

'Pretty posh hinterlands.' D'Arcy looked around at Jade's stark but luxurious black and white furnishings. 'Now if I described our elegant quarters in Mozambique you'd *know* hinterlands.'

Noel laughed affectionately. 'Don't let her fool you, Jade. For an American princess who used to live in a castle, this kid did all right. She acted like going to do her business in an outhouse that wasn't more than a hole in the ground was a joy forever. I have to admit it, she did me proud.' And his pride was a near tangible thing, Jade thought. It was in his voice, in his eyes, in his touch. His pride and his love. It was a glowing force that lit up her chic but cold living room, and a lump as big as a fist formed in her throat. How wonderful that D'Arcy, who couldn't have Rud, had found Noel. It was more than wonderful, it was awesome. 'I'm so proud of you both I could burst! You make the rest of us look bad.'

'Oh, really?' D'Arcy jeered. 'Look at Miss Big Movie Star here eating humble pie. Of course we haven't seen your movies yet but Mother has and she raved! She wrote that you not only looked like a dream but were a great actress too! She said she was very proud of you, Jade. That you had a very special quality . . . just like your mother.'

That made Jade feel like crying. *How generous of Frankie!*

'And we're proud of you too. Aren't we, Noel?'

His eyes crinkled at Jade. 'Very much so.'

'Well, I thank everyone kindly but, really, it's not much of a contribution to what the two of you have done.'

'Everything's a contribution,' Noel said. 'We all do what we can and what we're good at, hopefully. And we really enjoyed those two pieces you did with Joe Goodman.'

'You saw those? In Mozambique?'

'Frankie sent them to us. We thought they were great. We were hoping you'd do more.'

Jade shrugged. 'I was planning on it but— Well, I met Paul . . . Paul Frizon . . . he's my director and producer and there was no time. . . . But now Joe doesn't do that kind of thing anymore either. He's into much more serious work. You know, really *heavy* stuff. Joe says he wants his pictures to work for everyone – he says there has to be an awareness before anything gets done. . . .'

'He sounds terrific, Jade, doesn't he, Noel? We want to meet him while we're here and that's only for a couple of days. What about tonight? We could all have dinner together.'

'He's not around,' Jade said wistfully. 'He's in Belfast covering the trouble there. Actually, I don't get to see that much of Joe anymore.'

'Why?' D'Arcy demanded, as if disappointed.

'Oh, you know how it is. Joe's busy and I'm busy and he and Paul really don't hit it off—'

'What's Paul got to do with it? Joe's your friend and Paul's your director. Or is there more to it than what you've written to me? Is Paul your lover?'

'D'Arcy!' Noel protested.

D'Arcy waved him away. 'Well, is he?'

Jade laughed uneasily. It was all too complicated to explain and she was embarrassed to discuss it all in front of Noel. What could she say? That Paul had made her a star in her mother's image and wanted to marry her, and Joe said Paul didn't want to marry her so much as he wanted to own her and Paul said Joe was a bad influence and her friendship with him couldn't possibly do her career any good and Joe said Paul didn't care one damn about the real Jade . . . all he wanted to do was turn her into some kind of mindless doll who talked and walked, sang and danced in a dead woman's image. And they wrangled over her, Paul forbidding her to see Joe who kept her from concentrating on her career, with Joe insisting she'd do better to concentrate on who she really was and what kind of a person she wanted to be. . . .

'I wish you could meet Paul. He's really quite . . . well, interesting. But I'm afraid he's away too. He's in Rome this week, doing some pre-production stuff for my next movie.'

'Well, I would rather have met Joe,' D'Arcy said. 'He gets my vote.'

Jade tried to laugh. 'Really, D'Arcy, this isn't a political race and Joe's just my friend. A very good one, the best, but only a *friend*.'

'I don't care,' D'Arcy tossed her head. 'From everything you've written he sounds wonderful. He sounds almost as good as Noel.'

And the three of them laughed at that but Jade could see what D'Arcy meant, and the similarity wasn't physical. Noel was darkhaired and dark-eyed, and Joe had grey eyes and sandy coloured hair. Also, Noel was tall and lanky and Joe was shorter, more compact and muscular. No, the similarity was more a matter of spirit, an external humorous wryness with an earnest, clear-cut honesty underneath as if they both understood that it was fine to laugh and make jokes as long as one remembered that the basics of life were what was really important. And there was that essential goodness and kindness underlying everything they said and did. . . .

'Seriously speaking, though, Jade, don't you think Noel would make a terrific political candidate?'

Jade wasn't sure whether D'Arcy was kidding or not, but she did see a shadow cross Noel's face. 'Well, I don't know. What kind of a candidate are we talking about? A Congressman or what?'

'Congressman? I'm not talking lightweight here. I'm talking heavy, like presidential material.'

Jade laughed. D'Arcy *was* just kidding around. And Noel laughed, but uneasily. 'My wife insists that I'm just wasting my time aspiring to be a teacher . . . a historian. She insists she wants me to be the President. Would you mind telling her, Jade, that she's a little bit crazy? That I'm not exactly presidential material.'

'Of course you are! You're the most *decent* person I know and that's more than most presidential aspirants can say. Look at him, Jade! Is he not Lincolnesque?'

Jade could hardly say he wasn't . . . Lincolnesque. . . . She could only hope that D'Arcy and Noel weren't heading for trouble, at loggerheads over Noel's future.

Jade drove them to the airport, hating to see them go.

'I wish you could have stayed a little longer.'

'Me too. But I want to be with my mother for the election. She's pretty much alone. And I hate to see you here, so alone.'

'But I'm not. I have Paul and I have Joe.'

'You can't have them both,' D'Arcy said. 'You're going to have to choose.'

But Jade thought D'Arcy didn't understand. Joe and Paul were separate identities. One relationship didn't have any bearing on the other.

'Since you're so free with your advice, Mrs Rankin, you won't mind if I give you some – let Noel be. Let him be whatever he wants to be. . . .' And then D'Arcy thought Jade didn't understand. That Noel was such a great person, the country needed him. He was twice the person . . . ten times the person . . . that Rud Stanton was, and that she herself needed Noel to best Rud Stanton, that she would never be able to rest until he did.

'When are you coming home?'

'I'm not sure. Soon . . . maybe.'

'For God's sake, will you try and hurry?'

Jade laughed. D'Arcy was always so impatient. She always wanted everything to happen yesterday.

And then they were gone and she felt incredibly lonely. And she wished Joe would come home from Belfast. What was the point in his being there, after all? With him or without him, that business there was never going to be resolved. . . .

6.

By the time they moved back to Boston from Newport, Abby was pregnant once again. She had followed Judith's advice. Counter to her own inclinations, she'd courted Rud and seduced him. That part hadn't been difficult since Rud always rose to the occasion – with him it was as natural as breathing. But she knew that was as far as it went – it really didn't change anything.

When Abby told Judith she was pregnant but that she didn't think it made

367

Rud love her any the more, Judith made little of it. 'Love is a very nebulous thing. There are all kinds of love. I'm sure Rud loves you. But what kind of love are you talking about? Romantic love? That's for high school girls, Abby. But you're all grown up. You're an educated woman, and a rich one, and you should know better than to moon after romantic love. Of course Rud loves you. Why shouldn't he? You're his wife, his helpmate, the mother of his children. Love just means each person getting what he needs from the relationship. And you know what Rud needs from you. A wife who will help him attain his goals, who will stand by him while you *both* climb to the top. That's love, Abby. Respect and mutual goals. Romantic Love . . . sexual love – they're transient. But if you nurture your kind of love, it will do you well for the rest of your life.'

'But what do I do? Do I have to keep on courting Rud, seducing him so that he'll make love to me?' she asked with resentment.

Judith looked at her curiously. 'Well, you tell me, Abby. How do you feel about making love? For that matter, how do you truly feel about Rud? Are you mad to make love with him? Does the sex thrill you?'

Abigail was bewildered. She had never anticipated Judith cross-examining her. She wasn't prepared. But she knew that if she told Judith that she had more resentment against Rud than anything else, or that the sex with Rud was more mechanical than anything else, Judith wouldn't feel quite the same way about *her* again. It didn't matter to Judith how much or in what way Rud loved her, Abby, but it would matter how she felt about Rud. Judith wanted everyone's unquestioning love for Rud. And she herself needed Judith's love.

'You know I adore Rud. And of course I'm thrilled when we make love. How can you ask such a thing?'

'Well, since you love him so much I suggest you keep on doing just what you're doing. Make love to him, make babies, and campaign for him. The election isn't until November. You still have a couple of months to prove how invaluable you are. Speak at women's groups, clubs, churches, synagogues. Pour tea wherever they'll have you. Make a series of coffees in our house, one a week. Wherever you go be utterly charming and tell everybody how you and Rud have the sweetest little boy at home and another on the way. They'll love you and then you'll see how much Rud loves you too.'

At first Abigail was very bad at making speeches, her natural reticence getting the best of her. Her projection was poor, her well-bred modulated tones against her. But with coaching, she got better, began to get the hang of it, and the better she did, the more she enjoyed it, and once she started to enjoy it, she was off and running. It got so that when she came off a platform, the first thing she asked her staff was how did they rate her performance. And when they told her she was terrific, a chill ran down her spine, and she experienced a thrill far greater than sex could have provided. She even became good at 'pressing the flesh,' the practice which she had at first abhorred.

And then when it was finally all over – Election Day – she was sad even though victory was theirs. At the party Judith threw at the Copley for all of Rud's friends, supporters, staff and volunteer workers, when the band played, 'Happy Days Are Here Again,' Abby felt like they were playing her swan song. What was she going to do now that it was all over?

She asked Judith this, hoping that, as usual, Judith would have an answer, and Judith, flushed with the first triumph, did. First Abby would have her second child and then it would be spring – the perfect time for them to make their move to Washington where'd they'd be spending most of the year from now on. Of course they'd still keep the Boston house – that was Rud's home base – but Rud had to be a very real part of the Washington scene now that he was a Representative. He couldn't be running back and forth to Boston every other day. Everyone knew where the real deals in Washington were made, where a congressman could nail down a choice committee, make the right friends. On the party circuit. And giving the best parties in town, the power parties, instead of merely attending them, was even a surer ticket to success. High visibility!

'You'll be the best hostess in town, Abby. And *the* most visible of all the wives in Washington. Then when it comes time to go on the campaign trail again, there you'll be, leading the pack. And in the meantime, in between campaigns, you can have another baby, which will only enhance your worth as a campaigner. Doesn't that all sound exciting?'

'It did! Oh, it did! But why did she really have to keep on having babies? Two children were really an ideal number. More would only be bound to keep her tied down. But she didn't have to tell Judith that now. The last thing she wanted to do right now was argue with Judith . . . Judith who had made all things possible.

7.

D'Arcy, down from Boston with baby Cranston (named for Noel's father) and Noel for Thanksgiving, strolled along the beach with her mother. 'When you take a house in Washington, Ms Senator, just make sure you have two guestrooms because Noel and I plan on visiting you often and I hope Cranston is going to have a brother or sister by this time next year.'

'D'Arcy! For God's sake, Cranston is only two months old. What's your hurry?'

D'Arcy laughed. 'I forgot to whom I was talking – the esteemed proponent of planned parenthood. What is it you believe in again – one and a half babies per couple, or is it 1.34?'

'Really, D'Arcy, you're not funny. And you know darn well I'm not for population control. I think it's fine for people to have as many babies as long as they want them and can take—'

'— care of them. And I'm all for that and I think it's wonderful that you're a senator now and can be instrumental in getting a national programme for planned parenting going. . . . But since Noel and I want a whole house full of children and can take care of them, that's not our problem.'

'Well, since we're talking about a whole house full of children maybe I had better rent a house in Washington with three guestrooms . . . four, or maybe five!' She threw up her hands to the sky.

'Or better still, Mother, why don't you sell La Casa del Presidente, get a small house here or a condo, maybe, and get yourself something really super in Washington.'

Francesca stopped walking. 'Sell our house? Why, I couldn't do that! It's our home. You grew up there!'

'But, Mother, it's really not a home any more, is it? I mean, I live in Boston now. And Daddy's never coming back here. It's really over. You said so yourself. This summer you finally got it through your head that it was really and finally over between you and him. That asshole!'

'D'Arcy, don't you *dare* speak of your father that way!'

'I'm sorry but I can't help it. When I think of how you went to Newport to beg him to come back and he chose to stay with Judith the Witch! Well, what can I possibly say about him?'

'Say that you're still his daugher and that whatever happens between him and me has nothing to do with you. Marriages, as you can see, can come to an end, but that which is between a parent and child never ceases to be, no matter what.'

'No matter what covers too much ground, as far as I'm concerned. But anyway, I hope you'll at least *think* about selling the house. I hate to think of your staying there all by yourself in that great big castle. It's an anachronism. How many people keep houses like that any more? And even that dumb name.'

'D'Arcy, D'Arcy . . .' Francesca reproached her softly.

'Well, it *is* a dumb name. Dumb and pretentious. The house of the President! The only house of the President is the White House and I dare say the ex-king of Florida, now of Boston and Newport, just ain't going to make it there anymore. And if you sold it, you could get a house in Washington big enough to hold us all when Noel and I get to Washington in '72.'

'I wish you'd forget about that idea of Noel running for the House. When you came back last year and I asked you to live here with me, Noel said he had his heart set on getting his doctorate at Harvard. So why don't you just let him?'

D'Arcy picked up a pebble and threw it into the ocean, watching it disappear. 'I am. He's working on his doctorate, isn't he?'

'But I know you, D'Arcy. You're just humouring him. But in the meantime you're working on him.'

'But you don't understand, Mother. Noel has so much to offer. Why, he'd make ten times the President Mr Rud Stanton would. Noel really believes in people. What or who does Rud believe in?'

'But this isn't about Rud. Or is it?'

D'Arcy rolled her eyes. 'Really, Mother. I'm a big girl now. I'm a mother and a wife and I love my husband very much. I only want for Noel to be the greatest. . . .'

'Don't you think we should define what the greatest means? And what about what Noel wants? To be in politics, to be *anything* from Congressman up to the President, you have to want it very much, so much, more than anything else in the world. . . .'

Which had Bill wanted more? Carlotta? His son Rud . . . the Oval Office? Certainly not Judith . . .

'I assure you, Mom, by the time '72 rolls around, Noel will want very much to be part of the government of the people.'

'I hope so . . . for your sake, D'Arcy.'

D'Arcy laughed. 'And what do you hope for Noel's sake?'

'For Noel's sake, all I can hope is that he be happy.'

'Honestly, Mother. We all hope for *that*. As for you, I hope you'll seriously consider dumping your house of the President since no President you know is going to live there. It's only an albatross around your neck and you should be ready for a whole new great life! You're Senator Sheridan now, and screw the past! Frankie Sheridan and all the Rankins are going into the future . . . the very greatest of futures, and don't you forget it!'

XII
1971

1.

Rud was furious when he heard about Judith's purchase of a sixty-acre estate in McLean, Virginia not far away from Ethel Kennedy's Hickory Hill, and he didn't give a shit that it was, as Abby described it, 'a showplace, the perfect showcase for a young man with his eye fixed firmly on the Oval Office, grand enough to entertain royalty, grand enough to give the biggest and best parties Washington has ever seen. . . .' He recognized the language, it was Judith's, only related to him through Abby.

Even more than taking his seat in Congress, he had been looking forward to being on his own in Washington . . . getting his own place at the posh Watergate complex which was so large it afforded a man a lot of anonymity. The high visibility which Bill and Judith kept talking about would be reserved for the House floor.

Faced with the *fait accompli* of Judith's plan for a communal set-up in Fairfax County, Virginia, Rud said, 'No way.'

'Don't be ridiculous,' Judith told him. She had provided a way . . . the only way, to go.

Rud couldn't very well say he didn't want his family with him. Actually, it was Judith even more than Abby he wanted to leave behind for at least a part of the time. God! How he'd been looking forward to that. But all he could reasonably object to was living with his family in Judith's house. And why should Judith come to Washington, anyway?

'No, Mother. A man – a Congressman – has to at least appear to be the head of his own household. He can't go on living in his mother's house forever.'

Surprisingly enough, Judith agreed. 'You're right. But I think you should be the one to break it to Abby that she can't make the move to Washington, after all . . . that she has to be left behind in Boston. But be sure to tell her that you'll be back periodically to check in.'

Ah, so that was it. He made the only response to that that he could make. 'Just because we're not moving in with you, Judith, doesn't mean Abby has to stay behind. We'll get our own place just like everyone else. I daresay that there aren't too many Congressmen who live with their mothers but they all manage.'

'Good. Wanting to be independent is very admirable of you. Why don't we call Abby in here right now and you can tell her all about your admirable independence. I'm sure she'll be thrilled.'

Abby, big with child, came into the study apprehensively. She knew Rud would make a fuss about the house. She'd anticipated it from the start. Now Judith cried, 'Well, Rud, tell Abby how you and she are going to get your own home in Washington.'

'That's it, Abby. We are not moving into Mother's Stantonwood. We're going to set up housekeeping on our own.'

'But Rud, that house is big enough for everybody. Why, it's big enough for a dozen families. And it has two swimming pools – one for learners, which will be wonderful for the children. And stables. It's magnificent!'

He smiled tightly. 'I think we'll manage with something a trifle smaller, a trifle less magnificent.'

'Of course you can, Abby!' Judith agreed. 'You don't really need two pools. You certainly don't need sixty acres or bridle-paths. Heavens, the staff necessary just to maintain that place is enough to make one's head swim. I'm sure you can manage with whatever you and Rud can afford. How much do you think you *can* afford to spend on a house, Rud? On monthly maintenance?'

Rud shrugged. Finances were not his strong point. He'd leave that to Abby. 'I haven't thought about it.'

'Well, maybe you had better think about it. You don't expect me to give you the money for a home when I've just bought one for all of us and you refuse to live there, do you?'

No, he didn't. But this time he was prepared for her. This time he had a hole card and was prepared to use it, and if Abby didn't go along with him and took Judith's side against him, well that would be her choice, and she'd be stuck with it. That would be it. This was her big chance to be either his wife or his mother's daughter. Abby had her own money and money bought freedom for those who really wanted it.

'No, Mother, I don't expect you to do anything. But I think it's fair to expect my wife to cough up some of her money. What about it, Abby?'

For the first time Abby was pleased with the terms of her inheritance. 'But you know I can't touch my money, Rud! Not the principal! All I can ever put my hands on in my lifetime is the income. You know that!'

It was as if he'd been a big balloon and she had stuck a pin in him. 'No, I didn't know that! You never told me!'

'Of course I did! You never listen! You're always too busy thinking of yourself!'

He looked at Judith. *Did she know?* Of course she knew! He was the only fool in the family. Everybody else knew everything!

He didn't even know how much money was in Abby's trust. Several million? Whatever it was it couldn't begin to compare to Judith's fortune. Rumour had it that his mother was worth close to a billion. But he himself wouldn't know. He'd always been kept in the dark. Judith had always told him not to concern himself with things like money, to concentrate on his career, his future. He laughed bitterly. He probably would never know how much money there was. Not even after Judith died. She probably would leave everything in trust just like Abby's so that she'd be able to control him even from the grave.

'How much income is there a year?' he asked Abby dully, knowing already that whatever it was, it wouldn't be enough.

'Before taxes, or after?' Abby asked caustically. Oh, she knew what he had in mind. He wanted to take her income and combine it with his salary as a congressman and stick them in a little house in one of the less desirable Washington suburbs where there wouldn't be room enough to keep a maid, much less a nanny or a cook which they wouldn't be able to afford anyway.

Some tacky little house where she wouldn't be able to give a dinner party for six, much less a party which would set Washington on its ear.

She looked at Judith and Judith obliged. 'Of course there are a hundred ways to economize but I don't have to tell you, Abby. I'm sure you know them all. Like a nanny. That's not a must. I suppose you *will* need a nurse at first when the baby's born, but you can cut that down to a week. And you'll be able to save on your wardrobe. It's not like you'll be entertaining much or running around Washington to teas or luncheons or speaking somewhere. And for those P.T.A. meetings at the public schools the children will have to attend, well, you can wear any old thing. No one expects a young mother struggling along on a congressman's salary to dress like Jackie Kennedy. Of course, you, Rud, will have to keep up appearances more since you'll be out in the world. But I read that Congressman Hasting's wife cuts his hair to cut down on their expenses. Maybe you could learn to do that, Abby.'

Rud had to laugh. 'OK, Mother, we get the picture,' and Abby could have killed Judith. As usual, Judith was overdoing it. She was about as subtle as a sledge hammer. Rud had laughed! That wasn't what they wanted – to leave Rud laughing!

But Rud had just thought of someone who wouldn't mind helping him out . . . someone who treated him like a son, someone who was always telling him he'd be there for him. Of course Bill was Judith's friend and in many ways was dependent on her but Bill wouldn't mind helping him if they kept it a secret from Judith. Who could live in Judith's house, accept her favours and not want to bite her hand a little?

'I'd like to help you out, Rud, but I simply don't have the kind of money you need,' Bill said apologetically, miserable to see the disbelief in Rud's face. He rushed to explain that when he and Frankie got their divorce, Frankie insisted that instead of splitting their assets down the middle, the bulk of their fortune go into a trust for D'Arcy and her family.

'I won't go into our personal problems, but I felt compelled to go along with whatever she wanted. So we both kept enough to guarantee an adequate income for the rest of our lives but that's about it. As a gentleman I had to let her keep the house in Palm Beach.'

He could hardly tell Rud that Frankie had insisted they divest themselves of the fortune that had been built on the foundation of the money Judith had given him to get out of Boston so many years ago, or that to her it was poetic justice that Rud's half sister should end up with the bulk of their money.

Instead of money he gave Rud some advice. 'Where a man lives and with whom he lives doesn't have to define the borders of his independence . . . of his true existence. That's all up here,' he pointed to his head, 'and here.' He placed a hand on his heart.

Rud shook Bill's hand politely, thinking: 'Easy for you to spout that fancy bullshit. Your political struggles are behind you, you've got enough money to be independent if you choose to, and Judith to see to all your physical needs, which I'm sure includes fucking. But you should watch your step. Maybe the fucking you're getting ain't worth the fucking you're getting. . . .'

In the end, they all moved into Stantonwood with its stables, two pools, championship north/south tennis courts, its own lake, even a children's petting zoo. As it was pointed out to him by Abby, how could he be so selfish as to deny his children and wife the good life they were entitled to? He couldn't but on the other hand, Rud also felt that he had settled all accounts with Abby, leaving nothing in the debits column. Actually, since it was she who was better at figures, it was she who had done it all – she had established where her loyalties lay for all their future together. He owed her nothing!

2.

Then Judith planned the first party to be held at Stantonwood. It had to be very special. It had to be very grand. What could be more special, grander than a wedding? Nothing she could think of, and who could disagree with that? Not even Bill. . . .

Did he have a choice? Bill ruminated. Judith said they could no longer live under the same roof without benefit of sacrament . . . that people would talk, give the breath of scandal to their household, the household of a man that was going to be President. After all, how much longer could his 'continued convalescence' serve as an excuse? If he said no to Judith, he'd have to take up residence elsewhere . . . be alone . . . on the outside of Rud's life and career. Who would he have? What would he have? Certainly not D'Arcy. He barely heard from her. Not that he blamed her. Girls always sided with their mothers. Frankie. . . . He had closed that door for all time that day in Newport.

D'Arcy did not attend her father's wedding, although she and her husband and son were invited. She was too offended by the upcoming nuptials to even call her father to tell him that as she was newly pregnant, she wasn't up to the trip, not feeling all that great. Rather she wrote a stiff little note, barely wishing him the best.

How could she go? she asked Noel. It was just too much to see her father married to the woman who had as good as stolen him away, who had broken her mother's heart, who was not, by any stretch of the imagination, a nice person. What she didn't tell Noel was that she herself held Judith responsible, along with her son, for the abortion that she couldn't forget, not even if she had a hundred other children.

Still, when it was all over, she read the account of the wedding in several newspapers since Bill's and Judith's wedding at Stantonwood received extensive coverage in all the metropolitan papers, as well as those foreign capitals where the fashionable gathered. How not? Washington, which probably saw more entertaining than any other city in the world, seldom enjoyed the *best* parties, especially with the Nixon administration in charge of the social scene, since they didn't believe in putting too much emphasis on those things social. And now the Stanton-Sheridan nuptials, set against its magnificent backdrop, gave promise of a return to elegance Washington hadn't seen since Jackie Kennedy had reigned at the White House. It also gave hint that 'fun' parties would be 'in' once again just as they had been when Ethel and Bobby had entertained at Hickory Hill. What society editor wouldn't feature the story?

The article that D'Arcy read with the most interest, and which she cut out to send to Jade, was a column by a famous redhaired New York gossip-society columnist:

'Darlings, don't miss a word or you'll be sorry. The groom is the former gov of Florida and still a most attractive man even though he did his 'I do's' in a wheelchair. (More about *that* later.) In Florida, he was known as 'The King' and lived in a castle by the sea in Palm Beach, and was expected at one time to make a run for the presidency. Now, get *this*. Ex-kingie was formerly married to the newly elected senator from the State of the Big Orange, Frankie Sheridan, who herself was . . . is . . . (oh, does it really matter?) a former governor of Florida and just coincidentally, the aunt . . . yes, I said *aunt* . . . of the bride who is no shrinking violet herself. I should say not!

She (the bride) is that Judith Tyler Stanton, of Boston and Newport, and only *très* recently of Washington, DC, and reputedly one of the world's richest women, said to have a *bil*, which spells *pretty darn rich!* It is said by those in the know that Judy has come to Washington to push the career of her bully boy, Rud Stanton, also a recent imigré, he being the latest from Massachusetts in the way of a hot congressman, and I do mean hot! Let me tell you, boys and girls, Ruddy boy is probably the most excruciatingly handsome thing Washington has seen in years. Frankly, in more years than I care to count. Well, back to Mommy, the bride.

Judy was previously married to Rud's daddy, financier Dudley Stanton, who died such a long time ago and was at least half-a-century older than the still attractive present Mrs Sheridan. But the interesting thing (if macabre) is that when the then innocent Judy married old Dudley, he did *his* 'I do's' in a wheelchair too. *Isn't that uncanny?* Only old Dudley was a longtime invalid (Judith was his nurse, you see) and came by the wheelchair honestly enough while the current groom is only a relative newcomer to *his* wheelchair, having been the victim of a would-be assassination.

Although the would-be-assassin was never truly identified by those men in blue (do they still wear blue? – I haven't seen one in years), they believe that it was a gangland hit! Pow!

Don't go away, there's more. Coincidentally, a few days after that would-be assassination, Trace Boudin, well-known gambler and general man about town (the towns being Hollywood and Vegas) was shot as *he* sat in the living room of his girlfriend, an alleged madam, believe it or not, and *that* assassination (no would-be this time) was also alleged to be connected with gangland, since Trace worked for Ross Scott, who is currently awaiting sentencing for various wrongdoings.

But the best part of *that* story in connection with *our* story is that Trace Boudin knew Bill Sheridan and Judith Stanton way back when in Boston when all were young and gay. (No, kiddies, not *that* kind of gay.) At that time, Trace Boudin, no mean looker himself, caught the eye of Carlotta Collings, who was – now don't get mixed up – the gorgeous sister of Frankie Collings Sheridan, who *was* married to Bill Sheridan, who today married Judith, which of course, made the divine Carlotta Judith's aunt too *and* Bill Sheridan's sister-in-law. Whew! Are you following all this?

Sources in Boston who are willing to admit that they're *that* old enough to remember, say that Carlotta Collings, who married Whitman Truesdale (scion of a really proper Boston family) first had a fling with Bill Sheridan, who, they say, was mad about the girl, before she eventually went to Hollywood to marry our same Trace Boudin and become a movie star. You all remember Carlotta Boudin, whose loveliness lit up the screen back in the fifties before she met an untimely end while she was driving a red Rolls, under the influence, as they say?

If you think *this* is the end of the story, you don't really *deserve* to know the ending. Well, all right, I'll tell you anyway. Stunning Rud Stanton, who, they say likes the girls almost as much as they like him, is married to none other than the former Abigail Truesdale, daughter of the lovely late Carlotta and her late Boston hubby, blue blood Truesdale, which makes the brainy (yes, that's what they say) Abby the half-sister to foreign film star, Jade Boudin, who is really all American and who is not only gorgeous but a dead ringer for her mom, Carlotta, she – Jade – being the progeny of the Carlotta-Trace Boudin union.

So, children, if you unravel all this to its saccharine-sweet conclusion, you will see that the delicious Rud is also cousin to his sweetie of a wife Abby, who is known to give great speeches as a great little campaigner, and to her half-sister, Jade, who is a very sweet piece of work – so much so everybody wishes she'd come home and be a movie star here because we all need some old time glamour in our lives – and finally our boy Rud is also cousin to D'Arcy Sheridan Rankin of Boston, who is none other than Bill Sheridan's daughter by way of Frankie Sheridan, which now makes her also lovable Rud's stepsister, *I think*.

Incidentally, Bill Sheridan's daughter is married to Noel Rankin, allegedly some kind of a graduate student at Harvard about whom, believe it or not, no one knows *anything*, which is really quite strange, considering.

Whew! As for the list of guests who wouldn't have missed any of it all for the world, they even included a large segment from the Republican side of DC society even though Ruddy-Rud is a Demo and his mom is a long-time supporter thereof, although the groom, who started out a Democrat (he *is* Boston Irish, after all) continued to be one in Florida until the Johnson-Goldwater race back in '64. But as they say, old friends, thereby hangs another tale, one which because of space limitations, we cannot possibly even consider at this time. Otherwise, we wouldn't begin to tell you who was there, and that's what you really want to know.

Pat and Dick came for a couple of hours, which tells you how much fun was being had by all since they had only planned staying for one hour, intimates say. And those cuties, Erlichman and Haldeman were there, which is also saying a lot since they don't do the party circuit very often. Henry K. was there, which *was* a relief! Without Hunky Henry (yes, that's what the girls call him) it really wouldn't have been a real Washington party since everyone knows that Hank is the only bright light on the rather lacklustre Nixon administration scene, which only means perhaps that Nixonites are a more serious-minded group.

Oh well, who really cares? The good times are back and I, for one, say let them roll!

Yes, Ole Blue Eyes was there, along with the two Warrens – yes, *that* Warren, plus the Chief Justice. Also Julie and David, and Princess Grace happened to be in town and I suppose a quick invite was arranged. The Henry

Fords and the Annenbergs, and Bella . . . Abzug, that is. I think the Alsops were there plus practically every ambassador in town. As for the ones who weren't invited, shame-shame on them.

At least half the Senate was in attendance, and about a quarter of the House, along with Washington's leading journalistic lights. (Is it possible that the new bride and her daughter-in-law like a little publicity?) Well, why not? Washington, which is my kind of town, thrives on it, *n'est ce pas?*

Liz Taylor came to dance and why wouldn't she? Peter Duchin, who as it happens, played at Bill Sheridan's Sweet Sixteen Party for daughter D'Arcy, who by the by, was *not* among those present which gives pause, also did the musical honours at the wedding. George Romney was among those present, as were Spiro and *his* Judy.

Spiro, I must tell you, looked very natty. When it comes to dressing, it's no secret that he surpasses his boss.

Oh yes, the groom's ex, the senator lady, Frankie, was *not* present although the bride said that she'd been invited but couldn't make it. They're all great friends – one of those friendly divorces, heaven help us – and why shouldn't they be? It's all one happy family, as you can see.

As for the food, yummy! Even the hors d'oeuvres, which is the real test because everyone knows that Washington hors d'oeuvres aren't usually very interesting. . . .'

Judith and Abby read every single article and column written about the wedding. Judith told Abby to disregard the nasty columnist from that New York paper. 'The thing is, Abby, in politics one mustn't get mad, one must only get even.'

'But how do you do that?'

'You'll learn. I assure you, you'll learn.'

In general they exulted – all the other columns were impressive, made the family sound impressive, even splendid. Someone described Abby as a bright new vision on the Washington landscape, and Abby was heartened enough to tell Judith that she thought she should have her own publicist and social secretary if she were to do Rud any real good. She didn't tell Judith that when she went upstairs during the reception to check with baby Judy's nurse, she saw Rud come out of one of the multitude of bedrooms, tucking his shirt into his pants, and that all she herself did was turn away quickly before Rud saw her.

Judith would have made a thing of it, would have told her that she should have questioned Rud gently but firmly to get all the facts before she made a judgement. But the truth was she didn't want to question Rud, didn't want any confrontations. All she wanted was to ignore the whole thing and keep her mind free to focus on that which was important to her. The truth also was that she was bored with hashing things out with Judith.

Rud read only the New York columnist and he found it unsettling although he knew he shouldn't – it was such a bitchy bit of business no one could really take it seriously. Still . . . it made them all sound so . . . trivial, and he himself the most trivial of all. The article was bitchy and malicious but was it the truth? Was he himself only the sum of these parts? Maybe, he thought, and he determined right there and then that he would do better. He'd clean up his act. He'd try to anyway. . . .

Bill didn't get completely through the syndicated columnist's report. He had to stop when he got to the part about Dudley Stanton sitting in a wheelchair at his wedding, as the flood of memories washed over him leaving him almost gasping for air. . . .

That day . . . the day of Judith's wedding to Dudley was the first time he had met Judith, when Carlotta and Frankie had taken him there as their guest. Carlotta had laughed at Dudley sitting in his wheelchair, not because of the wheelchair but because of Dudley's fancy get-up. 'He looks silly. Judith has gussied the poor thing up, trying to gild a tired old lily,' and then she had placed her hand on his thigh and that was all it had taken to give him a visible erection and he'd been embarrassed. . . . But mostly he had felt pity for poor old Dudley, that tired gilded lily in a wheelchair, because he was carrying a determined, grim-lipped Judith instead of lovely, luscious Carlotta. . . .

And now, here he was almost thirty years later, old and tired and sitting in a wheelchair, married to the very same Judith. What goes around usually comes around, he reminded himself. Still, he found it difficult to breathe. . . .

After D'Arcy had cut out the column, she decided not to send it to Jade after all. Maybe she too would find it upsetting. Instead she called her mother in Washington. Her mother was sure to have read it. If she herself had missed it, someone would have surely called her attention to it. That was the way people were. But she was told that Frankie wasn't in Washington. She was in Palm Beach, so D'Arcy called her there. 'What are you doing in Palm Beach?—'

They never got to talk about the nasty column because once Francesca told her daughter that she was taking her advice – putting La Casa del Presidente on the market – there didn't seem much point in talking about what was, after all, old news . . . even ancient history.

3.

With the remake of *Born to be Bad* in the can, Paul was already considering Jade's next vehicle. But Jade was tired, emotionally if not physically drained by doing her mother's biggest success. She didn't want to think about doing another picture.

'I think I'd like to take sometime off,' she told Paul as they sat in Harry's Bar on Rome's Via Veneto. It was mid afternoon and she was wearing a pair of jeans, a loose jacket, a striped polo and her usual oversized sunglasses.

Paul, reading a New York newspaper, looked at her over the paper. 'Why? Are you tired? We'll go to Marbella for a couple of weeks.' Then, as if he were seeing her for the first time that day, he asked, 'Why are you wearing jeans?'

An old argument. Jade sighed. 'Because I'm relaxing and jeans are what I like to wear when I'm relaxing.'

'Not you. You're a star. You have to look like one. See these people walking by? They recognize you. They expect you to look like a star, a glamorous one, not just like everyone else. You must keep up the image at all times!'

'But I don't want to keep up the image, Paul, and I don't want to go to Marbella for a couple of weeks. I just want *to be*. I need more time than two weeks.'

He lowered his paper to look at her again and she thought that he was a symphony in grey. Dark gray suit, medium grey tie, beautifully barbered silver-grey hair, pale gray eyes made even paler in contrast to the evenly bronzed face. His eyes were the colour of steel, she thought. Joe had gray eyes too but his were different than Paul's. Joe's eyes were flecked with yellow, as if reflecting the sun.

'How much time are you talking about?'

She shrugged, the red hair falling over one eye, the *Born to be Bad* hairstyle. 'Six months maybe.'

'Why would you need six months?'

'To think.'

He laughed then and spoiled the pattern of grey on grey since his teeth weren't grayish at all but blindingly white against the bronze of his skin . . . as white as Bruno's had been, balanced against his olive complexion, as white as Trace's against his perpetual California tan.

'You're not paid to think,' Paul said. 'All you have to do is act, project an image. Leave the thinking to me.'

Suddenly, the white wine she was drinking tasted incredibly sour on her tongue, turned to acid in her stomach, and she ordered a vermouth instead – the sweet Italian vermouth.

He lifted an urbane eyebrow. 'How many times must I tell you that a sophisticated woman does not drink sweet wine.'

'What would you have me drink – martinis?' she asked tartly.

'You're free to drink whatever you like, I'm sure, as long as you don't overdo it. We don't want you to get puffy, do we?' He forced a smile.

Then she saw that the smile didn't reach his eyes . . . just like Trace, she thought, just like Scotty. Eyes like steel unwarmed by the sun.

'Here's something for you to read.' He handed her a page from his paper. 'There, that column.' He flicked it with a manicured nail.

Jade read a couple of lines before she realized what she was reading! She read some more, and felt sick, but she read through it to the bitter end. Then she thought that really she did need something stronger than vermouth, which now tasted nauseatingly sweet. . . . It was as if the writer had exposed them all . . . all of them . . . to the world, held them up for public scrutiny and scorn . . . to be ridiculous and sordid, even Carlotta who was dead. *It's terrible to do that to the dead!*

'I think you're right about not going to Marbella. What I think we should do right now is get married and take a trip to Hollywood. This article leads me to believe that we're ready to make our move to the other side of the Atlantic, release our movie there. With this kind of publicity I think the American public will be very eager to take Carlotta's daughter to their hearts. There's nothing like gossip, and such fascinating gossip, to make the American public's pulse beat faster. . . .'

At that moment Jade saw exactly who Paul Frizon was . . . more than a superbly talented director, more than the producer extraordinaire, more than the skilled lover. Oh, she knew him well, how could she not? She'd been there before. And then she looked into his eyes and saw herself reflected there, and to wash that image away, she picked up the glass of too-sweet vermouth and flung its contents into Paul Frizon's face.

4.

Joe didn't let Jade off the hook that easily. When she told him that she wanted to work with him, full time, he insisted that she commit herself totally to what they were doing and that she be sure that this was what she wanted to do . . . be a real journalist. 'This is the real world and frankly, Miss Boudin, at this stage of the game you're little more than an amateur.'

'I take umbrage at that, sir. I'm not a complete amateur. I *have* worked with the great photojournalist, Joe Goodman.'

'Right, but we're not talking about fluff anymore. Not shots of a budding actress showing what she's got on a beach in Brighton and not cute capers on the Cote d'Azur.'

'That's not fair, Joe. Those were your ideas and now you're using them to make fun of me.'

'I'm not making fun of you, Jade. I'm dead serious. Those articles were my idea and they were fun to do with you and I'm glad we did them but my point is that I've moved on since then and I think what I'm doing now is more important. And since I do feel it's important, showing the world how it really is, bringing home the hard facts, I want to be sure you're as serious as I am, *before* I put myself on the line for you, before I break my ass training you and developing a working relationship with you.'

'I'm serious.'

'Committed?'

'Committed.'

'No dilletanting around?'

'Christ, Joe! What do you want me to do? Sign an affidavit in blood?'

But she knew what he wanted her to confirm – that she was finished with the Paul Frizons of the world, was through trying to bring Carlotta back to life. Joe always had been wiser than she and he knew that you couldn't make the dead rise again.

'God knows, the last thing in the world I want is your blood,' he laughed now.

'What *do* you want of me, Joe?'

He sobered but didn't answer, only gazed at her speculatively. Maybe it wasn't a fair question, she thought.

'I just want to make sure you know what you're getting yourself into – dirty situations, even dangerous ones. You'll see things that will make you retch, make you cry, break your heart. . . .'

'I'm game.'

'Why?'

'Oh, my God, you're too much. *Why? Why?* I don't know why. Before, you said that you've moved on. Well, that's what I want to do too . . . move on.'

'And you won't miss being a Movie Star, in quotes?'

'No. That's all in the past. And you can quote me on that.'

They were off and running, a team. It was all the things Joe said it would be – hard, often dirty and dangerous, frequently sad, and she did indeed see things that made her retch, cry and broke her heart. But there were good times too, the times they laughed together and had wonderful long conversations, sometimes sharing confidences, even dreams. He was her teacher and always her friend and occasionally she wondered if he would ever be more.

384

There was that time in Pakistan. It had been a long, difficult, depressing day and when they went back to their hotel she asked him if he wanted to come to her room for a nightcap – she was famous for her martinis. He told her he didn't drink martinis any more.

'Did you ever?'

'No, not really. But once I did think about taking them up.'

'And?'

'And I decided they were too strong for my own good.'

'I could mix you a weak one. . . .'

'Nah,' he said. 'If I can't drink like the big boys, I'd rather not drink at all.'

Sometimes Joe could be enigmatic but this time Jade thought she knew exactly what Joe was talking about and she asked herself the question – weren't they missing out by being only friends and never lovers? But she decided she'd have to leave that one up to Joe to answer. He was without a doubt much smarter than she.

XIII
1975

1.

Jade and Joe had been in Vietnam several times and it had always been sad and terrible and violent, but when they arrived in Saigon that April they knew it was absolutely the worst of times. It was in the air . . . all of the city felt it – the more than a thousand Americans who were still there, along with the many thousands of Vietnamese who had been promised they'd never be left to the mercy of the enemy.

'I don't know if I'm up to this, Joe,' she said as they sat having drinks at the Hotel Continental.

'You are. Just forget the action . . . even the evacuation. The city is full of newspeople who will cover all that. You just tell the story of the human tragedy that you see all around you.'

'Must we concentrate only on the negative things? There has to be another story here, one of hope and faith and courage. Look at how everyone here is carrying on. They must be so frightened but yet, everything is calm and quiet, and it's business as usual. The restaurants are still serving decent food, the night clubs are still pouring beer and cokes, and you can still buy cigarettes in the lobby of the Eden building. Even the bookstalls are still selling books. Usually you're the one who wants to accentuate the positive.'

'Yes, but you still have to tell it like it is, Jade . . . both sides of the coin or else we won't ever learn from the past.'

Sometimes Joe just mixed her up, Jade thought. He was forever telling her that the past was only the past and now he was saying they had to learn from the past. He had a different set of rules when it came to her. . . .

He saw the anxiety in her green eyes. 'OK, so I told you to forget about the past and one should, but after one takes a good square look at it. Then, you can get on with the future.'

'She didn't know now if he were talking about Vietnam, or about her. But she dutifully chronicled that which Joe photographed, straining to capture the essence of Saigon in its final days before its inevitable fall. She described the women and children crowding the embassy to beg for 'out' . . . the women who were willing to stay behind if only the Americans would take their children to safety . . . the ancient crippled man who told them he was too old to leave and that it didn't matter, his whole family was dead. And she wrote about the pretty girls who placed their calls to their husbands or boyfriends who were already back in the States, telling them how good it was going to be when they joined them in the good old United States of America.

It was the bitter and the bittersweet. . . .

The end was creeping closer, day by day, when Joe told her to go over to the embassy – there was a delegation of congressmen who had just arrived, obviously unaware of how really desperate the situation was . . . how close it was to the end. 'Go hear what *they* have to say.'

'Aren't you coming with me?'

'No, thanks. I can always take pictures of congressmen. But it will be interesting for you to make contrasts with what they say and what you've seen.'

He put her in one of the blue and white checkered cabs that were still running, and then rode off on the Honda he'd bought from a Vietnamese girl who'd sung American rock songs in one of the cafés, who had managed to get herself evacuated and who was sure that once she got to the States, she would emerge as the new Janis Joplin. They had wondered but didn't ask if the girl knew that Janis was dead.

When Jade joined the other journalists at the embassy, she knew why Joe, in his infinite wisdom, or kindness, or madness, had insisted she go there alone, for looming above all the others, stood Congressman Rudyard Tyler Stanton. . . .

The other journalists were faintly surprised to see Jade Boudin, in her khakis, red hair flying, hurl herself at Rud Stanton, until some of them remembered that the two were related. Jade herself forgot everything in that moment, and Rud, pulse racing, tried desperately to remind himself that once he had gone out to buy this girl a present – a token of his love – and had returned to find her in another man's arms. But he lost the battle and wrapped *his* arms around her as if he would never let her go.

But finally he had to. Some of his colleagues were grinning while others seemed embarrassed, the newspeople were smirking and the photographers lost no time in capturing the embrace on film – an interesting highlight in the unfolding drama that was the fall of Saigon. . . . Jade stood back then, her eyes glistening, and Rud didn't know if the sparkle was tears. He tried to remember if those emerald eyes, green as grass, green as bottle glass, had always shone that way.

Then, unable to help himself, more or less out of control, he stepped forward and took her in his arms again. It was *his* Jade, the girl who'd been in his dreams for a thousand and one nights, and that other Jade, the one who had betrayed him with someone else, was a stranger, and that betrayal had happened ten years ago . . . a lifetime ago. As for the first time they had met, when she was fifteen and he but eighteen, that had to be an entire other millennium and this was *now*.

He turned to his associates. 'My sister-in-law,' he said in way of explanation. 'It's been ten years since we've seen each other and it's such a wonderful surprise.'

'I just bet it is,' one of them muttered under his breath but the congressman standing next to him thought the meeting *had* to be unexpected – who would pick this forlorn, terrible place rattling in its death throes as a trysting ground? Especially when the lovely in question was the glamorous, sexy Jade Boudin.

Jade, too, was conscious of the grins and looks and turned to *her* colleagues. 'He's my cousin and my brother-in-law. He's my sister's husband!'

And one of the two newswomen present who thought the Congressman from Massachusetts was a hunk like no other, murmured, 'Forget the sister!'

It was but a murmur but Jade heard. *Forget the sister?* That was the one thing she had to remember and keep on remembering. *Rud was her sister's husband. Abby's husband!*

Then she and Rud looked at each other again and it was as if they shared a single thought and Rud excused himself, saying to the others, 'I'm sure you'll get along without me for a while. . . .' Jade just smiled at everybody and then they left without another word even to each other.

For a few minutes they walked along not saying anything, as if words were unnecessary. And then their hands met as if of their own volition, and they strolled like any young lovers taking a springtime walk anywhere, oblivious to the din, the streets crowded with refugees who were pouring into the city, dreaming dreams of escape to a magical land where there was no war but laughter. Overhead, helicopters whirred, strange birds in the sky. For all Jade and Rud knew, it could have been April in Paris. . . .

Then, suddenly, they stopped walking, turned to speak at the same time, she asking, 'How's Abby?' and he, 'Why, Jade, why?'

The trucks with their cargoes of soldiers drove by, motorcycles, bicycles and cars. A boy on a passing scooter shouted at them, 'Americans go home!'

For a moment Rud was startled, then he laughed at the incongruity of it all. Jade said, 'Oh, I would if I could . . . if I knew where my home was.' He kissed her then, and she, kissing him back, thought she too was a refugee, dreaming of a magical land of escape.

They stopped for a drink on the terrace of the Continental Hotel but it was hard to ignore the begging children, the press of humanity who persisted in trying to sell them something. Rud was as amazed as she had been when she first arrived. What were all these people doing – the peddlers, the bartenders, the waiters? What were they waiting for, hoping for?

'They're doing the only thing they can do . . . they're carrying on.'

They ordered vodka and tonics, holding hands tightly across the table. 'I'll never forget that martini you made me that first night we met.'

She shook her head, smiling. 'I was fifteen and a very silly girl. I thought I knew all the answers.'

'It was the *best* martini. I've never had one as good since.'

She lowered her eyes, not wanting to look into his, so naked in their desire. She thought how *tender* they'd all been then . . . she, Abby, D'Arcy and Rud . . . tender and sweetly silly. Innocent. Innocent victims, each one of them. 'We were victims,' she said it aloud, not meaning to. 'Innocent victims, all of us.'

'Victims? What do you mean?' She was trying to tell him something, he thought . . . trying to explain why she had so betrayed him in Paris. He leaned forward, desperate to hear that there *had* been some reason, one that made sense. He had to hear that. . . . All those nights he'd lain awake, thinking he'd go insane if he didn't learn that there had been a reason other than that she didn't love him.

She saw the uncertainty in his eyes, the longing. He so wanted to believe, and she so wanted him to, too. But what could she tell him now that she couldn't tell him then? Something that he could accept? Certainly not that she wanted to send him home to Abby. 'I told you but you wouldn't listen to me. I told you that I couldn't endanger your career with my connections to Trace and Ross

391

Scott, but you just laughed. So I did the only thing that I could think of that would get through to you.'

It was the wrong thing to say. 'My God!' When he thought of what they hadn't had because of her desire to protect him he couldn't bear it! He wanted to scream but when his voice came out it was hoarse with frustration. 'Do you think that anything meant more to me than you did? My God! I loved you!'

He said he *loved* me, she thought. *Loved. . . . Past tense.*

'And I loved you.' She used the past tense too. How could it hurt now to tell him that she *had* loved him in the long ago past? *I love you, I loved you, I have loved you. . . .*

He was so overcome with longing for what could have been and hadn't he didn't even notice which tense she used. He stood up, pulled her out of her chair. 'Oh, Jade, I love you so!' The physical longing was so strong in him she could hear it in his voice. And she herself felt it so strong she couldn't bear to correct his conjugation. *Love, loved, have loved. . . .*

He crushed her to him, right there in the middle of the terrace of the Continental Hotel, crowded with its begging children and its peddlers of all manners of thing, with Saigon ready to fall, and she thought, I gave Abby a lifetime with him. Would it really be so terrible if I borrowed a few hours back?

The borrowing was convenient, the Continental was her hotel.

They stayed in her room the rest of the day and through the night. Joe, who had the room next door to hers, never came back to sleep. She knew that because never in their association had he failed to rap on her door when he came back from somewhere he'd been without her – to bid her a good night, to make sure she was all right, to let her know he was there just in case. . . .

Joe! He knew everything and had found himself another place to sleep.

They made love feverishly and with a certain poignancy, both knowing it had to last a lifetime. Never again would there be a place or a time for them. Later on, even years from now if they should chance to meet in some other corner of the earth, it would be the real world and in the real world, Jade knew exactly what her place was. And wherever she would be, there would always be a clock to tell her that it was too late, and she wouldn't question that. She had always known what time it was as far as Rud was concerned.

In the morning, Rud said that he'd join his delegation after breakfast. But after the girl had come to take away the dishes he changed it to after lunch. By the time they had eaten lunch they both knew that he wouldn't go away that day. And it didn't even occur to Jade that *she* had her own work to do. It was as if they both knew that once either of them went out the door, their borrowed time would be over.

'Tell me all about Abby,' she pleaded, feeling awkward even as she said it. It had to be the worst taste to ask a man about his wife when you were lying in bed with him wearing only a scrap of a silk robe.

'She never wrote to you, then? She always said she was going to—'

'No, she never has. I wrote to her several times, but—' A look of pain creased her brow. 'But I do understand. I really do. I think to Abby I represent my mother and she never truly accepted my explanation of why Carlotta had to give her up . . . leave her behind. All she can feel is the rejection – years of

392

rejection. And then when I had D'Arcy explain to her that I ran away because I didn't want her to fall into Trace's greedy hands, I guess she didn't accept that explanation either. So now she's rejecting me, and through me, Carlotta.'

'Well, she can afford to reject you,' he said bitterly. 'She doesn't need you. She doesn't need anyone except Judith.'

'Oh, Rud, you mustn't resent Abby loving your mother. Judith's been the only mother she's had.'

'You don't understand, Jade. At first it was that — she was my mother's daughter and she loved Judith more than anything in the world.'

'Oh, not more than you, I'm sure.'

He certainly could have given her an argument on that one but he let it go. 'But now it surpasses just love for Judith. It's as if Abby's turning *into* my mother.'

Jade laughed in disbelief. 'Abby? Like Judith? You don't mean it!'

'But I do. You wouldn't recognize Abby today. She's the epitome of sophistication . . . of ambition . . . for me . . . for herself. She wants to be *the* leader of Washington society. She's into power just like Judith. She belongs to dozens of organizations and committees. She *says*, of course, that it's only for my sake. And all she talks about is my future . . . how wonderful it's going to be when we make it to the White House. She's caught the presidential fever as much or more than anyone. . . . And she's into all the things that money can buy, just like Judith. Judith is much more than her mother now — she's her cohort, her associate, her partner, *and* the dispenser of the royal exchequer.'

'The dispenser of the royal exchequer? What do you mean?'

'You know I don't have a dime of my own. Judith has always kept the money just beyond my reach. Dangling it like a carrot to make me jump. OK, I could live with that. I was quite willing to go on my own like most people have to. I didn't have to live like a prince, and I was just as happy to go out and raise campaign money the way other politicians do. But Abby wouldn't go along. Why should we have to pinch pennies when Judith was there to give us everything we needed, more than we needed? Why waste time raising funds when Judith had all the money in the world to pay for the biggest and most lavish campaigns? And it takes *big* money to make it big in DC circles.'

'What about Abby's money? The money the Truesdales left her?'

'In trust. All she has is the income. That's all she'll ever have.' He laughed harshly. 'Do you think my mother would have let me marry a girl with access to money, money that my bride could actually spend which would make us independent of her?'

And then they both looked away remembering that once in Paris he had hoped to marry a girl without a cent in the world except for the money she earned and a collection of jewellery which reposed in a California vault.

'The thing is, once Judith manipulated Abby with motherly love. Now she's manipulating her with money just as she has always done with me. Then I was willing to break free but Abby wasn't.'

Jade was distraught. She loved this man just as she had loved the boy and she had sacrificed their love for the sake of Abby and now it seemed pointless. Clearly, Rud was unhappy. Could Abby be happy if he wasn't? And what about their children? If the mother and father weren't happy together, how could they be? Were they too doomed to be innocent victims?

Then Rud began to kiss her again, her lips, her throat, her breasts, and she couldn't give herself up to the joy of the moment, guilt winning out over ecstasy. *It was all her fault.*

Abby loved Rud but had Rud ever loved Abby enough? And probably Abby sensed that Rud didn't love her sufficiently, passionately, and turned to these other things for gratification – Judith, power, money, position. Wasn't she dreaming of the White House so that she would at least be the First Lady of the land, first somewhere . . . at last?

And it made sense that Rud couldn't give Abby enough love to satisfy her love-starved heart since he loved her, Jade, so much, too much. . . . Oh, she had heard the gossip from other newspeople about Rud's amatory exploits. One newsman had compared him to JFK whose sexual adventures were now part of the legend. Another journalist who covered the Washington scene had joked that Rud was the Congressman who had seen more DC bedrooms than a hotel chambermaid. And wasn't it she herself who had driven him into all those beds?

They were running out of time. She asked about Bill. Wasn't Bill's presence in Stantonwood a comfort to him, a source of aid and reassurance? Surely, Bill was a staunch ally. . . .

Rud was scornful. 'I *used* to respect him. I thought that, whatever else, he was a strong man and gutsy – the way he had gone after those bad guys. But once he let Judith get her hooks into him and then married her, I couldn't respect him. He's a wimp, a pussy-whipped wimp!' He shook his head. 'Imagine! He chose my mother over Francesca. What an asshole!'

'Frankie! Now there's a terrific woman! There isn't a man on the Hill who doesn't like her and respect her totally. Everyone says she's a woman of conviction and dedication. . . .'

Jade tried to put everything else out of her mind. Right now there were only these last few hours with Rud that would have to last forever. For all that, she still listened for Joe's footsteps that night, waited for his rap on her door, his voice, his reassurance that the world wasn't coming to an end and that everything was going to be all right. But again Joe didn't show. Did he sense that she needed a little more time?

She awoke early the next morning with a sense of urgency. She woke Rud. 'You must go. Everyone must be wondering what's become of you. We don't know what's happening out there and I have to go find Joe. He might need me.'

But he grinned at her. '*I* need you . . . now' and he reached for her. She thought, yes, one last time, one last act of love.

Then, just as she cried out in exultation and Rud whispered once again, 'I love you, Jade,' a thunderstorm broke. The monsoon season had arrived in Saigon. But then quickly the rain stopped and Jade said, 'Now you *must* go!'

'I'll only go if you come with me.'

She was frightened. She thought he understood that this was only an interlude, that they were on borrowed time. But then he said, 'If you think I'm going to leave you here with all hell about to break loose, you're crazy. I want to see you out of Saigon today.'

Then she was relieved. He was only concerned about her safety. He wasn't talking about anything else.

'Go and don't worry about me,' she told him. 'I'll be fine. I have Joe. He won't let anything bad happen to me.'

'Forget Joe. From here on in, I'm going to be the only man who takes care of you.'

'No. . . .' He *didn't* understand. She got out of the bed and started to back away. She was scared now. He had to go! She laughed uncertainly. 'But I can't forget Joe. And besides, you have enough things and people to take care of . . . to care about.'

He got out of the bed too and came after her. 'But I care about you most of all.'

He tried to pull her to him but she resisted, frantic. *Oh Rud, don't do this to us! Don't make me go through this again!*

'What about Abby? Your children? They need you!' she pleaded.

'The children will be fine.'

'Abby!' she said again. 'Your future—'

'Can't you get it through your head that nothing means anything to me if I can't have you?'

'You have responsibilities. . . .'

'To whom? To what? My major responsibility is to myself and to the woman I love. Children grow up no matter what . . . I grew up without a father. At least my children won't have to do that.'

He was wrong. He was wrong about everything. But how was she going to prove it?

'Think of Abby then.'

'I can't. But I tell you, it doesn't matter. What I feel for her is not enough. And God knows what she feels for me. If it's love, it's a tepid kind of love. Her passion lies elsewhere.'

'Oh no! She told me she loved you all those years ago and I know she's never stopped. If only you show her how much you love her, you'll see how she'll respond. That's what you must do! Show her that you love her, that she comes first with you and then, of course, you'll come first with her. That's how it works!'

She couldn't weaken. She didn't dare weaken. She had to be strong for all of them. There was too much at stake. She couldn't be the reason Abby lost her husband, the place she was making for herself. And if Rud left her, Judith would abandon her too and all Abby would have left would be her children to raise in a home where the father didn't live. She couldn't do this to Abby – be the reason for her bitterest rejection.

'Don't you love me, Jade?' His voice was quiet with desperation now. 'You said you did.'

'Oh I did! *Loved* you. But we were children then, really. There are all kinds of love and our love was a children's fantasy that wasn't meant to come true. It was a dream maybe. But now we're awake and we're not children anymore. We've moved on. I've moved on. I have another love now. An adult love.'

'Who?' His voice was cold.

'I thought you understood about Joe. I'm committed to him. He's a wonderful man, strong and compassionate and understanding.'

'And you love him? This adult?'

'Yes, I do. Very much.' And she knew that it was true. As she had just told Rud, there were all kinds of love.

'And what happened in this room? What was that?'

'It was part of the dream but now the dream is over.'

'And this great adult love of yours? Joe? Where was he while we were still dreaming?'

'I told you. He's a wonderful man and very understanding. And wise. Incredibly wise. He knew I had to dream a little more before I woke up.'

'You're right,' Rud said tonelessly. 'He is a wonderful, understanding man and if I were you, I'd hold on to him.' She couldn't tell for sure if he were being caustic, or sincere. But then again, it didn't matter.

She went to the window to look out at the strange golden light that bathed Saigon in the aftermath of the rain making it appear so tranquil, while Rud dressed quickly and left. She heard the door close softly and then she thought she heard the sound of artillery fire in the distance. And she waited for Joe to come back.

2.

At a little past six the end finally came not long after the latest and the last South Vietnamese president had been inaugurated. Jade heard the sound of anti-aircraft fire first, then she saw the people running madly in the streets. She looked up at the darkening sky and saw a plane . . . red flashes . . . and the noise grew louder and closer. Saigon was exploding all around her and she knew that Joe would be there at any second and she listened for his rap on her door.

XIV
1992

1.

The girls were out at a party, Joe was in Israel covering the troubles in the Gaza Strip, and Jade sat alone, watching the news on the TV. She was waiting for the report from the States on the primary race in New Hampshire and she was both tense and excited, rooting for Senator Stanton from Massachusetts to get the largest percentage of the Democratic vote. Rud, she knew, had been primed to enter the race in '88 but then had dropped out. D'Arcy, living in Washington and still very much immersed in all the political gossip, said that the word was that with all the Gary Hart business, Rud hadn't wanted to leave himself open to that kind of scrutiny. But this year he must be feeling confident that his personal life could pass muster and Jade was pleased about that.

When the telephone rang she ran to answer it, thinking it was the girls calling for their ride home. At fifteen and sixteen, so young and so pretty, Jake and Carlotta had their orders not to accept a lift home from any of the boys who might offer them one and she didn't care if they thought she was overprotective. But then Jade thought that it was probably too early for them to be ready to come home since they both adored a party, and it must be Joe – she'd been waiting for his call all day.

At first she argued with the caller. 'No, I don't believe you! You must be wrong! It's crazy! Joe's an American and we live in England. How can Joe be dead in a foreign land? It doesn't make sense! You'd better go back and check your facts!'

That was one of Joe's lines. But then when she hung up it did make sense. It made too much sense. Joe was exactly the kind of man who would throw himself on a terrorist's bomb left on a schoolbus full of innocent children. . . .

At first she damned him, angry with him, so angry she could have killed him if he weren't already dead.

Oh Joe, Joe! How could you do this to me, leave me all alone with two young daughters in a foreign land, homeless again?

For the first few days she went through the motions of carrying on. She had Carlotta and Jake to think of, and they were unfamiliar with death. She had to get them through this. She knew the terrain, she had been there before – this place of mourning, this time of grief.

At first it worked, the business of carrying on, but then there was the memorial service and the fact that she didn't even have a body to bury hit her. Joe, all the wonder of him, had been blown to bits, destroyed by offal who were willing to blow up children. She went home and could think of nothing but Joe. She found it incredible that she would never kiss him again or lie with him at night, feel him inside her. She'd never listen to his wonderful laugh again, never again hear him trying to explain the meaning of life to his daughters, never feel his lips against her ear murmuring sweet nothings.

Oh not nothings, Joe! Sweet but never nothings! Rather they were words of beauty, they were the sustenance of life.

She sat in his study for hours wanting to feel the impression his body had left in the old leather chair, listening to his collection of old records, recalling where they had been when they heard this song or thinking how they had made love listening to that one. Sometimes she would even caress his cameras, knowing that his hands had touched them lovingly.

And then she thought of all the men she had made love with while she had known Joe, men of no consequence and false prophets and of course . . . Rud, and she was filled with sorrow and regret. How many years of their time together had she wasted before she had known what time it was?

Oh Joe, you always knew what time it was. . . .

They had been back in London for three weeks when Jade knew that she was facing an age-old question – what to do about an unplanned pregnancy. Oh, such a hard question . . . the hardest. A question made even more complicated by the fact that love had been present at the conception. And sometimes as she lay awake pondering the question, she thought she could actually hear the baby's heart beating within her even though she knew that at this stage, it had to be her imagination.

Her friend Joe had watched her go through the days of agonizing until finally, not knowing the source of her anguish he asked, 'Can I help?'

Jade looked at the man who had come for her in Saigon, who had asked no questions and who had so wisely not taken her to safety but down to the river port of Khanh Hoi where they and others worked to help load the refugees onto barges which would hopefully take most of them to safety. They had worked desperately, racing against the clock and there had been no time to talk of matters of the heart. So she hadn't spoken that night to Joe of what she had learned in the room at the Continental Hotel . . . that there were many kinds of love and that she had a heart full of it for him. And then after that, there never seemed to be a right time to tell him all about her discovery and she thought she'd wait for him to tell her what she already knew.

And now that she knew she was pregnant with Rud's child, it was too late to talk of love to Joe. It wouldn't be fair. 'Just trying to make a decision, Joe.'

'Let's talk it over. They say two heads are better than one.'

'I think this is one time you can't help me.'

'Try me.'

'Well, I'm going to have a baby. Or rather, I'm with child and *maybe* I'm going to have a baby . . . *if* I decide to have it.'

Joe barely paused before he said, 'That doesn't seem like such a terrible problem. Solvable. What does your heart tell you?'

'Oh my heart says yes. It's my head that says no. My head tells me not to repeat the mistakes of the past. Another child of doubtful parentage. Me . . . my sister Abby . . . Rud. Only D'Arcy wasn't born with this particular cloud hanging overhead but she suffered just the same because of Rud's cloud.'

'Always listen to your heart,' Joe said softly. 'Your heart tells you true,' he said almost banteringly as if that would somehow make the gravity of their conversation more bearable.

400

'But the heart speaks purely . . . with love and valour.'

'But don't they say that discretion is the better part of valour? Which voice does one listen to when discretion is a priority?'

'You listen to your heart and you wrap your child in love and cover it with a most discreet name.'

'But wouldn't that be perpetuating the past too? Still, a child of doubtful parentage. . . .'

'That's the catch. You marry a man . . . the one with the discreet name, like Goodman, who will love your child so much . . . almost as much as he loves its mother . . . that there is no room for doubt as to its parent.'

Her eyes searched his. He had never before spoken of his love for her and yet she had never doubted that it was there. She felt it now stronger than she had ever felt it before . . . as she felt her own for him. A love full of passion as she had felt for Rud? She wasn't sure about that but there were all kinds of passion just as there were all kinds of love, and it had been an unreasoning passion that had, in the end, destroyed Carlotta.

It was a matter of strength, she thought, and Joe was a strong man, not one who was afraid of the past . . . her past. Strong enough that he would never feel threatened by it.

Still, she asked, 'Are you sure, Joe?'

'As sure as I am of my love for you, of your love for me.'

'Oh, Joe! You know that? That I do love you! But how long have you known? And why did you wait so long to tell me you loved me?'

'Just waiting for you to grow up and come out of that past . . . to join me in the future.'

'Oh Joe, you're so smart.'

'I know. I'm terrific.'

She laughed. 'Oh you! You Joe you!' And she went into the arms he held out to her, knowing that she was no longer refugee or expatriate. She had found her home.

Jade wandered through the house – her and Joe's house – looking for him upstairs, downstairs, in all the corners, in the shadows. When in more rational a moment, she realized that no matter how hard she searched, she wasn't going to find him, she didn't know where to turn. She didn't know how she was ever going to accept Joe's death. It was Joe who had finally made her truly accept her mother's death. . . .

When her daughter was born in January, Jade had been rueful about the baby's fuzz of red hair. 'I hope those blue eyes don't turn green. I think there have been enough green-eyed redheads in this family.' But then again, she didn't want the blue eyes to turn violet-blue either.

'Personally, I don't think it would be bad at all if our daughter has green eyes and red hair like her mother and grandmother. You can never have enough of a good thing,' Joe had said.

'Well, I'd just as soon she looked like nobody but herself. What shall we name her?'

Joe didn't hesitate a moment. 'What about Carlotta? It's such a pretty name.'

Jade was startled. 'No, Joe, that name belongs in the past. And you're the one who told me I have to come out of the past.'

'Yes, I did but I never told you to *forget* the past. If you did, you wouldn't really be a whole person, would you? I know how much you loved your mother and I know how hard you've struggled to redeem her memory, and I know how many sad things you had to cope with in this struggle. But what about the wonderful things, the good things, you loved about Carlotta? You don't want to forget those. What about standing up proud to the past, taking the best from it? We'll name our daughter Carlotta and then we'll raise her to be the very best part of that first Carlotta – beautiful of face and form, to be sure, but beautiful of spirit too. Just like you. What do you say to that?'

'Oh, Joe, what can I say? You make me cry! And I think that Carlotta Goodman has the most beautiful ring to it, and I think that Carlotta Goodman is a very lucky girl to have such a beautiful father.'

She made up her mind then to have another child right away – Joe's child. And she hoped it would be a girl so that, this time, there would be two sisters close in age who could grow up together, who would stay close, be friends forever. . . .

And that was the way it had turned out. Jake had been born a year later, almost to the very date, and more than anyone, she resembled her older sister.

'We named Carlotta after my mother,' Jade told Joe. 'Now it's your mother's turn. You've always told me what a wonderful woman JK was. But I don't think I want to call a baby by a set of initials. What did the JK stand for?'

Joe had laughed. 'You're not going to like this. Her name was Judith.'

'Oh no!'

'I was afraid you were going to say that.'

'What did the K stand for?'

'Katherine.'

'Then that's what we'll call her. Unless we just call her Jake.'

And then it was just as she had hoped. One could scarcely tell one sister from the other, and only guess which girl was the older. Carlotta was a bit taller than Jake, and Jake laughed just a bit more than Carlotta. But the important thing was that they were friends, as close as could be. . . .

Oh, they'd been so happy. Jade tried to console herself with that thought . . . that she and Joe had had seventeen years of happiness. Even when she had told Joe that she no longer wanted to go rushing around the world with him . . . that she wanted to stay home and watch her garden – the girls – grow, it hadn't changed anything. Not really. She and Joe had stayed as close as ever too. . . . He'd go away for a little while and then when he came back it was the four of them who were close.

The first time Joe went off without her, he asked: 'What will you do while I'm gone besides taking care of the girls?'

At first she didn't understand. 'What do you mean? Don't you think I'll have enough to do?'

'Well, here I've turned you into a top-notch writer. I don't want you to go rusty on me.'

'Aha,' she said, seeing what he was getting at. She smiled slyly. 'Remember that story I was writing when I first met you? About that girl who peeled beets?'

'My God, how could I forget!'

'Well, I've been thinking about that story. About reworking it and I've come to the conclusion that you were right. I'm going to make some changes and see how it goes. I'm definitely going to have that girl *scraping* beets instead of peeling them. How does that sound?'

'It sounds pretty good. I wouldn't be a bit surprised if the girl in your story is a girl whose time has come. . . .'

Like she herself. . . .

Two years later, she had published her first novel.

She tried to tell herself she had that . . . her writing which was as much her legacy from Joe as her daughters were. Still she was inconsolable and she went to bed, not caring when and if she would ever get up again.

Carlotta and Jake didn't know what to do about their mother. They admitted friends and neighbours, showed them upstairs to Jade's room but she turned her face to the wall until they were gone. By the time they thought of calling D'Arcy, they discovered that she was already on her way.

When Jade, face to the wall, heard that unmistakable Southern drawl in its ripest affectation – Well, ah do declare! Look who's lying there gasping out her 'lil ole last breath while she still manages to look more beautiful than the rest of us who are simply getting older,' she *had* to turn around. She was even forced to laugh.

'D'Arcy Sheridan Rankin, you second-rate Scarlett O'Hara, what do you think you're doing here?'

'What do you *think* I'm doing here, you ole asshole? I came here to straighten out my little ole kissin' cousin, that's what!' And she jumped into the bed to cover Jade's face with kisses while Jade protested, 'Will you stop acting like some crazy kid? We're too old for your nonsense, D'Arcy!' But D'Arcy didn't desist until Jade was laughing almost uncontrollably and then burst into racking uncontrollable sobs.

'What do you mean you can't accept Joe's death? You don't have any choice. There are Joe's daughters to think of. Here they've lost their daddy and now they see their mama slipping away too. Hell, Jade, you're scaring those poor kids to death, and two more darling girls I've never seen. They remind me so much of you that first time I saw you. They're *almost* as beautiful as you were. . . .'

'I don't care if they're beautiful. I just want them to be happy.'

'Well, then, maybe you'd better start pulling yourself together, don't you think?'

She talked Jade into coming down to dinner, and things started to look a little better, and after the girls went to bed they talked far into the night.

'I feel so guilty taking you away from Noel and the boys.'

'Well, don't. You forget that those four boys are pretty much grown up, that Cranston will be graduating from college this June. As for Noel, he's the one who *pushed* me on that plane. He knows better than I that if it hadn't been for you we probably wouldn't even be married today, or if we were . . . it would be one lousy marriage. Hell, Jade, you didn't only save our marriage, you saved our lives.'

Jade murmured automatic protests while her thoughts drifted back, remembering when she had finally decided that sometimes it was more crucial to divulge a secret than to keep it.

*

She was so excited that D'Arcy and Noel, along with their four sons, were finally coming to visit with them. Noel had finally been elected to fill the House Seat Rud had vacated by being elected to the Senate and they were taking a little vacation before the new Congress convened. 'Do you realize that this is the first time I'm going to see D'Arcy in the flesh in years?' she asked Joe the rhetorical question. 'The last time I saw her she was pregnant with Cranston, and now there's Thomas and Abraham and Franklin. I wonder if she's sorry now she didn't name Cranston George after the father of our country,' she giggled.

She realized later that Joe had been concerned even then that she was going to be upset by the changes in D'Arcy since he had gone to Washington several years earlier to cover the Watergate hearings, and at Jade's behest had visited with D'Arcy and Noel and her Aunt Frankie, and had reported to Jade that D'Arcy was constantly on her husband's back about his political career. 'Even her mother kept telling her to lay off but she didn't stop. To tell the truth, I don't think she's capable of stopping. She's a woman consumed.'

But that had been in '73, six years earlier, and Jade was sure that now that Noel was officially Congressman Rankin, D'Arcy would be much more mellow. 'It's going to be so much fun. And at last D'Arcy will get to see Carlotta and Jake. The pictures I sent her really didn't do either one of them justice.' But as soon as she said those words, she started to worry. Would D'Arcy be able to tell . . . guess her secret? That while they were Carlotta and Jake Goodman, there *was* a difference?

Joe, seeing the sudden anxiety reflected in her eyes, quickly reassured her – the two people Carlotta and Jake looked most like were each other, and the third person was Jade herself. . . .

But once Noel and D'Arcy and their four sons arrived, Jade saw that she needn't have worried – D'Arcy immediately pronounced the girls darlings, and launched into a blow-by-blow account of that '78 election. As for her own reaction to D'Arcy and Noel and their sons, Jade was more upset by the changes she saw in Noel than by anything else. Noel looked as if he had really aged and the man she remembered was gone. The old Noel had been sweet and even-tempered, had laughed a lot and had humoured D'Arcy when she had badgered him. Today's Noel didn't laugh much and mostly, he fought back. Between them, D'Arcy and Noel turned their home into a miniature war zone.

That particular night D'Arcy and Noel managed to argue over so small a matter as whether or not Cranston had to eat the second lamb chop on his plate. D'Arcy said he had to and Noel said he didn't, and then D'Arcy had snapped, '*That's* your problem. You're too soft. Too soft on everybody. Maybe if you had more backbone you'd be sitting in the Senate now instead of Rud Stanton, and *he'd* still be in the House.'

'I'm sick to death of hearing about your cousin Rud Stanton. Maybe *he's* sitting in the Senate because that's where he wants to be and he doesn't have a wife at home who's telling him he should be somewhere else.'

'Oh, great! Maybe you'd like to switch wives!'

'D'Arcy!' Jade gasped, although she had promised Joe, and herself for that matter, that she wouldn't get into the middle of the fights that had been going on non-stop since they arrived.

D'Arcy had lashed out at Jade then. 'Oh, you too? You're taking up for poor, itty-bitty Noel against me? Just like my mother. Mother's always taking up for Noel too. Poor Noel! His wife is such a nasty, ambitious wretch! Nobody's on my side. Not my mother and certainly not my father. Does my father care that his only daughter has a husband in politics? Does he care to extend a helping hand? Oh no! All he's interested in is his wife's son. . . . That bitch's insufferable—'

'D'Arcy! The children!' Jade protested.

Noel laughed bitterly. 'Oh, please, Jade, don't mention children to D'Arcy. She has no time for children. She's much too busy mapping out the next election. Talk about Bill Sheridan! If anybody is her father's daughter, it's our D'Arcy!'

'Would you mind not talking about me in the third person? And would you mind not saying in front of my children what a bad mother I am?'

Jade thought it would never end and finally Joe got up from the table to take all the children into another room for storytime.

When they were alone in their bedroom that night, Jade broke down and cried. 'I knew that D'Arcy was bitter but I didn't have any idea. . . . I don't even know why they came here to visit. They could have stayed home to fight. In fact, I don't even know why they stay together. When I think how much they were in love . . . how sweet and gentle Noel was. And D'Arcy! Granted she wasn't your sweet and gentle type, she was fun and warm and loving. What's going to happen to them, Joe?'

'I don't know. Maybe if D'Arcy could see the light – what she's doing to both of them. . . .'

'It's just this overwhelming resentment against Rud. She just can't rest until she sees Noel beat him and the thing is, he never will, will he?'

'No, he won't. His heart isn't in it, and that's what makes the difference.'

'I can't help but wonder. . . . If D'Arcy knew the truth . . . that Rud was her brother, wouldn't that make a difference to her?'

'It might . . . if it isn't too late already.'

'But they were so happy! It *can't* be too late, not for happiness.'

'Are you thinking what I think you're thinking?'

'I don't know. What do you think? It will be terrible but isn't it worth it – to try and save their marriage? Their lives?'

'That's a hard question. I would tend to think that it would be her mother's place to tell D'Arcy the truth, not yours.'

'But I don't know that Francesca knows the truth. And even if she did, she'd never tell. She would protect Bill no matter that they're divorced, and then she would want to protect the relationship between Bill and D'Arcy. She probably knows that D'Arcy would never forgive Bill.'

'But there doesn't seem to be much of a relationship left *there* to protect and it's always possible that that relationship would do better too if it saw the light of truth. . . .'

'Don't you see what you're doing, D'Arcy? You must let this obsession with Rud go!'

'Do you think that's so easy? If only I could! But I can't! Maybe I wouldn't hate Rud so much if I hadn't loved him so much in the first place.'

405

D'Arcy was breaking her heart and there was nothing to be done, Jade thought, but to go with the truth no matter how devastating it might be. She herself had struggled so long with the truth, but maybe in the end, that's all any of them really had.

'He's your brother, D'Arcy. You're Rud's half-sister.' She said it as gently as she possibly could, still it was terrible and Jade was grateful that Joe and Noel had taken the children out for the day.

They moved into the kitchen where Jade made pot after pot of tea.

'How long have you known?'

'A very long time. I knew even when we saw each other for the first time at your party. I knew ever since my mother died and I found her diaries hidden away.'

'But my mother? Does she know?'

'I don't know if she knows now. She didn't know then . . . those days we spent together in Palm Beach.'

'I can't believe that you knew all these years and you didn't tell me! All these years and we were friends. My God, Jade, why didn't you tell me?'

'I thought about it but I wasn't sure what the right thing to do was. And there was your mother. In case she still didn't know I wanted to protect her. And then . . . before we became real friends, I had no idea how strongly you felt about Rud. I thought it was just a teenage infatuation . . . that it wouldn't come to anything. That Judith would keep you and Rud apart. And then . . . after you told me about how you and Rud were – about the abortion, well, it was already too late. And there was still your mother to think about and your relationship with your father. I didn't want to make that worse than it already was. . . .'

D'Arcy nodded. 'But I think my mother *must* know. When she and my father divorced, she made him give me most of the money. Why would she have done that unless she knew that my father had taken Judith's money to—' She couldn't bring herself to say the words. 'And maybe even my saintly mother was not above making him pay penance. . . .'

Then she smiled crookedly. 'Just think, besides giving me a brother, Judith has inadvertently made me a rich woman. Although of course I've spent an awful lot of money on Noel's campaigns. On campaigns for political office that he never wanted! What a joke! But it's more a joke on poor Noel than on me, isn't it? I had the abortion but it's been poor Noel who has paid the price. Oh God, Jade! What torture I've put Noel through. And you know something? I haven't seen Noel really laugh in a long time. And my kids! Noel was right about that! I have neglected them! Not physically of course but I haven't really been there for them anymore than I was there for Noel . . . caring about what he wanted. Oh no, I was too preoccupied with my own madness. . . .

'So tell me, Jade, who else do you think knows Rud is my brother besides you and me and Joe and,' she laughed, 'Judith and good old Dad? Rud?'

'No, I don't think so.' But of course she knew for a fact he didn't . . . at least as of the fall of Saigon he hadn't known. . . .

'But that's only a guess.'

'Of course.'

'What about Abby? Do you think she knows? You didn't tell her that time in Palm Beach?'

406

'No. I wouldn't tell her your and Rud's secret. I didn't even tell her the secret about her own birth. And if I didn't tell her, who else would? My mother is dead and so is Trace. That leaves only Judith and Bill and they certainly wouldn't tell, why would they? This is one secret they're guarding with their lives.'

'So what do I do now, Jade? Do *I* tell Rud?'

'That's up to you, D'Arcy. If it will help you. . . .'

'No, not really. And what's the point now? It would only hurt him and I feel enough pain for both of us. You know what the funny part of all this is and believe me, I use the word *funny* advisedly – all along I had the feeling that Rud had been manipulated by Judith . . . that he would have come to the hospital to see me if she hadn't— Well, that isn't important now, is it?'

'Well, it *is* the past. And Rud, well he was just a victim of the past as you were. As for that abortion . . . under the circumstances it was for the best, wasn't it? It's all in the past, D'Arcy, and now, as Joe would say, it's time to get on with it. Now there's only the present and the future . . . your sons and Noel.'

'Oh my God! My poor Noel. I have a lot of making up to do.'

Several weeks later she got a call from D'Arcy. Since the good people of his district had elected Noel, he had decided to do the best job he could do for them for the next two years, and then he would seek a teaching position at a university, preferably at George Washington University in Washington so they could live in the area and be close to Frankie.

Jade thought of that last line from Fitzgerald's *The Great Gatsby*— ' . . . So we beat on, boats against the current, borne back ceaselessly into the past.'

Without a doubt, it was she herself and D'Arcy, Abby and Rud who had been ceaselessly borne back into the past. But maybe for her and D'Arcy the struggle against the current was over.

But that had been quite some time ago and now she knew that her own personal struggle with the past wasn't over.

'It was the past that killed Joe, you know,' Jade said suddenly.

'Now that's the silliest thing I ever heard.'

'It's not silly if you think about it. They've been fighting in Israel . . . Palestine . . . for years, hundreds and hundreds of years. And if it weren't for all that trouble in the past, that bomb wouldn't have been placed on that bus and Joe wouldn't have been destroyed saving those children.'

'That's pretty farfetched reasoning, Jade. I mean, that's *really* reaching.'

'No, I don't think so. It's the past's reaching . . . reaching out to get you every time.'

'Jade, when I was in trouble you told me that I had to give up my obsession with Rud, and you were right. Now, I'm telling you – you must give up this obsession with the past. And I want you to pack up your daughters and come home where you belong.'

'*This* is my home.'

'But you once told me home was where the heart was. And Joe's not here anymore, Jade. You just have to face that and come home where there are people who love you.'

407

Oh no, Jade thought. D'Arcy doesn't know what she's talking about. If I went back, then the past would surely reach out again and grab me up again in its terrible claws.

'No, I can't . . .'

But D'Arcy thought she was making progress . . . that the best thing was just to keep Jade talking. Wasn't that what the shrinks did? Just kept you talking until certain truths were torn out of your own consciousness, and then – presto! You were cured! No, that wasn't the word they used. Not cured. Rather, the truth was revealed to you and then you were able to live with what was bothering you in the first place. . . .

Jade was laughing as she told D'Arcy about the time she and Joe had found themselves in a remote village in Africa and they saw a tremendous cauldron of water boiling merrily away, and they both were really scared out of their wits but she told Joe not to worry – she had researched this tribe and there hadn't been *one* word about their being cannibals. Then Joe had asked her if there had been one word about their *not* being cannibals. 'But I tell you when the ladies of the village brought out their collective laundry and dumped it in the pot, were we relieved! Then, of course, we both claimed that we knew all along that they were simply boiling water to do the laundry.'

D'Arcy laughed hard and long before she said seriously, 'That's what you have to think about, Jade. All the good times you shared. And you know what? I don't think Joe would want you to stay here with the girls and be so alone.'

'Really, D'Arcy. I won't be alone. I have a lot of friends.'

'Friends aren't the same as family. If you came to live in Washington, you'd have family all around you. Think about it. Don't you owe that to your daughters?' And she thought of Abby. Of course Abby was part of the past Jade was obsessed with, but on the other hand she could use Abby to convince Jade where her place was. 'There's Abby, you know. *She* could use a friend.'

Jade looked at her suspiciously. 'First of all, Abby obviously wants nothing to do with me. She's rejected me constantly through the years. And why are you concerned with Abby suddenly? You haven't exactly been one of Abby's biggest fans.'

'But that's because she rejected me every time I made an overture, just as she rejected you. But she does need a friend.'

Jade averted her eyes. 'From everything I read she seems to be doing fine. She's been on the campaign trail for Rud. She's everywhere and I always see her name in the Washington papers. . . .'

'That doesn't mean she's happy, does it? She's not even the same person she used to be. She's so much in Judith's grip. Everyone knows her marriage is in trouble. Even Mother says so and you know she doesn't gossip.'

'But how does your mother know?'

'She hears things like everyone else. And besides she's pretty friendly with Rud on a certain level.'

'What? You never told me that.'

'I can't remember to tell you everything. But you know Mother's been either majority or minority leader of the Senate for years, and she often works closely with Rud. . . .'

Jade shook her head. 'It's so strange how things work out. Your mother and Rud friends. . . . I wonder how friendly they'd be if your mother knew that Rud was your father's—'

'She *does* know, Jade. Just recently we finally talked about it. It seems she's known for a long time now.'

'And—?'

'And she doesn't hold it against Rud. She says it's not Rud's fault who his father is.'

'She's a very generous woman,' Jade sighed, remembering how Frankie had forgiven her for what she had done thirty years before. . . .

'I'll say she is. She doesn't even hold any resentment against my father and if anyone deserved being resented— Oh well, let's not get into that. Let's get back to Abby. Jade, you have to come back to Washington to try and save Abby from Judith, to help save her marriage!'

Jade's eyes blazed. 'For God's sake, will you stop that?' Her voice was sharp and loud. 'I can't do anything more for Abby's marriage and I can't go to Washington! Can't you get that through your head? That the best thing I can do for Abby's marriage is stay away!'

D'Arcy was startled. So violent a reaction! And just then Carlotta and Jake walked into the house, home from school and she looked at them as Jade struggled to get herself under control. They came over to kiss Jade and then she herself. The two girls so alike they were like two peas in a pod, except for their eyes . . . Carlotta's, the colour of turquoise–bluish green, and Jake's, the colour of a grayish-green sea. Joe's eyes had been gray, of course but— And then everything clicked into place. D'Arcy could almost hear the click go off in her head.

As the girls went off to the kitchen to find something to eat, D'Arcy said softly, 'Oh, Jade, you too!' But she knew she had hit on the right answer to a larger question. . . .

'You know somehow, I think I always sensed it. Right from the start. But I guess I never wanted to think about it, so I pushed it away. But there's only one thing I don't understand. If you loved him, why did you let Abby have him?'

'Because she was my sister and she never felt our mother's love, and she loved him.'

'No. I don't think so.'

'D'Arcy! She *told* me she loved him.'

'I'm sorry, Jade, but that was a lie.'

'How can you say that? How can you possibly know? You've hardly been in her confidence.'

'Oh, come off it, Jade. She doesn't *act* like a woman in love. Anyone who knows her knows she's more in love with Judith or with Judith's money and power than she is with her husband. If she really loved him, she wouldn't give a good goddamn for Judith or her lousy money. She would have loved him and told Judith to go to hell a long time ago. If she ever loved him, it was a very feeble kind of love. And if you must know, I think the truth is that *you* never loved him all that much either, not with an all consuming burning passion!'

But she had! Oh, she had! Still, Jade leaned forward as if to hear better. 'Why do you say that, D'Arcy?'

'Because if you had loved him terribly, you wouldn't have given him up to Abby, no matter what. Even in the beginning you wouldn't have accepted that little lie of Abby's . . . that she loved him. You would have seen through that. And then later. . . . Oh, if you had loved him so, do you think you would have given him up so easily? Sacrificed so great a love like it was no more than a hunk of jewellery?'

Jade's eyes were large. 'But it wasn't *just* Abby. I would have been bad for him . . . for his career. The man who was my father was a mob figure . . . he—'

D'Arcy shook her head sadly. 'Oh, Jade, that's just more bull. You were just kidding yourself. If you loved Rud desperately, with every fibre of your being, you would have said fuck it all! You would have given up your place in paradise for him. More, you would have given up *his* place in paradise so that you could be together. Oh, Jade, I know! *I've* been there!'

'Oh, D'Arcy!' Jade whispered in commiseration. Still, her heart raced. Was D'Arcy right? Was D'Arcy speaking the truth? Oh God, she hoped so! And she realized that the real reason she had taken to her bed unable to accept Joe's death was not because she had loved him so much – oh, she had! – but because she was afraid that she had cheated him in life, by not loving him first, by not loving him best. But if what D'Arcy said was really true, that it was Rud whom she hadn't loved madly . . . sufficiently, then it had always been Joe whom she had loved best, first.

She reached out her hand to D'Arcy, her cousin and her friend. 'Thank you for coming, D'Arcy, and thank you for what you've said. . . . It makes a difference.'

'It's only fair. Now we're even-steven, cuz.'

And Jade thought that although she and Abby were sisters, and Rud was D'Arcy's brother, she and D'Arcy were closer now than any blood ties could ever bind them.

She drove D'Arcy to the airport. 'This is beginning to be a habit. Saying goodbye.'

'But we're not going to say goodbye. This time I'm only going to say *au revoir*. Deal?'

'Deal. But before you go, I have two more questions to ask you. Are you game?'

'Gee, Jade, you make it sound like it's going to hurt. But go ahead.'

'Do you think you'll ever make it up with your father? Will you ever forgive him for—?'

'For Rud? I can forgive him for Rud, but what I can't forgive him for is not telling me, letting me get hurt, as if I didn't even count, and then, finally, for choosing Rud over me. He did, you know, he did. And while Rud was his son, he should have remembered that I was his daughter, and that I counted too.'

'And Rud? Does it *still* hurt?'

'Sometimes. I guess it's like a toothache that goes away and then suddenly, when you least expect it, it gives you a bad twinge.'

'Do you think it will ever go away completely?'

'I'm not sure. Maybe if some time we could talk it out and kind of cry on each other's shoulder. But he'd have to know that he's my brother before we could do that, and one thing I know for sure is that I'm not the one to tell him.

It's quite possible he'll never know,' she said with regret in her voice. 'But in the meantime, I'm rooting for him to win the nomination even if he doesn't know it. And you, you think about coming home, you hear? It will be all right, Jade, I swear. No one would ever guess that Carlotta and Jake didn't have the same father. . . .'

Jade walked back to her car.

' . . . *So we beat on, boats against the current, borne back ceaselessly into the past.*'

Maybe someday they would beat it, if they all just kept beating on. . . .

2.

When the California attorney's letter arrived in June informing Jade that Ross Scott had died in prison and left her the house in which she, Carlotta and Trace had lived as a family but to which Ross had owned title, plus a large sum of money . . . an enormous sum of money! . . Jade could only reflect that sometimes life itself . . . events and circumstance pointed the way . . . illuminated the road for the confused to follow.

Ever since D'Arcy had left, she'd been pondering her future. *Was* it time for her to go home? Was it safe for her to go home? Could she, indeed, help Abby if she did? . . . Could she help both Rud and Abby? Herself? If indeed she had sacrificed for Abby didn't she owe it to all of them – Rud, Abby, and herself – to try and make that sacrifice good, make it work? If only Joe could send her a message, she thought, as to what she should do. Joe had been so wise.

She took Scotty's death and his bequest as a sign . . . a light in the labyrinth of life. It was meant for her to go home . . . the time had come. And along with the house and the money Scotty had left her, there was the matter of Carlotta's jewellery which was still waiting in that California bank vault for her to collect, just gathering dust since she was twenty-one and it was hers to pick up.

And she decided not to waste time speculating as to why Scotty had chosen her as his chief beneficiary. It *could* mean he thought she was his daughter, or it could mean that out of all the people he knew, she was the only one to whom he felt some kind of human connection. Even the Scottys of the world needed that . . . the human connection.

No matter, the California story was finally over for her. All she had to do now was dispose of the house, pick up the jewellery, decide what to do about the money Scotty had left her, and then she could write The End. And one thing Joe had taught her was that every story had to have a definite ending, and a fitting one. . . .

Four weeks later Jade sat in a suite at the Beverly Hills Hotel, her eyes glued to the television, watching the Democratic Convention taking place in downtown Los Angeles, while Carlotta and Jake demanded that they take a ride out to Zuma Beach which they had heard was probably the surfing capital of the world.

'Really, Jade! What's so fascinating on the telly that we have to sit here inside a hotel room while outside the sun is shining and the real world awaits!' Carlotta declared dramatically.

It didn't help that Jade told them it was *their* cousin who was capturing the

411

nomination on the very first ballot. To them Rud Stanton was only a name . . . a name without a face. 'And if you must know,' Jade said, piqued, 'when I was a girl we much preferred Surfrider's Beach at the pier to Zuma Beach, so there!'

Then, giving up on Jade who sat tensely waiting for the newly-nominated candidate to make his official appearance at the convention along with his wife and children, Carlotta and Jake put on their bikinis and went down to the hotel pool where they arranged to have themselves paged while they caught a few rays wearing their brand new Wayfarer shades which they'd been told were the right sunglasses to be wearing when in L.A.

A few days later, going along with Jade to the great pink house in the hills of Bel-Air where she had grown up, they couldn't understand why she was selling it.

'But it's so beautiful, Mum, and it would be so much fun to live here with Hollywood only a few minutes away to the left of us, and the beach a few minutes more away to the right,' Carlotta pouted and Jake wailed, 'Who would rather live in Washington?'

But then her daughers were today's children who couldn't understand why she couldn't live with the ghosts that dwelled in the house of her past, and for that Jade was grateful.

3.

Judith handed Bill his usual pre-dinner drink – a double bourbon straight up. He held the glass up to the light as if he saw something magical in the amber coloured liquid. 'Have you heard? The latest polls have Rud ahead by almost ten per cent. What do you have to say to that, Judith? It looks like we're going to sail into the White House with flying colours.' He took a healthy swallow of his drink.

'It certainly looks that way.' She sipped her wine slowly, contemplatively. 'I think it's high time we started thinking about *your* future.'

He looked at her over the rim of his glass. He never took even one word his wife said less than seriously, and he waited for her to continue.

'I believe it's time we decided which role is going to be yours once we move into the White House.'

'Not the same role I've had all along – confidant, advisor, researcher, number one man in the kitchen cabinet?'

'Does that satisfy you? It doesn't satisfy me. It's not enough. It's time you came out of the kitchen into the parlour with a title of your own . . . a title with all the importance and dignity you've earned.'

The little hairs on the back of his neck stood up, and he felt a little chill course through him. He knew Judith wasn't talking just to hear herself talk. 'What title are you talking about?'

'Secretary of State.'

This time Judith was joshing him. 'You're not serious, after all.'

'I've never been more serious. Why not?' Her voice now had that steely quality with which he was well familiar. 'I think Rud owes it to us and *I* want you to have it. If it weren't for us where would he be today? Are you content to be chief nose wiper for the rest of your life?'

Chief nose wiper. The words stung as they were meant to.

'But it won't work, Judith. Even if we could talk Rud into it, I'd never be confirmed. They'd scream nepotism. And they'd question my credentials which even you and I must admit *are* questionable. I haven't held a public office in—'

'I can count, Bill. And I say so what? Who has been prepping Rud all these years? Who knows every facet of government better than you? Foreign as well as domestic. Who's better briefed on all the issues? Not one of all the incompetents who surround us in Washington.'

'There's my age—'

'What about it? It would be of pertinence if you wanted to be President or Vice-President. But as Secretary of State, I would say age equals wisdom, and except for that wheelchair, you look as fit as anyone. You're still a damn goodlooking man. . . .'

Unconsciously Bill's hand smoothed his full head of hair, an artful blend of silver and black, moved down to his throat, which was smooth and taut, as much so as Judith's own. Eight months before he had undergone plastic surgery at Judith's insistence. She had this in mind all along, he thought.

She smiled at him. 'I'd say King Sheridan looks almost as good as he ever did.'

King Sheridan! God, it would feel good to be a man of real power again. Secretary of State! The respect! God damn, he was tired of being chief nose wiper!

'But how could we possibly swing it?'

'Shame on you, Bill. Have you suddenly forgotten how to launch a campaign? We swing it like we've always swung things, you and I. We do our homework, lots of spade work, and we spend a lot of money making a lot of the right people happy, and where the money doesn't work, we squeeze . . . massage . . . and apply a little pressure to the crucial joints. . . .'

She had no intention of sitting in a rocker next to Bill's wheelchair put out to pasture in a back garden of the White House. And once the idea she'd just planted in Bill's head started to sprout, well, she didn't think he'd like that picture any more than she did. She glanced at him now, staring into the fire that burned in the hearth. Dreaming new dreams of possible glory? Or old dreams of the past? He wasn't absolutely convinced yet but he would be . . . as they'd all be when she was through. She hadn't got to where she was by accepting other people's determinations of what was possible. . . .

Rud, back in Washington for the weekend after two weeks of campaigning in the South, was tired. He had told his staff to get lost for the weekend too. He just wanted to relax if Abby would let him. She had her own schedule and he knew she had a couple of social things lined up which, of course, weren't really social at all but just another form of campaigning. But in the end he knew he'd give in to her demands. He owed it to her to do that – she was the most tireless of campaigners and when he was finally in the White House, he would have to accord her a lot of the credit. Still, he wished she'd let up once in a while. And Bill too. Even now, as he sat in the library, just having a drink, Bill was at him, wanting to hear every detail of the last two weeks . . . how big the crowds were who had come to hear him talk, which politicians in which state had been really supportive.

'And you're keeping your nose clean?'

The question irritated him. He pretended he didn't know what Bill was talking about and he poured himself another drink.

'Hey, boy, you're talking to Bill Sheridan now. We're too close to the big day to have you do a Gary Hart on us.'

'But I'm not Gary Hart. I'm Rud Stanton, remember?' He was, as Bill put it, keeping his nose clean but it didn't have anything to do with anyone – not Gary Hart and not his stepfather. It didn't even have anything to do with Abby or being found out. It only had to do with him wanting to be the kind of man who would be worthy of the honour he wanted the American people to bestow on him, and he didn't need anyone to prod him . . . not Judith and not Bill. He had made up his mind about that several years ago, and all on his own.

'Have you been doing any more thinking about your Cabinet?' Bill asked, trying to appear nonchalant.

Rud wanted to laugh and would have if he had the energy to get into that kind of conversation but he didn't. Judith and Bill were working up to something and they weren't being very subtle. Subtlety was not their strong suit.

'It's still a little premature for that, isn't it? I haven't been elected yet.'

'Shit!' Bill said. 'Everyone knows it's in the bag.'

Every once in a while Rud wished that he was going to lose the election just to give the three of them a jolt – Judith, Bill and Abby.

Abby, dressing for the evening, tried to decide which gown would be the most suitable, when Judith came in and immediately vetoed the dress she was trying on.

And Rud thinks he has problems! God, she wasn't looking forward to having Judith and Bill move into the White House with them. What was really funny was that Rud thought she was. If he only knew how tired she was of having Judith dictate every damn move! And now Judith was leaning on her, trying to get her to lean on Rud to get him to agree to Bill being his Secretary of State, and Election Day was still three weeks off! And it was such a ridiculous idea! They'd be the laughing stock of Washington. Bill Sheridan as Secretary of State!

Judith plucked a gown from the wardrobe. 'Wear this one! It makes you look like a queen.' It was a white gown, studded with brilliants, and it had been a special gift from Judith. 'And why wouldn't it?' Judith asked. 'It cost a queen's ransom. But then again, I'm not going to let *my* daughter be put in the shade by anyone.' She laughed. 'You're going to be the First Lady who puts everyone else in the shade, even when it comes to fashion. You're going to make Nancy and Jackie look like amateurs!'

Abby sighed. She knew she shouldn't be caught up in Judith's games, but once she got going, Judith could spin a web which was almost irresistible.

She wondered what Judith would have to say if she knew that Jade had called her, insisted that she wanted to meet with her after all these years. Well, she wouldn't bring it up. She wasn't up to one of Judith's long counselling sessions. But then Judith said, 'I've heard that your sister is in Washington. Perhaps you ought to see her. See what it is she's up to. . . .'

'Is she necessarily up to something?'

'Of course. Haven't you learned, Abby, that everyone is always up to something?'

Rud had agreed to go to the reception at the Italian Embassy on the condition that they wouldn't stay more than an hour . . . an hour and a half at most and Abby had agreed. Compromise was the name of the game, and she wanted to use the time in the limousine when they'd be alone except for the driver to effect another compromise. 'I thought that *if* you do win the election, and you *are* going to, would it really hurt so much if you let Bill be the Secretary of State for a while?'

'*Let? For a while?* What do you think we're talking about here? Some child's game? Some make-believe never-never land? I won't even discuss it.'

'Do it for me, Rud. You owe me something too, you know. I've stuck it out with you through . . . well, through everything. And it hasn't been easy. Never! This is the one thing I'm asking of you.'

'I know, Abby, I know. But must it be this?'

'Yes. It's the only thing that is going to satisfy Judith, and it might be the only thing that will keep her from moving into the White House with us.'

He turned to look at her. Was she serious? She wanted him to trade the Secretary of State position for the privilege of not having the Sheridans living with them in the White House? And was this some new Abby? An Abby who wanted to throw her adored mother out into the cold? He looked out the window of the car. He decided to resist the temptation to remind her that it was she who through all the years of their marriage had chosen to live with Judith, had insisted on it. It would hardly be fair. He had changed. He had grown up. What right did he have to question Abby's growth?

He wished he could oblige her. He would have liked to do something for her. 'Does it matter that much?'

'It does. I know that I was the one who always insisted— But it has come to the point where I'm suffocating. Can you understand that?'

Yes, he could. He knew the feeling well.

'Can't you just tell her then? That you don't want her in the White House with us?' he said softly.

'It's too late for that . . .' she said, and he didn't argue with her. He too knew that it was too late.

4.

Jade sat across the table from Abby in Washington's Aux Beaux Champs, her hands shaking slightly as she lifted the glass of wine to her lips. Abby was drinking only fizzy water but she held her own glass aloft. 'We must make a toast, Jade. "Let us join hands and go into the future together." That's Rud's slogan.'

Jade clinked her glass against Abby's. 'Sounds good. I'll drink to that.'

'I remember when you made that martini for Rud at D'Arcy's Sweet Sixteen. I was *so* impressed,' Abby laughed. 'There I was, sixteen, but a child really. In that awful pink dress. And there you were, fifteen, but a woman, dressed like the movie star you eventually became. And you were so breathtakingly

415

beautiful! I thought you had to be the most beautiful, fifteen-year-old woman in the whole world. . . .'

They both laughed and Jade was pleased. Laughing together had to be an icebreaker. They were sisters and blood was supposedly thicker than water but time and distance and estrangement was a thinner of blood like nothing else.

Jade hadn't really recognized Abby when she came into the restaurant, wouldn't have at all except that she herself was already seated and watching for her. And then when she saw the ultrafashionable woman vaguely in her forties enter – black hair drawn tightly back, pearl and diamond earrings, black designer dress – she knew it had to be her sister Abby. Still, she was surprised. She had kept this vision of Abby in her head as she last remembered her – big, frightened eyes, wet as if on the verge of tears, long wavy dark hair falling to below the shoulders, awkward in her total lack of self-confidence.

This Abby had rushed over to the table, displaying a big smile with the gloss of professionalism about it and swiftly bent to peck her cheek, 'Jade, dear, dear Jade! I couldn't mistake that hair anywhere. And it's still *so* red! How *do* you manage? You haven't ordered a drink? Well, we must take care of that at once!'

She'd summoned the *maître d'hôtel* himself with a barely perceptible flick of the finger, addressed him by name, asked Jade what she would have, and said, 'I never drink anything but bottled water at lunch myself. Campaigning – all those women's lunches and teas – require a clear head, I can tell you!'

All this in about five seconds. And then as soon as they'd given the order for the drinks, she gestured to the head waiter to take their food order.

'You don't mind if we order right away, do you?' she half-asked Jade. I'm terribly pressed for time.' She glanced at her slim wristwatch, set with small discreet daytime diamonds. 'I'm meeting with my campaign manager at two-thirty.'

'*Your* campaign manager? I thought it was Rud's campaign.' Jade laughed a little.

Abby's responding smile was that of a stern teacher humouring a somewhat naughty child. 'Really, Jade, campaigning is serious business.'

She ordered only asparagus with a lime vinaigrette, after questioning the waiter extensively about the asparagus, wanting to know if they were the first of the season and if they were really tender, and suggested Jade try the *escalopes* of monkfish in a saffron sauce. 'It's a house specialty.'

Jade felt as if there was a gauze curtain between them. How was she to tear it away so that instantly, magically, they could be friends and she could tell her sister what she had come here to tell her? How much easier it had been to tear away the years that separated them when first they'd met . . . when *they'd* been sweet and tender, the very first of the season.

Now Abby was forking into her asparagus as if she were really starved, and sneaking covert glances at her watch. It didn't look like there was going to be time for all the things that had to be said, Jade reflected.

'Abby, I have something to tell you and something to give you, but it's so busy here and there are so many people here who know you, and you keep looking at your watch, which makes me very nervous—' Jade began, wanting to suggest that they go someplace else to talk.

416

'*You* nervous? That's a laugh. I thought you were the height of poise and self-assurance when I met you. And I was so thrilled that you were being so nice to me. But then of course you ended up running away from me, didn't you?' Still, having said *that* with a caustic edge, Abby kept smiling as if there were a wall of ice around her that didn't let anything really get to her, and the smile was only the glittering icicles that hung suspended, a decoration.

Jade was desperate. She felt that Abby might never again find the time to meet with her and all the words that had to be spoken were never going to get said.

'But D'Arcy explained to you that I ran away because I didn't want you exposed to my father, that it wouldn't be good for you. . . . And I wrote to you explaining—'

Abby dabbed delicately at the corner of her lips with her napkin. 'Come now, Jade. Did you really expect me to believe that? I may have been young and naive but I wasn't stupid. What could he have done to me? He might have been greedy but my money was tied up in trust.'

'But he didn't know that. None of us knew that then. And you didn't know him. He had his ways.'

'Legally, he couldn't have done a thing. He really wasn't anything to me except a kind of stepfather, which wasn't even true since Carlotta was already dead. No, Jade, I'm afraid your story didn't hold water then and it doesn't now. What you did was exactly what Carlotta did. Cut and run,' Abby said crisply.

Jade first looked around, then leaned across the table to try and take Abby's hand, but Abby pulled hers away.

'You don't understand, Abby. Carlotta did what she did for the same reason I did! To save you from Trace Boudin!'

Abby managed to look both bored *and* disgusted. 'I don't know why you're bringing up all this unpleasantness now, Jade. We're only days away from Election Day and I must keep my concentration. Why are you doing this?'

'Because you have to know the truth.'

'Oh, very well. Let's get this over with since I see you're going to persist. What is this truth you feel you must divulge?'

'Abby, Trace Boudin wasn't your stepfather – he was your father. Your real father!'

Jade didn't know what she expected. That Abby would drop her glass of fizzy water . . . that she'd faint or scream. She never dreamed that Abby would laugh . . . nastily, but laugh!

'Well, if this isn't the most malicious thing I've ever heard! Judith was right about you. What is it you want, Jade? Why did you pop up again after thirty years? To blackmail us with your ugly fabrications? If you were left badly off when your husband died, all you had to do was ask. You didn't have to wait until almost election day to try and extort money from us. Or is it just that you want to embarrass us? Or is this something you and D'Arcy have concocted to—? I know what it is – you're jealous! Is that it? You were always the beautiful one, and the one, of course, Carlotta chose to keep. Well, why wouldn't she? You're two of a kind. But now you're not such a big deal anymore, are you? No longer the film star, and you're getting on, and that career of yours as a journalist is over and all you have left now are those little books of yours that you manage to get published. Actually, you're pretty much of a nobody these days and you can't bear it, can you, that *I'm* going to be the First Lady, the one in the limelight. That's it, right?'

Her words seared Jade's consciousness. Her sister was so full of resentment and spite. She had had no idea. But then, she couldn't really blame Abby. She had been with Judith so long, and it was she herself who had sent her there. As good as sold her to Judith.

'Please, Abby, don't say any more! I only told you this because you had to know that your mother loved you as I did . . . that there was a valid reason for what you still see as abandonment. But you have to see that it wasn't – that it was an act of love! And I came here not to blackmail you but to bring you this – the proof of your mother's love.'

Jade reached for her handbag and withdrew a cashier's cheque and handed it to Abby. Abby looked at it blankly. 'What *is* this?'

'You can see for yourself. It's a cheque for over seven million dollars. . . .'

Abby looked again. The cheque was for $7,052,049.35 and it was made out to her! To Abigail Truesdale Stanton!

Abby's limousine took them to Jade's house so that they could talk. As they drove up the long winding driveway to the mansion – that was the only word to describe it, Abby thought – she was flabbergasted. First the cheque, and now this house in Georgetown where just a good townhouse went in the millions. . . .

Abby laughed. 'What have you been doing, Jade, robbing banks?'

'That cheque for seven million is rightfully yours. It's not a gift from me. It comes from the sale of Carlotta's jewellery which she meant for you. She just left it in my name trusting me . . . that I would pass it on to you, her elder daughter. I put the collection up for auction in California. I imagine it was worth a couple of million when Carlotta died, but that's a long time ago. The Duchess of Windsor's collection brought more than forty million, I understand, when it went under the hammer—'

'Fifty,' Abby corrected automatically. 'I believe that *was* the amount the Duchess's collection brought,' and Jade laughed. She should have known that when it came to money, Abby would be much better informed than she.

Abby looked at the cheque again, looked all around the living room that was filled with expensive furnishings, fingered the cheque, studied it, and then finally, Jade saw a single tear trickle down her sister's cheek.

'She really left her jewellery to me?'

'Yes, Abby,' Jade lied, not feeling any guilt whatsoever about lying. 'It was an act of love.'

Abby laughed, the first real laugh of the day. 'It's more than an act of love. What this cheque is is a blow for freedom and not just mine!'

Jade smiled complacently. That was exactly what she had hoped it would be. Abby caught on fast. It wasn't only truth that set people free – money did too.

'I accept that Trace Boudin was my father. Only I must admit it doesn't really register. Maybe I've just been Abigail Truesdale Stanton so long that I can't really conceive of being Trace Boudin's daughter. It's so . . . alien. And to think that Judith knew all along! *That's* what is really inconceivable. And you, does it bother you, Jade, that you're not sure who your father is?'

'No. Not really. But then I've known the question of that for so long a time. You might say I've grown up *not* knowing. But I certainly didn't want Ross Scott's bloody money, and I thought it was only right that most of the money went to doing some good. There didn't seem much point to burning it when it could buy a lot of housing for the homeless.'

'So that's what you've done?'

'Yes. Forty million dollars can cover a lot of ground.'

'Forty million dollars? Wow!'

'And that's only what he left me. I guess, crime paid.'

Abby laughed. 'I'll say but I think it's great that it's going to do so much good. And this house? It's so grand.'

'Well, I sold the house we all lived in . . . Carlotta and me and Trace. I certainly couldn't have lived there. It was so full of ghosts. And real estate being what it is in Bel-Air, California, it went for several million dollars. That, plus the furnishings and the paintings. . . . Well, it amounted to a lot of money and I wanted my daughters to have this as *their* heritage . . . from their grandmother.'

'Carlotta. . . . So she left us both free. . . .' And then finally, Abby cried.

'I stopped loving Judith a long time ago, if love was ever the proper term for what I felt. And that's not really any tribute to my intelligence. It really didn't take much of a brain to figure out what Judith was all about once I took off my rose-coloured glasses. She's really not very subtle. It's do what I say or off with your head! Rud always knew this but I refused to listen to him until it was too late.'

'But it's *not* too late, Abby. It's never too late.'

Abby laughed. 'You sound like such a Pollyanna. Like me thirty years ago before I learned the facts of life. You can't keep a sapling alive without plenty of water and nourishment. Our little sapling – Rud's and mine – never really had a chance.'

'But you loved him, Abby. You told me so.'

'Oh, Jade, Jade! I told you what I thought you wanted to hear. I felt what I thought Judith wanted me to feel.'

'You mean you *never* really loved him?'

D'Arcy was right, after all, Jade thought, and she was filled with despair.

'Oh, I loved him. Of course, I loved him. Who couldn't love charming Rud? If nothing else, there were always those looks! And he was always so sweet to me. I think I must have loved him like a big brother. An adorable older brother. . . .'

It was quite a joke on them all, the four of them, Jade thought. Abby had loved him like a brother, and D'Arcy who *should* have loved him like a brother, had loved him with all the passion of a Juliet, a Heloise, a Camille. . . . And how had she herself loved him? Second best? After Abby?

After Joe? Would she ever really know? But did it really matter? She *had* loved. . . .

'The funny thing is, the more intimate we became and the more Judith pushed, the less, I think, I felt towards Rud, and the less he felt for me. Judith pushing us together, always pushing, was the kiss of death. And then later on, she was the one in the middle, coming between us. Well, that's the way it is. Do you know what I would really like? For Rud and me to be wonderful friends the way we were in the beginning. And if Judith and Bill weren't always around, it could happen. Do you want to hear something really amusing? I was never really into sex. And when Rud and I—'

Jade put her finger to Abby's lips. 'I don't think you should tell me this—'

'It's OK. I wasn't about to give you any juicy details. All I was going to say was that I always wondered what the big fuss was all about. I had friends who talked about having multiple orgasms, and ones who didn't have any at all and were ready to kill themselves because of it, and even today I know women who only think about who's going to be their next lover. And then, knowing that at least half the women Rud met were dying to climb into bed with him, I thought there had to be something wrong with *me*. And the conclusion I came to was that it was because of my proper Truesdale blood! Now, is that a laugh? And now, here I am, with racy Trace's hot blood!'

Abby said she really had to go. The election! But as she was leaving, she asked, 'And you didn't keep *anything* of Carlotta's?'

'Yes, I did. I kept Mother's portrait. I haven't hung it yet.' She sighed. Did she have to give that up too? 'Do you want it, Abby?'

'Oh no! You should have it. And what about Carlotta's clothes? Did you keep them?'

'I wasn't going to— But then my daughters – you'll have to meet them – they carried on so, I finally agreed to let them have them . . . all of it, the gowns and the furs. But your daughter is Carlotta's granddaughter too. Do you think she'd like to have a few gowns? A fur?'

Abby considered a second. 'Why not? As you say, she's Carlotta's granddaughter too, and Carlotta was pretty special, wasn't she?'

Abby was almost out the door. 'Rud will be dying to see you, I'm sure. The minute he has a chance. To tell the truth, I always thought Rud had a crush on you that time in Palm Beach. D'Arcy was hot after him but I think he had eyes only for you. It's funny how things work out, isn't it? You were so beautiful and D'Arcy was so pretty and cute, and I, shy little Abby Truesdale ended up with the prize.'

'Abby, you *will* try, won't you? To make it work out with you and Rud?'

'I'll try but maybe we've got out of the habit, if ever there was one. But we do have an understanding, you know. But I *will* try and if Rud's elected, I intend to be the best damn First Lady this country's ever seen. I owe that much to Rud, and to the country.'

'Great! Who's going to be your role model?' Jade laughed. 'Jackie or Nancy?'

'Are you kidding? I intend to emulate Eleanor Roosevelt who really made a difference.'

420

Jade gave Abby one last hug. 'Good for you.'

5.

Jade went over to D'Arcy's and Noel's to watch the election returns coming in. Carlotta and Jake went with her but not surprisingly they were more interested in fooling around with their cousins, D'Arcy's boys, finding the election proceedings pretty much boring, even if it was their cousin who appeared to be winning. It didn't mean much to them since they had never met him. But they thought it was great that their mother and D'Arcy and Noel were taking it so to heart, that their mother was so excited and happy and having such a good time with her cousins D'Arcy and Noel and her Aunt Frankie who was surprisingly nice considering her age and the fact that she'd been in politics for years and years. Everyone always said that American politicians were in a class of their own . . . kind of peculiar . . . but she wasn't at all, unless you considered crying a lot peculiar. She had hugged their mother so hard and for so long and then had hugged them just as hard, crying the whole time and murmuring over and over how much they reminded her of their grandmother Carlotta. . . .

The projections came in early and it was Rud Stanton for sure, but it was very late when it was all over and official, and the cameras moved to Boston to show the newly-elected President and his family at their election headquarters there. . . . Rud, Abby, their son and daughter, the mother of the President and her husband Bill in his wheelchair.

The lights were dimmed in the Rankin den and no one saw anyone else's tears, and no one spoke until Rud finished making his acceptance speech. Then Noel said, 'He's going to make a fine President,' and Francesca said with a catch in her voice, 'I'm sure of it.'

'I think so too,' D'Arcy said tremulously, 'but you do know, Jade, that if Mother hadn't been Rud's aunt, they would have run her as V.P.?'

'Oh, hush,' Francesca told her. 'Now's no time to think of ifs, or what might have beens. . . .'

Jade agreed with her completely. No ifs . . . no might have beens. As far as she was concerned, Abby looked very much like a First Lady . . . the first and the best, and Rud? He looked like he was born to be the President. . . .

6.

Judith sent a servant to summon Rud to the library. It was the last day of the year, and she wanted this whole thing settled, clearing the slate so to speak before the new year dawned. It was absurd – here they were so close to the Inauguration and Rud had announced all his choices for the Cabinet save for the Secretary of State. 'I want it done with!' she told Bill. 'What does he think he's doing? Playing games with us?'

'Maybe he's saving it as a kind of surprise . . .' Bill appeased her, convinced now by Judith that all things *were* possible, but still apprehensive about a direct confrontation with Rud. 'Maybe we shouldn't push now. Let him do it in his own time. Maybe he wants to pretend that it was all *his* idea. After all,

Judith, he is the President now and he wants to think that he's making all his own decisions.'

'If that's the case, let him look in the mirror every morning and tell himself he's making all the decisions. But I'm not going to be satisfied until he tells the whole country who the Secretary of State is going to be.'

Bill knew that once Judith was in this kind of mood, there was no arguing with her, and he rolled himself over to the window to wait for Rud to come running in answer to his mother's summons, but he pushed his shoulders back, tried to sit up taller in his chair, conscious that as he grew older, he was losing height, shrinking into himself. And although he'd been in his chair for almost twenty-five years, he once again silently cursed his fate and reflected, not for the first time certainly, on how Trace Boudin had managed in a fashion to have the last laugh. . . .

When Rud walked into the library, having a pretty good idea of why he'd been sent for, seeing Bill over by the window almost in the shadows since it was a dark, grey day outside, and Judith standing in front of the fireplace, arms folded across her chest, he couldn't help feeling not like the President-Elect he was but more like a schoolboy sent for by the principal to answer to an accusing teacher. But who was the teacher here, and who the administrator? No question. . . .

In spite of her militant stance, Judith started off coolly enough, even pleasantly, but with a positive accent. 'Bill and I have decided that there's no point in playing footsie anymore with this Secretary of State announcement. We appreciate that you're trying to do this in the most politic manner, but all you're doing is drawing more attention to the announcement than it's worth. The best way is just to grab the bull by the horns and do it! If you're going to be a forceful President and I think that we all agree that is the kind of President you want to be, you have to learn to do what you want, say what you want, and leave it to the others to cope with it. Let it be *their* problem! My dear Rud, how are you going to be an effective President if you don't make strong decisions and stick by them? Now I want you to call in your press representatives and make the announcement that you want William Sheridan, a man you have complete faith in, as your Secretary of State, and do it without any more delay. You can let the writers fill in all the blanks, reasons . . . etc.'

So this was it, Rud thought. The old showdown at the old corral.

He glanced over at Bill, who had his shoulders hunched almost as if he were waiting for a blow. He didn't want to hurt Bill's feelings . . . he'd been waiting with the announcement, putting it off, for that reason. But Judith was right – the best thing was to do it with a clean, sure stroke, getting it over with. An effective President couldn't afford to hesitate . . . water down the drinks. That didn't change the results – it just made it all take longer.

Still, he couldn't bring himself to do it *that* cleanly. He did have some measure of affection for Bill. More he felt sorry for him. Bill was a man who had missed the big chance in more ways than one. Did Bill really think he had chosen the better woman? When he thought of what Frankie had accomplished in her years in the Senate – of all the really important legislation she'd pushed through and had still remained what she'd always been – a warm, caring person, he was only filled with pity for the man who had married Judith, could not help thinking that he was no more than a fool. More, he was out of it . . . living in some different phase of time. How could he dream of being Secretary of State? But then he was only dreaming. It was Judith who dared that he aspire to that position. . . .

But Judith was standing in the centre . . . in front of the fireplace, and Bill was over by the window. Whom did he address?

He turned to Bill. '*You* must know that it's out of the question. You haven't been active in any form of government for thirty years. *You* know what kind of uproar there'd be. . . . Even if I were to name you you'd never be confirmed. . . .'

Bill said nothing but Judith's voice snapped out: '*You* name him and let *me* worry about the confirmation.'

Rud turned to Judith, the woman who had given him life and then taken that life away from him . . . bit by bit . . . year by year, ever since he could remember. 'What are you going to do, Mother? Buy up all the votes for confirmation? Did it ever occur to you that there are people who *can't* be bought, no matter what?'

Judith laughed, more a sneer really. 'A few . . . maybe. But those you can't buy, you squeeze.'

'Is that what you did to me? Did you buy me, or did you just squeeze?'

Judith laughed again, this time with contempt. 'Perhaps I did a little bit of both. And don't you get self-righteous with me now. You're not a little boy any longer. You're forty-eight years old and hardly the innocent virgin. You know the score and you know exactly what I've done for you and how I did it and *you* let me do it, and don't you forget it! No, my sonny-boy, your hands aren't that clean, and no one gets off scot-free. There's always a price to pay.'

In spite of himself, Rud was appalled. He had always known what kind of a person Judith was . . . that she bought and sold people . . . used people to get what she wanted, but he had never doubted that she loved him in her fashion. But now he saw that she didn't! Not really. Had she ever loved him? When he was a baby and she had held him in her arms and had sworn to herself that he was going to be the President, had she loved him then? Or had she loved only herself and her dreams of glory? Had she ever loved him for himself?

He shook his head as if to clear it.

'Be that as it may, Mother, I am the President now, and I intend to be the best President I can possibly be, and I have to follow my own conscience as to what and whom is good for the country and I don't feel that Bill has the right qualifications to—'

A strange animal cry sounded from Judith's throat and Bill's voice finally rang out like a shot, 'Judith, don't!' But it was too late.

'You pompous, self-righteous ass! You stupid ingrate! Don't you give me that crap about what you can and cannot do, carry on about Bill's qualifications. *I* made you! *I* manufactured you! *I* bore you and *I* wiped your behind every step of the way! And yes, I bought you just the way I bought your father. And you're just like him and don't you forget it! You *are* your father! You are Bill!'

Rud looked from Judith whose face was screwed up with venom to Bill who was as if collapsed in his chair, and he didn't have to hear any more to know that Judith was speaking the truth. He didn't have to hear any more and he didn't want to—

It was just like people said – how when one was dying one's life passed in front of one's eyes. And he thought of all the years growing up when he never had a father and how he had so yearned for one. How he had only Judith and how he longed for a father that would have been his friend and his ally. And then, when Bill had come into his life, he had thought that at last he had a man who *acted* like a father, who was his friend, but then, of course, in the end, he hadn't been that . . . he had been only Judith's man . . . *her* ally, her lackey. No, Bill hadn't been a real father. Where had he been when he needed him?

And then Rud thought of D'Arcy! And it was then that he wanted to cry. D'Arcy. . . . Bill had left both of them, D'Arcy and him, his son, to dangle in the wind! And now, even if he could have forgiven Bill for himself, how could he ever forgive him for D'Arcy? He was sick to think what he and Judith, between them, had done to D'Arcy. . . .

He realized that Judith was still talking. . . . ' . . . So just you keep in mind, what I make I can break and I guess you know me well enough to know that I mean what I say. . . .'

'I know it, Mother. I believe it, and I intend to take everything you say under advice and I will let you know what I decide.'

Yes, he knew what he had to do. No matter how he had grown up, no matter what it had taken to get him elected to the presidency of the United States, once a man *was* President there was only one way to go. They said that the job made the man and he hoped that it was true, for whatever else he would be, he was determined that he would be his own man. . . . That was the very least a President could be. . . .

EPILOGUE
The Inaugural Ball
January, 1993

The Army band played 'Hail to the Chief' when Rudyard Tyler Stanton – tall, still spectacularly handsome and looking every inch the President, entered the grand ballroom of the Mayflower Hotel with his First Lady on his arm, she resplendent in a ballgown of rustling green taffeta chosen to set off her diamond and emerald necklace. (The gown was going to the Smithsonian, she told the press, but absolutely not the necklace! That had been her mother's, the famous Carlotta Boudin's. It was a joke of course since no one expected her to give the necklace away, still the statement was said with a lot of pride.) Behind the presidential couple were their son and daughter, Will and Judy, he shorter than his father by a couple of inches, she blond and blue-eyed like her Dad, with a head of unruly curls. They were surrounded by a cordon of Secret Service men also in formal attire.

There were five other balls that evening to accommodate the thousands of excited and jubilant friends and supporters who wanted to celebrate with and greet the new President. Rud Stanton had already been at the Hilton, the Regency, the Sheraton, the Watergate as well as the Smithsonian to address the crowds there, shake hands, to throw his head back in his famous laugh.

The Mayflower was his last stop of the evening. Here, he and his wife and children would meet up with the rest of the family.

Abby had made the plans. Instead of having all the family at one ball, all the members of the Supreme Court at another, and all the new Cabinet members at still another, she had mixed it all up so that each ball would enjoy its share of each group, as well as the celebrities who had stomped for Rud and were in town for the festivities. Only Judith, with Bill in his wheelchair, was already seated in the box reserved for the presidential party. Judith, in black velvet and diamonds with pearls, was slightly annoyed that she and Bill had been delegated only to attend this ball rather than making the rounds with Rud and Abby and the children. But she was somewhat mollified by the thought that by the time the evening was over, Bill would be named as Secretary of State, so sure was she that after Rud had thought it all out carefully, with Abby's help and advice, he'd do the right thing by all of them. After all, he was his mother's son and his father's ... he'd do that which in the end would be to his advantage. He would keep in mind that there was a life *after* the presidency and if he wanted to live it in comfort, he'd just better shape up.

As for Abby, whose idea it had been for her and Bill to come only to this ball, explaining 'I'm only thinking of Bill who should be spared the embarrassment of being wheeled into each ball, ball after ball, and especially into the Mayflower since that's where Rud is making the big announcement,' she had always proven herself a practical woman, who knew which side her bread was buttered on, who wanted her and Bill living with them in the White House to help ease her way.

Oh yes, between the two of them, they'd do the right thing. She'd bet the whole Stanton fortune on it! Actually it would all prove very effective . . . saving the Secretary of State announcement for tonight. It lent a sense of drama to the occasion. It would be a fitting climax to all the years of planning. It would be a triumph!

Instead of proceeding directly to his box, the President moved through the crowd who were cheering, applauding, even stomping their feet and rushing forward to offer their congratulations. But even as he shook hands, stopping to talk to this one, waving to that one, making jokes and laughing, his eyes swept the room like an actor counting the house. Although Jade and her daughters had been in Washington for almost three months, he hadn't seen her yet but Abby had told him that the three of them would be here tonight. And D'Arcy. . . . Finally, after all these years.

His eyes moved to the presidential box . . . to his mother and Bill. He had avoided them both ever since the confrontation but he couldn't help wondering what his mother expected tonight, she who prided herself on never being taken by surprise.

Abby's eyes too kept moving to the entrance. She saw Barbra Streisand coming in with a whole group. But it wasn't her appearance Abby was nervous about although the crowd seemed elated that Barbra was there. *Where is everyone?* They were all late – D'Arcy and Noel and their sons. Frankie. Jade and the girls. This was supposed to be reunion after all, as well as an Inaugural Ball!

Rud saw D'Arcy first and his first impulse was to tear through the crowd to get to her so that they could have at least a couple of minutes alone. But how was he going to manage that with the Secret Service ready to sprint if he did? Why had he waited until tonight?

'Oh, thank God, there's Frankie now!' Abby said, relieved. 'Now, if only Jade would get here. I should have sent a car for them. The traffic tonight is horrendous! But I don't want you to speak until they're here. I want us all to be together before we start. . . .'

Rud patted her arm to reassure her. 'We'll wait until they get here. . . .' Why not? Hadn't he spent the larger part of his life waiting for Jade?

D'Arcy waved to him from across the room and he felt this terrible lump in his throat. He waved back. And then she raised clasped hands above her head, and he laughed, throwing back his head. D'Arcy! She *was* a champ.

Francesca looked over to the presidential box. Judith looked regal, quite the Queen Mother, she thought. She was relieved that she felt nothing . . . no rancour, no resentment. Nothing. As if she and Judith were strangers. Then she looked at Bill, and her heart turned over. So many times she had told herself that her heart would never do that again! And yet, fifty years from that first time here it was, acting up. She saw Judith give him a little push, and saw Bill sit up straighter. And those gestures made her feel even sadder and she turned away to speak to the French Ambassador who was her escort for the evening. 'Doesn't the room look beautiful?'

She tried to concentrate on the decorations . . . everything in pastel shades – the balloons matching the profusion of flowers, shade for shade – yellow and pink, the blues and the mauves and the apricots. . . . 'It's January and so cold outside, but in here it looks like spring.'

'Just like you, Francesca. A lovely spring flower in your pretty yellow gown.'

'Me?' she laughed. 'I'm hardly a spring flower.' But she was pleased. Say what you would about the French, they sure knew how to turn a woman's head. 'Come with me,' she told the ambassador. 'This yellow spring flower is going to introduce you to her grandsons.'

There was a stir at the entrance and all heads turned to see who was entering. Again Abby was disappointed. She had thought the stir would mean Jade was there in one of Carlotta's movie star gowns, a knock-out. But it was only Liz Taylor in bright red velvet and enough diamonds to knock your eyes out, with Beatty and Nicholson in tow.

'She was 'at D'Arcy's Sweet Sixteen. Remember?' she murmured to Rud who was shaking hands with Gary Hart. 'But look at her! She looks as good as ever.'

'Why not?' Rud answered. 'So do you.'

Does he mean it? Or is he just being charming . . . polite? 'Thank you, Sir. Now *you* look better than ever! Being President becomes you. . . .'

They couldn't wait any longer, they'd have to start without Jade. . . .

There was a deafening roar as Rud and Abby, Will and Judy stepped into the presidential box, Rud carefully not looking at his mother and Bill. Rud held up his hand to the crowd but the clapping went on for several minutes. Finally he was able to speak, 'No speeches tonight. To tell the truth, this past year I've made enough speeches to last a lifetime.'

There was more cheering and applause and he waited for it to die down before continuing. And then Abby tugged at his arm and he saw her – not the Jade who had come to D'Arcy's Sweet Sixteen in her mother's satin and furs, the bright red hair falling over one eye; and not the glamorous Parisian model he had made love to in a narrow single bed. Nor was she the wild-haired, sad-eyed but still lovely young woman who had told him she loved him but it was all a dream. . . . No, this was a Jade all grown up, her bright red hair piled on top of her head, serene and beautiful in a simple white gown and no jewellery, as if she had planned her appearance with a purpose – not to compete with the evening's leading lady . . . the First Lady. But then if she were different, so was he. He was all grown up too. He was the President.

Then he saw the two red-headed girls standing behind her . . . obviously her daughters, so much like Jade when he first saw her that he would have recognized them any place in the world, and he laughed. *They* were the ones in Carlotta's movie star clothes with the fall of red hair covering an eye!

He turned back to the crowd.

'As I said, no speeches tonight. Tonight we're only going to drink, make merry and dance. But I do want to thank you all for coming tonight . . . for being my friends and my supporters, and for accompanying me as we all go into the future together. And now I'd like to introduce my wife who, I think, is even better known to you than I am since she's done more actual campaigning than I have.'

The crowd laughed and cheered Abby, and then Will and Judy. And then the President introduced his mother, which was par for the course, and then his friend and aide, the former governor of Florida, Bill Sheridan. He managed to do this without looking at them.

And then it was time to name his choice for Secretary of State, and Abby placed her hand on his arm, as if to reassure him.

'And now I'd like to introduce you to our new Secretary of State, someone who needs little introduction since this person has been on the political scene longer than I . . . who has served the country long and well. . . .'

He took a breath, could feel the tension in the box, could *feel* Judith readying herself to push Bill's chair forward.

'Frankie Sheridan, will you please come up and take a bow?'

Even with all the din and cheering, D'Arcy's voice could be heard screaming, 'Mother!' as Francesca made her way to the presidential box. No one could hear Judith hiss at her daughter-in-law, 'You'll be sorry for this.'

Abby turned to her and said steadily, 'Please, Mother! Frankie's going to speak and we don't want to do anything to spoil Rud's inaugural ball after we've all waited so long for this moment!'

'You're not going to get away with this!'

'You'll have to control yourself, Mother, or you'll have to leave. . . .'

Before Frankie spoke she turned to Bill, who was slumped in his chair. 'I'm really sorry . . .' she whispered.

He managed to smile and stuck out his hand, 'Don't be. I always said you were the best. . . .'

The best what? She stepped to the mike. 'My President has just said this is not a night for speeches. So all I will say is that it's a pleasure to be here with you all tonight, and that I'm going to do my best to serve President Stanton and the nation.'

Rud took back the microphone to say, 'And now folks, let's see some dancing! This is supposed to be a ball!'

Judith pulled at him, unable to contain herself. 'You're going to regret this for the rest of your life. This is going to be the sorriest day of your life!'

He looked into her eyes. 'This is one time you're wrong, Judith. This is the best day of my life in more ways than one. And now, if you'll excuse me, I have to dance with my First Lady.'

But the crowd was surging towards the box. It was bedlam, and Abby murmured to Rud, 'You go down there and mix. . . . I'll be along in a couple of minutes.' She turned back to Judith.

'Really, it would be best if you and Bill left now. I'll have a car brought around for you.'

Judith sneered. 'I'm quite capable of ordering a car. I'm the one who taught *you* how.'

'Well, good. Then I suggest that you do just that and make sure the car takes you back to Stantonwood. I don't think there's going to be room for you and Bill at the White House, after all.'

Judith's head snapped back. This was a double blow. But she recovered quickly. It was her way. 'Oh, you're feeling strong right now, Abby. But you won't be feeling so strong tomorrow, or next week, or next year. . . . You'll change your mind.'

'I'll be fine . . . next week and the week after that . . . I won't change my mind, be assured.'

And then Judith was convinced. 'You bitch! You viper! How can you do this to me, after everything I did for you?'

'How, Judith? Because you taught me how to do it, and you were a marvellous teacher. The best!'

'I want you to go up to your father and just give him a big hug, D'Arcy. And I don't want to hear any arguments.'

'OK, Frankie. I wouldn't dream of arguing with the Secretary of State. I'll do it!' But her eyes were locked with Rud's. And his eyes were wet, and only then did her own eyes fill with tears.

At the very same moment, they went towards each other. He opened up his arms and she went into them and laid her head against his shoulder. 'D'Arcy,' he said, and she sighed and said into the fabric of his dinner jacket, 'Rud . . . oh, Rud!' And then she lifted her head and said, 'Into the future together, bro.'

He kissed the top of her head. D'Arcy was . . . always would be, special.

When Rud danced off with Abby, D'Arcy squared her shoulders. Now she would do what her mother wanted, but only because it *was* what Frankie wanted. She looked around for her father. Even in this mob she couldn't miss him. He was a standout in his chair with the queen bee beside him. But she couldn't spot him. He had already left. But tomorrow *was* another day. . . .

Rud danced Abby over to the edge of the floor where Jade and her daughters waited. Now that he looked again close up, he realized that Jade's daughters, while he'd be able to recognize them anywhere, wouldn't really fool him. He'd never really mix them up with the fifteen-year-old Jade he remembered, or even the slightly older Jade in Paris. He could tell them from the original. There'd never be another Jade!

Abby spun herself around. 'Well, how am I doing, sister?'

'You're looking good. I think Mother would be very proud. I know I am.'

And then the President held out his arm to his sister-in-law. 'Will you do me the honour?'

'My pleasure, Mr President.'

And they danced off as Abby welcomed her nieces home, took them to meet their cousins, Will and Judy.

Rud and Jade didn't dance cheek to cheek, their bodies barely touched, still there was an intimacy between them that would never change, would never be diminished. For the rest of their eternity it would be there . . . part of their shared past. And Jade knew that just as there were many kinds of love, there were certain loves that never died, and that was as it should be. Love was the best part of the past, and the best could not ever be forgotten. Rather, you treasured it, a golden good-luck charm, guaranteed to ensure a many-splendoured future . . .

And then their eyes met, and suddenly, for a few moments the years melted away and it could have been thirty years earlier . . . the night they first met. She had been only fifteen but already an enchantress, and he had been the eighteen-year-old prince of the realm with the predestined future, and they had fallen in love . . . a love fated to last throughout the years. Their eyes, shining wetly, acknowledged this and that, finally, was the last secret . . . their secret . . . to be kept and shared and cherished. . . .